Hooky

VOLUME 2

MÍRIAM BONASTRE TUR

CLARION BOOKS
IMPRINTS OF HARPERCOLLINSPUBLISHERS

CLARION BOOKS IS AN IMPRINT OF HARPERCOLLINS PUBLISHERS.
HARPERALLEY IS AN IMPRINT OF HARPERCOLLINS PUBLISHERS.

HOOKY VOLUME 2
ISBN 978-0-35-869309-3 PAPERBACK
ISBN 978-0-35-869310-9 HARDCOVER
ISBN 978-0-06-327362-7 SIGNED EDITION

LETTERING BY NATALIE FONDRIEST

22 23 24 25 26 RTLO 10 9 8 7 6 5 4 3 2 1

FIRST EDITION
A DIGITAL VERSION OF HOOKY WAS ORIGINALLY PUBLISHED ON
WEBTOON IN 2015.

CHAPTER 33

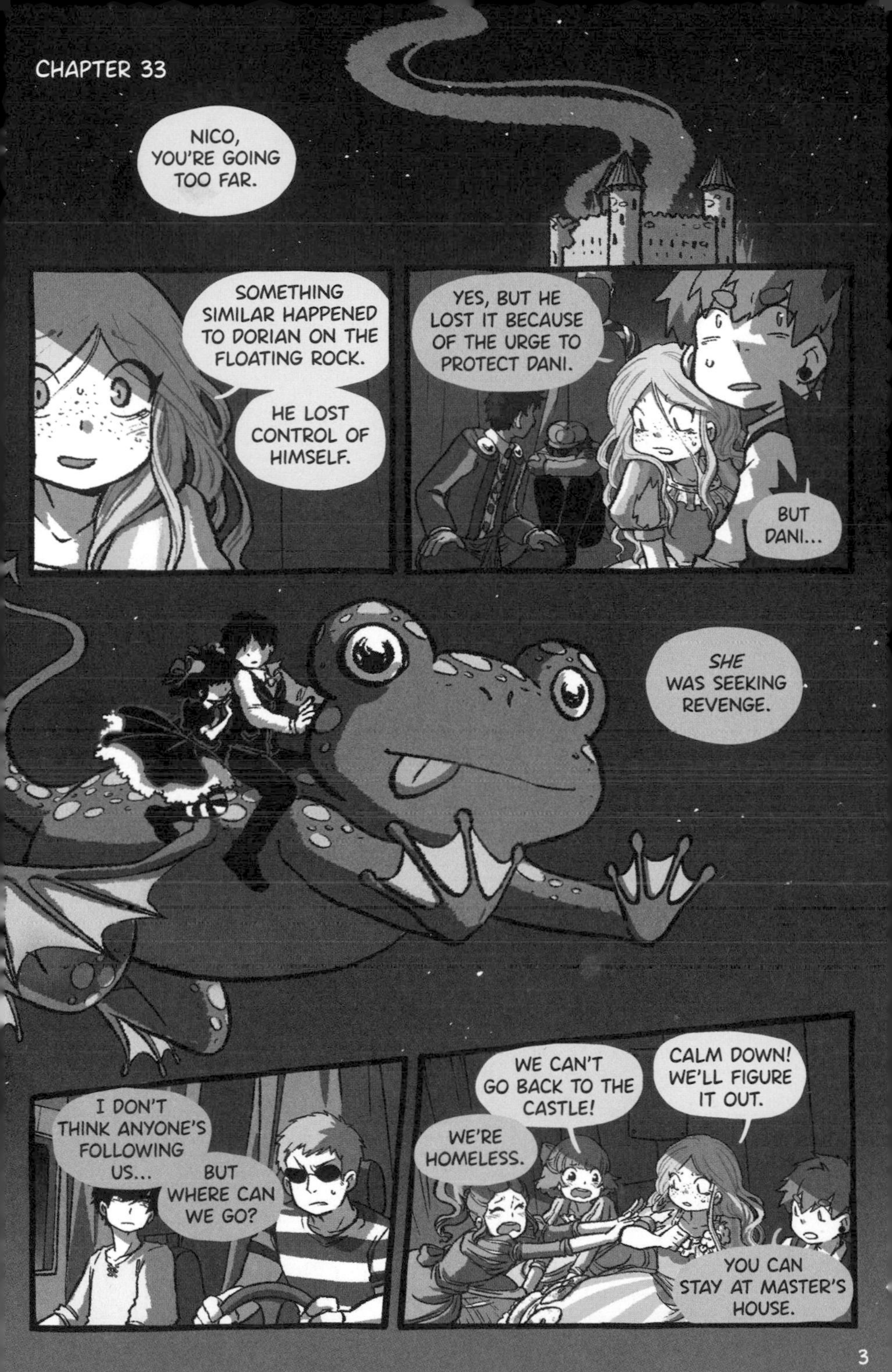
NICO, YOU'RE GOING TOO FAR.
SOMETHING SIMILAR HAPPENED TO DORIAN ON THE FLOATING ROCK.
HE LOST CONTROL OF HIMSELF.
YES, BUT HE LOST IT BECAUSE OF THE URGE TO PROTECT DANI.
BUT DANI...
SHE WAS SEEKING REVENGE.
I DON'T THINK ANYONE'S FOLLOWING US...
BUT WHERE CAN WE GO?
WE CAN'T GO BACK TO THE CASTLE!
WE'RE HOMELESS.
CALM DOWN! WE'LL FIGURE IT OUT.
YOU CAN STAY AT MASTER'S HOUSE.

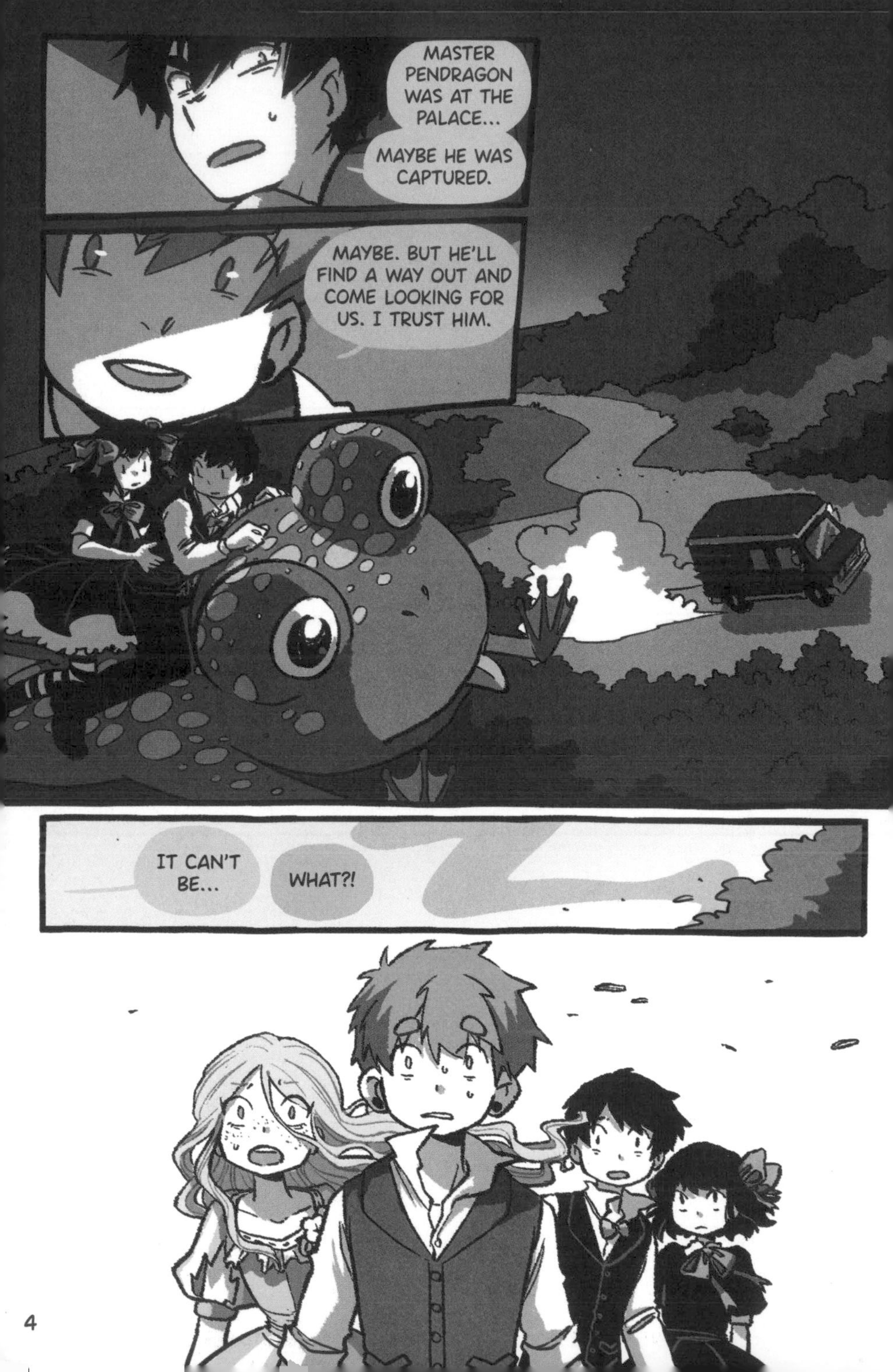
MASTER PENDRAGON WAS AT THE PALACE...
MAYBE HE WAS CAPTURED.
MAYBE. BUT HE'LL FIND A WAY OUT AND COME LOOKING FOR US. I TRUST HIM.
IT CAN'T BE...
WHAT?!

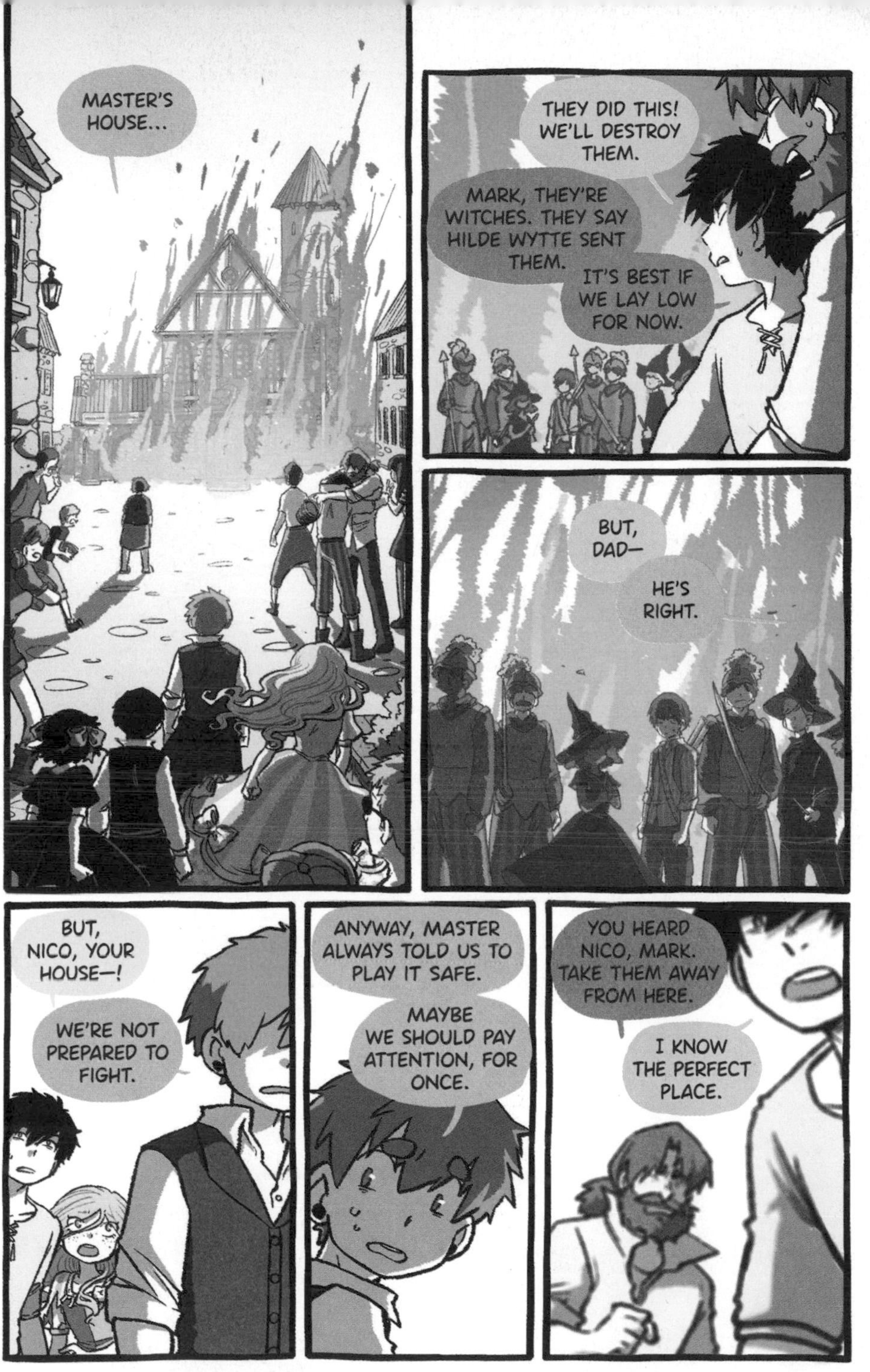
MASTER'S HOUSE...
THEY DID THIS! WE'LL DESTROY THEM.
MARK, THEY'RE WITCHES. THEY SAY HILDE WYTTE SENT THEM.
IT'S BEST IF WE LAY LOW FOR NOW.
BUT, DAD—
HE'S RIGHT.
BUT, NICO, YOUR HOUSE—!
WE'RE NOT PREPARED TO FIGHT.
ANYWAY, MASTER ALWAYS TOLD US TO PLAY IT SAFE.
MAYBE WE SHOULD PAY ATTENTION, FOR ONCE.
YOU HEARD NICO, MARK. TAKE THEM AWAY FROM HERE.
I KNOW THE PERFECT PLACE.

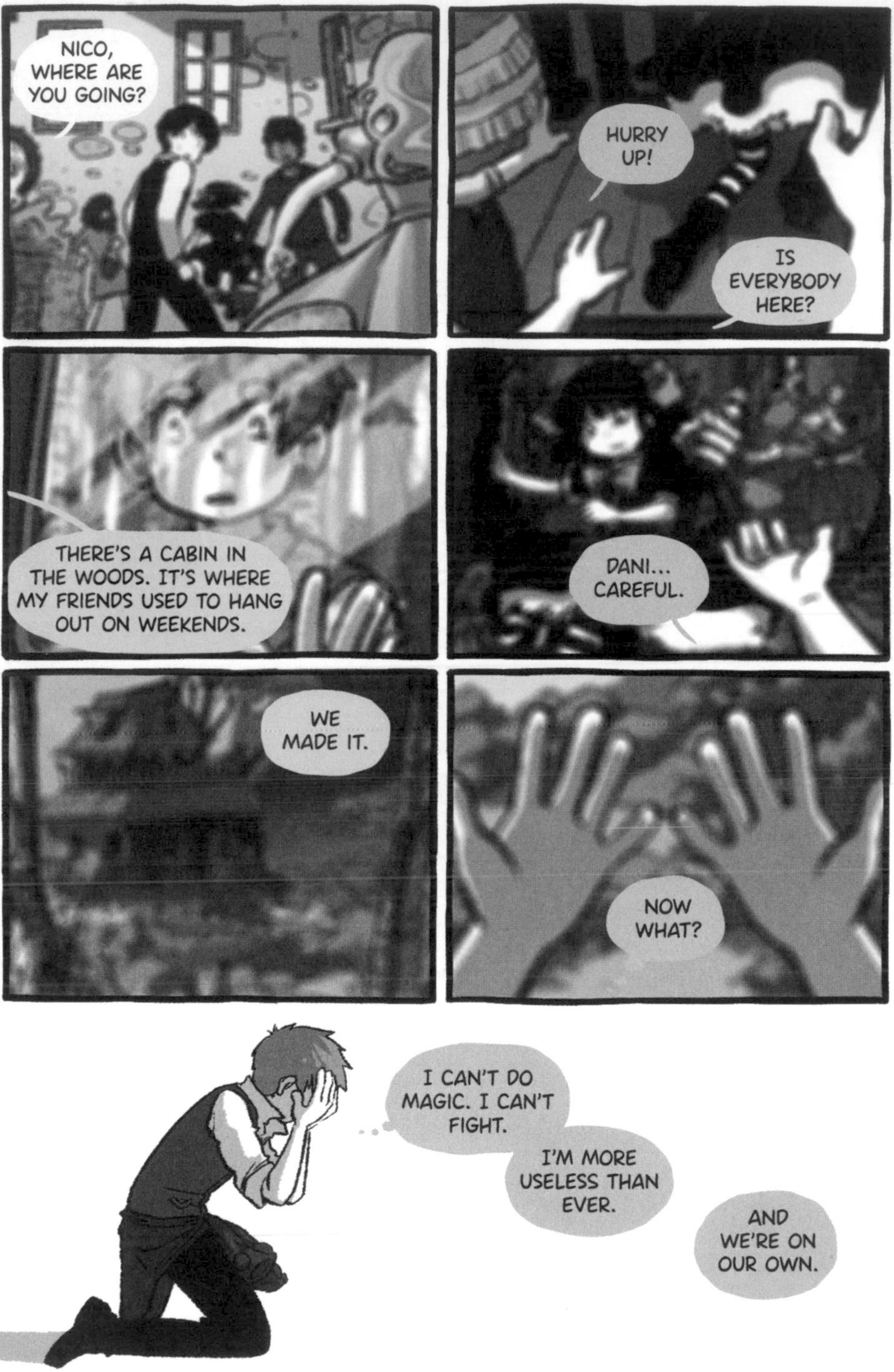
NICO, WHERE ARE YOU GOING?
HURRY UP!
IS EVERYBODY HERE?
THERE'S A CABIN IN THE WOODS. IT'S WHERE MY FRIENDS USED TO HANG OUT ON WEEKENDS.
DANI... CAREFUL.
WE MADE IT.
NOW WHAT?
I CAN'T DO MAGIC. I CAN'T FIGHT.
I'M MORE USELESS THAN EVER.
AND WE'RE ON OUR OWN.

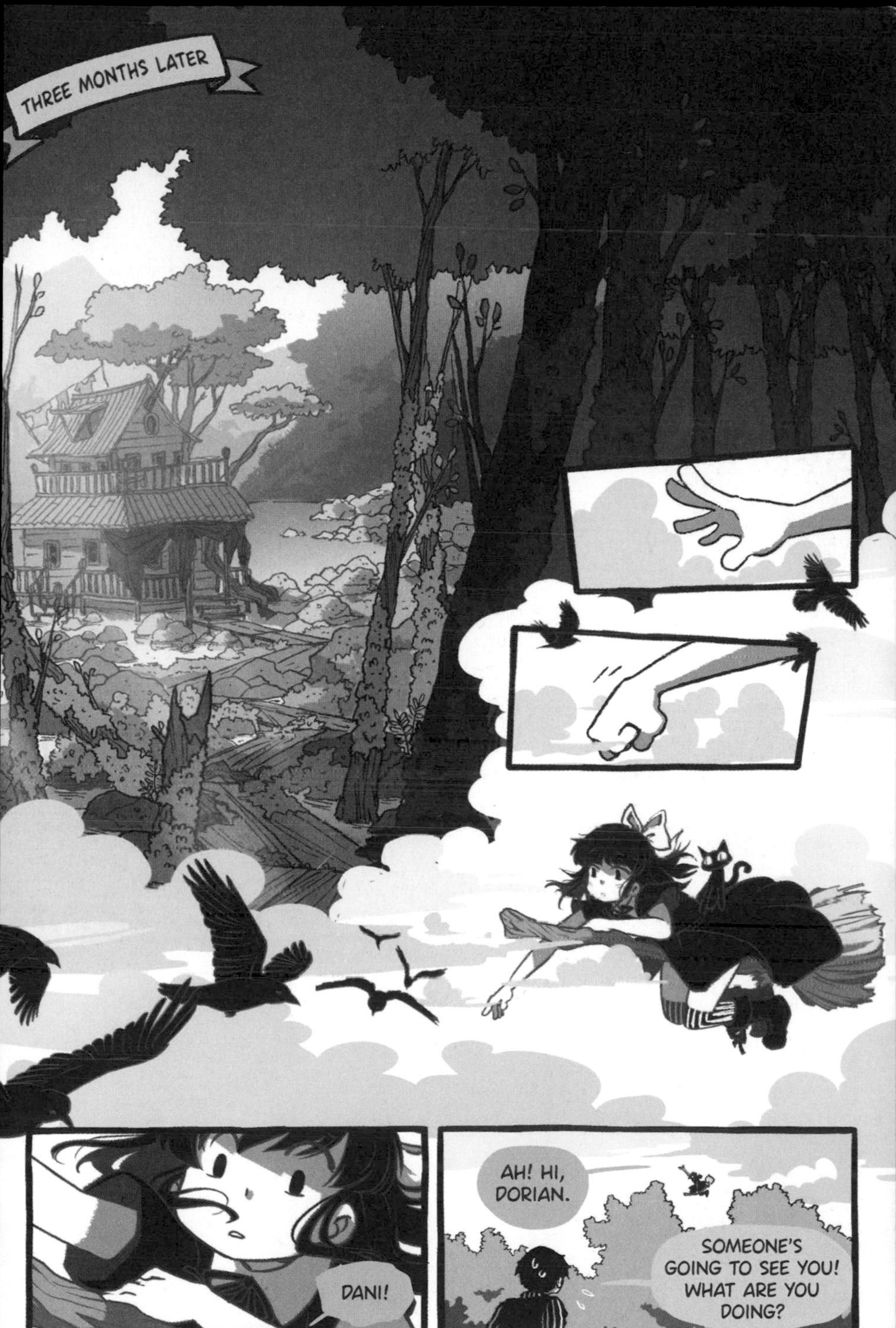
THREE MONTHS LATER
DANI!
AH! HI, DORIAN.
SOMEONE'S GOING TO SEE YOU! WHAT ARE YOU DOING?

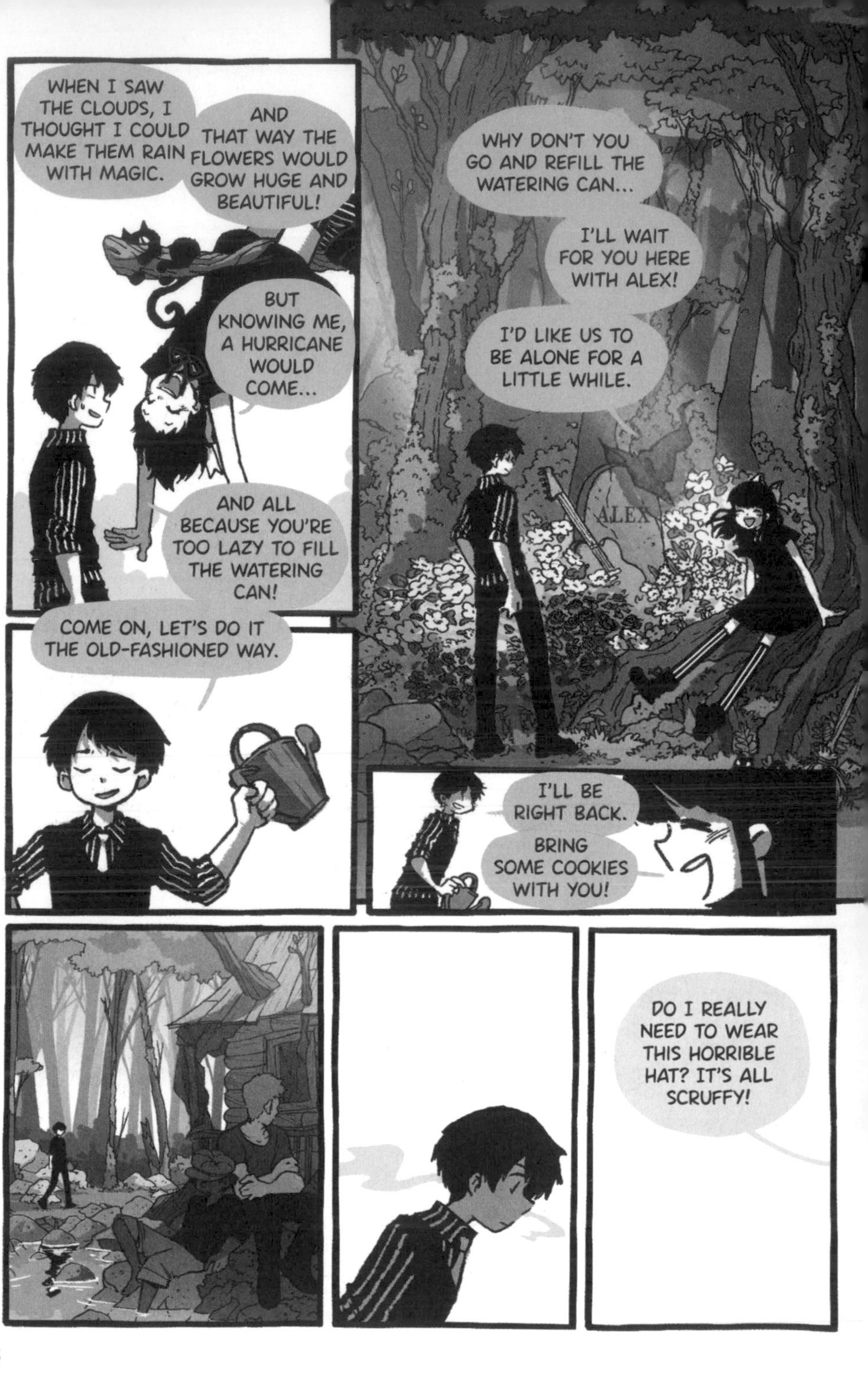
WHEN I SAW THE CLOUDS, I THOUGHT I COULD MAKE THEM RAIN WITH MAGIC.
AND THAT WAY THE FLOWERS WOULD GROW HUGE AND BEAUTIFUL!
BUT KNOWING ME, A HURRICANE WOULD COME...
AND ALL BECAUSE YOU'RE TOO LAZY TO FILL THE WATERING CAN!
WHY DON'T YOU GO AND REFILL THE WATERING CAN...
I'LL WAIT FOR YOU HERE WITH ALEX!
I'D LIKE US TO BE ALONE FOR A LITTLE WHILE.
ALEX
COME ON, LET'S DO IT THE OLD-FASHIONED WAY.
I'LL BE RIGHT BACK.
BRING SOME COOKIES WITH YOU!
DO I REALLY NEED TO WEAR THIS HORRIBLE HAT? IT'S ALL SCRUFFY!

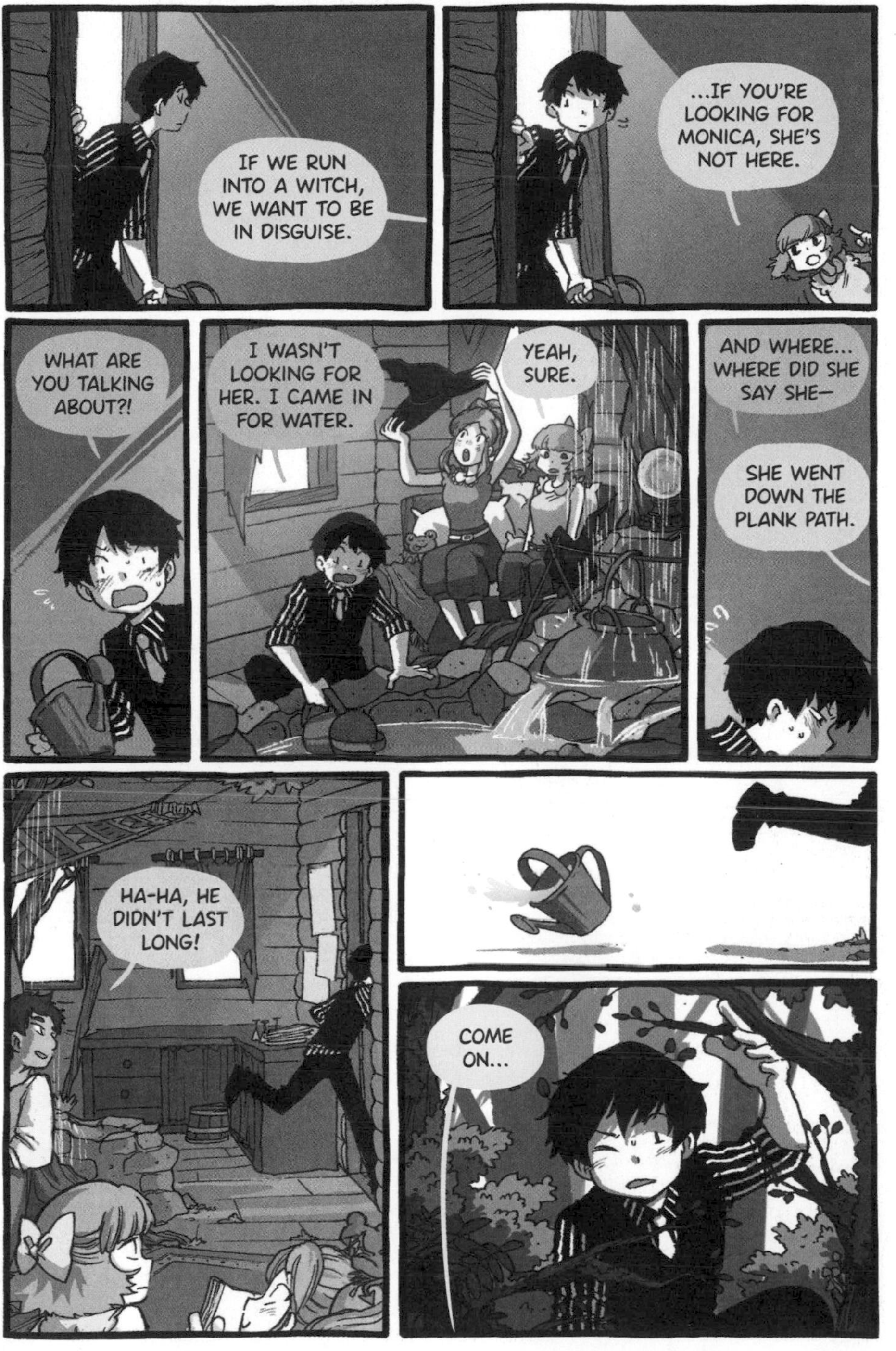
IF WE RUN INTO A WITCH, WE WANT TO BE IN DISGUISE.
...IF YOU'RE LOOKING FOR MONICA, SHE'S NOT HERE.
WHAT ARE YOU TALKING ABOUT?!
I WASN'T LOOKING FOR HER. I CAME IN FOR WATER.
YEAH, SURE.
AND WHERE... WHERE DID SHE SAY SHE—
SHE WENT DOWN THE PLANK PATH.
HA-HA, HE DIDN'T LAST LONG!
COME ON...

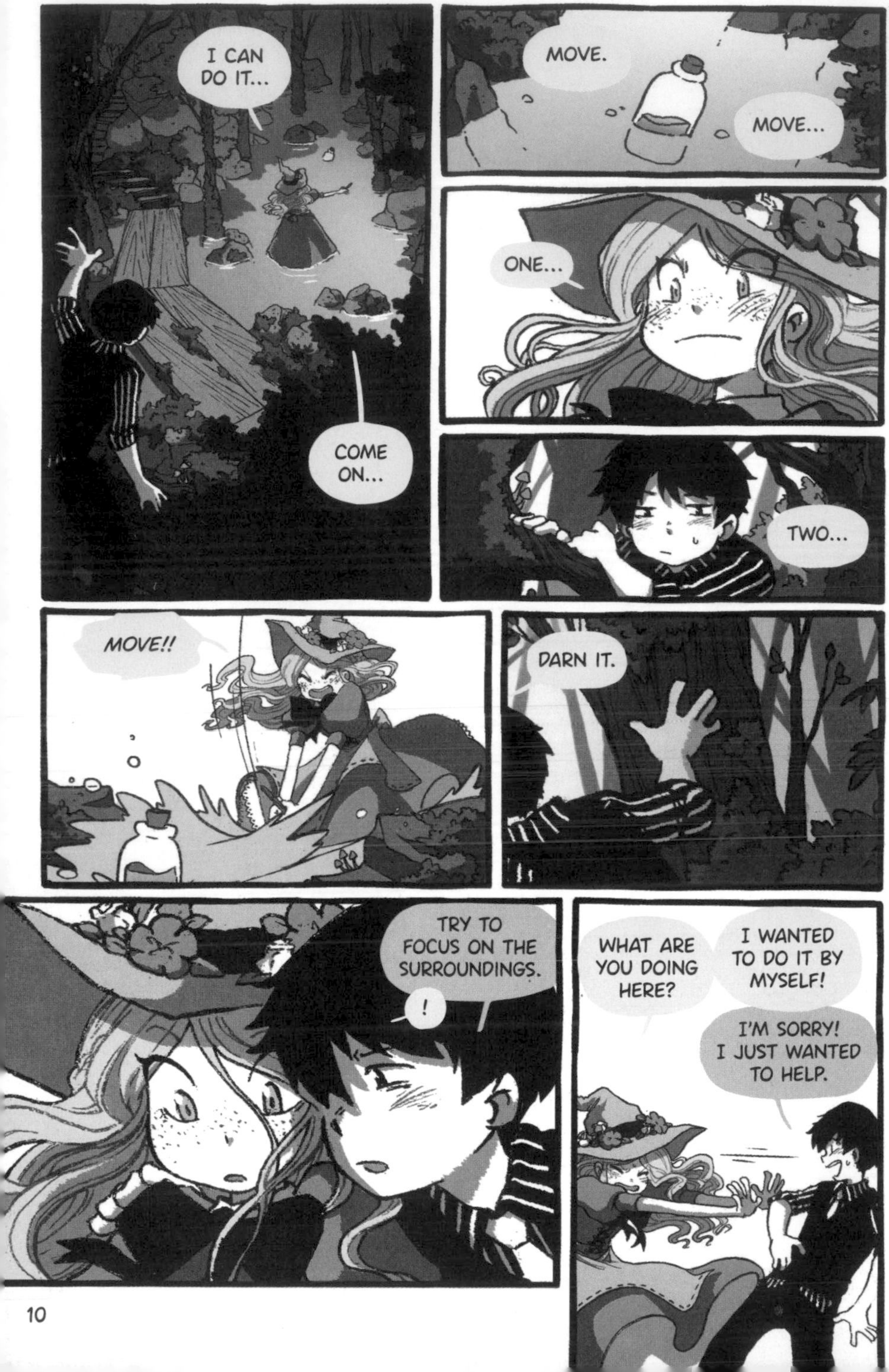
I CAN DO IT...
COME ON...
MOVE.
MOVE...
ONE...
TWO...
MOVE!!
DARN IT.
TRY TO FOCUS ON THE SURROUNDINGS.
!
WHAT ARE YOU DOING HERE?
I WANTED TO DO IT BY MYSELF!
I'M SORRY! I JUST WANTED TO HELP.

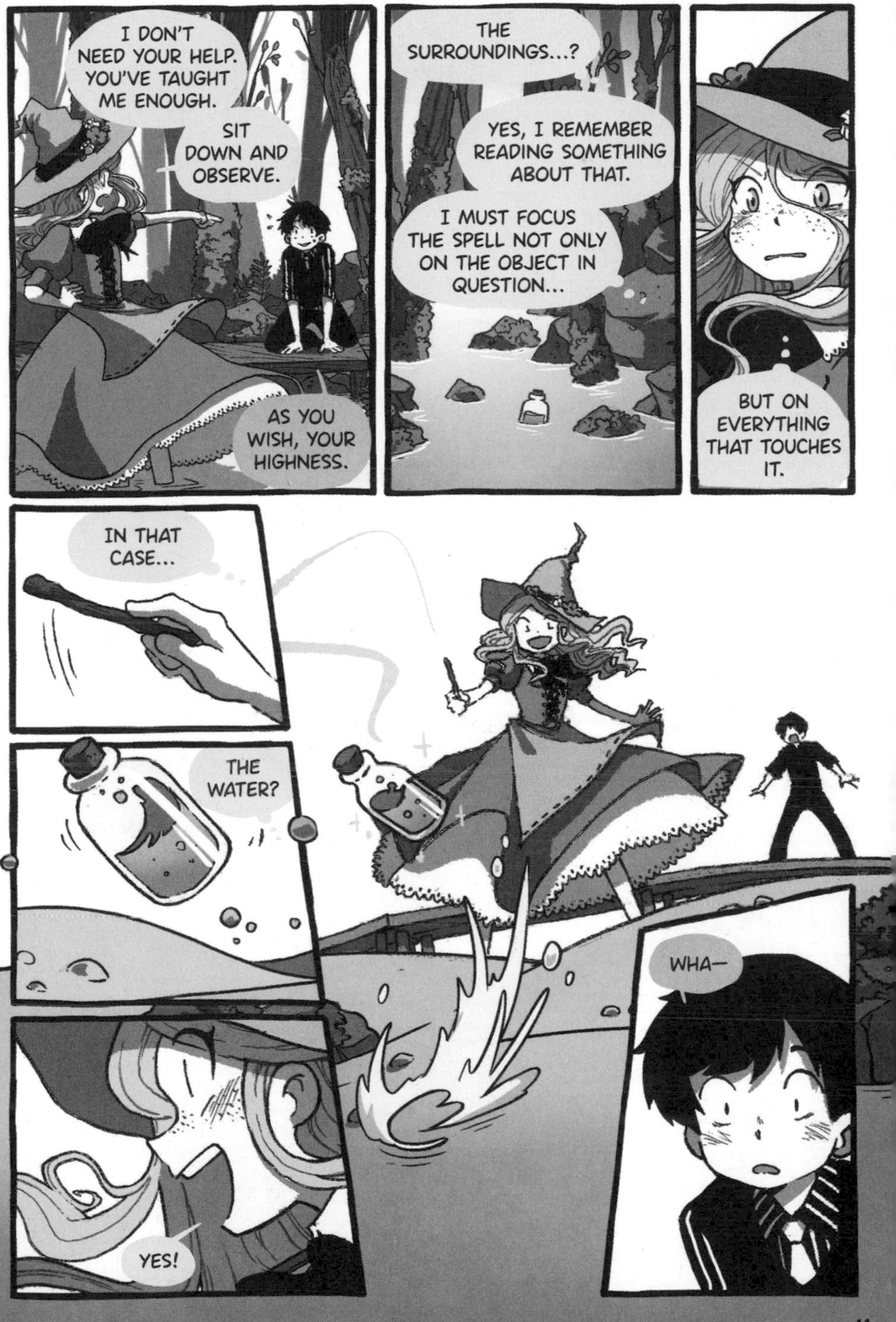
I DON'T NEED YOUR HELP. YOU'VE TAUGHT ME ENOUGH.
SIT DOWN AND OBSERVE.
AS YOU WISH, YOUR HIGHNESS.
THE SURROUNDINGS...?
YES, I REMEMBER READING SOMETHING ABOUT THAT.
I MUST FOCUS THE SPELL NOT ONLY ON THE OBJECT IN QUESTION...
BUT ON EVERYTHING THAT TOUCHES IT.
IN THAT CASE...
THE WATER?
YES!
WHA—

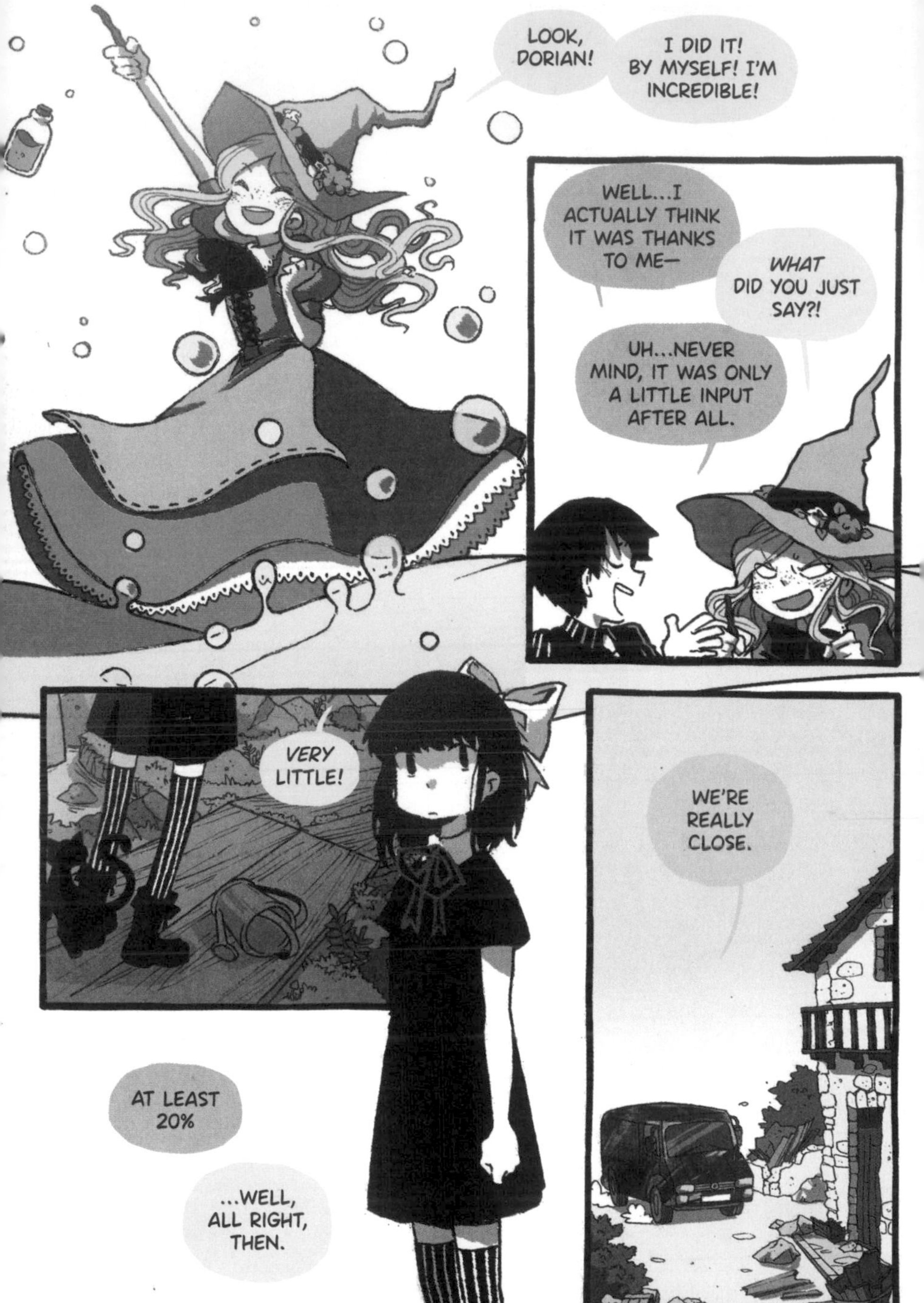
LOOK, DORIAN!
I DID IT! BY MYSELF! I'M INCREDIBLE!
WELL...I ACTUALLY THINK IT WAS THANKS TO ME—
WHAT DID YOU JUST SAY?!
UH...NEVER MIND, IT WAS ONLY A LITTLE INPUT AFTER ALL.
VERY LITTLE!
AT LEAST 20%
...WELL, ALL RIGHT, THEN.
WE'RE REALLY CLOSE.

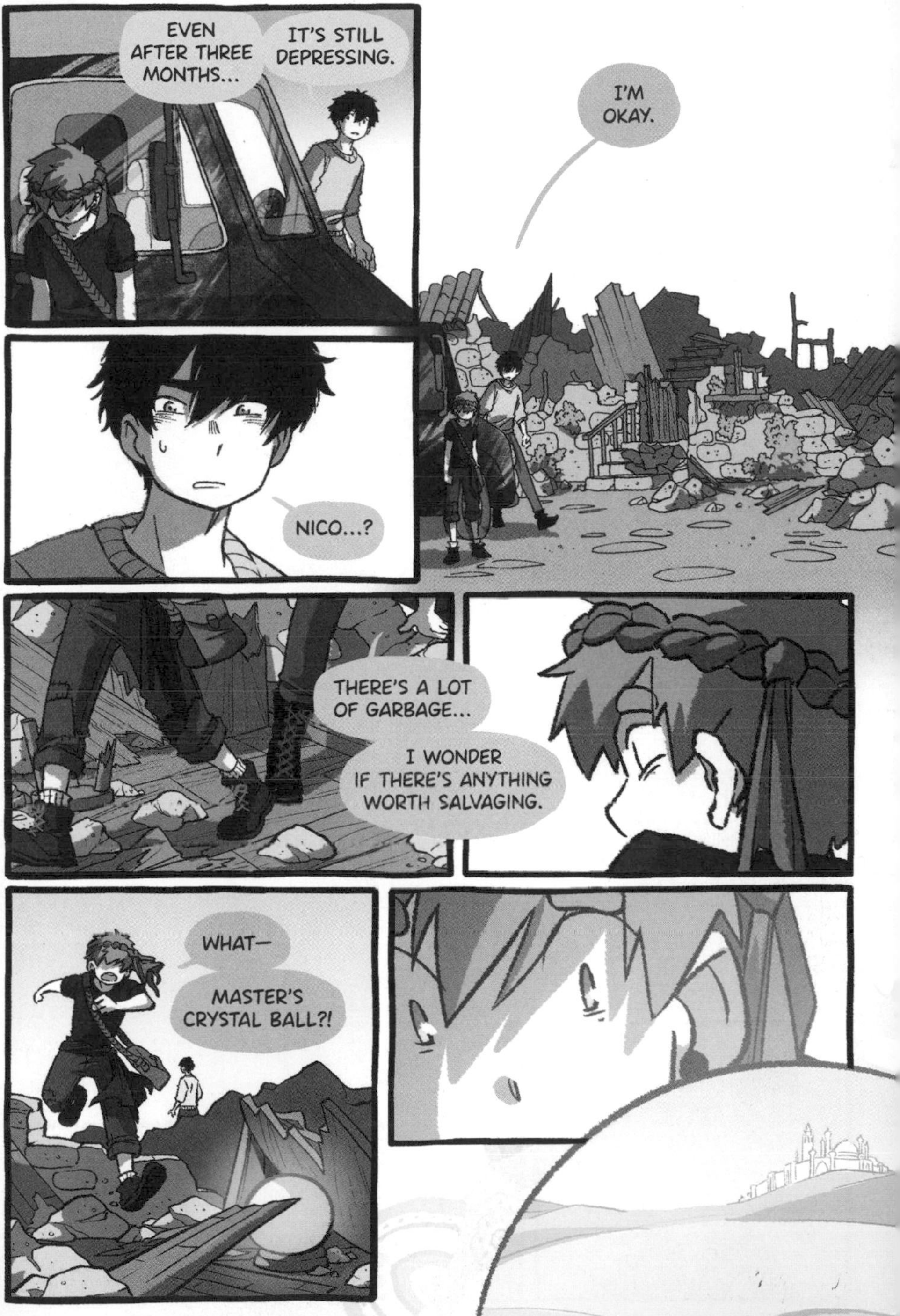
EVEN AFTER THREE MONTHS...
IT'S STILL DEPRESSING.
I'M OKAY.
NICO...?
THERE'S A LOT OF GARBAGE...
I WONDER IF THERE'S ANYTHING WORTH SALVAGING.
WHAT—
MASTER'S CRYSTAL BALL?!

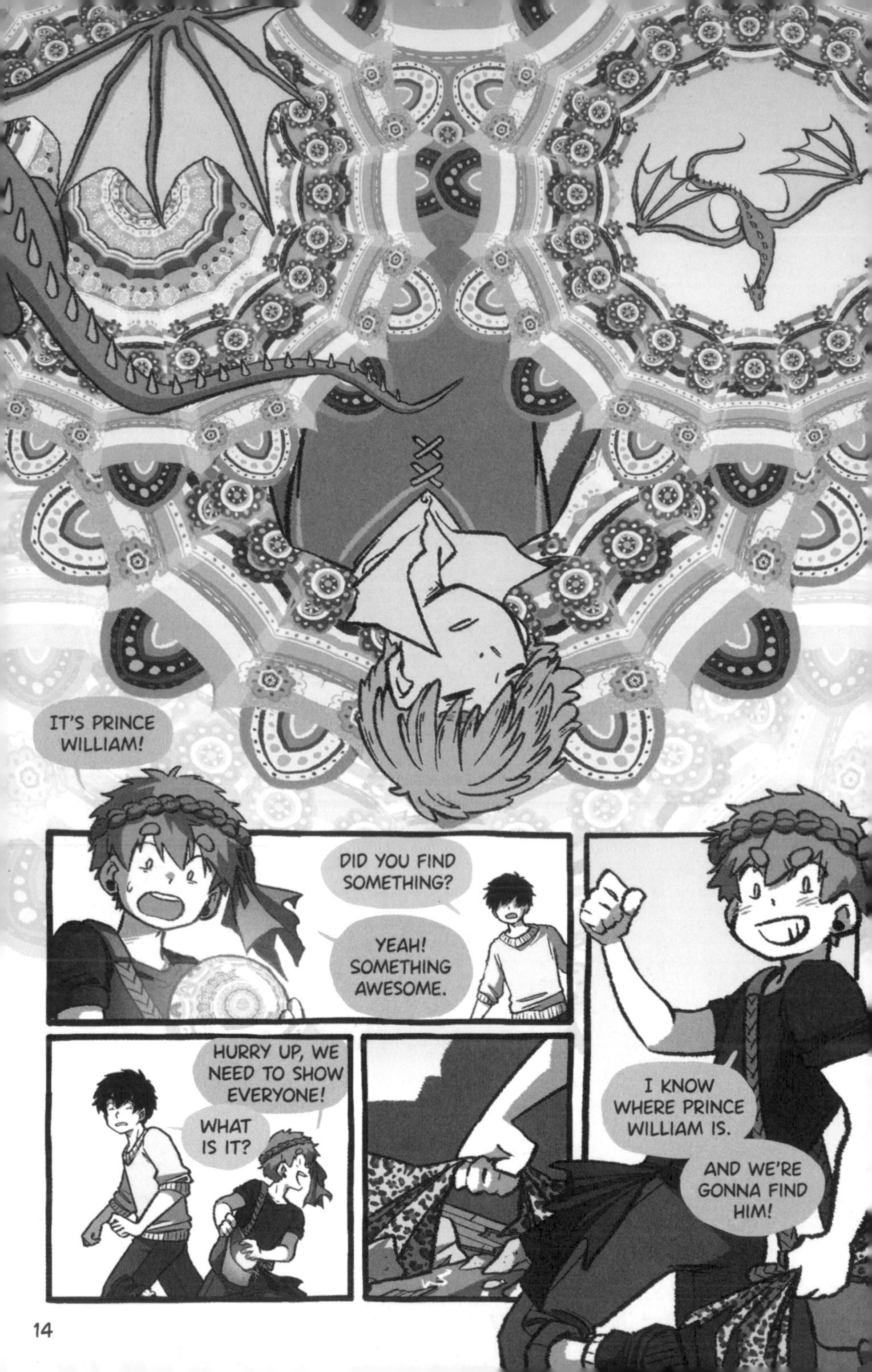
IT'S PRINCE WILLIAM!
DID YOU FIND SOMETHING?
YEAH! SOMETHING AWESOME.
HURRY UP, WE NEED TO SHOW EVERYONE!
WHAT IS IT?
I KNOW WHERE PRINCE WILLIAM IS.
AND WE'RE GONNA FIND HIM!

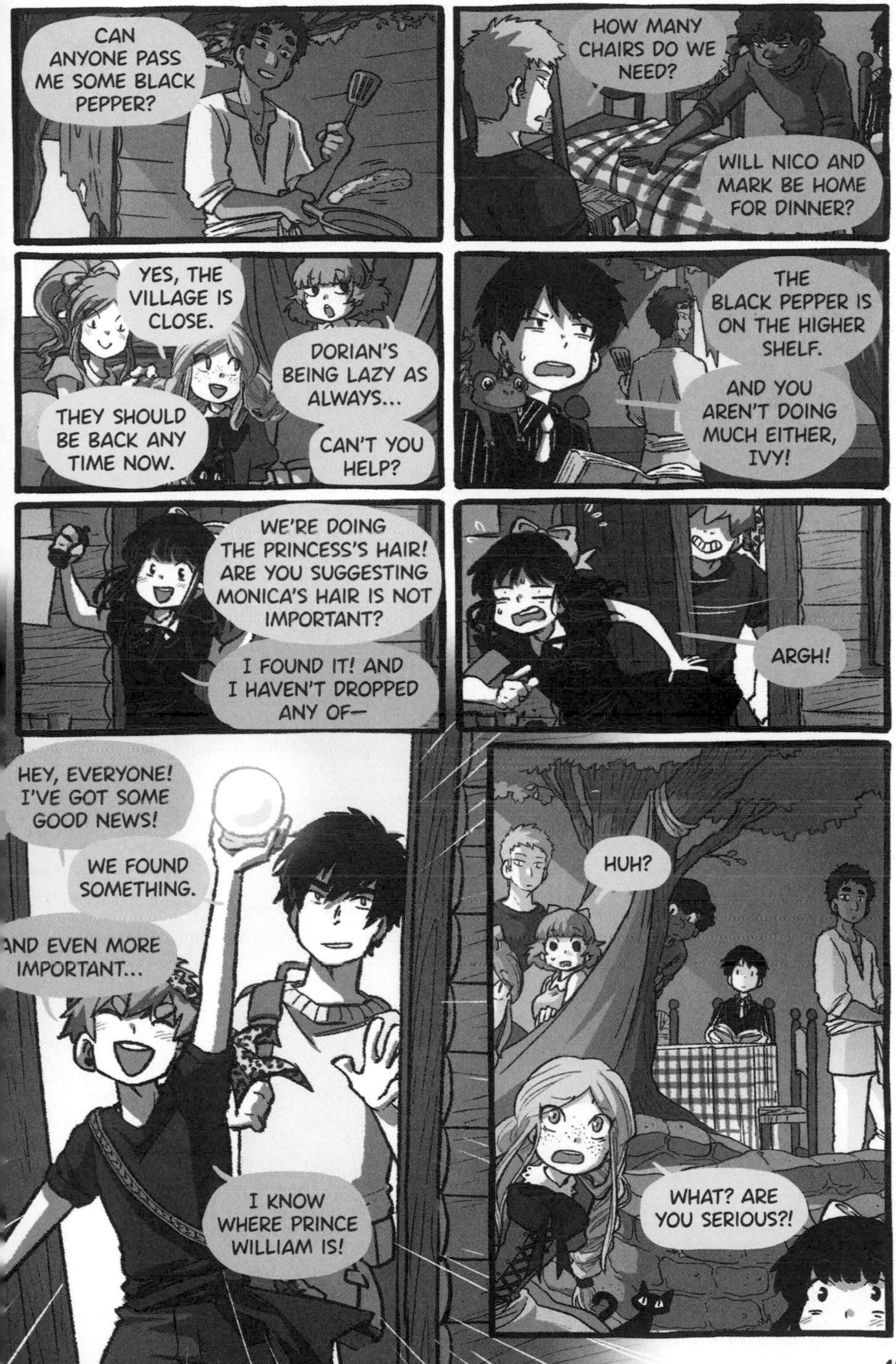
CAN ANYONE PASS ME SOME BLACK PEPPER?
HOW MANY CHAIRS DO WE NEED?
WILL NICO AND MARK BE HOME FOR DINNER?
YES, THE VILLAGE IS CLOSE.
THEY SHOULD BE BACK ANY TIME NOW.
DORIAN'S BEING LAZY AS ALWAYS...
CAN'T YOU HELP?
THE BLACK PEPPER IS ON THE HIGHER SHELF.
AND YOU AREN'T DOING MUCH EITHER, IVY!
WE'RE DOING THE PRINCESS'S HAIR! ARE YOU SUGGESTING MONICA'S HAIR IS NOT IMPORTANT?
I FOUND IT! AND I HAVEN'T DROPPED ANY OF—
ARGH!
HEY, EVERYONE! I'VE GOT SOME GOOD NEWS!
WE FOUND SOMETHING.
AND EVEN MORE IMPORTANT...
I KNOW WHERE PRINCE WILLIAM IS!
HUH?
WHAT? ARE YOU SERIOUS?!

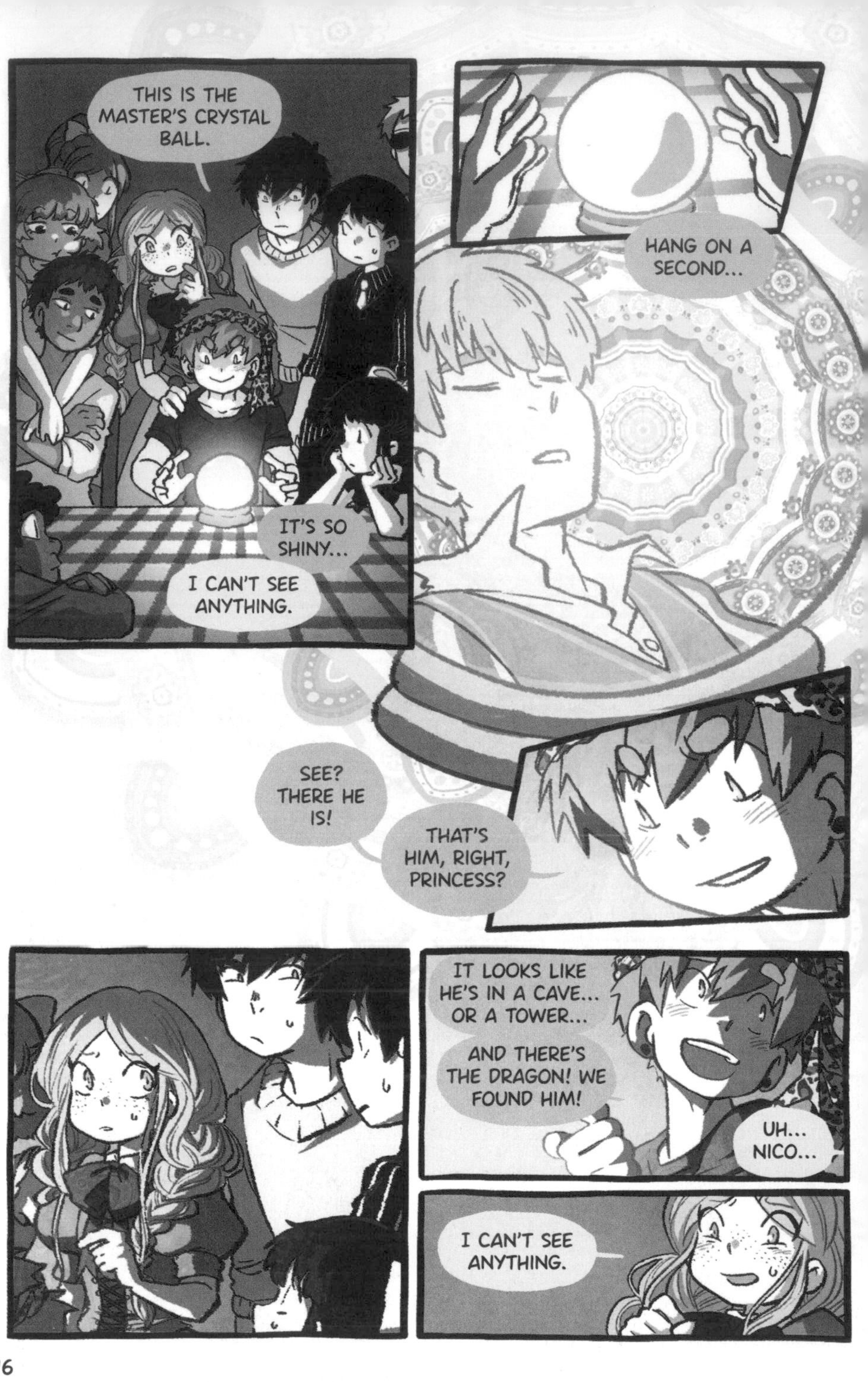
THIS IS THE MASTER'S CRYSTAL BALL.
IT'S SO SHINY...
I CAN'T SEE ANYTHING.
HANG ON A SECOND...
SEE? THERE HE IS!
THAT'S HIM, RIGHT, PRINCESS?
IT LOOKS LIKE HE'S IN A CAVE... OR A TOWER...
AND THERE'S THE DRAGON! WE FOUND HIM!
UH... NICO...
I CAN'T SEE ANYTHING.

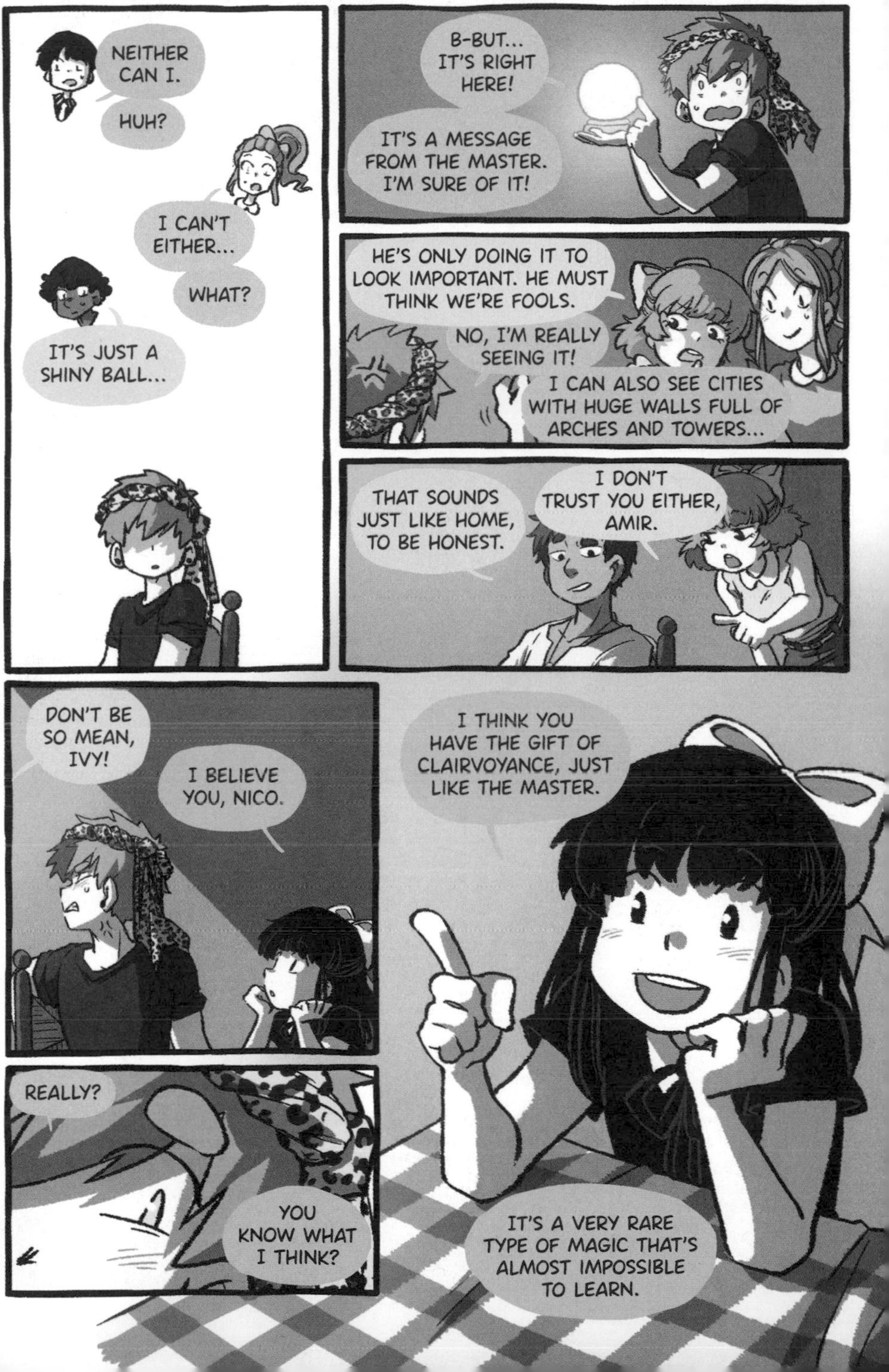
NEITHER CAN I.
HUH?
I CAN'T EITHER...
WHAT?
IT'S JUST A SHINY BALL...
B-BUT... IT'S RIGHT HERE!
IT'S A MESSAGE FROM THE MASTER. I'M SURE OF IT!
HE'S ONLY DOING IT TO LOOK IMPORTANT. HE MUST THINK WE'RE FOOLS.
NO, I'M REALLY SEEING IT!
I CAN ALSO SEE CITIES WITH HUGE WALLS FULL OF ARCHES AND TOWERS...
THAT SOUNDS JUST LIKE HOME, TO BE HONEST.
I DON'T TRUST YOU EITHER, AMIR.
DON'T BE SO MEAN, IVY!
I BELIEVE YOU, NICO.
REALLY?
YOU KNOW WHAT I THINK?
I THINK YOU HAVE THE GIFT OF CLAIRVOYANCE, JUST LIKE THE MASTER.
IT'S A VERY RARE TYPE OF MAGIC THAT'S ALMOST IMPOSSIBLE TO LEARN.

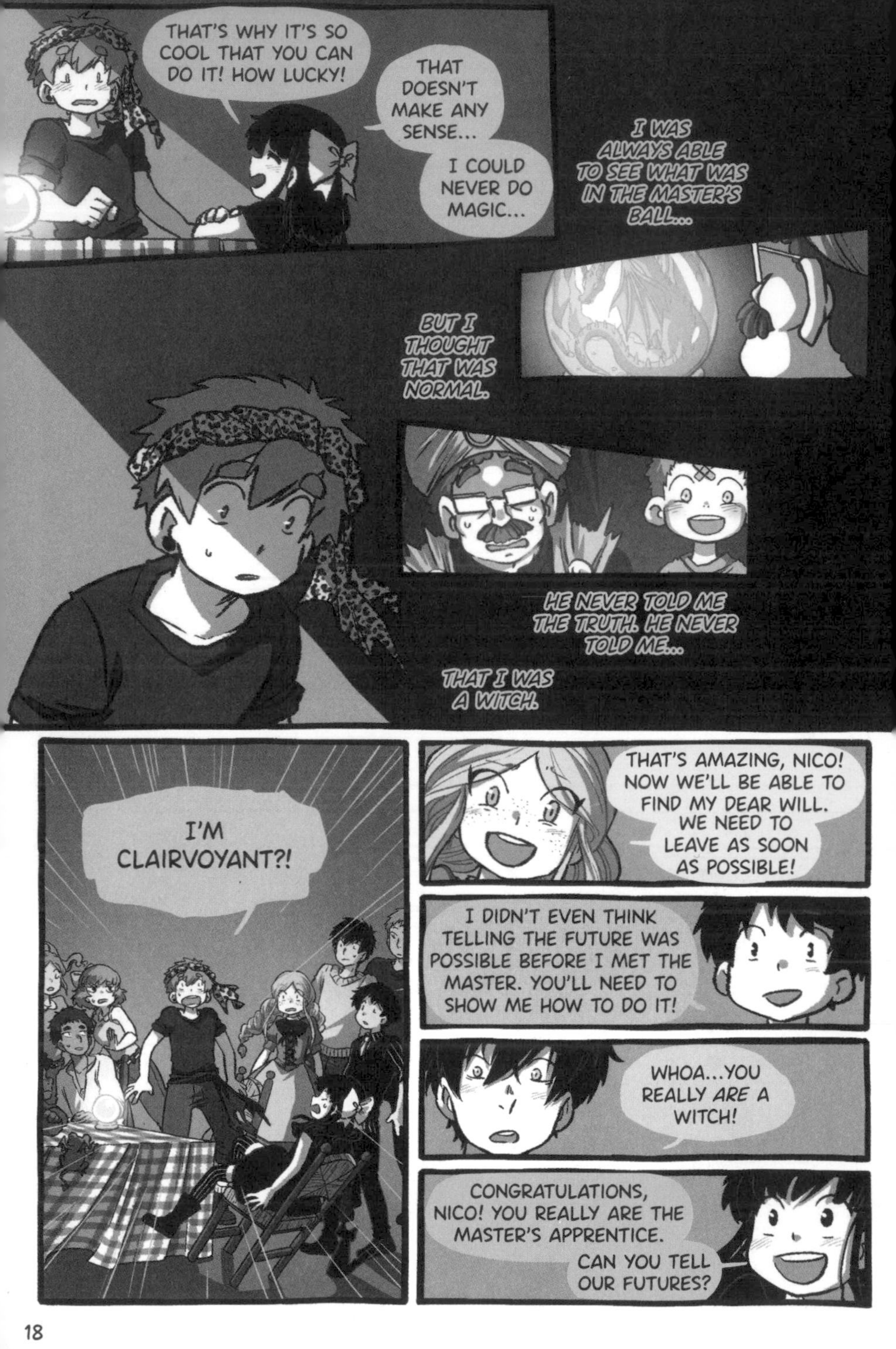
THAT'S WHY IT'S SO COOL THAT YOU CAN DO IT! HOW LUCKY!
THAT DOESN'T MAKE ANY SENSE...
I COULD NEVER DO MAGIC...
I WAS ALWAYS ABLE TO SEE WHAT WAS IN THE MASTER'S BALL...
BUT I THOUGHT THAT WAS NORMAL.
HE NEVER TOLD ME THE TRUTH. HE NEVER TOLD ME...
THAT I WAS A WITCH.
I'M CLAIRVOYANT?!
THAT'S AMAZING, NICO! NOW WE'LL BE ABLE TO FIND MY DEAR WILL. WE NEED TO LEAVE AS SOON AS POSSIBLE!
I DIDN'T EVEN THINK TELLING THE FUTURE WAS POSSIBLE BEFORE I MET THE MASTER. YOU'LL NEED TO SHOW ME HOW TO DO IT!
WHOA...YOU REALLY ARE A WITCH!
CONGRATULATIONS, NICO! YOU REALLY ARE THE MASTER'S APPRENTICE.
CAN YOU TELL OUR FUTURES?

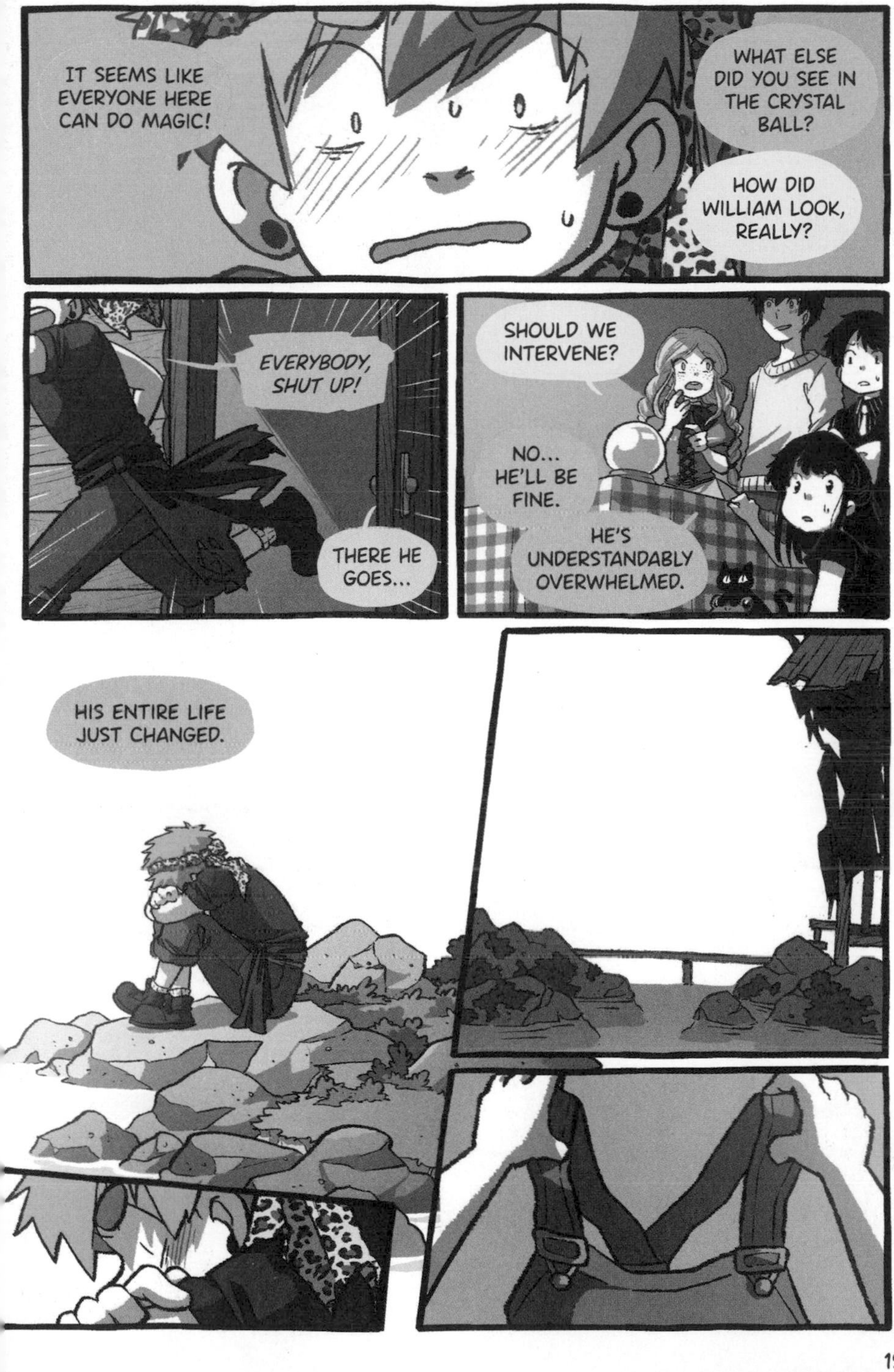
IT SEEMS LIKE EVERYONE HERE CAN DO MAGIC!
WHAT ELSE DID YOU SEE IN THE CRYSTAL BALL?
HOW DID WILLIAM LOOK, REALLY?
EVERYBODY, SHUT UP!
THERE HE GOES...
SHOULD WE INTERVENE?
NO... HE'LL BE FINE.
HE'S UNDERSTANDABLY OVERWHELMED.
HIS ENTIRE LIFE JUST CHANGED.

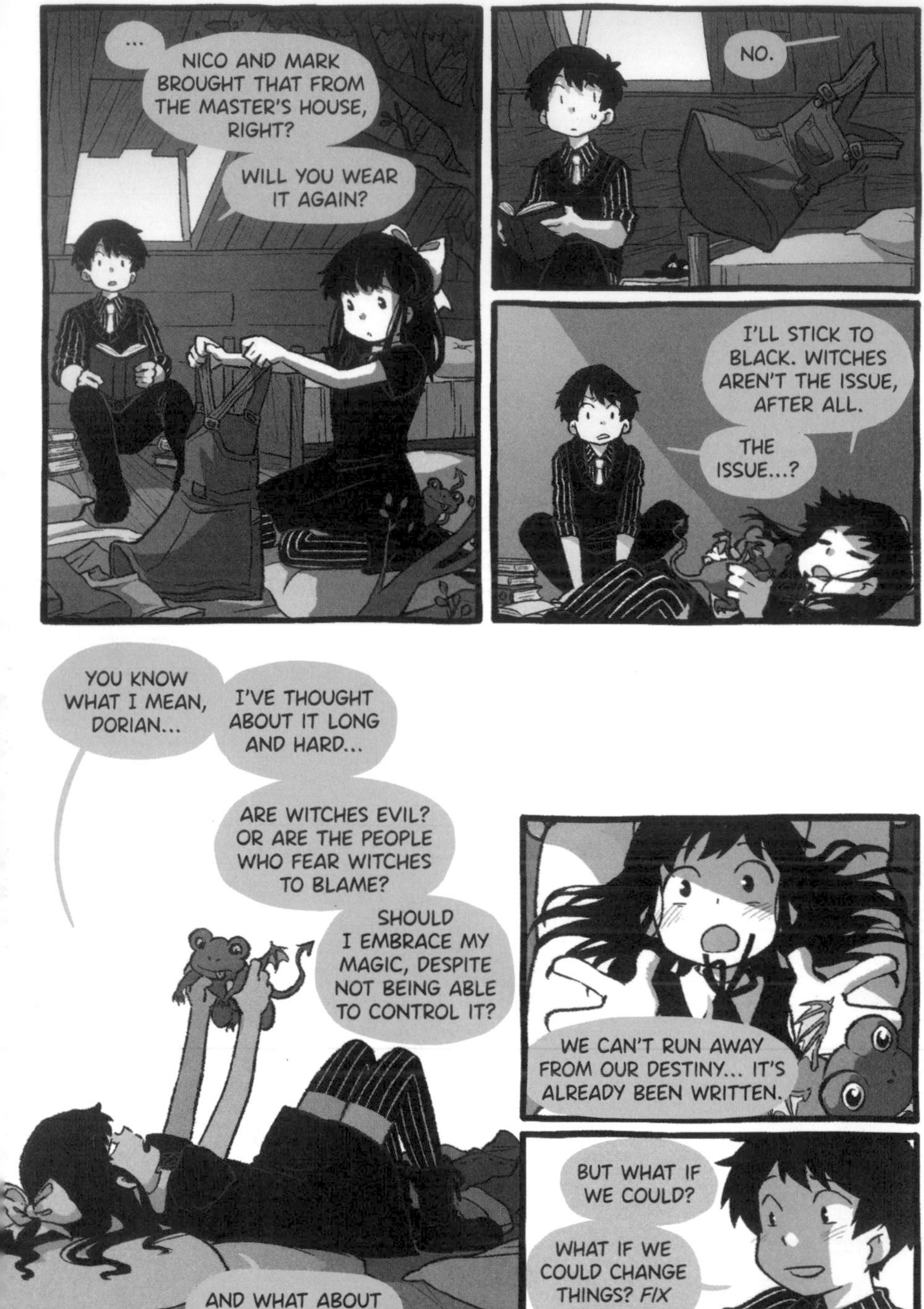
...
NICO AND MARK BROUGHT THAT FROM THE MASTER'S HOUSE, RIGHT?
WILL YOU WEAR IT AGAIN?
NO.
I'LL STICK TO BLACK. WITCHES AREN'T THE ISSUE, AFTER ALL.
THE ISSUE...?
YOU KNOW WHAT I MEAN, DORIAN...
I'VE THOUGHT ABOUT IT LONG AND HARD...
ARE WITCHES EVIL? OR ARE THE PEOPLE WHO FEAR WITCHES TO BLAME?
SHOULD I EMBRACE MY MAGIC, DESPITE NOT BEING ABLE TO CONTROL IT?
AND WHAT ABOUT THE PROPHECIES...?
WE CAN'T RUN AWAY FROM OUR DESTINY... IT'S ALREADY BEEN WRITTEN.
BUT WHAT IF WE COULD?
WHAT IF WE COULD CHANGE THINGS? *FIX* THINGS?

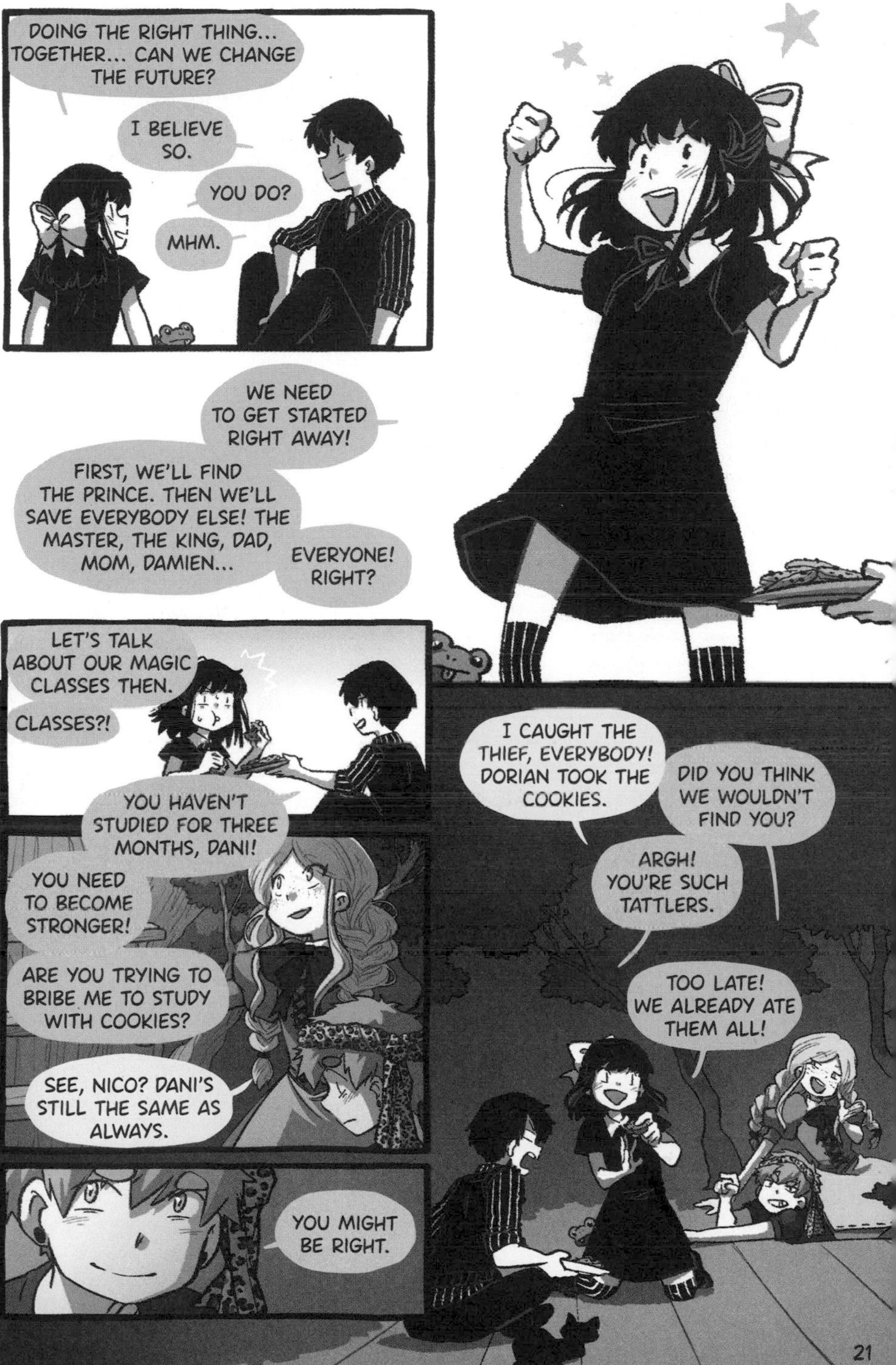
DOING THE RIGHT THING... TOGETHER... CAN WE CHANGE THE FUTURE?
I BELIEVE SO.
YOU DO?
MHM.
WE NEED TO GET STARTED RIGHT AWAY!
FIRST, WE'LL FIND THE PRINCE. THEN WE'LL SAVE EVERYBODY ELSE! THE MASTER, THE KING, DAD, MOM, DAMIEN...
EVERYONE! RIGHT?
LET'S TALK ABOUT OUR MAGIC CLASSES THEN.
CLASSES?!
YOU HAVEN'T STUDIED FOR THREE MONTHS, DANI!
YOU NEED TO BECOME STRONGER!
ARE YOU TRYING TO BRIBE ME TO STUDY WITH COOKIES?
SEE, NICO? DANI'S STILL THE SAME AS ALWAYS.
YOU MIGHT BE RIGHT.
I CAUGHT THE THIEF, EVERYBODY! DORIAN TOOK THE COOKIES.
DID YOU THINK WE WOULDN'T FIND YOU?
ARGH! YOU'RE SUCH TATTLERS.
TOO LATE! WE ALREADY ATE THEM ALL!

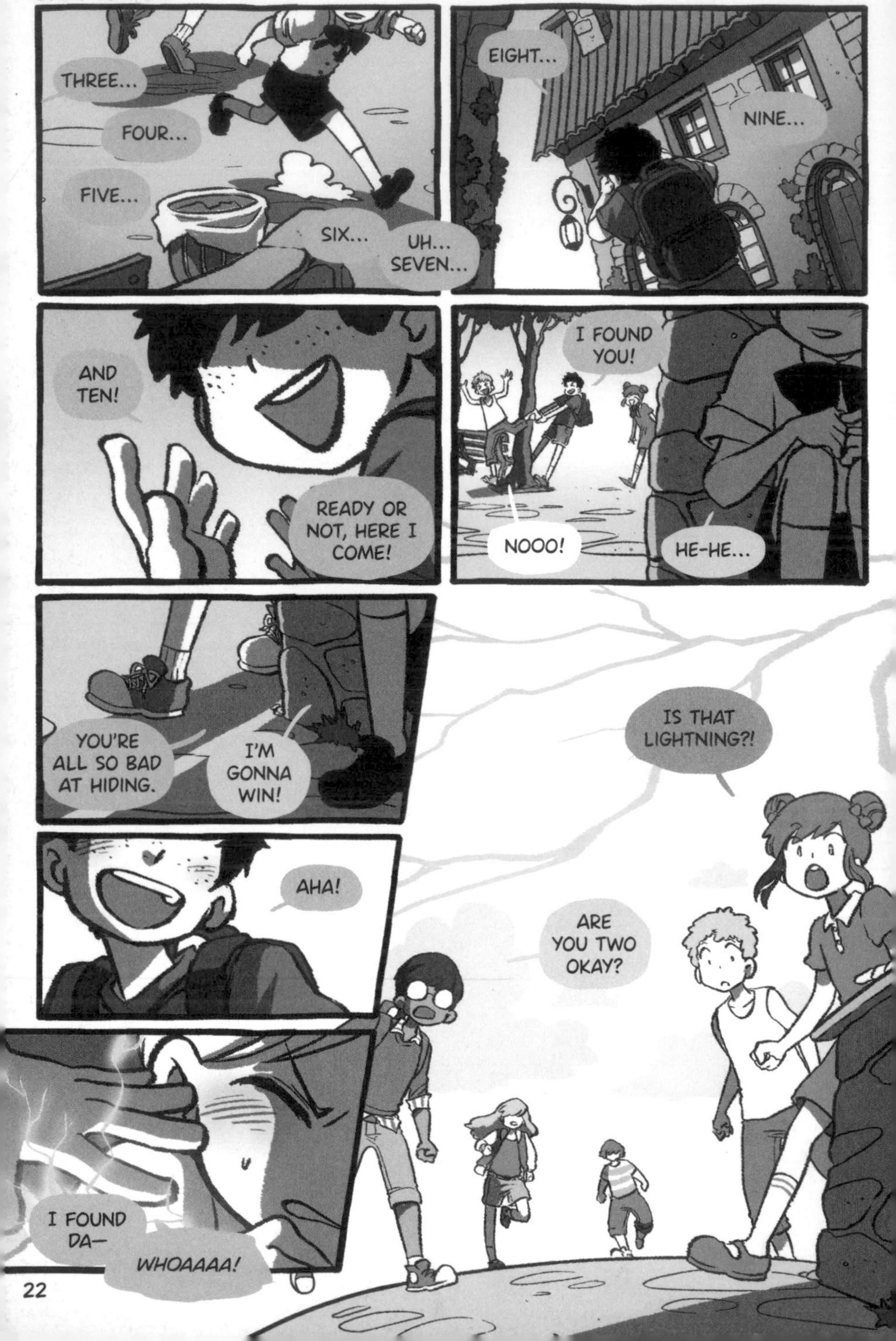
THREE...
FOUR...
FIVE...
SIX...
UH... SEVEN...
EIGHT...
NINE...
AND TEN!
READY OR NOT, HERE I COME!
I FOUND YOU!
NOOO!
HE-HE...
YOU'RE ALL SO BAD AT HIDING.
I'M GONNA WIN!
AHA!
I FOUND DA—
WHOAAAA!
IS THAT LIGHTNING?!
ARE YOU TWO OKAY?

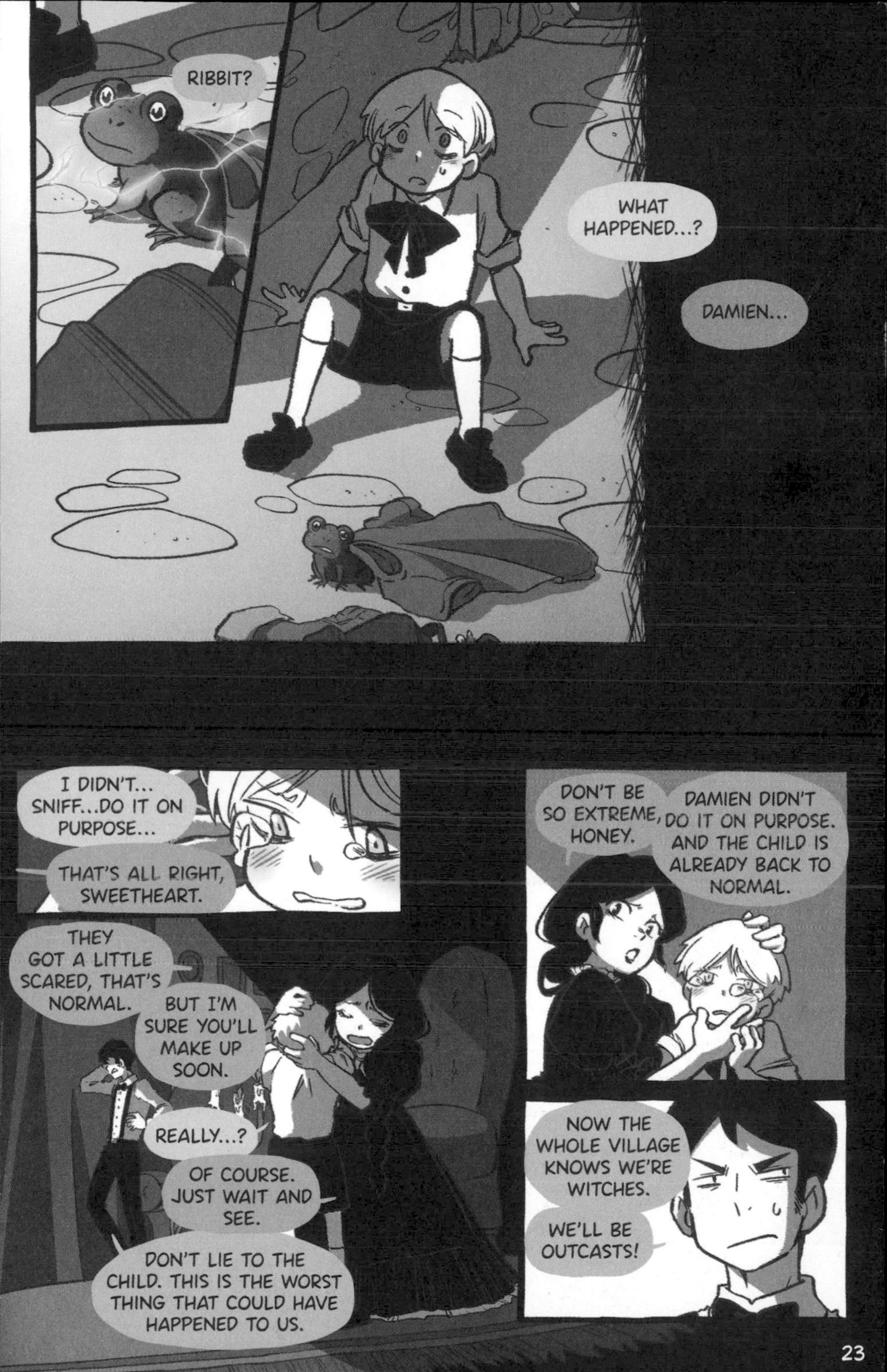
RIBBIT?
WHAT HAPPENED...?
DAMIEN...
I DIDN'T... SNIFF...DO IT ON PURPOSE...
THAT'S ALL RIGHT, SWEETHEART.
DON'T BE SO EXTREME, HONEY.
DAMIEN DIDN'T DO IT ON PURPOSE. AND THE CHILD IS ALREADY BACK TO NORMAL.
THEY GOT A LITTLE SCARED, THAT'S NORMAL.
BUT I'M SURE YOU'LL MAKE UP SOON.
REALLY...?
OF COURSE. JUST WAIT AND SEE.
DON'T LIE TO THE CHILD. THIS IS THE WORST THING THAT COULD HAVE HAPPENED TO US.
NOW THE WHOLE VILLAGE KNOWS WE'RE WITCHES.
WE'LL BE OUTCASTS!

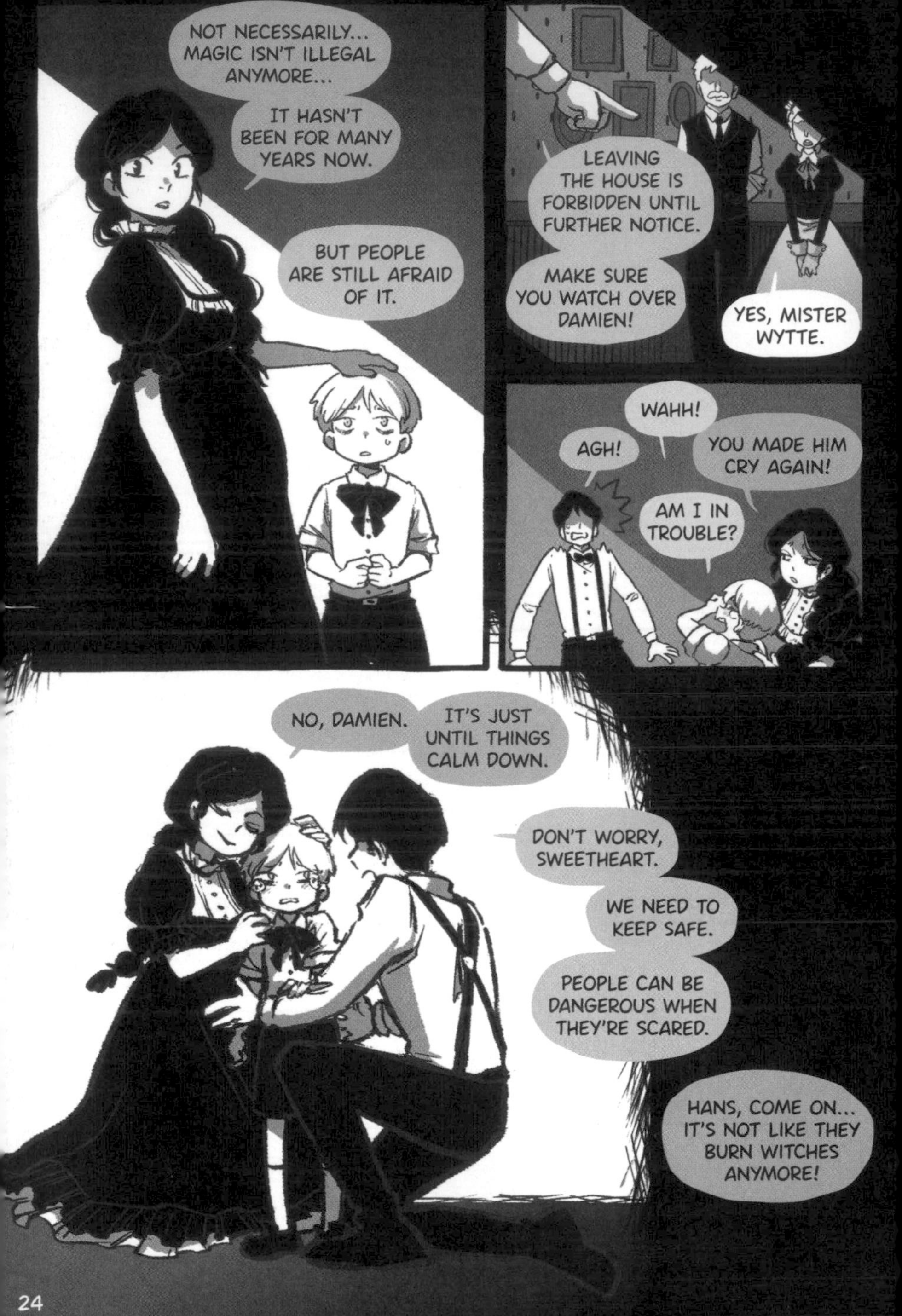
NOT NECESSARILY... MAGIC ISN'T ILLEGAL ANYMORE...
IT HASN'T BEEN FOR MANY YEARS NOW.
BUT PEOPLE ARE STILL AFRAID OF IT.
LEAVING THE HOUSE IS FORBIDDEN UNTIL FURTHER NOTICE.
MAKE SURE YOU WATCH OVER DAMIEN!
YES, MISTER WYTTE.
WAHH!
AGH!
YOU MADE HIM CRY AGAIN!
AM I IN TROUBLE?
NO, DAMIEN.
IT'S JUST UNTIL THINGS CALM DOWN.
DON'T WORRY, SWEETHEART.
WE NEED TO KEEP SAFE.
PEOPLE CAN BE DANGEROUS WHEN THEY'RE SCARED.
HANS, COME ON... IT'S NOT LIKE THEY BURN WITCHES ANYMORE!

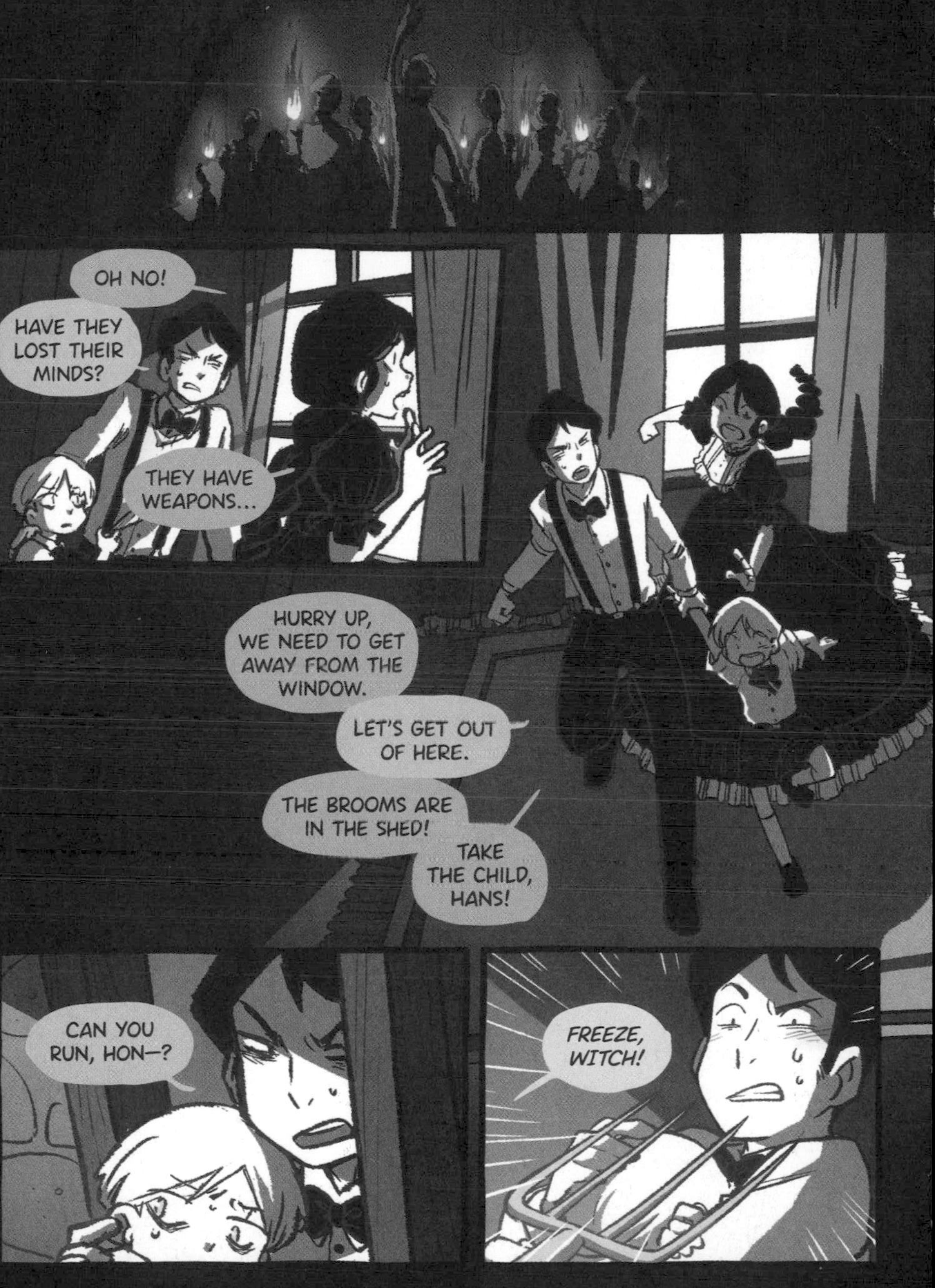
OH NO!
HAVE THEY LOST THEIR MINDS?
THEY HAVE WEAPONS...
HURRY UP, WE NEED TO GET AWAY FROM THE WINDOW.
LET'S GET OUT OF HERE.
THE BROOMS ARE IN THE SHED!
TAKE THE CHILD, HANS!
CAN YOU RUN, HON—?
FREEZE, WITCH!

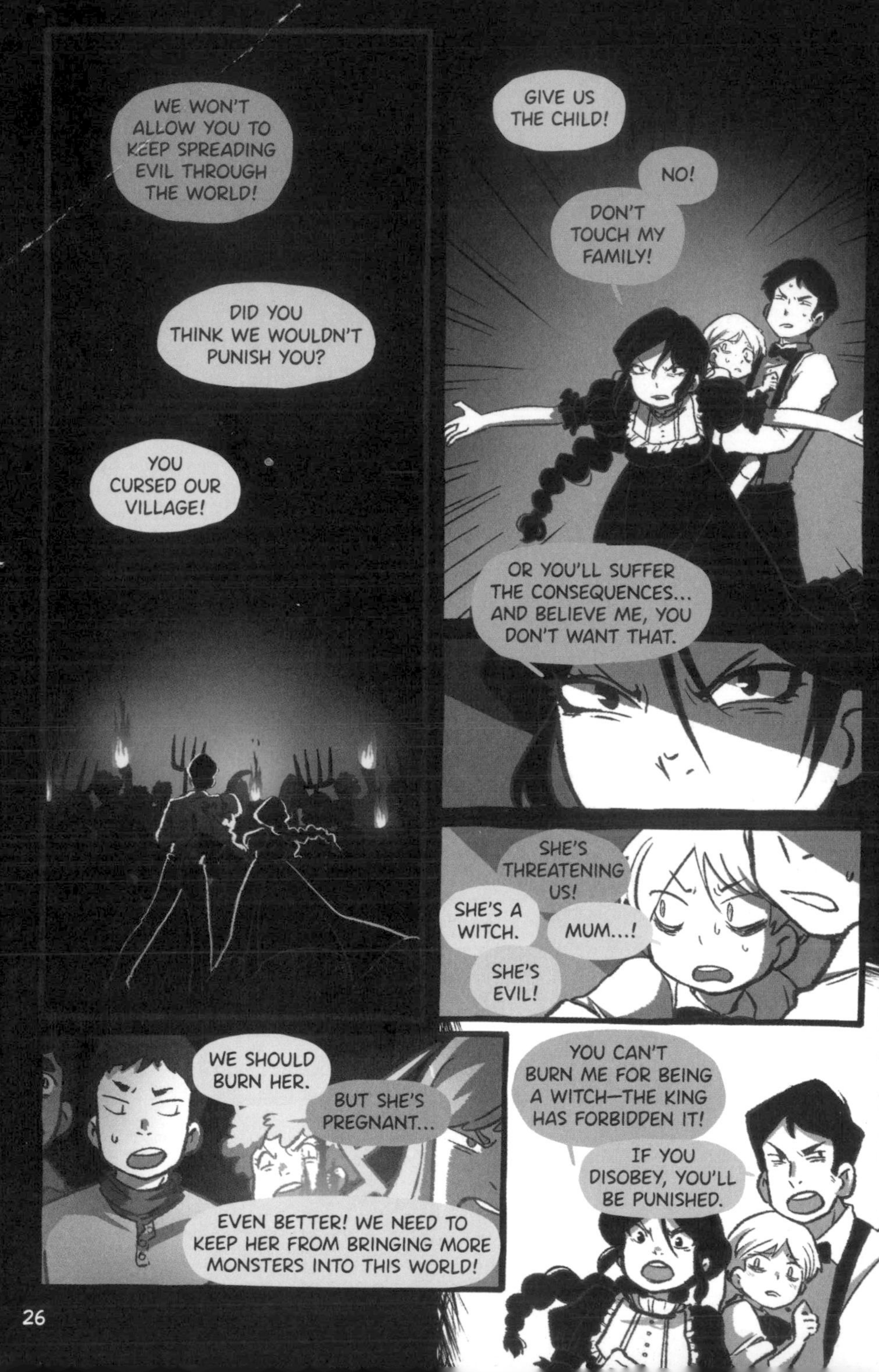
WE WON'T ALLOW YOU TO KEEP SPREADING EVIL THROUGH THE WORLD!
DID YOU THINK WE WOULDN'T PUNISH YOU?
YOU CURSED OUR VILLAGE!
GIVE US THE CHILD!
NO!
DON'T TOUCH MY FAMILY!
OR YOU'LL SUFFER THE CONSEQUENCES... AND BELIEVE ME, YOU DON'T WANT THAT.
SHE'S THREATENING US!
SHE'S A WITCH.
MUM...!
SHE'S EVIL!
WE SHOULD BURN HER.
BUT SHE'S PREGNANT...
EVEN BETTER! WE NEED TO KEEP HER FROM BRINGING MORE MONSTERS INTO THIS WORLD!
YOU CAN'T BURN ME FOR BEING A WITCH—THE KING HAS FORBIDDEN IT!
IF YOU DISOBEY, YOU'LL BE PUNISHED.

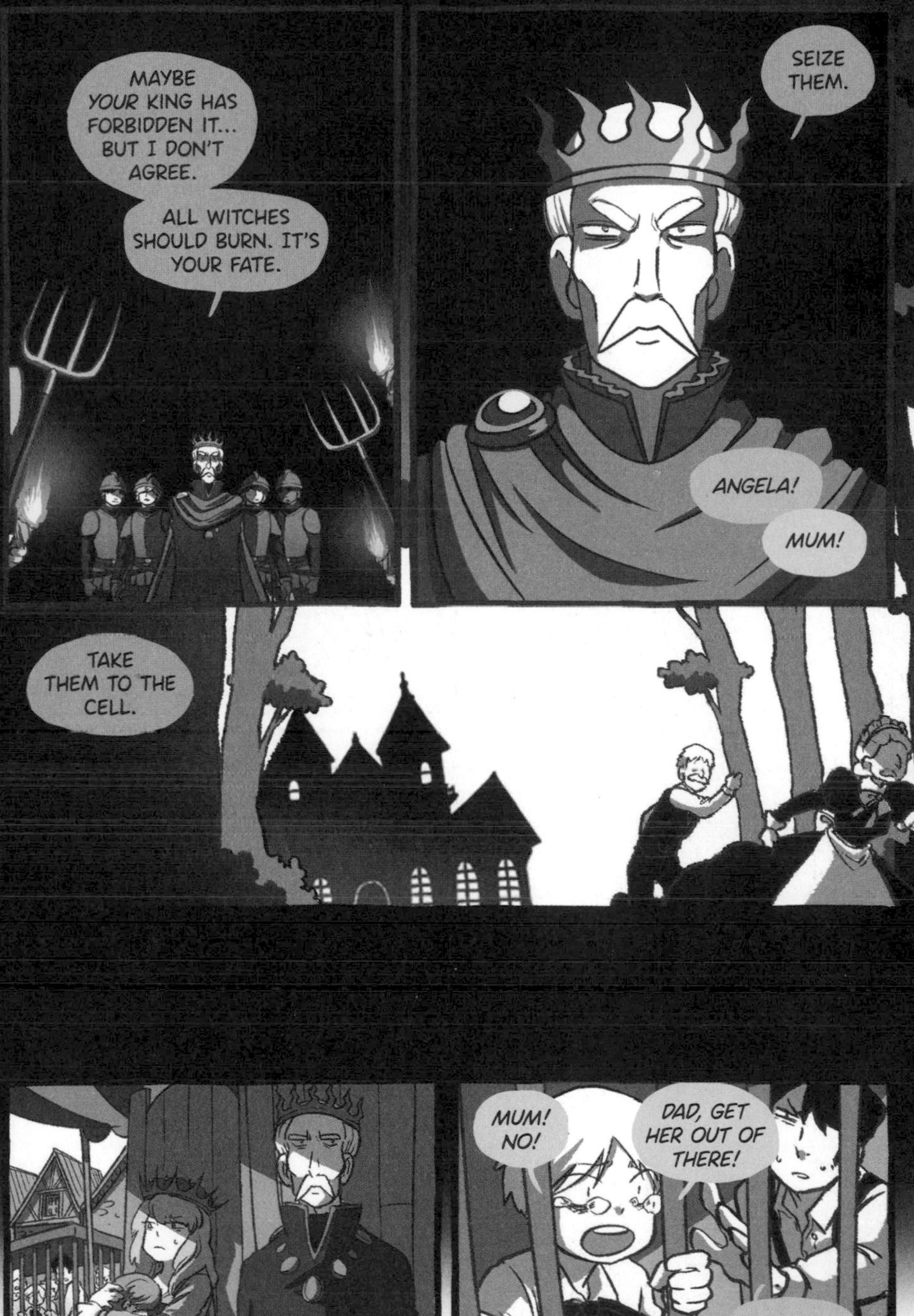
MAYBE YOUR KING HAS FORBIDDEN IT... BUT I DON'T AGREE.
ALL WITCHES SHOULD BURN. IT'S YOUR FATE.
SEIZE THEM.
ANGELA!
MUM!
TAKE THEM TO THE CELL.
MUM! NO!
DAD, GET HER OUT OF THERE!
DAMIEN...

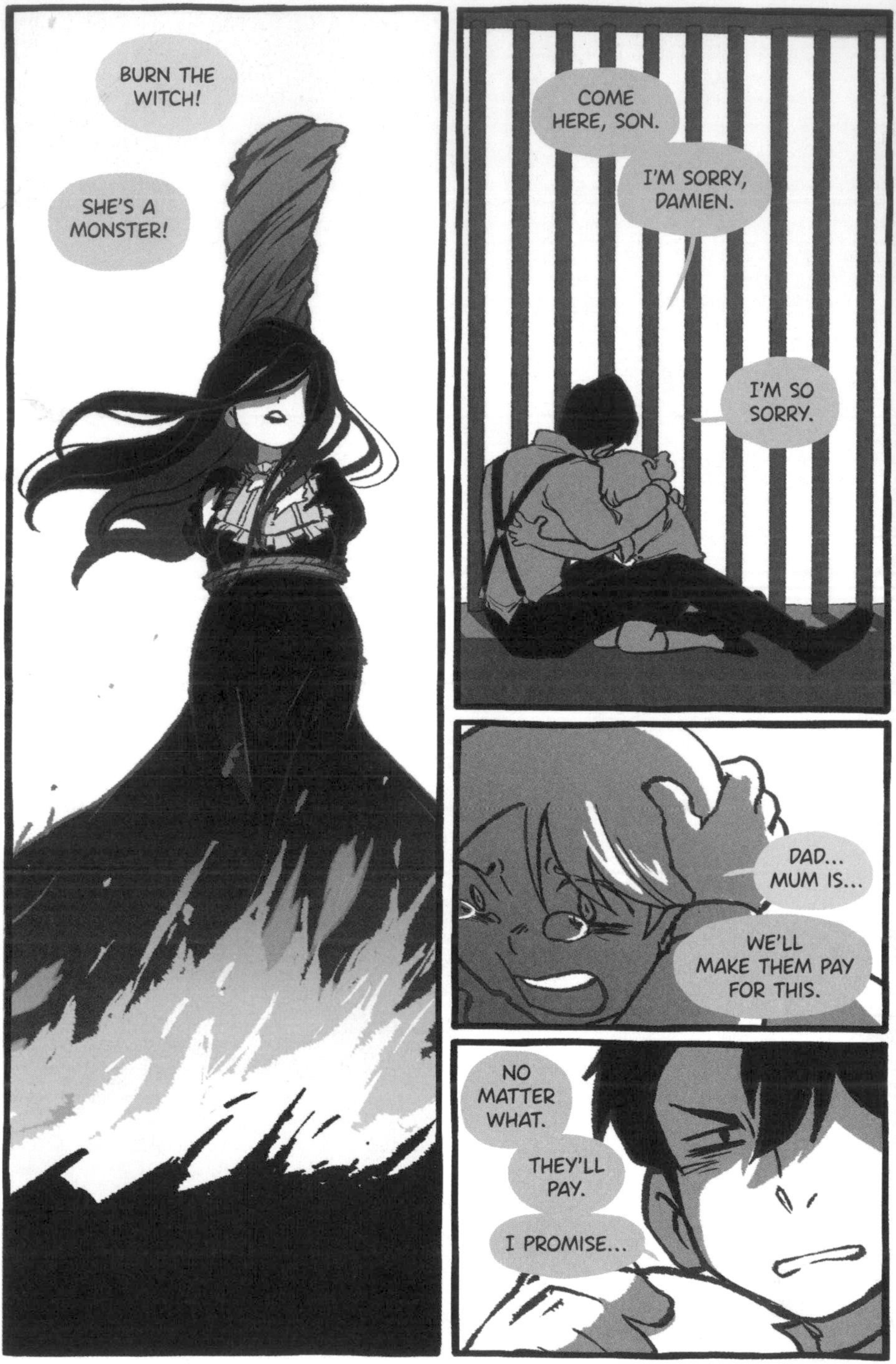
BURN THE WITCH!
SHE'S A MONSTER!
COME HERE, SON.
I'M SORRY, DAMIEN.
I'M SO SORRY.
DAD... MUM IS...
WE'LL MAKE THEM PAY FOR THIS.
NO MATTER WHAT.
THEY'LL PAY.
I PROMISE...

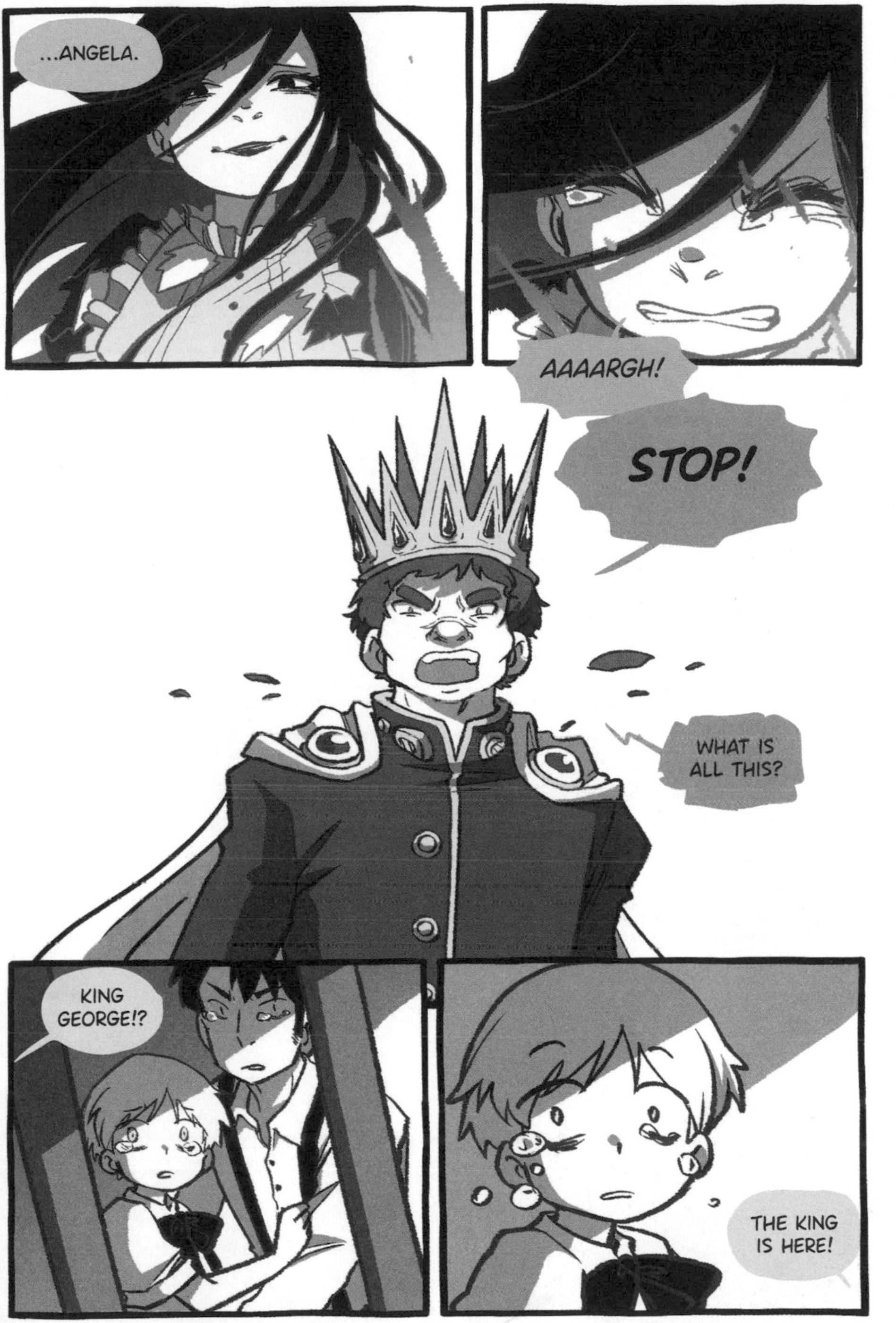
...ANGELA.
AAAARGH!
STOP!
WHAT IS ALL THIS?
KING GEORGE!?
THE KING IS HERE!

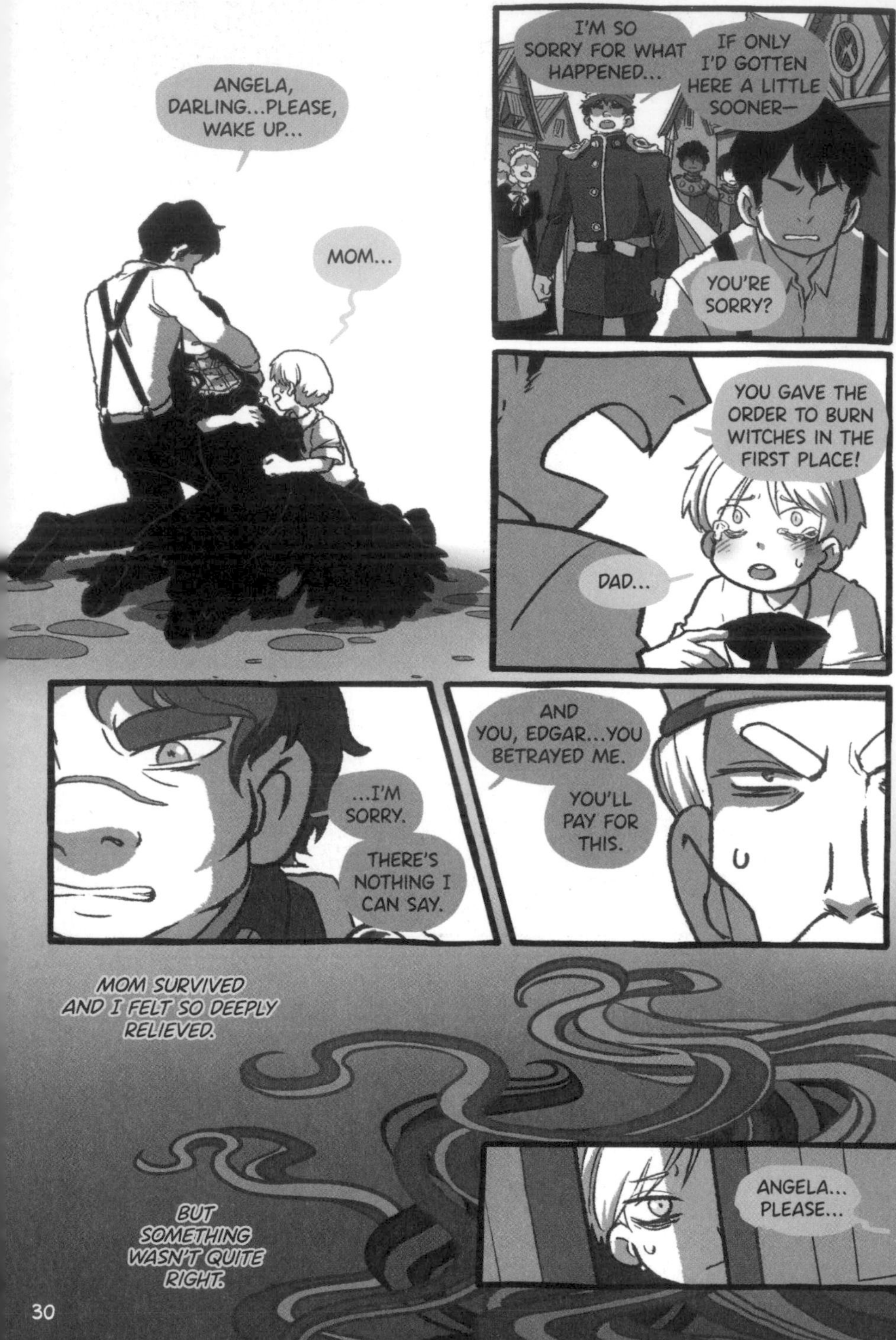
ANGELA, DARLING...PLEASE, WAKE UP...
MOM...
I'M SO SORRY FOR WHAT HAPPENED...
IF ONLY I'D GOTTEN HERE A LITTLE SOONER—
YOU'RE SORRY?
YOU GAVE THE ORDER TO BURN WITCHES IN THE FIRST PLACE!
DAD...
...I'M SORRY.
THERE'S NOTHING I CAN SAY.
AND YOU, EDGAR...YOU BETRAYED ME.
YOU'LL PAY FOR THIS.
MOM SURVIVED AND I FELT SO DEEPLY RELIEVED.
BUT SOMETHING WASN'T QUITE RIGHT.
ANGELA... PLEASE...

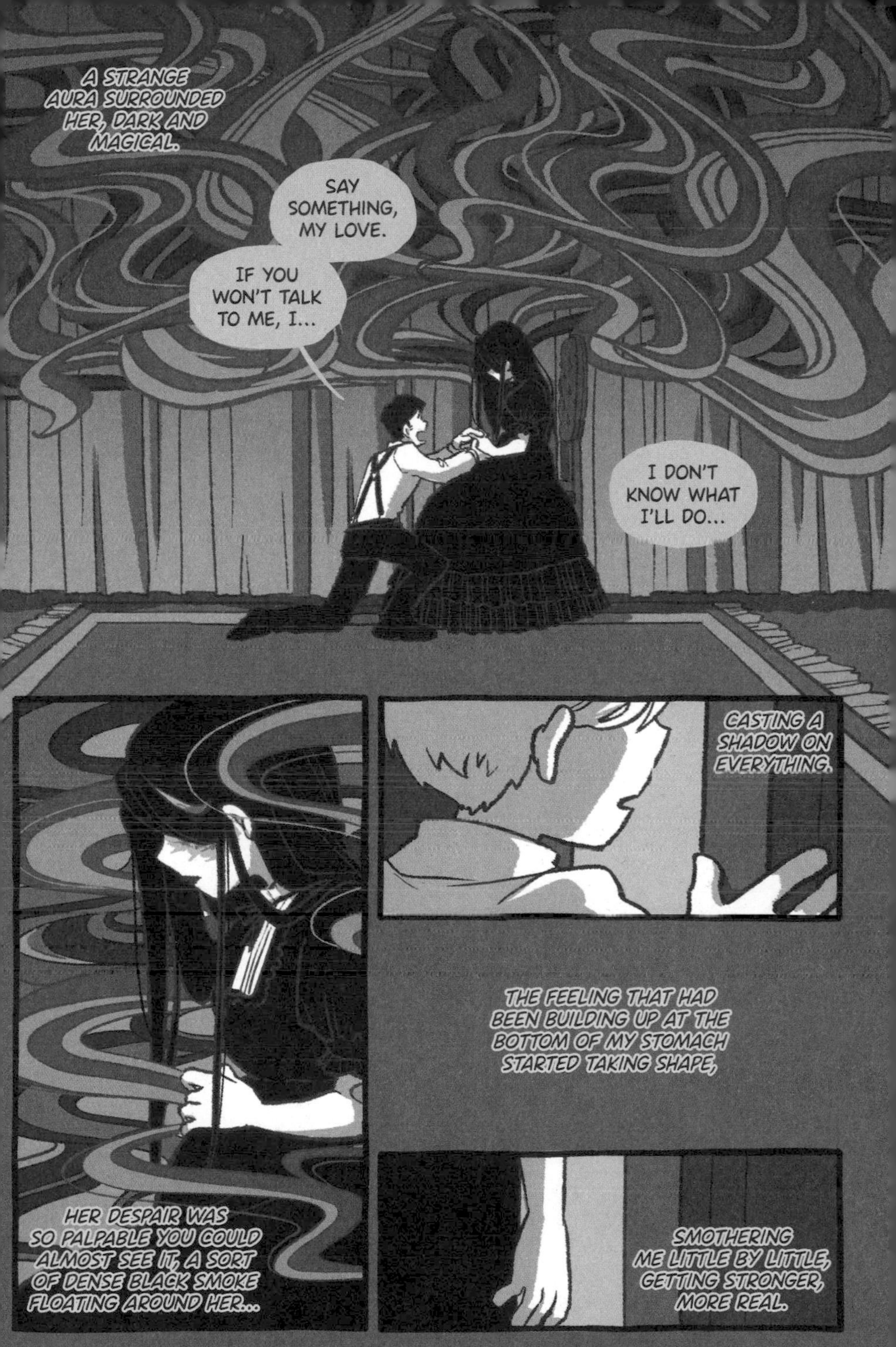
A STRANGE AURA SURROUNDED HER, DARK AND MAGICAL.
SAY SOMETHING, MY LOVE.
IF YOU WON'T TALK TO ME, I...
I DON'T KNOW WHAT I'LL DO...
HER DESPAIR WAS SO PALPABLE YOU COULD ALMOST SEE IT, A SORT OF DENSE BLACK SMOKE FLOATING AROUND HER...
CASTING A SHADOW ON EVERYTHING.
THE FEELING THAT HAD BEEN BUILDING UP AT THE BOTTOM OF MY STOMACH STARTED TAKING SHAPE,
SMOTHERING ME LITTLE BY LITTLE, GETTING STRONGER, MORE REAL.

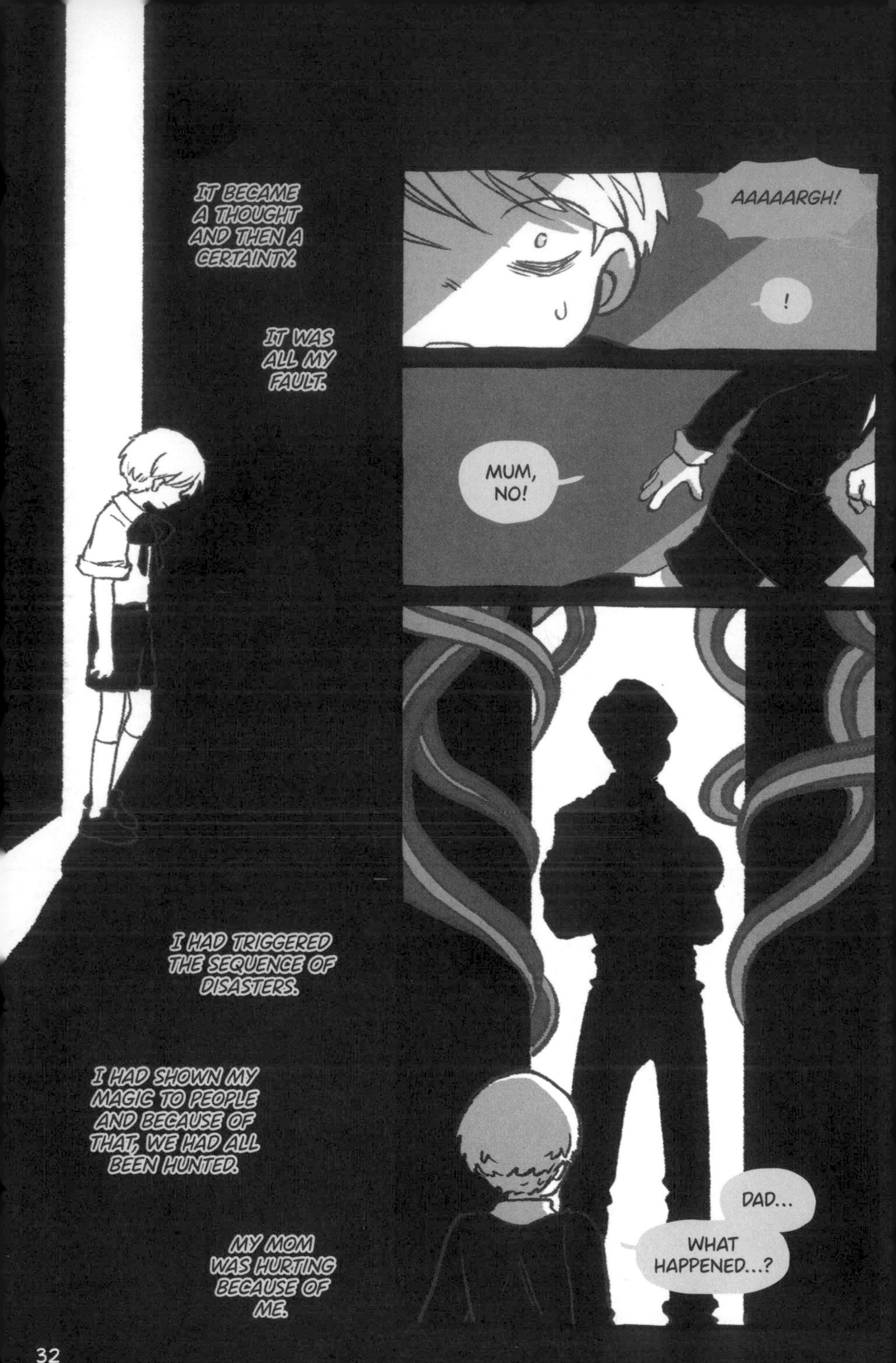
IT BECAME A THOUGHT AND THEN A CERTAINTY.
AAAAARGH!
!
IT WAS ALL MY FAULT.
MUM, NO!
I HAD TRIGGERED THE SEQUENCE OF DISASTERS.
I HAD SHOWN MY MAGIC TO PEOPLE AND BECAUSE OF THAT, WE HAD ALL BEEN HUNTED.
MY MOM WAS HURTING BECAUSE OF ME.
DAD...
WHAT HAPPENED...?

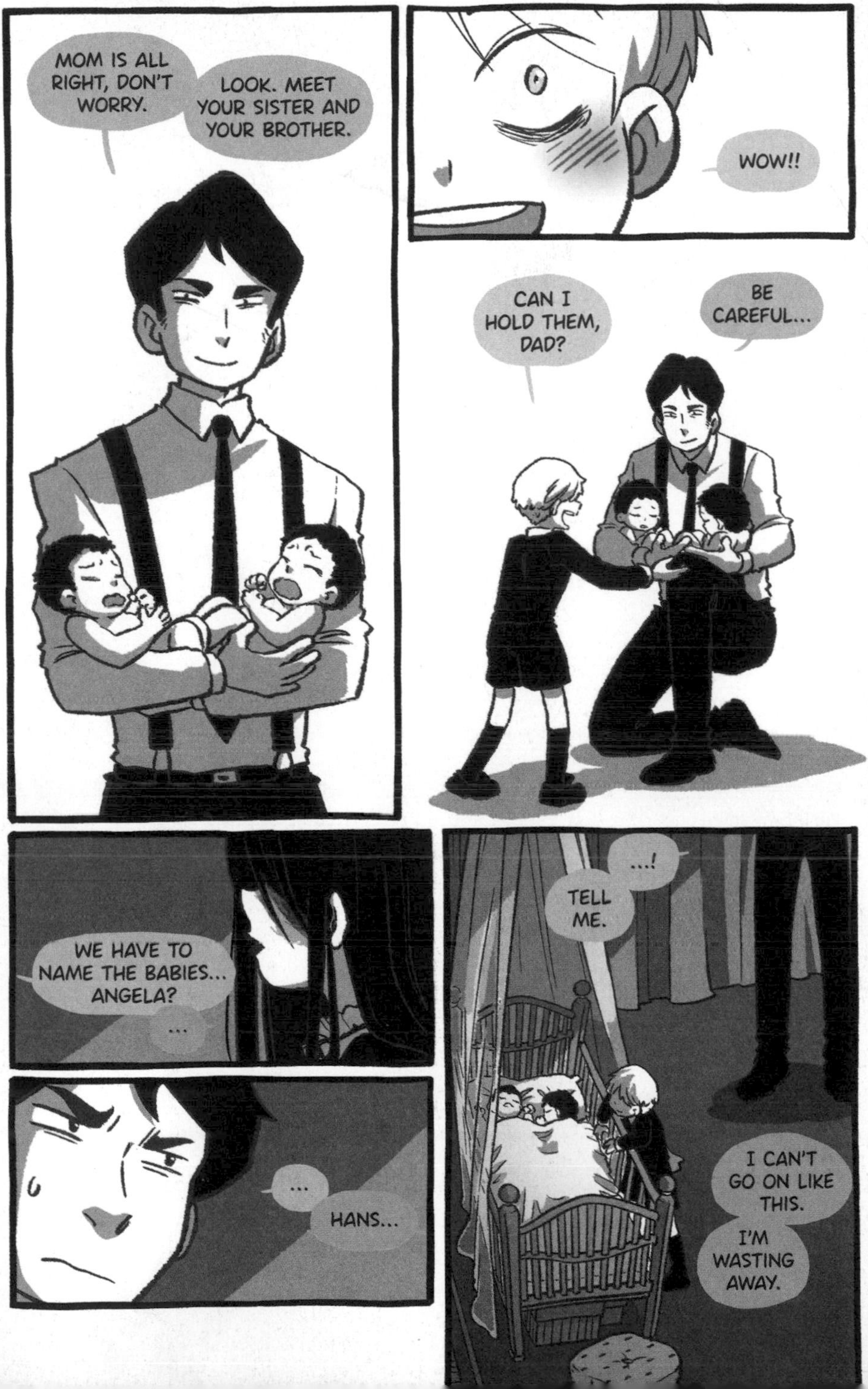
MOM IS ALL RIGHT, DON'T WORRY.
LOOK. MEET YOUR SISTER AND YOUR BROTHER.
WOW!!
CAN I HOLD THEM, DAD?
BE CAREFUL...
WE HAVE TO NAME THE BABIES... ANGELA?
...
...
HANS...
...!
TELL ME.
I CAN'T GO ON LIKE THIS.
I'M WASTING AWAY.

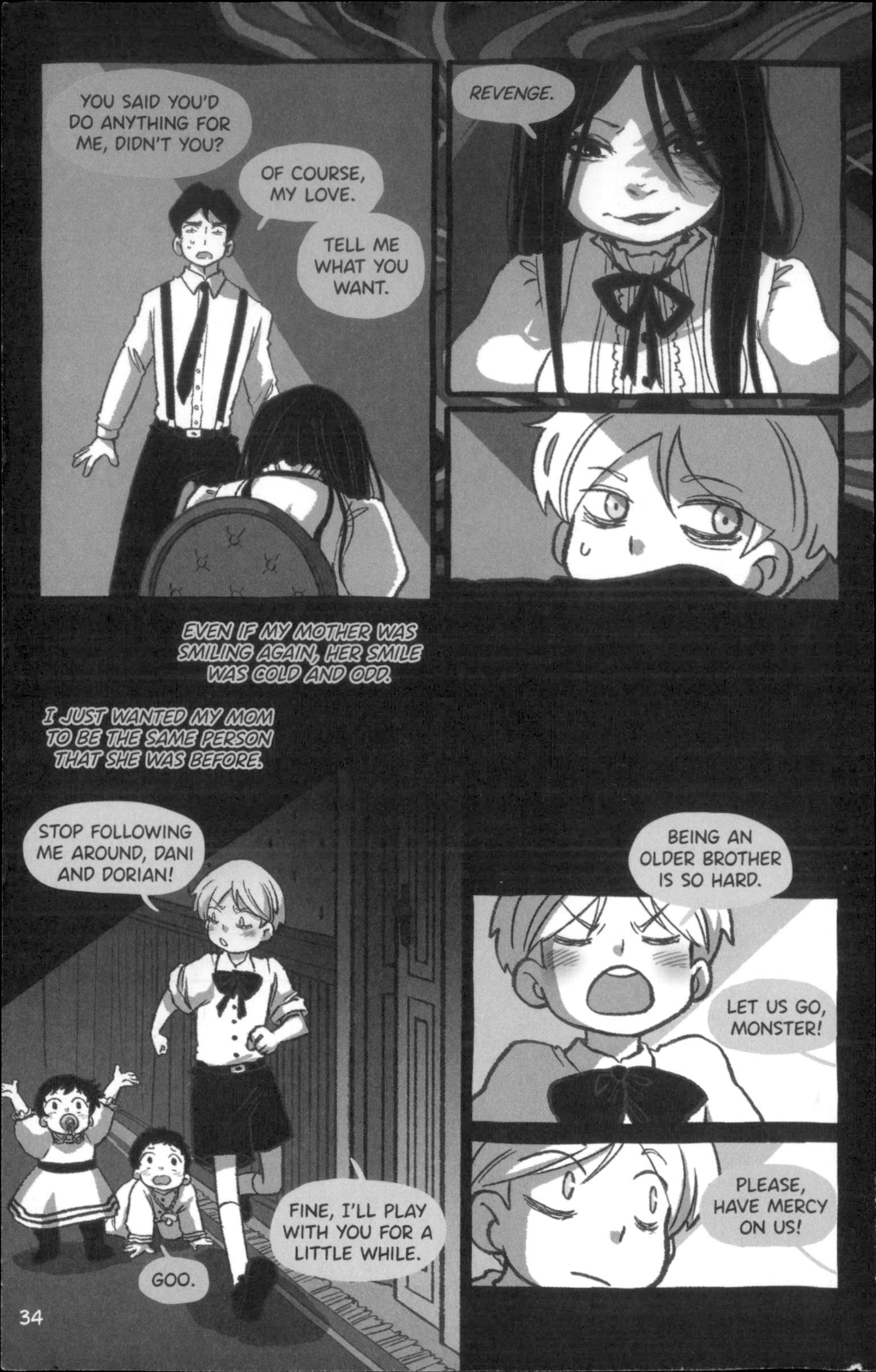
YOU SAID YOU'D DO ANYTHING FOR ME, DIDN'T YOU?
OF COURSE, MY LOVE.
TELL ME WHAT YOU WANT.
REVENGE.
EVEN IF MY MOTHER WAS SMILING AGAIN, HER SMILE WAS COLD AND ODD.
I JUST WANTED MY MOM TO BE THE SAME PERSON THAT SHE WAS BEFORE.
STOP FOLLOWING ME AROUND, DANI AND DORIAN!
GOO.
FINE, I'LL PLAY WITH YOU FOR A LITTLE WHILE.
BEING AN OLDER BROTHER IS SO HARD.
LET US GO, MONSTER!
PLEASE, HAVE MERCY ON US!

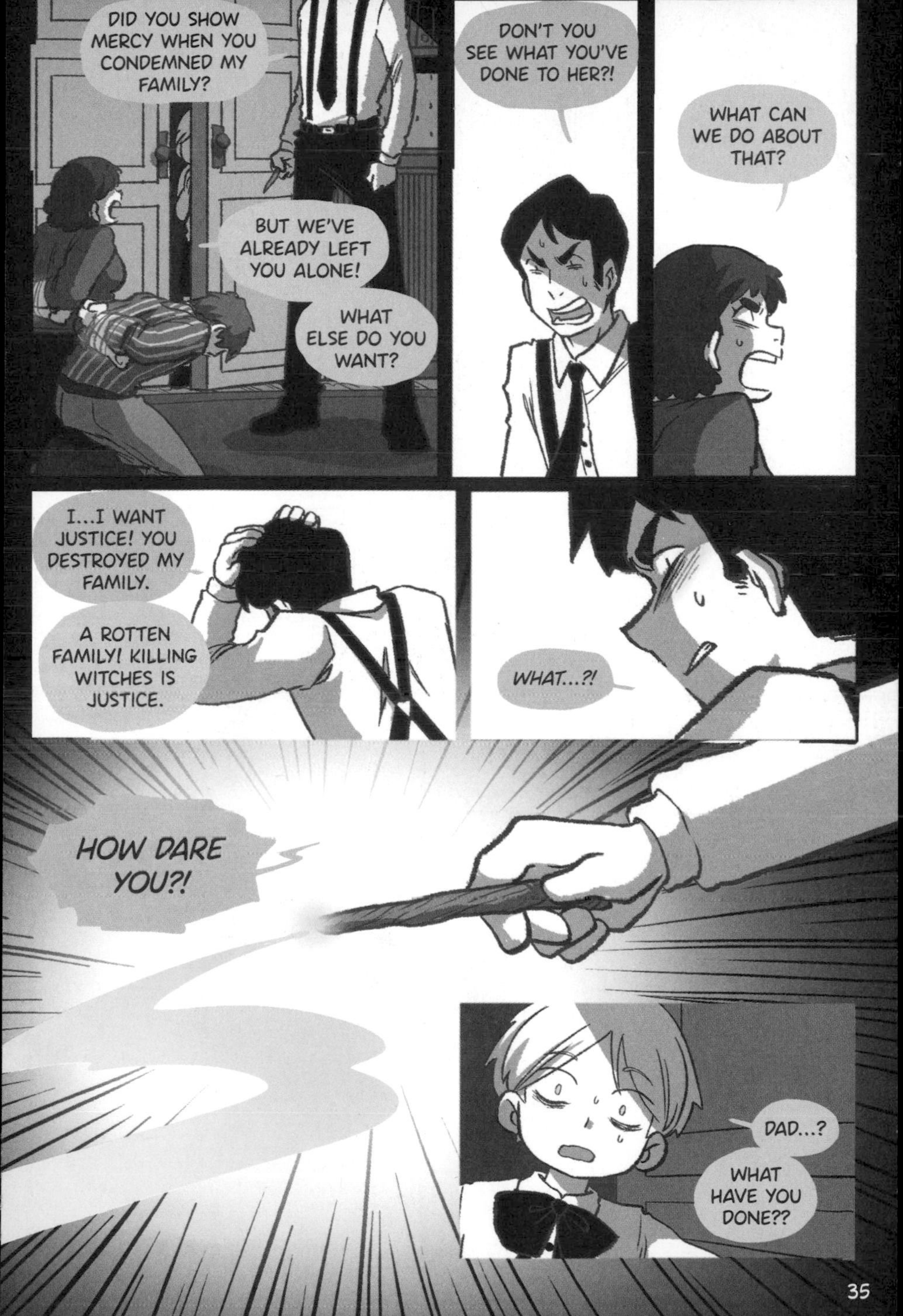
DID YOU SHOW MERCY WHEN YOU CONDEMNED MY FAMILY?
BUT WE'VE ALREADY LEFT YOU ALONE!
WHAT ELSE DO YOU WANT?
DON'T YOU SEE WHAT YOU'VE DONE TO HER?!
WHAT CAN WE DO ABOUT THAT?
I...I WANT JUSTICE! YOU DESTROYED MY FAMILY.
A ROTTEN FAMILY! KILLING WITCHES IS JUSTICE.
WHAT...?!
HOW DARE YOU?!
DAD...?
WHAT HAVE YOU DONE??

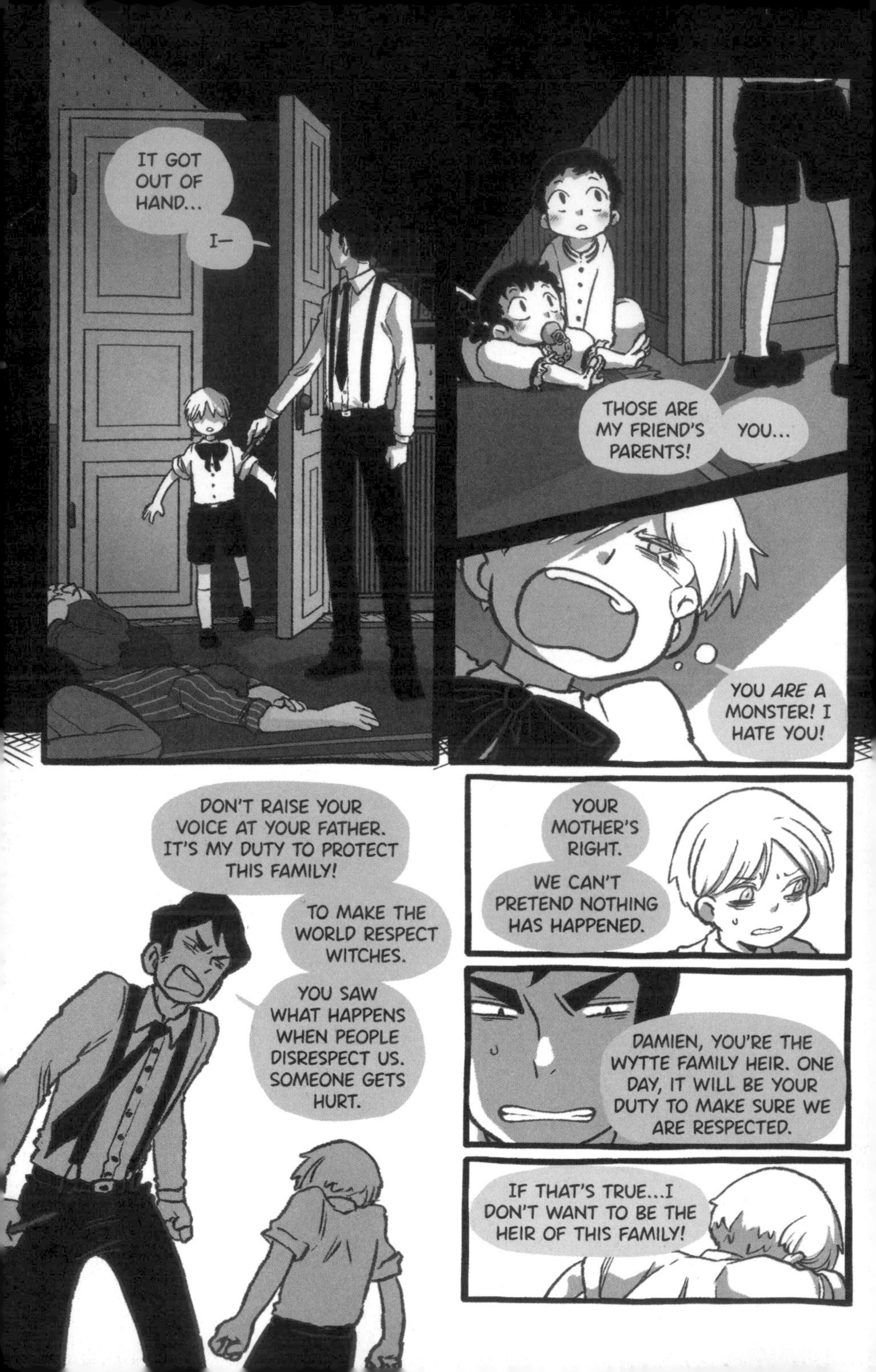
IT GOT OUT OF HAND...
I—
THOSE ARE MY FRIEND'S PARENTS!
YOU...
YOU *ARE* A MONSTER! I HATE YOU!
DON'T RAISE YOUR VOICE AT YOUR FATHER. IT'S MY DUTY TO PROTECT THIS FAMILY!
TO MAKE THE WORLD RESPECT WITCHES.
YOU SAW WHAT HAPPENS WHEN PEOPLE DISRESPECT US. SOMEONE GETS HURT.
YOUR MOTHER'S RIGHT.
WE CAN'T PRETEND NOTHING HAS HAPPENED.
DAMIEN, YOU'RE THE WYTTE FAMILY HEIR. ONE DAY, IT WILL BE YOUR DUTY TO MAKE SURE WE ARE RESPECTED.
IF THAT'S TRUE...I DON'T WANT TO BE THE HEIR OF THIS FAMILY!

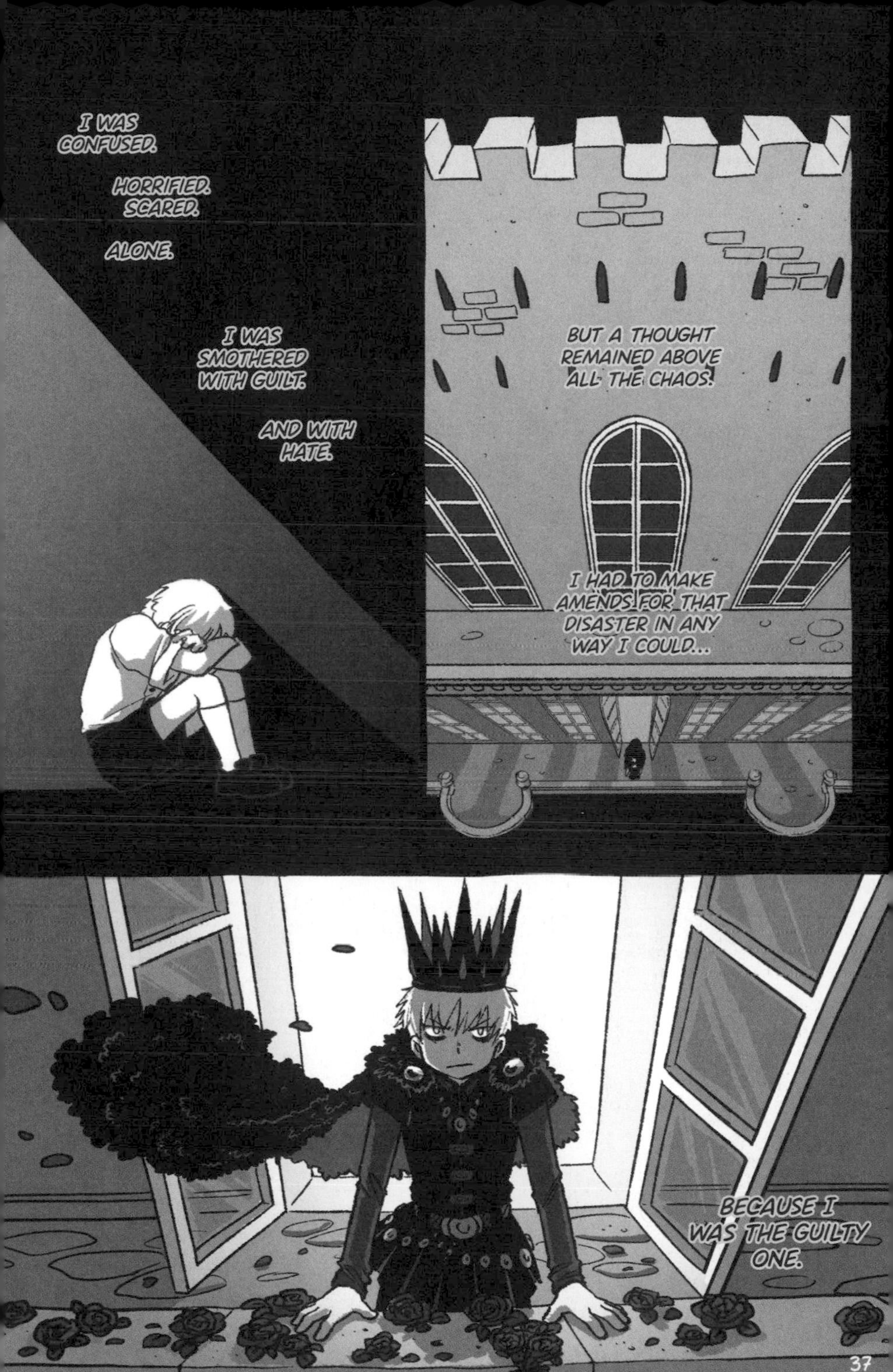
I WAS CONFUSED.
HORRIFIED. SCARED.
ALONE.
I WAS SMOTHERED WITH GUILT.
AND WITH HATE.
BUT A THOUGHT REMAINED ABOVE ALL THE CHAOS.
I HAD TO MAKE AMENDS FOR THAT DISASTER IN ANY WAY I COULD...
BECAUSE I WAS THE GUILTY ONE.

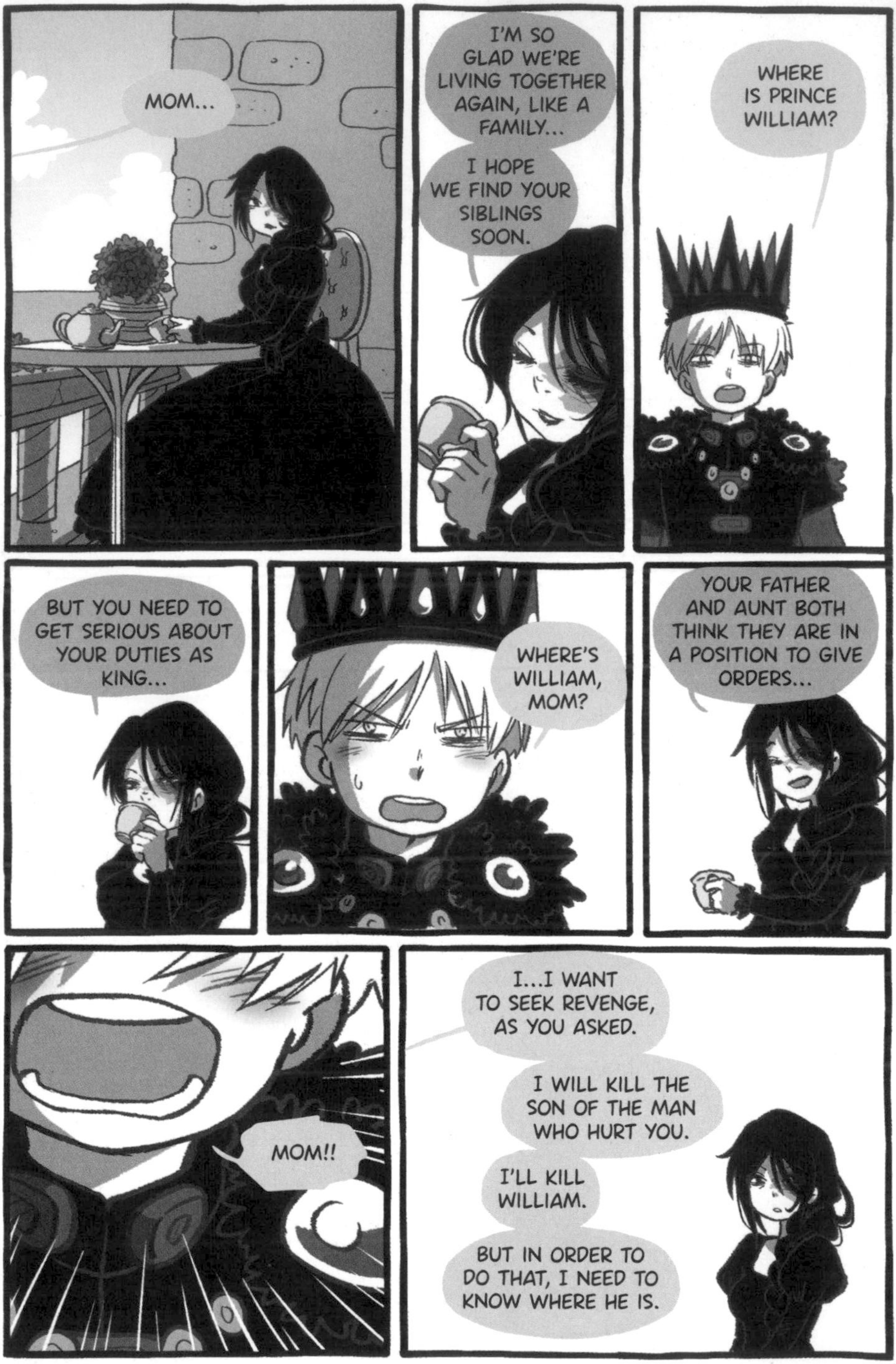
MOM...
I'M SO GLAD WE'RE LIVING TOGETHER AGAIN, LIKE A FAMILY...
I HOPE WE FIND YOUR SIBLINGS SOON.
WHERE IS PRINCE WILLIAM?
BUT YOU NEED TO GET SERIOUS ABOUT YOUR DUTIES AS KING...
WHERE'S WILLIAM, MOM?
YOUR FATHER AND AUNT BOTH THINK THEY ARE IN A POSITION TO GIVE ORDERS...
MOM!!
I...I WANT TO SEEK REVENGE, AS YOU ASKED.
I WILL KILL THE SON OF THE MAN WHO HURT YOU.
I'LL KILL WILLIAM.
BUT IN ORDER TO DO THAT, I NEED TO KNOW WHERE HE IS.

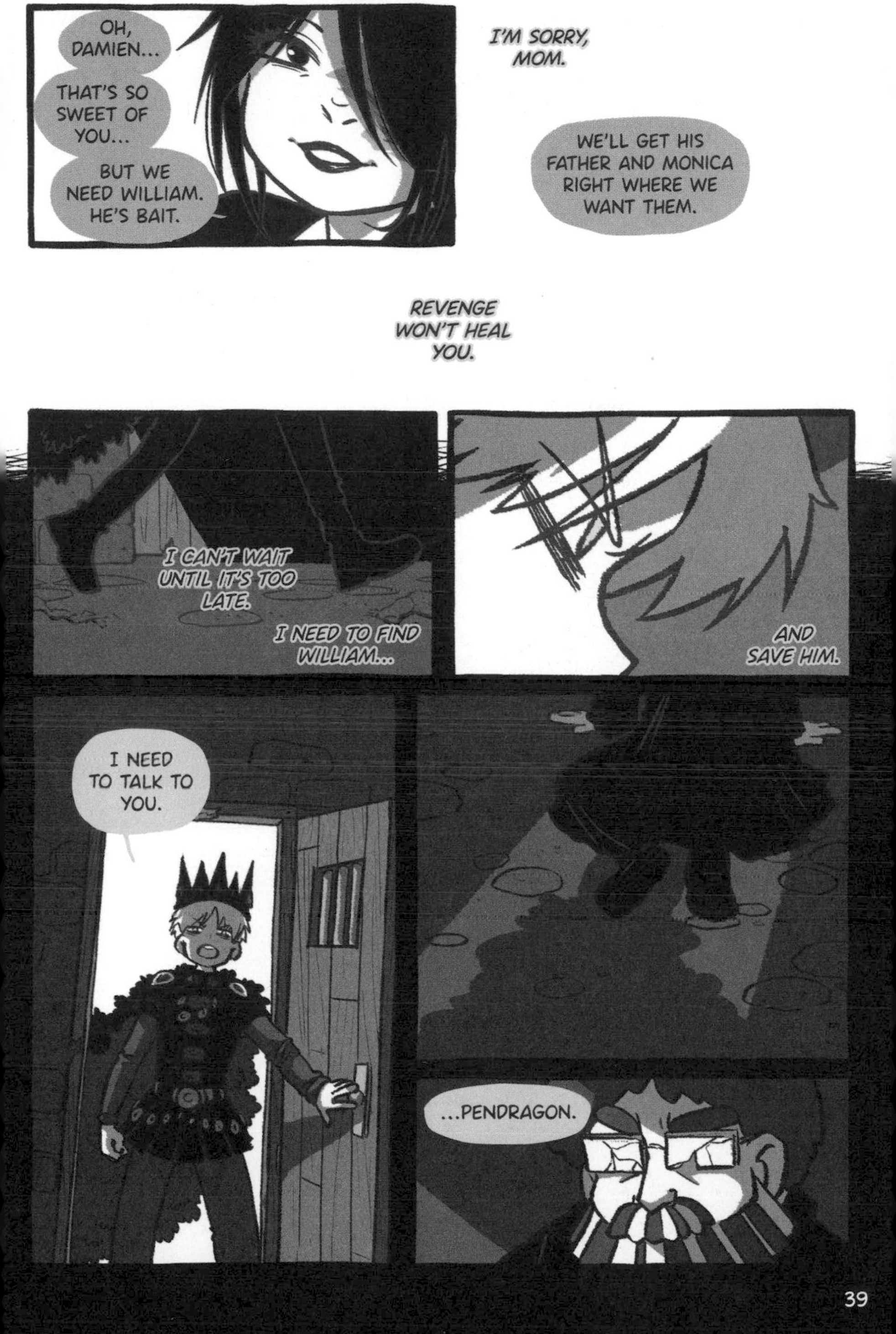

OH, DAMIEN...
THAT'S SO SWEET OF YOU...
BUT WE NEED WILLIAM. HE'S BAIT.
I'M SORRY, MOM.
WE'LL GET HIS FATHER AND MONICA RIGHT WHERE WE WANT THEM.
REVENGE WON'T HEAL YOU.
I CAN'T WAIT UNTIL IT'S TOO LATE.
I NEED TO FIND WILLIAM...
AND SAVE HIM.
I NEED TO TALK TO YOU.
...PENDRAGON.

CHAPTER 35

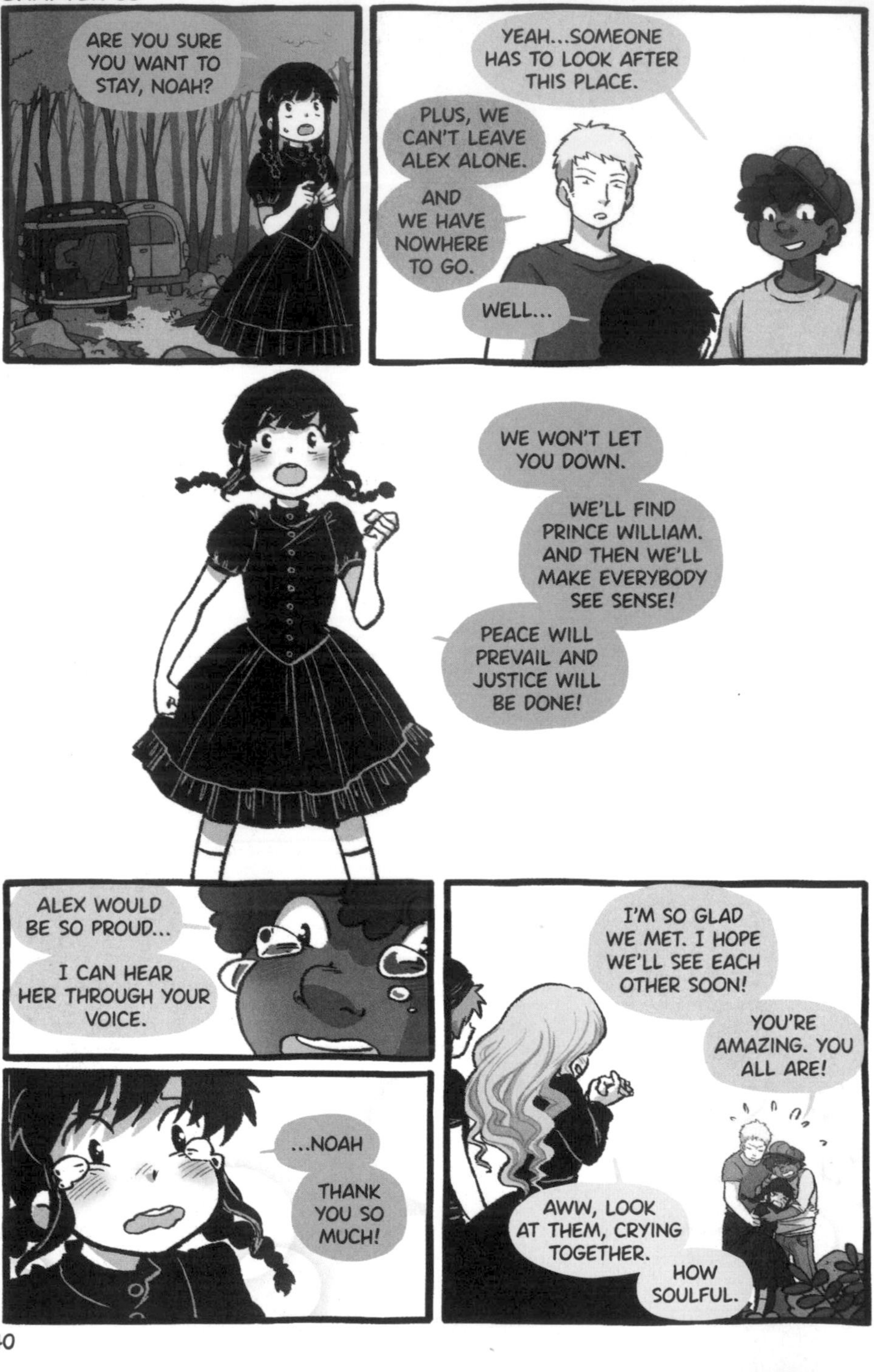
ARE YOU SURE YOU WANT TO STAY, NOAH?
YEAH...SOMEONE HAS TO LOOK AFTER THIS PLACE.
PLUS, WE CAN'T LEAVE ALEX ALONE.
AND WE HAVE NOWHERE TO GO.
WELL...
WE WON'T LET YOU DOWN.
WE'LL FIND PRINCE WILLIAM. AND THEN WE'LL MAKE EVERYBODY SEE SENSE!
PEACE WILL PREVAIL AND JUSTICE WILL BE DONE!
ALEX WOULD BE SO PROUD...
I CAN HEAR HER THROUGH YOUR VOICE.
...NOAH
THANK YOU SO MUCH!
I'M SO GLAD WE MET. I HOPE WE'LL SEE EACH OTHER SOON!
YOU'RE AMAZING. YOU ALL ARE!
AWW, LOOK AT THEM, CRYING TOGETHER.
HOW SOULFUL.

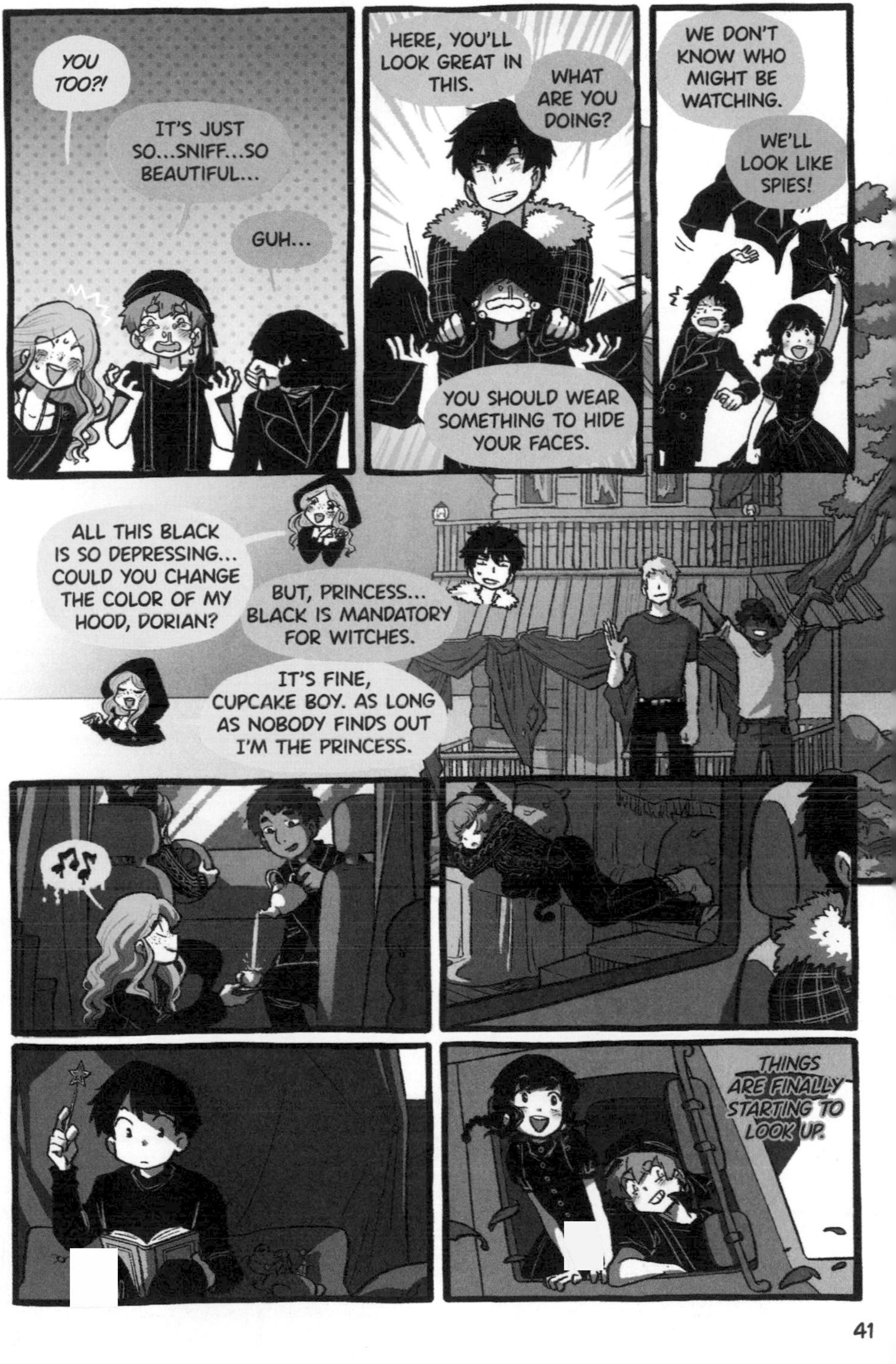
YOU TOO?!
IT'S JUST SO...SNIFF...SO BEAUTIFUL...
GUH...
HERE, YOU'LL LOOK GREAT IN THIS.
WHAT ARE YOU DOING?
YOU SHOULD WEAR SOMETHING TO HIDE YOUR FACES.
WE DON'T KNOW WHO MIGHT BE WATCHING.
WE'LL LOOK LIKE SPIES!
ALL THIS BLACK IS SO DEPRESSING... COULD YOU CHANGE THE COLOR OF MY HOOD, DORIAN?
BUT, PRINCESS... BLACK IS MANDATORY FOR WITCHES.
IT'S FINE, CUPCAKE BOY. AS LONG AS NOBODY FINDS OUT I'M THE PRINCESS.
THINGS ARE FINALLY STARTING TO LOOK UP.

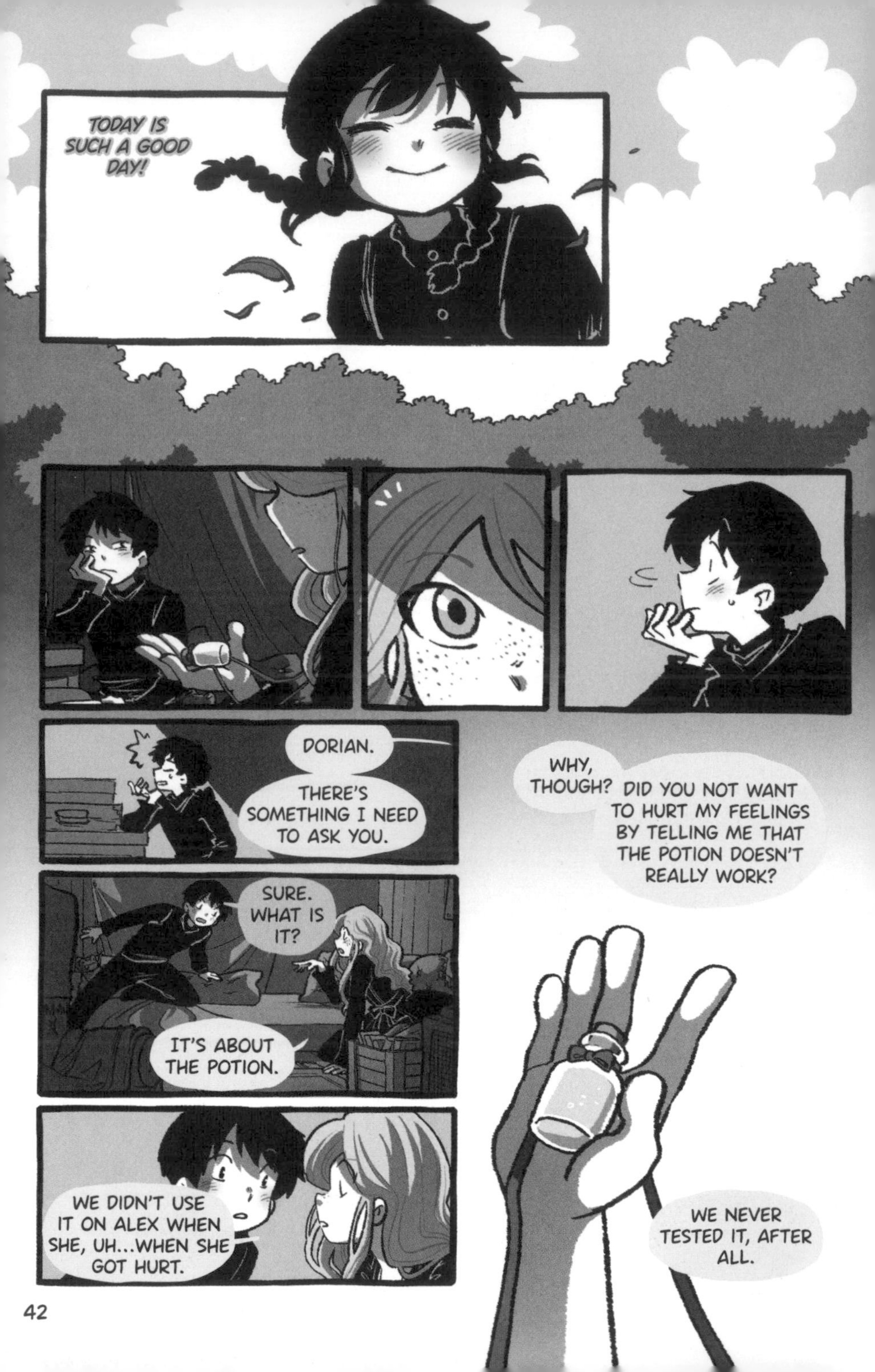
TODAY IS SUCH A GOOD DAY!
DORIAN.
THERE'S SOMETHING I NEED TO ASK YOU.
SURE. WHAT IS IT?
IT'S ABOUT THE POTION.
WE DIDN'T USE IT ON ALEX WHEN SHE, UH...WHEN SHE GOT HURT.
WHY, THOUGH?
DID YOU NOT WANT TO HURT MY FEELINGS BY TELLING ME THAT THE POTION DOESN'T REALLY WORK?
WE NEVER TESTED IT, AFTER ALL.

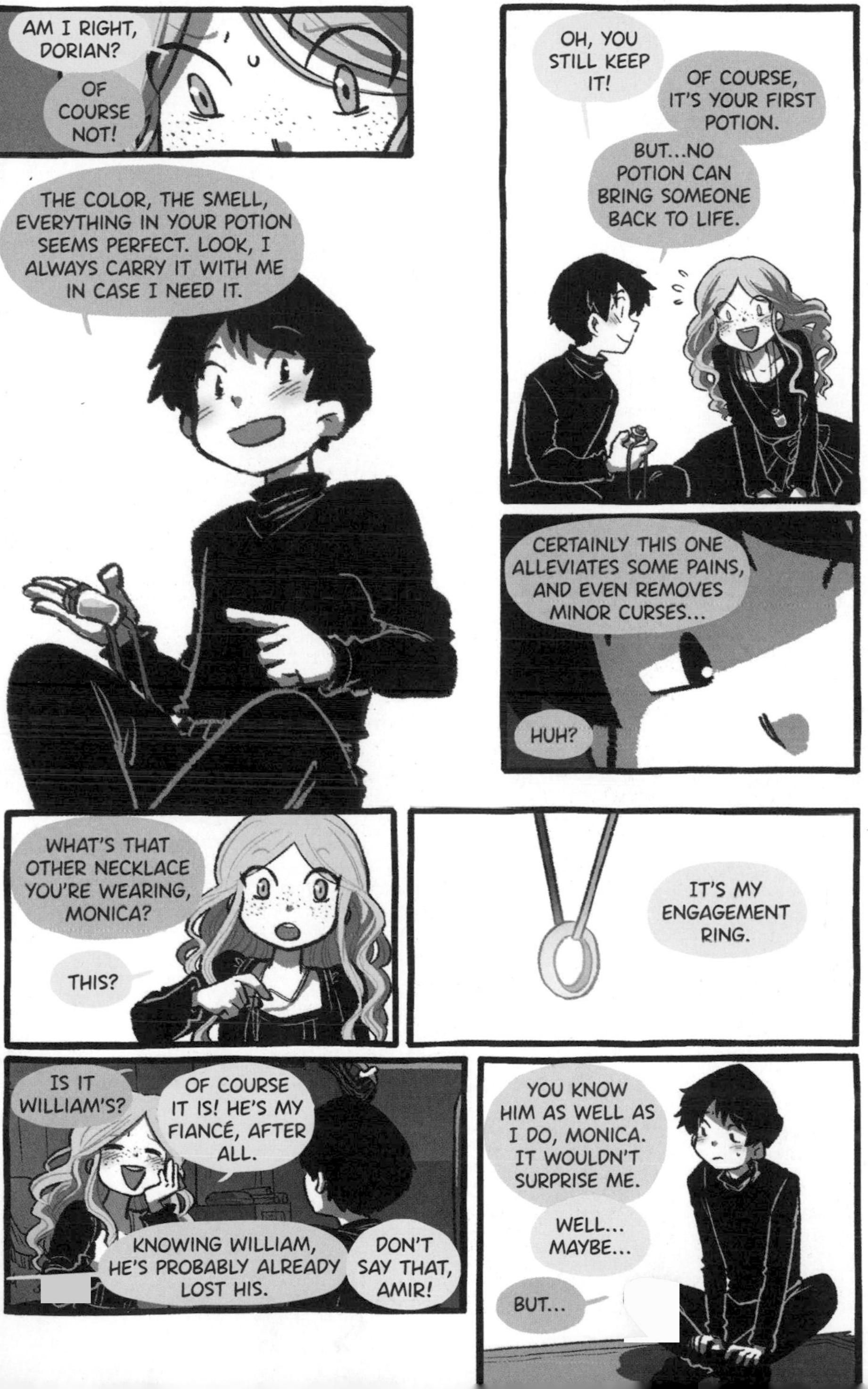
AM I RIGHT, DORIAN?
OF COURSE NOT!
OH, YOU STILL KEEP IT!
OF COURSE, IT'S YOUR FIRST POTION.
BUT...NO POTION CAN BRING SOMEONE BACK TO LIFE.
THE COLOR, THE SMELL, EVERYTHING IN YOUR POTION SEEMS PERFECT. LOOK, I ALWAYS CARRY IT WITH ME IN CASE I NEED IT.
CERTAINLY THIS ONE ALLEVIATES SOME PAINS, AND EVEN REMOVES MINOR CURSES...
HUH?
WHAT'S THAT OTHER NECKLACE YOU'RE WEARING, MONICA?
THIS?
IT'S MY ENGAGEMENT RING.
IS IT WILLIAM'S?
OF COURSE IT IS! HE'S MY FIANCÉ, AFTER ALL.
KNOWING WILLIAM, HE'S PROBABLY ALREADY LOST HIS.
DON'T SAY THAT, AMIR!
YOU KNOW HIM AS WELL AS I DO, MONICA. IT WOULDN'T SURPRISE ME.
WELL... MAYBE...
BUT...

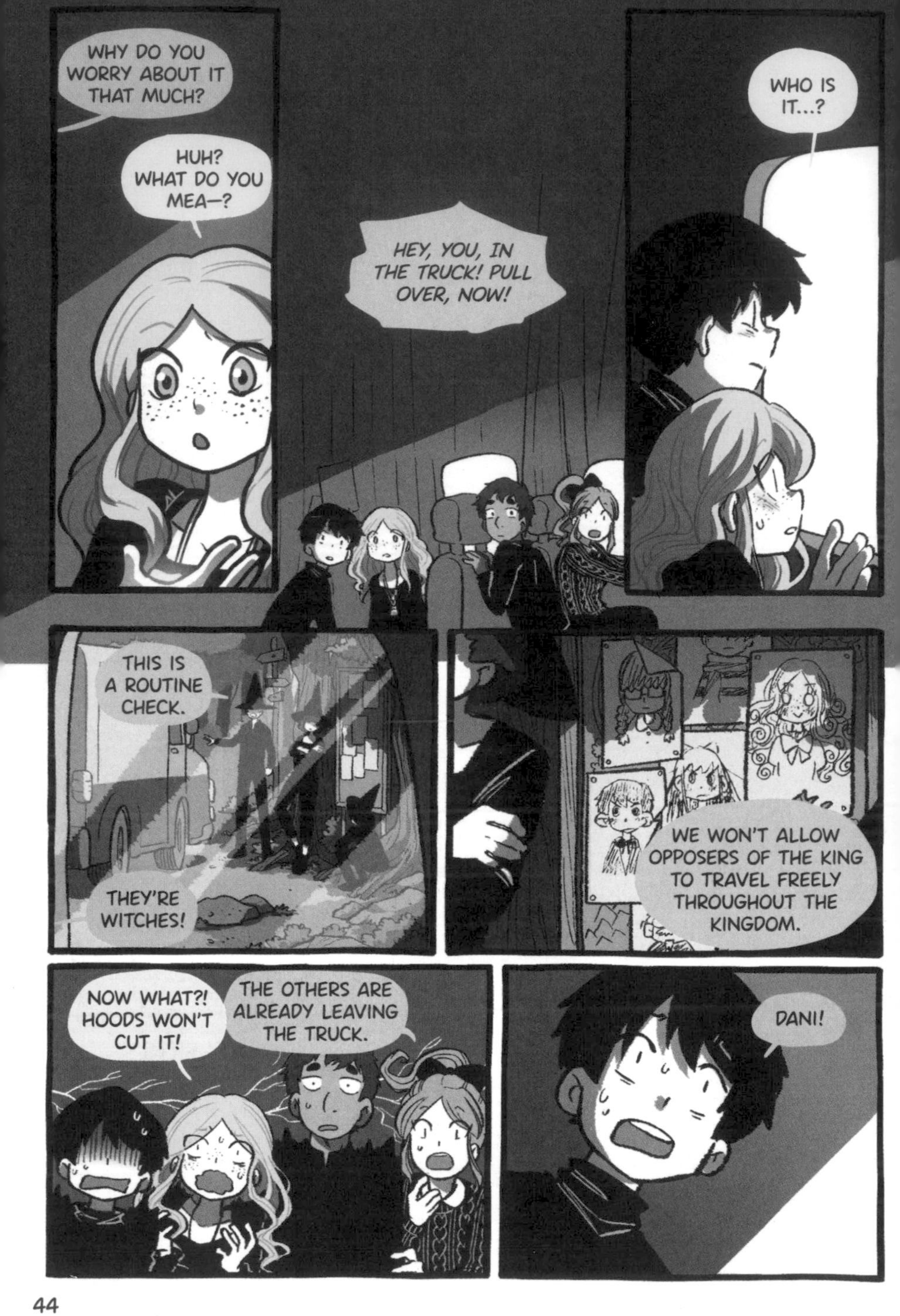
WHY DO YOU WORRY ABOUT IT THAT MUCH?
HUH? WHAT DO YOU MEA—?
HEY, YOU, IN THE TRUCK! PULL OVER, NOW!
WHO IS IT...?
THIS IS A ROUTINE CHECK.
THEY'RE WITCHES!
WE WON'T ALLOW OPPOSERS OF THE KING TO TRAVEL FREELY THROUGHOUT THE KINGDOM.
NOW WHAT?! HOODS WON'T CUT IT!
THE OTHERS ARE ALREADY LEAVING THE TRUCK.
DANI!

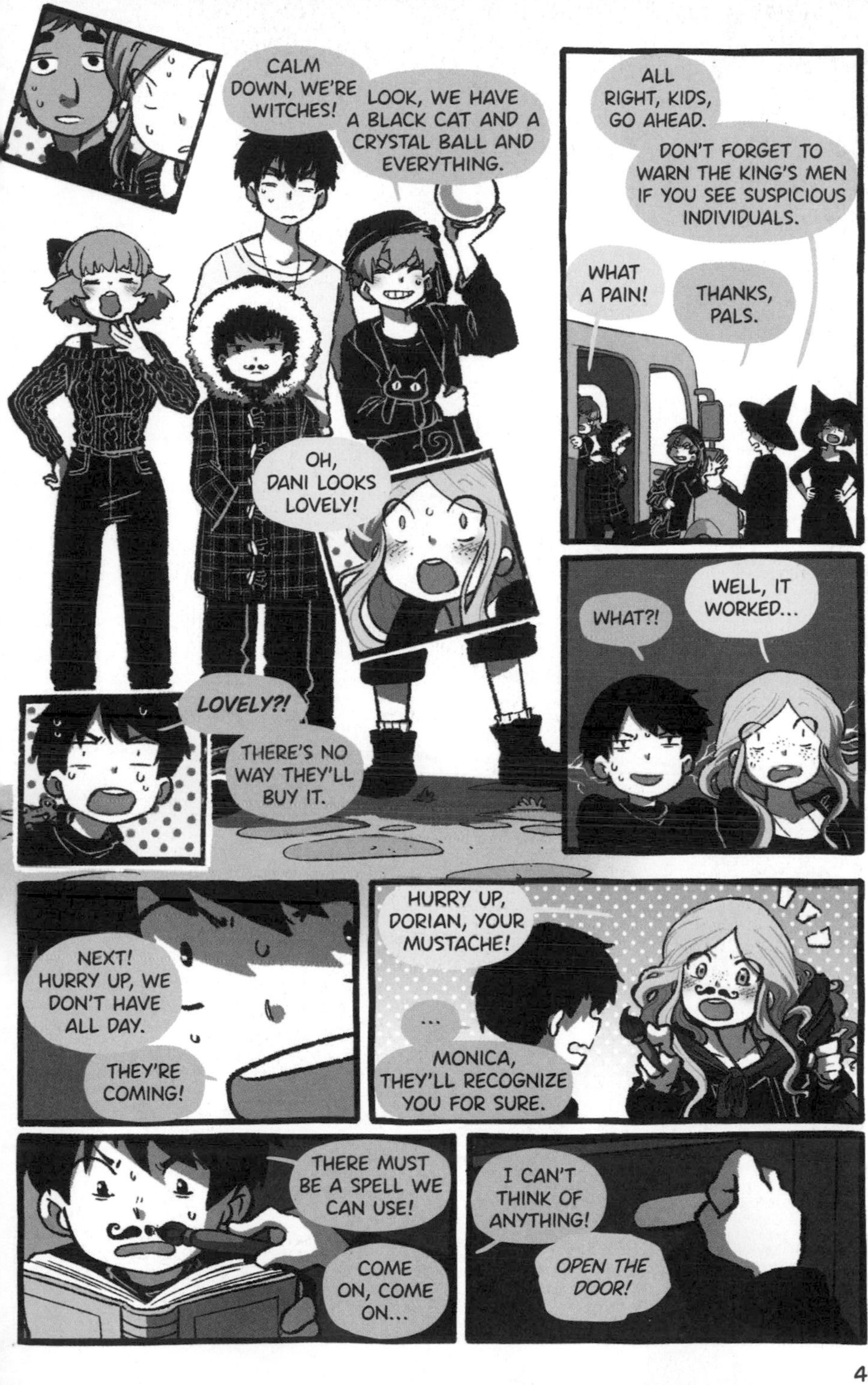
CALM DOWN, WE'RE WITCHES!
LOOK, WE HAVE A BLACK CAT AND A CRYSTAL BALL AND EVERYTHING.
OH, DANI LOOKS LOVELY!
LOVELY?!
THERE'S NO WAY THEY'LL BUY IT.
ALL RIGHT, KIDS, GO AHEAD.
DON'T FORGET TO WARN THE KING'S MEN IF YOU SEE SUSPICIOUS INDIVIDUALS.
WHAT A PAIN!
THANKS, PALS.
WHAT?!
WELL, IT WORKED...
NEXT! HURRY UP, WE DON'T HAVE ALL DAY.
THEY'RE COMING!
HURRY UP, DORIAN, YOUR MUSTACHE!
...
MONICA, THEY'LL RECOGNIZE YOU FOR SURE.
THERE MUST BE A SPELL WE CAN USE!
COME ON, COME ON...
I CAN'T THINK OF ANYTHING!
OPEN THE DOOR!

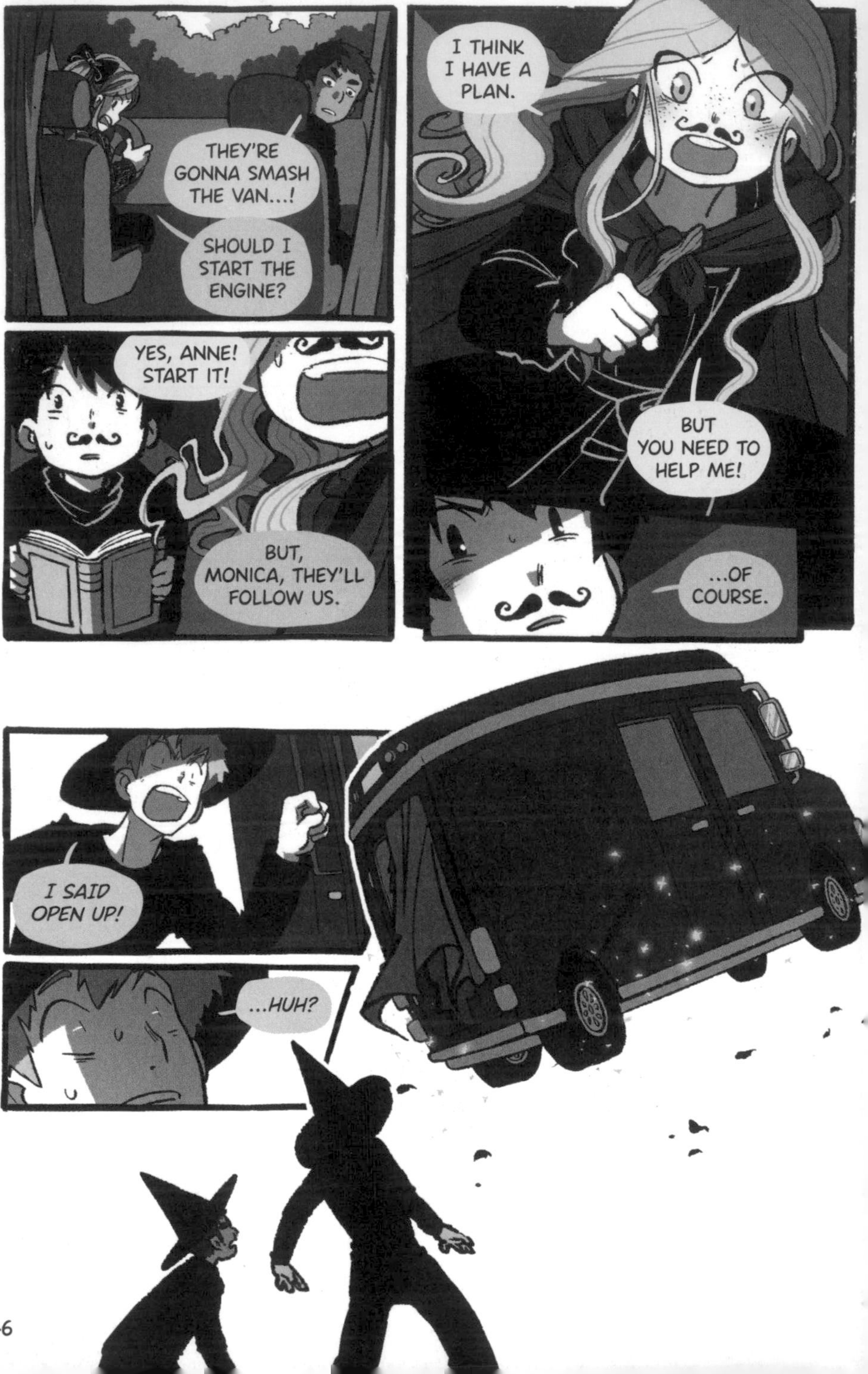
THEY'RE GONNA SMASH THE VAN...!
SHOULD I START THE ENGINE?
I THINK I HAVE A PLAN.
YES, ANNE! START IT!
BUT, MONICA, THEY'LL FOLLOW US.
BUT YOU NEED TO HELP ME!
...OF COURSE.
I SAID OPEN UP!
...HUH?

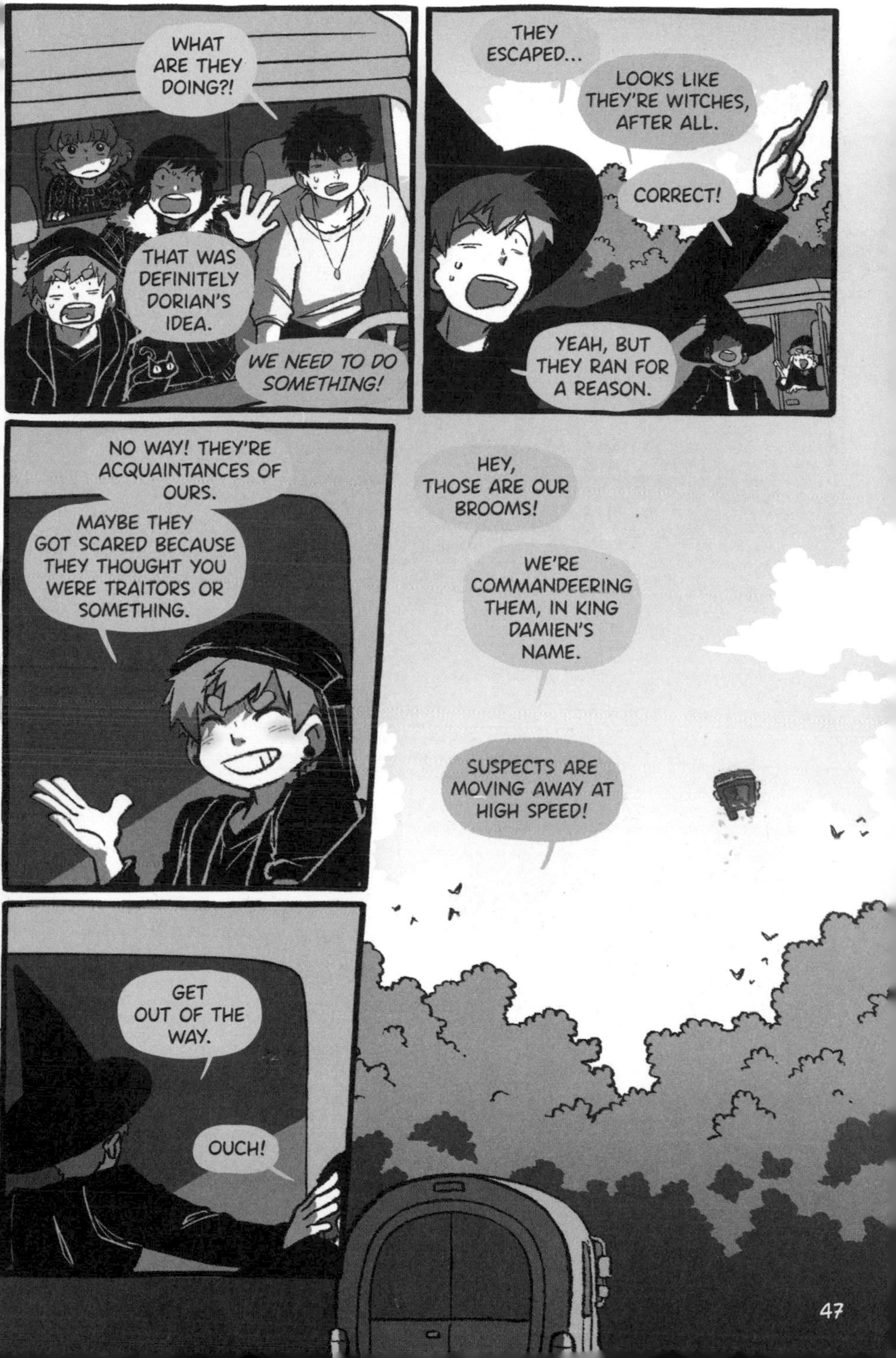
WHAT ARE THEY DOING?!
THAT WAS DEFINITELY DORIAN'S IDEA.
WE NEED TO DO SOMETHING!
THEY ESCAPED...
LOOKS LIKE THEY'RE WITCHES, AFTER ALL.
CORRECT!
YEAH, BUT THEY RAN FOR A REASON.
NO WAY! THEY'RE ACQUAINTANCES OF OURS.
MAYBE THEY GOT SCARED BECAUSE THEY THOUGHT YOU WERE TRAITORS OR SOMETHING.
HEY, THOSE ARE OUR BROOMS!
WE'RE COMMANDEERING THEM, IN KING DAMIEN'S NAME.
SUSPECTS ARE MOVING AWAY AT HIGH SPEED!
GET OUT OF THE WAY.
OUCH!

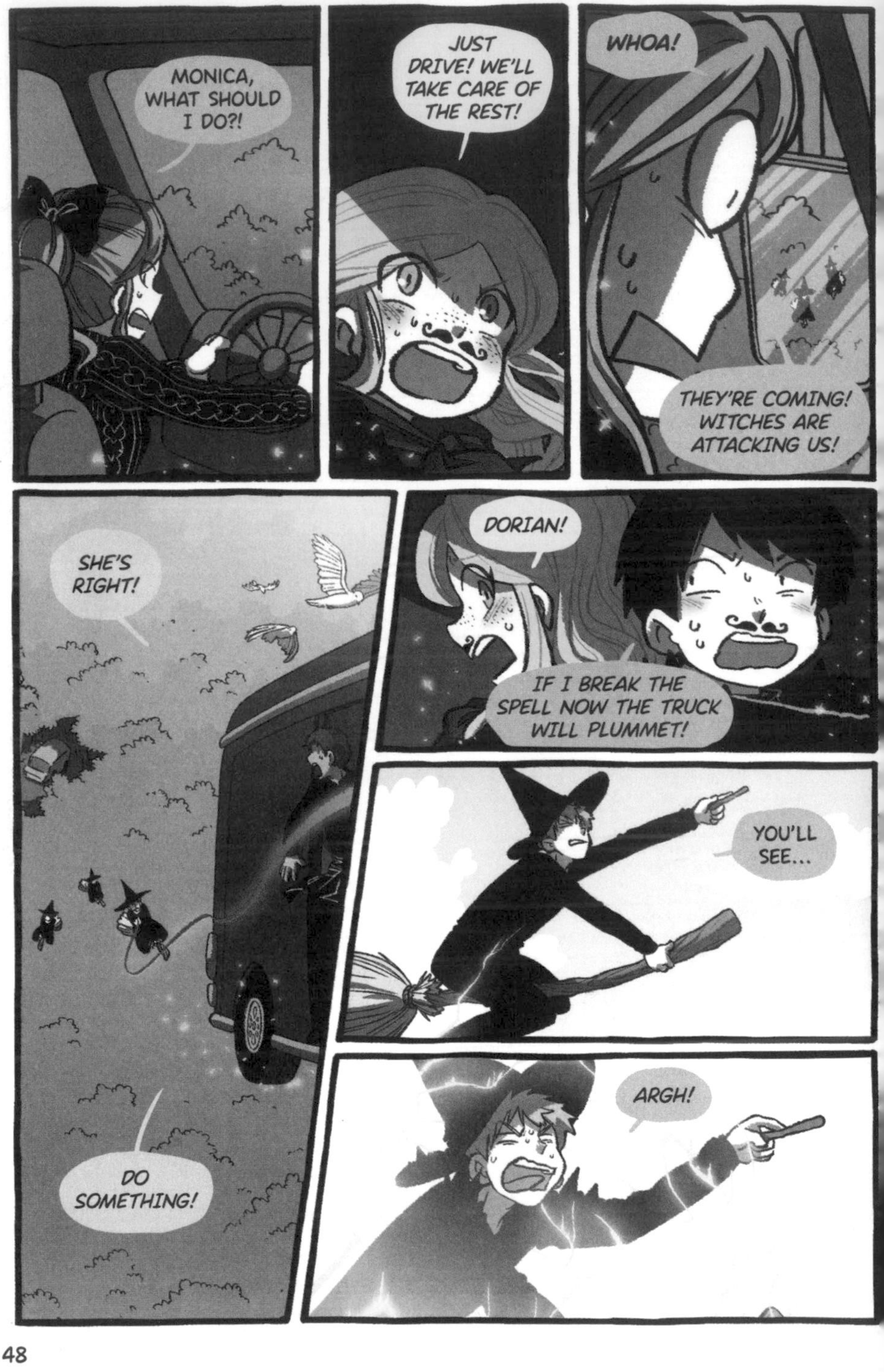
MONICA, WHAT SHOULD I DO?!
JUST DRIVE! WE'LL TAKE CARE OF THE REST!
WHOA!
THEY'RE COMING! WITCHES ARE ATTACKING US!
SHE'S RIGHT!
DO SOMETHING!
DORIAN!
IF I BREAK THE SPELL NOW THE TRUCK WILL PLUMMET!
YOU'LL SEE...
ARGH!

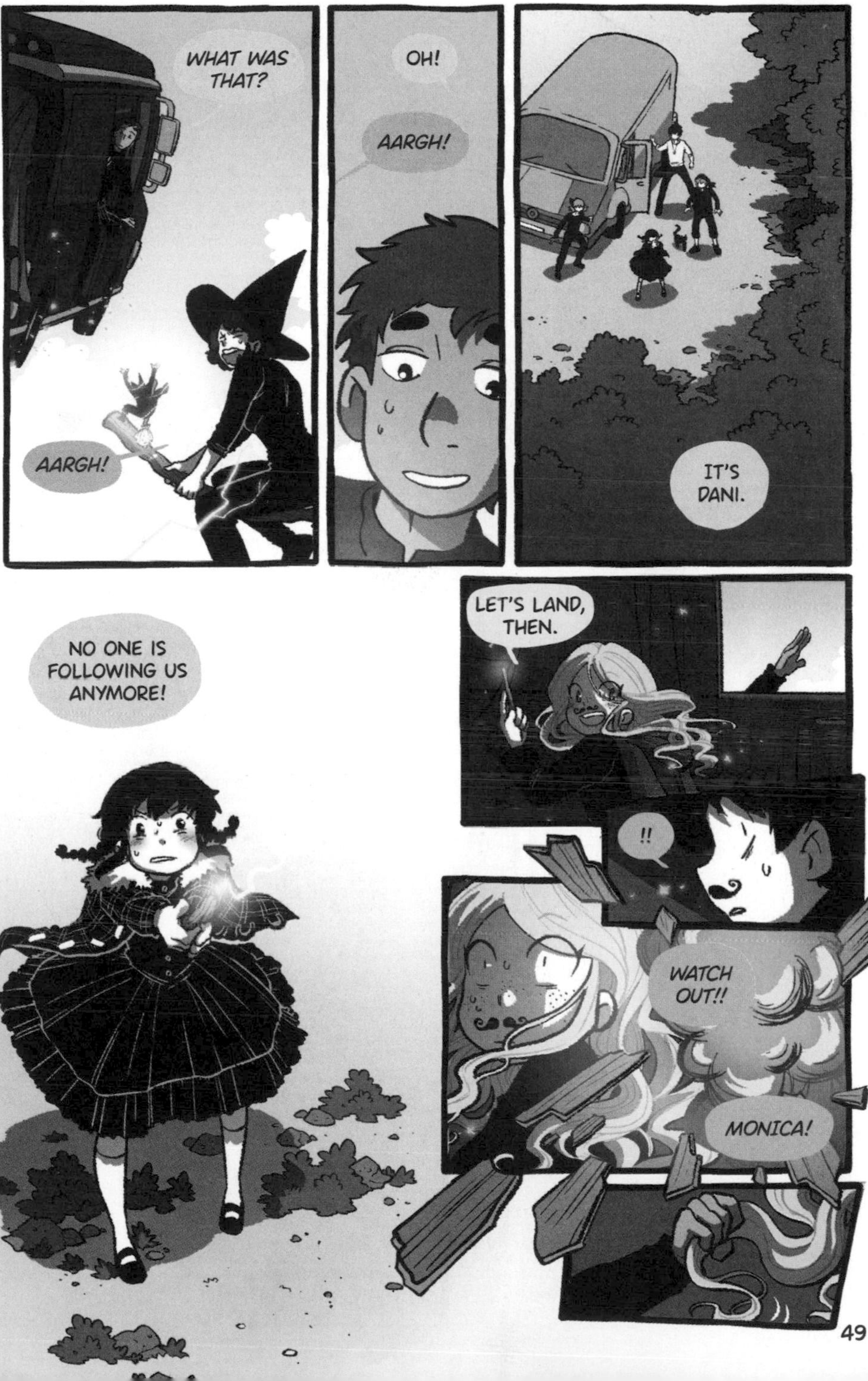
WHAT WAS THAT?
AARGH!
OH!
AARGH!
IT'S DANI.
NO ONE IS FOLLOWING US ANYMORE!
LET'S LAND, THEN.
!!
WATCH OUT!!
MONICA!

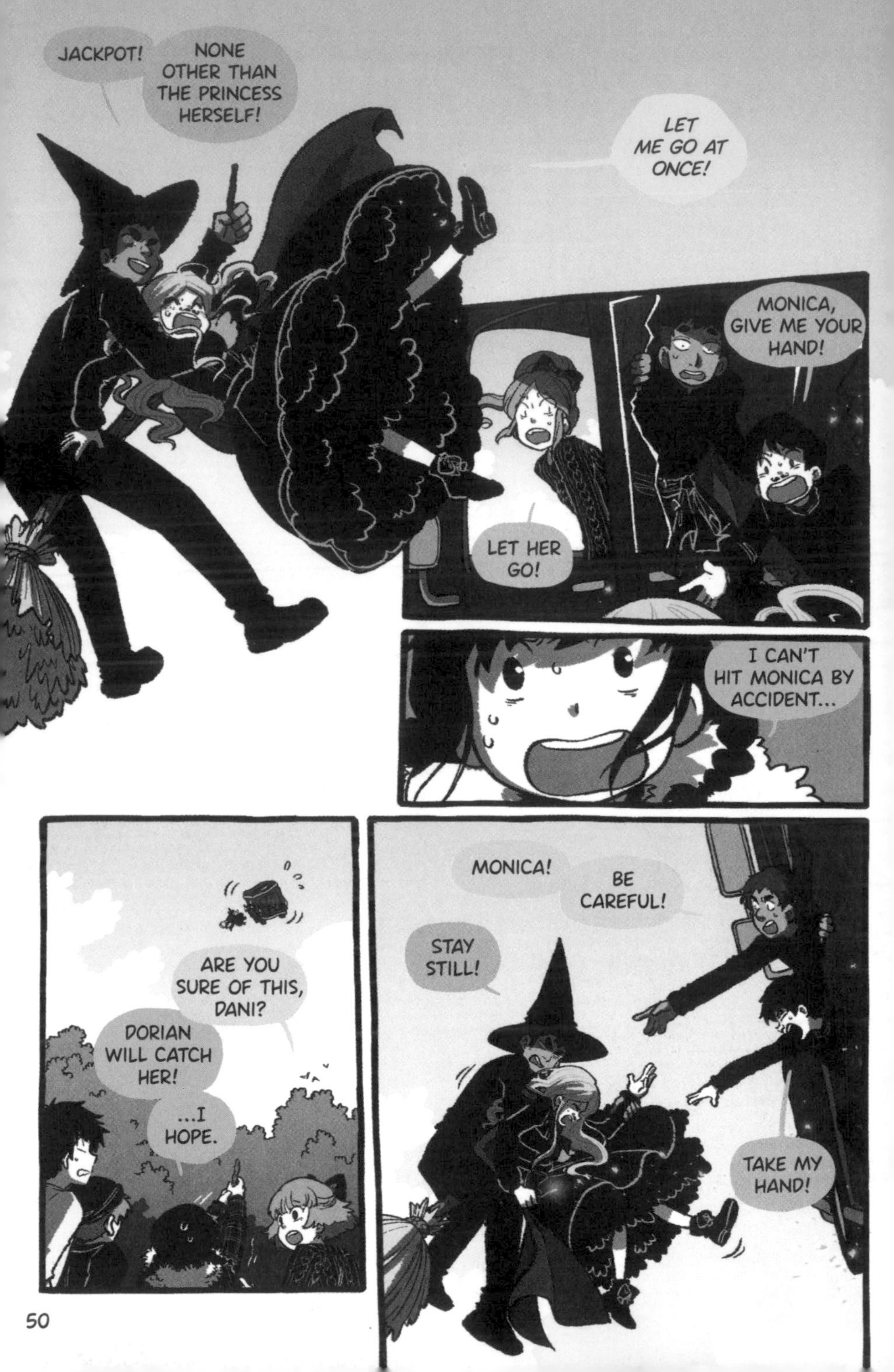
JACKPOT!
NONE OTHER THAN THE PRINCESS HERSELF!
LET ME GO AT ONCE!
MONICA, GIVE ME YOUR HAND!
LET HER GO!
I CAN'T HIT MONICA BY ACCIDENT...
ARE YOU SURE OF THIS, DANI?
DORIAN WILL CATCH HER!
...I HOPE.
MONICA!
BE CAREFUL!
STAY STILL!
TAKE MY HAND!

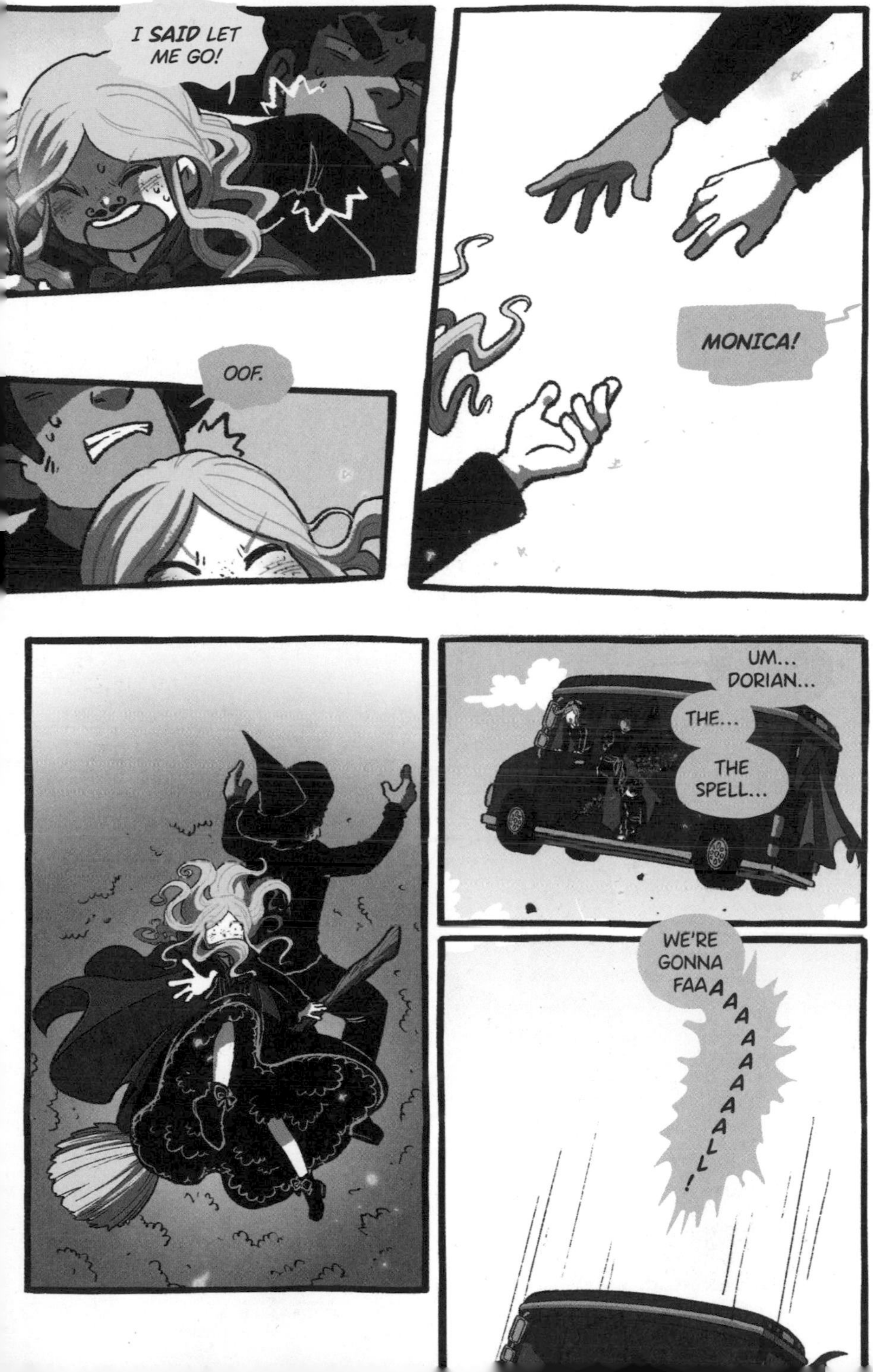
I SAID LET ME GO!
MONICA!
OOF.
UM... DORIAN...
THE...
THE SPELL...
WE'RE GONNA FAAAAAAAAAAALL!

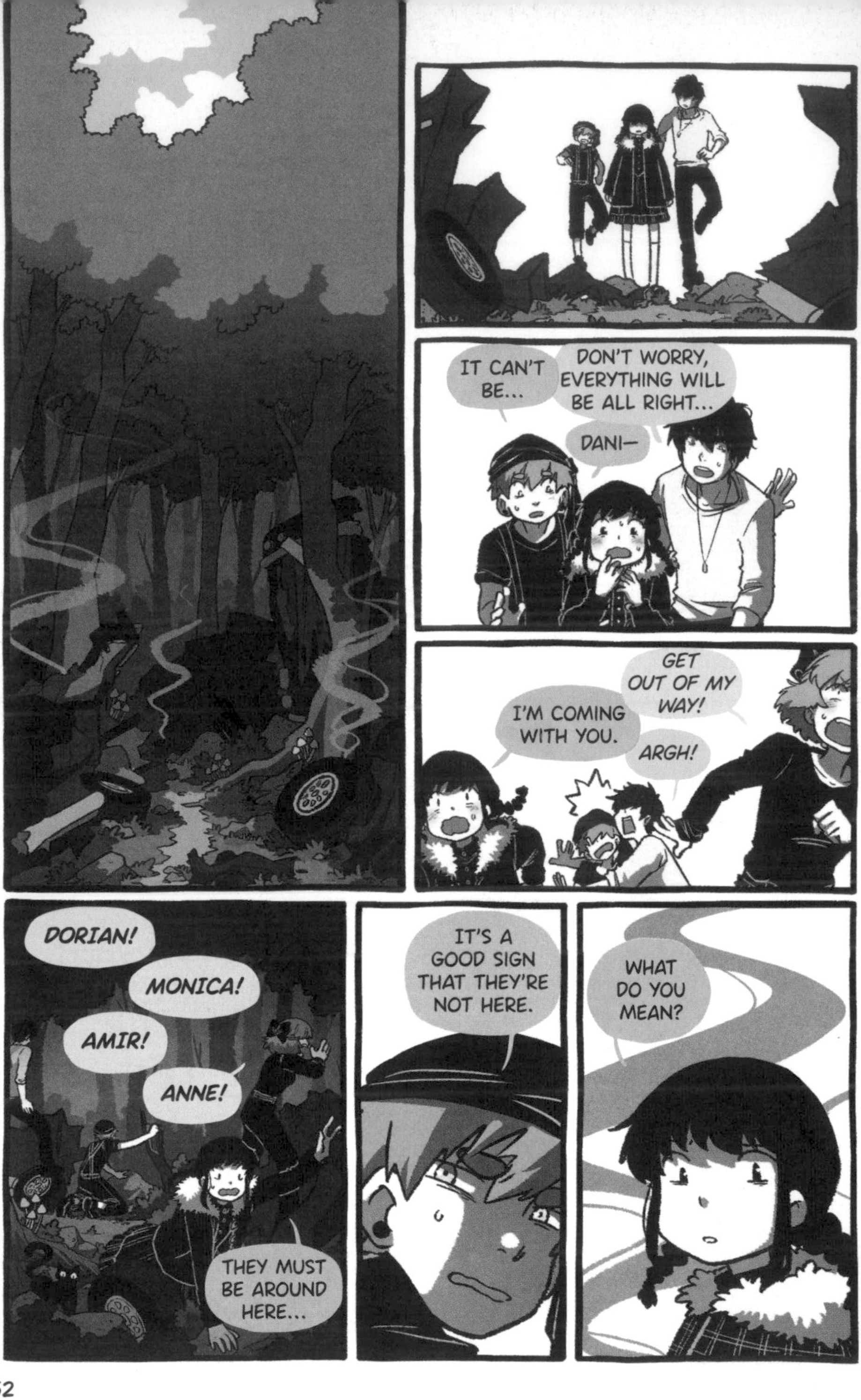
IT CAN'T BE...
DON'T WORRY, EVERYTHING WILL BE ALL RIGHT...
DANI—
GET OUT OF MY WAY!
I'M COMING WITH YOU.
ARGH!
DORIAN!
MONICA!
AMIR!
ANNE!
THEY MUST BE AROUND HERE...
IT'S A GOOD SIGN THAT THEY'RE NOT HERE.
WHAT DO YOU MEAN?

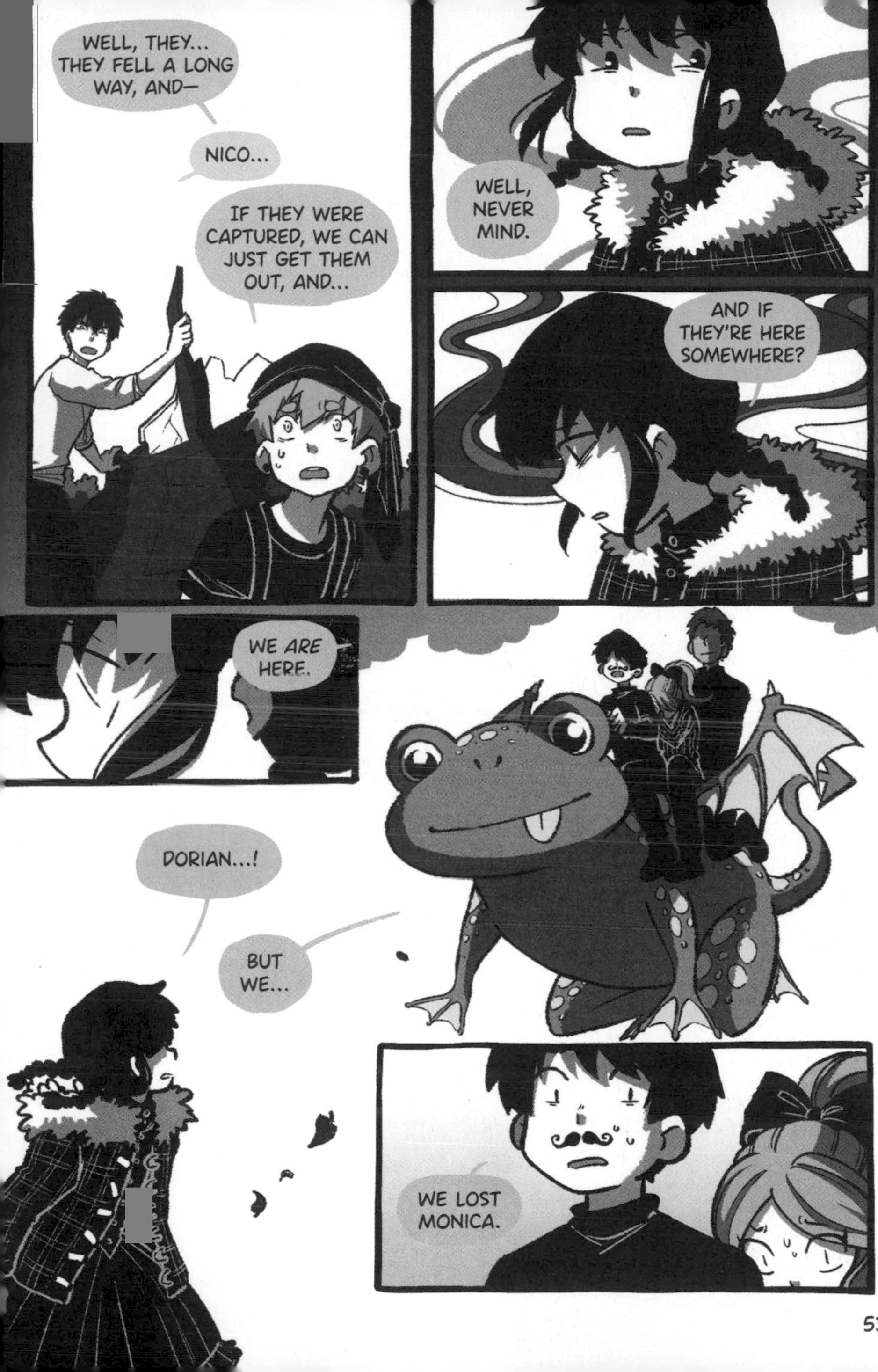
WELL, THEY... THEY FELL A LONG WAY, AND—
NICO...
IF THEY WERE CAPTURED, WE CAN JUST GET THEM OUT, AND...
WELL, NEVER MIND.
AND IF THEY'RE HERE SOMEWHERE?
WE ARE HERE.
DORIAN...!
BUT WE...
WE LOST MONICA.

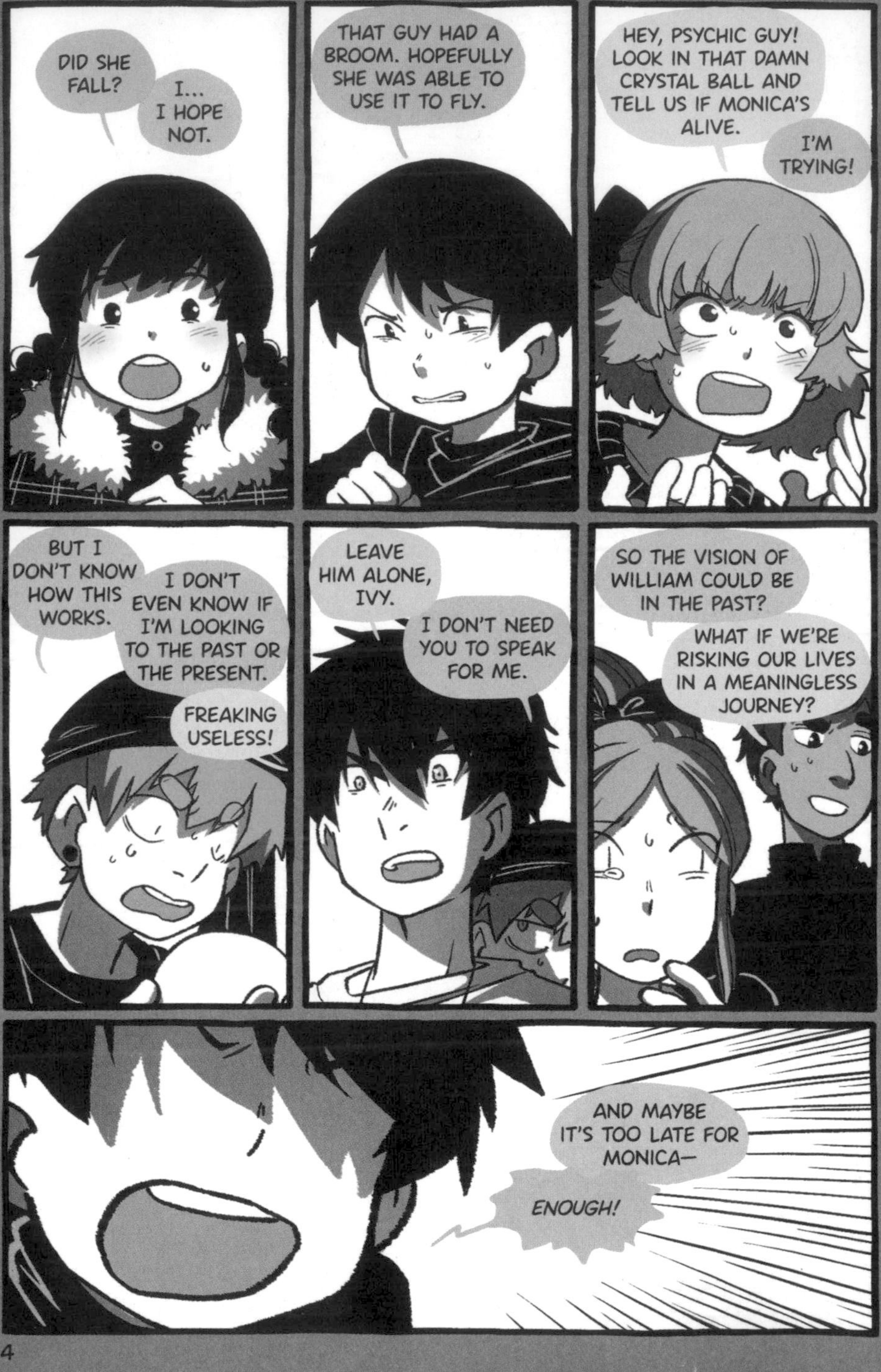
DID SHE FALL?
I... I HOPE NOT.
THAT GUY HAD A BROOM. HOPEFULLY SHE WAS ABLE TO USE IT TO FLY.
HEY, PSYCHIC GUY! LOOK IN THAT DAMN CRYSTAL BALL AND TELL US IF MONICA'S ALIVE.
I'M TRYING!
BUT I DON'T KNOW HOW THIS WORKS.
I DON'T EVEN KNOW IF I'M LOOKING TO THE PAST OR THE PRESENT.
FREAKING USELESS!
LEAVE HIM ALONE, IVY.
I DON'T NEED YOU TO SPEAK FOR ME.
SO THE VISION OF WILLIAM COULD BE IN THE PAST?
WHAT IF WE'RE RISKING OUR LIVES IN A MEANINGLESS JOURNEY?
AND MAYBE IT'S TOO LATE FOR MONICA—
ENOUGH!

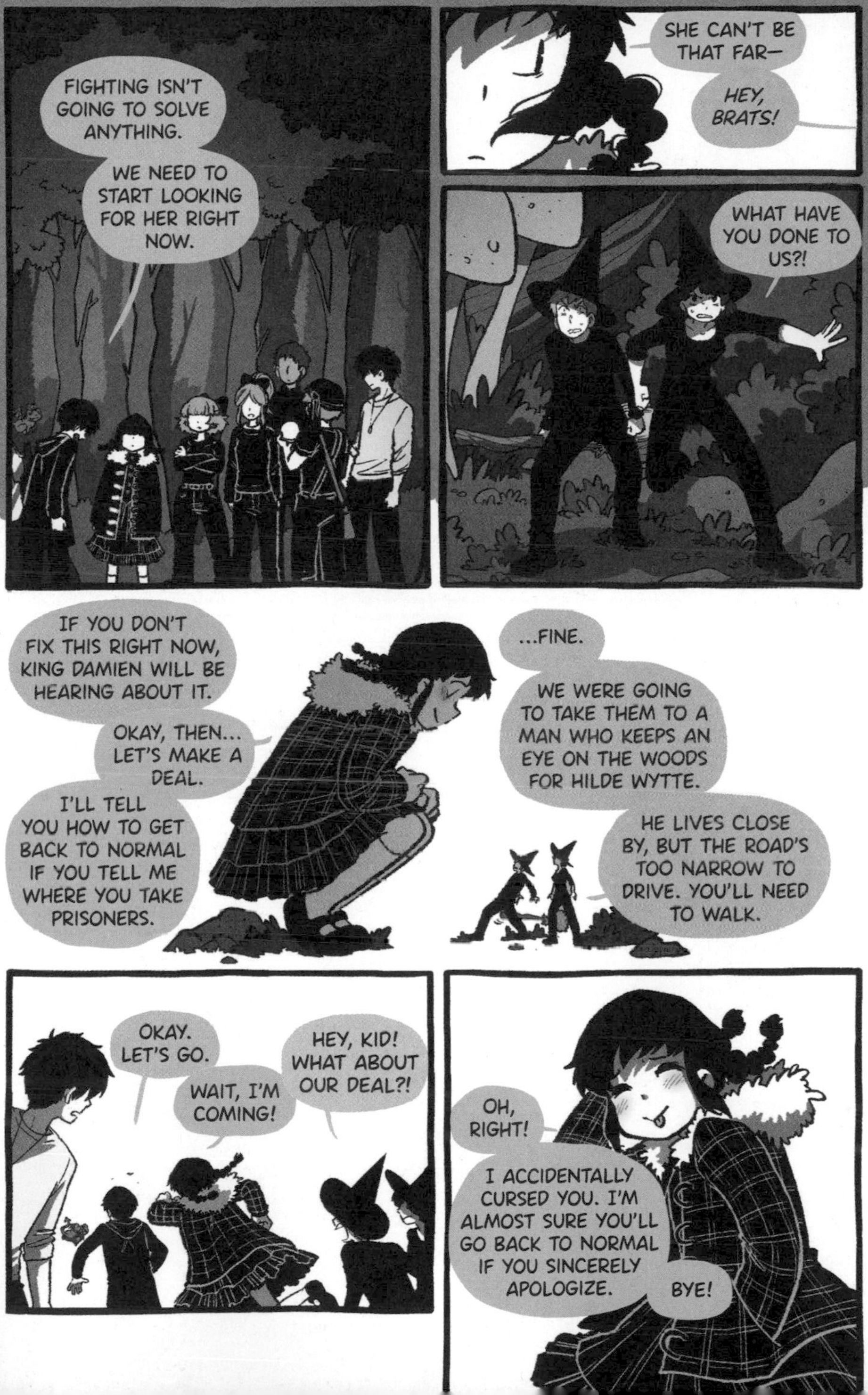
FIGHTING ISN'T GOING TO SOLVE ANYTHING.
WE NEED TO START LOOKING FOR HER RIGHT NOW.
SHE CAN'T BE THAT FAR—
HEY, BRATS!
WHAT HAVE YOU DONE TO US?!
IF YOU DON'T FIX THIS RIGHT NOW, KING DAMIEN WILL BE HEARING ABOUT IT.
OKAY, THEN... LET'S MAKE A DEAL.
I'LL TELL YOU HOW TO GET BACK TO NORMAL IF YOU TELL ME WHERE YOU TAKE PRISONERS.
...FINE.
WE WERE GOING TO TAKE THEM TO A MAN WHO KEEPS AN EYE ON THE WOODS FOR HILDE WYTTE.
HE LIVES CLOSE BY, BUT THE ROAD'S TOO NARROW TO DRIVE. YOU'LL NEED TO WALK.
OKAY. LET'S GO.
WAIT, I'M COMING!
HEY, KID! WHAT ABOUT OUR DEAL?!
OH, RIGHT!
I ACCIDENTALLY CURSED YOU. I'M ALMOST SURE YOU'LL GO BACK TO NORMAL IF YOU SINCERELY APOLOGIZE.
BYE!

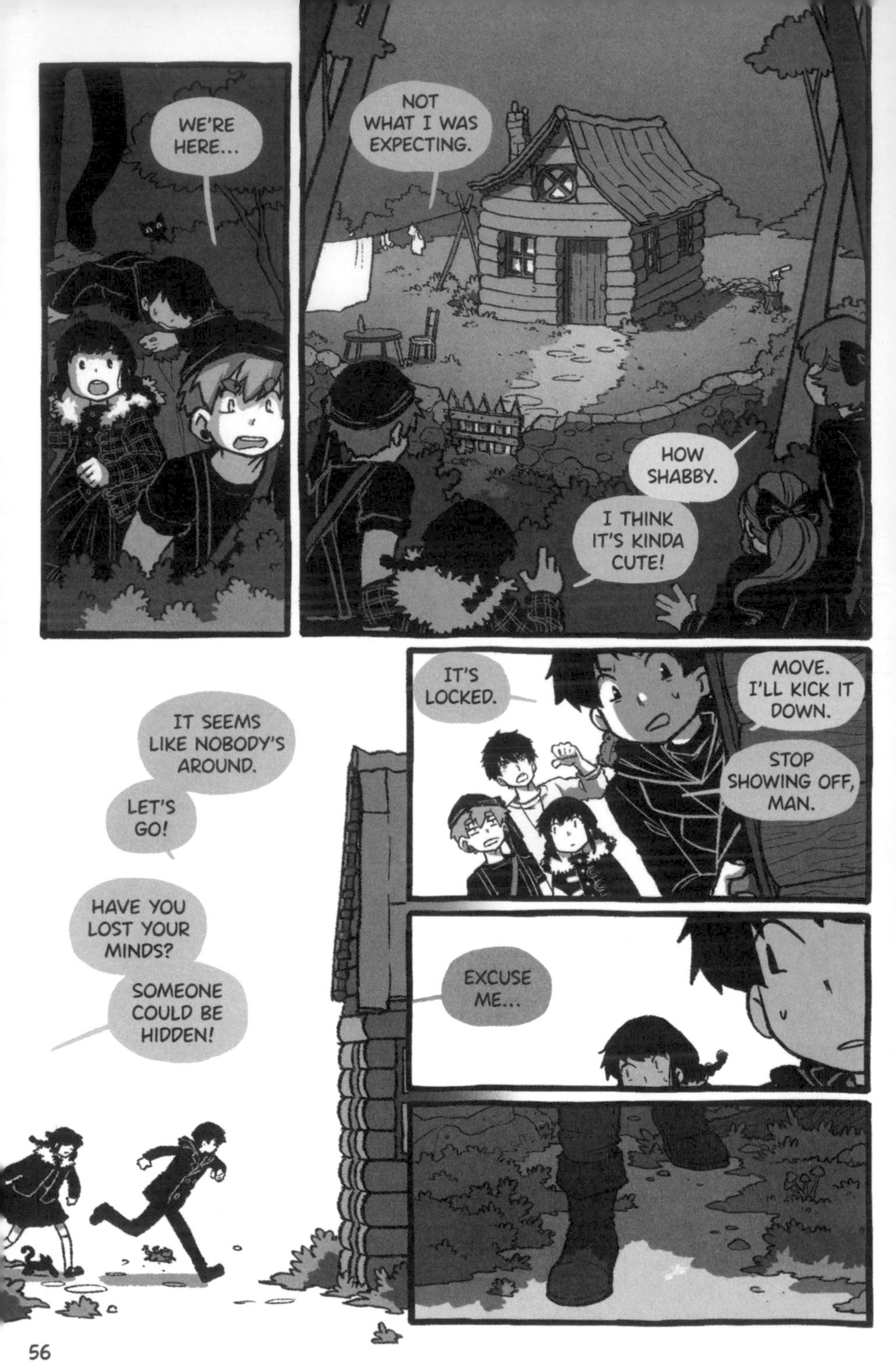

WE'RE HERE...
NOT WHAT I WAS EXPECTING.
HOW SHABBY.
I THINK IT'S KINDA CUTE!
IT SEEMS LIKE NOBODY'S AROUND.
LET'S GO!
HAVE YOU LOST YOUR MINDS?
SOMEONE COULD BE HIDDEN!
IT'S LOCKED.
MOVE. I'LL KICK IT DOWN.
STOP SHOWING OFF, MAN.
EXCUSE ME...

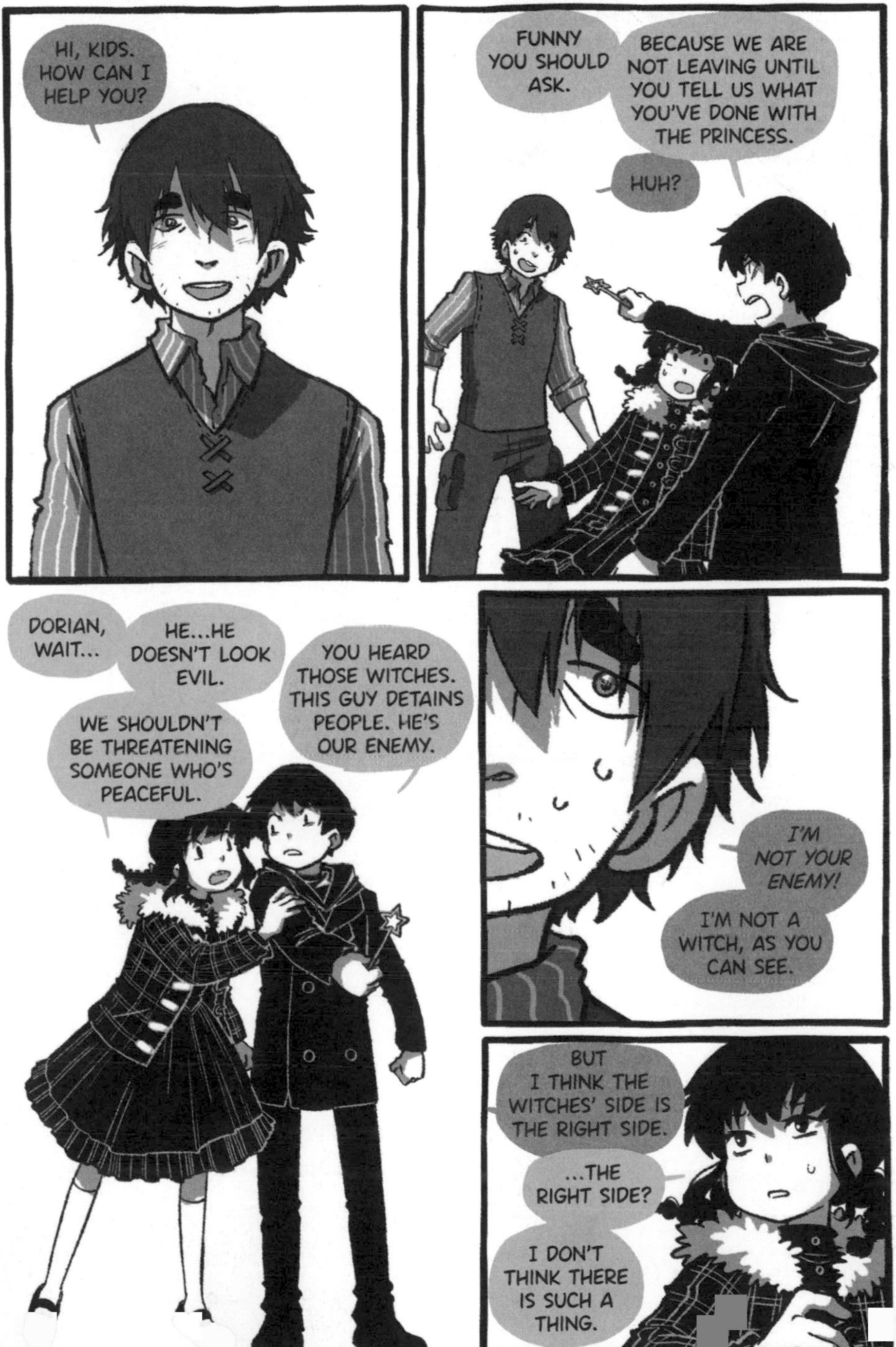
HI, KIDS. HOW CAN I HELP YOU?
FUNNY YOU SHOULD ASK.
BECAUSE WE ARE NOT LEAVING UNTIL YOU TELL US WHAT YOU'VE DONE WITH THE PRINCESS.
HUH?
DORIAN, WAIT...
HE...HE DOESN'T LOOK EVIL.
WE SHOULDN'T BE THREATENING SOMEONE WHO'S PEACEFUL.
YOU HEARD THOSE WITCHES. THIS GUY DETAINS PEOPLE. HE'S OUR ENEMY.
I'M NOT YOUR ENEMY!
I'M NOT A WITCH, AS YOU CAN SEE.
BUT I THINK THE WITCHES' SIDE IS THE RIGHT SIDE.
...THE RIGHT SIDE?
I DON'T THINK THERE IS SUCH A THING.

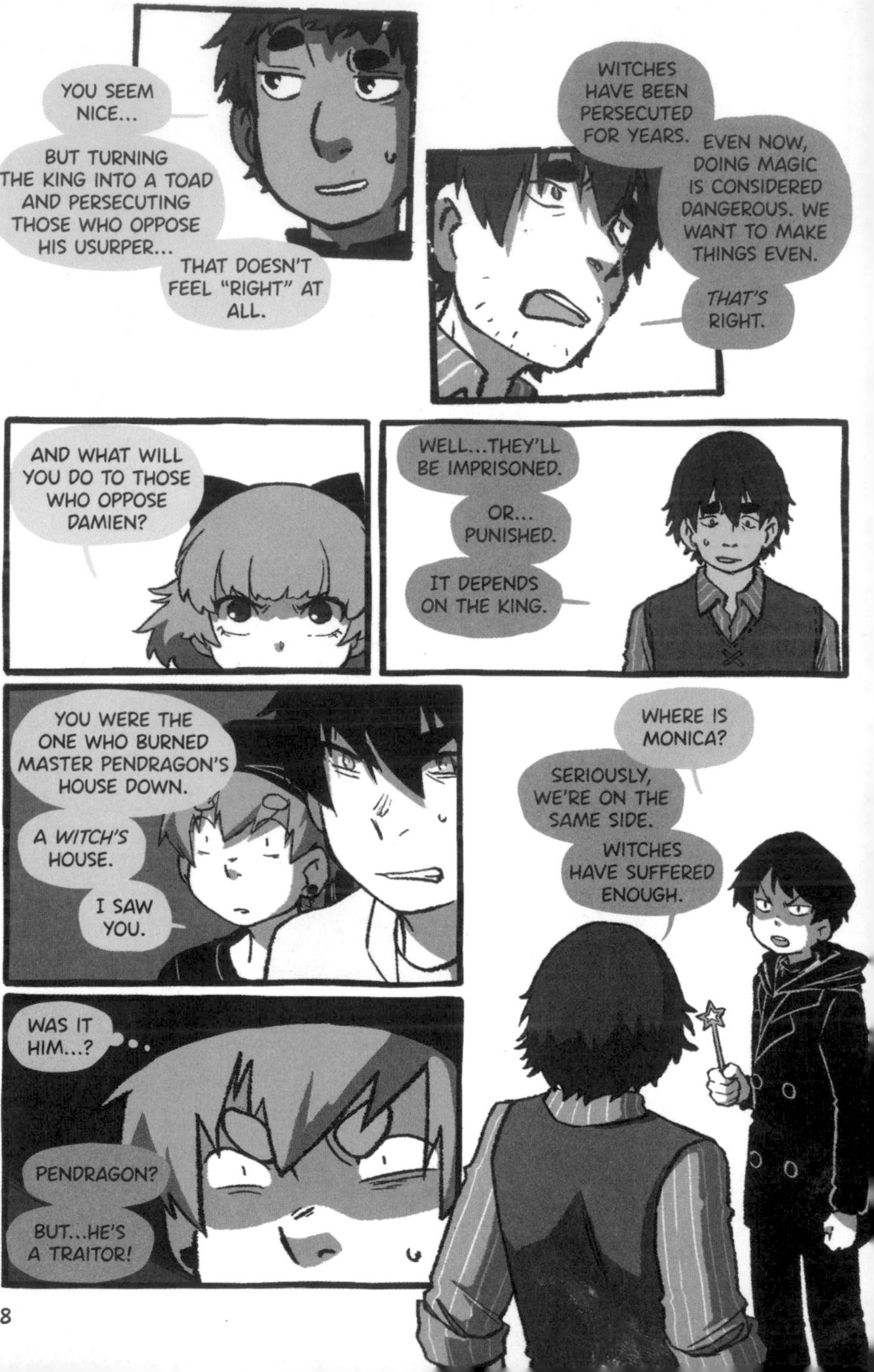
YOU SEEM NICE...
BUT TURNING THE KING INTO A TOAD AND PERSECUTING THOSE WHO OPPOSE HIS USURPER...
THAT DOESN'T FEEL "RIGHT" AT ALL.
WITCHES HAVE BEEN PERSECUTED FOR YEARS.
EVEN NOW, DOING MAGIC IS CONSIDERED DANGEROUS. WE WANT TO MAKE THINGS EVEN.
THAT'S RIGHT.
AND WHAT WILL YOU DO TO THOSE WHO OPPOSE DAMIEN?
WELL...THEY'LL BE IMPRISONED.
OR... PUNISHED.
IT DEPENDS ON THE KING.
YOU WERE THE ONE WHO BURNED MASTER PENDRAGON'S HOUSE DOWN.
A WITCH'S HOUSE.
I SAW YOU.
WHERE IS MONICA?
SERIOUSLY, WE'RE ON THE SAME SIDE.
WITCHES HAVE SUFFERED ENOUGH.
WAS IT HIM...?
PENDRAGON?
BUT...HE'S A TRAITOR!

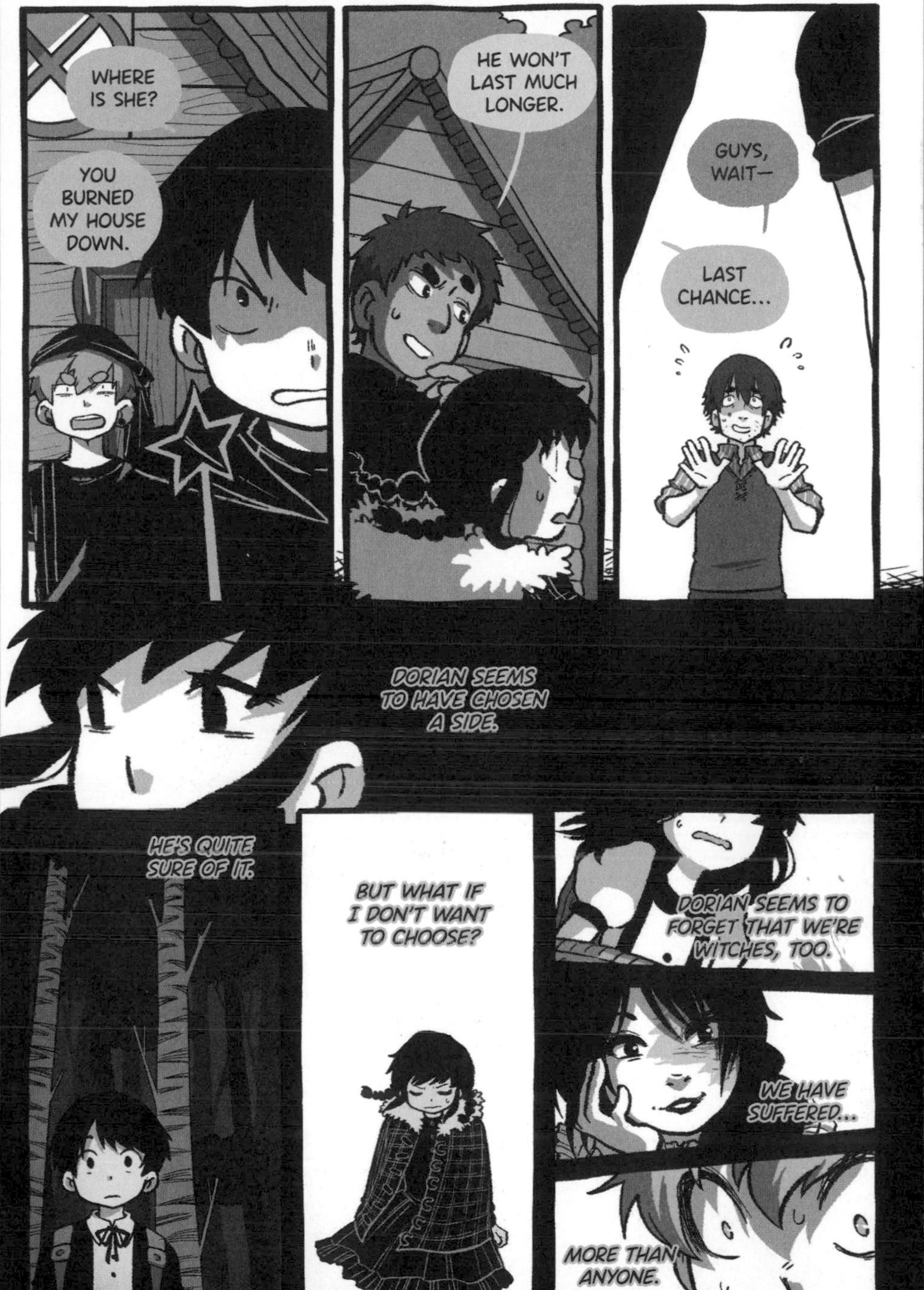
WHERE IS SHE?
YOU BURNED MY HOUSE DOWN.
HE WON'T LAST MUCH LONGER.
GUYS, WAIT—
LAST CHANCE...
DORIAN SEEMS TO HAVE CHOSEN A SIDE.
HE'S QUITE SURE OF IT.
BUT WHAT IF I DON'T WANT TO CHOOSE?
DORIAN SEEMS TO FORGET THAT WE'RE WITCHES, TOO.
WE HAVE SUFFERED...
MORE THAN ANYONE.

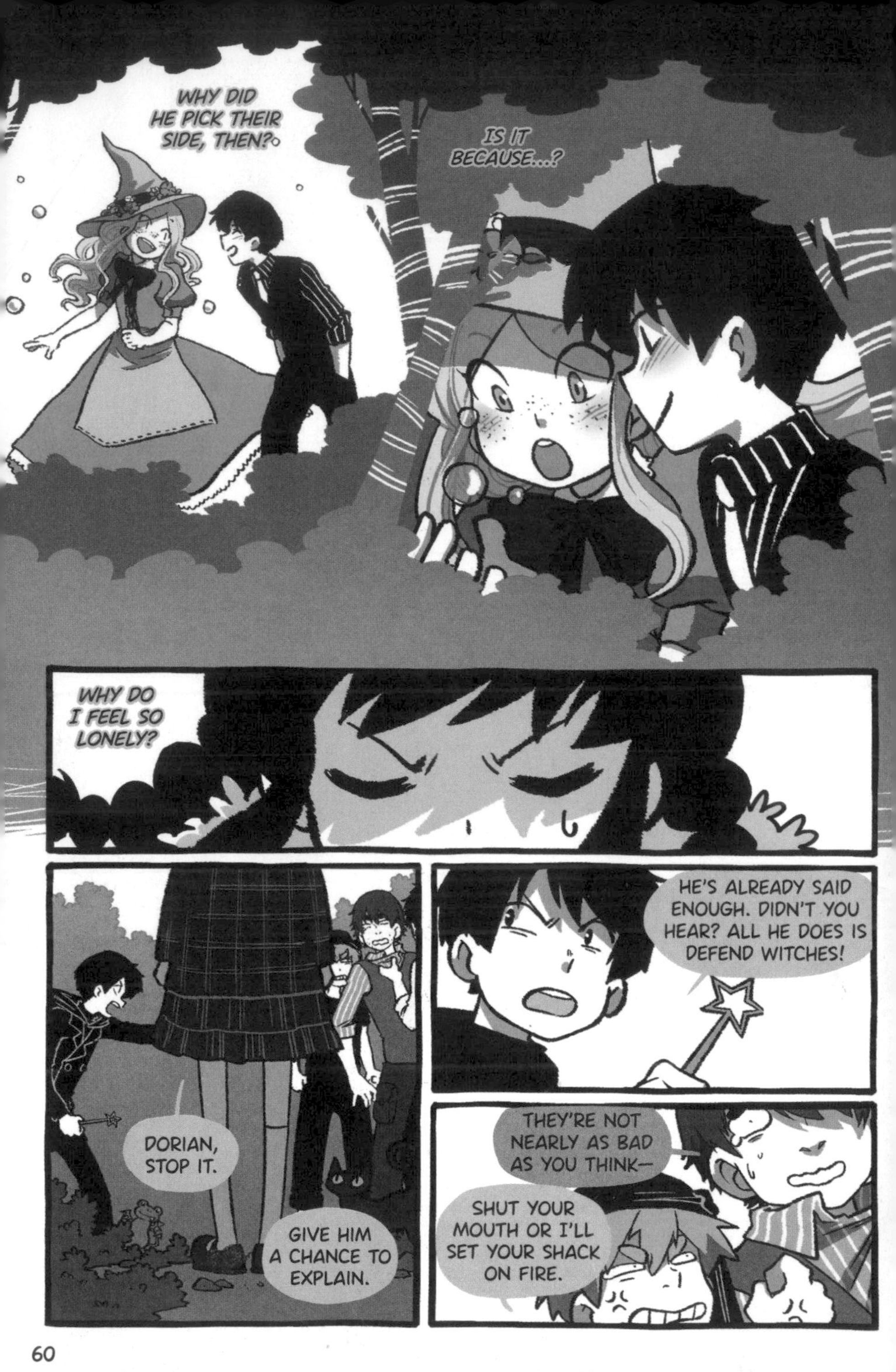
WHY DID HE PICK THEIR SIDE, THEN?
IS IT BECAUSE...?
WHY DO I FEEL SO LONELY?
DORIAN, STOP IT.
GIVE HIM A CHANCE TO EXPLAIN.
HE'S ALREADY SAID ENOUGH. DIDN'T YOU HEAR? ALL HE DOES IS DEFEND WITCHES!
THEY'RE NOT NEARLY AS BAD AS YOU THINK—
SHUT YOUR MOUTH OR I'LL SET YOUR SHACK ON FIRE.

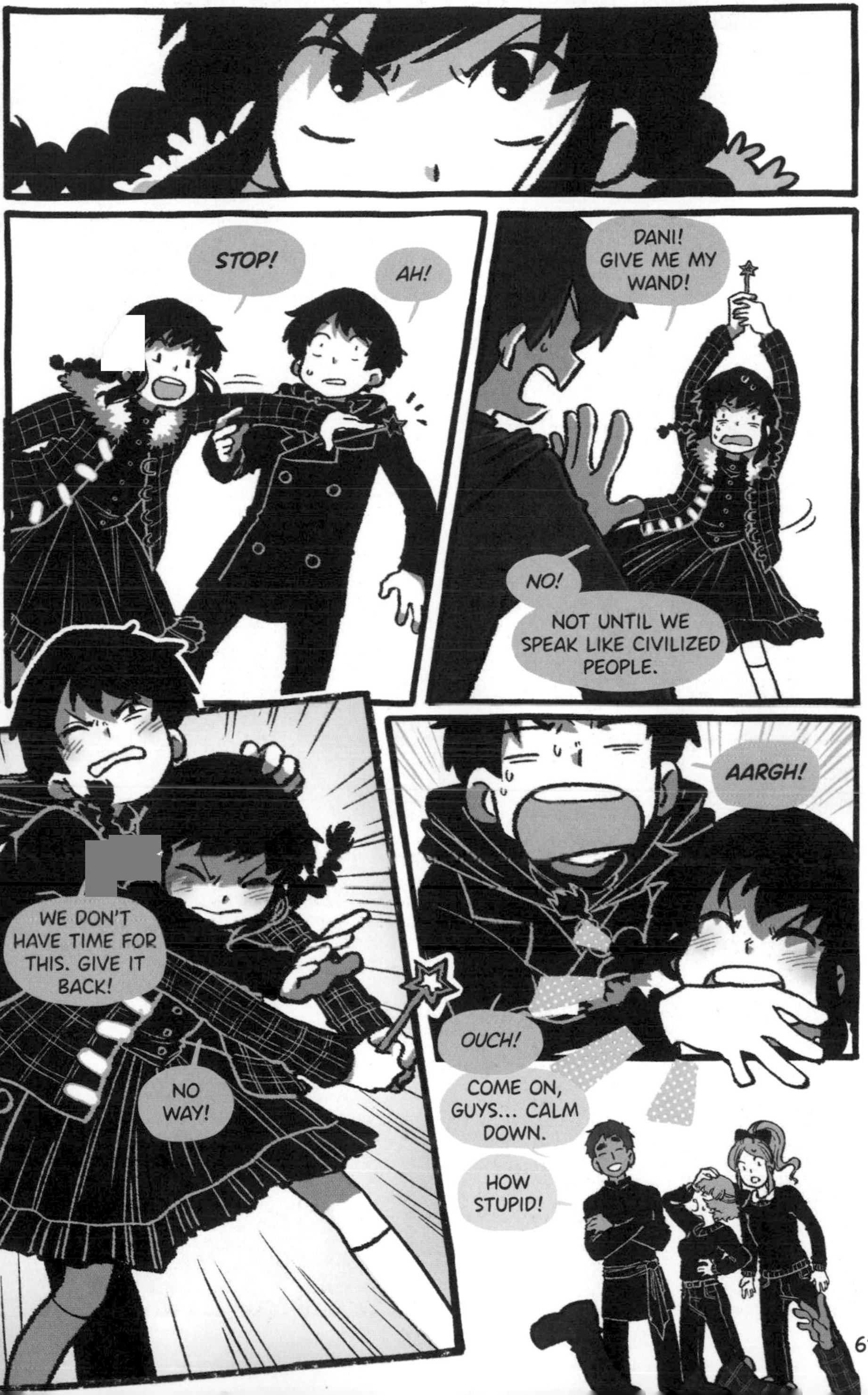
STOP!
AH!
DANI! GIVE ME MY WAND!
NO!
NOT UNTIL WE SPEAK LIKE CIVILIZED PEOPLE.
WE DON'T HAVE TIME FOR THIS. GIVE IT BACK!
NO WAY!
AARGH!
OUCH!
COME ON, GUYS... CALM DOWN.
HOW STUPID!

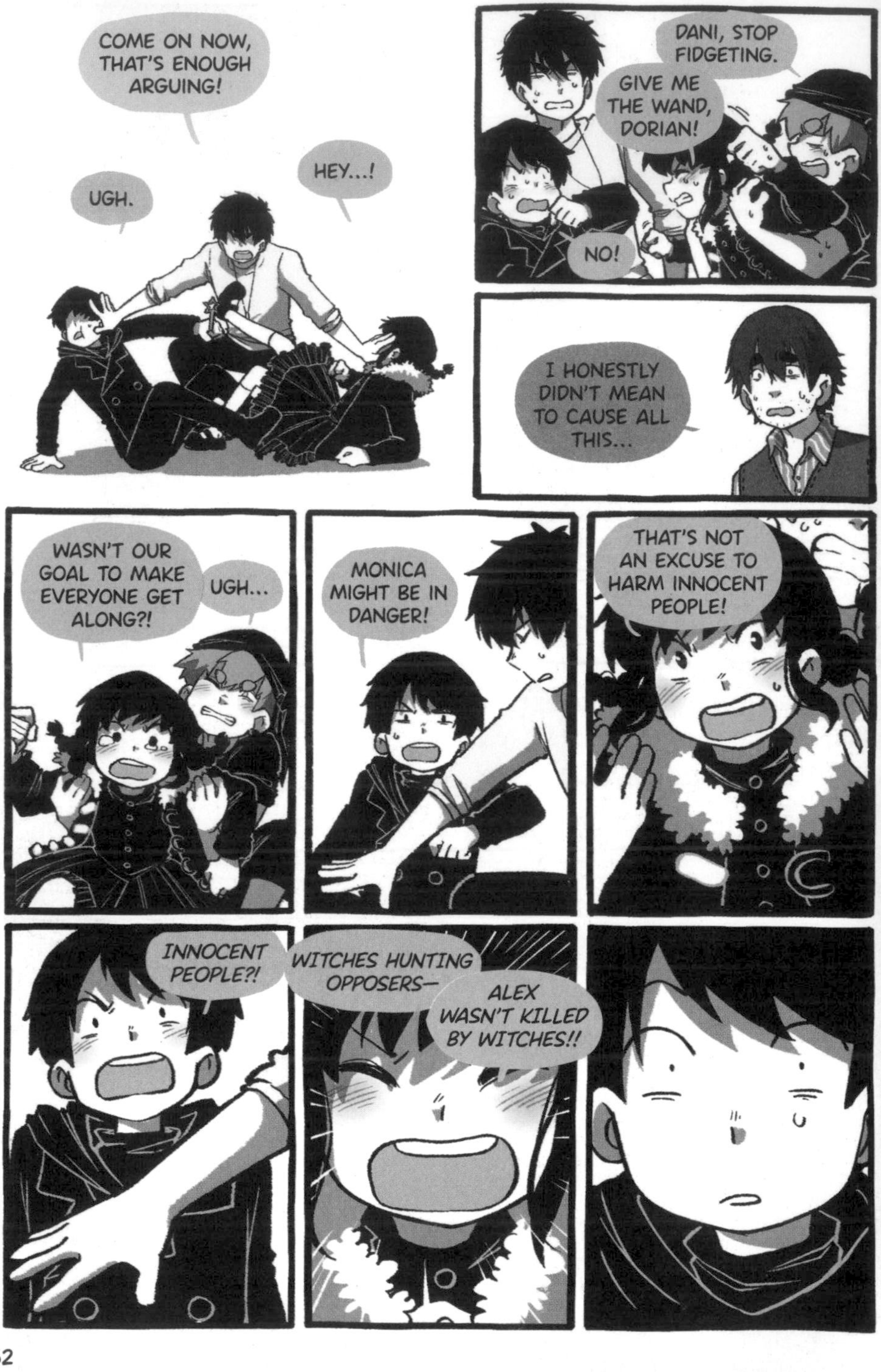
COME ON NOW, THAT'S ENOUGH ARGUING!
HEY...!
UGH.
DANI, STOP FIDGETING.
GIVE ME THE WAND, DORIAN!
NO!
I HONESTLY DIDN'T MEAN TO CAUSE ALL THIS...
WASN'T OUR GOAL TO MAKE EVERYONE GET ALONG?!
UGH...
MONICA MIGHT BE IN DANGER!
THAT'S NOT AN EXCUSE TO HARM INNOCENT PEOPLE!
INNOCENT PEOPLE?!
WITCHES HUNTING OPPOSERS—
ALEX WASN'T KILLED BY WITCHES!!

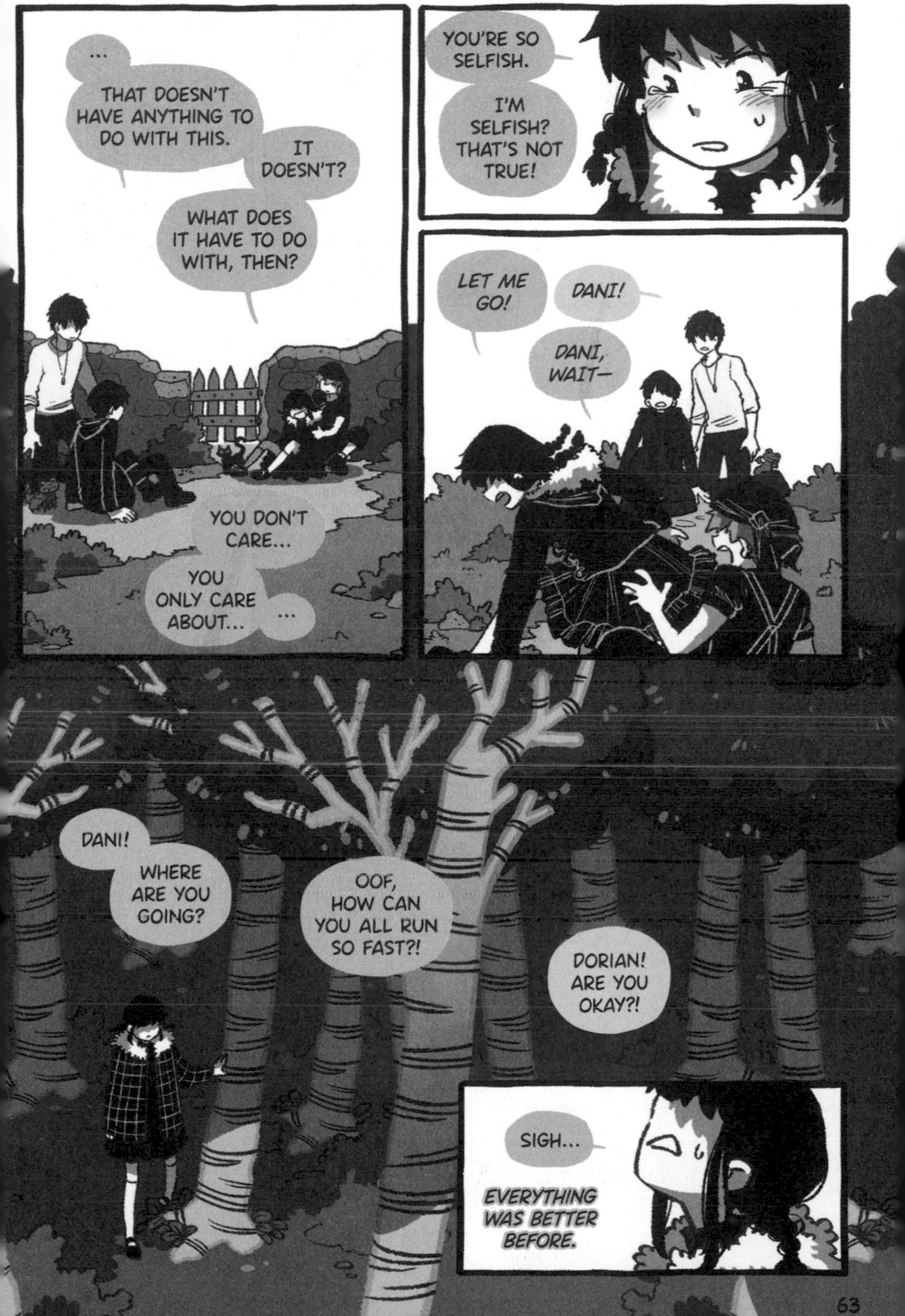
...
THAT DOESN'T HAVE ANYTHING TO DO WITH THIS.
IT DOESN'T?
WHAT DOES IT HAVE TO DO WITH, THEN?
YOU DON'T CARE...
YOU ONLY CARE ABOUT...
...
YOU'RE SO SELFISH.
I'M SELFISH? THAT'S NOT TRUE!
LET ME GO!
DANI!
DANI, WAIT—
DANI!
WHERE ARE YOU GOING?
OOF, HOW CAN YOU ALL RUN SO FAST?!
DORIAN! ARE YOU OKAY?!
SIGH...
EVERYTHING WAS BETTER BEFORE.

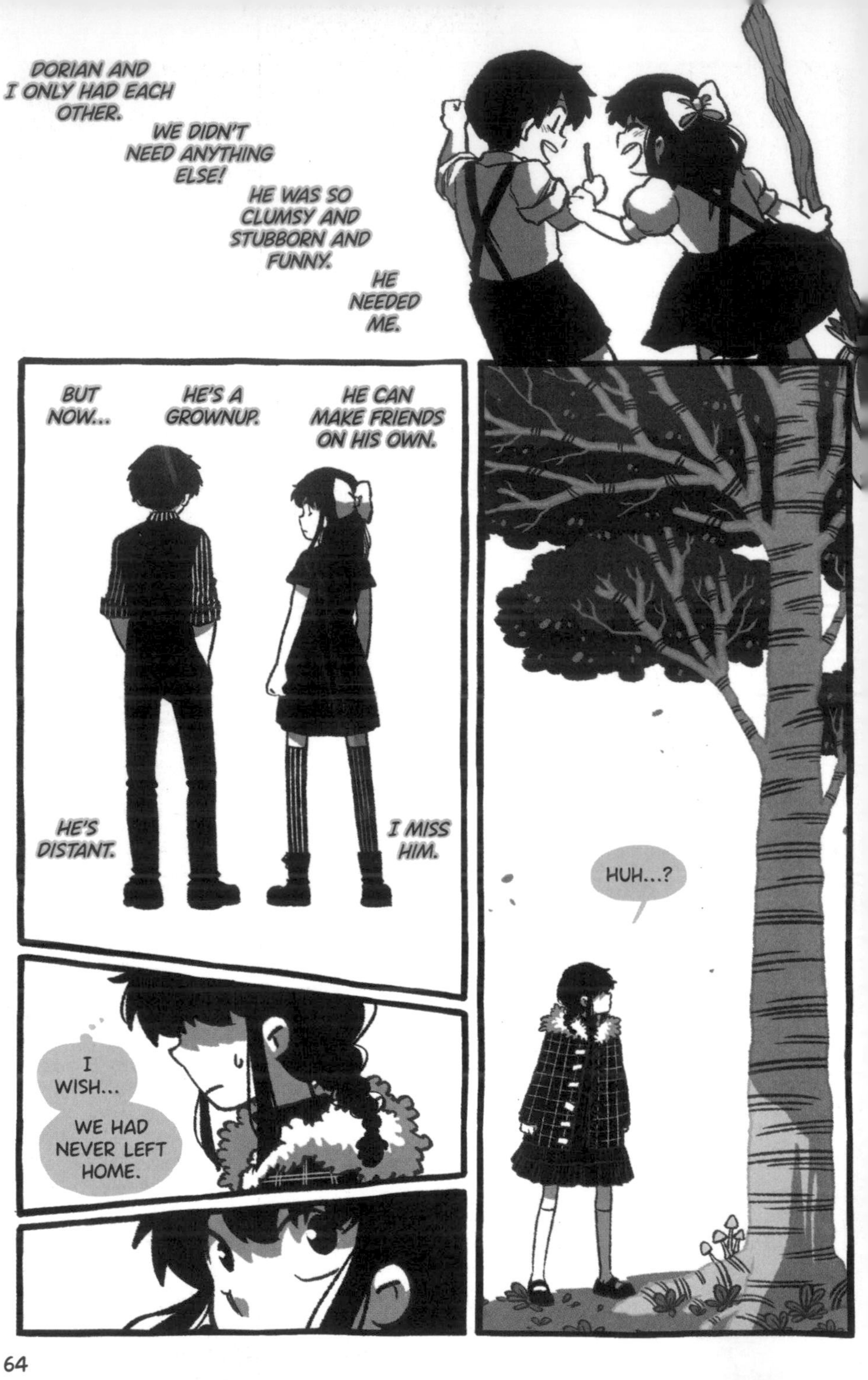
DORIAN AND I ONLY HAD EACH OTHER.
WE DIDN'T NEED ANYTHING ELSE!
HE WAS SO CLUMSY AND STUBBORN AND FUNNY.
HE NEEDED ME.
BUT NOW...
HE'S A GROWNUP.
HE CAN MAKE FRIENDS ON HIS OWN.
HE'S DISTANT.
I MISS HIM.
HUH...?
I WISH...
WE HAD NEVER LEFT HOME.

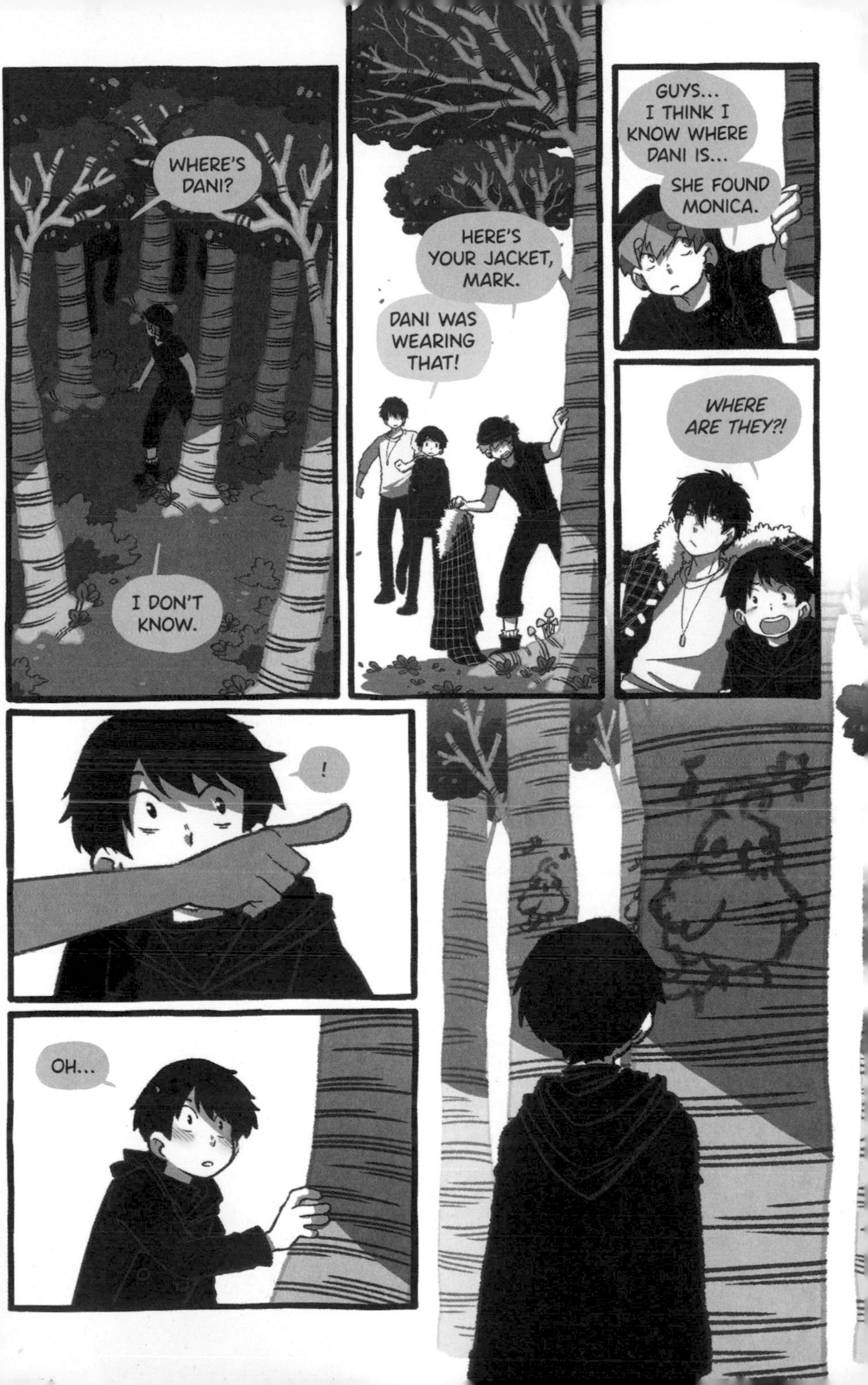
WHERE'S DANI?
I DON'T KNOW.
HERE'S YOUR JACKET, MARK.
DANI WAS WEARING THAT!
GUYS... I THINK I KNOW WHERE DANI IS...
SHE FOUND MONICA.
WHERE ARE THEY?!
!
OH...

CHAPTER 37

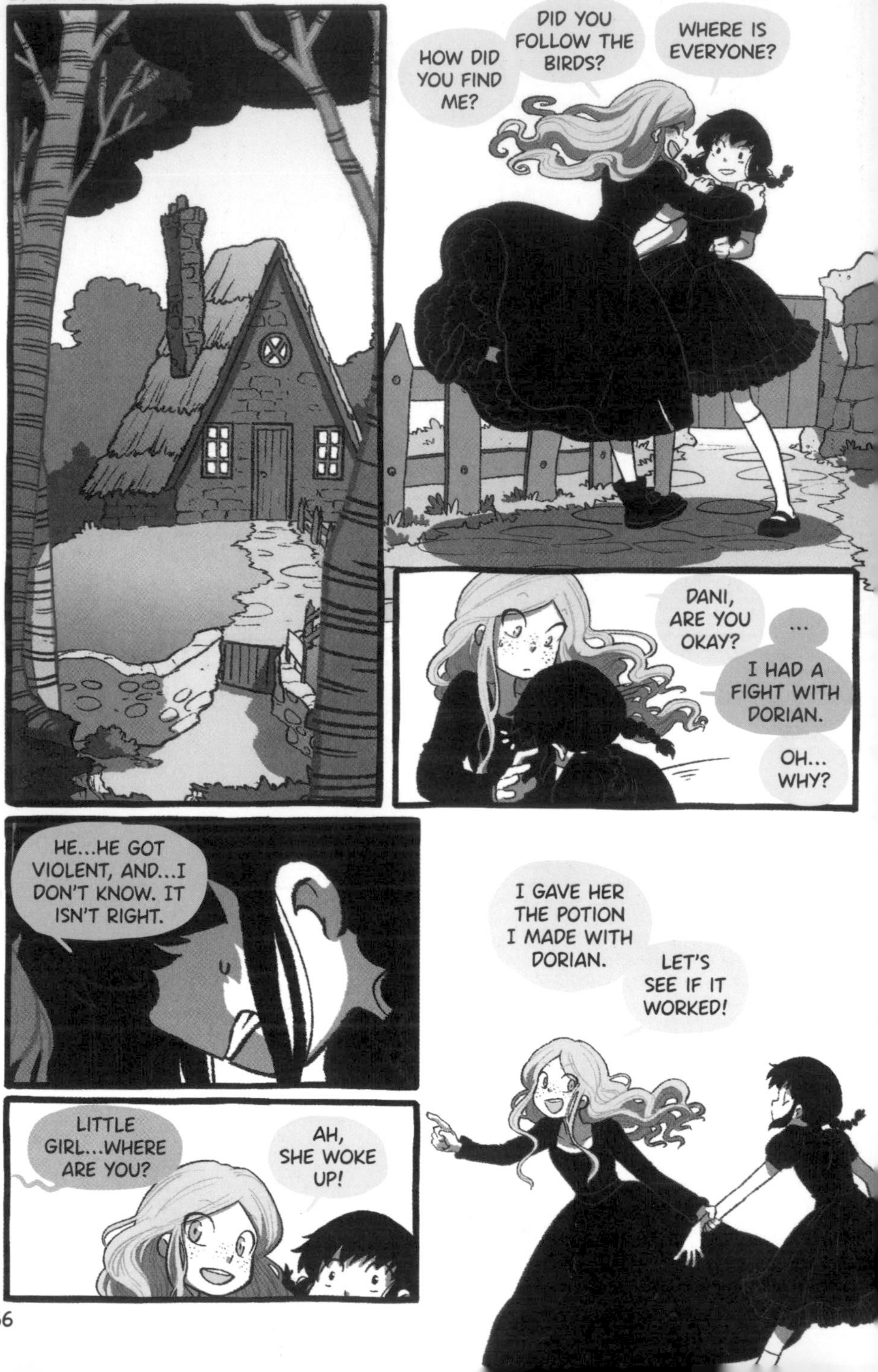
HOW DID YOU FIND ME?
DID YOU FOLLOW THE BIRDS?
WHERE IS EVERYONE?
DANI, ARE YOU OKAY?
...
I HAD A FIGHT WITH DORIAN.
OH... WHY?
HE...HE GOT VIOLENT, AND...I DON'T KNOW. IT ISN'T RIGHT.
LITTLE GIRL...WHERE ARE YOU?
AH, SHE WOKE UP!
I GAVE HER THE POTION I MADE WITH DORIAN.
LET'S SEE IF IT WORKED!

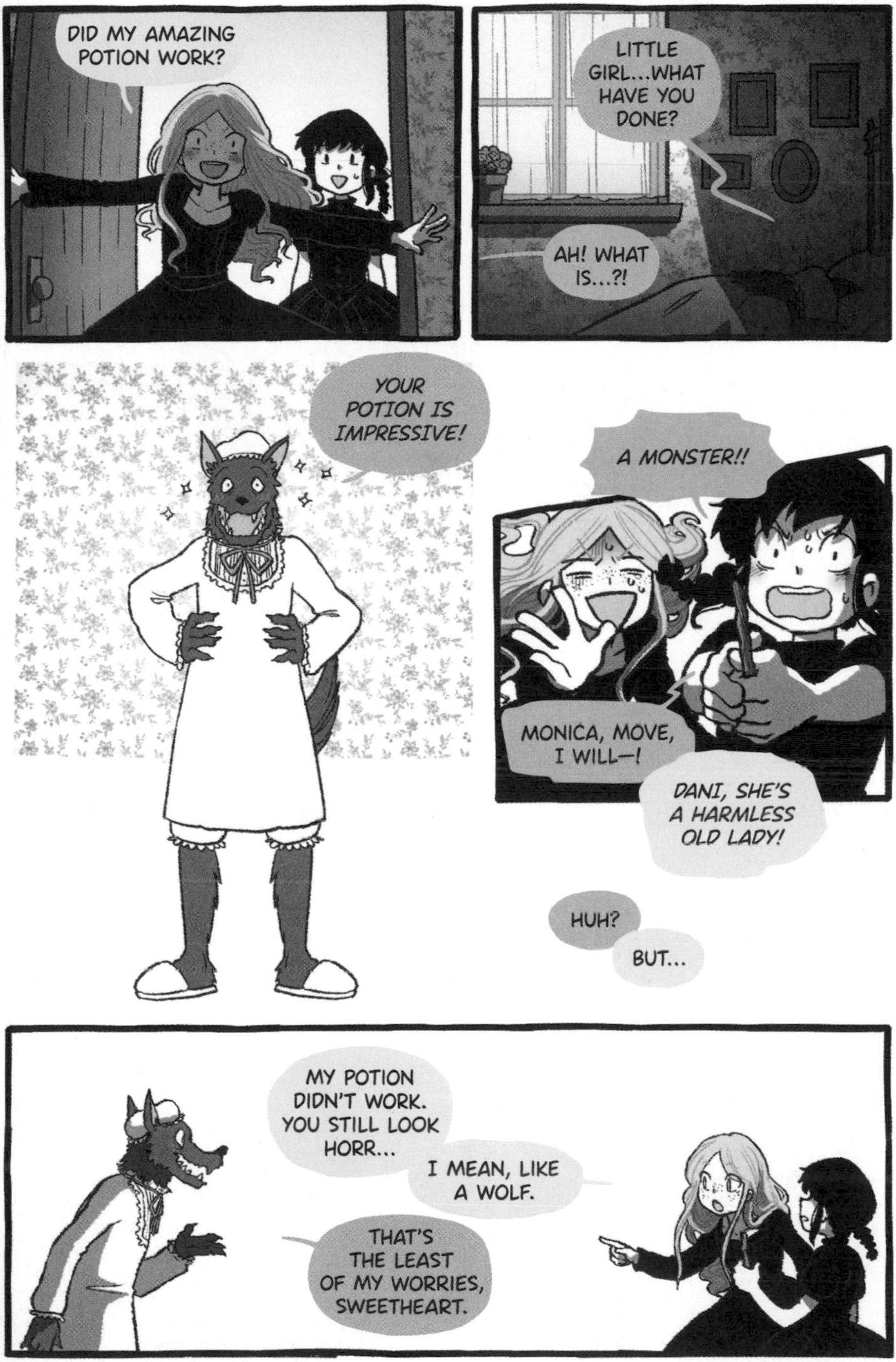
DID MY AMAZING POTION WORK?
LITTLE GIRL...WHAT HAVE YOU DONE?
AH! WHAT IS...?!
YOUR POTION IS IMPRESSIVE!
A MONSTER!!
MONICA, MOVE, I WILL—!
DANI, SHE'S A HARMLESS OLD LADY!
HUH?
BUT...
MY POTION DIDN'T WORK. YOU STILL LOOK HORR...
I MEAN, LIKE A WOLF.
THAT'S THE LEAST OF MY WORRIES, SWEETHEART.

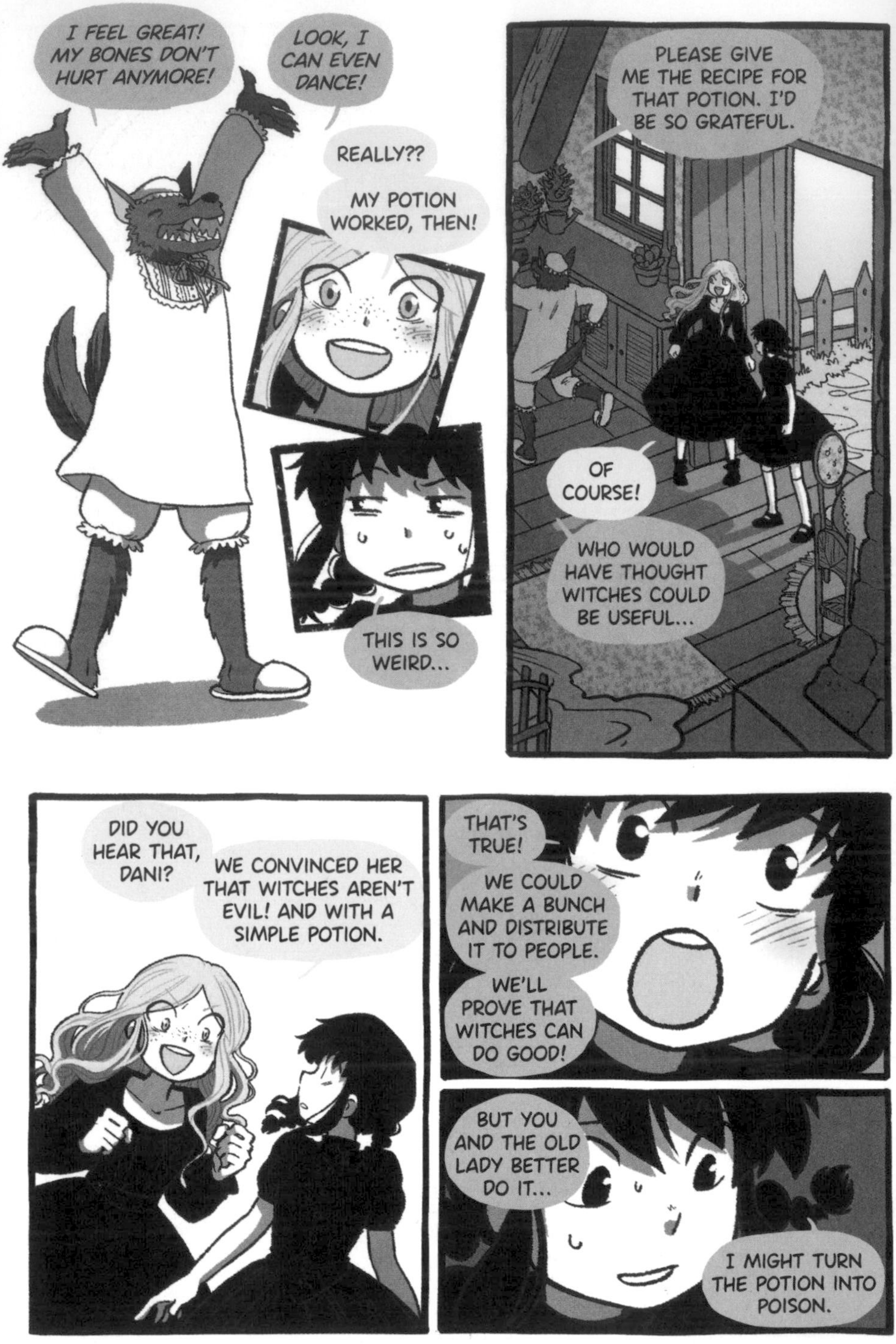
I FEEL GREAT! MY BONES DON'T HURT ANYMORE!
LOOK, I CAN EVEN DANCE!
REALLY??
MY POTION WORKED, THEN!
THIS IS SO WEIRD...
PLEASE GIVE ME THE RECIPE FOR THAT POTION. I'D BE SO GRATEFUL.
OF COURSE!
WHO WOULD HAVE THOUGHT WITCHES COULD BE USEFUL...
DID YOU HEAR THAT, DANI?
WE CONVINCED HER THAT WITCHES AREN'T EVIL! AND WITH A SIMPLE POTION.
THAT'S TRUE!
WE COULD MAKE A BUNCH AND DISTRIBUTE IT TO PEOPLE.
WE'LL PROVE THAT WITCHES CAN DO GOOD!
BUT YOU AND THE OLD LADY BETTER DO IT...
I MIGHT TURN THE POTION INTO POISON.

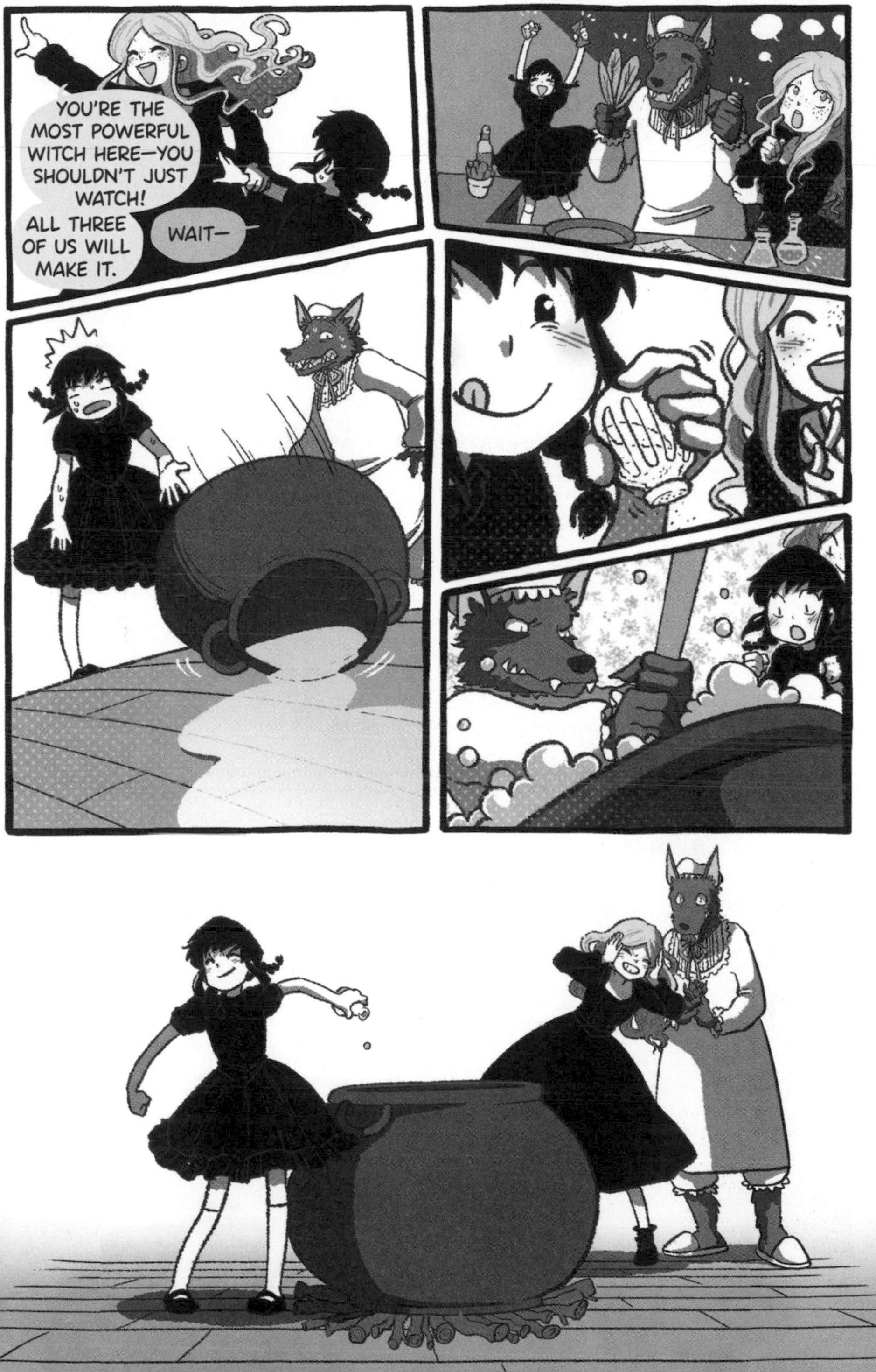
YOU'RE THE MOST POWERFUL WITCH HERE—YOU SHOULDN'T JUST WATCH!
ALL THREE OF US WILL MAKE IT.
WAIT—

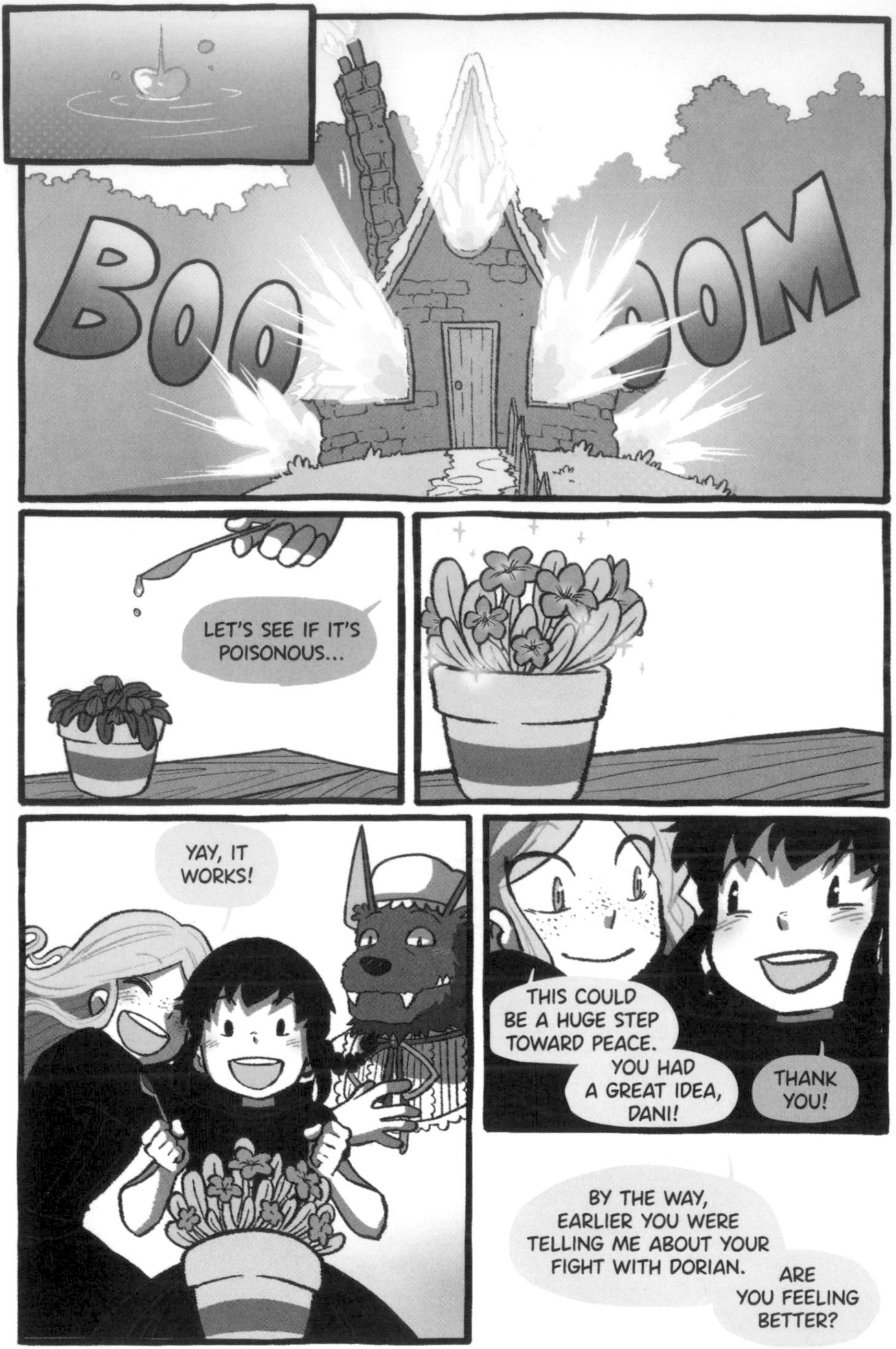
BOOOOM
LET'S SEE IF IT'S POISONOUS...
YAY, IT WORKS!
THIS COULD BE A HUGE STEP TOWARD PEACE.
YOU HAD A GREAT IDEA, DANI!
THANK YOU!
BY THE WAY, EARLIER YOU WERE TELLING ME ABOUT YOUR FIGHT WITH DORIAN.
ARE YOU FEELING BETTER?

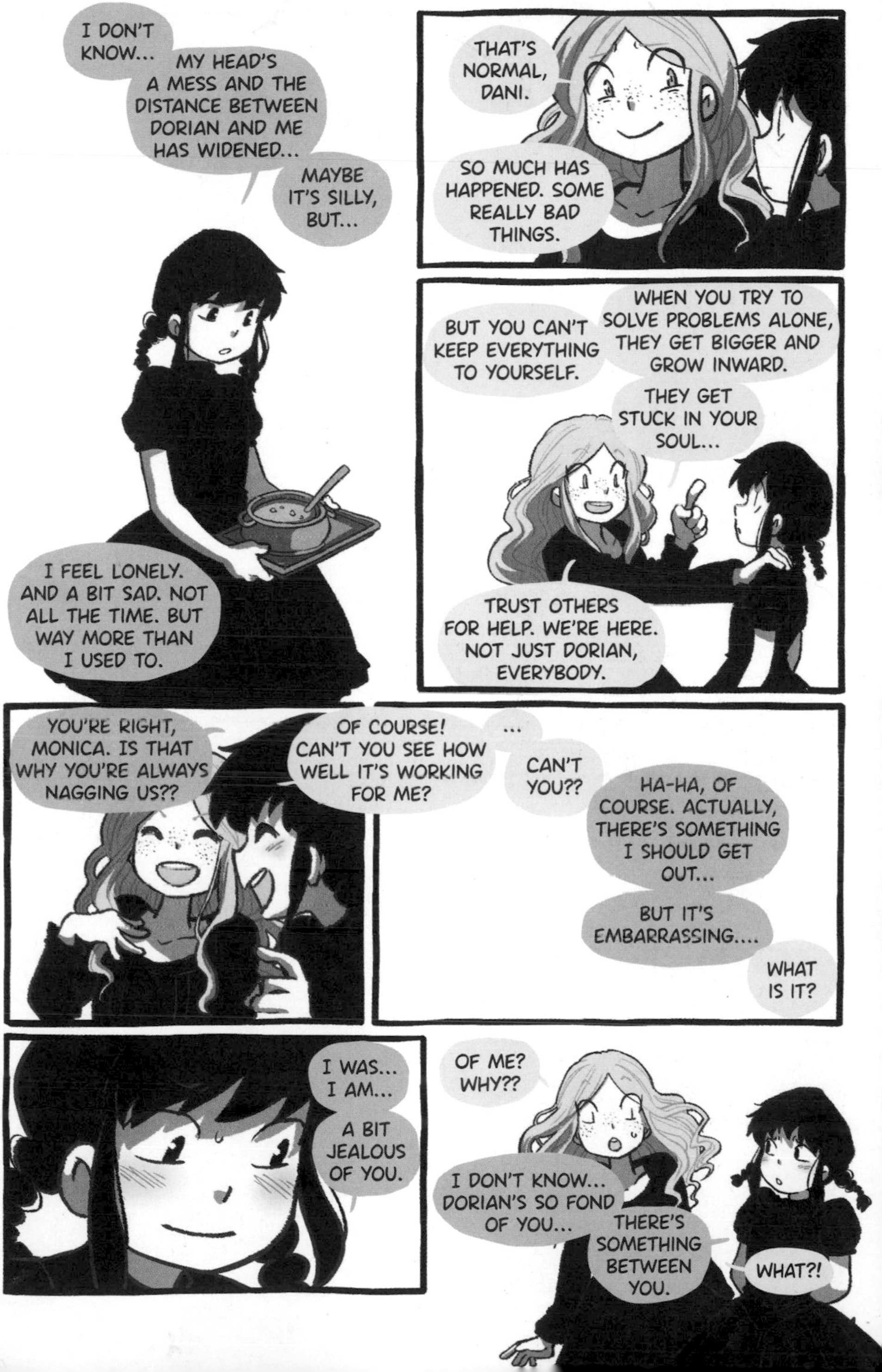
I DON'T KNOW...
MY HEAD'S A MESS AND THE DISTANCE BETWEEN DORIAN AND ME HAS WIDENED...
MAYBE IT'S SILLY, BUT...
I FEEL LONELY. AND A BIT SAD. NOT ALL THE TIME. BUT WAY MORE THAN I USED TO.
THAT'S NORMAL, DANI.
SO MUCH HAS HAPPENED. SOME REALLY BAD THINGS.
BUT YOU CAN'T KEEP EVERYTHING TO YOURSELF.
WHEN YOU TRY TO SOLVE PROBLEMS ALONE, THEY GET BIGGER AND GROW INWARD.
THEY GET STUCK IN YOUR SOUL...
TRUST OTHERS FOR HELP. WE'RE HERE. NOT JUST DORIAN, EVERYBODY.
YOU'RE RIGHT, MONICA. IS THAT WHY YOU'RE ALWAYS NAGGING US??
OF COURSE! CAN'T YOU SEE HOW WELL IT'S WORKING FOR ME?
...
CAN'T YOU??
HA-HA, OF COURSE. ACTUALLY, THERE'S SOMETHING I SHOULD GET OUT...
BUT IT'S EMBARRASSING....
WHAT IS IT?
I WAS... I AM...
A BIT JEALOUS OF YOU.
OF ME? WHY??
I DON'T KNOW... DORIAN'S SO FOND OF YOU...
THERE'S SOMETHING BETWEEN YOU.
WHAT?!

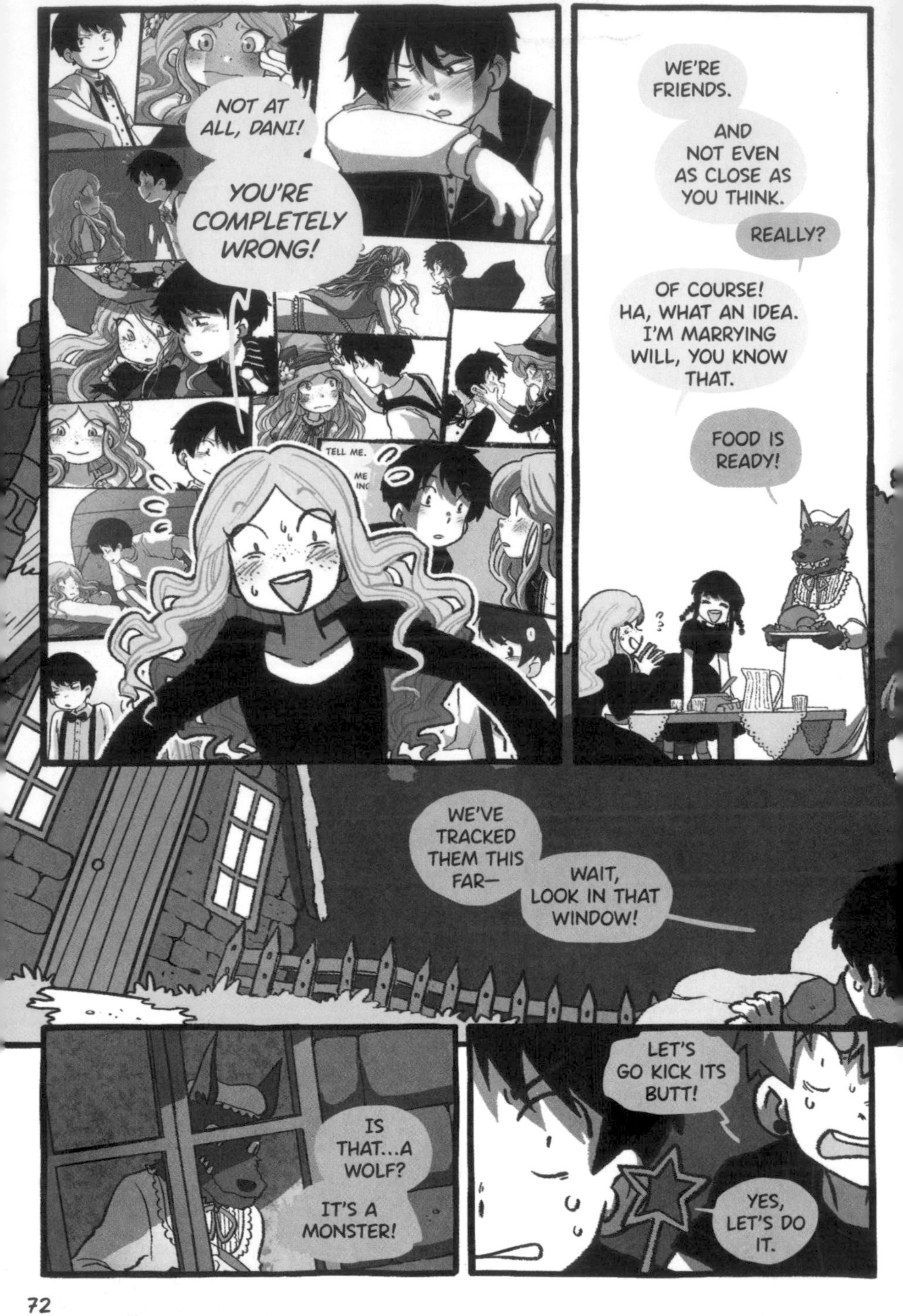
NOT AT ALL, DANI!
YOU'RE COMPLETELY WRONG!
TELL ME.
WE'RE FRIENDS.
AND NOT EVEN AS CLOSE AS YOU THINK.
REALLY?
OF COURSE! HA, WHAT AN IDEA. I'M MARRYING WILL, YOU KNOW THAT.
FOOD IS READY!
WE'VE TRACKED THEM THIS FAR—
WAIT, LOOK IN THAT WINDOW!
IS THAT...A WOLF?
IT'S A MONSTER!
LET'S GO KICK ITS BUTT!
YES, LET'S DO IT.

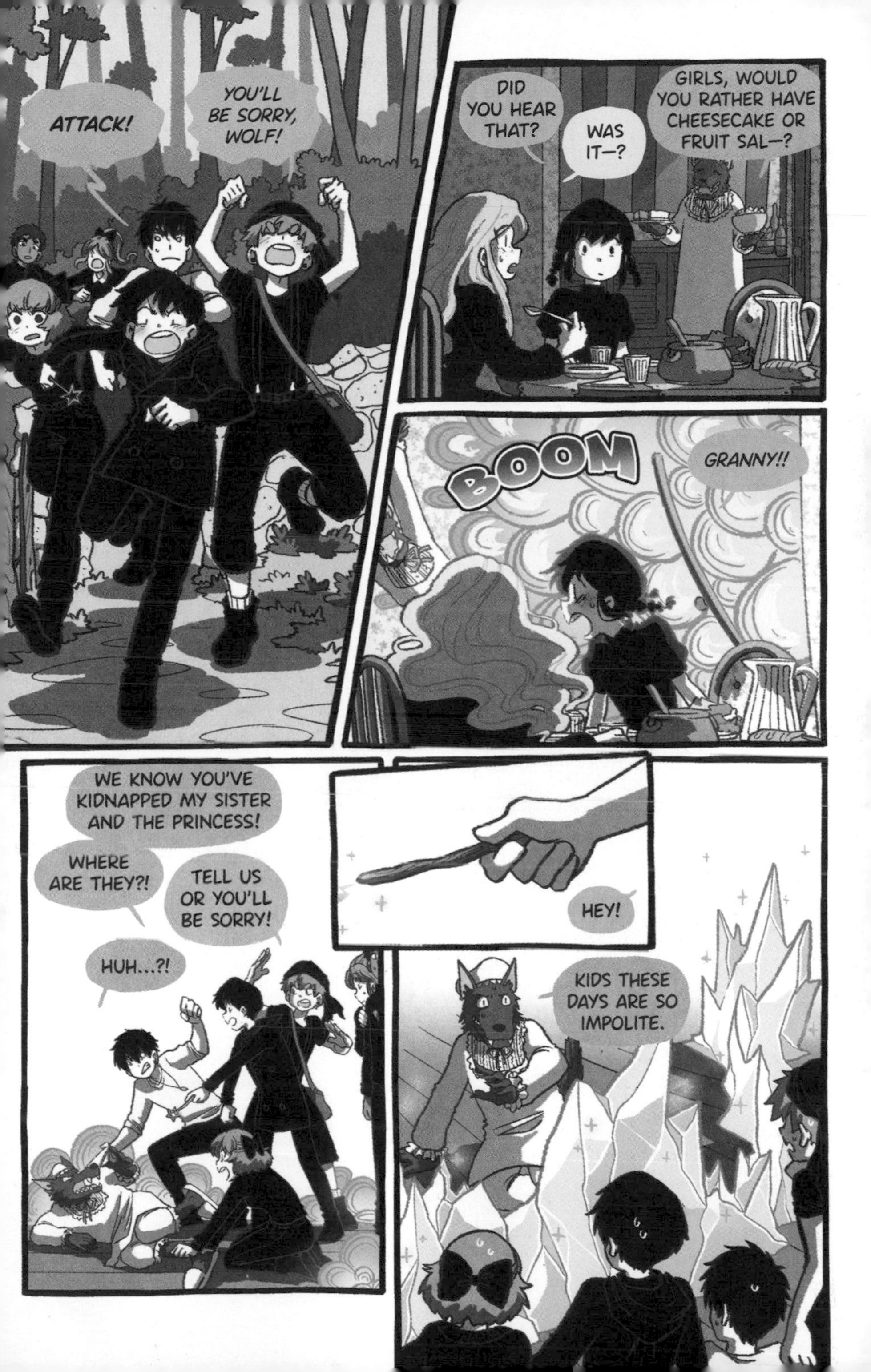
ATTACK!
YOU'LL BE SORRY, WOLF!
DID YOU HEAR THAT?
WAS IT—?
GIRLS, WOULD YOU RATHER HAVE CHEESECAKE OR FRUIT SAL—?
BOOM
GRANNY!!
WE KNOW YOU'VE KIDNAPPED MY SISTER AND THE PRINCESS!
WHERE ARE THEY?!
TELL US OR YOU'LL BE SORRY!
HUH...?!
HEY!
KIDS THESE DAYS ARE SO IMPOLITE.

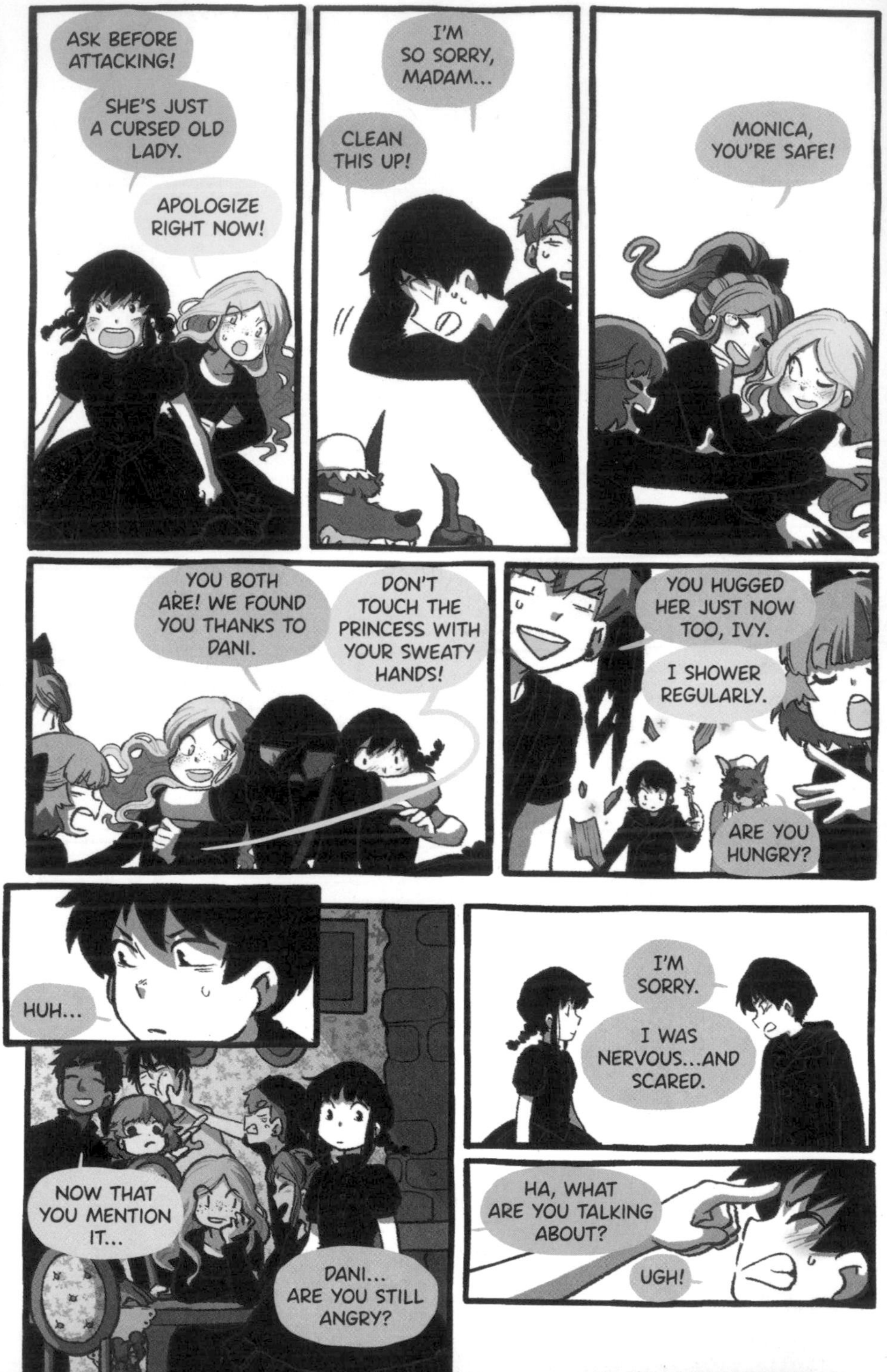
ASK BEFORE ATTACKING!
SHE'S JUST A CURSED OLD LADY.
APOLOGIZE RIGHT NOW!
I'M SO SORRY, MADAM...
CLEAN THIS UP!
MONICA, YOU'RE SAFE!
YOU BOTH ARE! WE FOUND YOU THANKS TO DANI.
DON'T TOUCH THE PRINCESS WITH YOUR SWEATY HANDS!
YOU HUGGED HER JUST NOW TOO, IVY.
I SHOWER REGULARLY.
ARE YOU HUNGRY?
HUH...
NOW THAT YOU MENTION IT...
DANI... ARE YOU STILL ANGRY?
I'M SORRY.
I WAS NERVOUS...AND SCARED.
HA, WHAT ARE YOU TALKING ABOUT?
UGH!

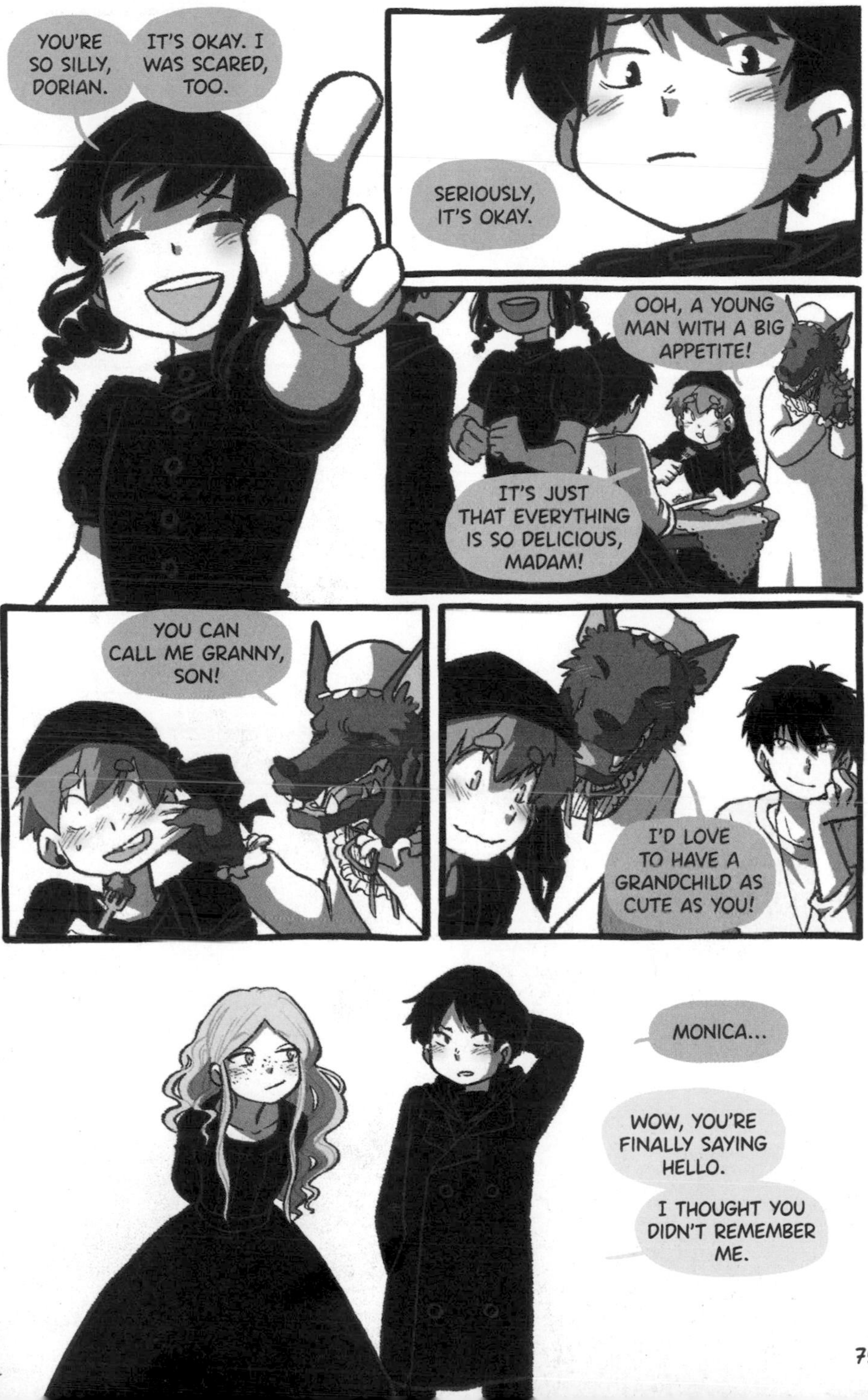
YOU'RE SO SILLY, DORIAN.
IT'S OKAY. I WAS SCARED, TOO.
SERIOUSLY, IT'S OKAY.
OOH, A YOUNG MAN WITH A BIG APPETITE!
IT'S JUST THAT EVERYTHING IS SO DELICIOUS, MADAM!
YOU CAN CALL ME GRANNY, SON!
I'D LOVE TO HAVE A GRANDCHILD AS CUTE AS YOU!
MONICA...
WOW, YOU'RE FINALLY SAYING HELLO.
I THOUGHT YOU DIDN'T REMEMBER ME.

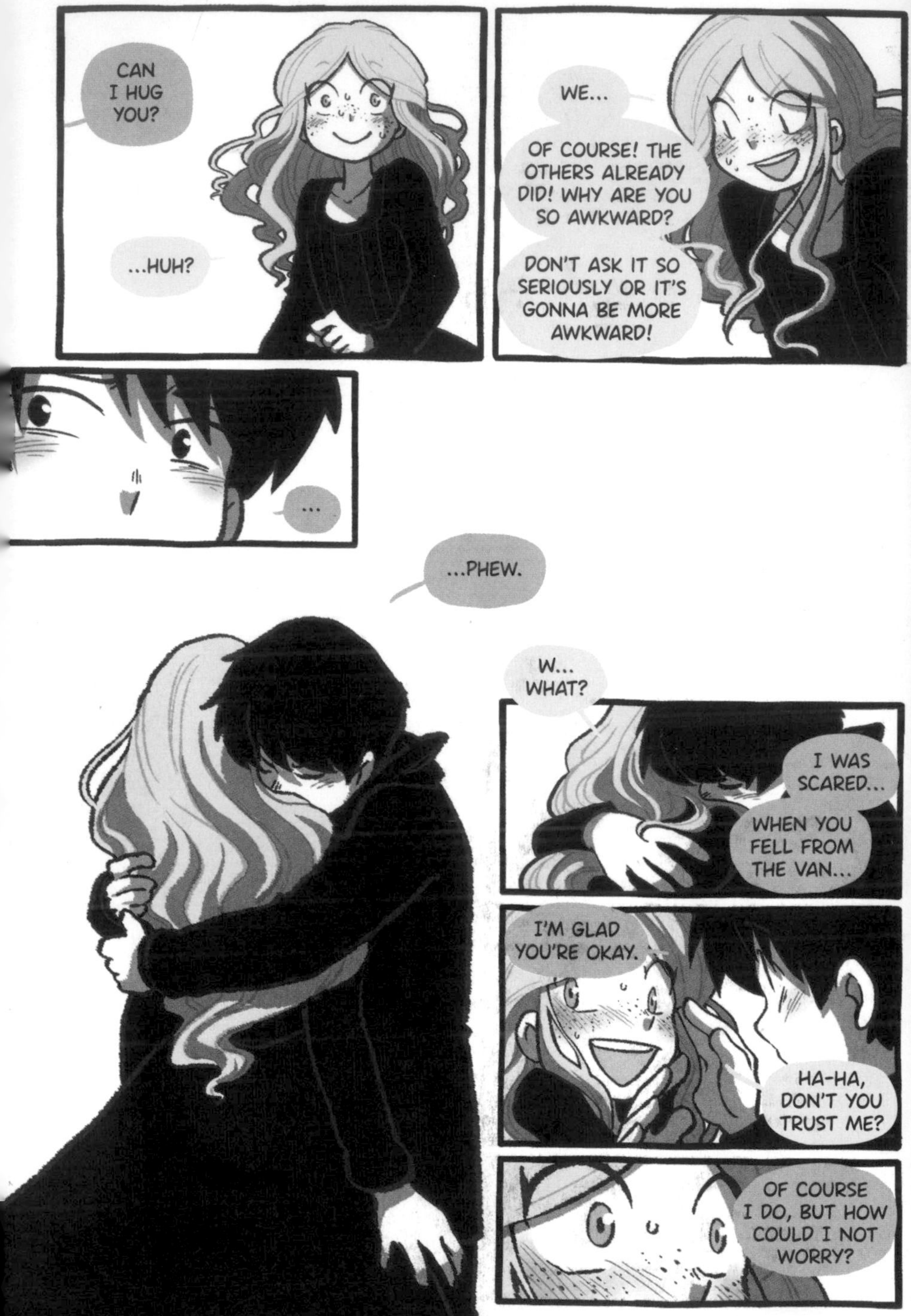
CAN I HUG YOU?
...HUH?
WE...
OF COURSE! THE OTHERS ALREADY DID! WHY ARE YOU SO AWKWARD?
DON'T ASK IT SO SERIOUSLY OR IT'S GONNA BE MORE AWKWARD!
...
...PHEW.
W... WHAT?
I WAS SCARED...
WHEN YOU FELL FROM THE VAN...
I'M GLAD YOU'RE OKAY.
HA-HA, DON'T YOU TRUST ME?
OF COURSE I DO, BUT HOW COULD I NOT WORRY?

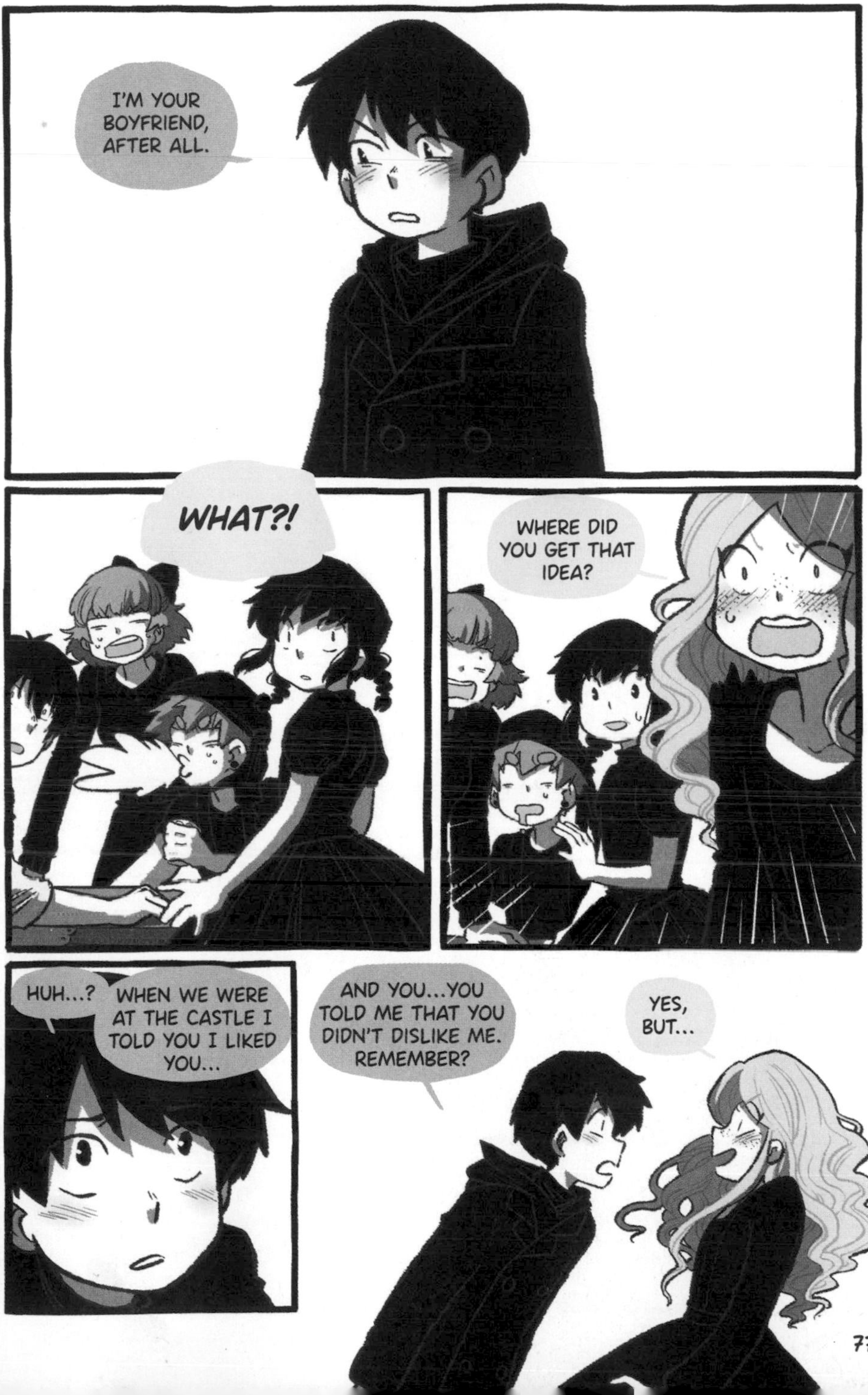
I'M YOUR BOYFRIEND, AFTER ALL.
WHAT?!
WHERE DID YOU GET THAT IDEA?
HUH...?
WHEN WE WERE AT THE CASTLE I TOLD YOU I LIKED YOU...
AND YOU...YOU TOLD ME THAT YOU DIDN'T DISLIKE ME. REMEMBER?
YES, BUT...

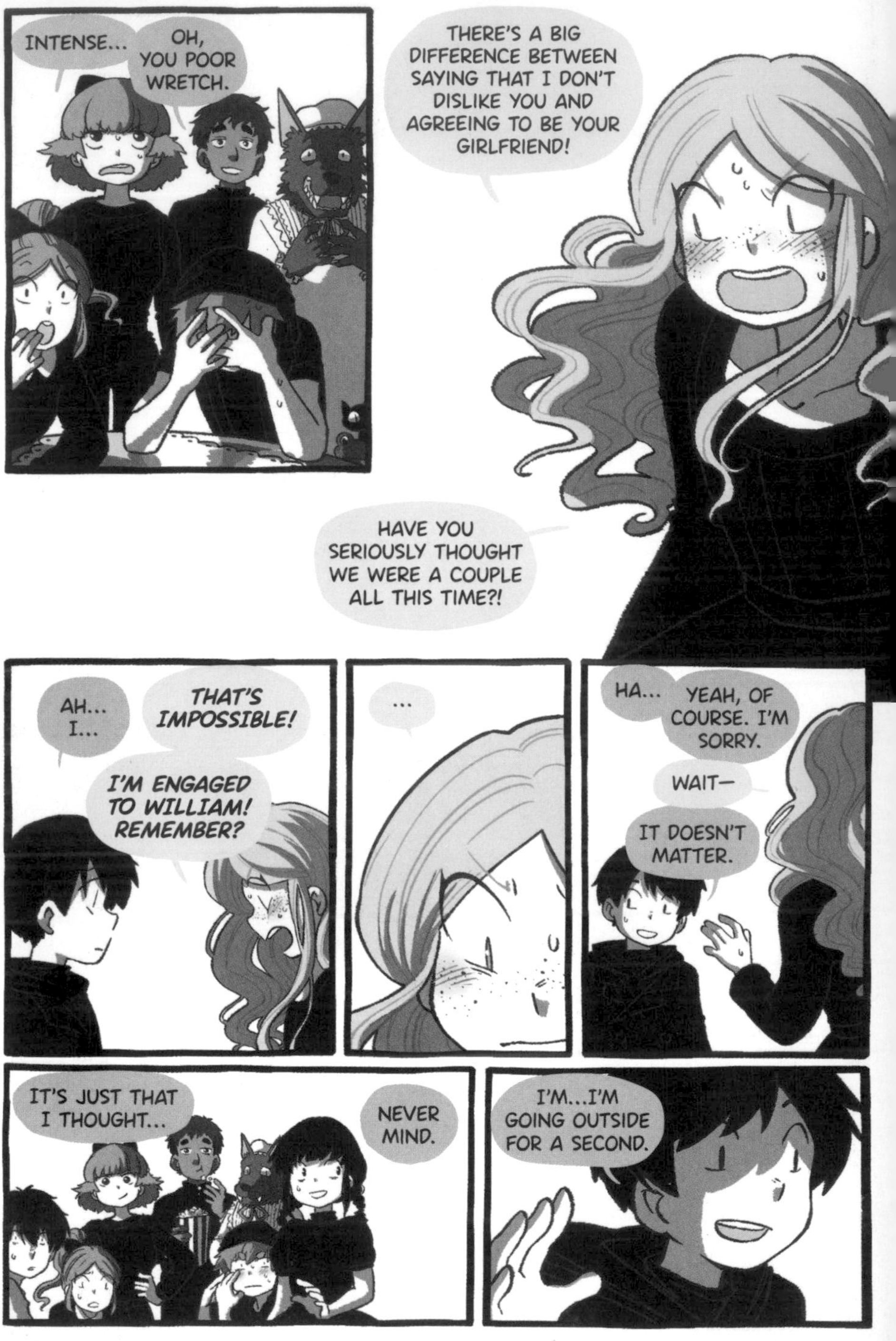
INTENSE...
OH, YOU POOR WRETCH.
THERE'S A BIG DIFFERENCE BETWEEN SAYING THAT I DON'T DISLIKE YOU AND AGREEING TO BE YOUR GIRLFRIEND!
HAVE YOU SERIOUSLY THOUGHT WE WERE A COUPLE ALL THIS TIME?!
AH... I...
THAT'S IMPOSSIBLE!
I'M ENGAGED TO WILLIAM! REMEMBER?
...
HA...
YEAH, OF COURSE. I'M SORRY.
WAIT—
IT DOESN'T MATTER.
IT'S JUST THAT I THOUGHT...
NEVER MIND.
I'M...I'M GOING OUTSIDE FOR A SECOND.

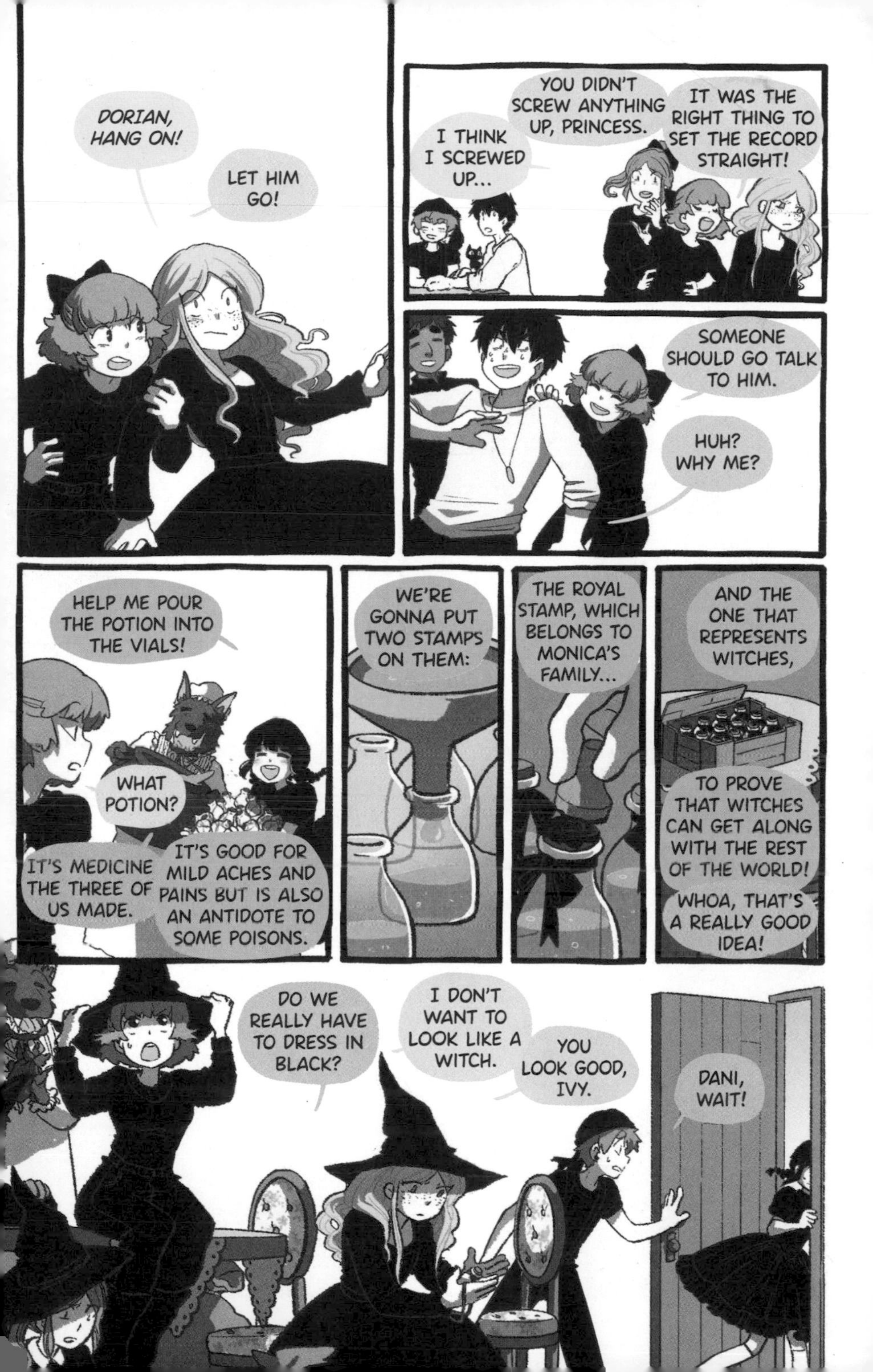

DORIAN, HANG ON!
LET HIM GO!
I THINK I SCREWED UP...
YOU DIDN'T SCREW ANYTHING UP, PRINCESS.
IT WAS THE RIGHT THING TO SET THE RECORD STRAIGHT!
SOMEONE SHOULD GO TALK TO HIM.
HUH? WHY ME?
HELP ME POUR THE POTION INTO THE VIALS!
WHAT POTION?
IT'S MEDICINE THE THREE OF US MADE.
IT'S GOOD FOR MILD ACHES AND PAINS BUT IS ALSO AN ANTIDOTE TO SOME POISONS.
WE'RE GONNA PUT TWO STAMPS ON THEM:
THE ROYAL STAMP, WHICH BELONGS TO MONICA'S FAMILY...
AND THE ONE THAT REPRESENTS WITCHES,
TO PROVE THAT WITCHES CAN GET ALONG WITH THE REST OF THE WORLD!
WHOA, THAT'S A REALLY GOOD IDEA!
DO WE REALLY HAVE TO DRESS IN BLACK?
I DON'T WANT TO LOOK LIKE A WITCH.
YOU LOOK GOOD, IVY.
DANI, WAIT!

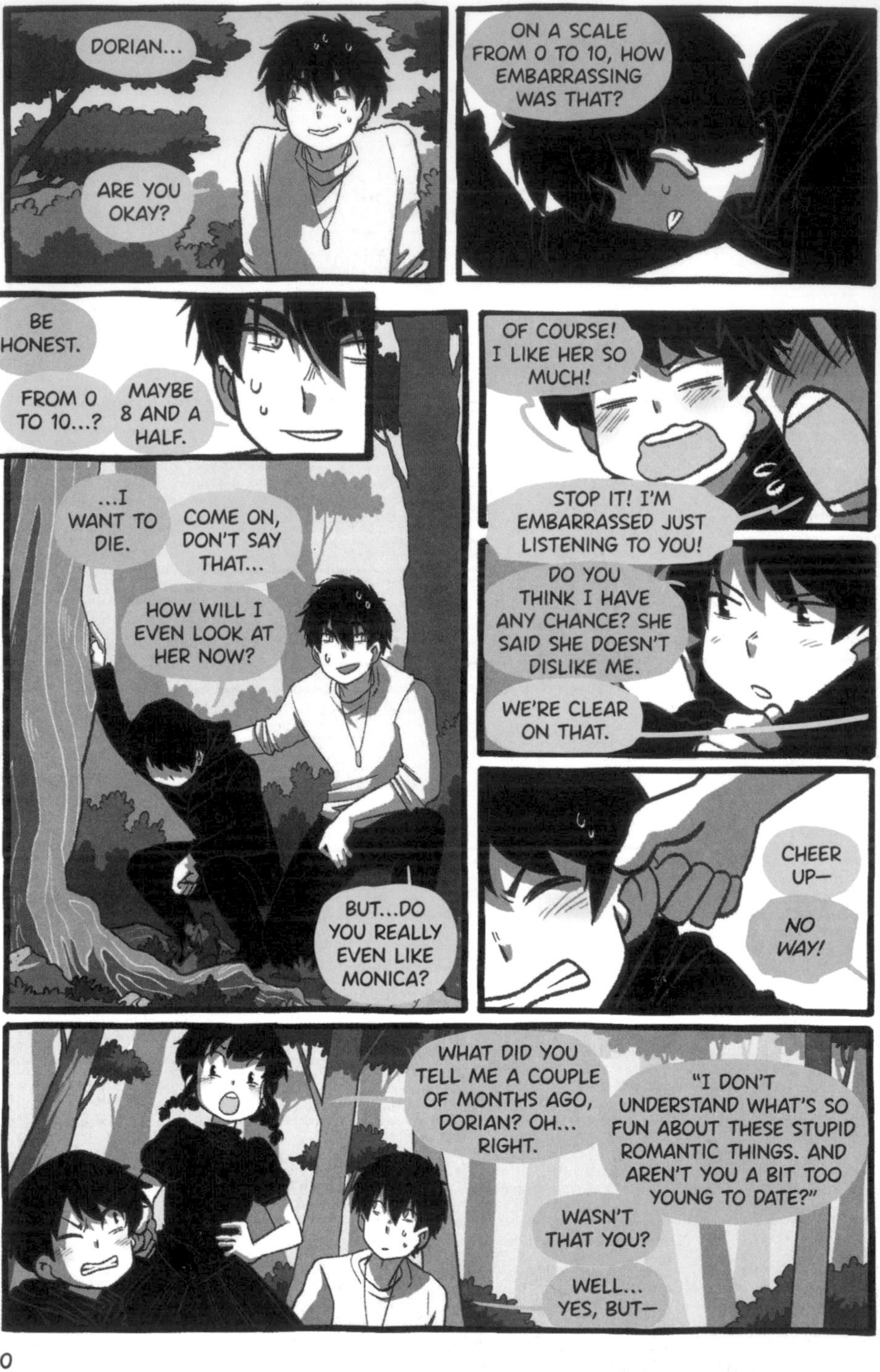
DORIAN...
ARE YOU OKAY?
ON A SCALE FROM 0 TO 10, HOW EMBARRASSING WAS THAT?
BE HONEST.
FROM 0 TO 10...?
MAYBE 8 AND A HALF.
...I WANT TO DIE.
COME ON, DON'T SAY THAT...
HOW WILL I EVEN LOOK AT HER NOW?
BUT...DO YOU REALLY EVEN LIKE MONICA?
OF COURSE! I LIKE HER SO MUCH!
STOP IT! I'M EMBARRASSED JUST LISTENING TO YOU!
DO YOU THINK I HAVE ANY CHANCE? SHE SAID SHE DOESN'T DISLIKE ME.
WE'RE CLEAR ON THAT.
CHEER UP—
NO WAY!
WHAT DID YOU TELL ME A COUPLE OF MONTHS AGO, DORIAN? OH... RIGHT.
"I DON'T UNDERSTAND WHAT'S SO FUN ABOUT THESE STUPID ROMANTIC THINGS. AND AREN'T YOU A BIT TOO YOUNG TO DATE?"
WASN'T THAT YOU?
WELL... YES, BUT—

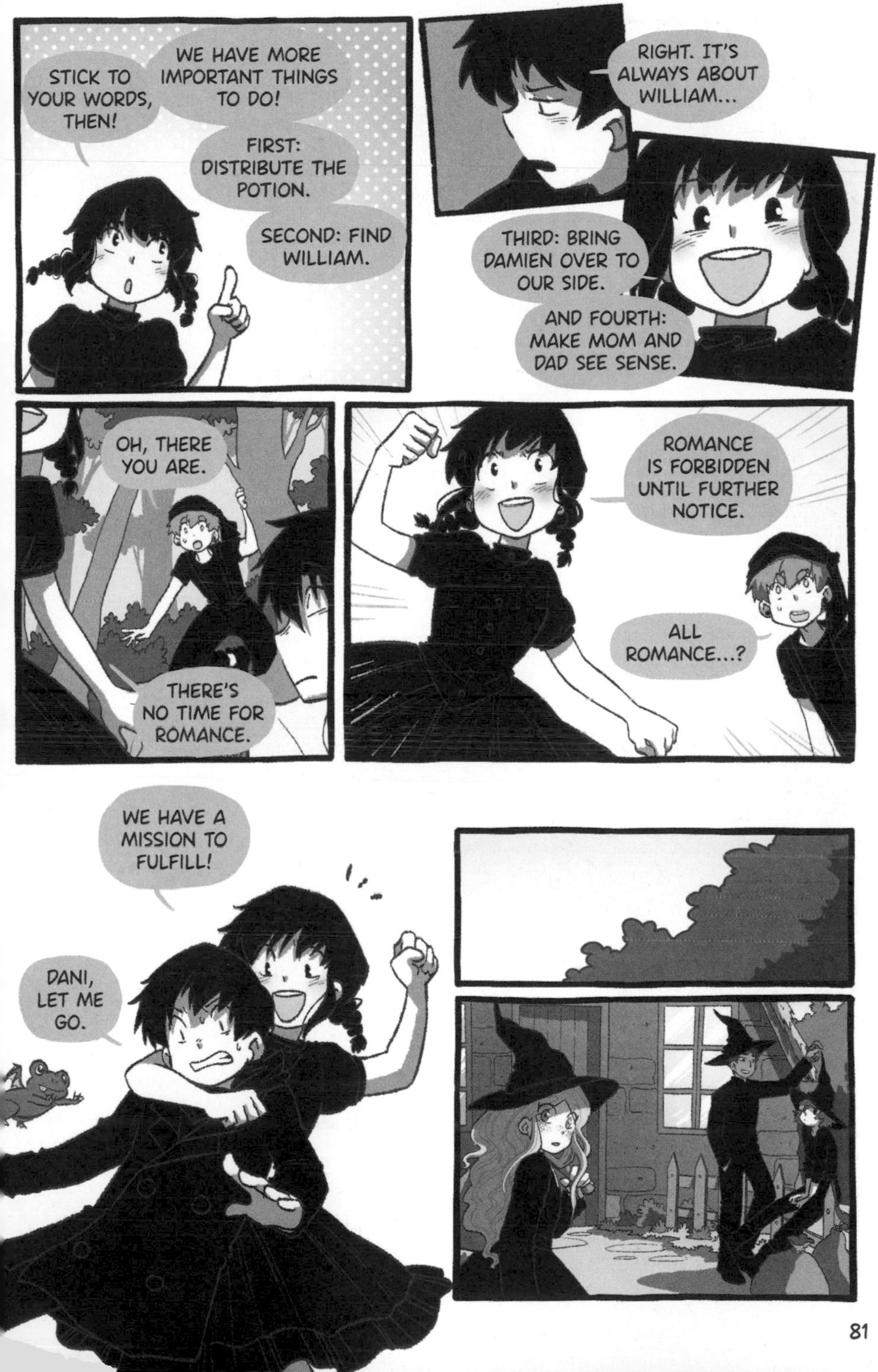

STICK TO YOUR WORDS, THEN!
WE HAVE MORE IMPORTANT THINGS TO DO!
FIRST: DISTRIBUTE THE POTION.
SECOND: FIND WILLIAM.
RIGHT. IT'S ALWAYS ABOUT WILLIAM...
THIRD: BRING DAMIEN OVER TO OUR SIDE.
AND FOURTH: MAKE MOM AND DAD SEE SENSE.
OH, THERE YOU ARE.
THERE'S NO TIME FOR ROMANCE.
ROMANCE IS FORBIDDEN UNTIL FURTHER NOTICE.
ALL ROMANCE...?
WE HAVE A MISSION TO FULFILL!
DANI, LET ME GO.

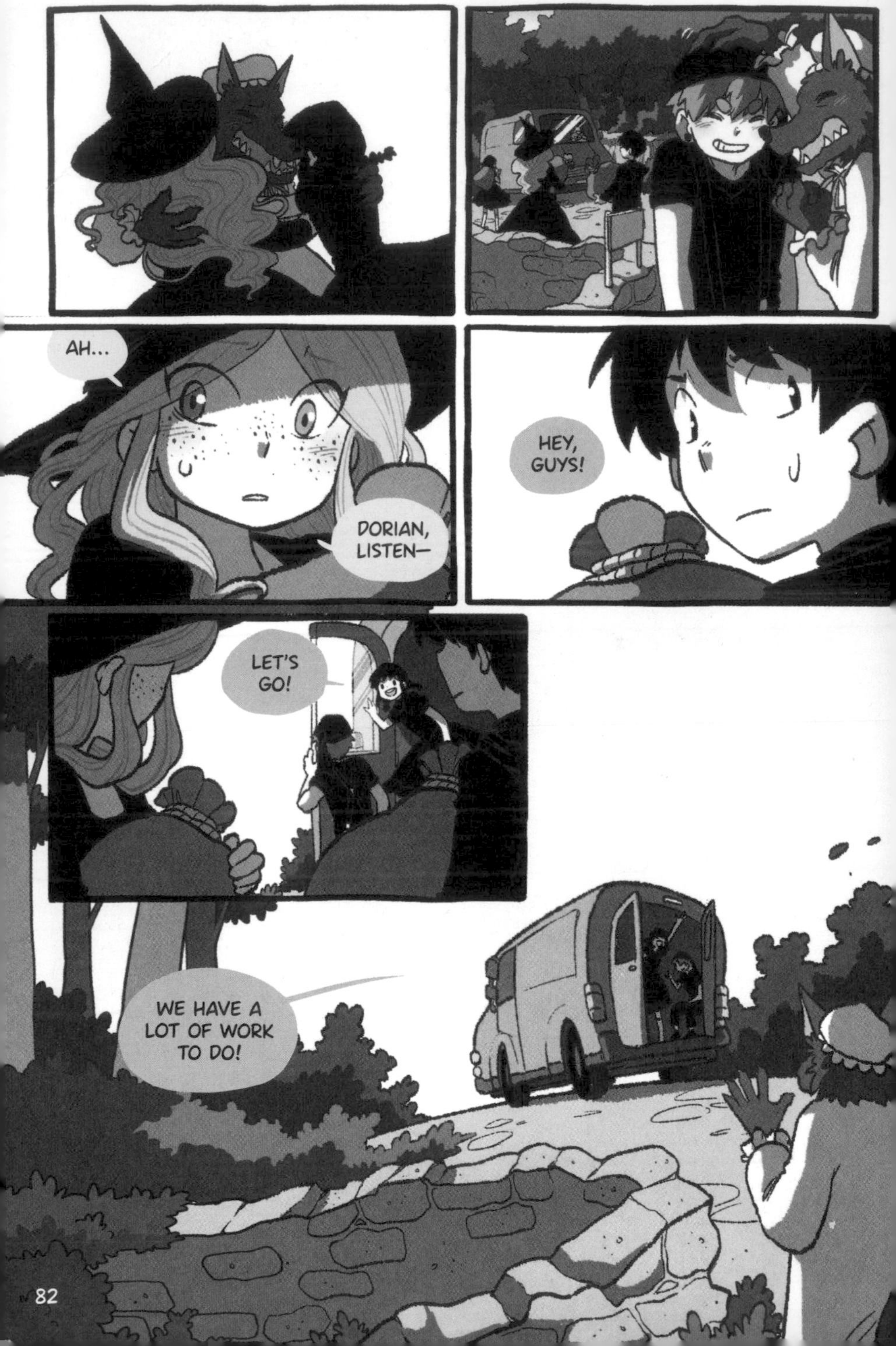
AH...
DORIAN, LISTEN—
HEY, GUYS!
LET'S GO!
WE HAVE A LOT OF WORK TO DO!

CHAPTER 38

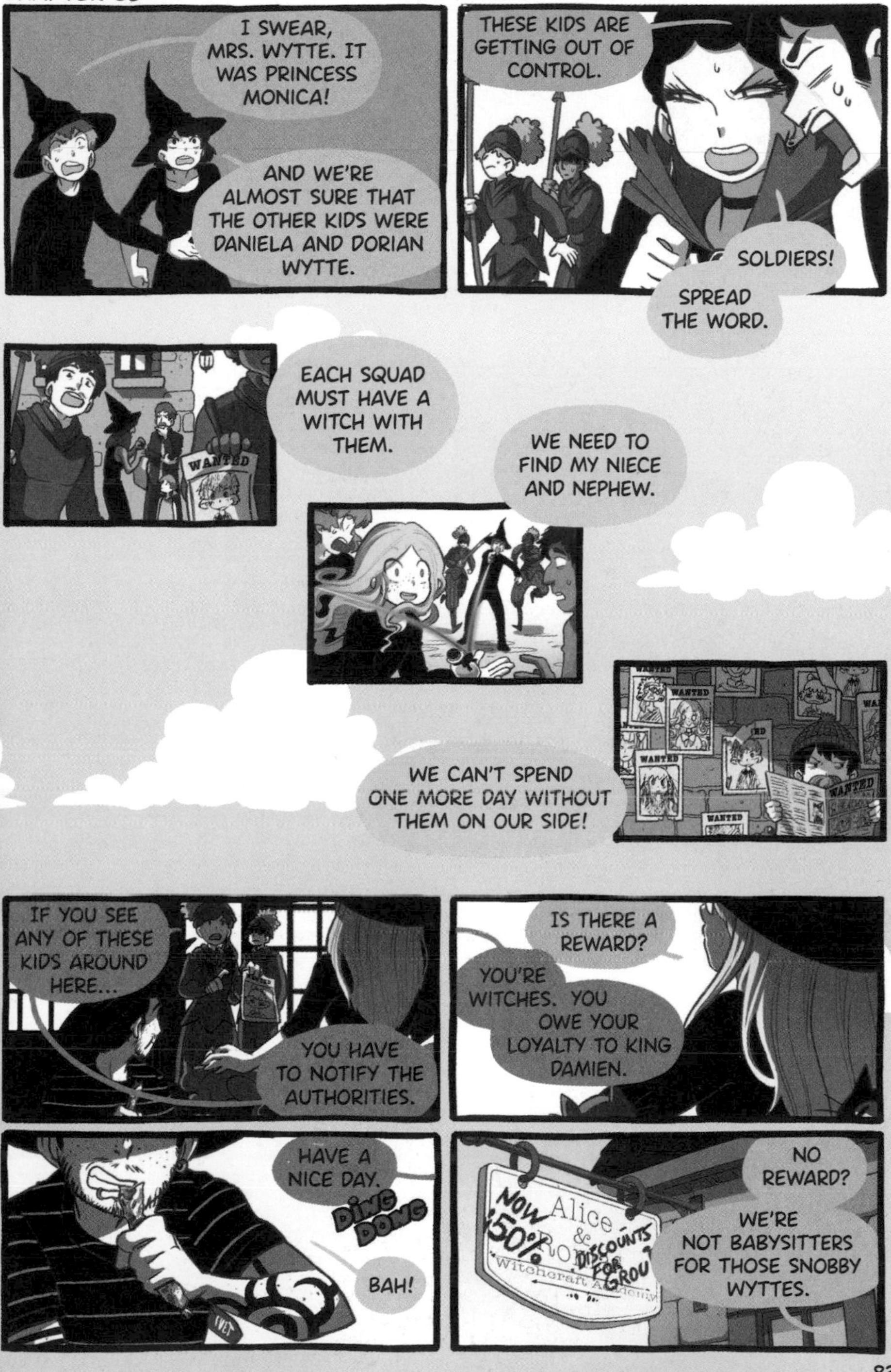

I SWEAR, MRS. WYTTE. IT WAS PRINCESS MONICA!
AND WE'RE ALMOST SURE THAT THE OTHER KIDS WERE DANIELA AND DORIAN WYTTE.
THESE KIDS ARE GETTING OUT OF CONTROL.
SOLDIERS!
SPREAD THE WORD.
EACH SQUAD MUST HAVE A WITCH WITH THEM.
WANTED
WE NEED TO FIND MY NIECE AND NEPHEW.
WE CAN'T SPEND ONE MORE DAY WITHOUT THEM ON OUR SIDE!
WANTED
IF YOU SEE ANY OF THESE KIDS AROUND HERE...
YOU HAVE TO NOTIFY THE AUTHORITIES.
IS THERE A REWARD?
YOU'RE WITCHES. YOU OWE YOUR LOYALTY TO KING DAMIEN.
HAVE A NICE DAY.
DING DONG
BAH!
NOW 50%
NO REWARD?
WE'RE NOT BABYSITTERS FOR THOSE SNOBBY WYTTES.

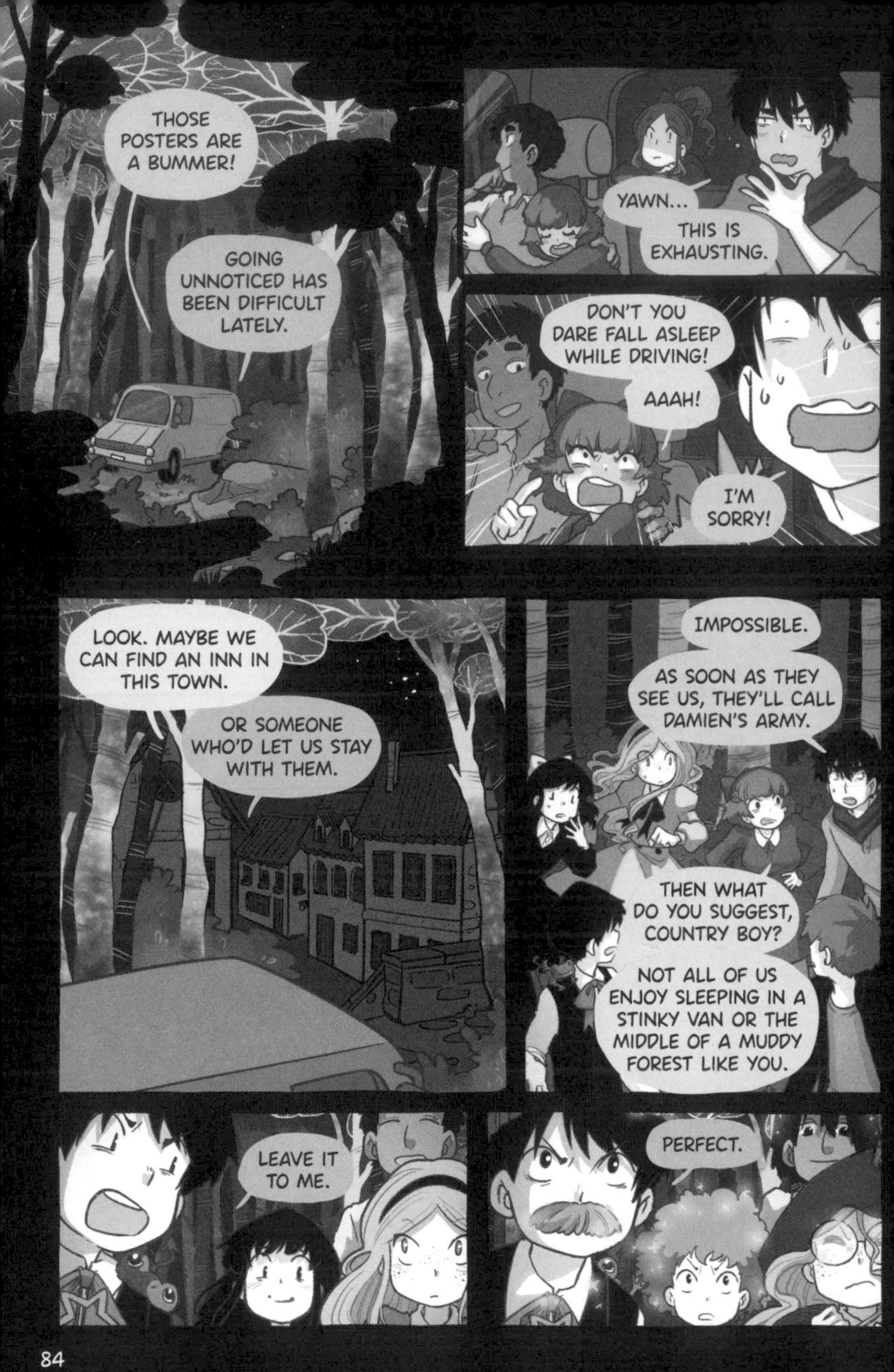
THOSE POSTERS ARE A BUMMER!
GOING UNNOTICED HAS BEEN DIFFICULT LATELY.
YAWN...
THIS IS EXHAUSTING.
DON'T YOU DARE FALL ASLEEP WHILE DRIVING!
AAAH!
I'M SORRY!
LOOK. MAYBE WE CAN FIND AN INN IN THIS TOWN.
OR SOMEONE WHO'D LET US STAY WITH THEM.
IMPOSSIBLE.
AS SOON AS THEY SEE US, THEY'LL CALL DAMIEN'S ARMY.
THEN WHAT DO YOU SUGGEST, COUNTRY BOY?
NOT ALL OF US ENJOY SLEEPING IN A STINKY VAN OR THE MIDDLE OF A MUDDY FOREST LIKE YOU.
LEAVE IT TO ME.
PERFECT.

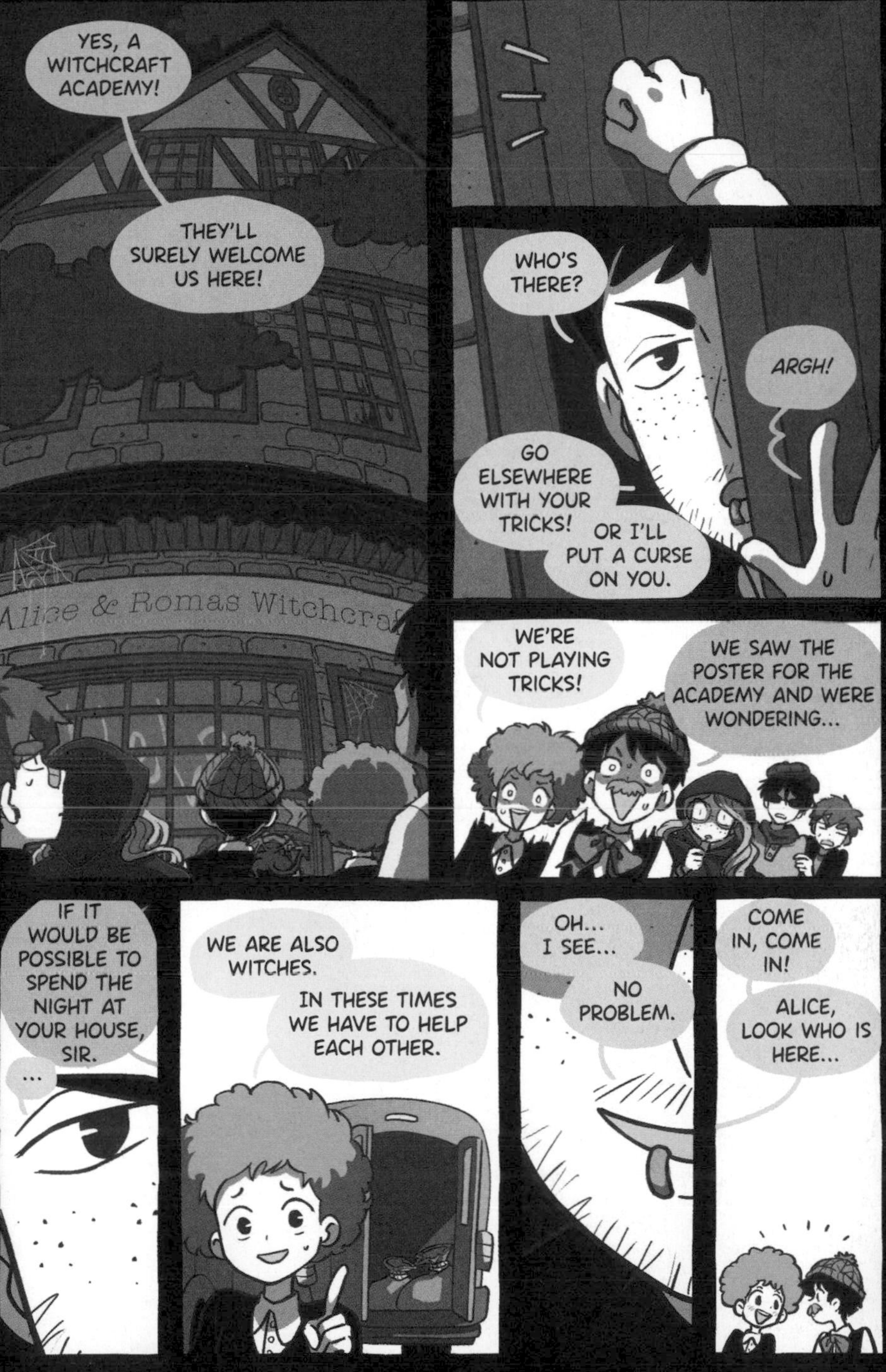
YES, A WITCHCRAFT ACADEMY!
THEY'LL SURELY WELCOME US HERE!
Alice & Romas Witchcraf
WHO'S THERE?
ARGH!
GO ELSEWHERE WITH YOUR TRICKS!
OR I'LL PUT A CURSE ON YOU.
WE'RE NOT PLAYING TRICKS!
WE SAW THE POSTER FOR THE ACADEMY AND WERE WONDERING...
IF IT WOULD BE POSSIBLE TO SPEND THE NIGHT AT YOUR HOUSE, SIR.
...
WE ARE ALSO WITCHES.
IN THESE TIMES WE HAVE TO HELP EACH OTHER.
OH... I SEE...
NO PROBLEM.
COME IN, COME IN!
ALICE, LOOK WHO IS HERE...

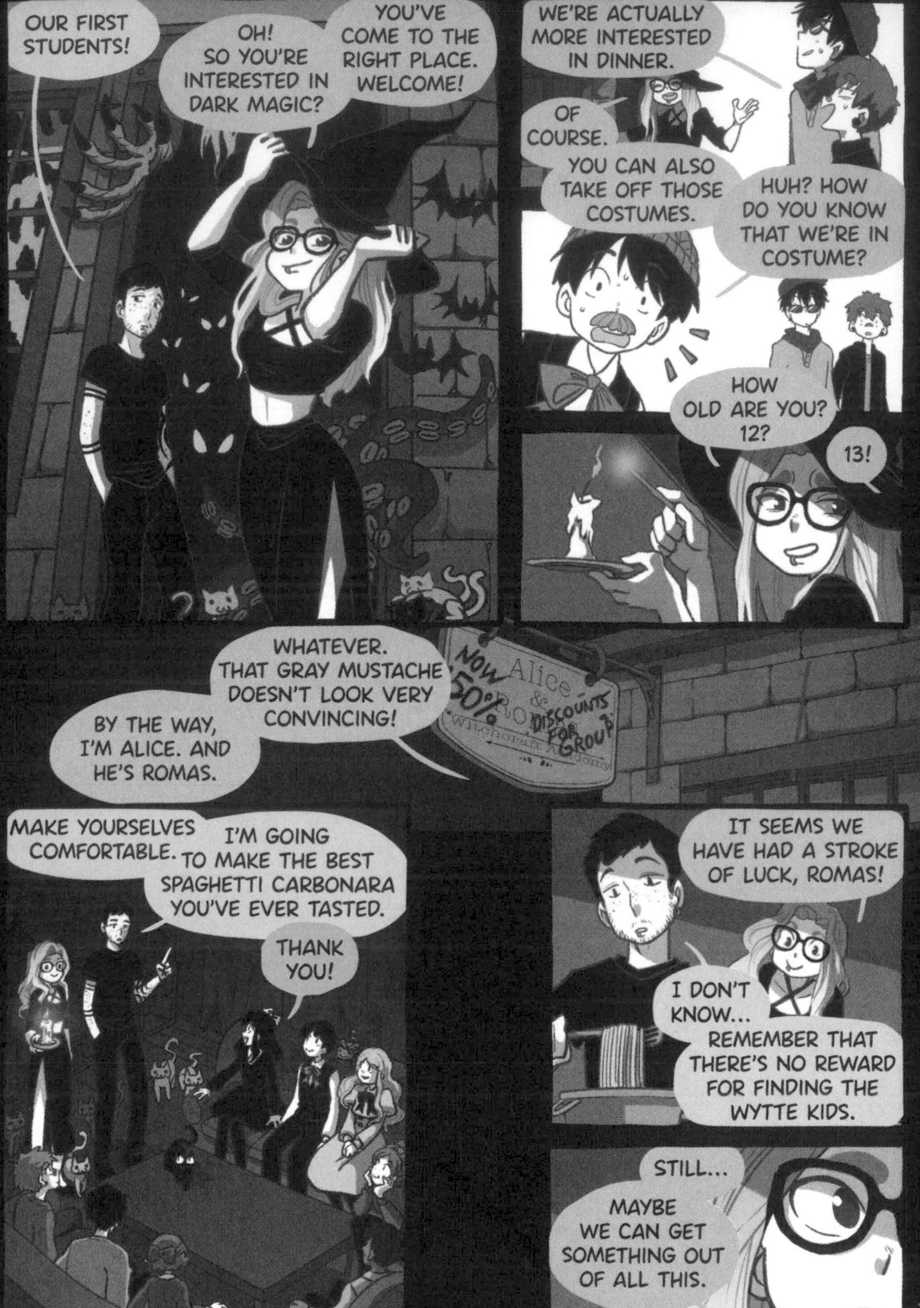

OUR FIRST STUDENTS!
OH! SO YOU'RE INTERESTED IN DARK MAGIC?
YOU'VE COME TO THE RIGHT PLACE. WELCOME!
WE'RE ACTUALLY MORE INTERESTED IN DINNER.
OF COURSE.
YOU CAN ALSO TAKE OFF THOSE COSTUMES.
HUH? HOW DO YOU KNOW THAT WE'RE IN COSTUME?
HOW OLD ARE YOU? 12?
13!
WHATEVER. THAT GRAY MUSTACHE DOESN'T LOOK VERY CONVINCING!
BY THE WAY, I'M ALICE. AND HE'S ROMAS.
NOW 50%
Alice & Romas
DISCOUNTS FOR GROUPS
MAKE YOURSELVES COMFORTABLE.
I'M GOING TO MAKE THE BEST SPAGHETTI CARBONARA YOU'VE EVER TASTED.
THANK YOU!
IT SEEMS WE HAVE HAD A STROKE OF LUCK, ROMAS!
I DON'T KNOW...
REMEMBER THAT THERE'S NO REWARD FOR FINDING THE WYTTE KIDS.
STILL...
MAYBE WE CAN GET SOMETHING OUT OF ALL THIS.

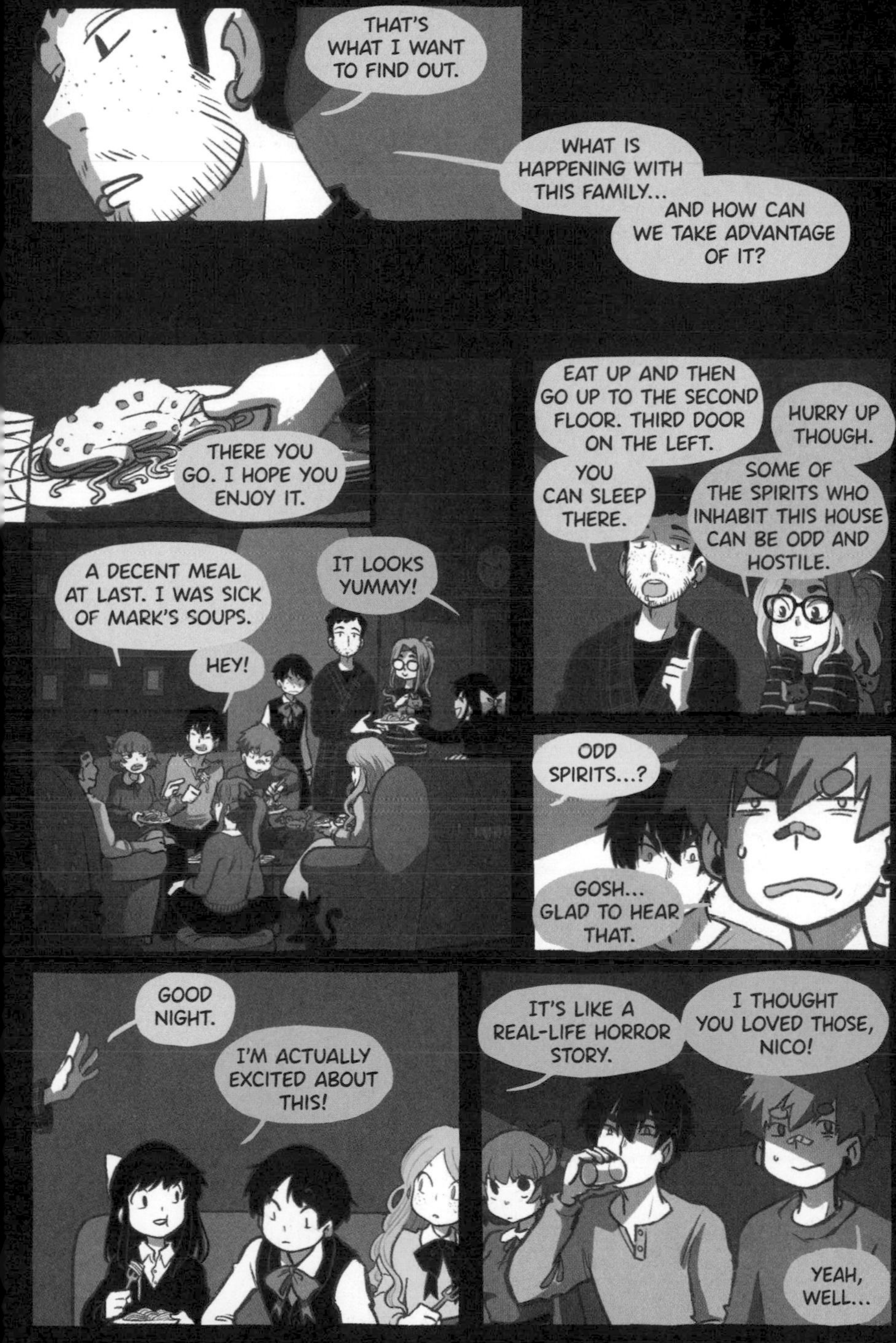
THAT'S WHAT I WANT TO FIND OUT.
WHAT IS HAPPENING WITH THIS FAMILY...
AND HOW CAN WE TAKE ADVANTAGE OF IT?
THERE YOU GO. I HOPE YOU ENJOY IT.
A DECENT MEAL AT LAST. I WAS SICK OF MARK'S SOUPS.
IT LOOKS YUMMY!
HEY!
EAT UP AND THEN GO UP TO THE SECOND FLOOR. THIRD DOOR ON THE LEFT.
YOU CAN SLEEP THERE.
HURRY UP THOUGH.
SOME OF THE SPIRITS WHO INHABIT THIS HOUSE CAN BE ODD AND HOSTILE.
ODD SPIRITS...?
GOSH... GLAD TO HEAR THAT.
GOOD NIGHT.
I'M ACTUALLY EXCITED ABOUT THIS!
IT'S LIKE A REAL-LIFE HORROR STORY.
I THOUGHT YOU LOVED THOSE, NICO!
YEAH, WELL...

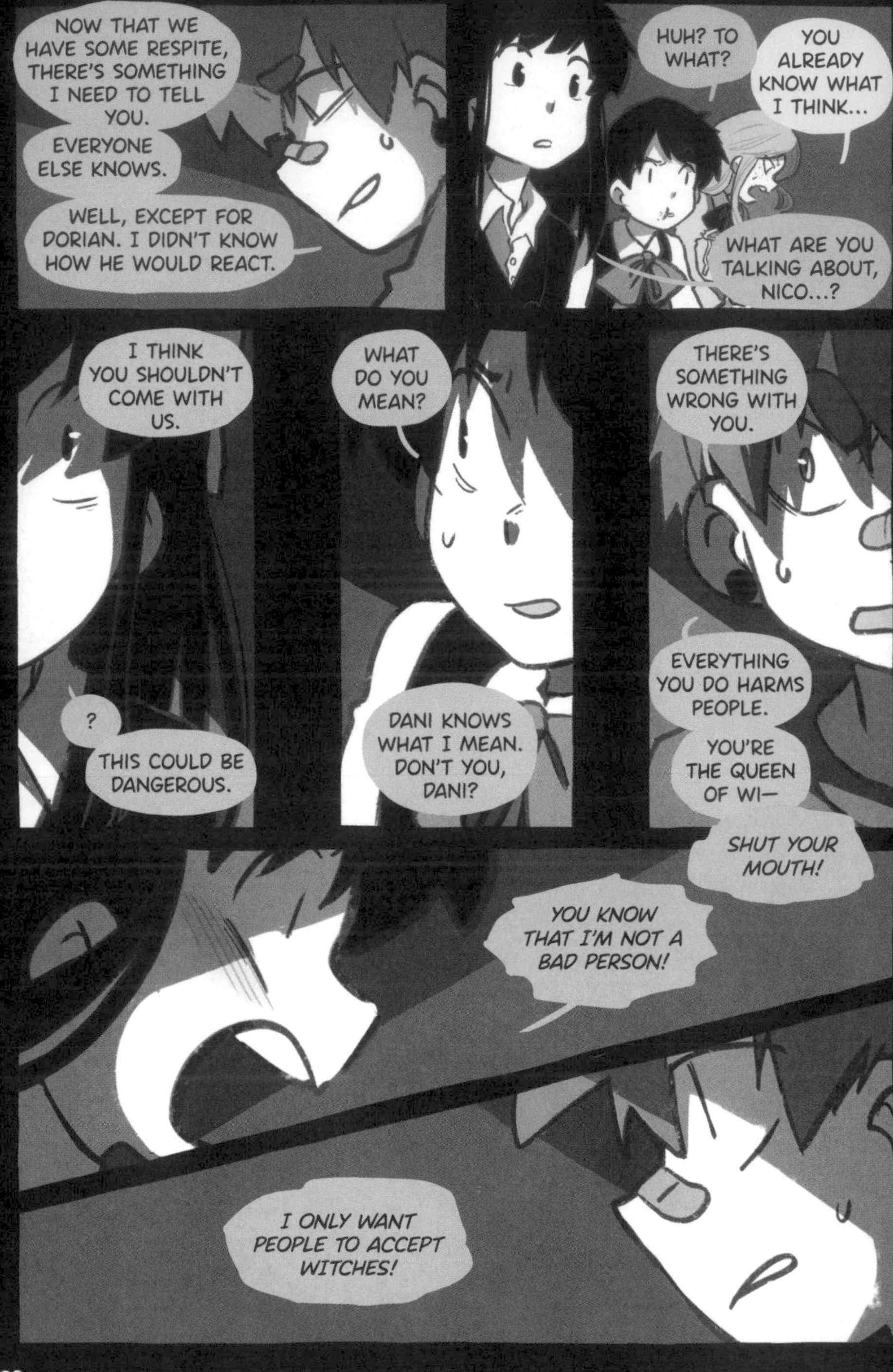
NOW THAT WE HAVE SOME RESPITE, THERE'S SOMETHING I NEED TO TELL YOU.
EVERYONE ELSE KNOWS.
WELL, EXCEPT FOR DORIAN. I DIDN'T KNOW HOW HE WOULD REACT.
HUH? TO WHAT?
YOU ALREADY KNOW WHAT I THINK...
WHAT ARE YOU TALKING ABOUT, NICO...?
I THINK YOU SHOULDN'T COME WITH US.
?
THIS COULD BE DANGEROUS.
WHAT DO YOU MEAN?
DANI KNOWS WHAT I MEAN. DON'T YOU, DANI?
THERE'S SOMETHING WRONG WITH YOU.
EVERYTHING YOU DO HARMS PEOPLE.
YOU'RE THE QUEEN OF WI—
SHUT YOUR MOUTH!
YOU KNOW THAT I'M NOT A BAD PERSON!
I ONLY WANT PEOPLE TO ACCEPT WITCHES!

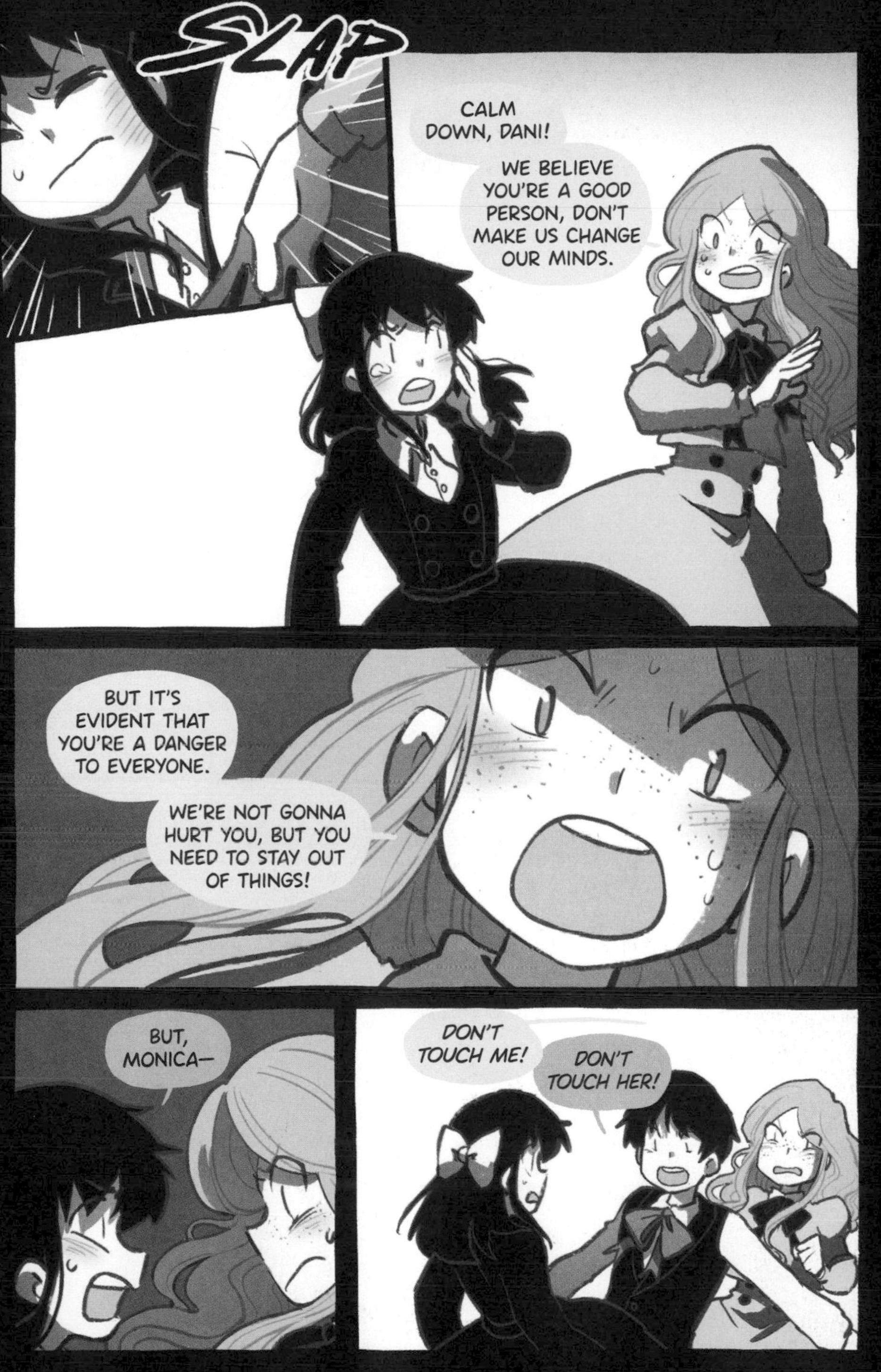
SLAP
CALM DOWN, DANI!
WE BELIEVE YOU'RE A GOOD PERSON, DON'T MAKE US CHANGE OUR MINDS.
BUT IT'S EVIDENT THAT YOU'RE A DANGER TO EVERYONE.
WE'RE NOT GONNA HURT YOU, BUT YOU NEED TO STAY OUT OF THINGS!
BUT, MONICA—
DON'T TOUCH ME!
DON'T TOUCH HER!

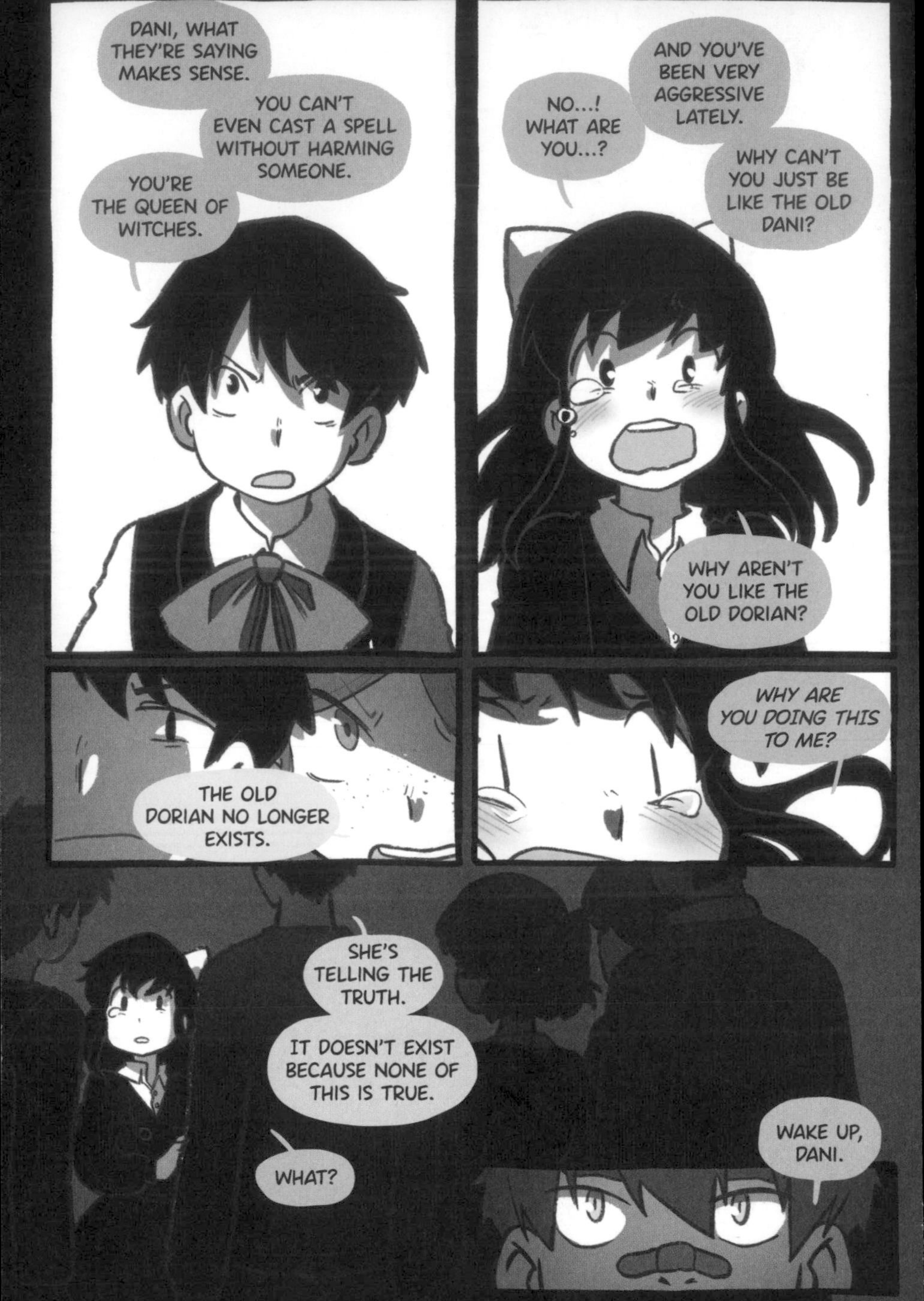

DANI, WHAT THEY'RE SAYING MAKES SENSE.
YOU CAN'T EVEN CAST A SPELL WITHOUT HARMING SOMEONE.
YOU'RE THE QUEEN OF WITCHES.
NO...! WHAT ARE YOU...?
AND YOU'VE BEEN VERY AGGRESSIVE LATELY.
WHY CAN'T YOU JUST BE LIKE THE OLD DANI?
WHY AREN'T YOU LIKE THE OLD DORIAN?
THE OLD DORIAN NO LONGER EXISTS.
WHY ARE YOU DOING THIS TO ME?
SHE'S TELLING THE TRUTH.
IT DOESN'T EXIST BECAUSE NONE OF THIS IS TRUE.
WHAT?
WAKE UP, DANI.

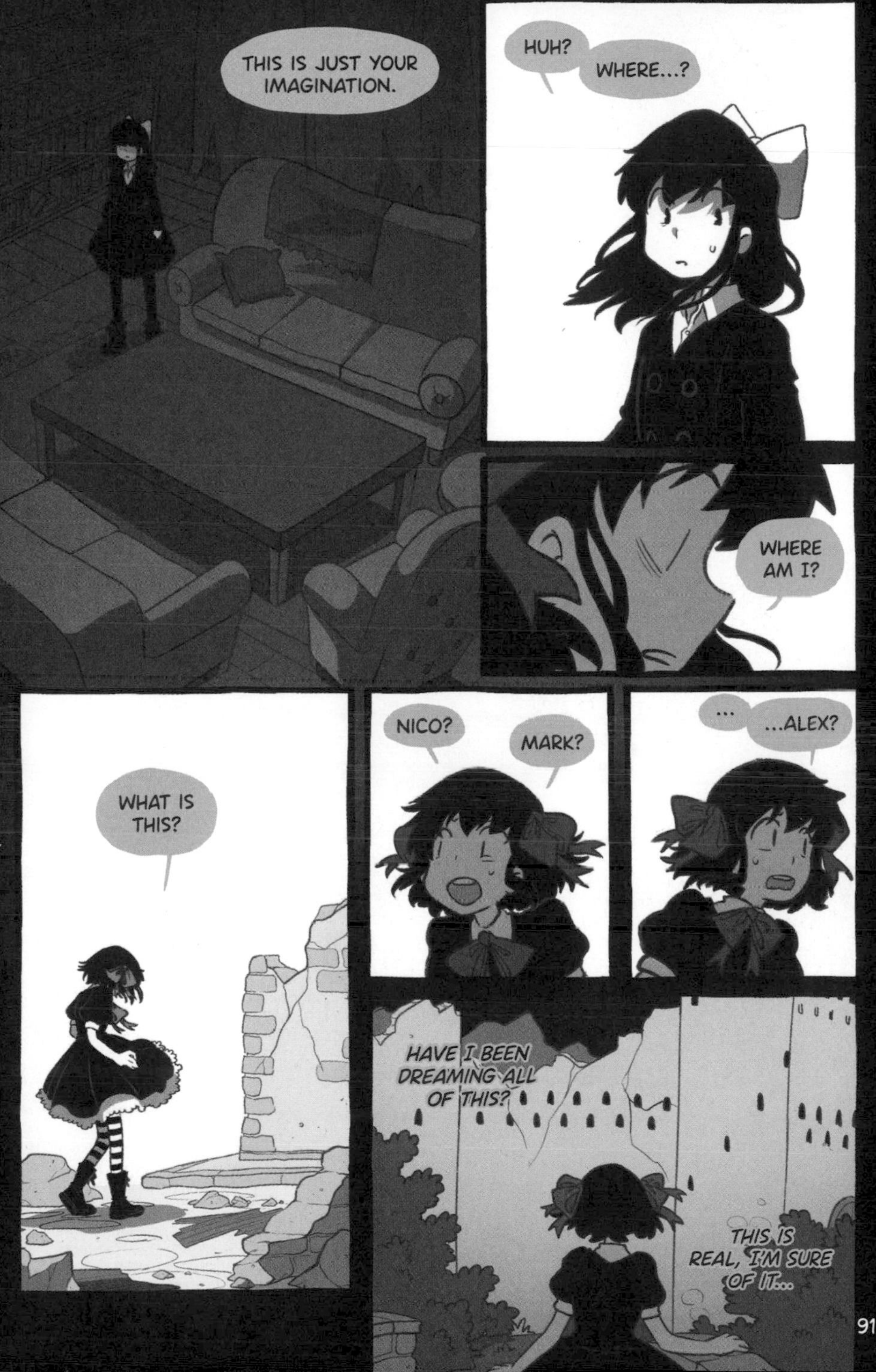
THIS IS JUST YOUR IMAGINATION.
HUH?
WHERE...?
WHERE AM I?
WHAT IS THIS?
NICO?
MARK?
...
...ALEX?
HAVE I BEEN DREAMING ALL OF THIS?
THIS IS REAL, I'M SURE OF IT...

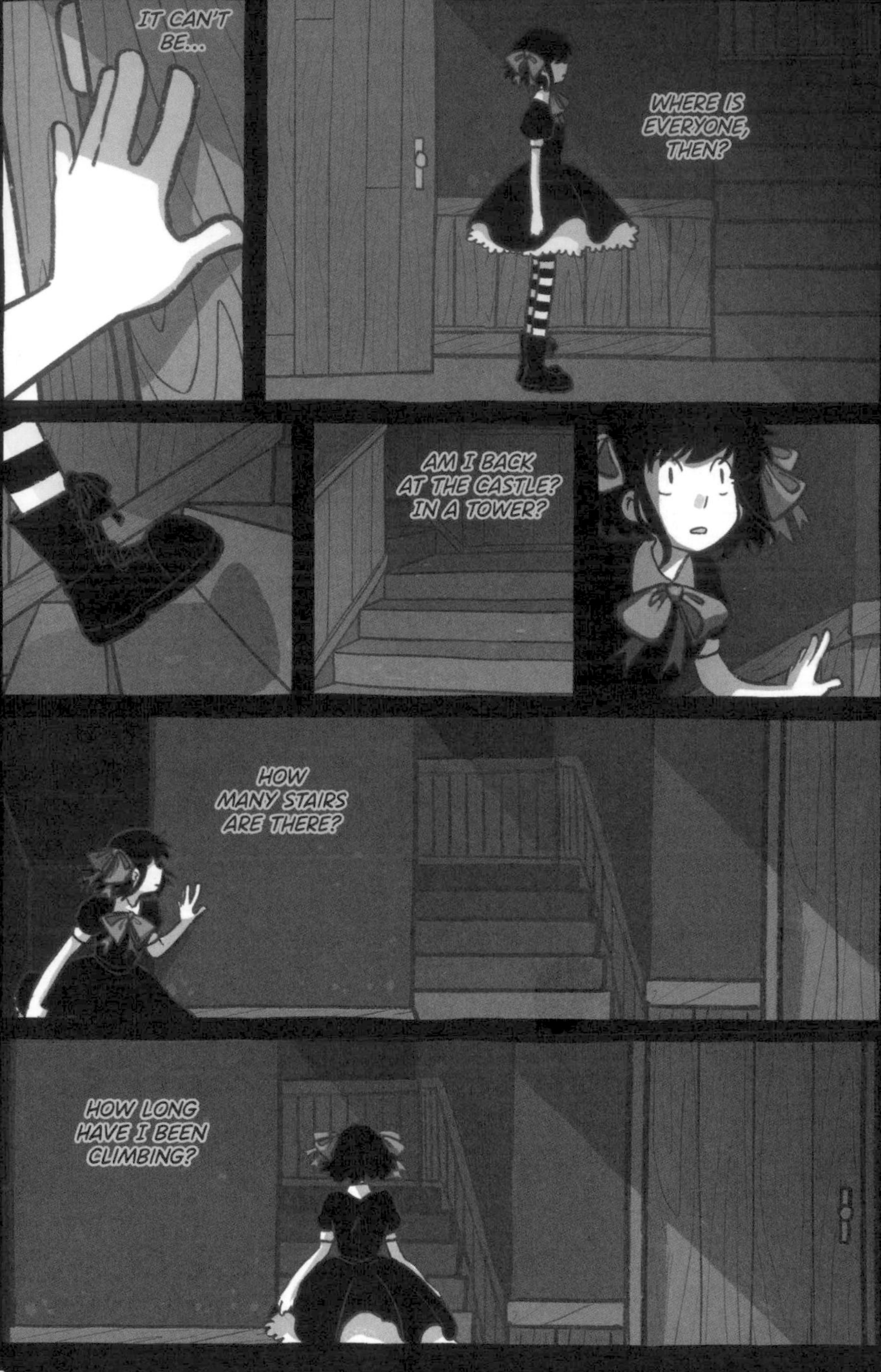
IT CAN'T BE...
WHERE IS EVERYONE, THEN?
AM I BACK AT THE CASTLE? IN A TOWER?
HOW MANY STAIRS ARE THERE?
HOW LONG HAVE I BEEN CLIMBING?

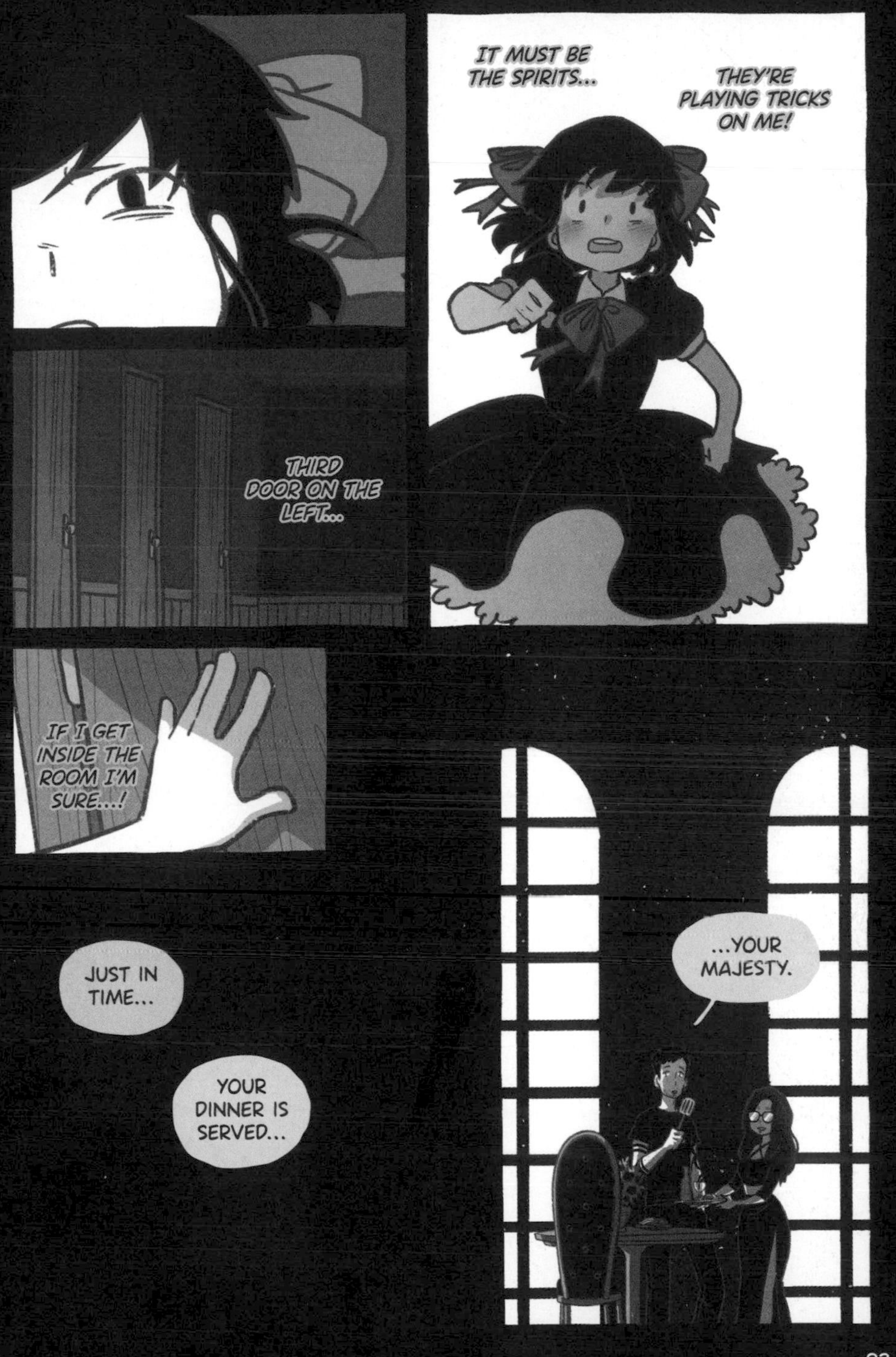
IT MUST BE THE SPIRITS...
THEY'RE PLAYING TRICKS ON ME!
THIRD DOOR ON THE LEFT...
IF I GET INSIDE THE ROOM I'M SURE...!
JUST IN TIME...
YOUR DINNER IS SERVED...
...YOUR MAJESTY.

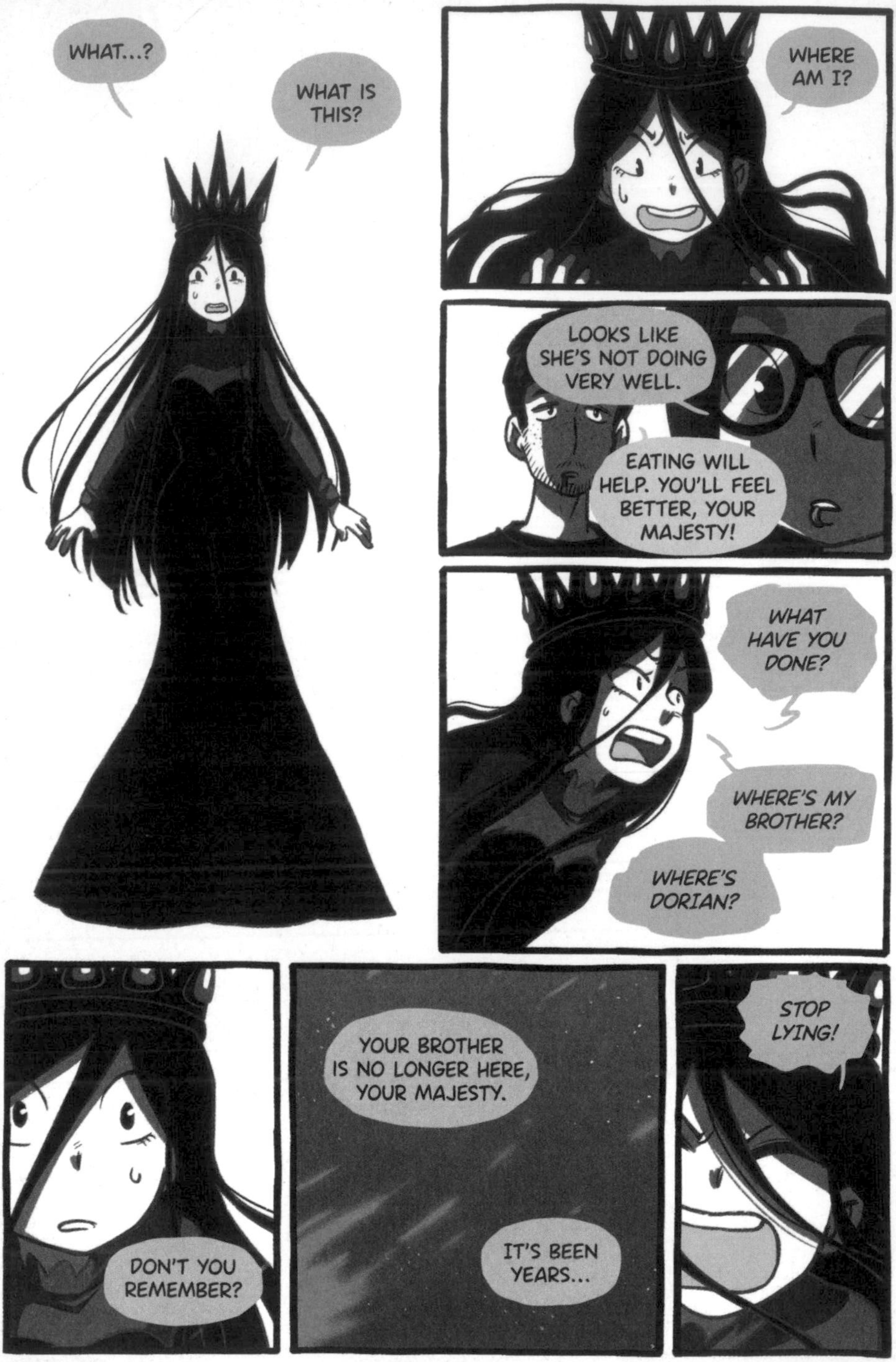
WHAT...?
WHAT IS THIS?
WHERE AM I?
LOOKS LIKE SHE'S NOT DOING VERY WELL.
EATING WILL HELP. YOU'LL FEEL BETTER, YOUR MAJESTY!
WHAT HAVE YOU DONE?
WHERE'S MY BROTHER?
WHERE'S DORIAN?
DON'T YOU REMEMBER?
YOUR BROTHER IS NO LONGER HERE, YOUR MAJESTY.
IT'S BEEN YEARS...
STOP LYING!

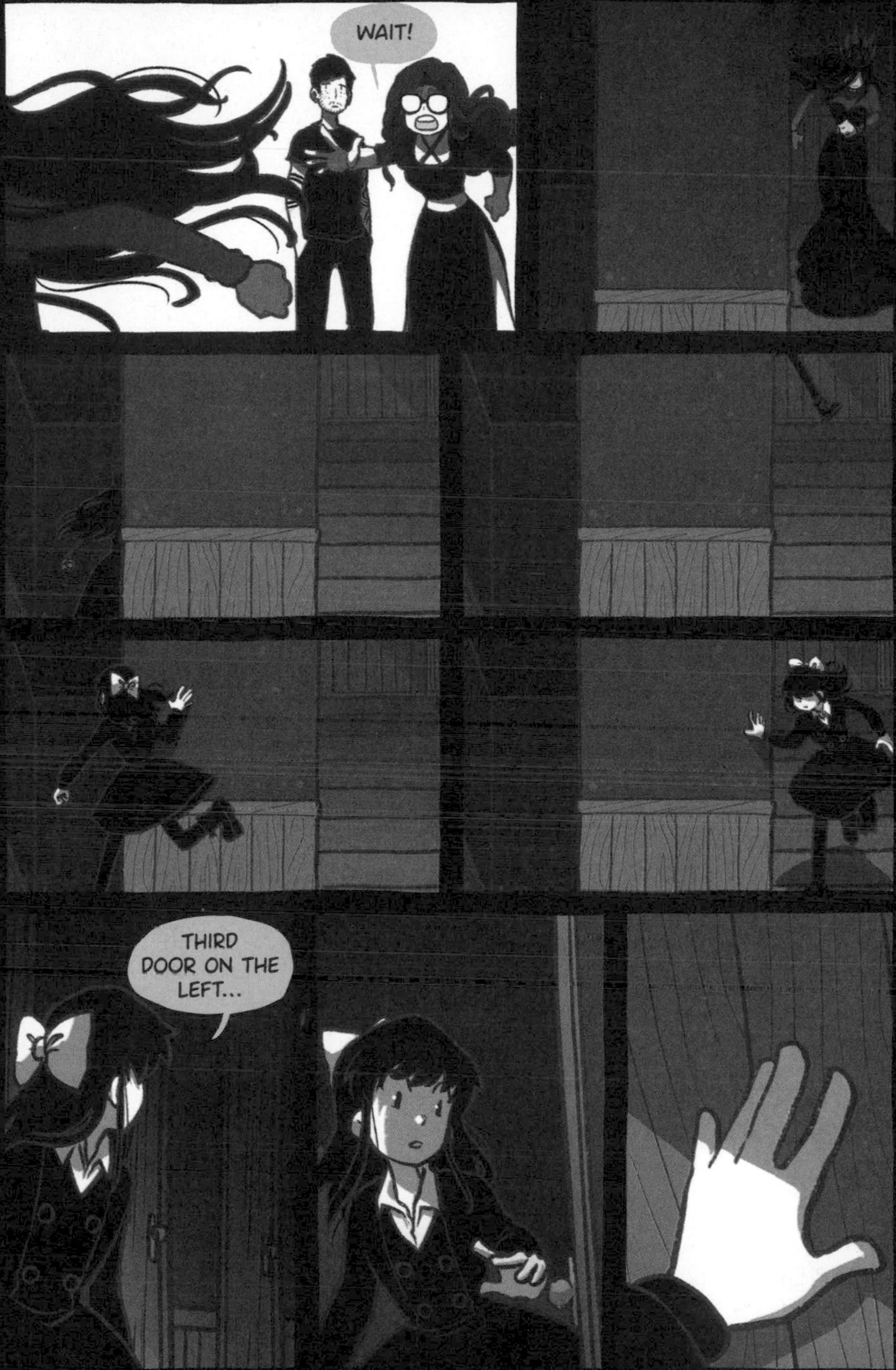
WAIT!
THIRD DOOR ON THE LEFT...

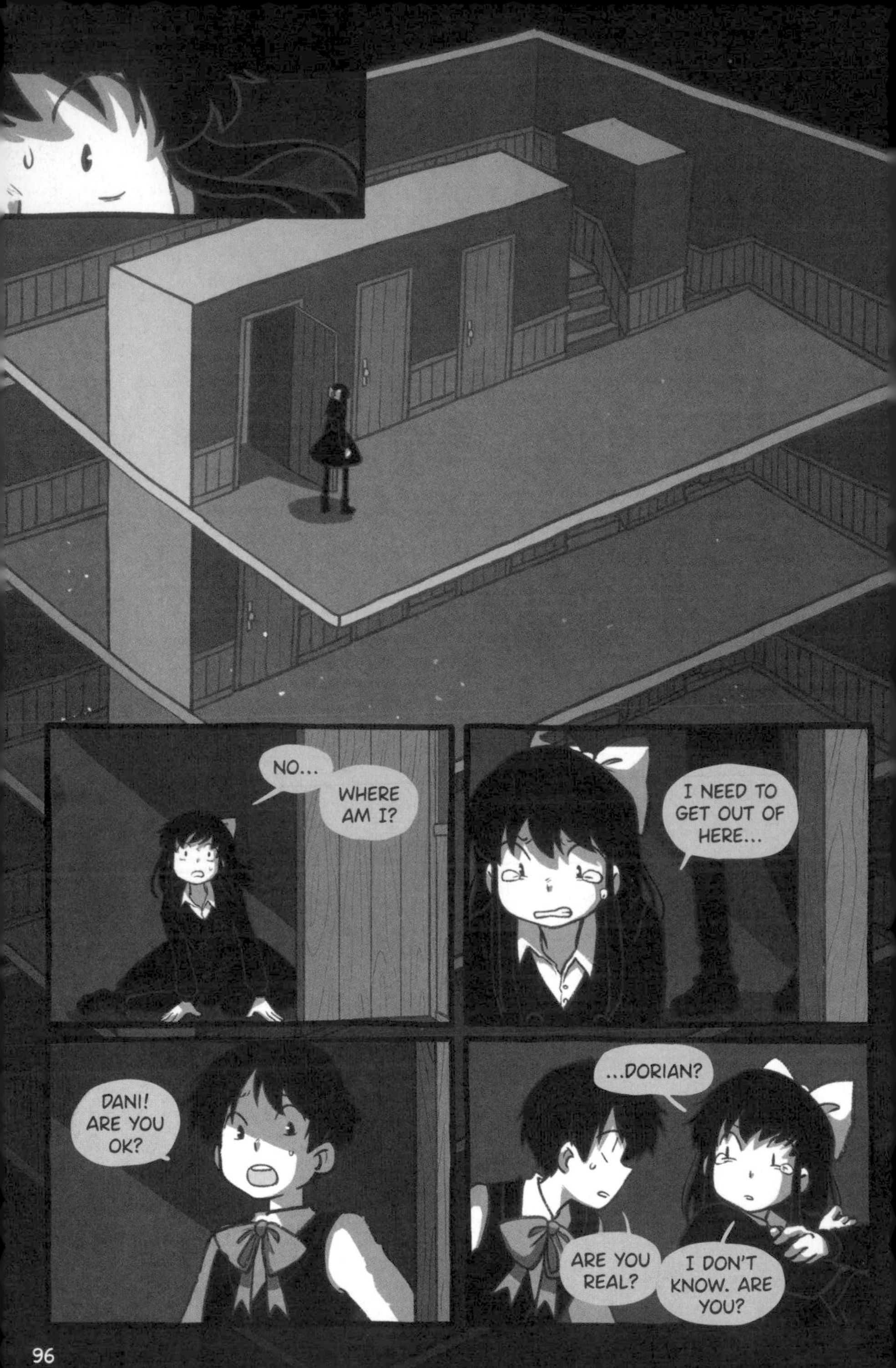
NO...
WHERE AM I?
I NEED TO GET OUT OF HERE...
DANI! ARE YOU OK?
...DORIAN?
ARE YOU REAL?
I DON'T KNOW. ARE YOU?

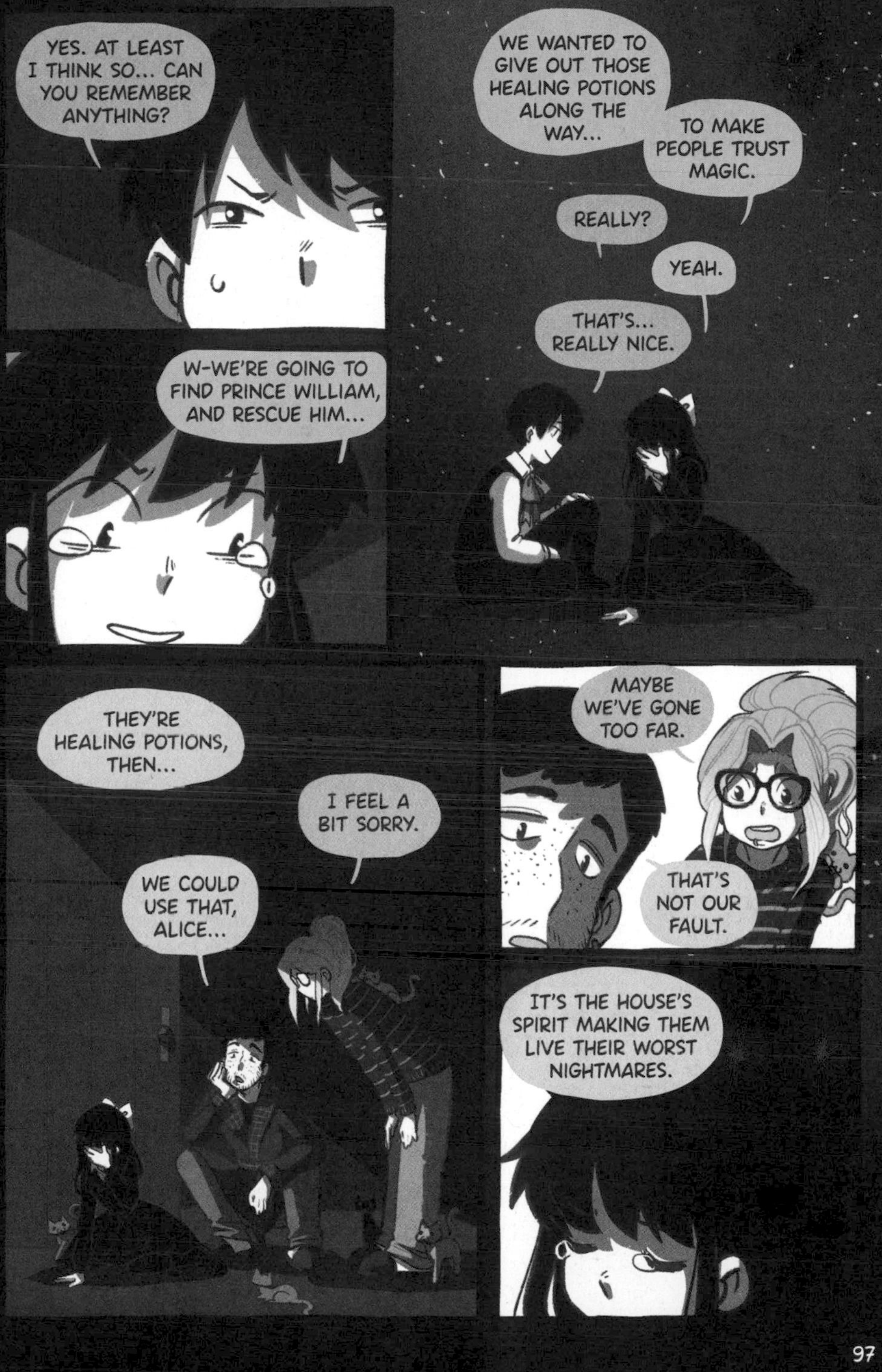
YES. AT LEAST I THINK SO... CAN YOU REMEMBER ANYTHING?
W-WE'RE GOING TO FIND PRINCE WILLIAM, AND RESCUE HIM...
WE WANTED TO GIVE OUT THOSE HEALING POTIONS ALONG THE WAY...
TO MAKE PEOPLE TRUST MAGIC.
REALLY?
YEAH.
THAT'S... REALLY NICE.
THEY'RE HEALING POTIONS, THEN...
I FEEL A BIT SORRY.
WE COULD USE THAT, ALICE...
MAYBE WE'VE GONE TOO FAR.
THAT'S NOT OUR FAULT.
IT'S THE HOUSE'S SPIRIT MAKING THEM LIVE THEIR WORST NIGHTMARES.

CHAPTER 39

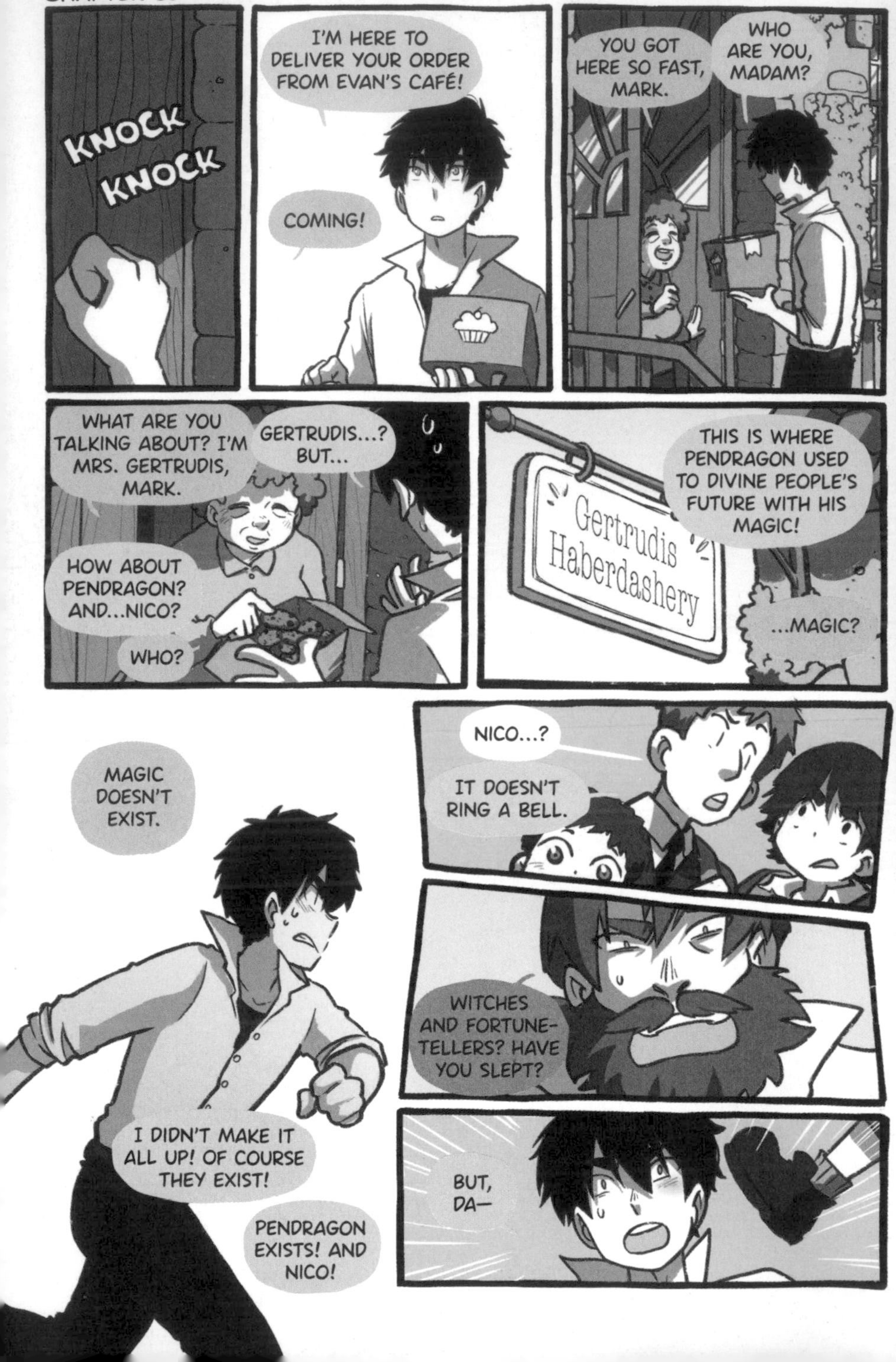
KNOCK
KNOCK
I'M HERE TO DELIVER YOUR ORDER FROM EVAN'S CAFÉ!
COMING!
YOU GOT HERE SO FAST, MARK.
WHO ARE YOU, MADAM?
WHAT ARE YOU TALKING ABOUT? I'M MRS. GERTRUDIS, MARK.
GERTRUDIS...? BUT...
HOW ABOUT PENDRAGON? AND...NICO?
WHO?
Gertrudis Haberdashery
THIS IS WHERE PENDRAGON USED TO DIVINE PEOPLE'S FUTURE WITH HIS MAGIC!
...MAGIC?
MAGIC DOESN'T EXIST.
NICO...?
IT DOESN'T RING A BELL.
WITCHES AND FORTUNE-TELLERS? HAVE YOU SLEPT?
I DIDN'T MAKE IT ALL UP! OF COURSE THEY EXIST!
PENDRAGON EXISTS! AND NICO!
BUT, DA—

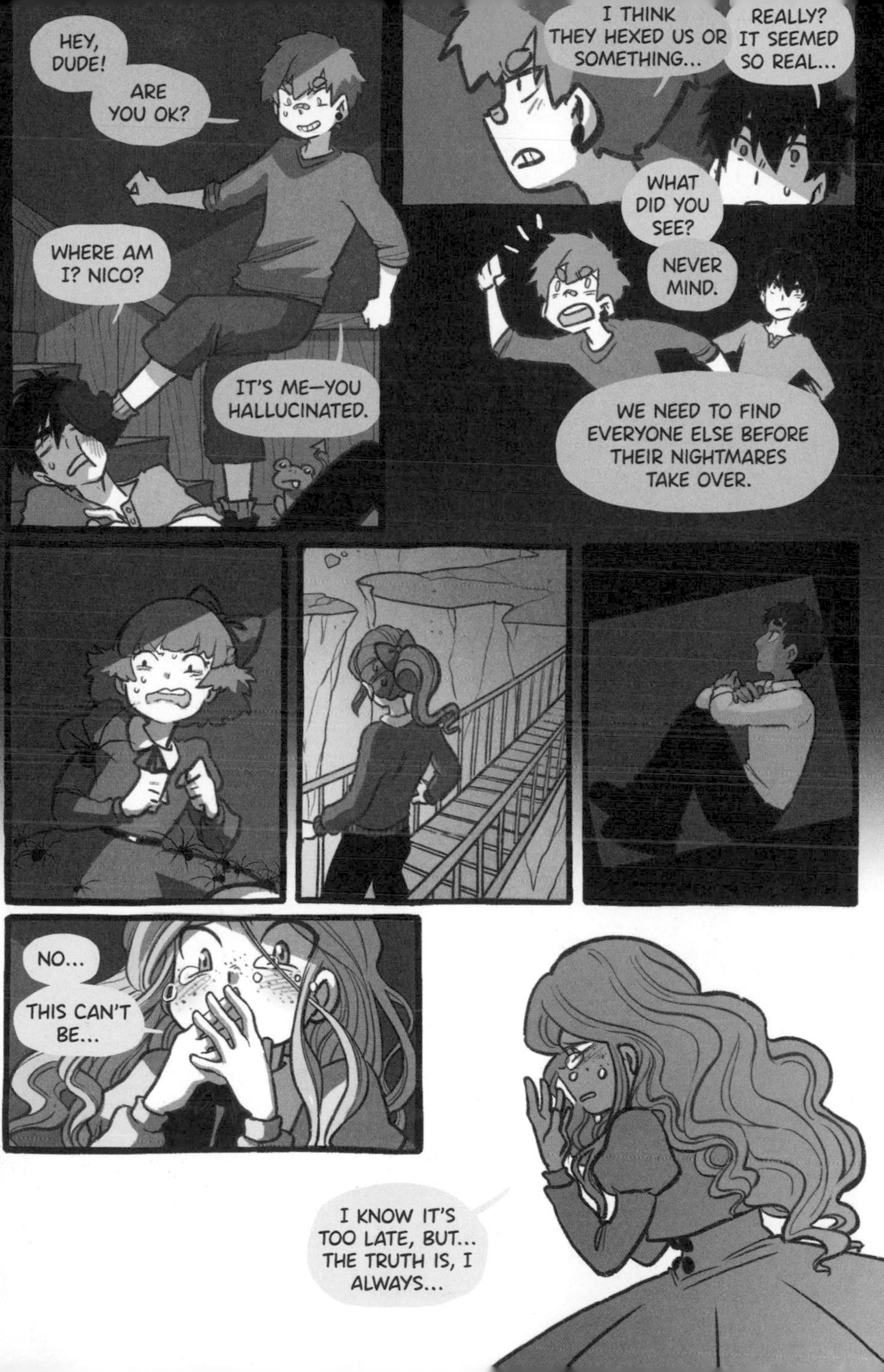

HEY, DUDE!
ARE YOU OK?
WHERE AM I? NICO?
IT'S ME—YOU HALLUCINATED.
I THINK THEY HEXED US OR SOMETHING...
REALLY? IT SEEMED SO REAL...
WHAT DID YOU SEE?
NEVER MIND.
WE NEED TO FIND EVERYONE ELSE BEFORE THEIR NIGHTMARES TAKE OVER.
NO...
THIS CAN'T BE...
I KNOW IT'S TOO LATE, BUT... THE TRUTH IS, I ALWAYS...

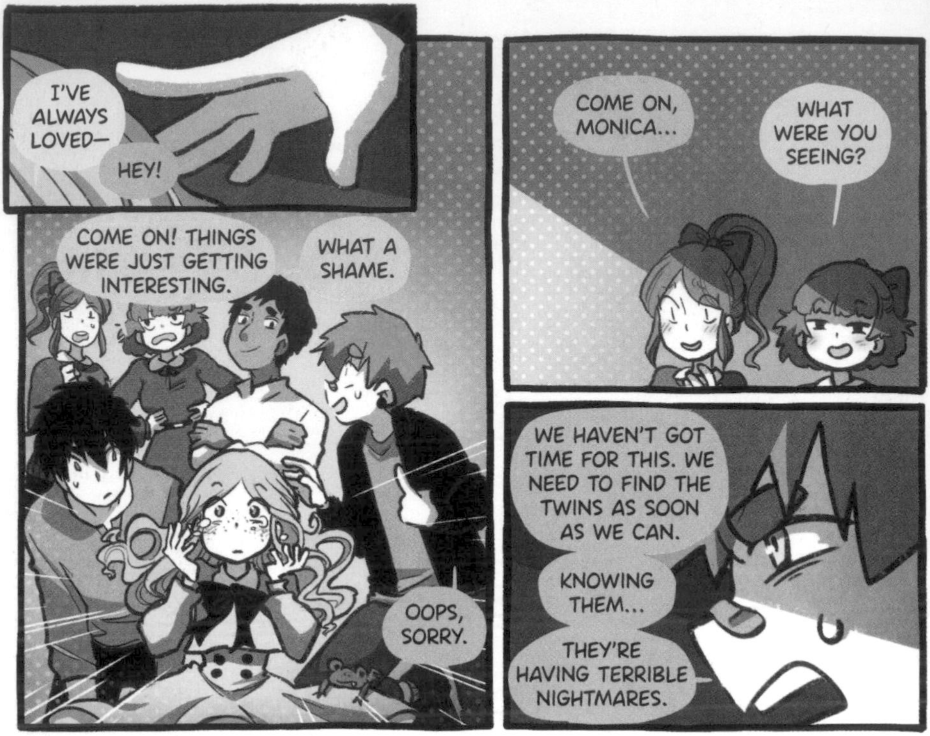
I'VE ALWAYS LOVED—
HEY!
COME ON! THINGS WERE JUST GETTING INTERESTING.
WHAT A SHAME.
OOPS, SORRY.
COME ON, MONICA...
WHAT WERE YOU SEEING?
WE HAVEN'T GOT TIME FOR THIS. WE NEED TO FIND THE TWINS AS SOON AS WE CAN.
KNOWING THEM...
THEY'RE HAVING TERRIBLE NIGHTMARES.

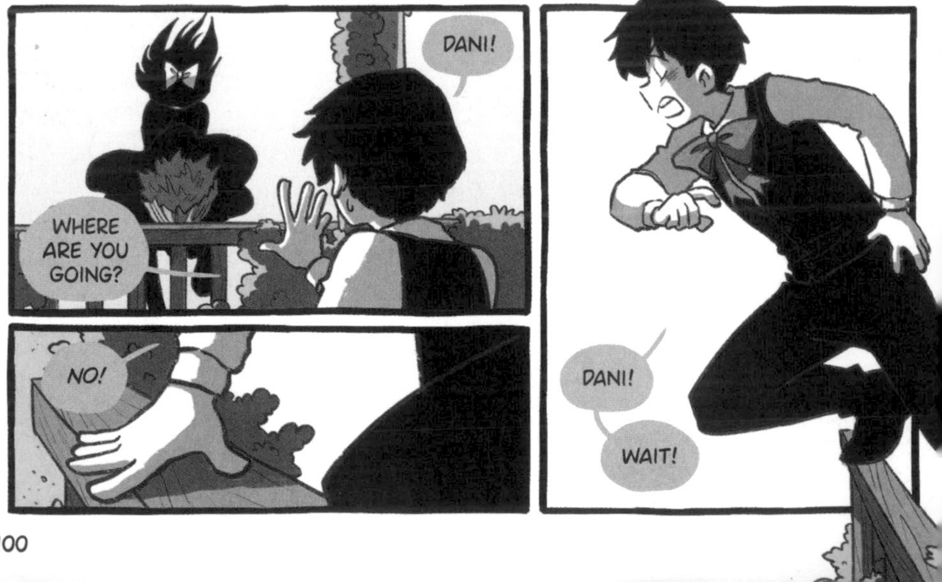
DANI!
WHERE ARE YOU GOING?
NO!
DANI!
WAIT!

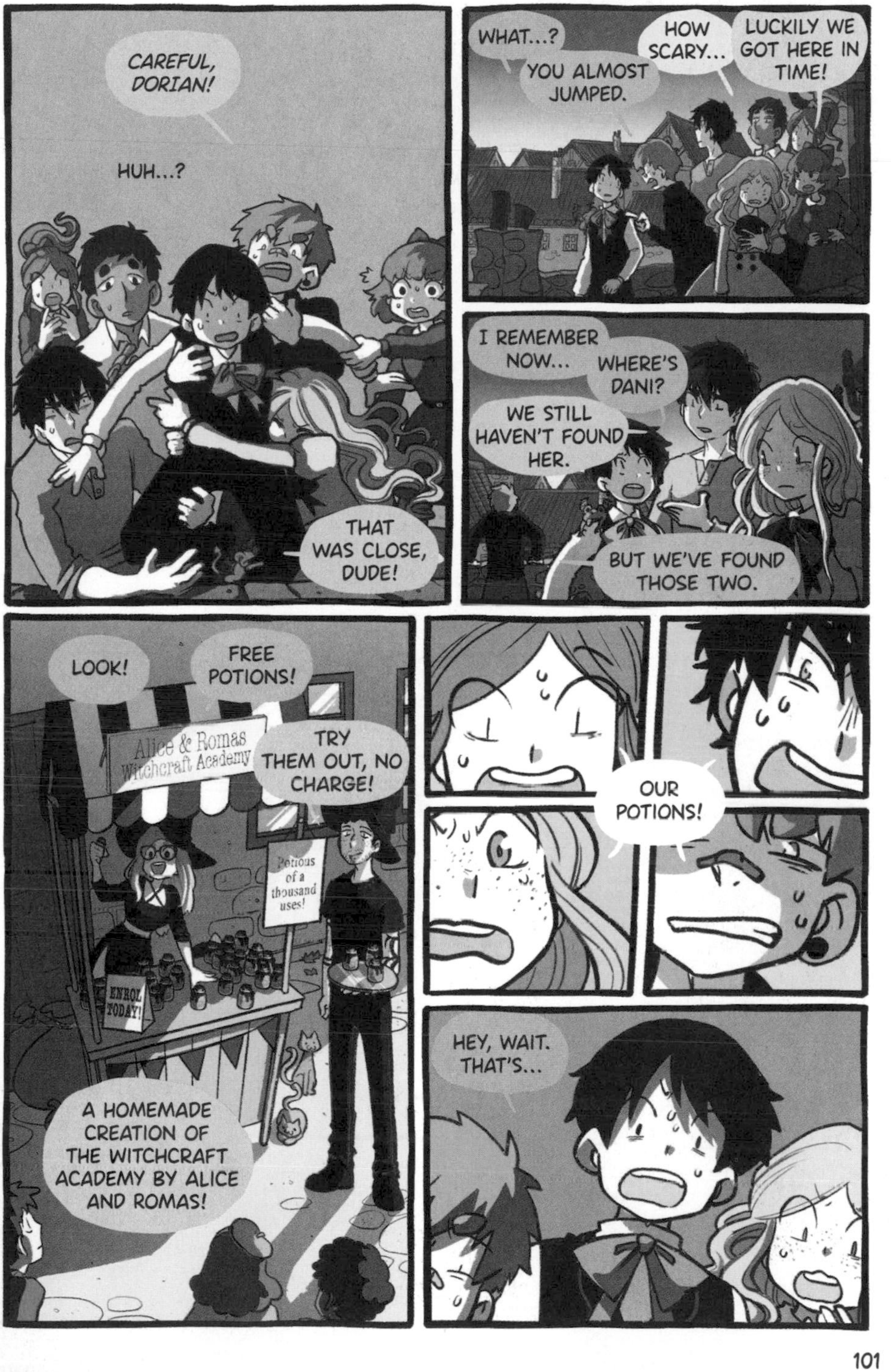
CAREFUL, DORIAN!
HUH...?
THAT WAS CLOSE, DUDE!
WHAT...?
YOU ALMOST JUMPED.
HOW SCARY...
LUCKILY WE GOT HERE IN TIME!
I REMEMBER NOW...
WHERE'S DANI?
WE STILL HAVEN'T FOUND HER.
BUT WE'VE FOUND THOSE TWO.
LOOK!
FREE POTIONS!
Alice & Romas Witchcraft Academy
TRY THEM OUT, NO CHARGE!
Potions of a thousand uses!
ENROL TODAY!
A HOMEMADE CREATION OF THE WITCHCRAFT ACADEMY BY ALICE AND ROMAS!
OUR POTIONS!
HEY, WAIT. THAT'S...

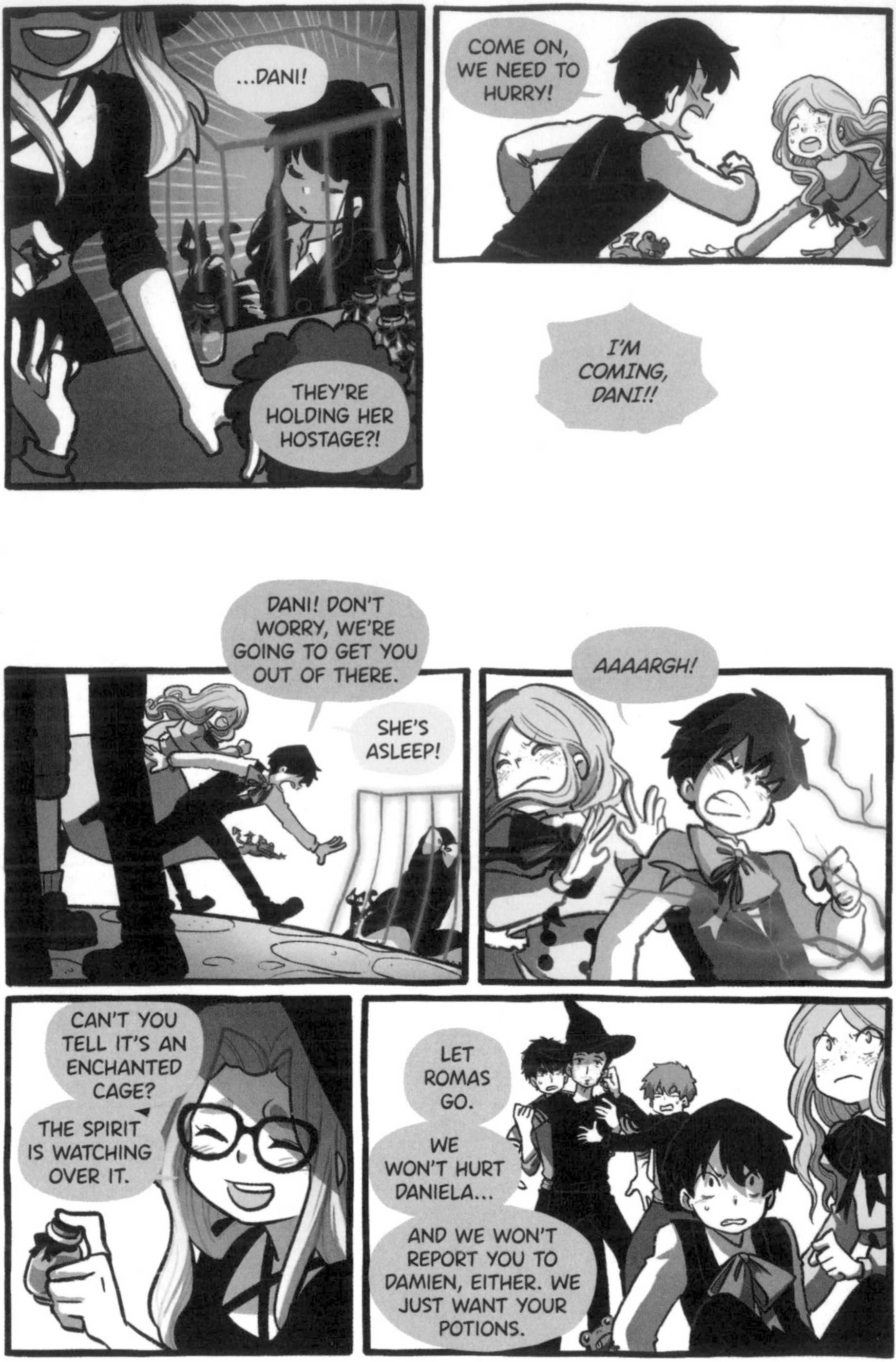
...DANI!
THEY'RE HOLDING HER HOSTAGE?!
COME ON, WE NEED TO HURRY!
I'M COMING, DANI!!
DANI! DON'T WORRY, WE'RE GOING TO GET YOU OUT OF THERE.
SHE'S ASLEEP!
AAAARGH!
CAN'T YOU TELL IT'S AN ENCHANTED CAGE?
THE SPIRIT IS WATCHING OVER IT.
LET ROMAS GO.
WE WON'T HURT DANIELA...
AND WE WON'T REPORT YOU TO DAMIEN, EITHER. WE JUST WANT YOUR POTIONS.

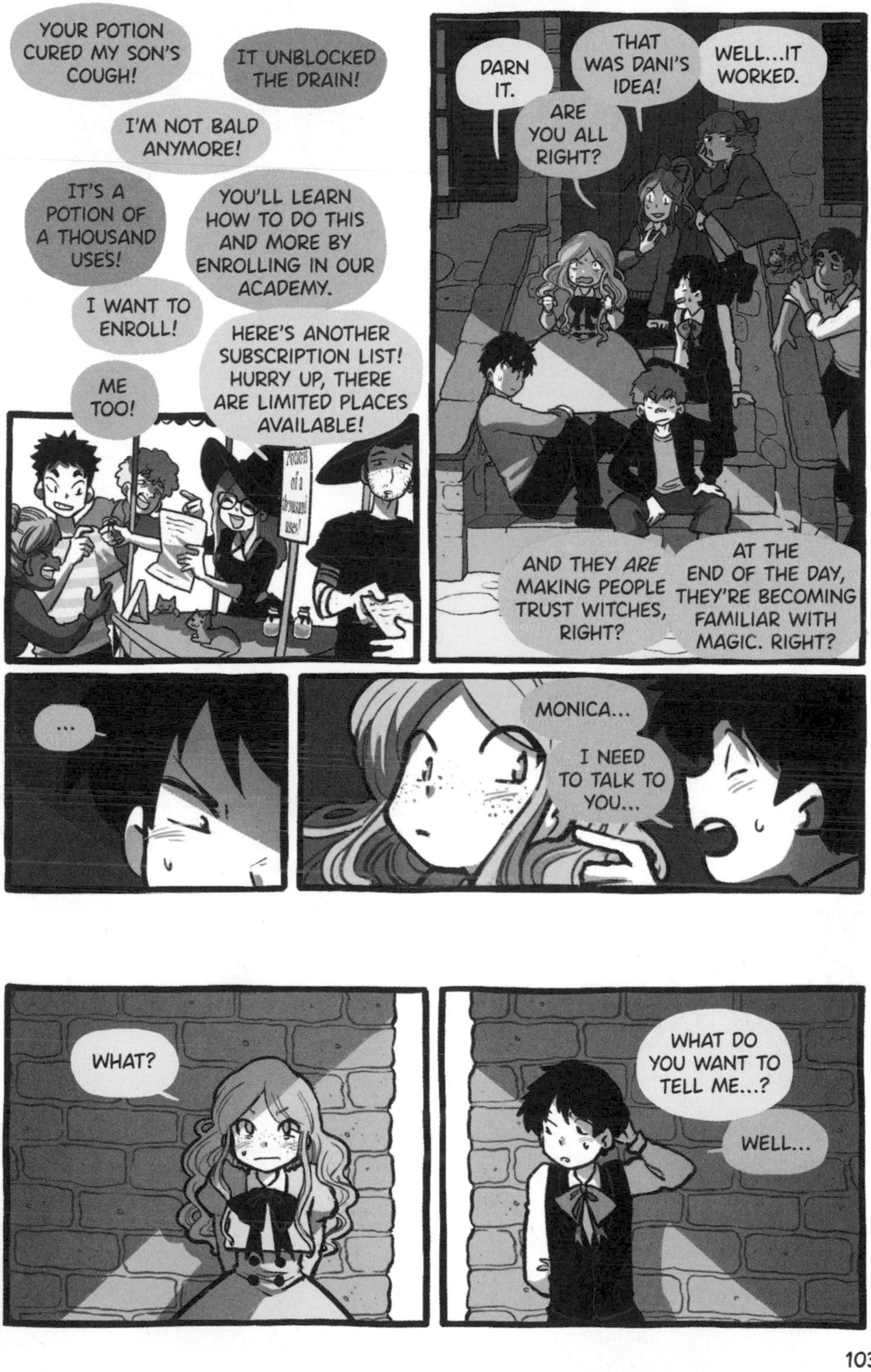
YOUR POTION CURED MY SON'S COUGH!
IT UNBLOCKED THE DRAIN!
I'M NOT BALD ANYMORE!
IT'S A POTION OF A THOUSAND USES!
YOU'LL LEARN HOW TO DO THIS AND MORE BY ENROLLING IN OUR ACADEMY.
I WANT TO ENROLL!
HERE'S ANOTHER SUBSCRIPTION LIST! HURRY UP, THERE ARE LIMITED PLACES AVAILABLE!
ME TOO!
Potion of a thousand uses!
DARN IT.
THAT WAS DANI'S IDEA!
WELL...IT WORKED.
ARE YOU ALL RIGHT?
AND THEY *ARE* MAKING PEOPLE TRUST WITCHES, RIGHT?
AT THE END OF THE DAY, THEY'RE BECOMING FAMILIAR WITH MAGIC. RIGHT?
...
MONICA...
I NEED TO TALK TO YOU...
WHAT?
WHAT DO YOU WANT TO TELL ME...?
WELL...

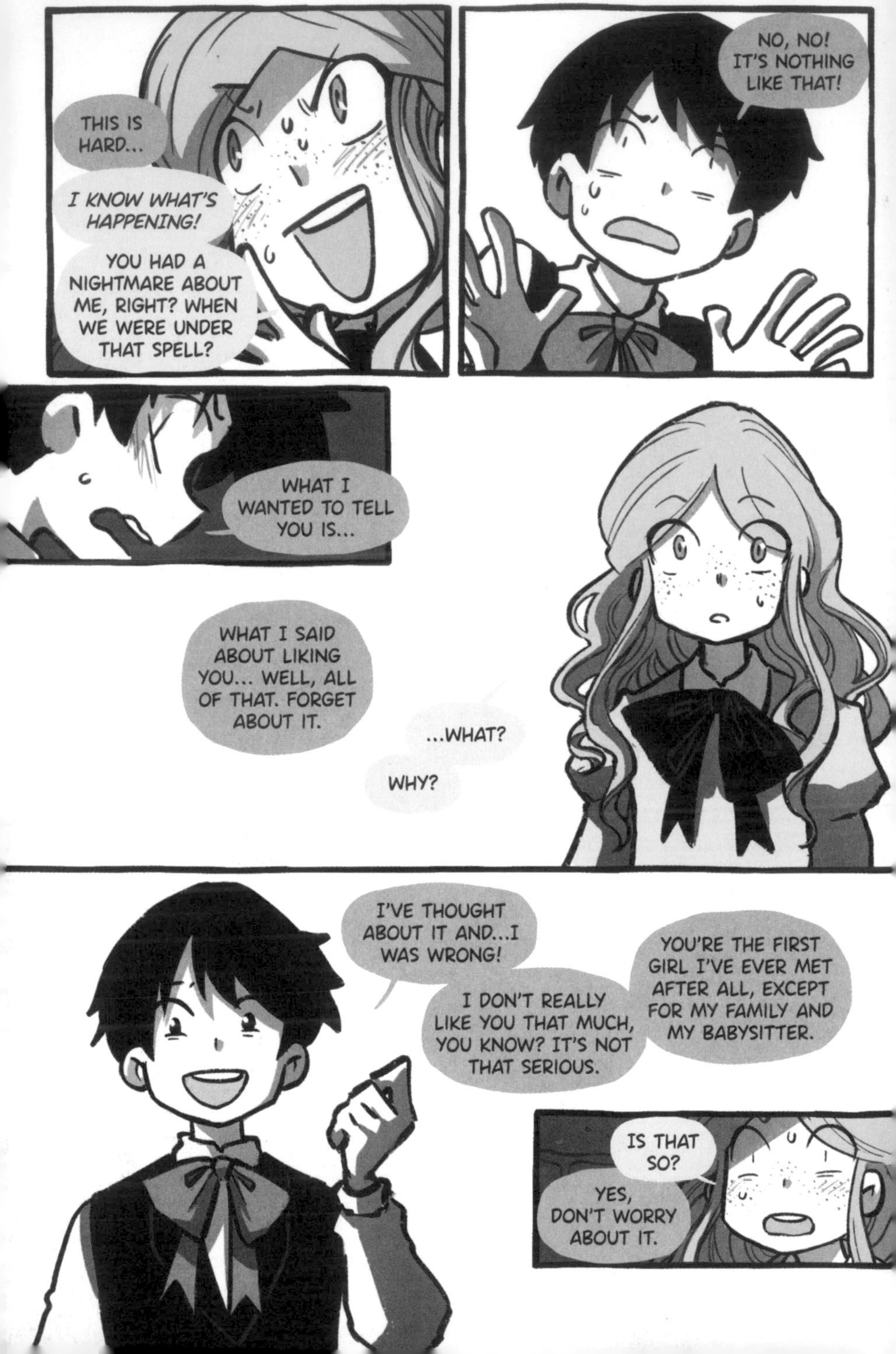
THIS IS HARD...
I KNOW WHAT'S HAPPENING!
YOU HAD A NIGHTMARE ABOUT ME, RIGHT? WHEN WE WERE UNDER THAT SPELL?
NO, NO! IT'S NOTHING LIKE THAT!
WHAT I WANTED TO TELL YOU IS...
WHAT I SAID ABOUT LIKING YOU... WELL, ALL OF THAT. FORGET ABOUT IT.
...WHAT?
WHY?
I'VE THOUGHT ABOUT IT AND...I WAS WRONG!
I DON'T REALLY LIKE YOU THAT MUCH, YOU KNOW? IT'S NOT THAT SERIOUS.
YOU'RE THE FIRST GIRL I'VE EVER MET AFTER ALL, EXCEPT FOR MY FAMILY AND MY BABYSITTER.
IS THAT SO?
YES, DON'T WORRY ABOUT IT.

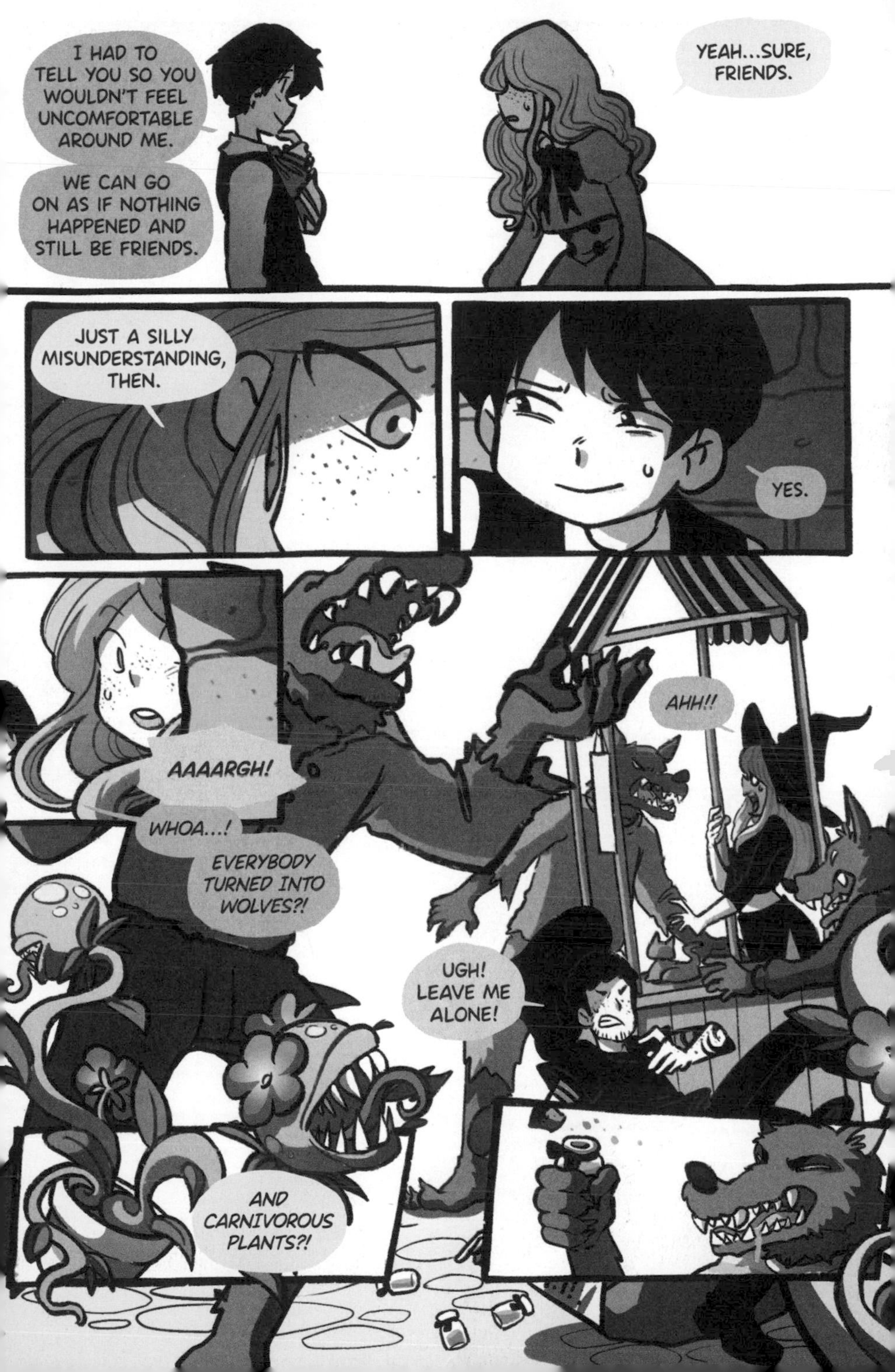

I HAD TO TELL YOU SO YOU WOULDN'T FEEL UNCOMFORTABLE AROUND ME.
WE CAN GO ON AS IF NOTHING HAPPENED AND STILL BE FRIENDS.
YEAH...SURE, FRIENDS.
JUST A SILLY MISUNDERSTANDING, THEN.
YES.
AAAARGH!
WHOA...!
EVERYBODY TURNED INTO WOLVES?!
AHH!!
UGH! LEAVE ME ALONE!
AND CARNIVOROUS PLANTS?!

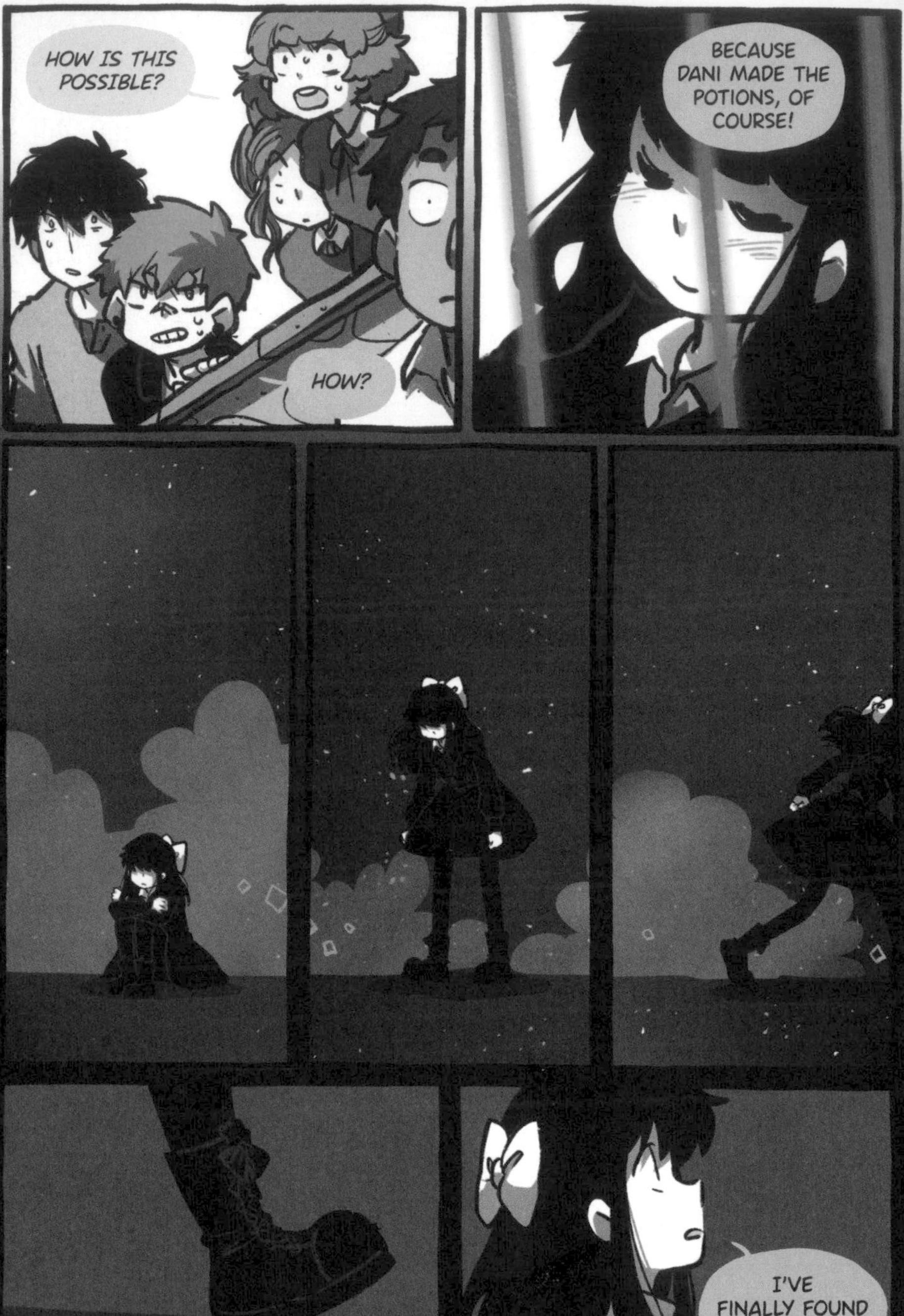
HOW IS THIS POSSIBLE?
HOW?
BECAUSE DANI MADE THE POTIONS, OF COURSE!
I'VE FINALLY FOUND YOU.

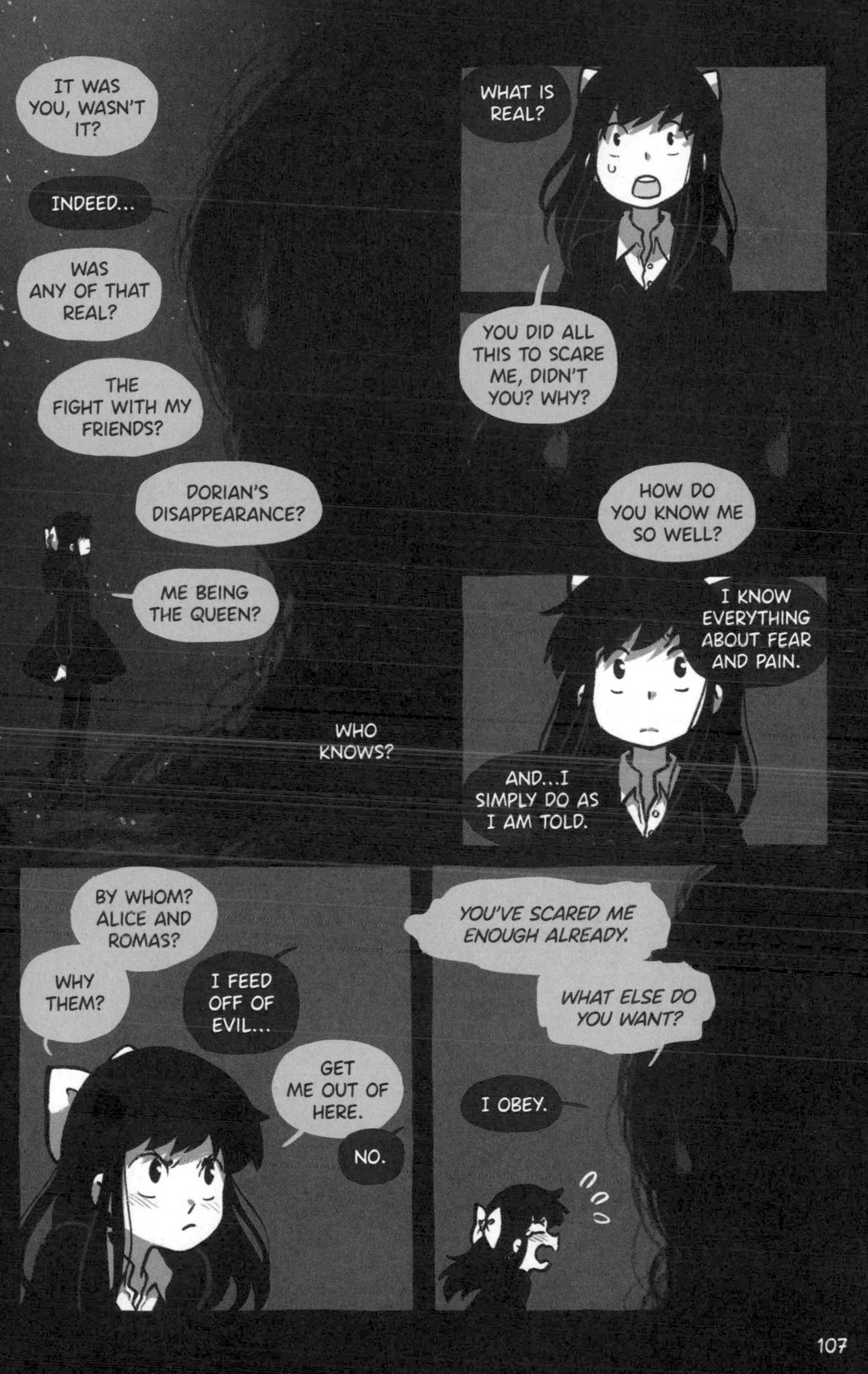
IT WAS YOU, WASN'T IT?
INDEED...
WAS ANY OF THAT REAL?
THE FIGHT WITH MY FRIENDS?
DORIAN'S DISAPPEARANCE?
ME BEING THE QUEEN?
WHO KNOWS?
WHAT IS REAL?
YOU DID ALL THIS TO SCARE ME, DIDN'T YOU? WHY?
HOW DO YOU KNOW ME SO WELL?
I KNOW EVERYTHING ABOUT FEAR AND PAIN.
AND...I SIMPLY DO AS I AM TOLD.
BY WHOM? ALICE AND ROMAS?
WHY THEM?
I FEED OFF OF EVIL...
GET ME OUT OF HERE.
NO.
YOU'VE SCARED ME ENOUGH ALREADY.
WHAT ELSE DO YOU WANT?
I OBEY.

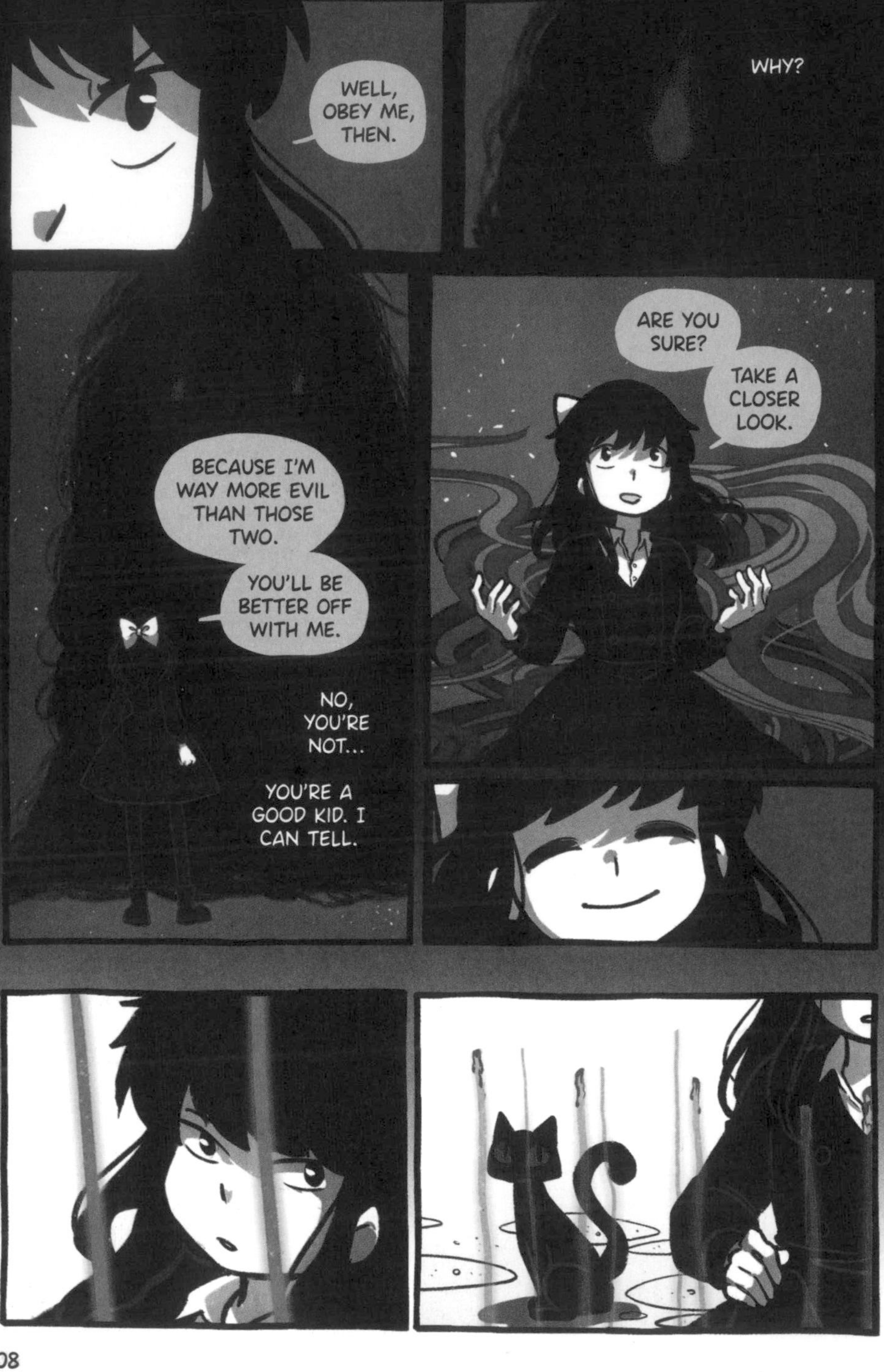
WELL, OBEY ME, THEN.
WHY?
BECAUSE I'M WAY MORE EVIL THAN THOSE TWO.
YOU'LL BE BETTER OFF WITH ME.
ARE YOU SURE?
TAKE A CLOSER LOOK.
NO, YOU'RE NOT...
YOU'RE A GOOD KID. I CAN TELL.

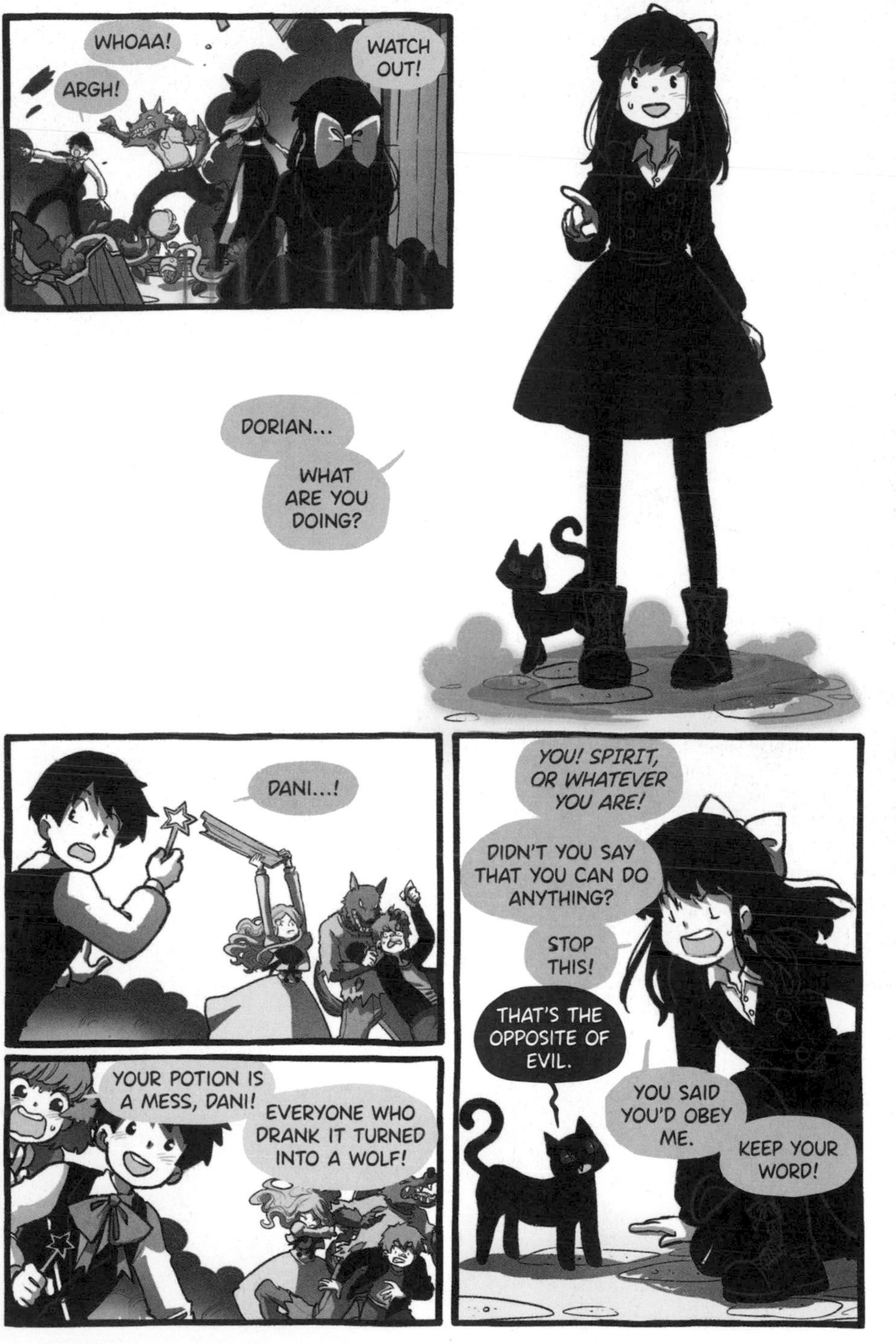
WHOAA!
ARGH!
WATCH OUT!
DORIAN...
WHAT ARE YOU DOING?
DANI...!
YOU! SPIRIT, OR WHATEVER YOU ARE!
DIDN'T YOU SAY THAT YOU CAN DO ANYTHING?
STOP THIS!
YOUR POTION IS A MESS, DANI!
EVERYONE WHO DRANK IT TURNED INTO A WOLF!
THAT'S THE OPPOSITE OF EVIL.
YOU SAID YOU'D OBEY ME.
KEEP YOUR WORD!

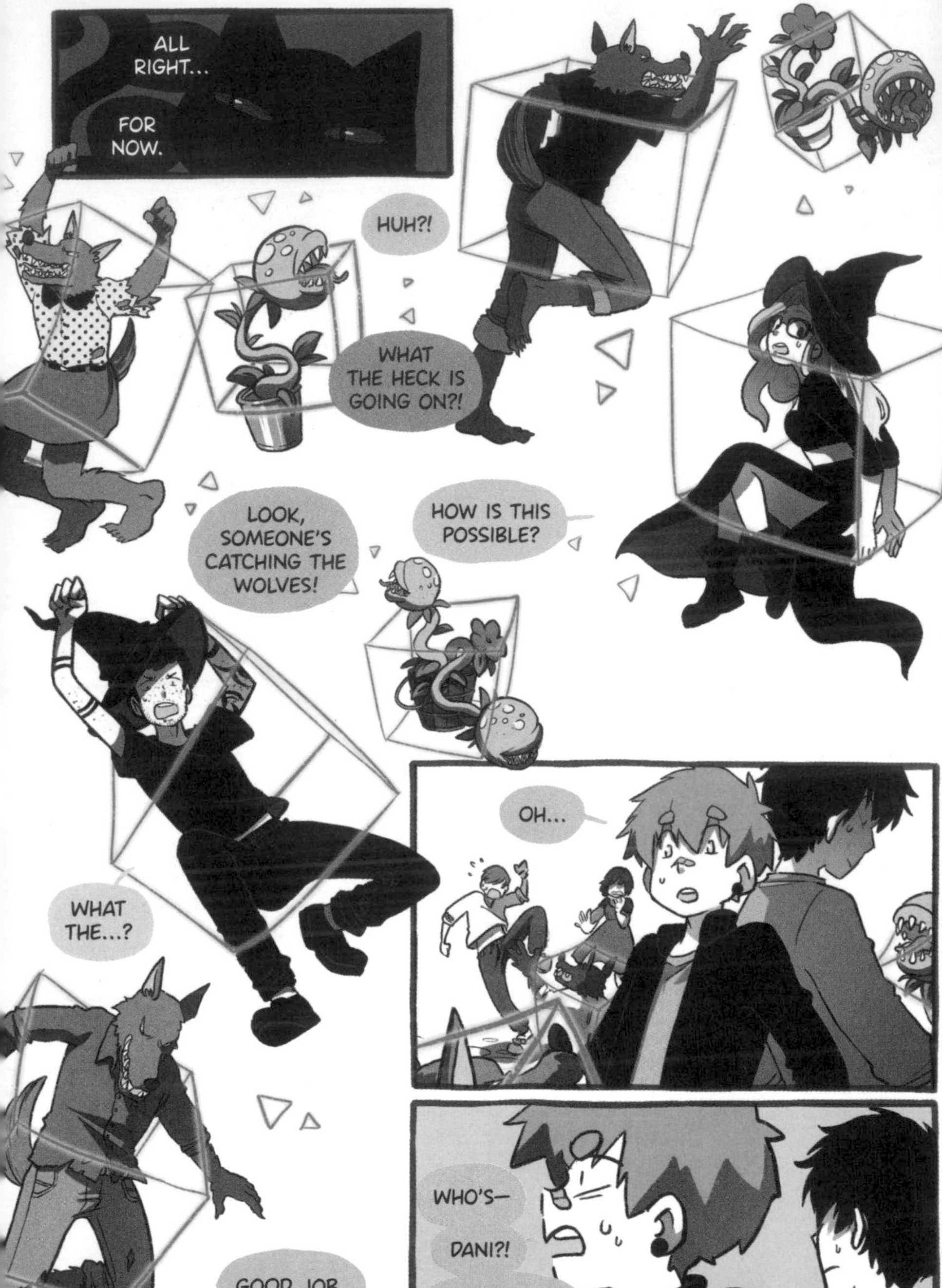
ALL RIGHT...
FOR NOW.
HUH?!
WHAT THE HECK IS GOING ON?!
LOOK, SOMEONE'S CATCHING THE WOLVES!
HOW IS THIS POSSIBLE?
WHAT THE...?
GOOD JOB, SPIRIT!
OH...
WHO'S—
DANI?!
HOW DID YOU DO THAT?!

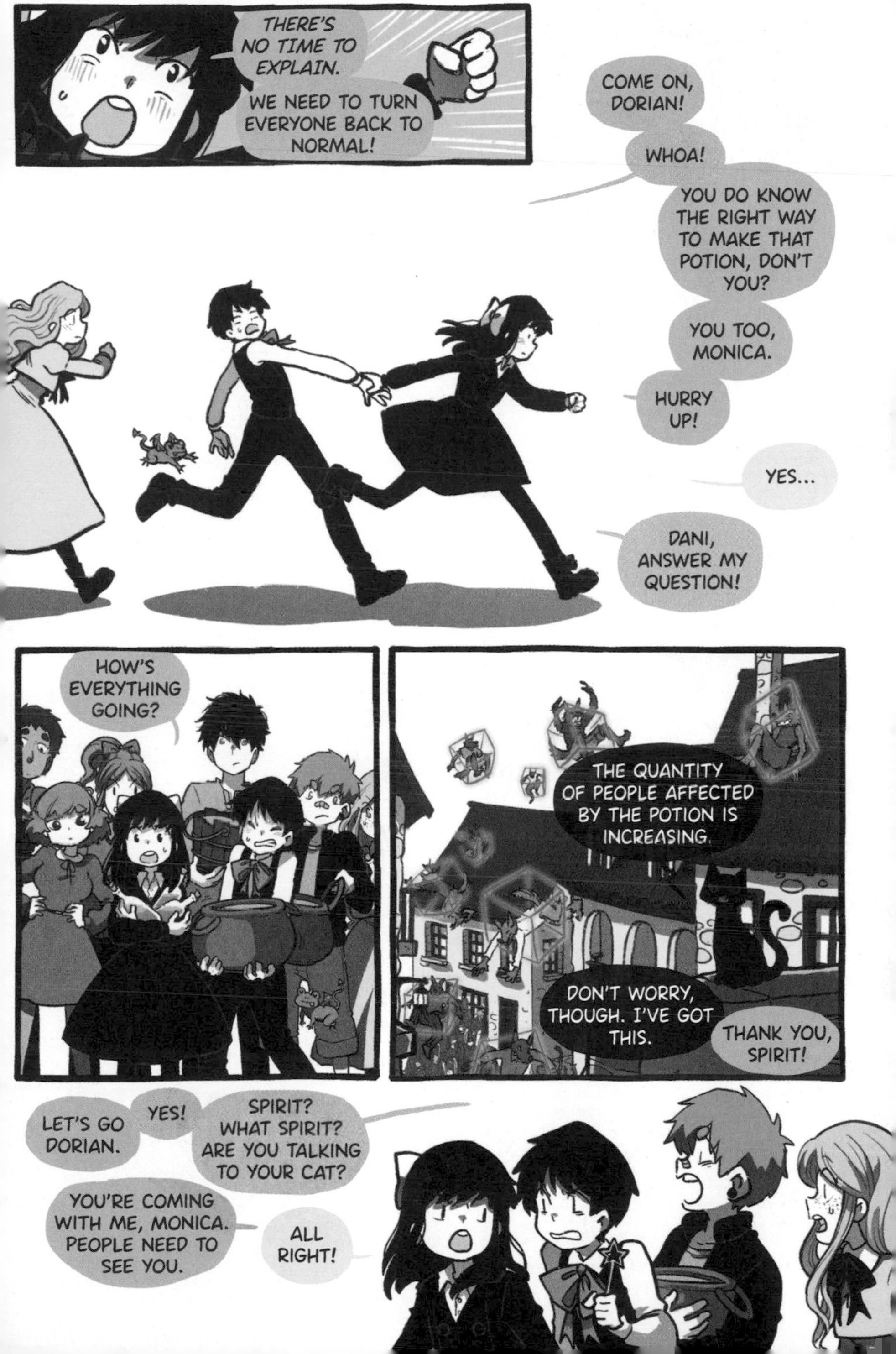
THERE'S NO TIME TO EXPLAIN.
WE NEED TO TURN EVERYONE BACK TO NORMAL!
COME ON, DORIAN!
WHOA!
YOU DO KNOW THE RIGHT WAY TO MAKE THAT POTION, DON'T YOU?
YOU TOO, MONICA.
HURRY UP!
YES...
DANI, ANSWER MY QUESTION!
HOW'S EVERYTHING GOING?
THE QUANTITY OF PEOPLE AFFECTED BY THE POTION IS INCREASING.
DON'T WORRY, THOUGH. I'VE GOT THIS.
THANK YOU, SPIRIT!
LET'S GO DORIAN.
YES!
SPIRIT? WHAT SPIRIT? ARE YOU TALKING TO YOUR CAT?
YOU'RE COMING WITH ME, MONICA. PEOPLE NEED TO SEE YOU.
ALL RIGHT!

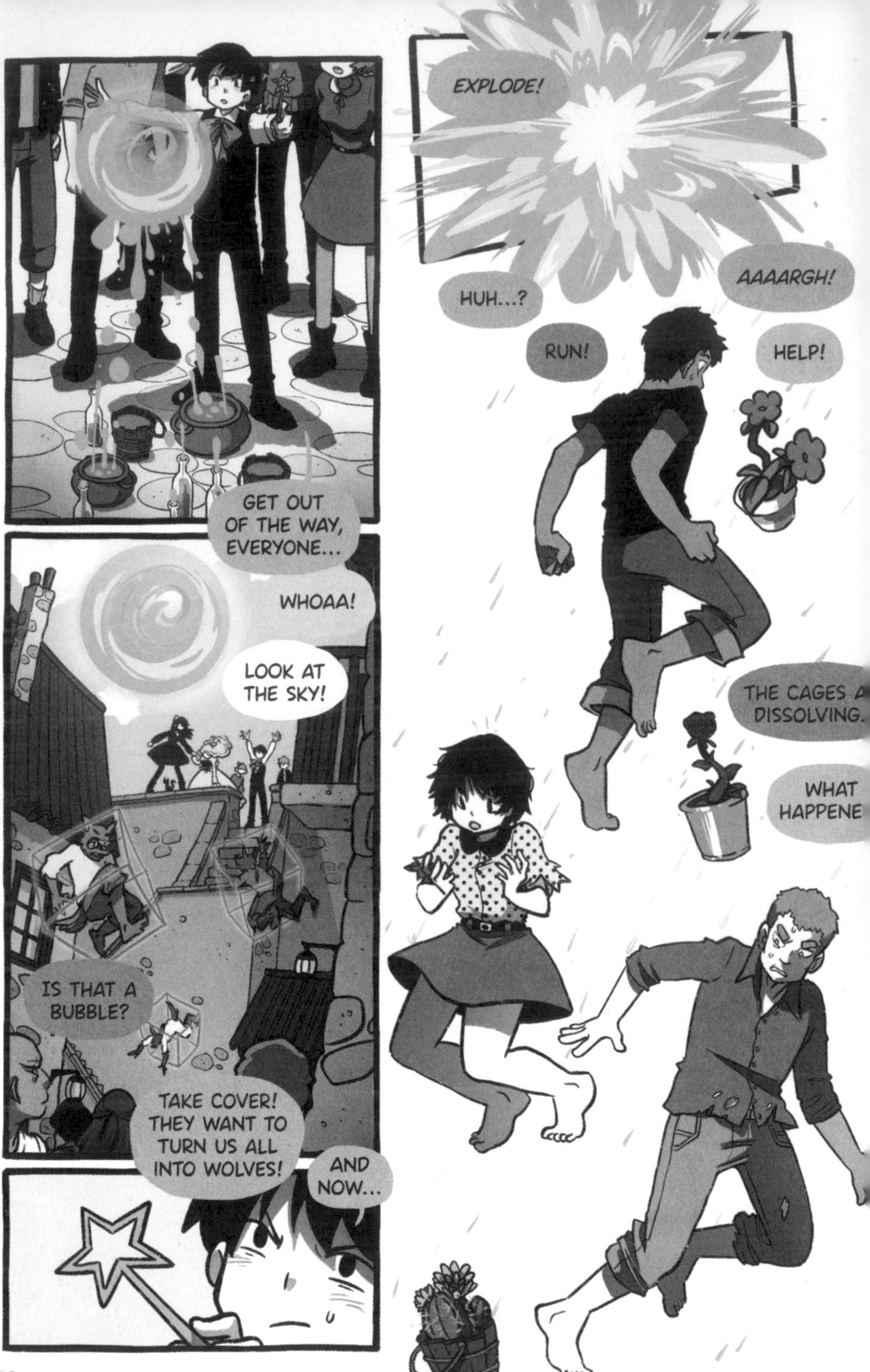
GET OUT OF THE WAY, EVERYONE...
WHOAA!
LOOK AT THE SKY!
IS THAT A BUBBLE?
TAKE COVER! THEY WANT TO TURN US ALL INTO WOLVES!
AND NOW...
EXPLODE!
HUH...?
AAAARGH!
RUN!
HELP!
THE CAGES A
DISSOLVING.
WHAT
HAPPENE

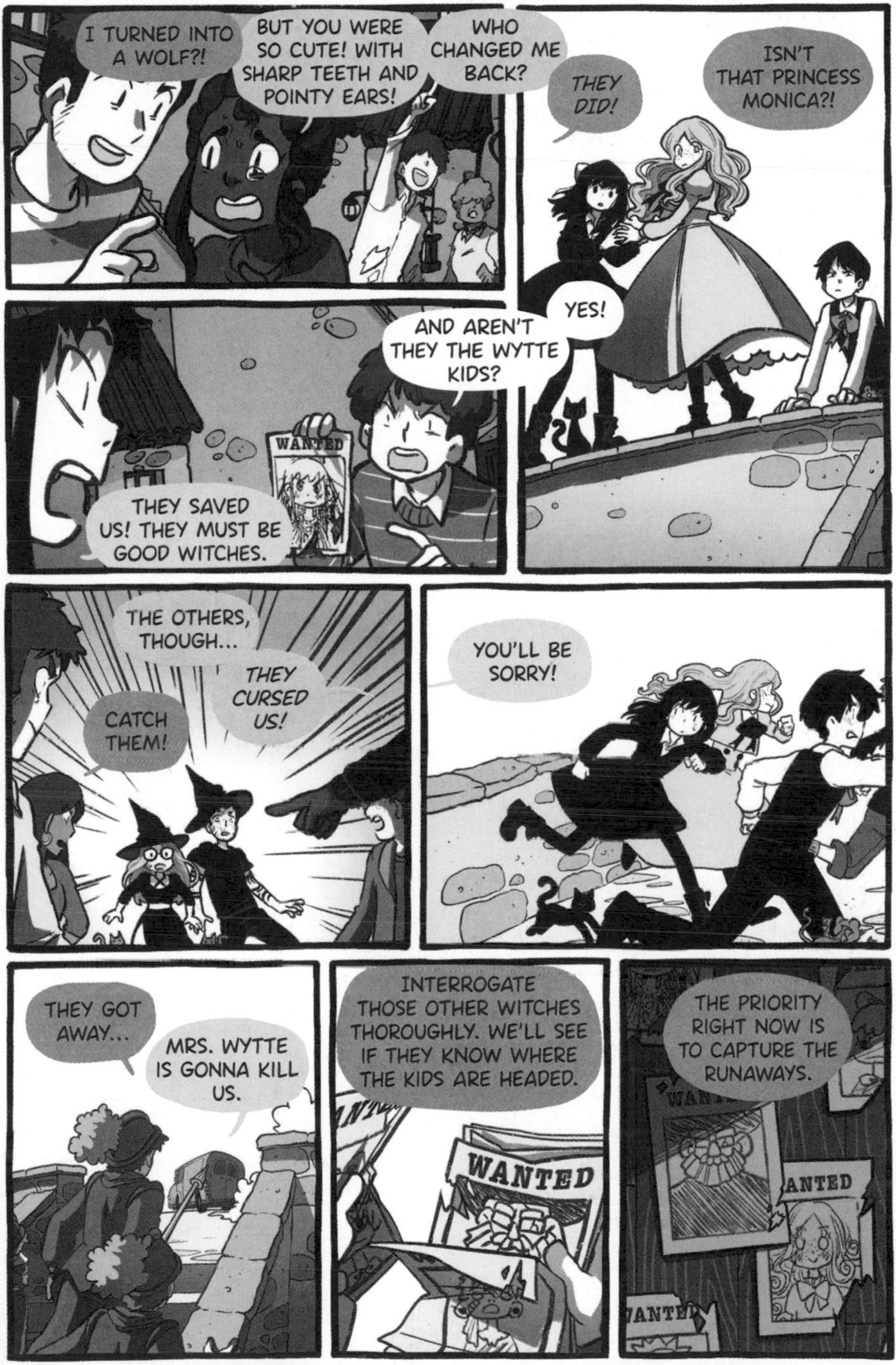
I TURNED INTO A WOLF?!
BUT YOU WERE SO CUTE! WITH SHARP TEETH AND POINTY EARS!
WHO CHANGED ME BACK?
THEY DID!
ISN'T THAT PRINCESS MONICA?!
AND AREN'T THEY THE WYTTE KIDS?
YES!
WANTED
THEY SAVED US! THEY MUST BE GOOD WITCHES.
THE OTHERS, THOUGH...
THEY CURSED US!
CATCH THEM!
YOU'LL BE SORRY!
THEY GOT AWAY...
MRS. WYTTE IS GONNA KILL US.
INTERROGATE THOSE OTHER WITCHES THOROUGHLY. WE'LL SEE IF THEY KNOW WHERE THE KIDS ARE HEADED.
WANTED
THE PRIORITY RIGHT NOW IS TO CAPTURE THE RUNAWAYS.
ANTED

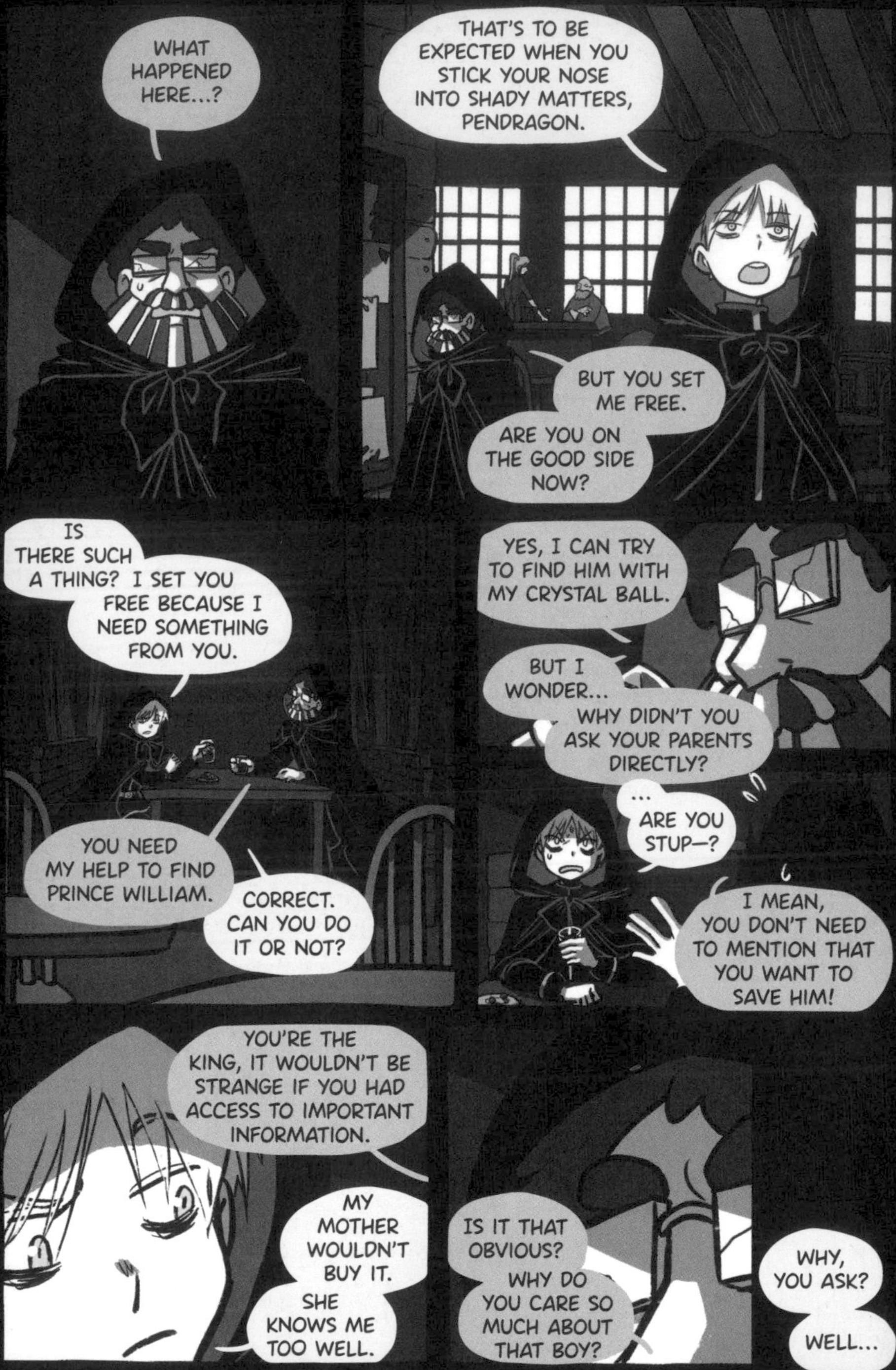
WHAT HAPPENED HERE...?
THAT'S TO BE EXPECTED WHEN YOU STICK YOUR NOSE INTO SHADY MATTERS, PENDRAGON.
BUT YOU SET ME FREE.
ARE YOU ON THE GOOD SIDE NOW?
IS THERE SUCH A THING? I SET YOU FREE BECAUSE I NEED SOMETHING FROM YOU.
YOU NEED MY HELP TO FIND PRINCE WILLIAM.
CORRECT. CAN YOU DO IT OR NOT?
YES, I CAN TRY TO FIND HIM WITH MY CRYSTAL BALL.
BUT I WONDER...
WHY DIDN'T YOU ASK YOUR PARENTS DIRECTLY?
... ARE YOU STUP—?
I MEAN, YOU DON'T NEED TO MENTION THAT YOU WANT TO SAVE HIM!
YOU'RE THE KING, IT WOULDN'T BE STRANGE IF YOU HAD ACCESS TO IMPORTANT INFORMATION.
MY MOTHER WOULDN'T BUY IT.
SHE KNOWS ME TOO WELL.
IS IT THAT OBVIOUS?
WHY DO YOU CARE SO MUCH ABOUT THAT BOY?
WHY, YOU ASK?
WELL...

CHAPTER 40

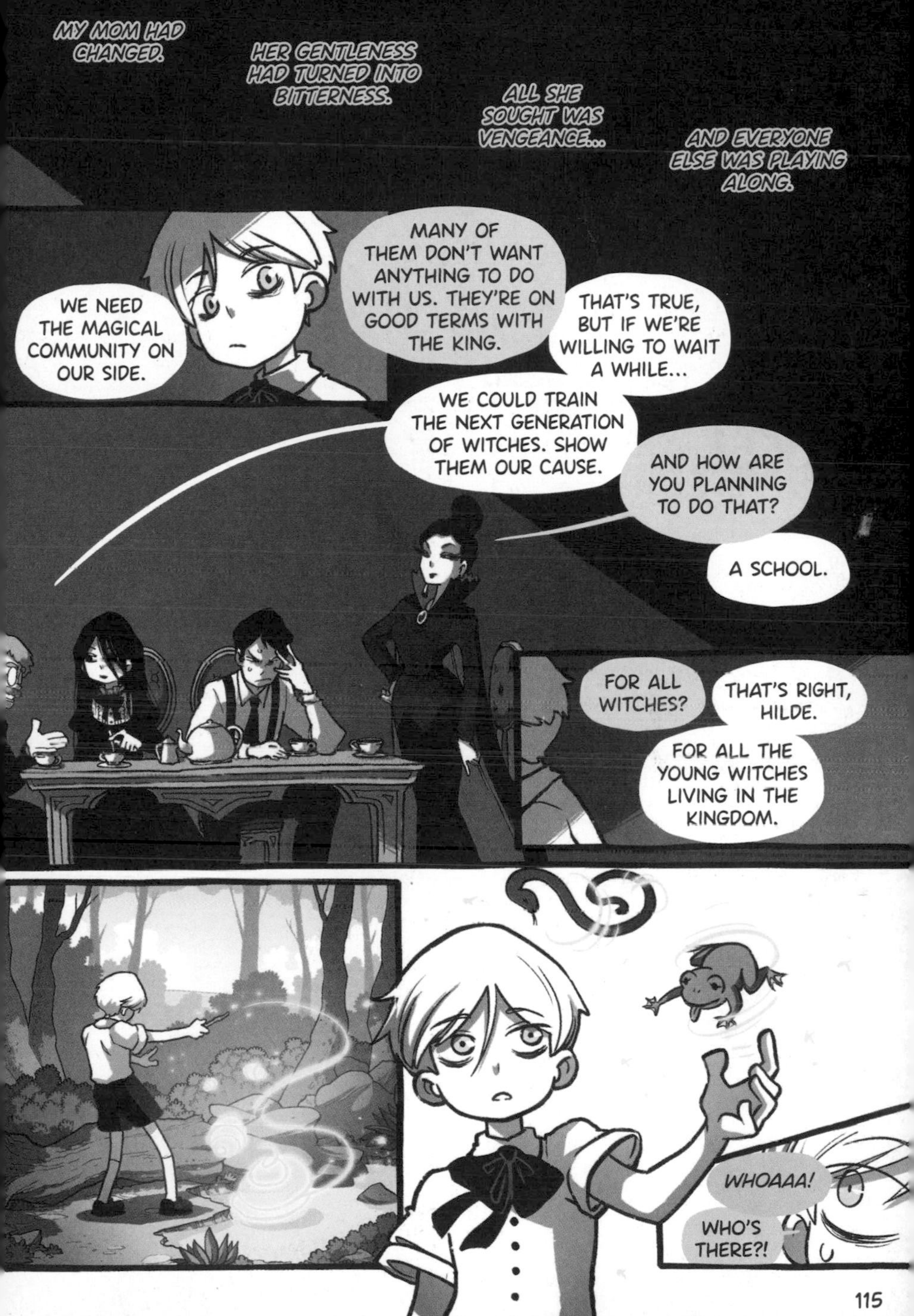

MY MOM HAD CHANGED.
HER GENTLENESS HAD TURNED INTO BITTERNESS.
ALL SHE SOUGHT WAS VENGEANCE...
AND EVERYONE ELSE WAS PLAYING ALONG.
WE NEED THE MAGICAL COMMUNITY ON OUR SIDE.
MANY OF THEM DON'T WANT ANYTHING TO DO WITH US. THEY'RE ON GOOD TERMS WITH THE KING.
THAT'S TRUE, BUT IF WE'RE WILLING TO WAIT A WHILE...
WE COULD TRAIN THE NEXT GENERATION OF WITCHES. SHOW THEM OUR CAUSE.
AND HOW ARE YOU PLANNING TO DO THAT?
A SCHOOL.
FOR ALL WITCHES?
THAT'S RIGHT, HILDE.
FOR ALL THE YOUNG WITCHES LIVING IN THE KINGDOM.
WHOAAA!
WHO'S THERE?!

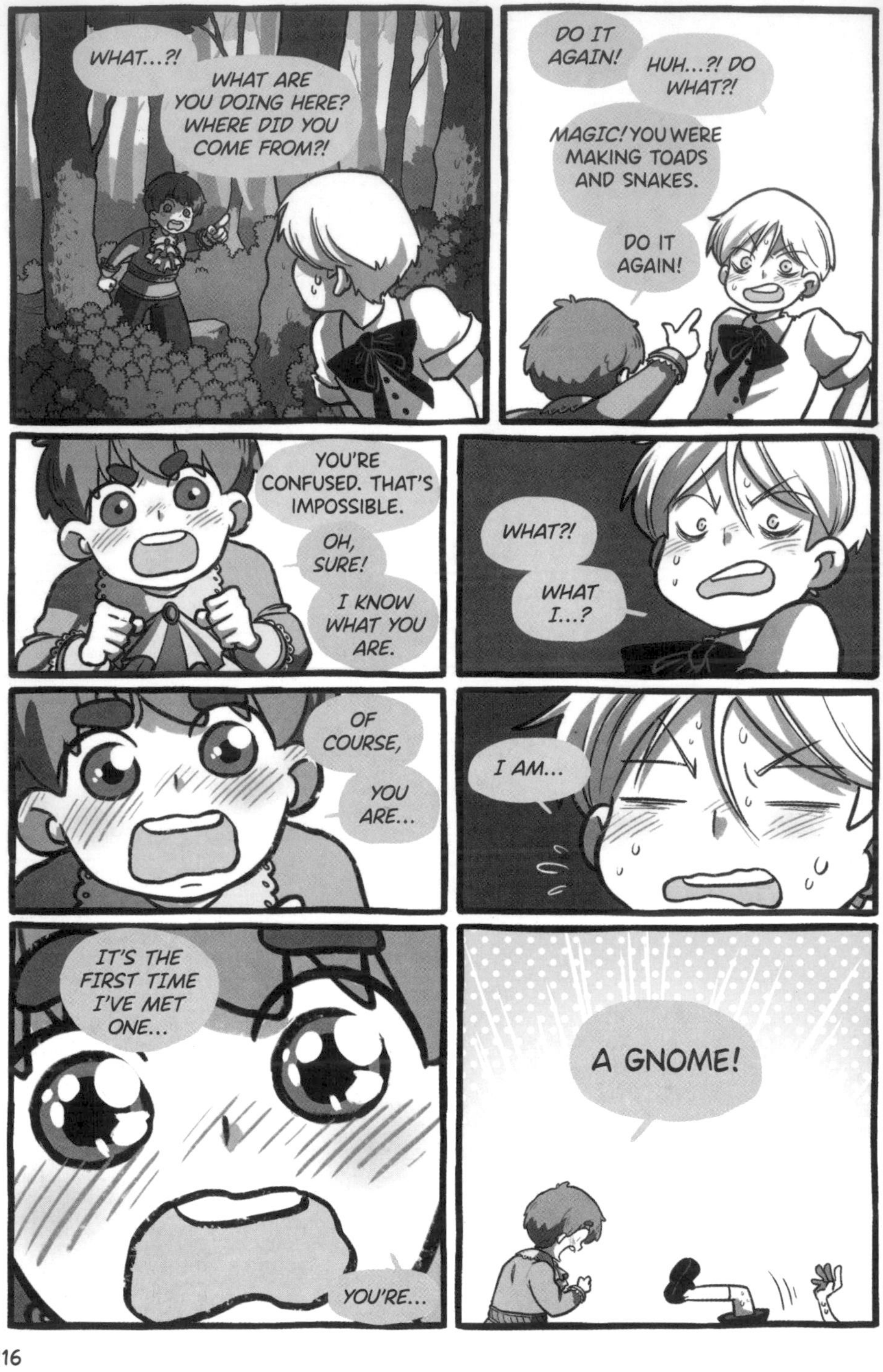
WHAT...?!
WHAT ARE YOU DOING HERE? WHERE DID YOU COME FROM?!
DO IT AGAIN!
HUH...?! DO WHAT?!
MAGIC! YOU WERE MAKING TOADS AND SNAKES.
DO IT AGAIN!
YOU'RE CONFUSED. THAT'S IMPOSSIBLE.
OH, SURE!
I KNOW WHAT YOU ARE.
WHAT?!
WHAT I...?
OF COURSE,
YOU ARE...
I AM...
IT'S THE FIRST TIME I'VE MET ONE...
YOU'RE...
A GNOME!

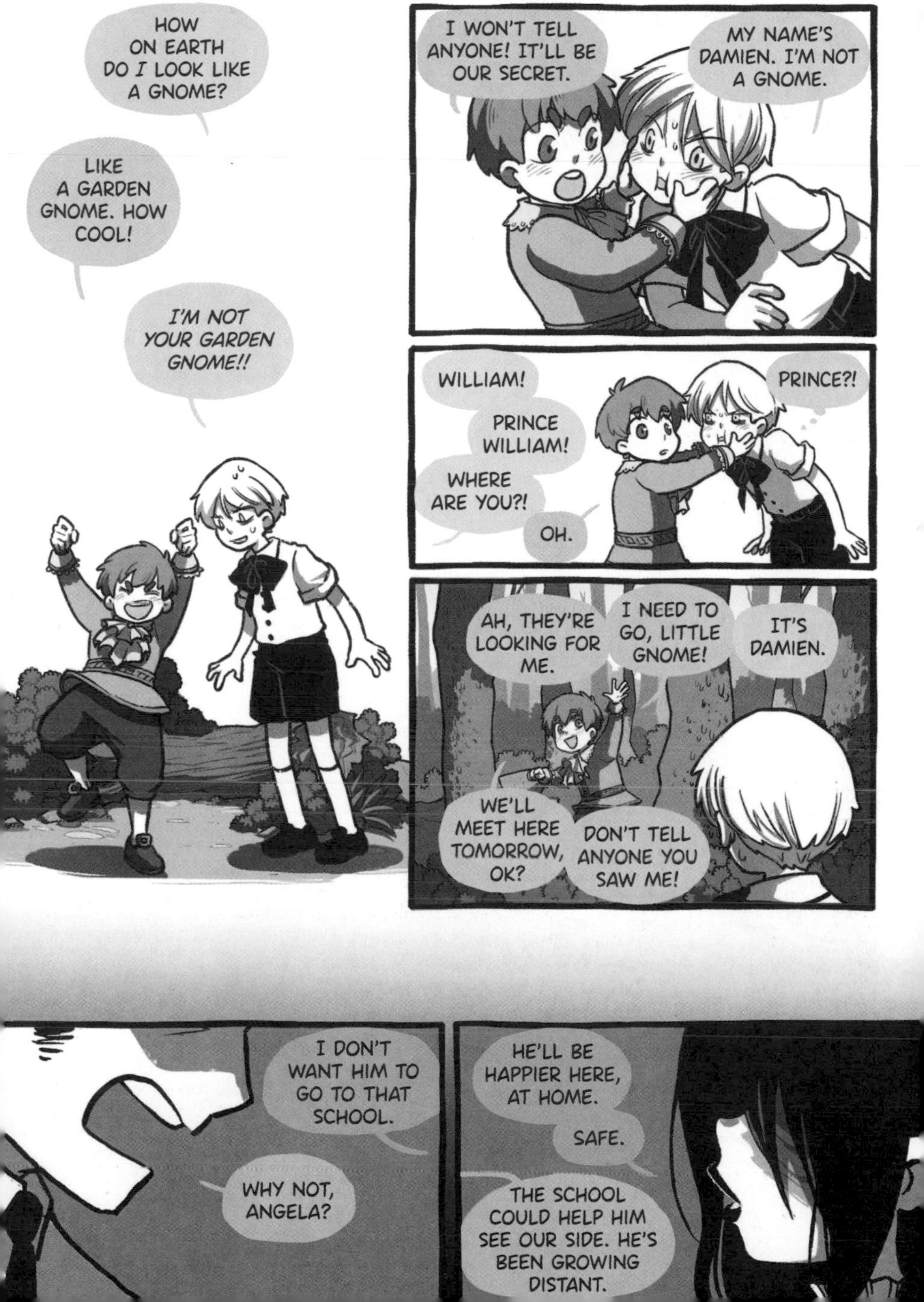
HOW ON EARTH DO *I* LOOK LIKE A GNOME?
LIKE A GARDEN GNOME. HOW COOL!
I'M NOT YOUR GARDEN GNOME!!
I WON'T TELL ANYONE! IT'LL BE OUR SECRET.
MY NAME'S DAMIEN. I'M NOT A GNOME.
WILLIAM!
PRINCE WILLIAM!
WHERE ARE YOU?!
OH.
PRINCE?!
AH, THEY'RE LOOKING FOR ME.
I NEED TO GO, LITTLE GNOME!
IT'S DAMIEN.
WE'LL MEET HERE TOMORROW, OK?
DON'T TELL ANYONE YOU SAW ME!
I DON'T WANT HIM TO GO TO THAT SCHOOL.
WHY NOT, ANGELA?
HE'LL BE HAPPIER HERE, AT HOME.
SAFE.
THE SCHOOL COULD HELP HIM SEE OUR SIDE. HE'S BEEN GROWING DISTANT.

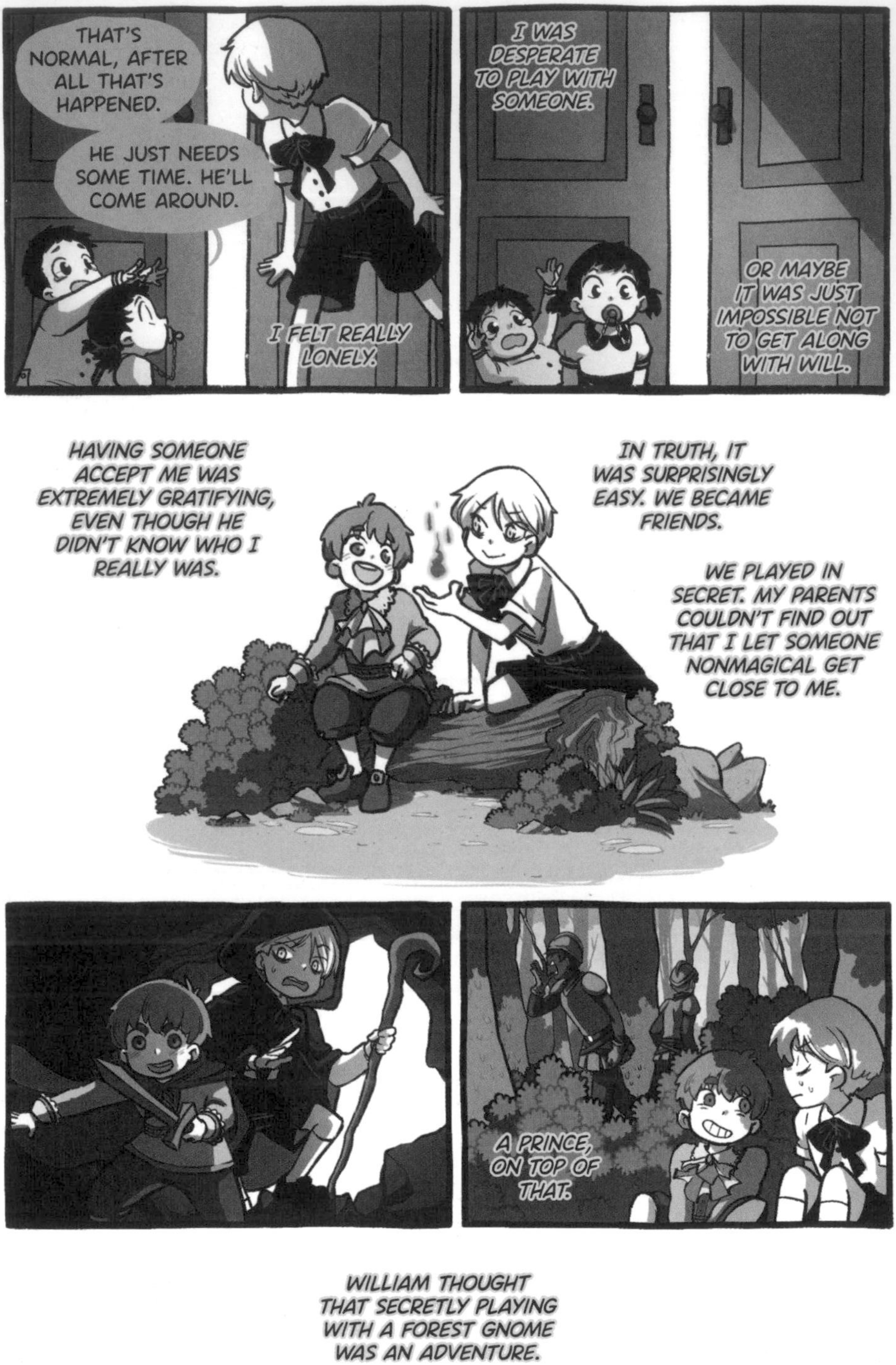
THAT'S NORMAL, AFTER ALL THAT'S HAPPENED.
HE JUST NEEDS SOME TIME. HE'LL COME AROUND.
I FELT REALLY LONELY.
I WAS DESPERATE TO PLAY WITH SOMEONE.
OR MAYBE IT WAS JUST IMPOSSIBLE NOT TO GET ALONG WITH WILL.
HAVING SOMEONE ACCEPT ME WAS EXTREMELY GRATIFYING, EVEN THOUGH HE DIDN'T KNOW WHO I REALLY WAS.
IN TRUTH, IT WAS SURPRISINGLY EASY. WE BECAME FRIENDS.
WE PLAYED IN SECRET. MY PARENTS COULDN'T FIND OUT THAT I LET SOMEONE NONMAGICAL GET CLOSE TO ME.
A PRINCE, ON TOP OF THAT.
WILLIAM THOUGHT THAT SECRETLY PLAYING WITH A FOREST GNOME WAS AN ADVENTURE.

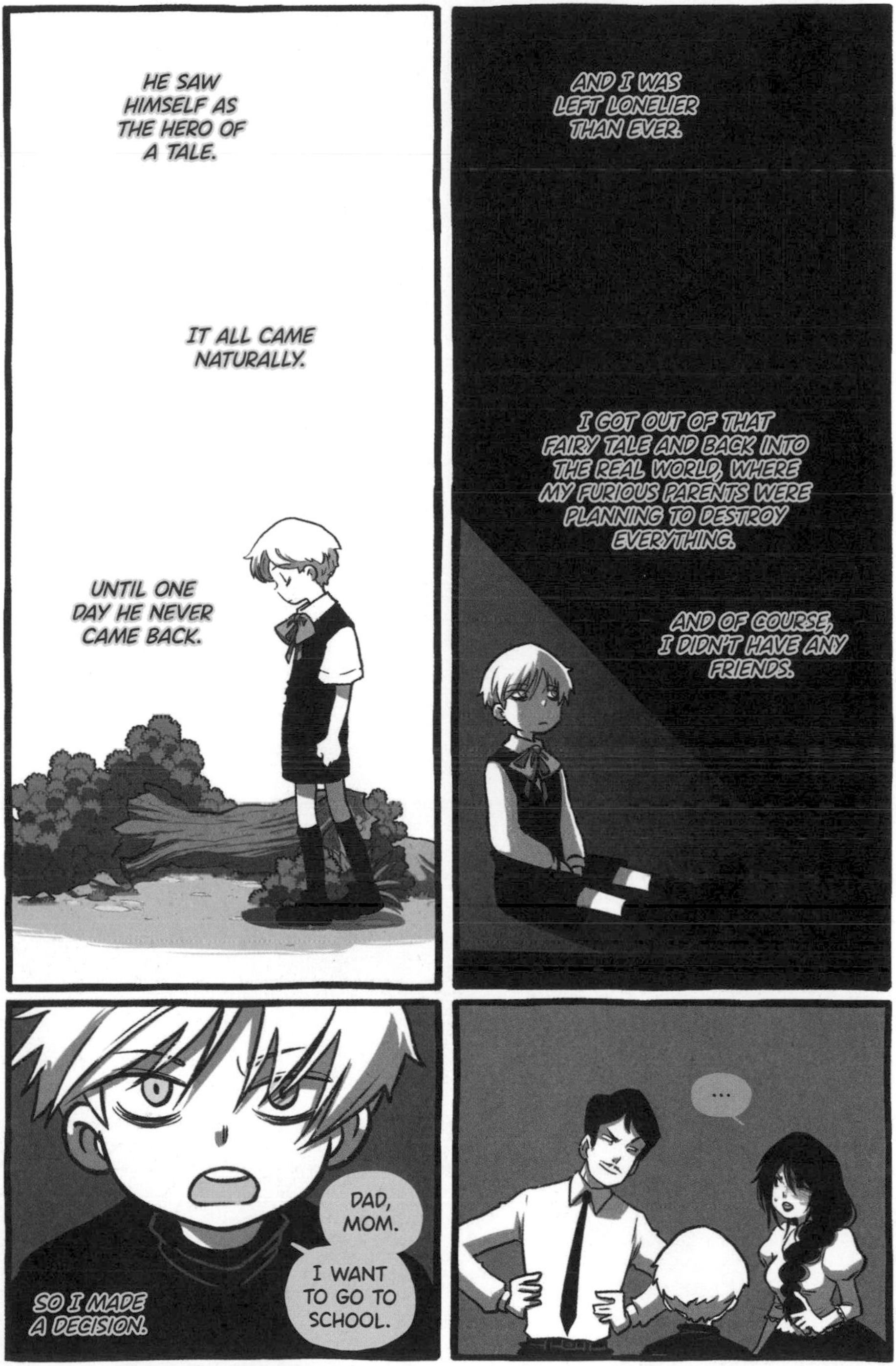
HE SAW HIMSELF AS THE HERO OF A TALE.
IT ALL CAME NATURALLY.
UNTIL ONE DAY HE NEVER CAME BACK.
AND I WAS LEFT LONELIER THAN EVER.
I GOT OUT OF THAT FAIRY TALE AND BACK INTO THE REAL WORLD, WHERE MY FURIOUS PARENTS WERE PLANNING TO DESTROY EVERYTHING.
AND OF COURSE, I DIDN'T HAVE ANY FRIENDS.
SO I MADE A DECISION.
DAD, MOM.
I WANT TO GO TO SCHOOL.
...

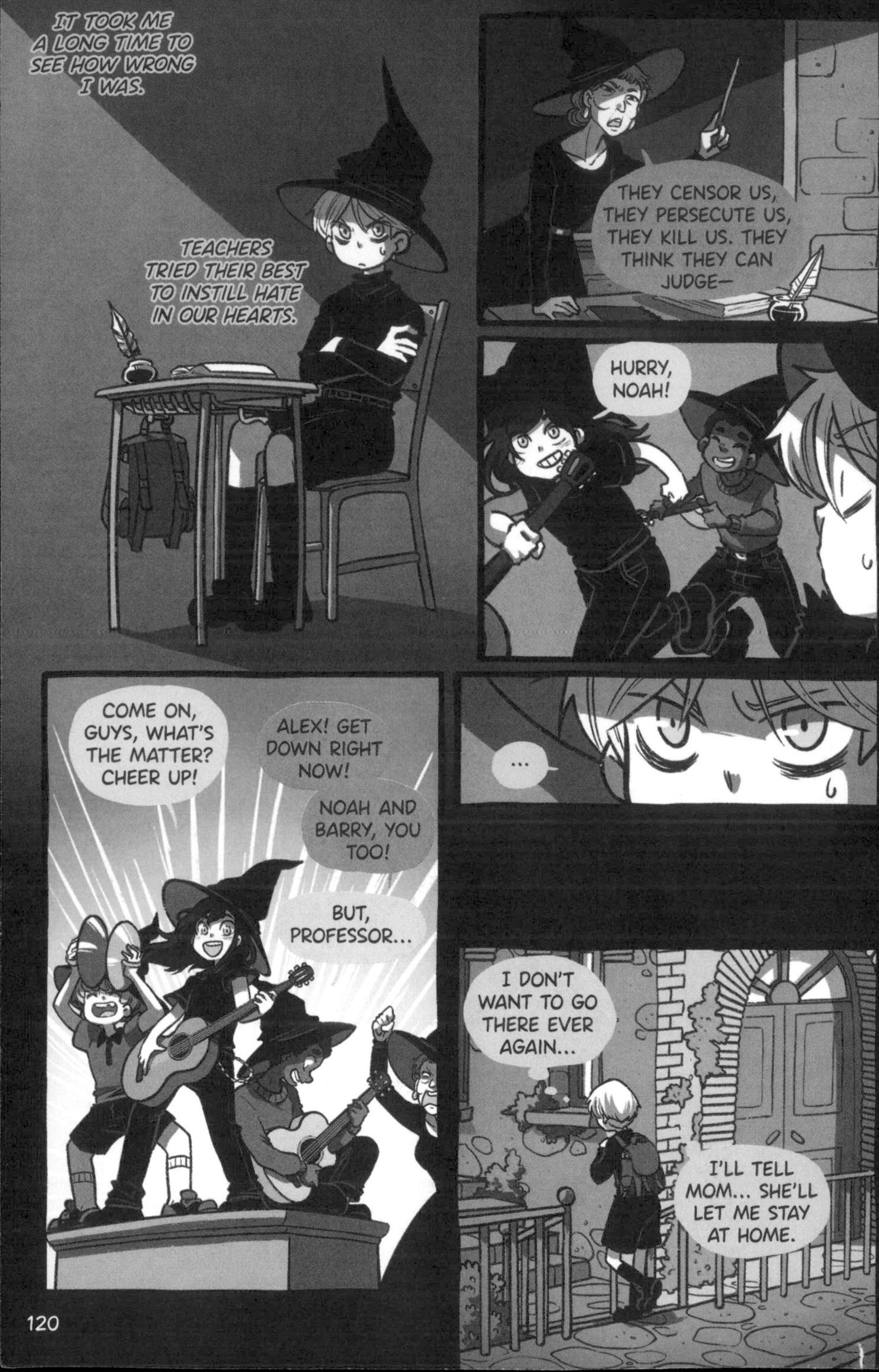
IT TOOK ME A LONG TIME TO SEE HOW WRONG I WAS.
TEACHERS TRIED THEIR BEST TO INSTILL HATE IN OUR HEARTS.
THEY CENSOR US, THEY PERSECUTE US, THEY KILL US. THEY THINK THEY CAN JUDGE—
HURRY, NOAH!
COME ON, GUYS, WHAT'S THE MATTER? CHEER UP!
ALEX! GET DOWN RIGHT NOW!
NOAH AND BARRY, YOU TOO!
BUT, PROFESSOR...
...
I DON'T WANT TO GO THERE EVER AGAIN...
I'LL TELL MOM... SHE'LL LET ME STAY AT HOME.

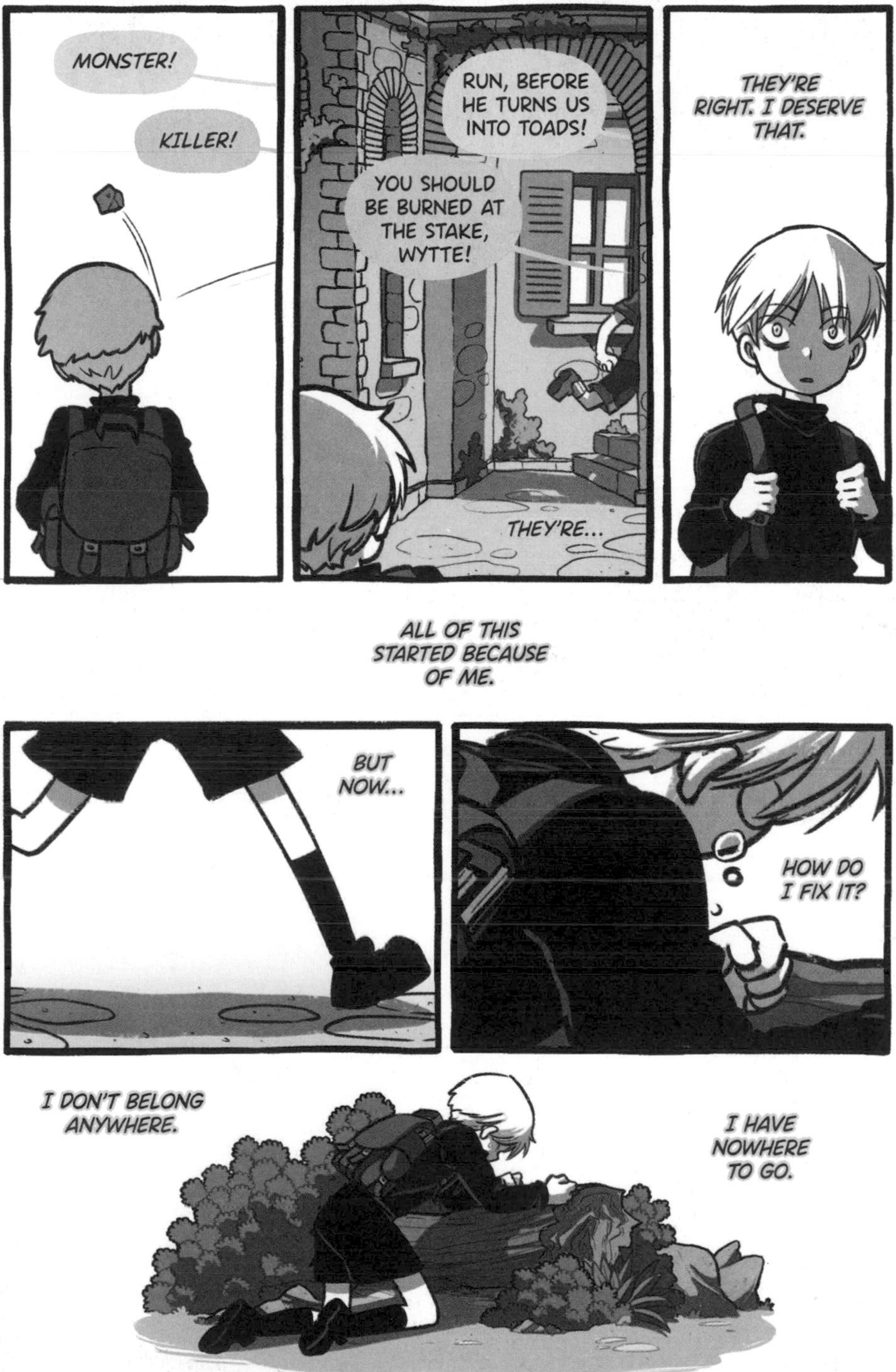
MONSTER!
KILLER!
RUN, BEFORE HE TURNS US INTO TOADS!
YOU SHOULD BE BURNED AT THE STAKE, WYTTE!
THEY'RE...
THEY'RE RIGHT. I DESERVE THAT.
ALL OF THIS STARTED BECAUSE OF ME.
BUT NOW...
HOW DO I FIX IT?
I DON'T BELONG ANYWHERE.
I HAVE NOWHERE TO GO.

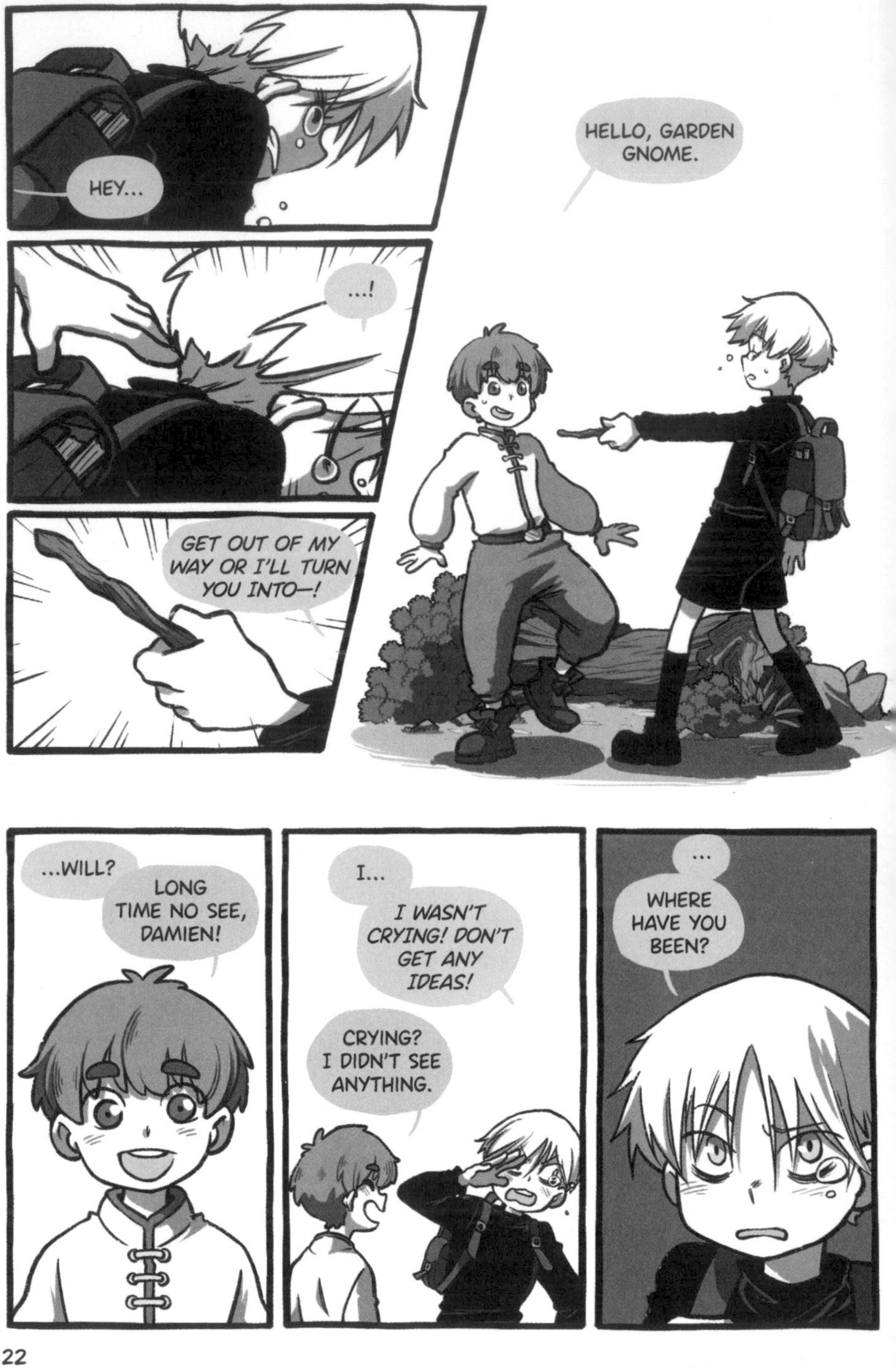
HEY...
HELLO, GARDEN GNOME.
...!
GET OUT OF MY WAY OR I'LL TURN YOU INTO—!
...WILL?
LONG TIME NO SEE, DAMIEN!
I...
I WASN'T CRYING! DON'T GET ANY IDEAS!
CRYING? I DIDN'T SEE ANYTHING.
...
WHERE HAVE YOU BEEN?

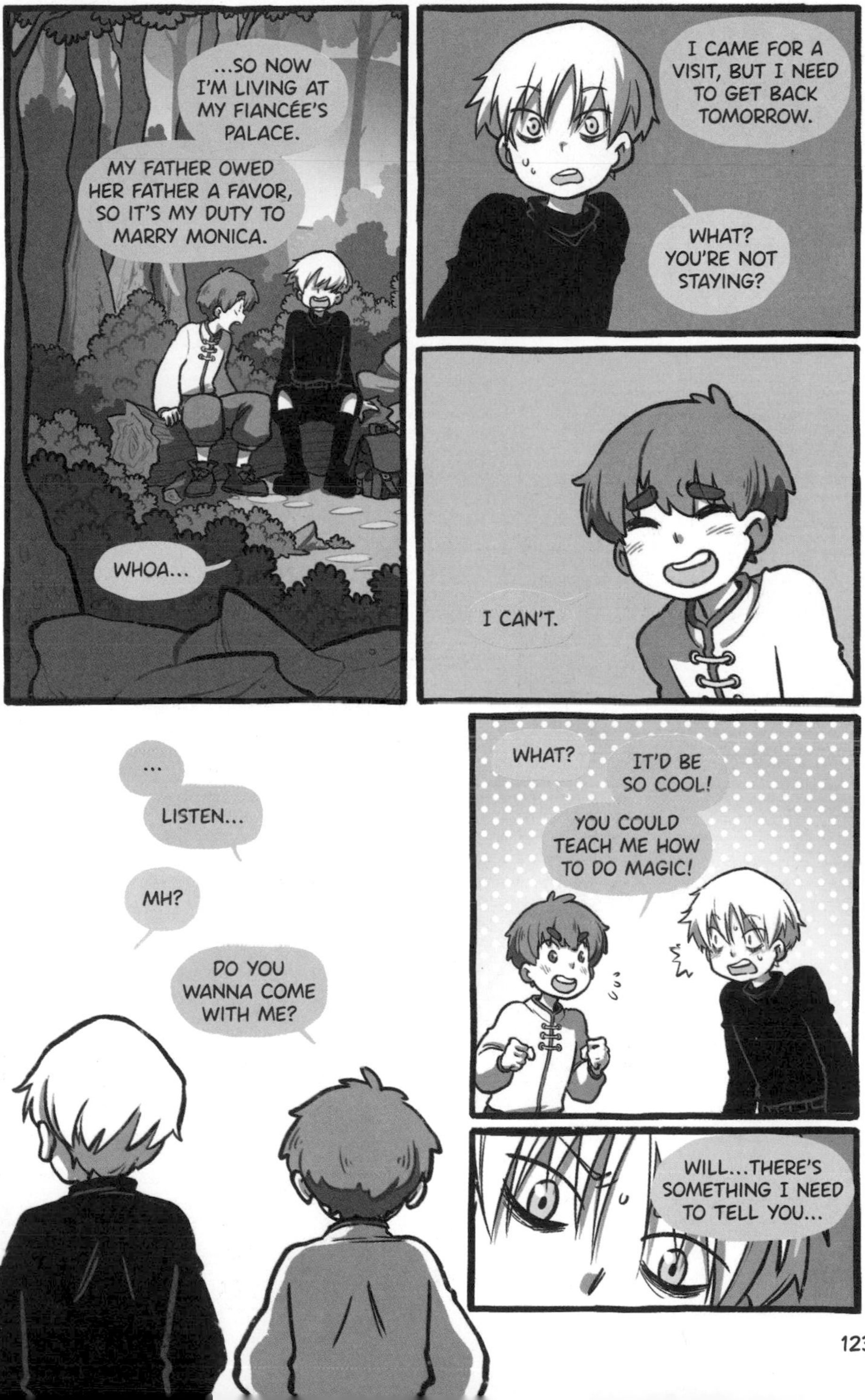
...SO NOW I'M LIVING AT MY FIANCÉE'S PALACE.
MY FATHER OWED HER FATHER A FAVOR, SO IT'S MY DUTY TO MARRY MONICA.
WHOA...
I CAME FOR A VISIT, BUT I NEED TO GET BACK TOMORROW.
WHAT? YOU'RE NOT STAYING?
I CAN'T.
...
LISTEN...
MH?
DO YOU WANNA COME WITH ME?
WHAT?
IT'D BE SO COOL!
YOU COULD TEACH ME HOW TO DO MAGIC!
WILL...THERE'S SOMETHING I NEED TO TELL YOU...

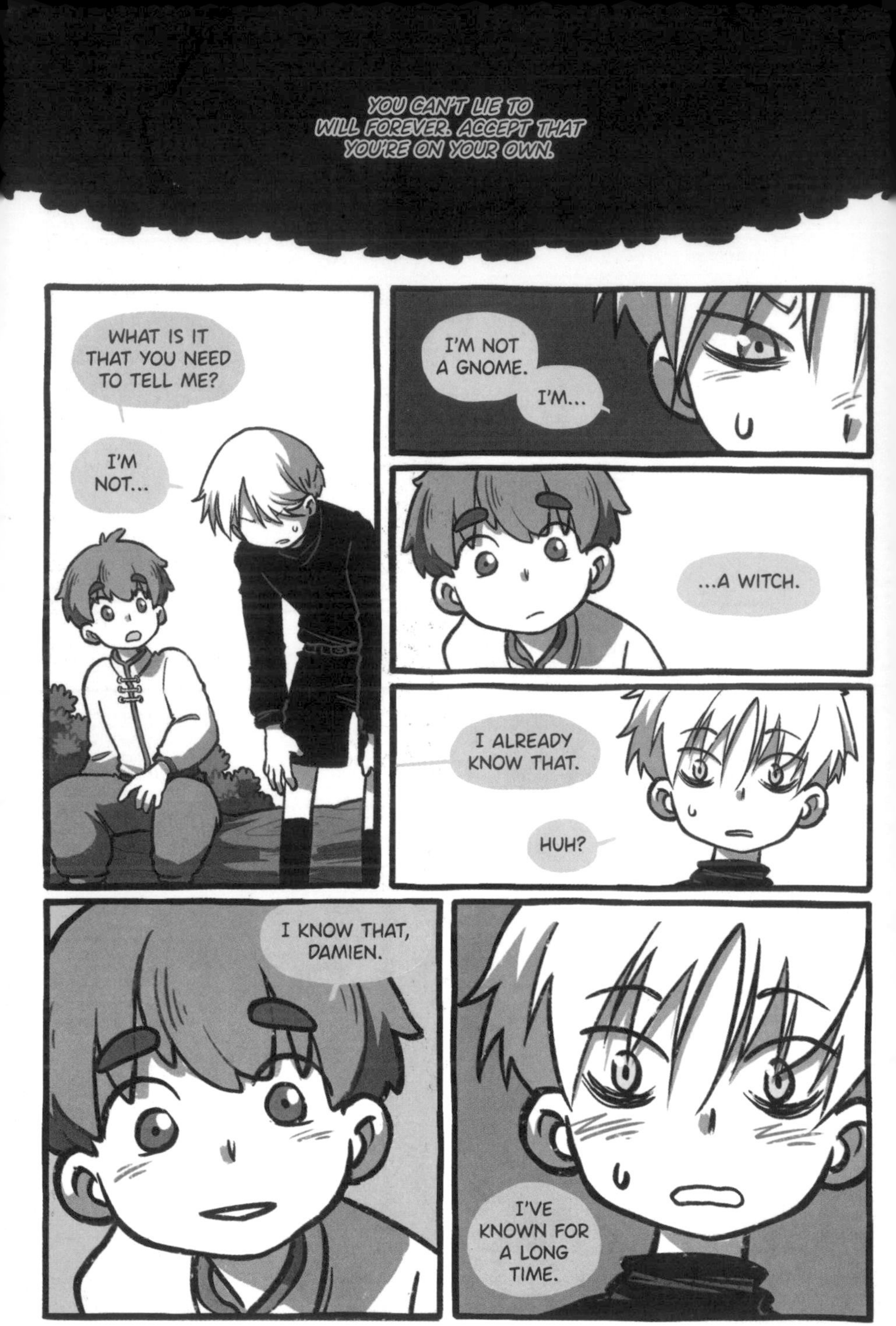
YOU CAN'T LIE TO WILL FOREVER. ACCEPT THAT YOU'RE ON YOUR OWN.
WHAT IS IT THAT YOU NEED TO TELL ME?
I'M NOT...
I'M NOT A GNOME.
I'M...
...A WITCH.
I ALREADY KNOW THAT.
HUH?
I KNOW THAT, DAMIEN.
I'VE KNOWN FOR A LONG TIME.

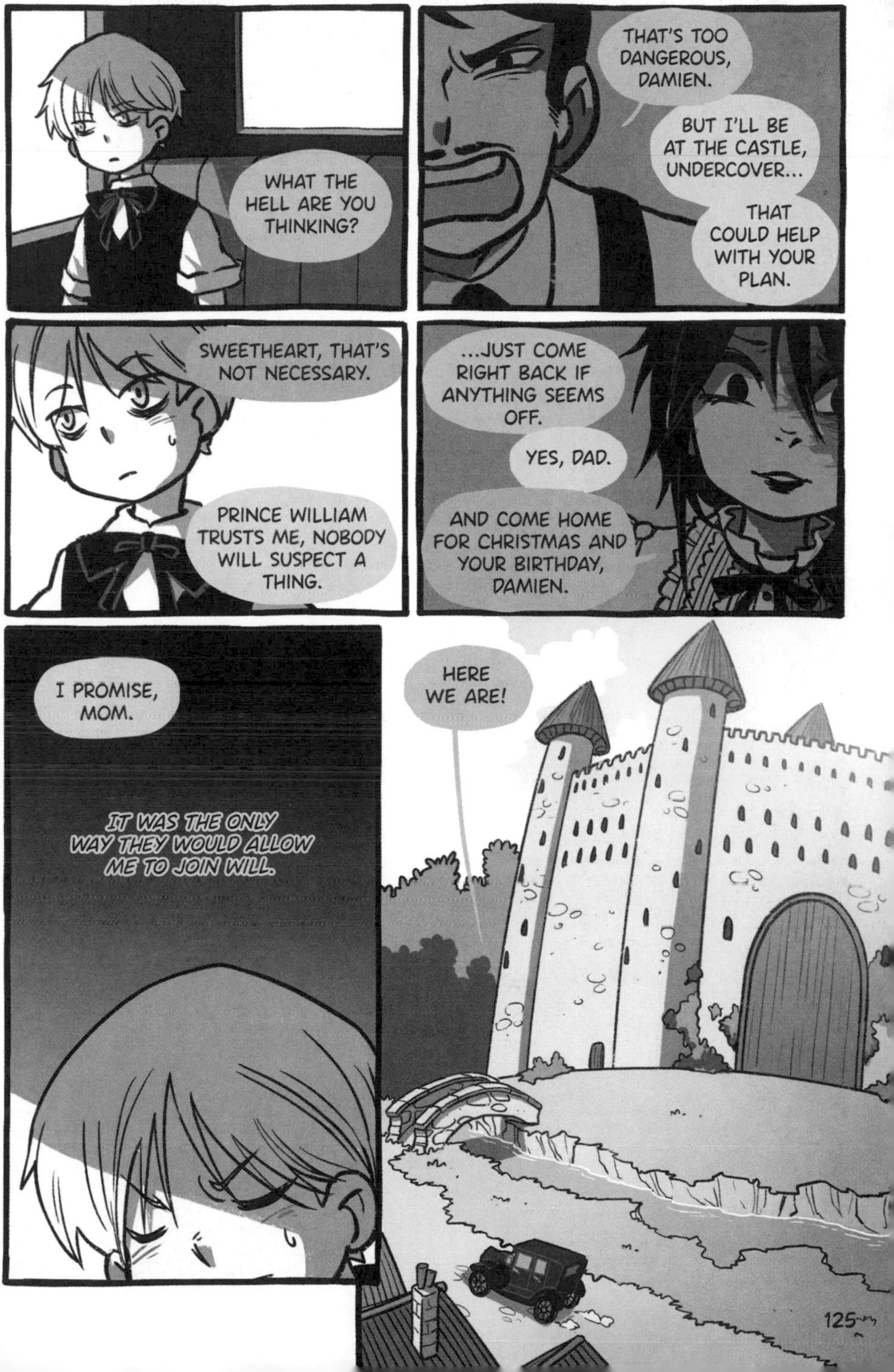
WHAT THE HELL ARE YOU THINKING?
THAT'S TOO DANGEROUS, DAMIEN.
BUT I'LL BE AT THE CASTLE, UNDERCOVER...
THAT COULD HELP WITH YOUR PLAN.
SWEETHEART, THAT'S NOT NECESSARY.
PRINCE WILLIAM TRUSTS ME, NOBODY WILL SUSPECT A THING.
...JUST COME RIGHT BACK IF ANYTHING SEEMS OFF.
YES, DAD.
AND COME HOME FOR CHRISTMAS AND YOUR BIRTHDAY, DAMIEN.
I PROMISE, MOM.
IT WAS THE ONLY WAY THEY WOULD ALLOW ME TO JOIN WILL.
HERE WE ARE!

AND THAT'S HOW MY LIFE AT THE PALACE BEGAN.

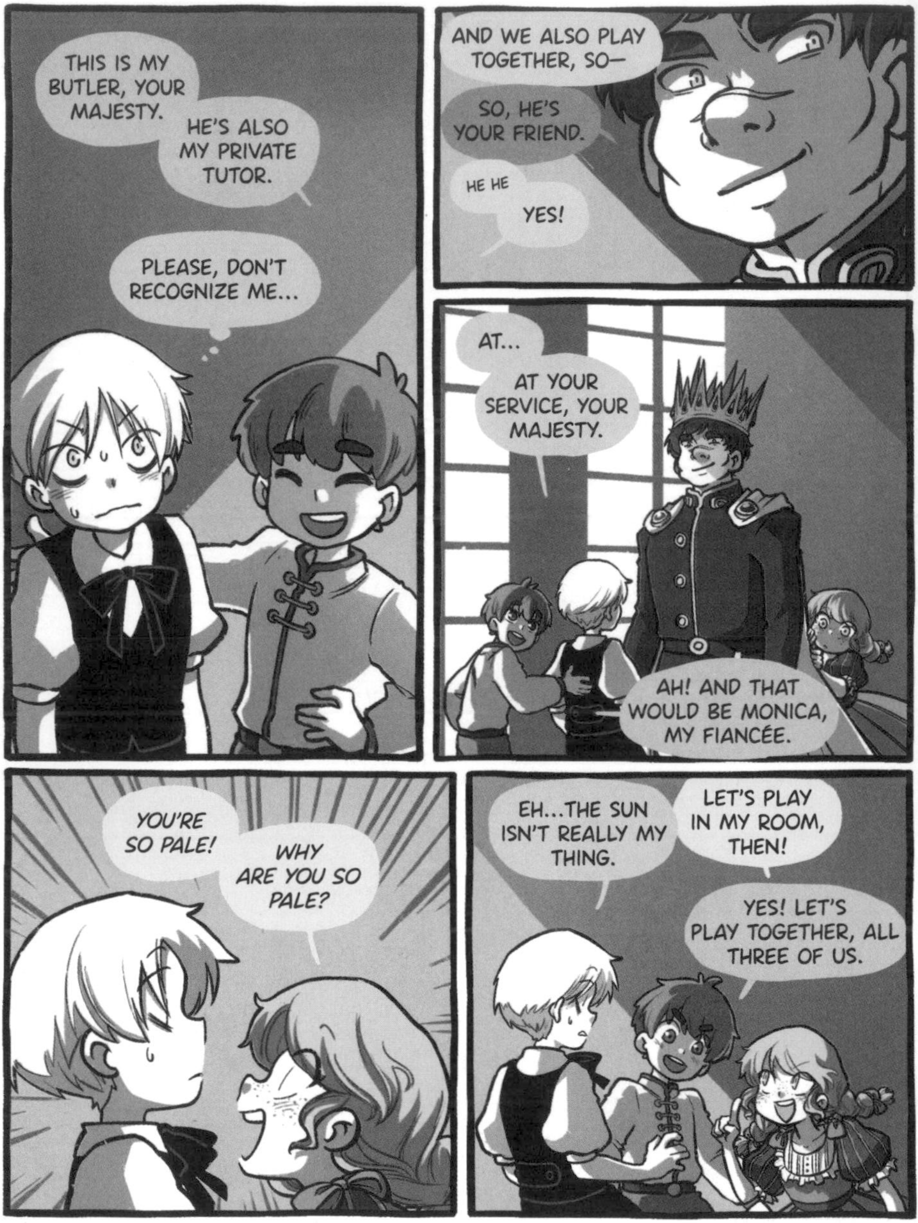
THIS IS MY BUTLER, YOUR MAJESTY.
HE'S ALSO MY PRIVATE TUTOR.
PLEASE, DON'T RECOGNIZE ME...
AND WE ALSO PLAY TOGETHER, SO—
SO, HE'S YOUR FRIEND.
HE HE
YES!
AT...
AT YOUR SERVICE, YOUR MAJESTY.
AH! AND THAT WOULD BE MONICA, MY FIANCÉE.
YOU'RE SO PALE!
WHY ARE YOU SO PALE?
EH...THE SUN ISN'T REALLY MY THING.
LET'S PLAY IN MY ROOM, THEN!
YES! LET'S PLAY TOGETHER, ALL THREE OF US.

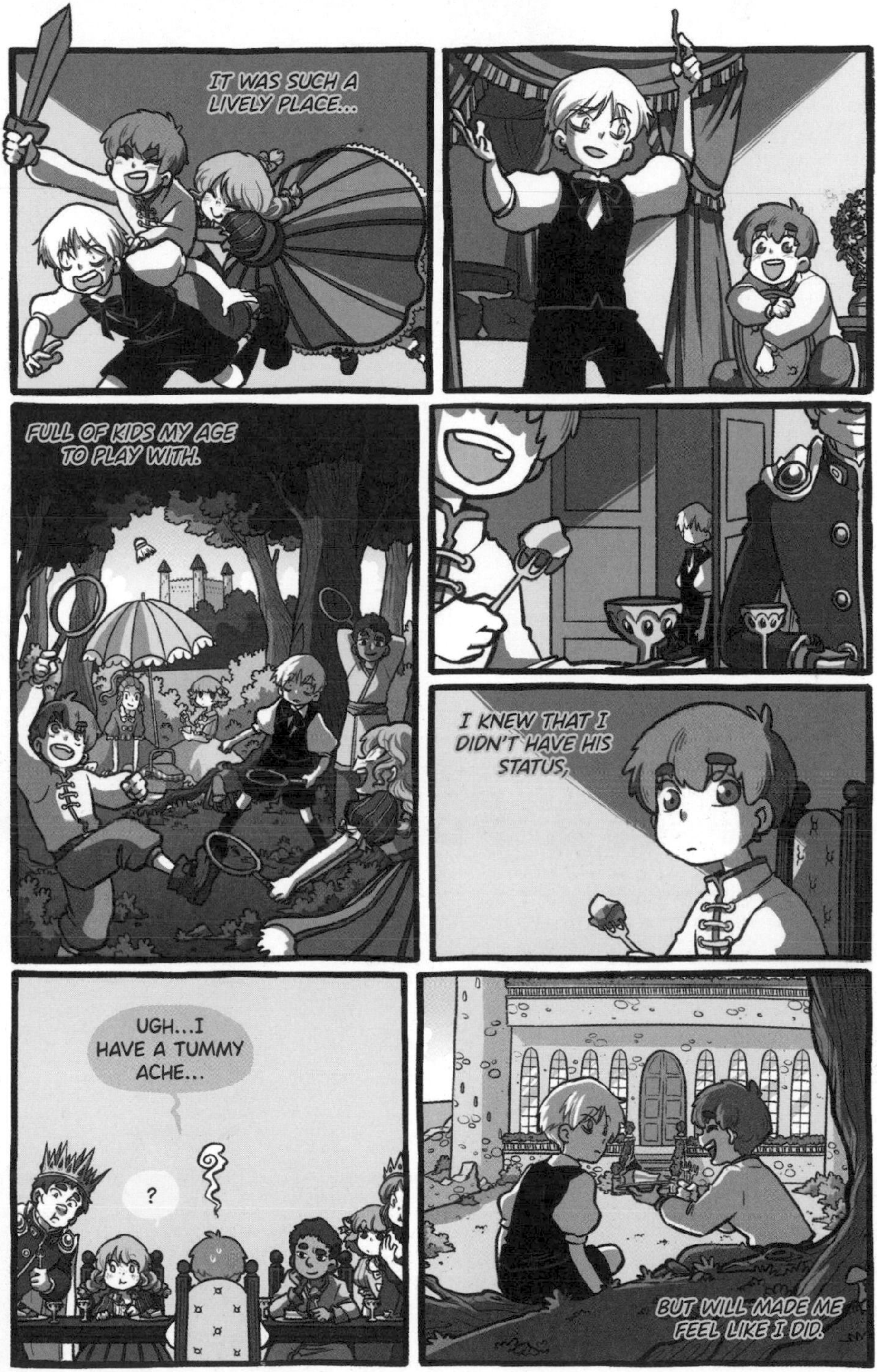
IT WAS SUCH A LIVELY PLACE...
FULL OF KIDS MY AGE TO PLAY WITH.
I KNEW THAT I DIDN'T HAVE HIS STATUS,
UGH...I HAVE A TUMMY ACHE...
?
BUT WILL MADE ME FEEL LIKE I DID.

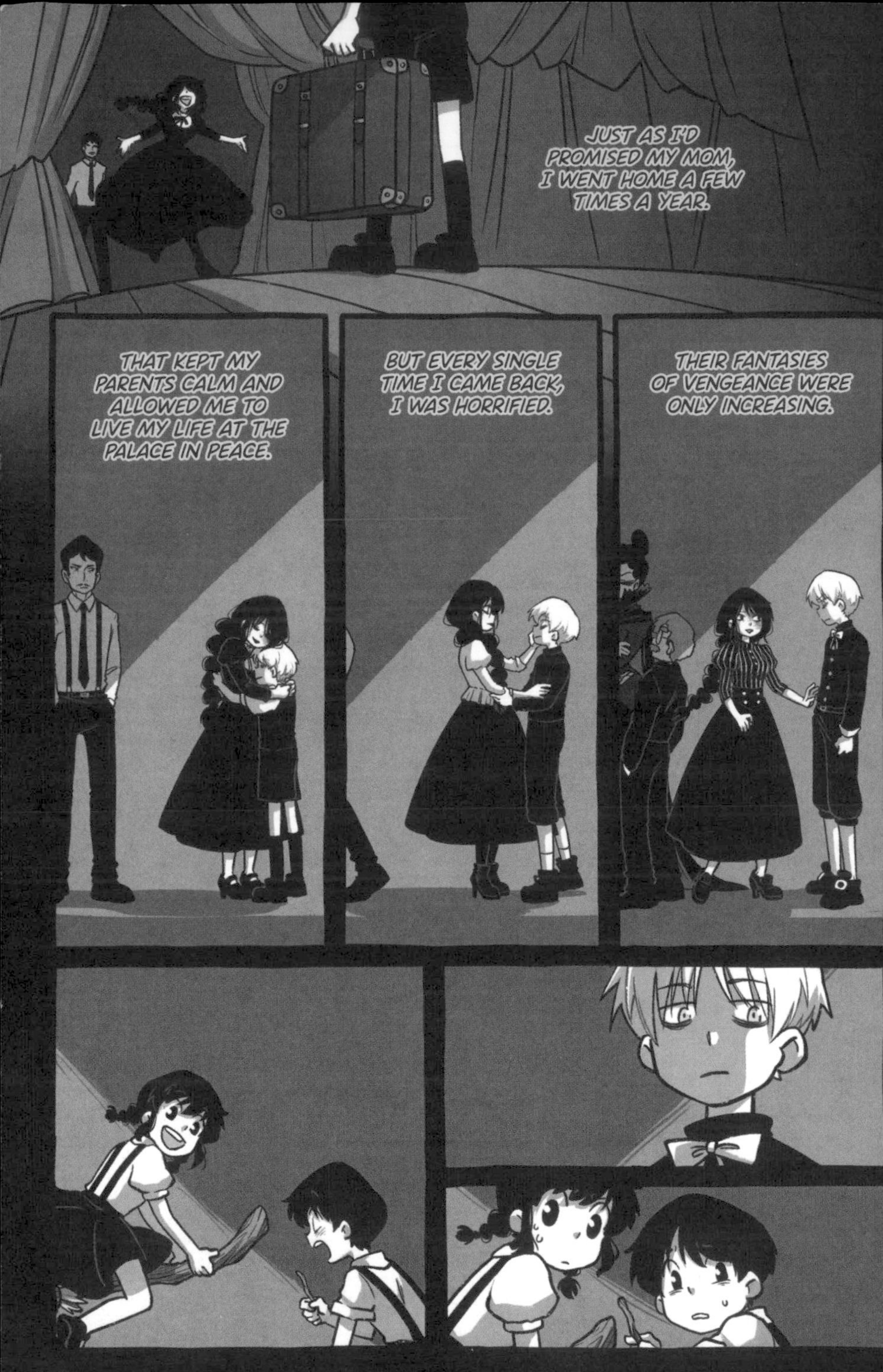

JUST AS I'D PROMISED MY MOM, I WENT HOME A FEW TIMES A YEAR.
THAT KEPT MY PARENTS CALM AND ALLOWED ME TO LIVE MY LIFE AT THE PALACE IN PEACE.
BUT EVERY SINGLE TIME I CAME BACK, I WAS HORRIFIED.
THEIR FANTASIES OF VENGEANCE WERE ONLY INCREASING.

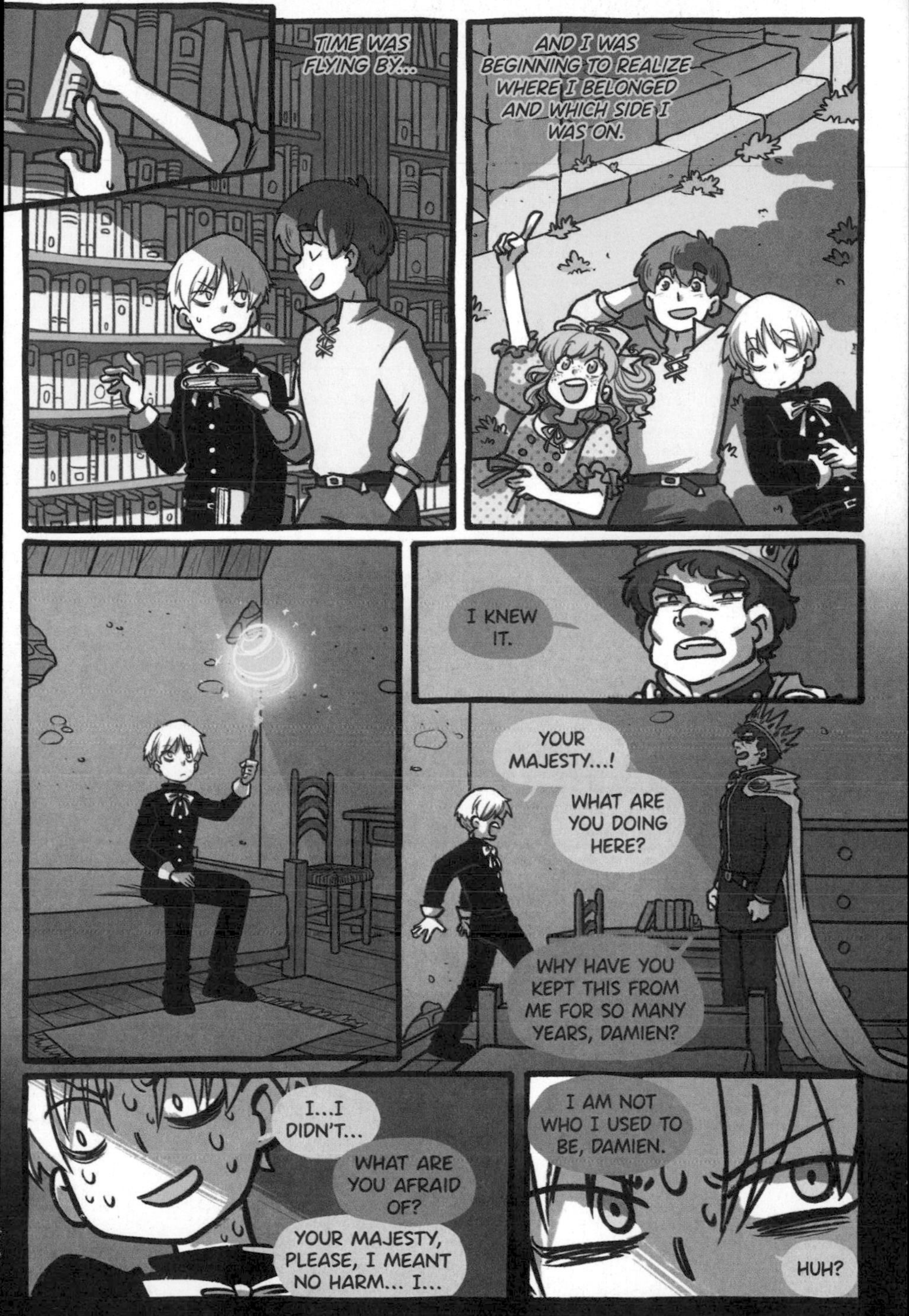
TIME WAS FLYING BY...
AND I WAS BEGINNING TO REALIZE WHERE I BELONGED AND WHICH SIDE I WAS ON.
I KNEW IT.
YOUR MAJESTY...!
WHAT ARE YOU DOING HERE?
WHY HAVE YOU KEPT THIS FROM ME FOR SO MANY YEARS, DAMIEN?
I...I DIDN'T...
WHAT ARE YOU AFRAID OF?
YOUR MAJESTY, PLEASE, I MEANT NO HARM... I...
I AM NOT WHO I USED TO BE, DAMIEN.
HUH?

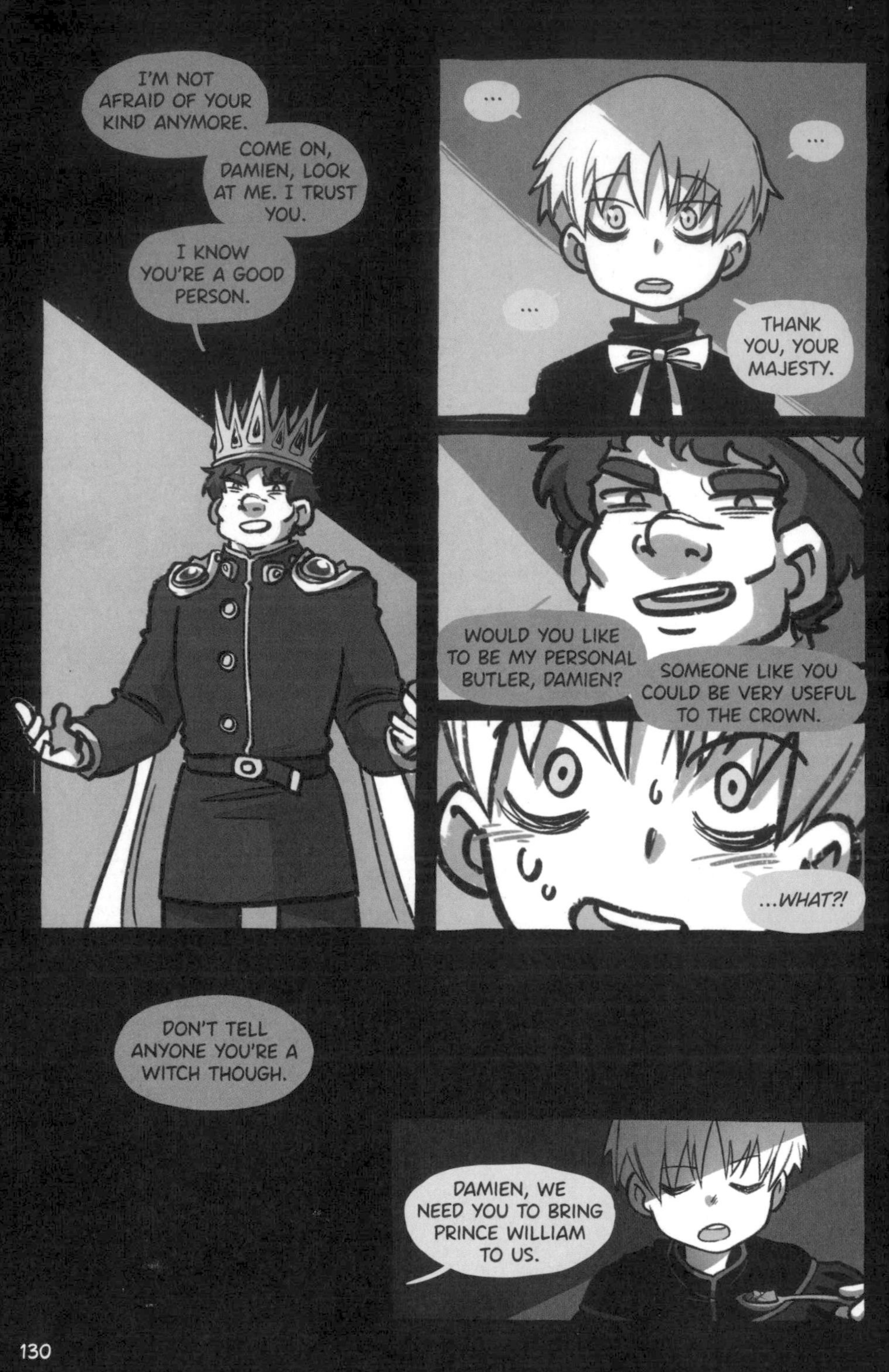
I'M NOT AFRAID OF YOUR KIND ANYMORE.
COME ON, DAMIEN, LOOK AT ME. I TRUST YOU.
I KNOW YOU'RE A GOOD PERSON.
...
...
...
THANK YOU, YOUR MAJESTY.
WOULD YOU LIKE TO BE MY PERSONAL BUTLER, DAMIEN?
SOMEONE LIKE YOU COULD BE VERY USEFUL TO THE CROWN.
...WHAT?!
DON'T TELL ANYONE YOU'RE A WITCH THOUGH.
DAMIEN, WE NEED YOU TO BRING PRINCE WILLIAM TO US.

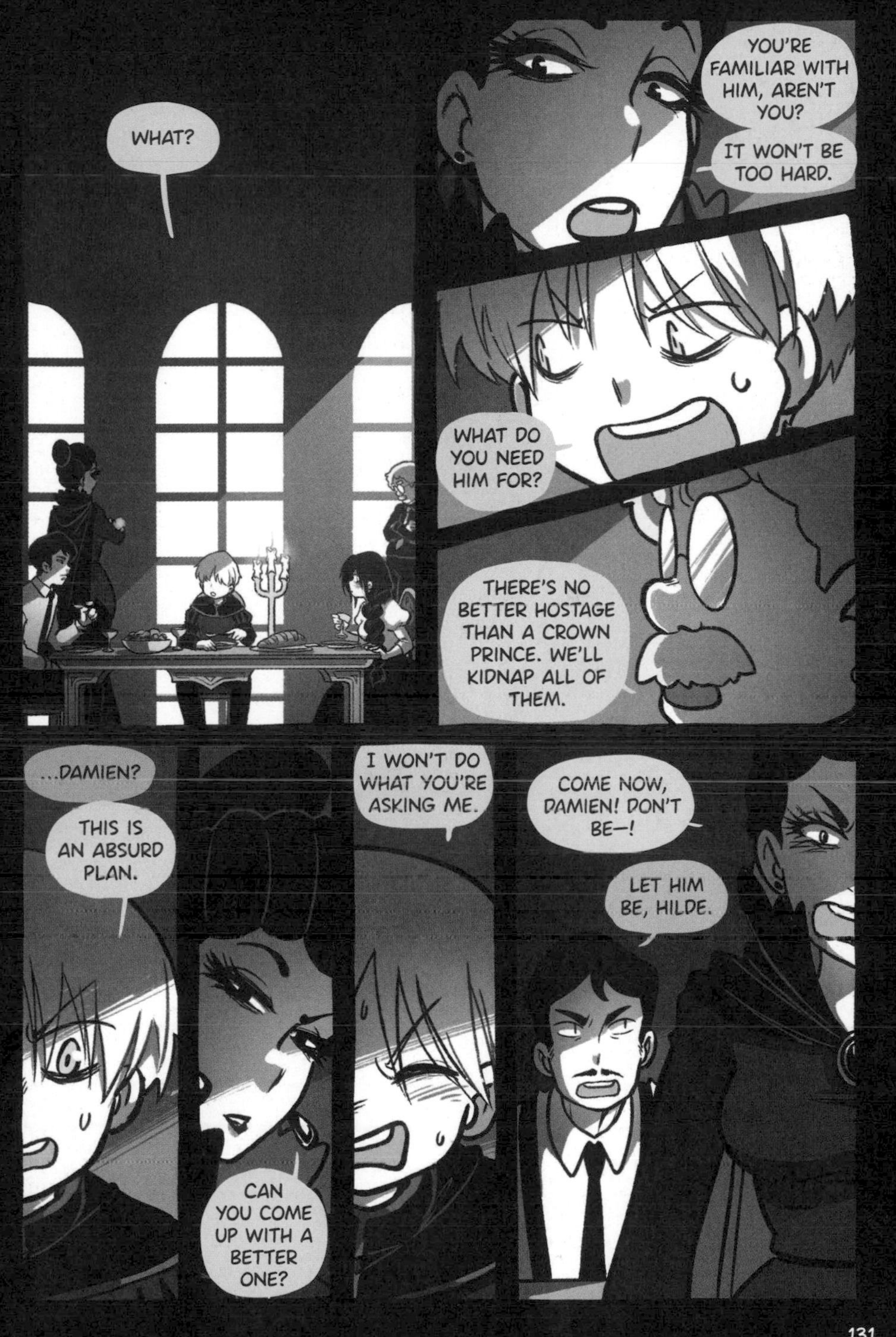
WHAT?
YOU'RE FAMILIAR WITH HIM, AREN'T YOU?
IT WON'T BE TOO HARD.
WHAT DO YOU NEED HIM FOR?
THERE'S NO BETTER HOSTAGE THAN A CROWN PRINCE. WE'LL KIDNAP ALL OF THEM.
...DAMIEN?
THIS IS AN ABSURD PLAN.
CAN YOU COME UP WITH A BETTER ONE?
I WON'T DO WHAT YOU'RE ASKING ME.
COME NOW, DAMIEN! DON'T BE—!
LET HIM BE, HILDE.

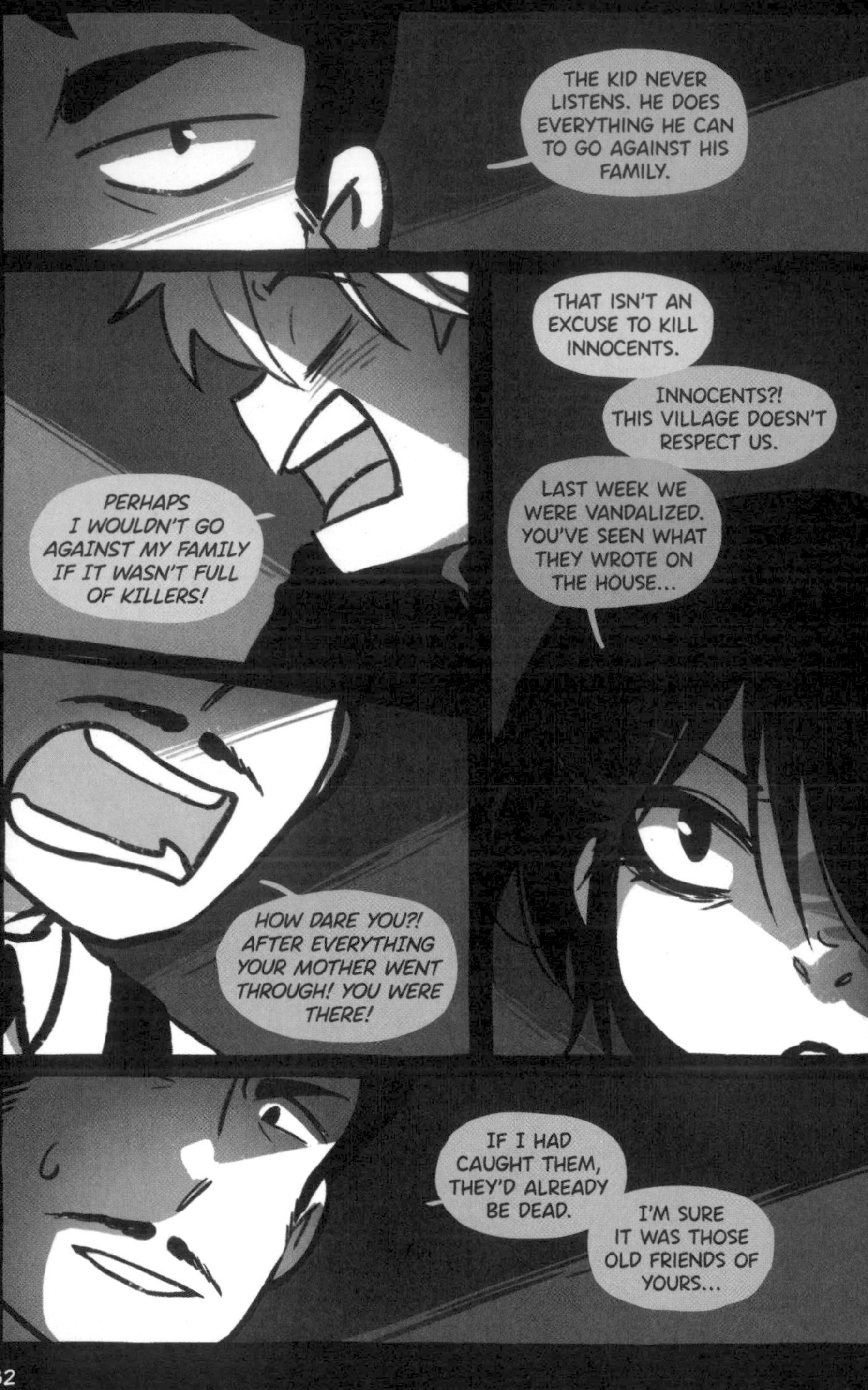
THE KID NEVER LISTENS. HE DOES EVERYTHING HE CAN TO GO AGAINST HIS FAMILY.
THAT ISN'T AN EXCUSE TO KILL INNOCENTS.
INNOCENTS?! THIS VILLAGE DOESN'T RESPECT US.
LAST WEEK WE WERE VANDALIZED. YOU'VE SEEN WHAT THEY WROTE ON THE HOUSE...
PERHAPS I WOULDN'T GO AGAINST MY FAMILY IF IT WASN'T FULL OF KILLERS!
HOW DARE YOU?! AFTER EVERYTHING YOUR MOTHER WENT THROUGH! YOU WERE THERE!
IF I HAD CAUGHT THEM, THEY'D ALREADY BE DEAD.
I'M SURE IT WAS THOSE OLD FRIENDS OF YOURS...

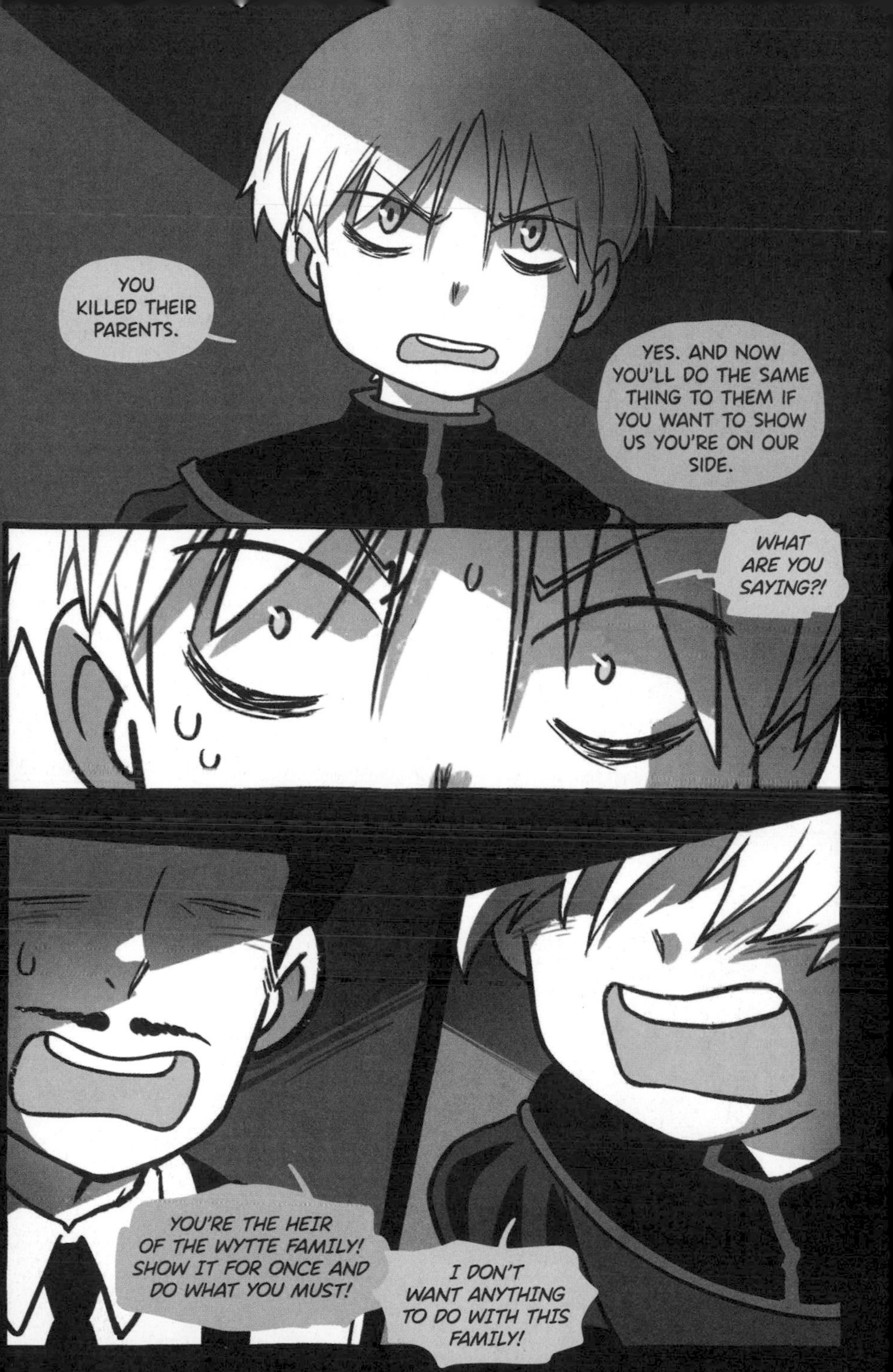
YOU KILLED THEIR PARENTS.
YES. AND NOW YOU'LL DO THE SAME THING TO THEM IF YOU WANT TO SHOW US YOU'RE ON OUR SIDE.
WHAT ARE YOU SAYING?!
YOU'RE THE HEIR OF THE WYTTE FAMILY! SHOW IT FOR ONCE AND DO WHAT YOU MUST!
I DON'T WANT ANYTHING TO DO WITH THIS FAMILY!

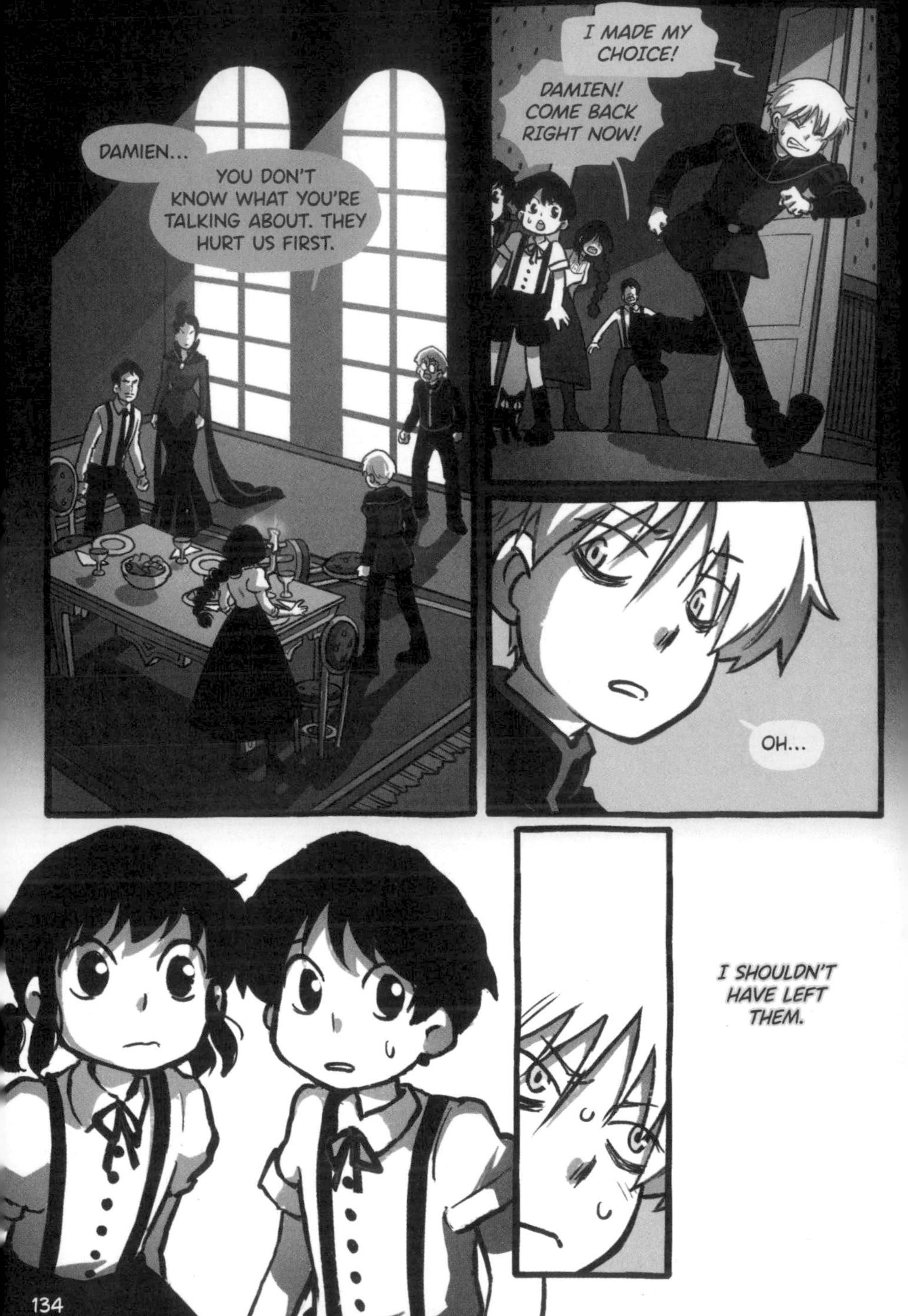
DAMIEN...
YOU DON'T KNOW WHAT YOU'RE TALKING ABOUT. THEY HURT US FIRST.
I MADE MY CHOICE!
DAMIEN! COME BACK RIGHT NOW!
OH...
I SHOULDN'T HAVE LEFT THEM.

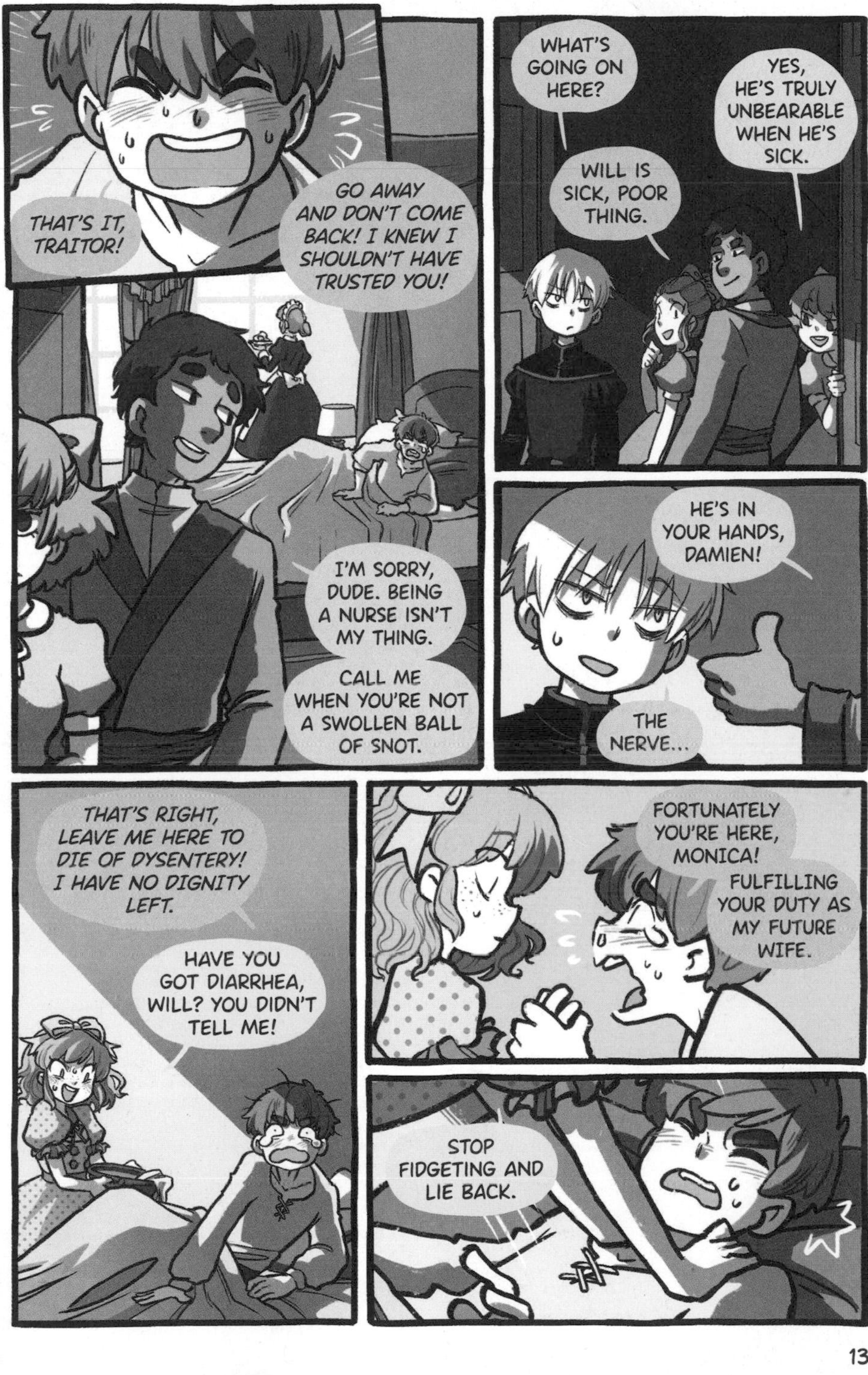
THAT'S IT, TRAITOR!
GO AWAY AND DON'T COME BACK! I KNEW I SHOULDN'T HAVE TRUSTED YOU!
I'M SORRY, DUDE. BEING A NURSE ISN'T MY THING.
CALL ME WHEN YOU'RE NOT A SWOLLEN BALL OF SNOT.
WHAT'S GOING ON HERE?
WILL IS SICK, POOR THING.
YES, HE'S TRULY UNBEARABLE WHEN HE'S SICK.
HE'S IN YOUR HANDS, DAMIEN!
THE NERVE...
THAT'S RIGHT, LEAVE ME HERE TO DIE OF DYSENTERY! I HAVE NO DIGNITY LEFT.
HAVE YOU GOT DIARRHEA, WILL? YOU DIDN'T TELL ME!
FORTUNATELY YOU'RE HERE, MONICA!
FULFILLING YOUR DUTY AS MY FUTURE WIFE.
STOP FIDGETING AND LIE BACK.

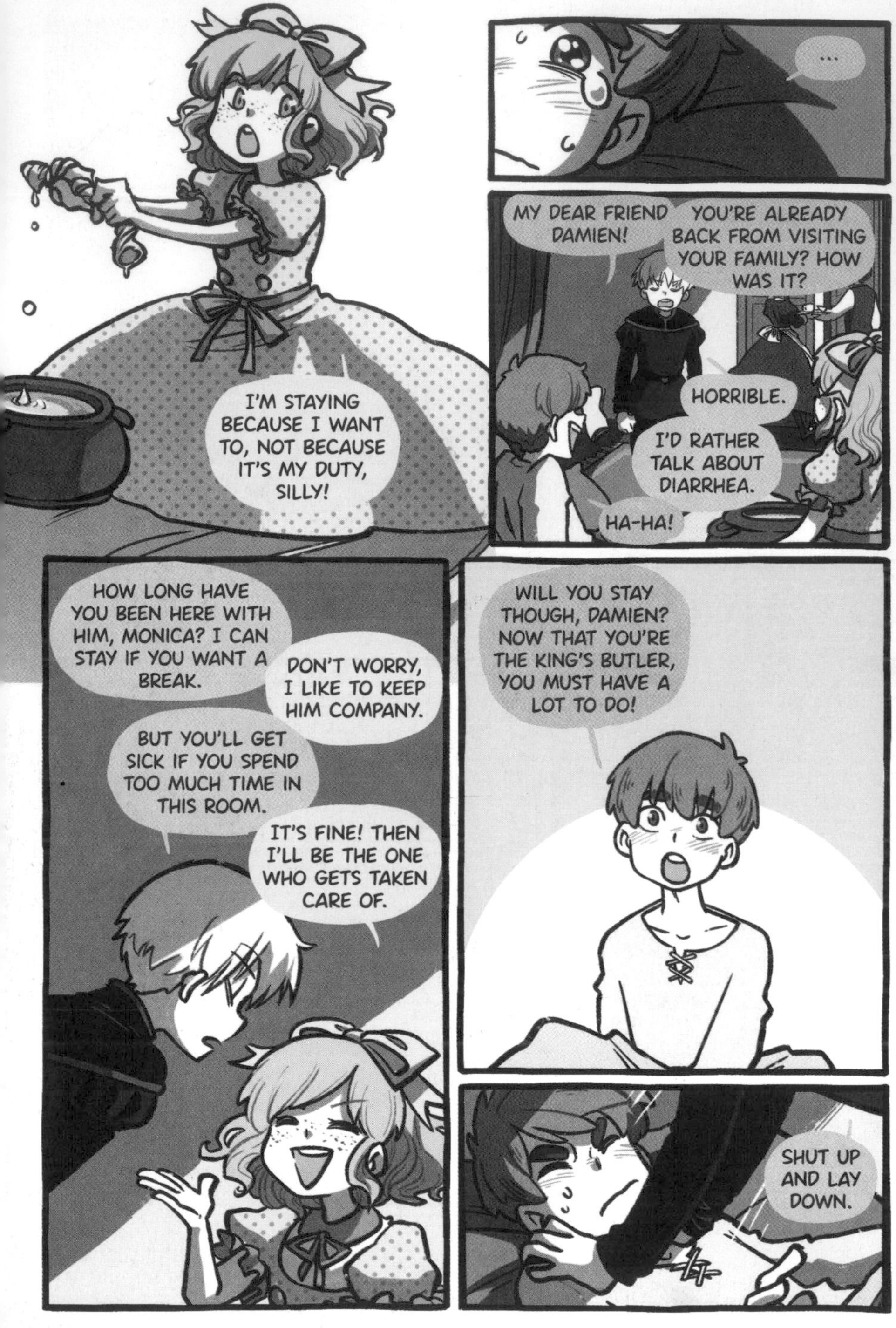

I'M STAYING BECAUSE I WANT TO, NOT BECAUSE IT'S MY DUTY, SILLY!
...
MY DEAR FRIEND DAMIEN!
YOU'RE ALREADY BACK FROM VISITING YOUR FAMILY? HOW WAS IT?
HORRIBLE.
I'D RATHER TALK ABOUT DIARRHEA.
HA-HA!
HOW LONG HAVE YOU BEEN HERE WITH HIM, MONICA? I CAN STAY IF YOU WANT A BREAK.
DON'T WORRY, I LIKE TO KEEP HIM COMPANY.
BUT YOU'LL GET SICK IF YOU SPEND TOO MUCH TIME IN THIS ROOM.
IT'S FINE! THEN I'LL BE THE ONE WHO GETS TAKEN CARE OF.
WILL YOU STAY THOUGH, DAMIEN? NOW THAT YOU'RE THE KING'S BUTLER, YOU MUST HAVE A LOT TO DO!
SHUT UP AND LAY DOWN.

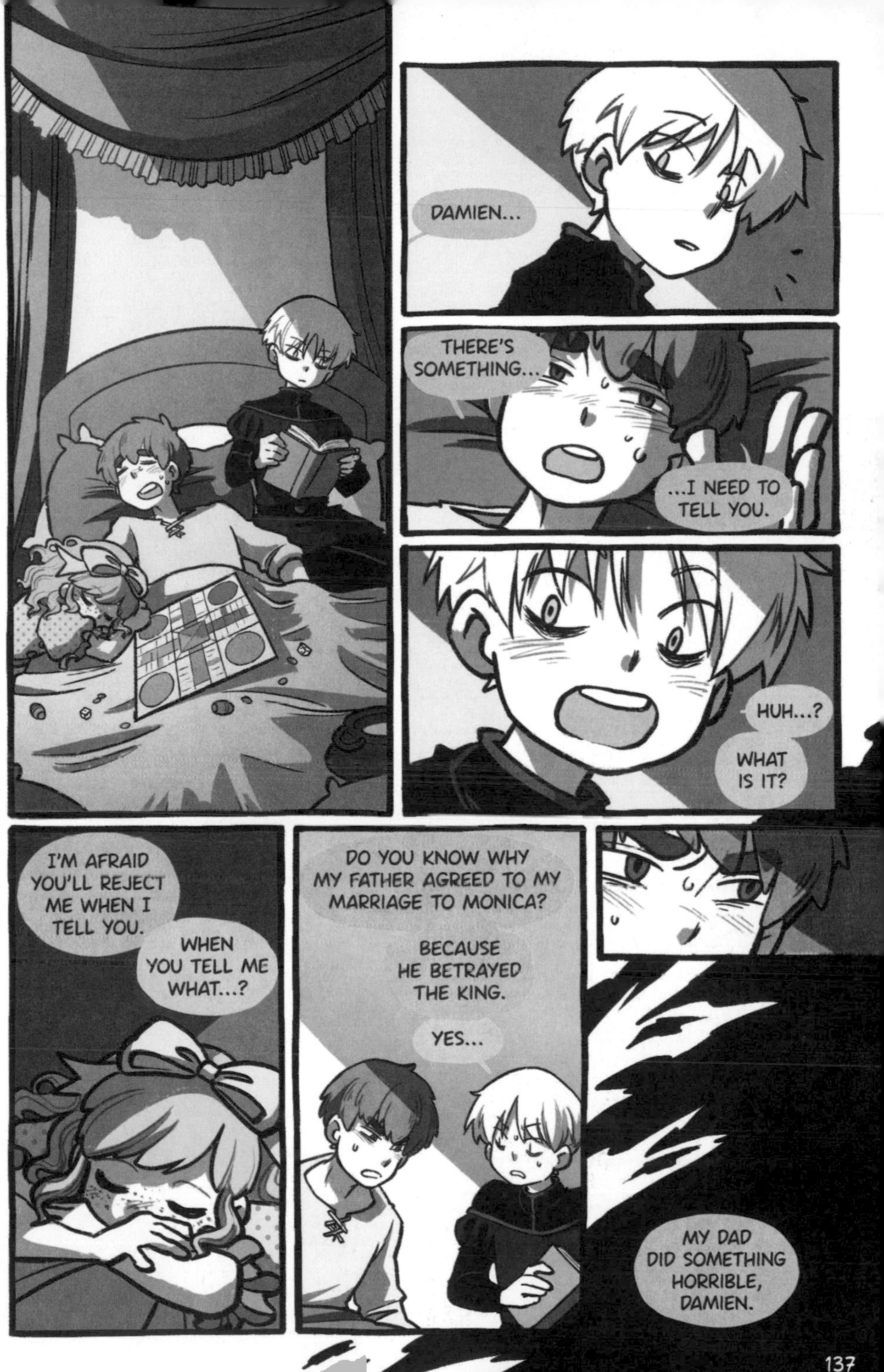
DAMIEN...
THERE'S SOMETHING...
...I NEED TO TELL YOU.
HUH...?
WHAT IS IT?
I'M AFRAID YOU'LL REJECT ME WHEN I TELL YOU.
WHEN YOU TELL ME WHAT...?
DO YOU KNOW WHY MY FATHER AGREED TO MY MARRIAGE TO MONICA?
BECAUSE HE BETRAYED THE KING.
YES...
MY DAD DID SOMETHING HORRIBLE, DAMIEN.

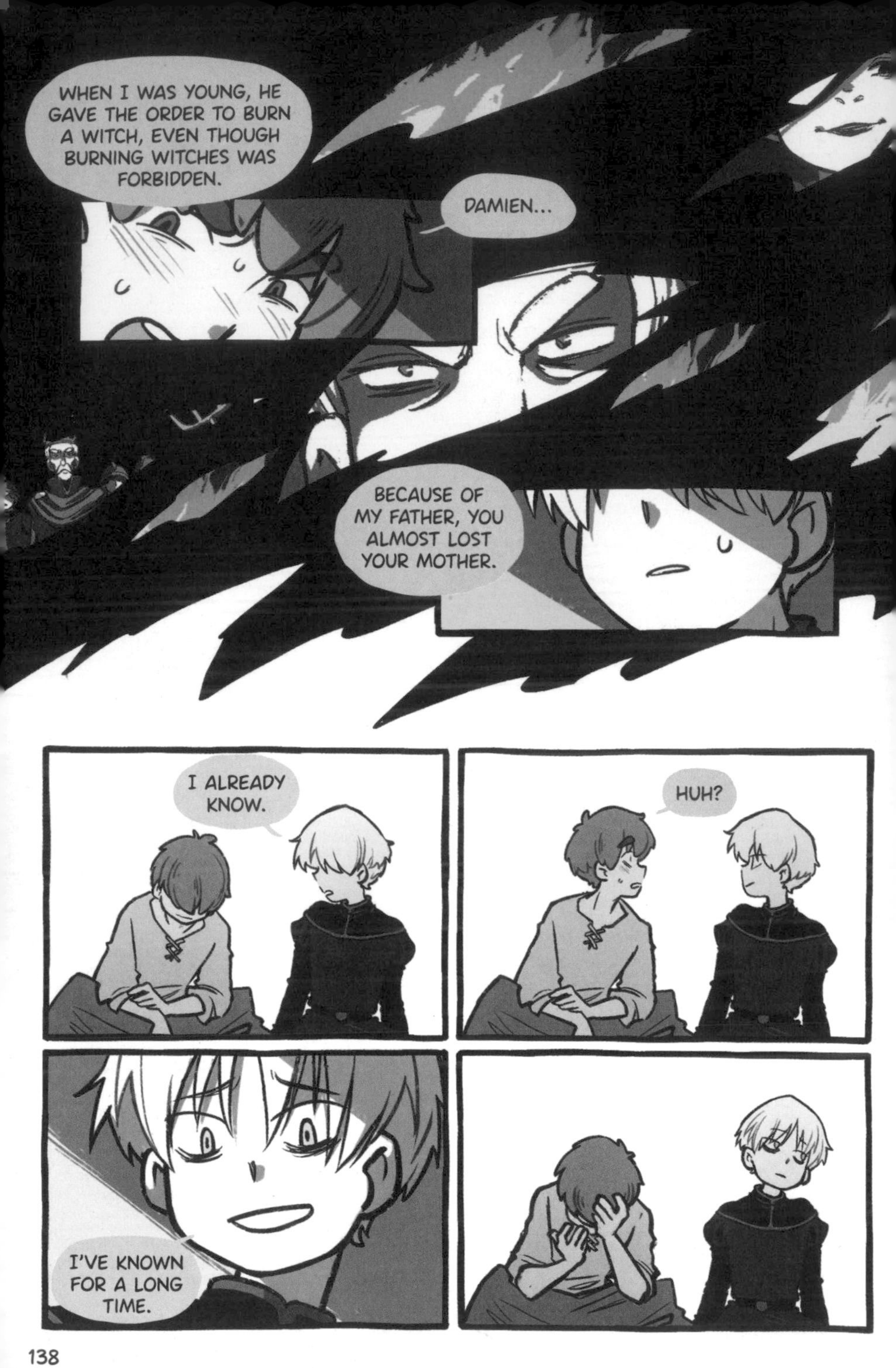
WHEN I WAS YOUNG, HE GAVE THE ORDER TO BURN A WITCH, EVEN THOUGH BURNING WITCHES WAS FORBIDDEN.
DAMIEN...
BECAUSE OF MY FATHER, YOU ALMOST LOST YOUR MOTHER.
I ALREADY KNOW.
HUH?
I'VE KNOWN FOR A LONG TIME.

CHAPTER 41

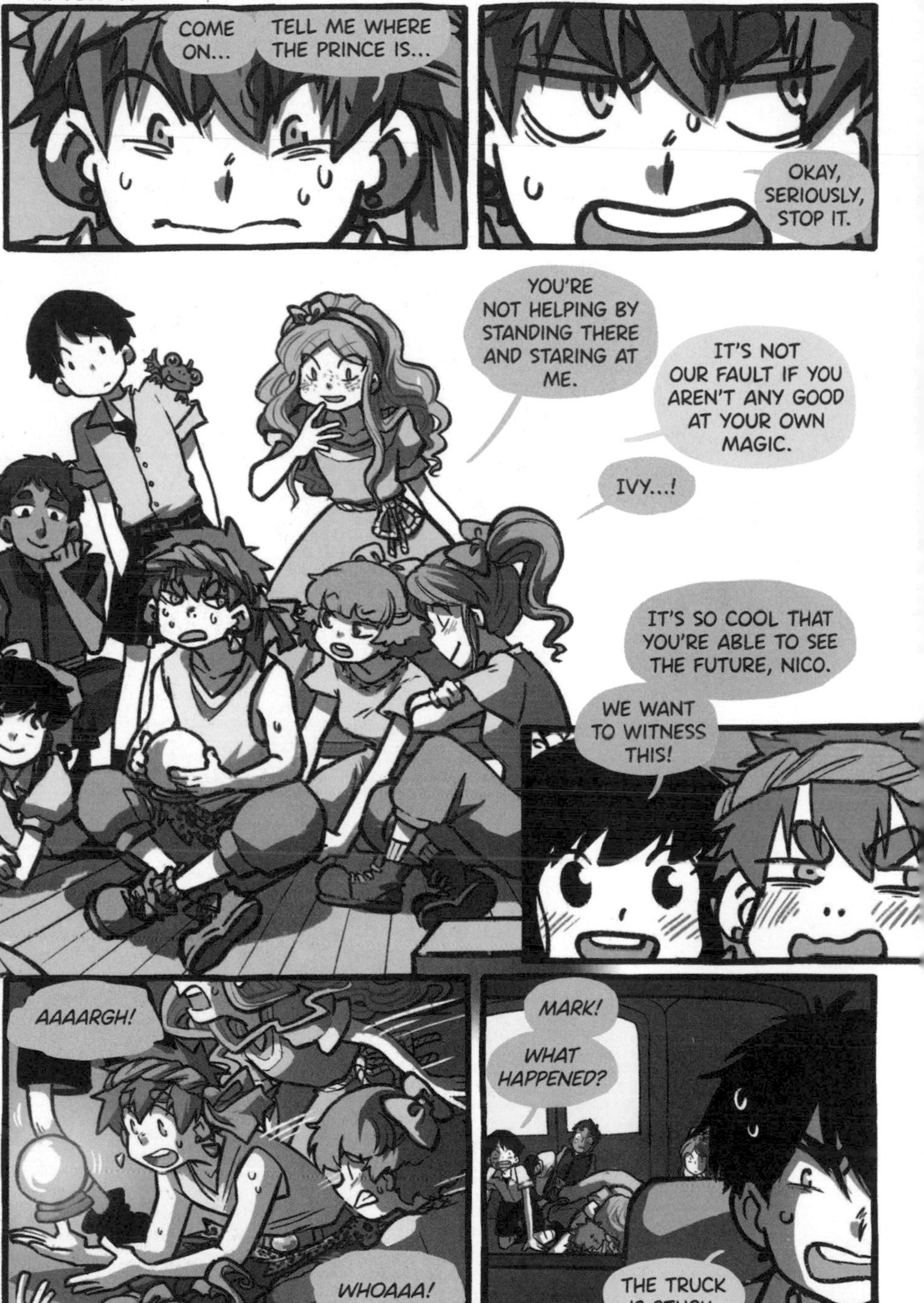
COME ON...
TELL ME WHERE THE PRINCE IS...
OKAY, SERIOUSLY, STOP IT.
YOU'RE NOT HELPING BY STANDING THERE AND STARING AT ME.
IT'S NOT OUR FAULT IF YOU AREN'T ANY GOOD AT YOUR OWN MAGIC.
IVY...!
IT'S SO COOL THAT YOU'RE ABLE TO SEE THE FUTURE, NICO.
WE WANT TO WITNESS THIS!
AAAARGH!
WHOAAA!
MARK!
WHAT HAPPENED?
THE TRUCK IS STUCK.

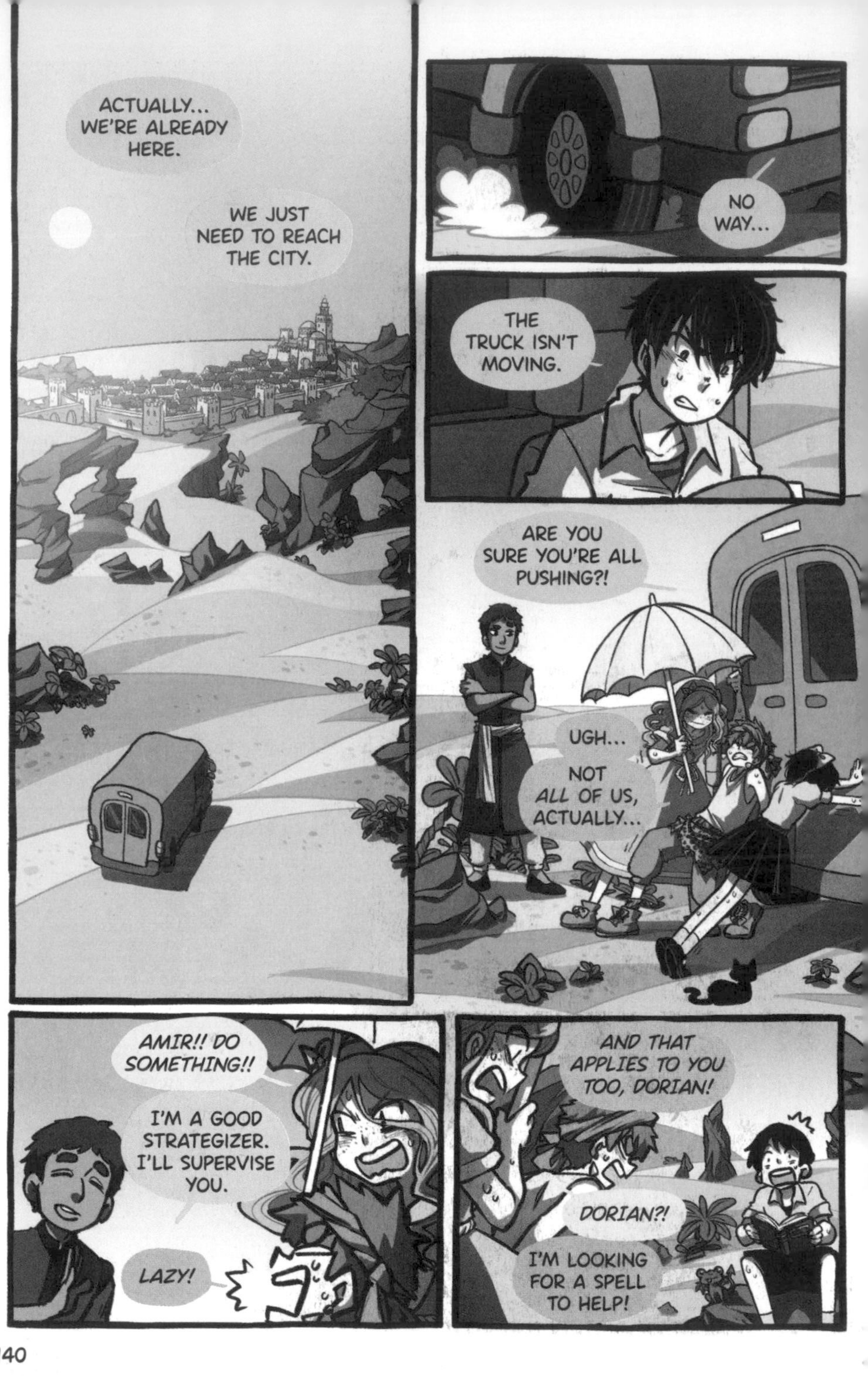
ACTUALLY... WE'RE ALREADY HERE.
WE JUST NEED TO REACH THE CITY.
NO WAY...
THE TRUCK ISN'T MOVING.
ARE YOU SURE YOU'RE ALL PUSHING?!
UGH...
NOT ALL OF US, ACTUALLY...
AMIR!! DO SOMETHING!!
I'M A GOOD STRATEGIZER. I'LL SUPERVISE YOU.
LAZY!
AND THAT APPLIES TO YOU TOO, DORIAN!
DORIAN?!
I'M LOOKING FOR A SPELL TO HELP!

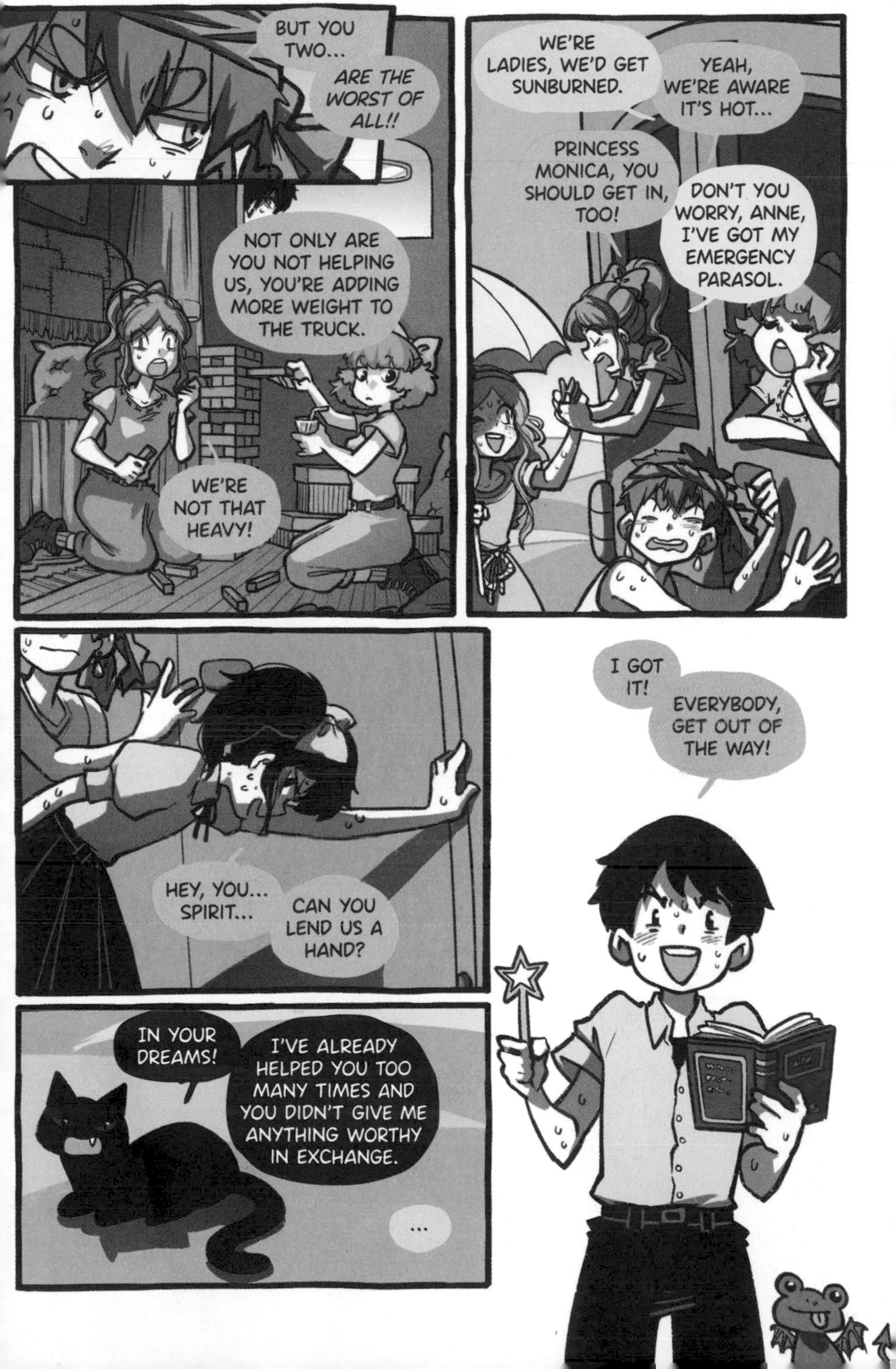
BUT YOU TWO...
ARE THE WORST OF ALL!!
WE'RE LADIES, WE'D GET SUNBURNED.
YEAH, WE'RE AWARE IT'S HOT...
NOT ONLY ARE YOU NOT HELPING US, YOU'RE ADDING MORE WEIGHT TO THE TRUCK.
WE'RE NOT THAT HEAVY!
PRINCESS MONICA, YOU SHOULD GET IN, TOO!
DON'T YOU WORRY, ANNE, I'VE GOT MY EMERGENCY PARASOL.
HEY, YOU... SPIRIT...
CAN YOU LEND US A HAND?
IN YOUR DREAMS!
I'VE ALREADY HELPED YOU TOO MANY TIMES AND YOU DIDN'T GIVE ME ANYTHING WORTHY IN EXCHANGE.
...
I GOT IT!
EVERYBODY, GET OUT OF THE WAY!

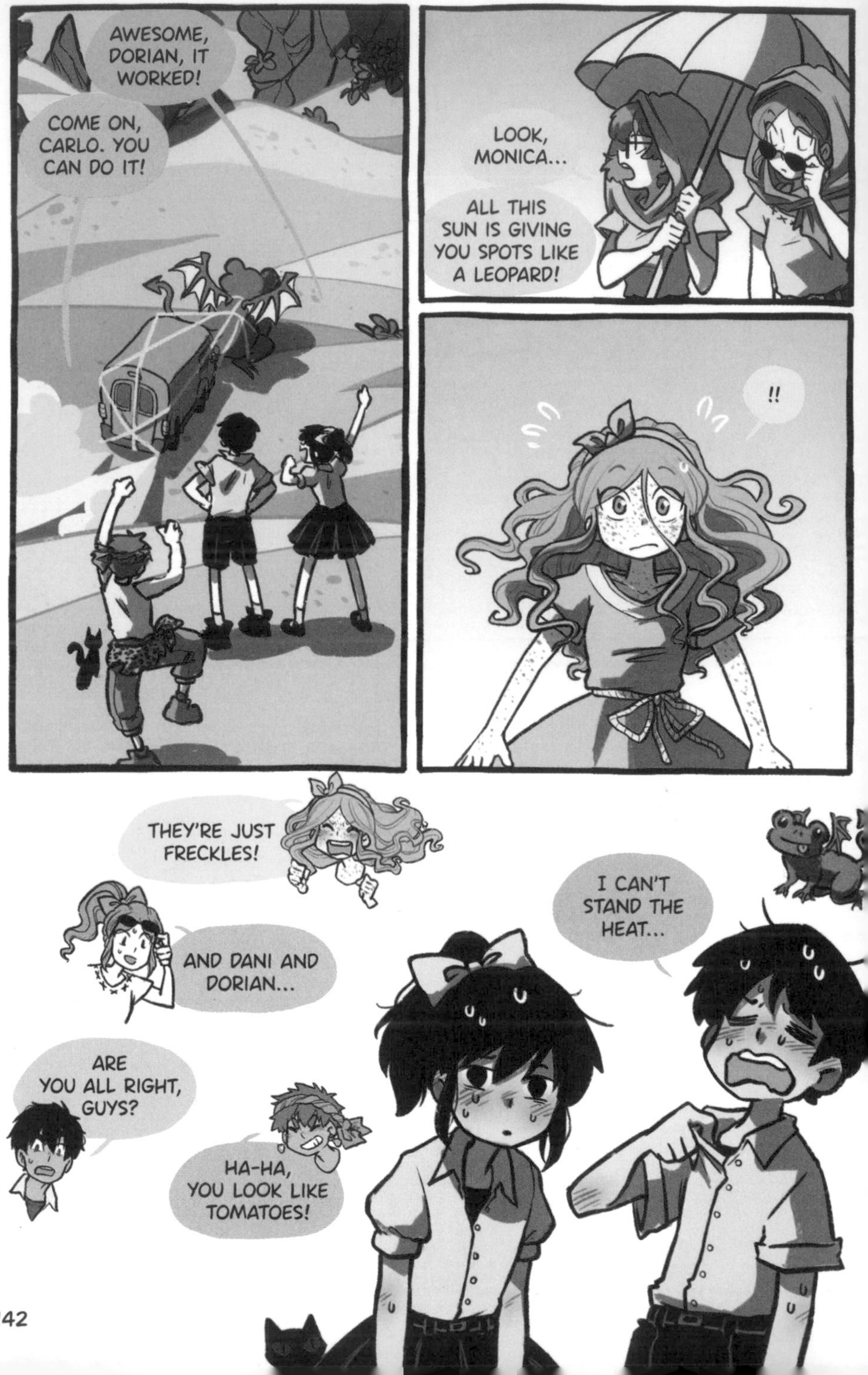

AWESOME, DORIAN, IT WORKED!
COME ON, CARLO. YOU CAN DO IT!
LOOK, MONICA...
ALL THIS SUN IS GIVING YOU SPOTS LIKE A LEOPARD!
!!
THEY'RE JUST FRECKLES!
AND DANI AND DORIAN...
I CAN'T STAND THE HEAT...
ARE YOU ALL RIGHT, GUYS?
HA-HA, YOU LOOK LIKE TOMATOES!

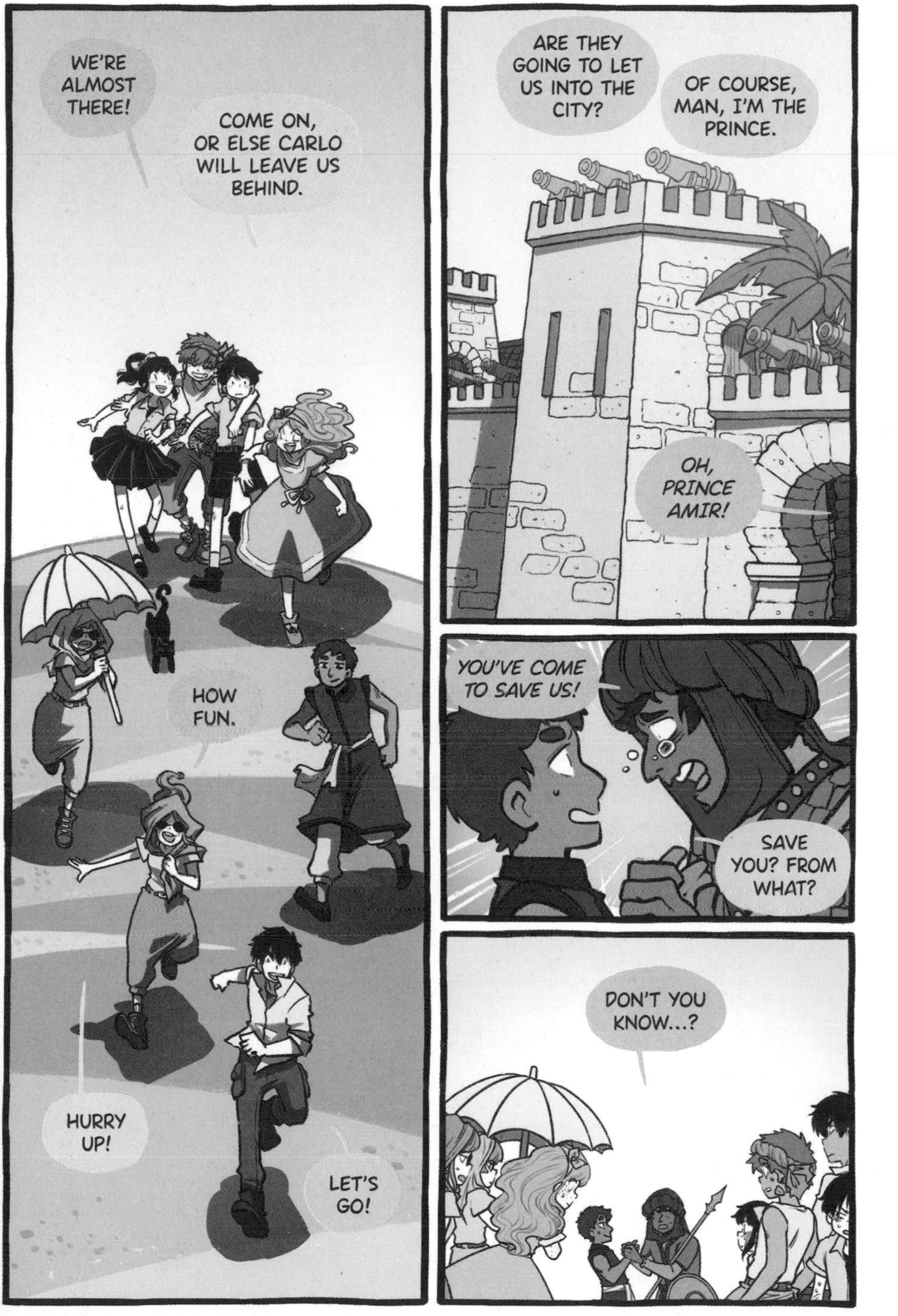
WE'RE ALMOST THERE!
COME ON, OR ELSE CARLO WILL LEAVE US BEHIND.
HOW FUN.
HURRY UP!
LET'S GO!
ARE THEY GOING TO LET US INTO THE CITY?
OF COURSE, MAN, I'M THE PRINCE.
OH, PRINCE AMIR!
YOU'VE COME TO SAVE US!
SAVE YOU? FROM WHAT?
DON'T YOU KNOW...?

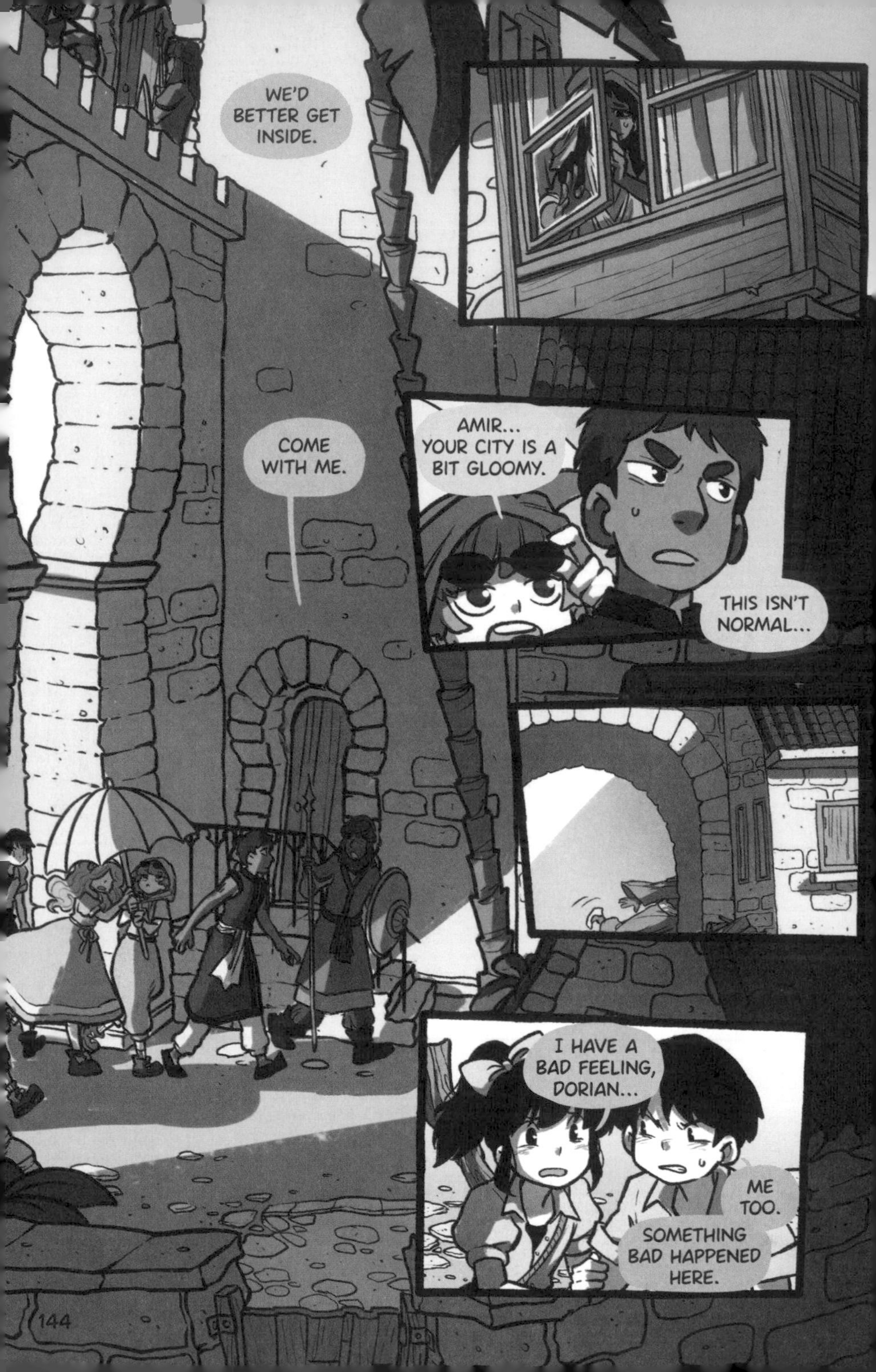
WE'D BETTER GET INSIDE.
COME WITH ME.
AMIR... YOUR CITY IS A BIT GLOOMY.
THIS ISN'T NORMAL...
I HAVE A BAD FEELING, DORIAN...
ME TOO.
SOMETHING BAD HAPPENED HERE.

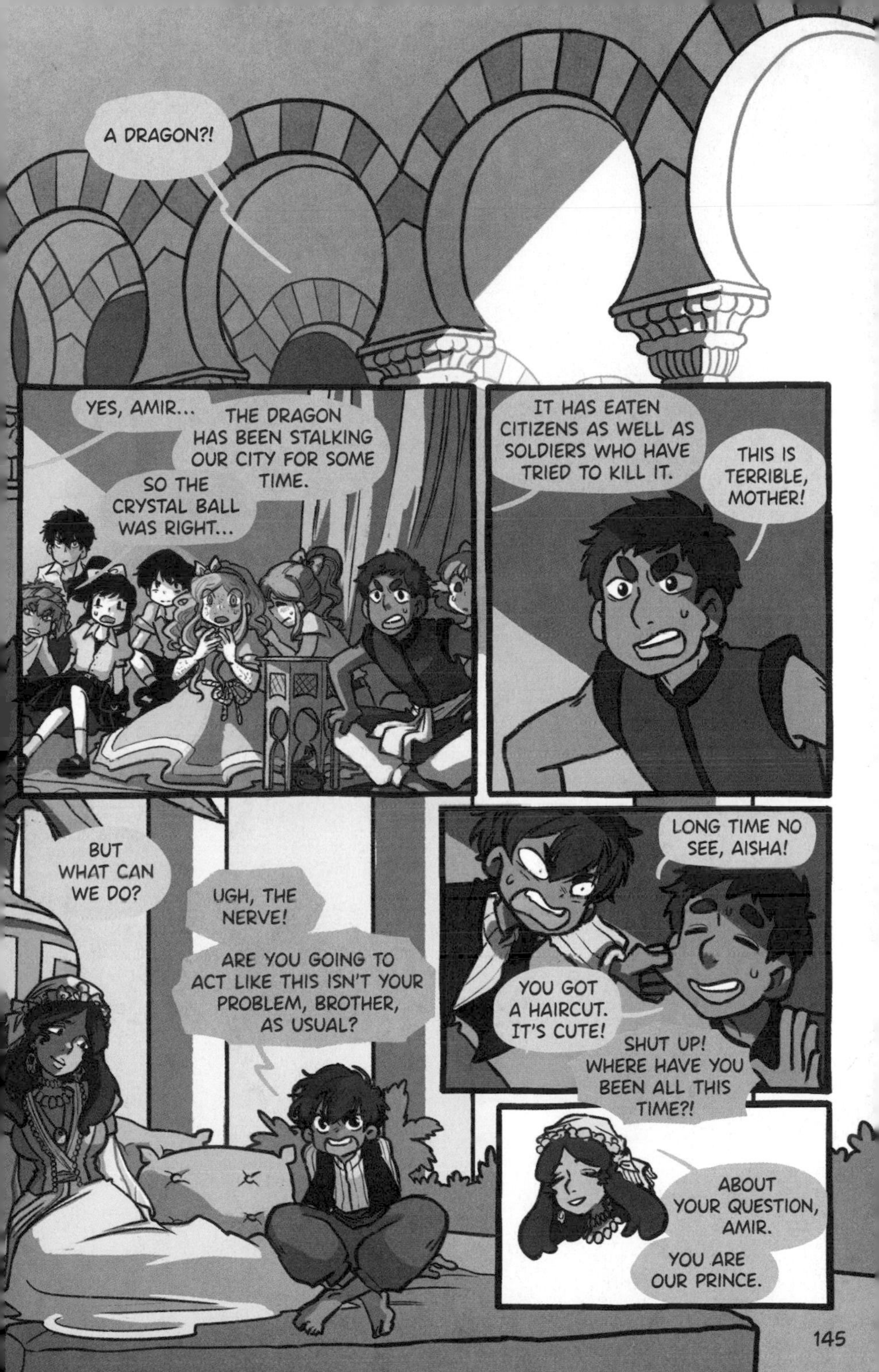
A DRAGON?!
YES, AMIR...
THE DRAGON HAS BEEN STALKING OUR CITY FOR SOME TIME.
SO THE CRYSTAL BALL WAS RIGHT...
IT HAS EATEN CITIZENS AS WELL AS SOLDIERS WHO HAVE TRIED TO KILL IT.
THIS IS TERRIBLE, MOTHER!
BUT WHAT CAN WE DO?
UGH, THE NERVE!
ARE YOU GOING TO ACT LIKE THIS ISN'T YOUR PROBLEM, BROTHER, AS USUAL?
LONG TIME NO SEE, AISHA!
YOU GOT A HAIRCUT. IT'S CUTE!
SHUT UP! WHERE HAVE YOU BEEN ALL THIS TIME?!
ABOUT YOUR QUESTION, AMIR.
YOU ARE OUR PRINCE.

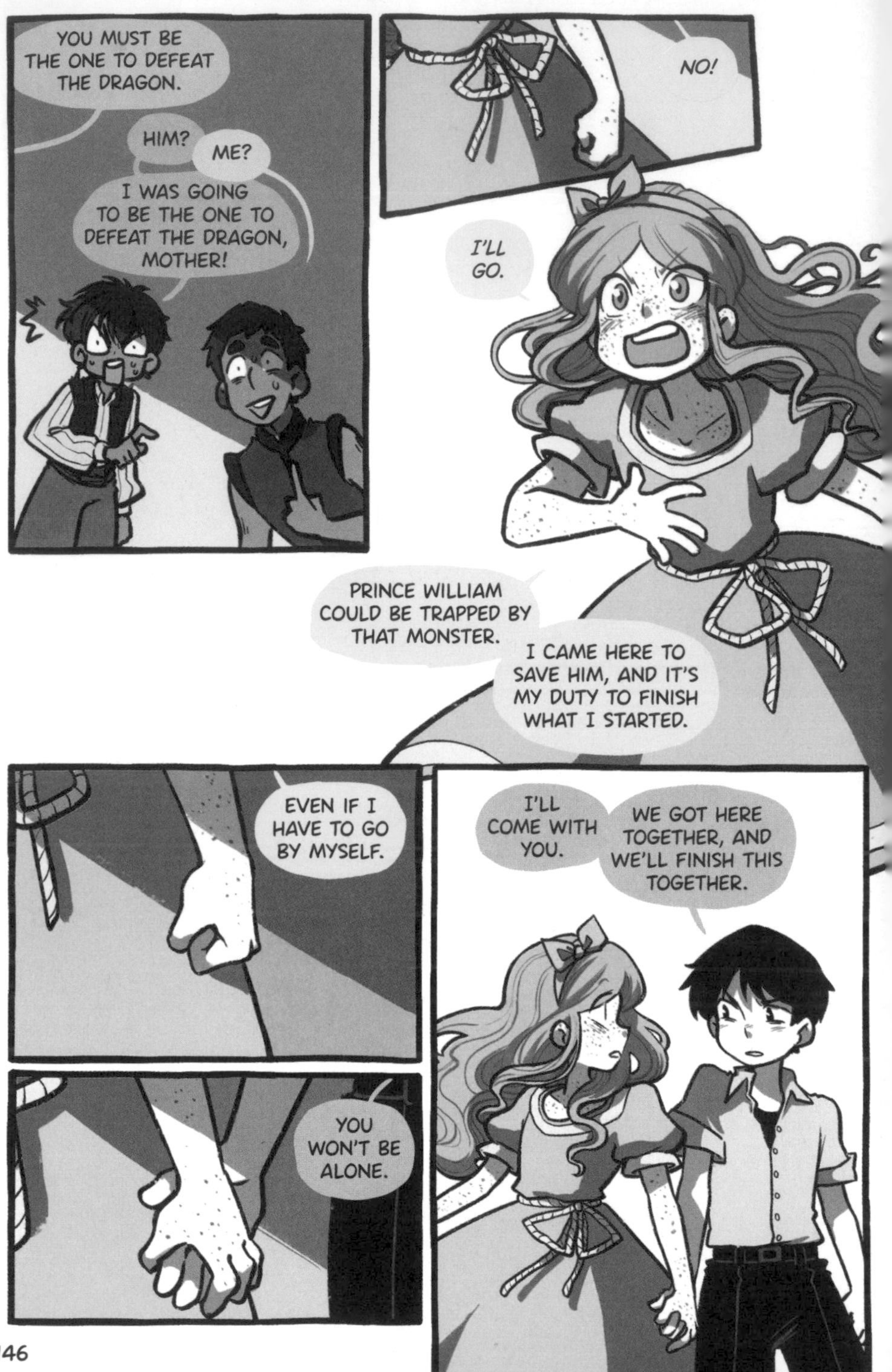
YOU MUST BE THE ONE TO DEFEAT THE DRAGON.
HIM?
ME?
I WAS GOING TO BE THE ONE TO DEFEAT THE DRAGON, MOTHER!
NO!
I'LL GO.
PRINCE WILLIAM COULD BE TRAPPED BY THAT MONSTER.
I CAME HERE TO SAVE HIM, AND IT'S MY DUTY TO FINISH WHAT I STARTED.
EVEN IF I HAVE TO GO BY MYSELF.
YOU WON'T BE ALONE.
I'LL COME WITH YOU.
WE GOT HERE TOGETHER, AND WE'LL FINISH THIS TOGETHER.

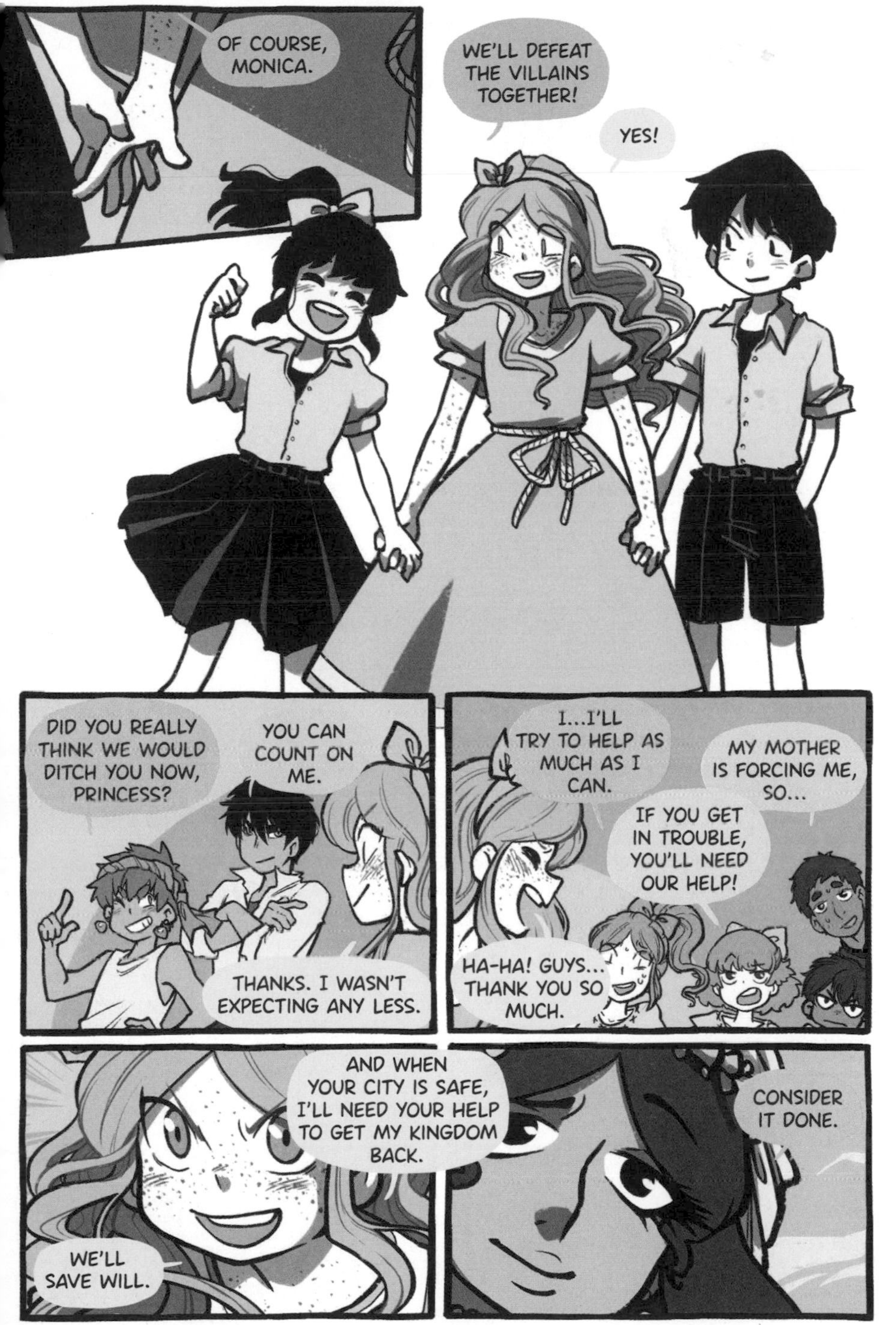
OF COURSE, MONICA.
WE'LL DEFEAT THE VILLAINS TOGETHER!
YES!
DID YOU REALLY THINK WE WOULD DITCH YOU NOW, PRINCESS?
YOU CAN COUNT ON ME.
THANKS. I WASN'T EXPECTING ANY LESS.
I...I'LL TRY TO HELP AS MUCH AS I CAN.
MY MOTHER IS FORCING ME, SO...
IF YOU GET IN TROUBLE, YOU'LL NEED OUR HELP!
HA-HA! GUYS... THANK YOU SO MUCH.
AND WHEN YOUR CITY IS SAFE, I'LL NEED YOUR HELP TO GET MY KINGDOM BACK.
WE'LL SAVE WILL.
CONSIDER IT DONE.

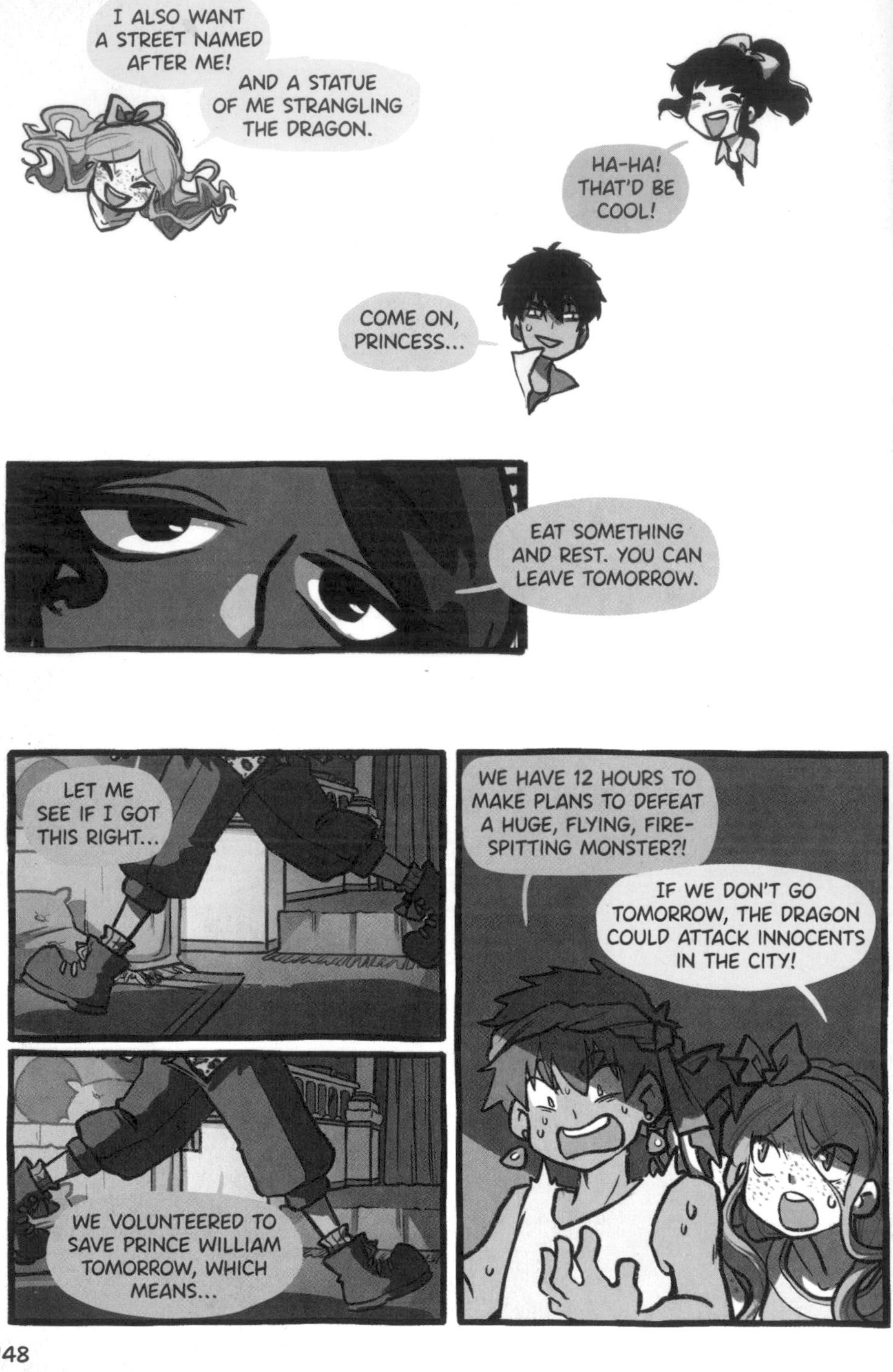
I ALSO WANT A STREET NAMED AFTER ME!
AND A STATUE OF ME STRANGLING THE DRAGON.
HA-HA! THAT'D BE COOL!
COME ON, PRINCESS...
EAT SOMETHING AND REST. YOU CAN LEAVE TOMORROW.
LET ME SEE IF I GOT THIS RIGHT...
WE VOLUNTEERED TO SAVE PRINCE WILLIAM TOMORROW, WHICH MEANS...
WE HAVE 12 HOURS TO MAKE PLANS TO DEFEAT A HUGE, FLYING, FIRE-SPITTING MONSTER?!
IF WE DON'T GO TOMORROW, THE DRAGON COULD ATTACK INNOCENTS IN THE CITY!

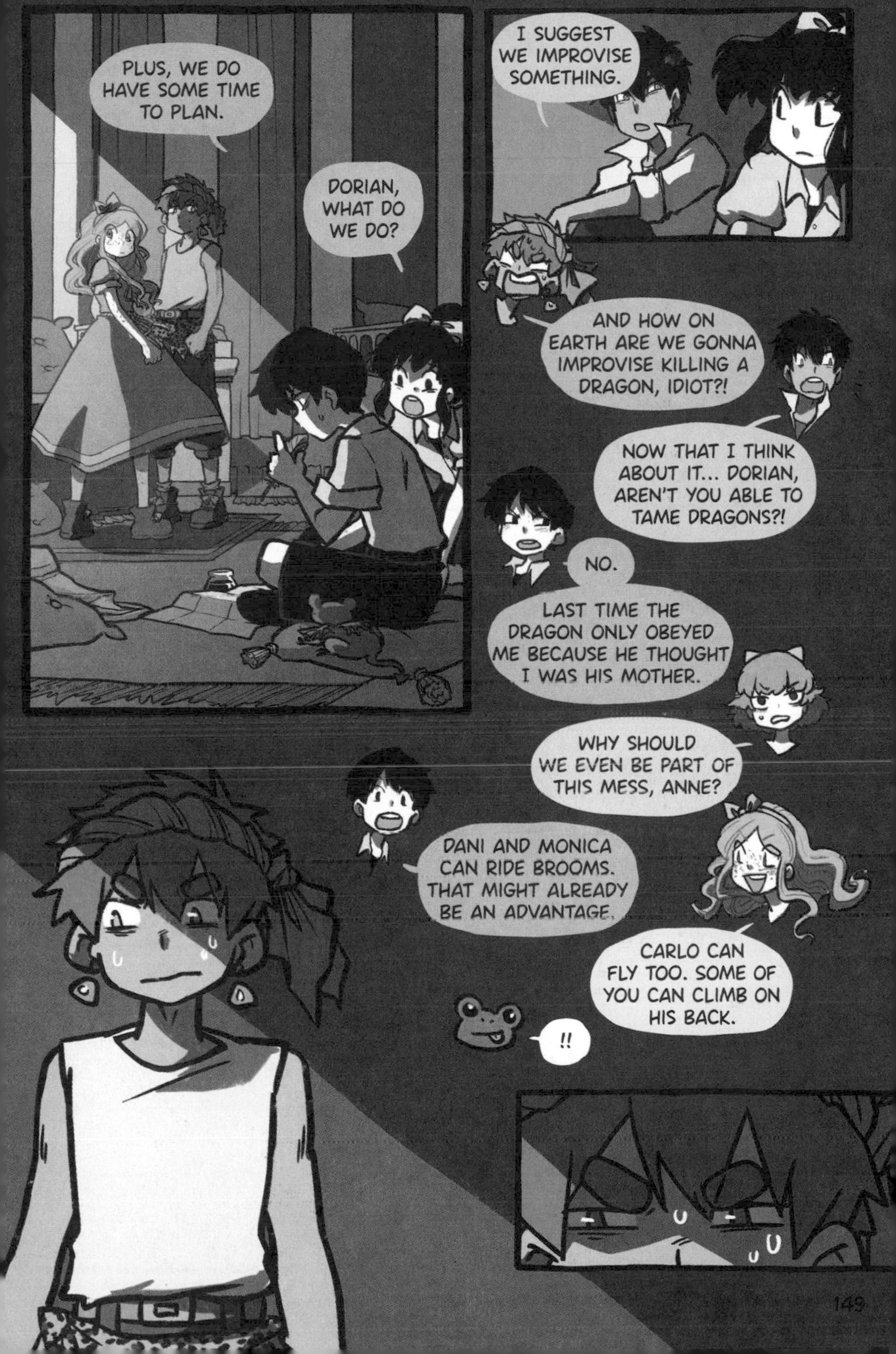
PLUS, WE DO HAVE SOME TIME TO PLAN.
DORIAN, WHAT DO WE DO?
I SUGGEST WE IMPROVISE SOMETHING.
AND HOW ON EARTH ARE WE GONNA IMPROVISE KILLING A DRAGON, IDIOT?!
NOW THAT I THINK ABOUT IT... DORIAN, AREN'T YOU ABLE TO TAME DRAGONS?!
NO.
LAST TIME THE DRAGON ONLY OBEYED ME BECAUSE HE THOUGHT I WAS HIS MOTHER.
WHY SHOULD WE EVEN BE PART OF THIS MESS, ANNE?
DANI AND MONICA CAN RIDE BROOMS. THAT MIGHT ALREADY BE AN ADVANTAGE.
CARLO CAN FLY TOO. SOME OF YOU CAN CLIMB ON HIS BACK.
!!

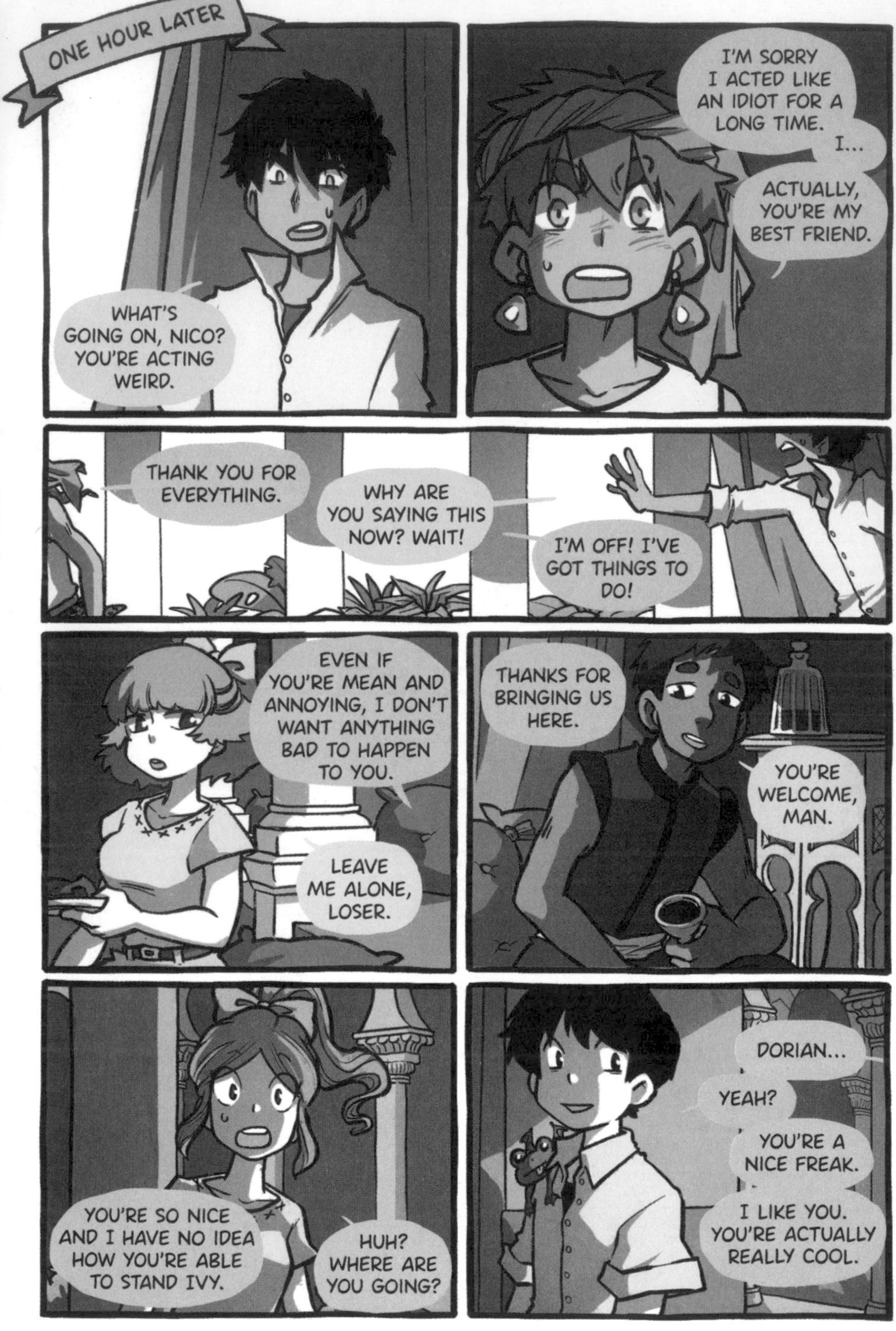
ONE HOUR LATER
WHAT'S GOING ON, NICO? YOU'RE ACTING WEIRD.
I'M SORRY I ACTED LIKE AN IDIOT FOR A LONG TIME.
I...
ACTUALLY, YOU'RE MY BEST FRIEND.
THANK YOU FOR EVERYTHING.
WHY ARE YOU SAYING THIS NOW? WAIT!
I'M OFF! I'VE GOT THINGS TO DO!
EVEN IF YOU'RE MEAN AND ANNOYING, I DON'T WANT ANYTHING BAD TO HAPPEN TO YOU.
LEAVE ME ALONE, LOSER.
THANKS FOR BRINGING US HERE.
YOU'RE WELCOME, MAN.
YOU'RE SO NICE AND I HAVE NO IDEA HOW YOU'RE ABLE TO STAND IVY.
HUH? WHERE ARE YOU GOING?
DORIAN...
YEAH?
YOU'RE A NICE FREAK.
I LIKE YOU. YOU'RE ACTUALLY REALLY COOL.

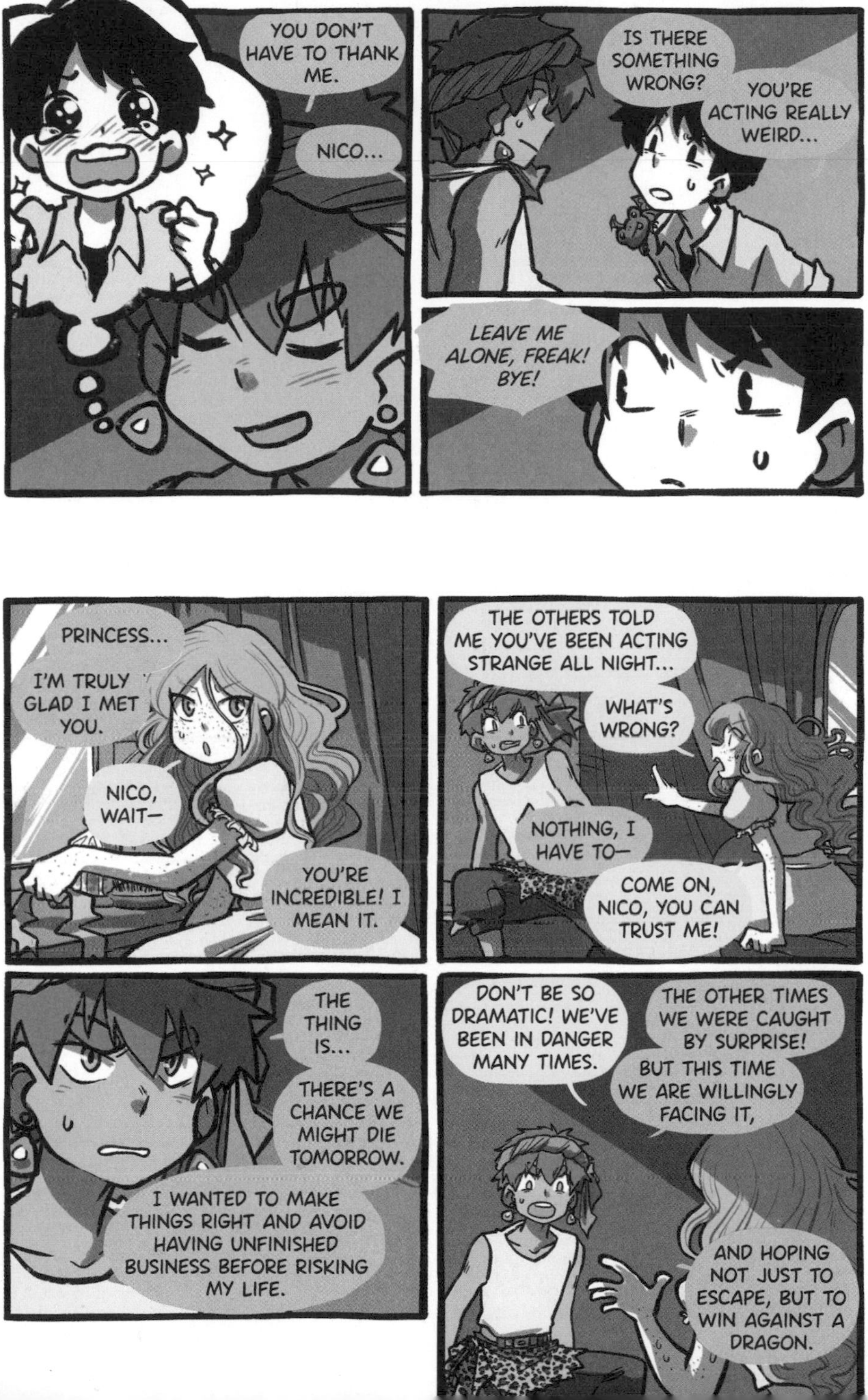

YOU DON'T HAVE TO THANK ME.
NICO...
IS THERE SOMETHING WRONG?
YOU'RE ACTING REALLY WEIRD...
LEAVE ME ALONE, FREAK! BYE!
PRINCESS...
I'M TRULY GLAD I MET YOU.
NICO, WAIT—
YOU'RE INCREDIBLE! I MEAN IT.
THE OTHERS TOLD ME YOU'VE BEEN ACTING STRANGE ALL NIGHT...
WHAT'S WRONG?
NOTHING, I HAVE TO—
COME ON, NICO, YOU CAN TRUST ME!
THE THING IS...
THERE'S A CHANCE WE MIGHT DIE TOMORROW.
I WANTED TO MAKE THINGS RIGHT AND AVOID HAVING UNFINISHED BUSINESS BEFORE RISKING MY LIFE.
DON'T BE SO DRAMATIC! WE'VE BEEN IN DANGER MANY TIMES.
THE OTHER TIMES WE WERE CAUGHT BY SURPRISE!
BUT THIS TIME WE ARE WILLINGLY FACING IT,
AND HOPING NOT JUST TO ESCAPE, BUT TO WIN AGAINST A DRAGON.

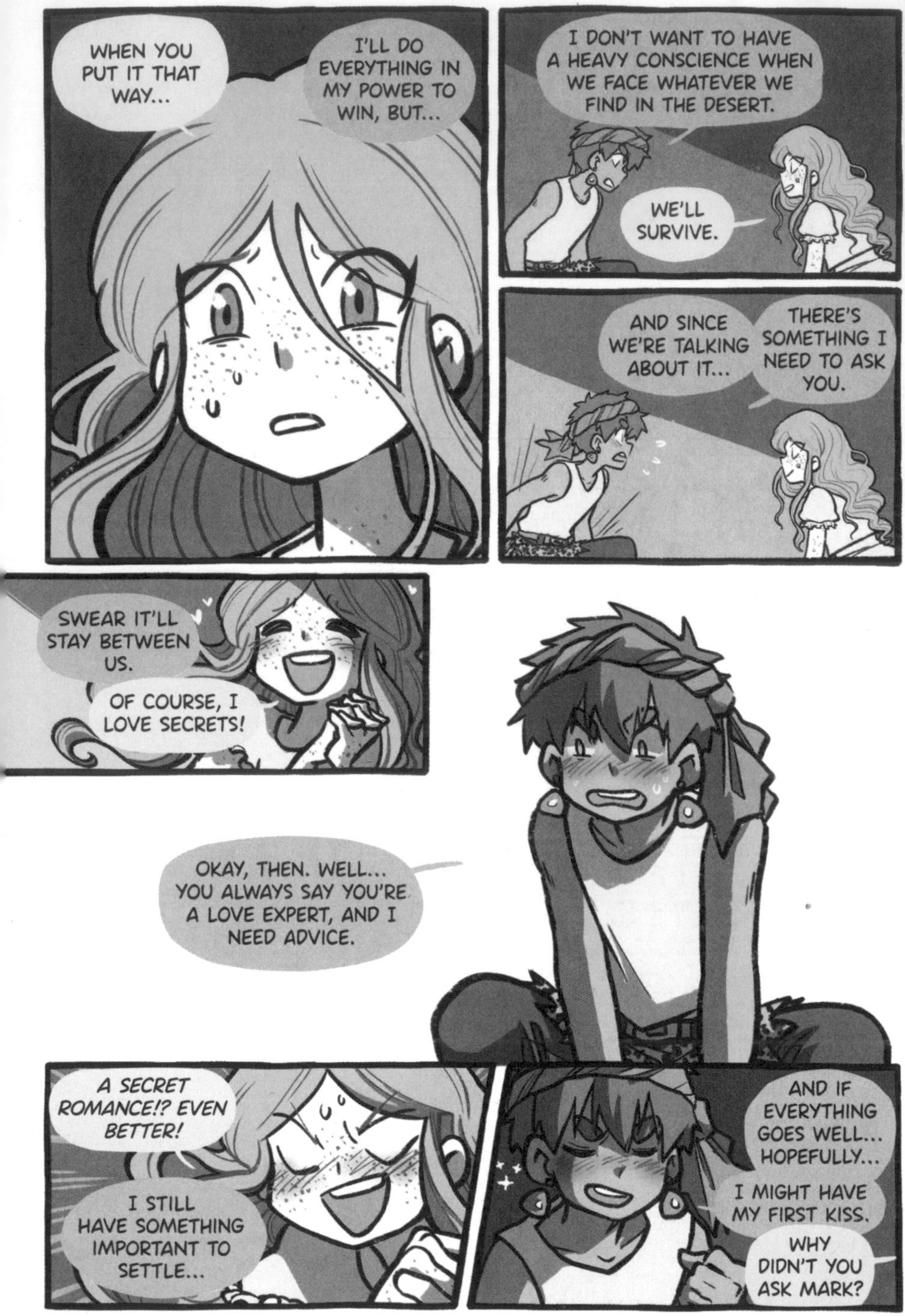
WHEN YOU PUT IT THAT WAY...
I'LL DO EVERYTHING IN MY POWER TO WIN, BUT...
I DON'T WANT TO HAVE A HEAVY CONSCIENCE WHEN WE FACE WHATEVER WE FIND IN THE DESERT.
WE'LL SURVIVE.
AND SINCE WE'RE TALKING ABOUT IT...
THERE'S SOMETHING I NEED TO ASK YOU.
SWEAR IT'LL STAY BETWEEN US.
OF COURSE, I LOVE SECRETS!
OKAY, THEN. WELL... YOU ALWAYS SAY YOU'RE A LOVE EXPERT, AND I NEED ADVICE.
A SECRET ROMANCE!? EVEN BETTER!
I STILL HAVE SOMETHING IMPORTANT TO SETTLE...
AND IF EVERYTHING GOES WELL... HOPEFULLY...
I MIGHT HAVE MY FIRST KISS.
WHY DIDN'T YOU ASK MARK?

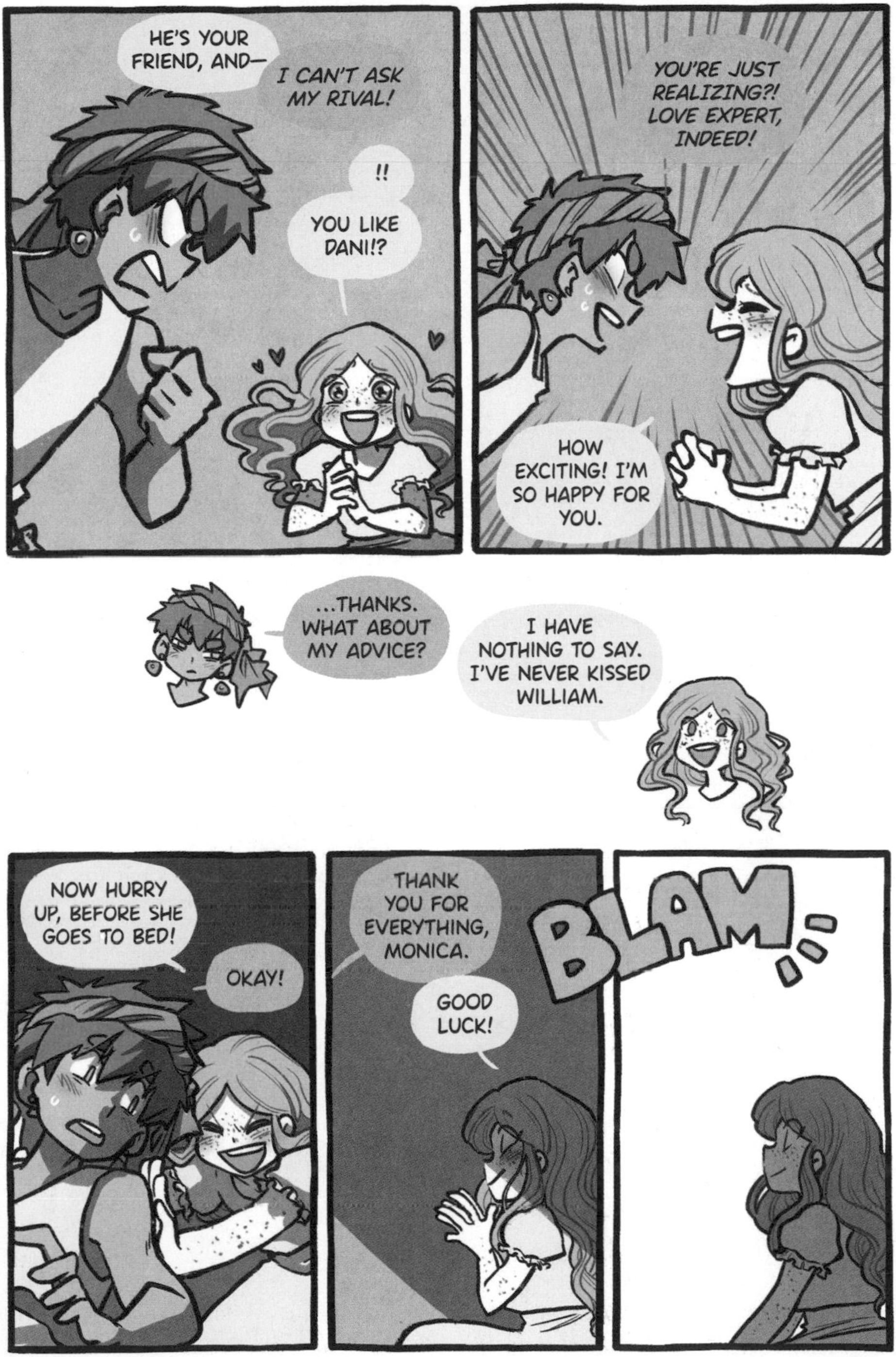
HE'S YOUR FRIEND, AND—
I CAN'T ASK MY RIVAL!
!!
YOU LIKE DANI!?
YOU'RE JUST REALIZING?! LOVE EXPERT, INDEED!
HOW EXCITING! I'M SO HAPPY FOR YOU.
...THANKS. WHAT ABOUT MY ADVICE?
I HAVE NOTHING TO SAY. I'VE NEVER KISSED WILLIAM.
NOW HURRY UP, BEFORE SHE GOES TO BED!
OKAY!
THANK YOU FOR EVERYTHING, MONICA.
GOOD LUCK!
BLAM

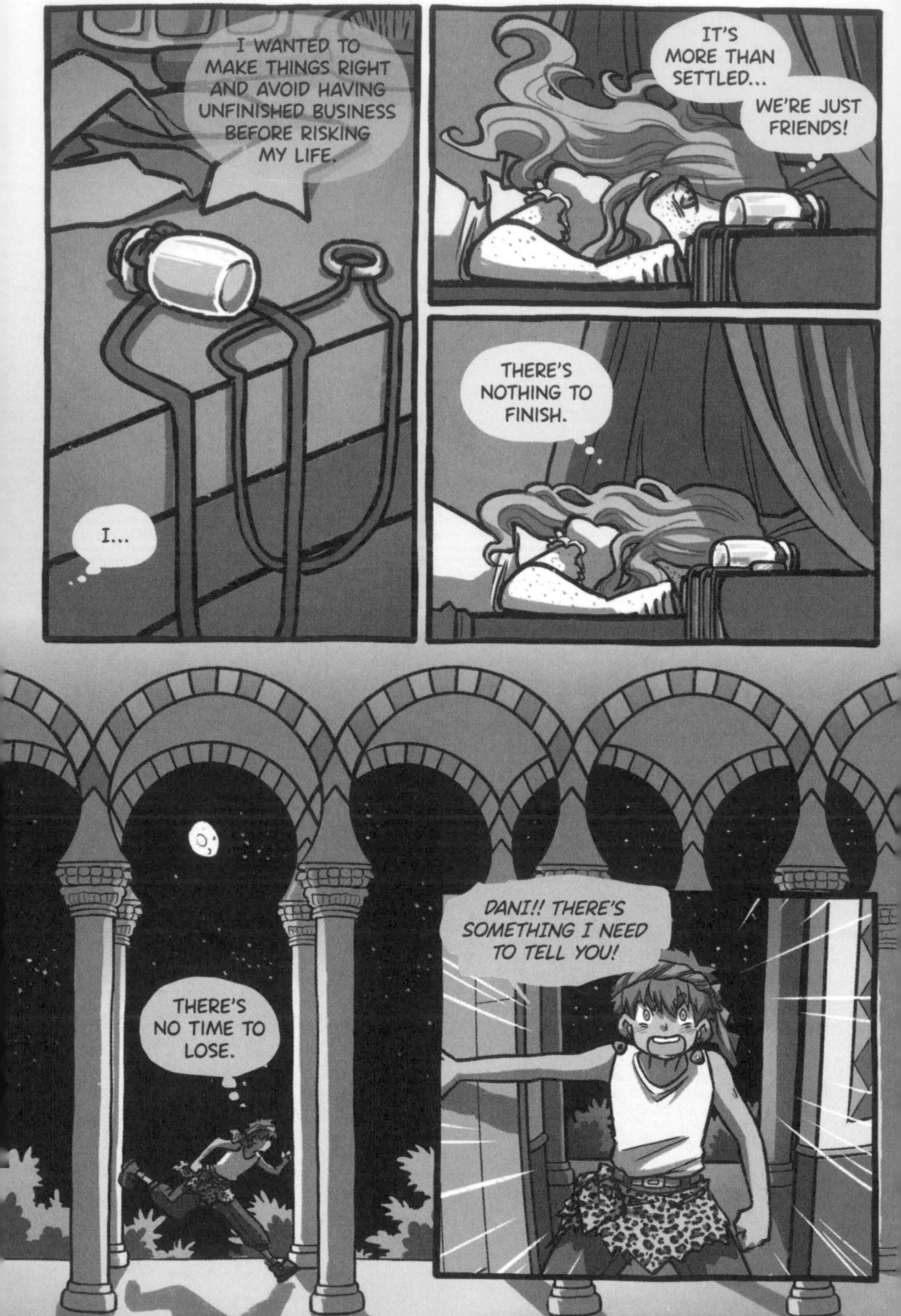
I WANTED TO MAKE THINGS RIGHT AND AVOID HAVING UNFINISHED BUSINESS BEFORE RISKING MY LIFE.
I...
IT'S MORE THAN SETTLED...
WE'RE JUST FRIENDS!
THERE'S NOTHING TO FINISH.
THERE'S NO TIME TO LOSE.
DANI!! THERE'S SOMETHING I NEED TO TELL YOU!

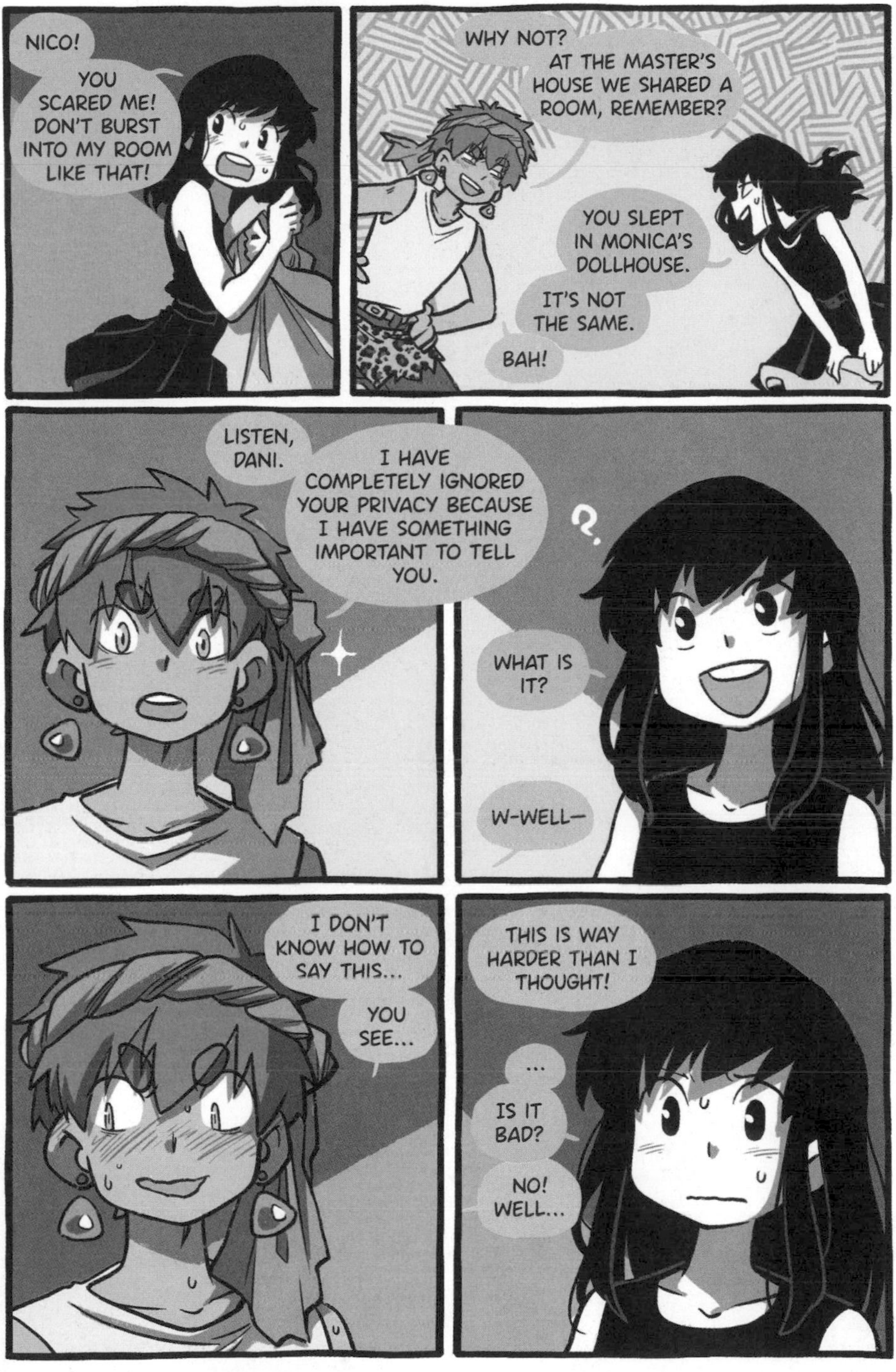
NICO!
YOU SCARED ME! DON'T BURST INTO MY ROOM LIKE THAT!
WHY NOT?
AT THE MASTER'S HOUSE WE SHARED A ROOM, REMEMBER?
YOU SLEPT IN MONICA'S DOLLHOUSE.
IT'S NOT THE SAME.
BAH!
LISTEN, DANI.
I HAVE COMPLETELY IGNORED YOUR PRIVACY BECAUSE I HAVE SOMETHING IMPORTANT TO TELL YOU.
?
WHAT IS IT?
W-WELL—
I DON'T KNOW HOW TO SAY THIS...
YOU SEE...
THIS IS WAY HARDER THAN I THOUGHT!
...
IS IT BAD?
NO! WELL...

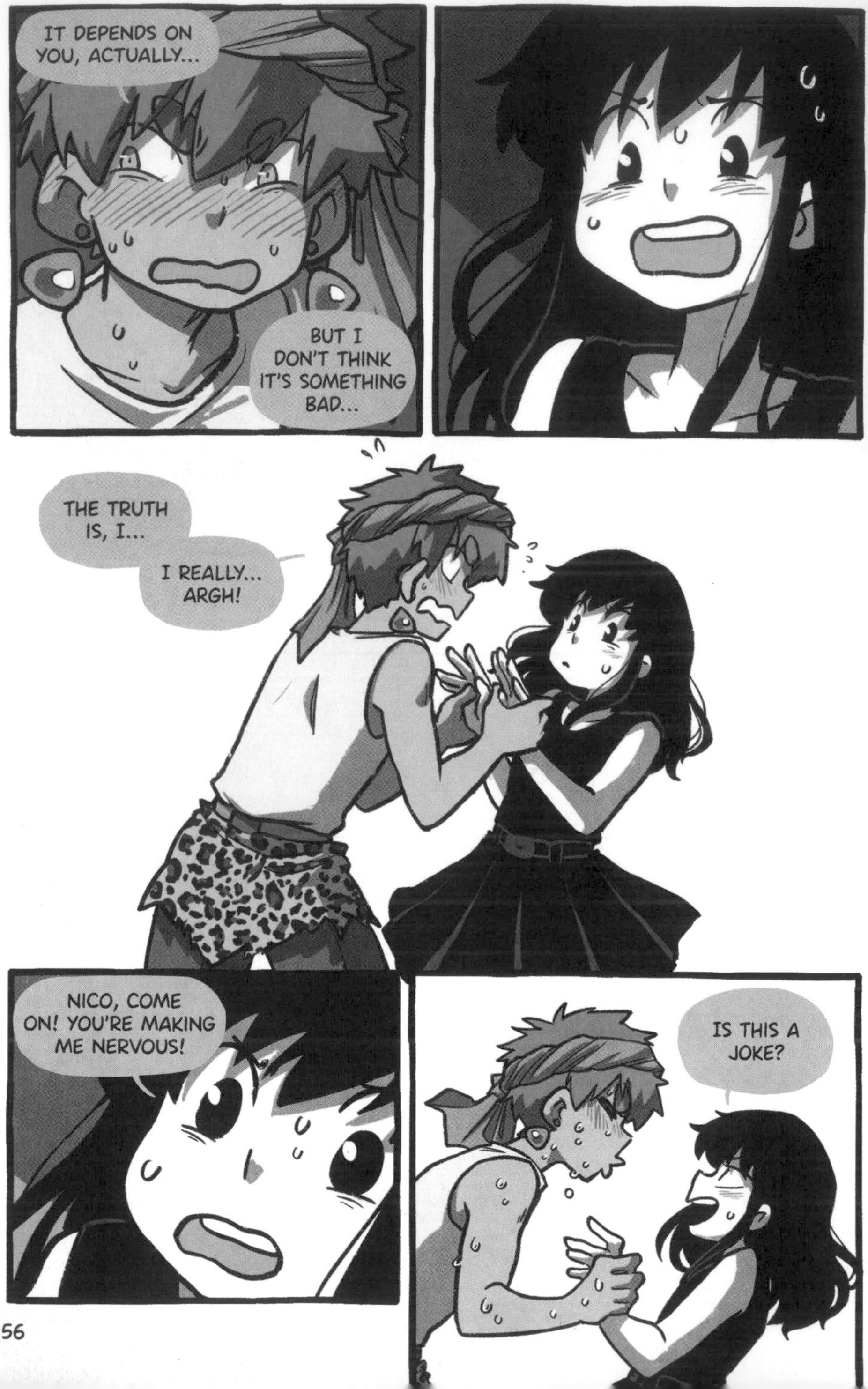
IT DEPENDS ON YOU, ACTUALLY...
BUT I DON'T THINK IT'S SOMETHING BAD...
THE TRUTH IS, I...
I REALLY... ARGH!
NICO, COME ON! YOU'RE MAKING ME NERVOUS!
IS THIS A JOKE?

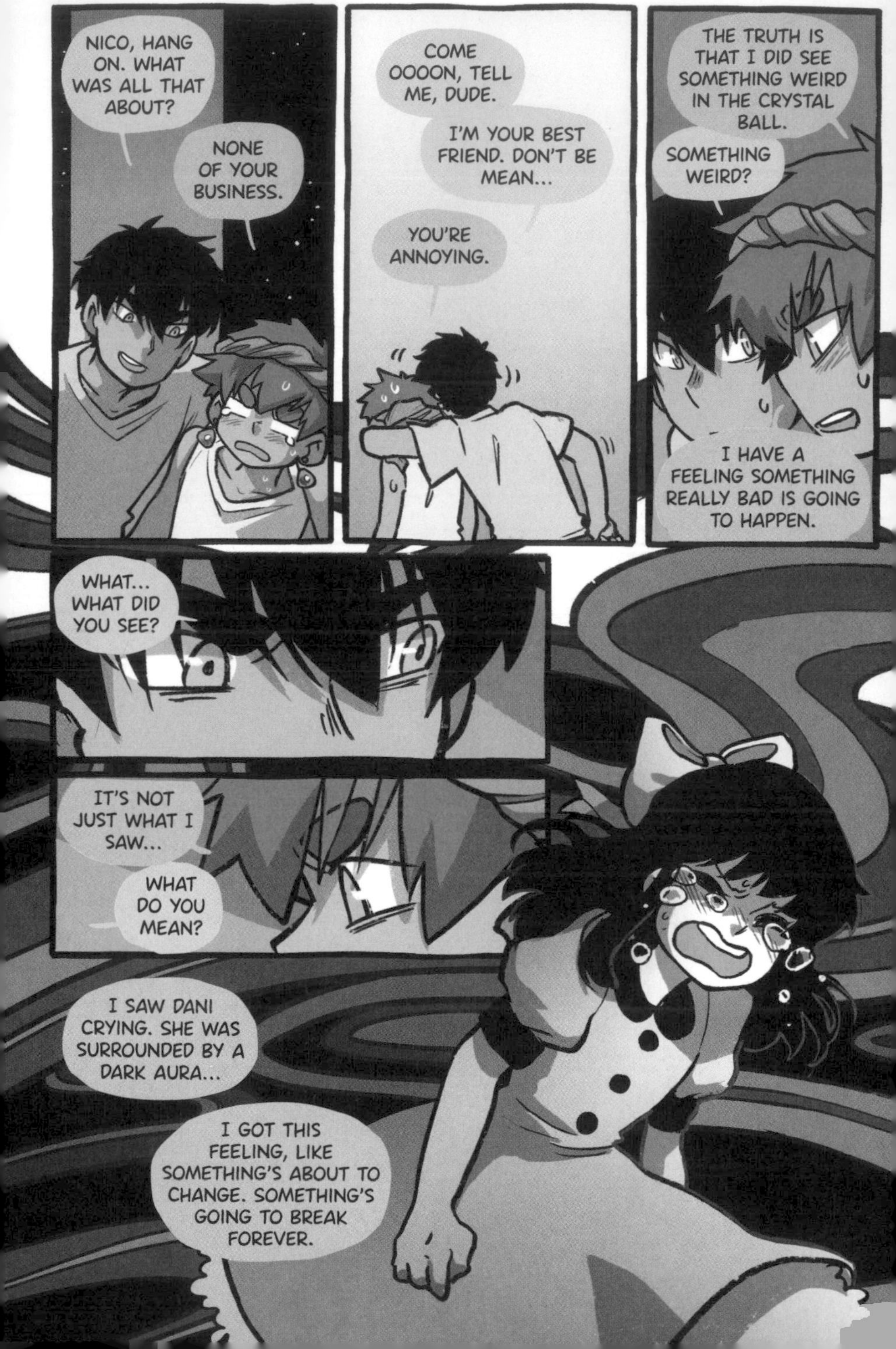
NICO, HANG ON. WHAT WAS ALL THAT ABOUT?
NONE OF YOUR BUSINESS.
COME OOOON, TELL ME, DUDE.
I'M YOUR BEST FRIEND. DON'T BE MEAN...
YOU'RE ANNOYING.
THE TRUTH IS THAT I DID SEE SOMETHING WEIRD IN THE CRYSTAL BALL.
SOMETHING WEIRD?
I HAVE A FEELING SOMETHING REALLY BAD IS GOING TO HAPPEN.
WHAT... WHAT DID YOU SEE?
IT'S NOT JUST WHAT I SAW...
WHAT DO YOU MEAN?
I SAW DANI CRYING. SHE WAS SURROUNDED BY A DARK AURA...
I GOT THIS FEELING, LIKE SOMETHING'S ABOUT TO CHANGE. SOMETHING'S GOING TO BREAK FOREVER.

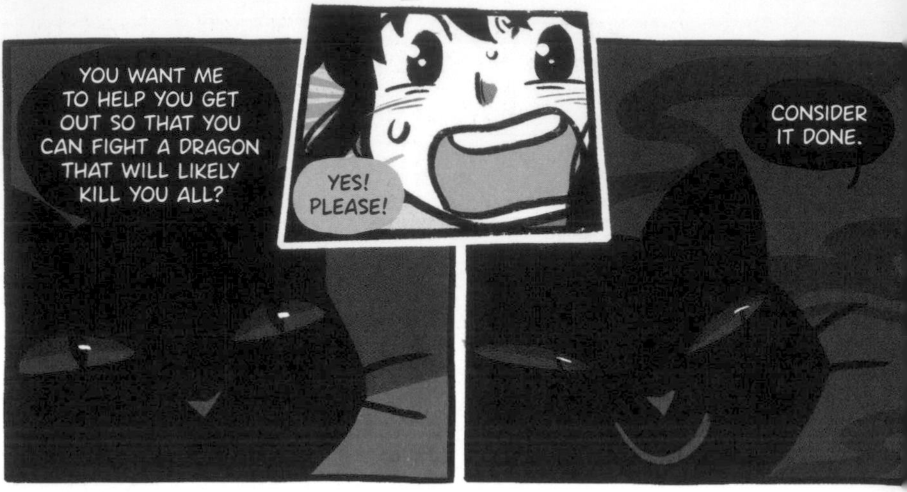
YOU WANT ME TO HELP YOU GET OUT SO THAT YOU CAN FIGHT A DRAGON THAT WILL LIKELY KILL YOU ALL?
YES! PLEASE!
CONSIDER IT DONE.

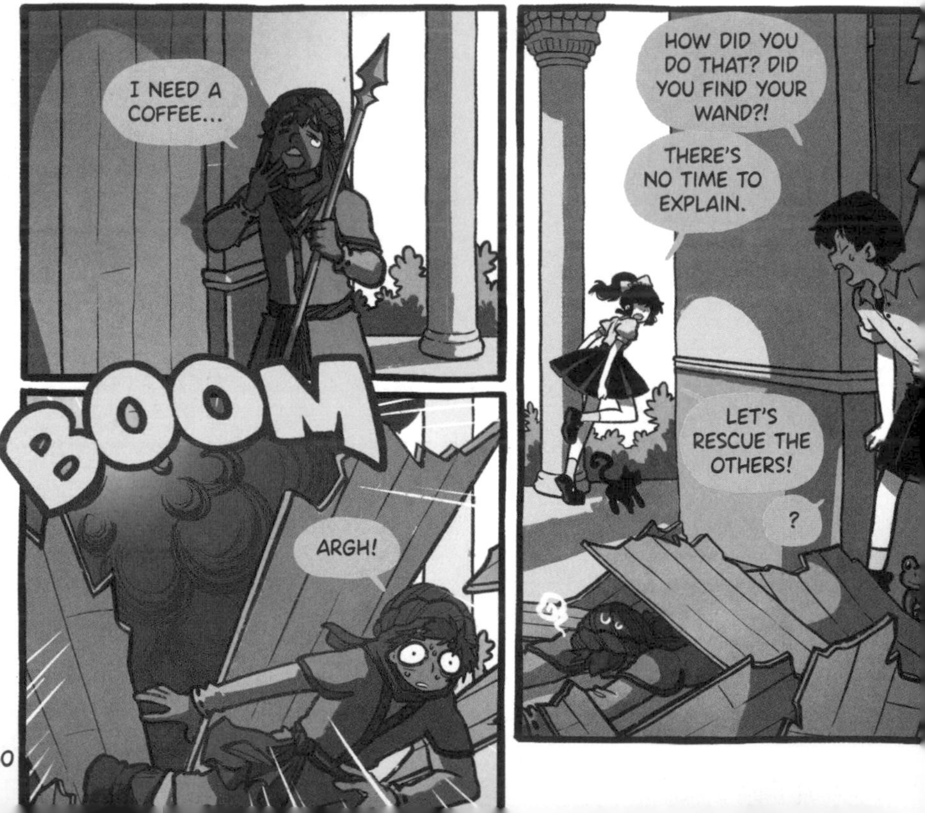
I NEED A COFFEE...
BOOM
ARGH!
HOW DID YOU DO THAT? DID YOU FIND YOUR WAND?!
THERE'S NO TIME TO EXPLAIN.
LET'S RESCUE THE OTHERS!
?

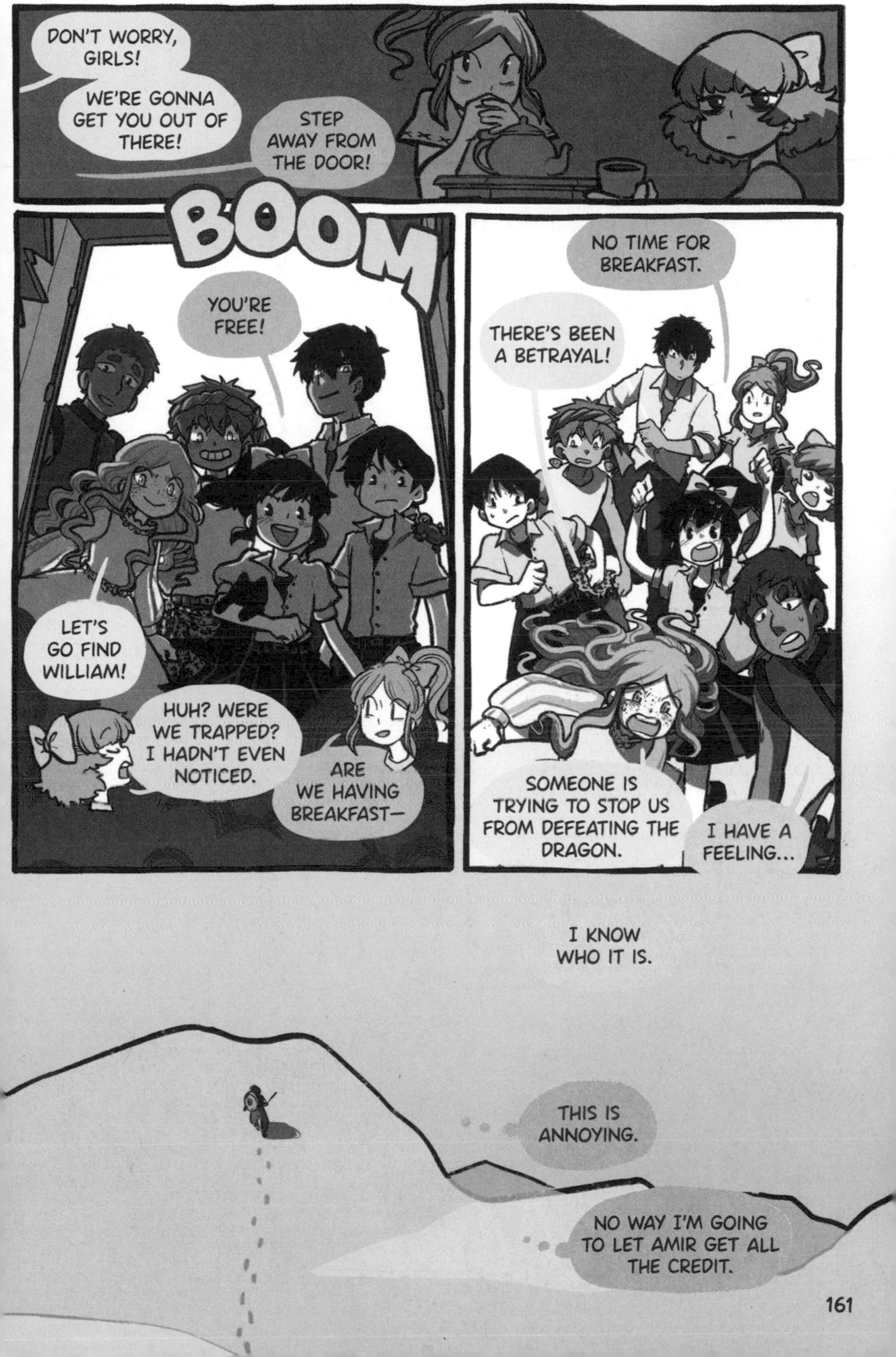
DON'T WORRY, GIRLS!
WE'RE GONNA GET YOU OUT OF THERE!
STEP AWAY FROM THE DOOR!
BOOM
YOU'RE FREE!
LET'S GO FIND WILLIAM!
HUH? WERE WE TRAPPED? I HADN'T EVEN NOTICED.
ARE WE HAVING BREAKFAST—
NO TIME FOR BREAKFAST.
THERE'S BEEN A BETRAYAL!
SOMEONE IS TRYING TO STOP US FROM DEFEATING THE DRAGON.
I HAVE A FEELING...
I KNOW WHO IT IS.
THIS IS ANNOYING.
NO WAY I'M GOING TO LET AMIR GET ALL THE CREDIT.

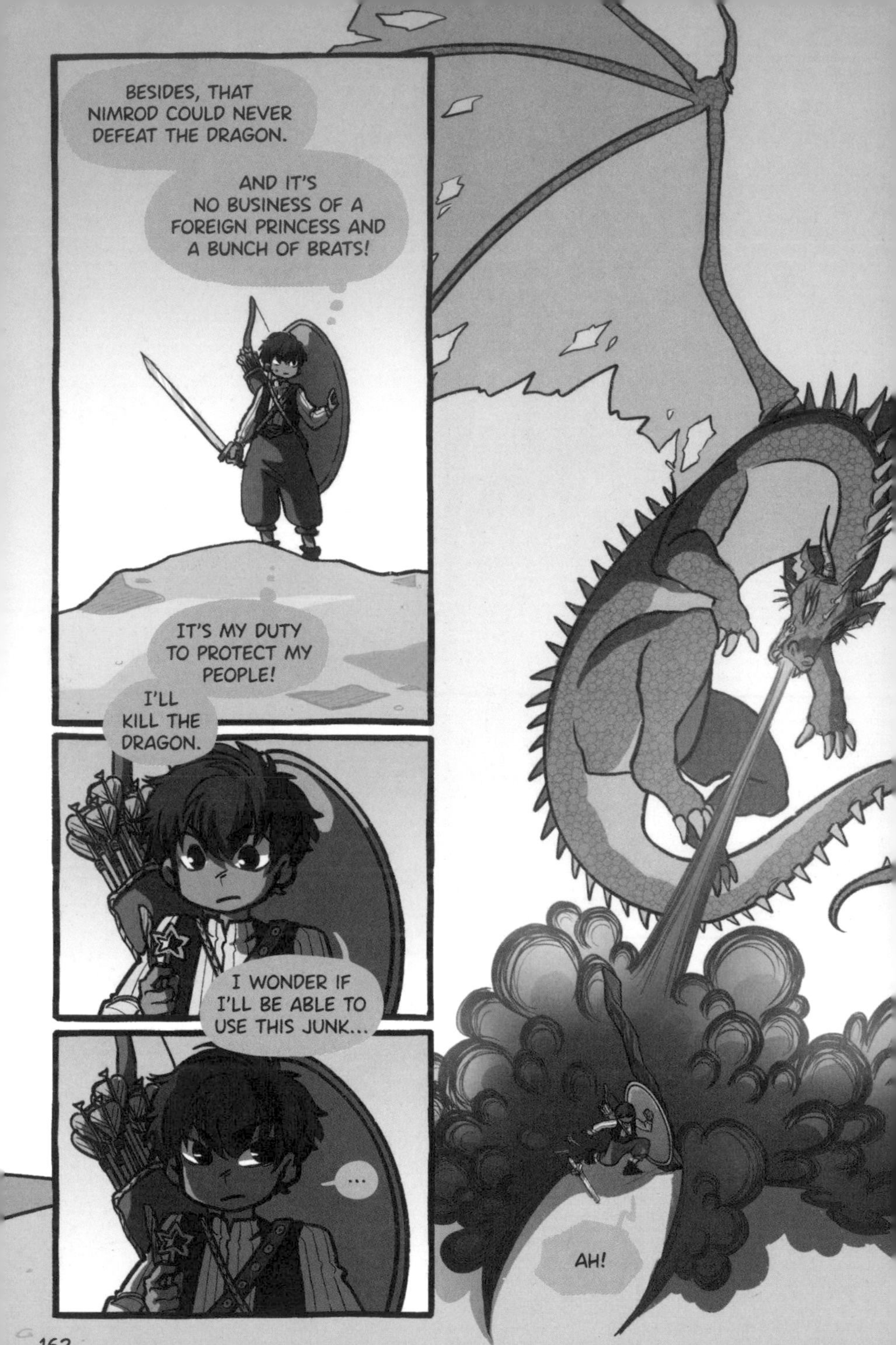
BESIDES, THAT NIMROD COULD NEVER DEFEAT THE DRAGON.
AND IT'S NO BUSINESS OF A FOREIGN PRINCESS AND A BUNCH OF BRATS!
IT'S MY DUTY TO PROTECT MY PEOPLE!
I'LL KILL THE DRAGON.
I WONDER IF I'LL BE ABLE TO USE THIS JUNK...
...
AH!

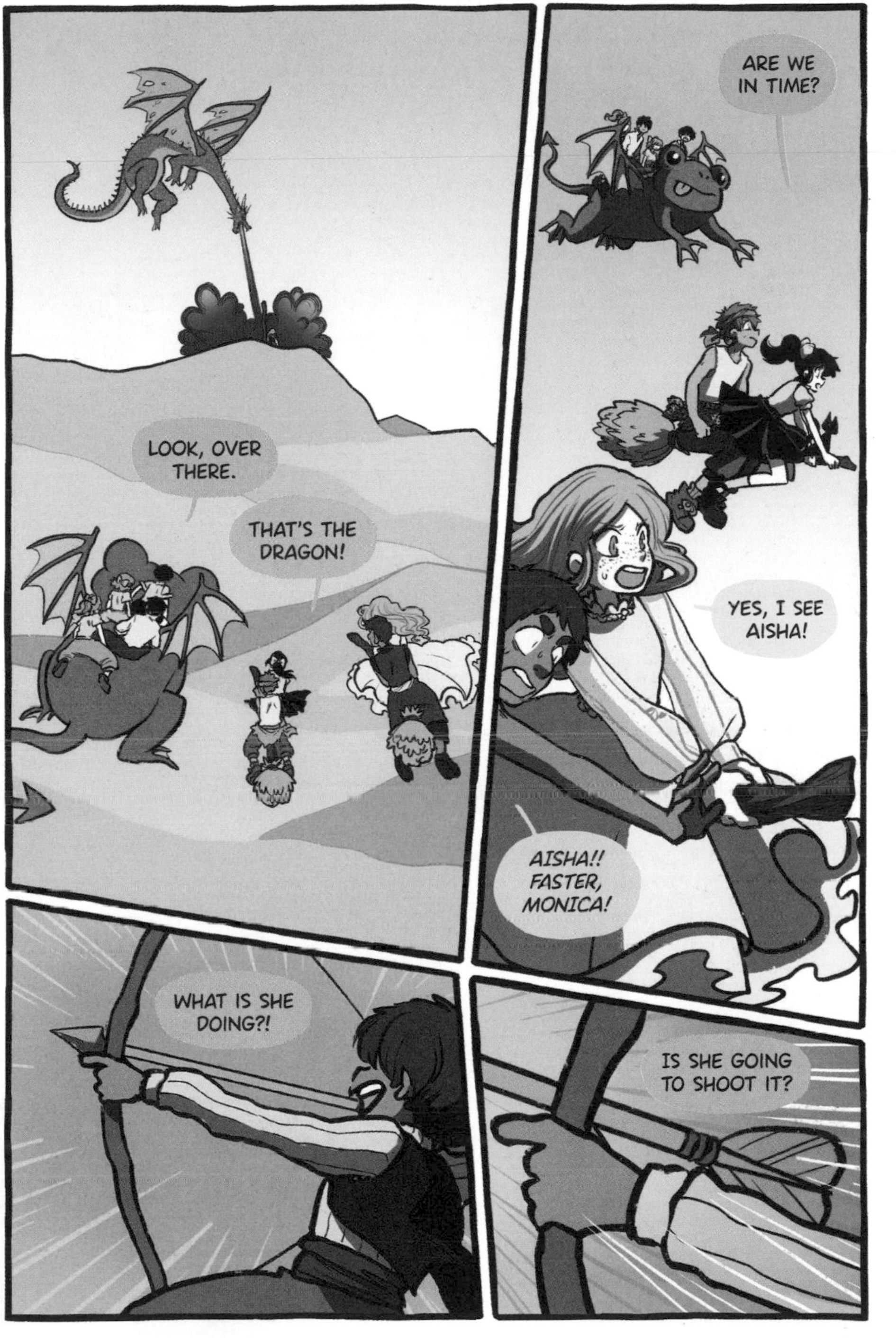
LOOK, OVER THERE.
THAT'S THE DRAGON!
ARE WE IN TIME?
YES, I SEE AISHA!
AISHA!! FASTER, MONICA!
WHAT IS SHE DOING?!
IS SHE GOING TO SHOOT IT?

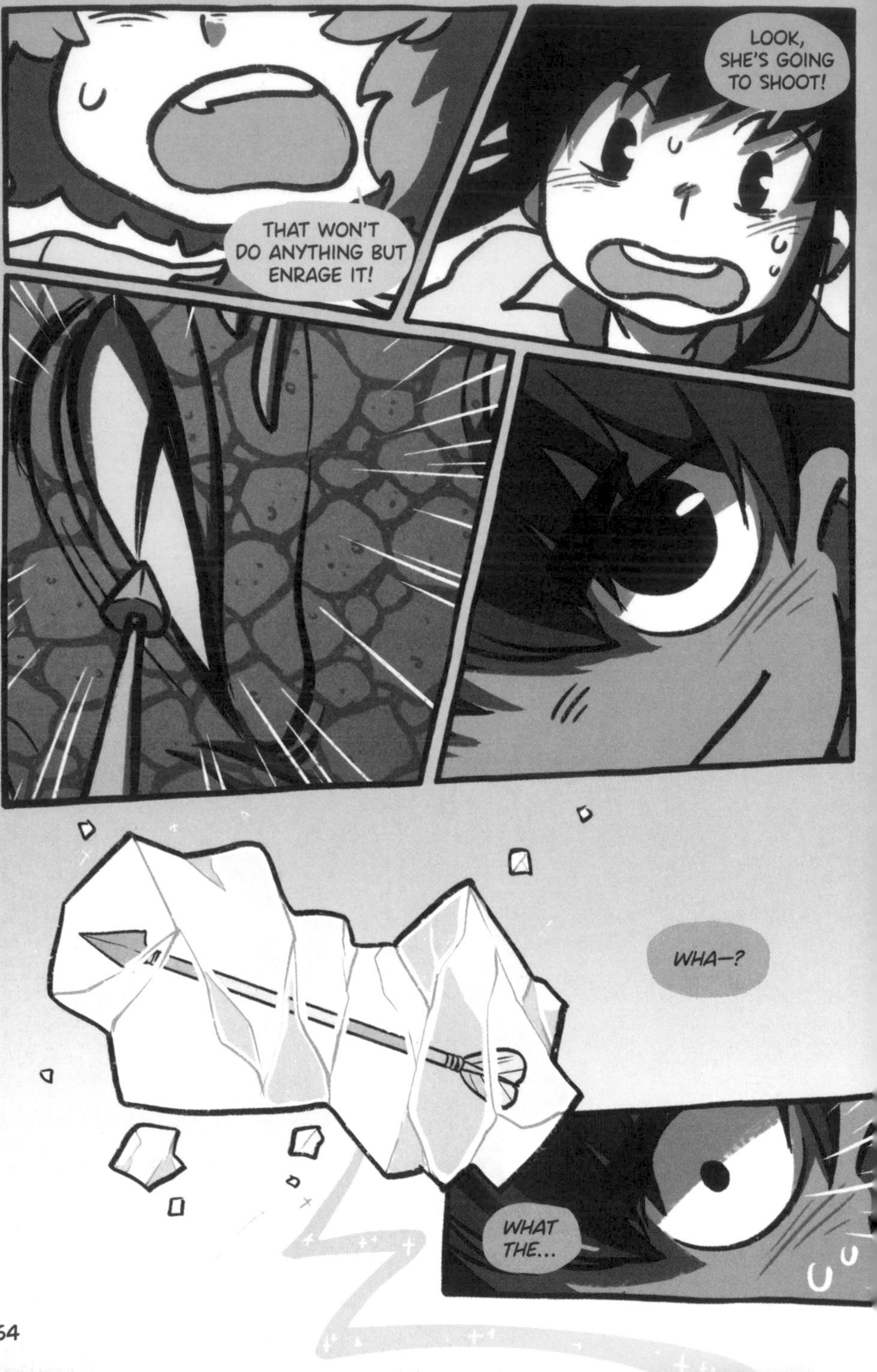
LOOK, SHE'S GOING TO SHOOT!
THAT WON'T DO ANYTHING BUT ENRAGE IT!
WHA–?
WHAT THE...

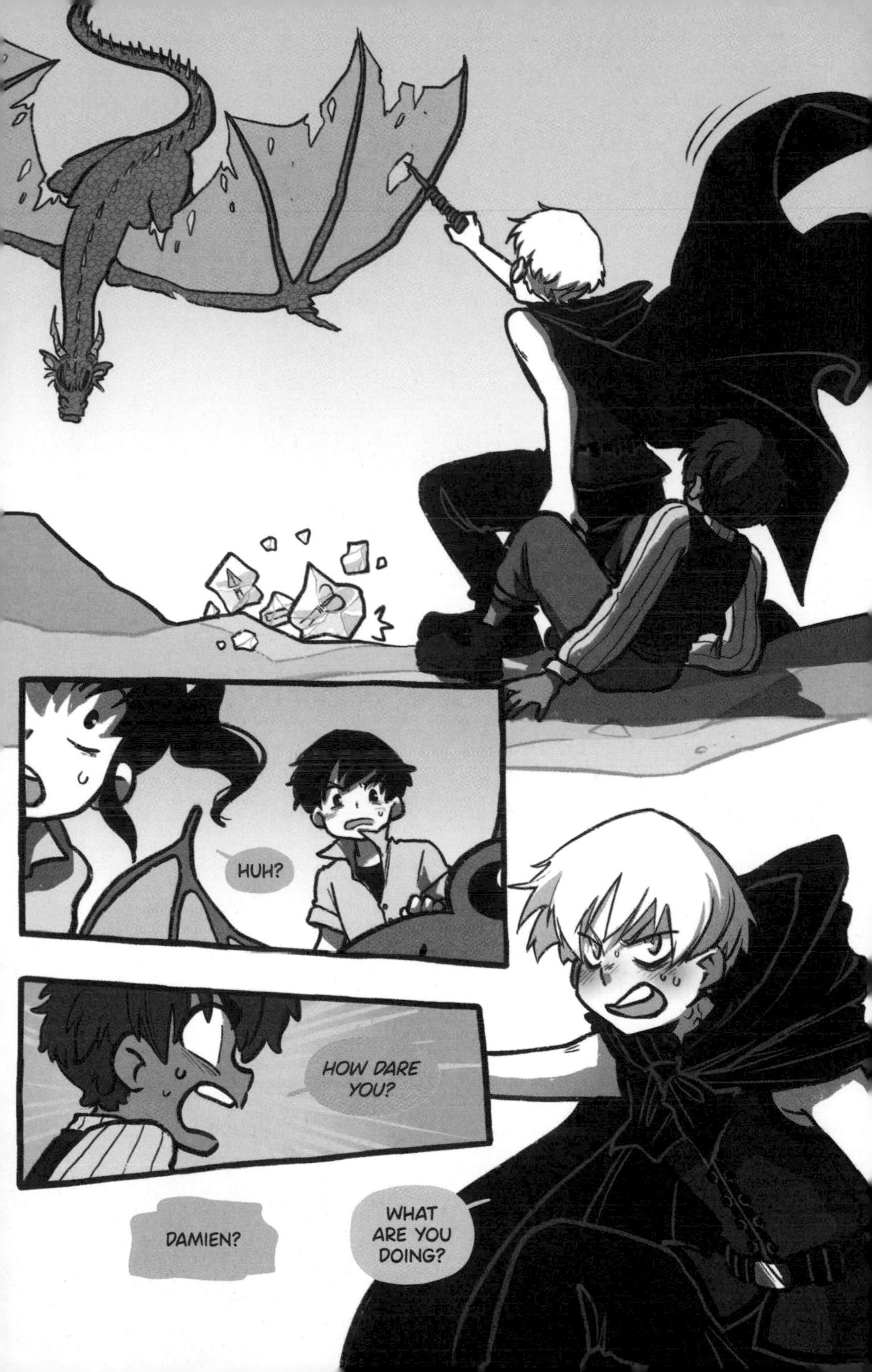
HUH?
HOW DARE YOU?
DAMIEN?
WHAT ARE YOU DOING?

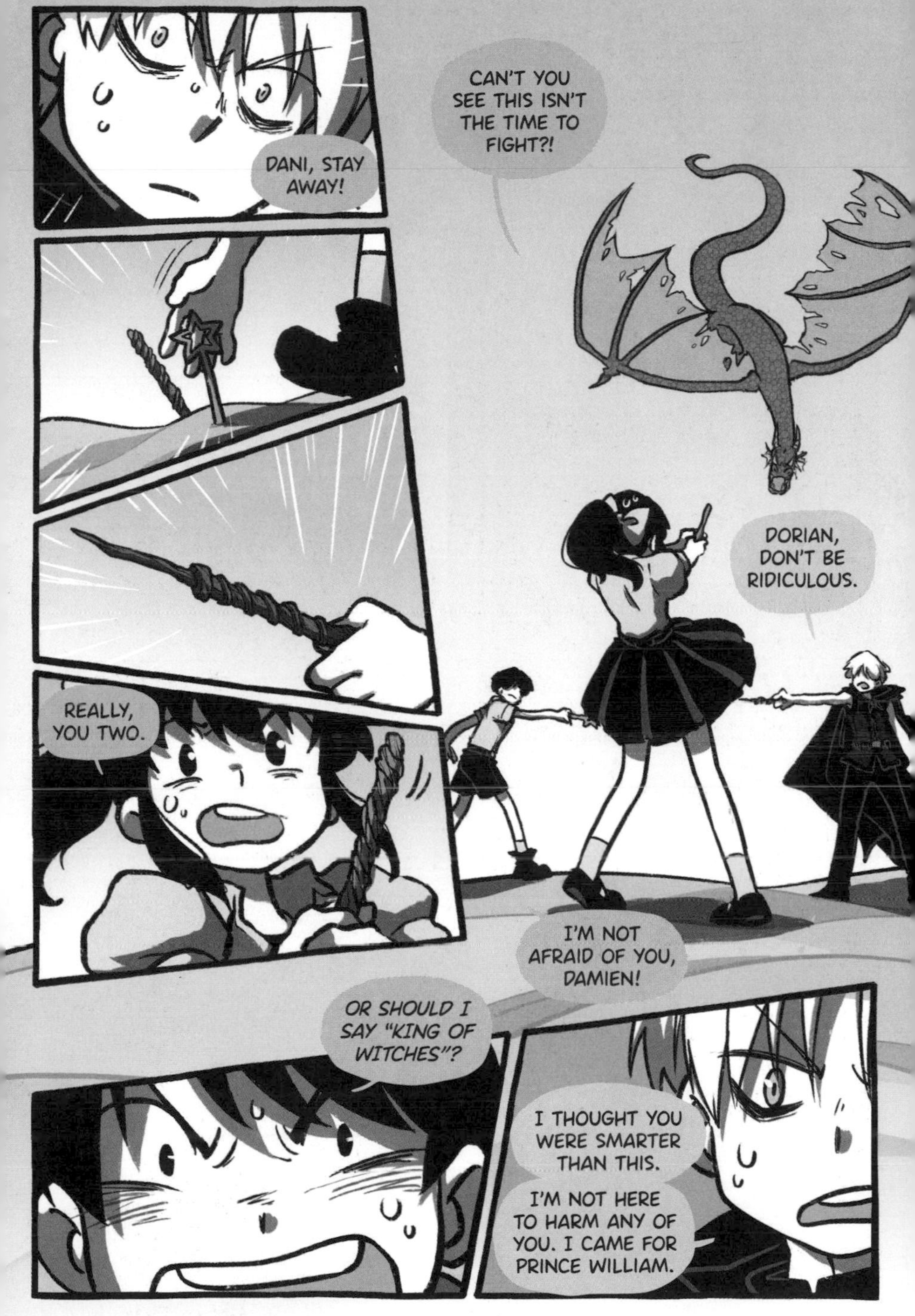
CAN'T YOU SEE THIS ISN'T THE TIME TO FIGHT?!
DANI, STAY AWAY!
DORIAN, DON'T BE RIDICULOUS.
REALLY, YOU TWO.
I'M NOT AFRAID OF YOU, DAMIEN!
OR SHOULD I SAY "KING OF WITCHES"?
I THOUGHT YOU WERE SMARTER THAN THIS.
I'M NOT HERE TO HARM ANY OF YOU. I CAME FOR PRINCE WILLIAM.

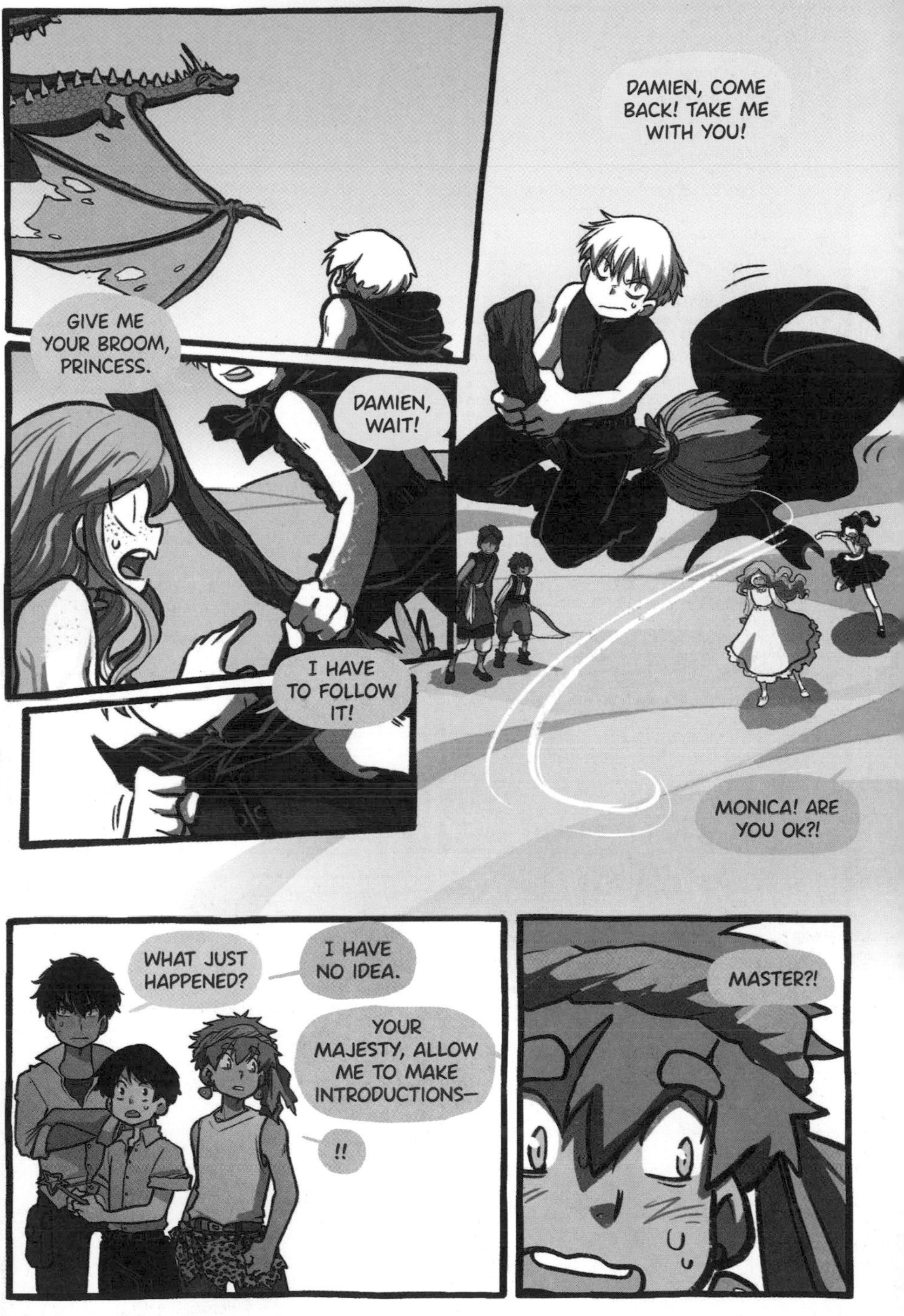
DAMIEN, COME BACK! TAKE ME WITH YOU!
GIVE ME YOUR BROOM, PRINCESS.
DAMIEN, WAIT!
I HAVE TO FOLLOW IT!
MONICA! ARE YOU OK?!
WHAT JUST HAPPENED?
I HAVE NO IDEA.
YOUR MAJESTY, ALLOW ME TO MAKE INTRODUCTIONS—
!!
MASTER?!

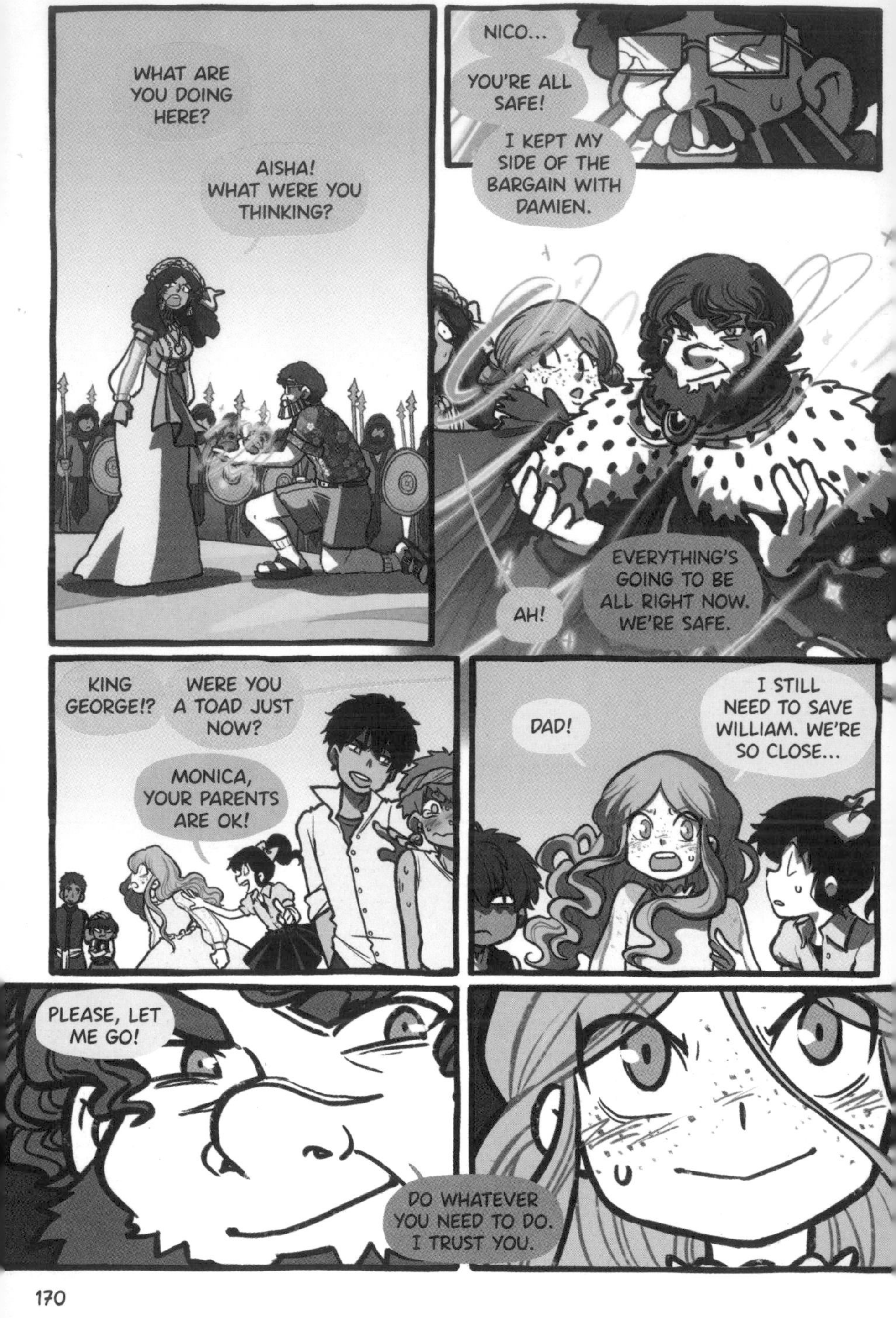
WHAT ARE YOU DOING HERE?
AISHA! WHAT WERE YOU THINKING?
NICO...
YOU'RE ALL SAFE!
I KEPT MY SIDE OF THE BARGAIN WITH DAMIEN.
AH!
EVERYTHING'S GOING TO BE ALL RIGHT NOW. WE'RE SAFE.
KING GEORGE!?
WERE YOU A TOAD JUST NOW?
MONICA, YOUR PARENTS ARE OK!
DAD!
I STILL NEED TO SAVE WILLIAM. WE'RE SO CLOSE...
PLEASE, LET ME GO!
DO WHATEVER YOU NEED TO DO. I TRUST YOU.

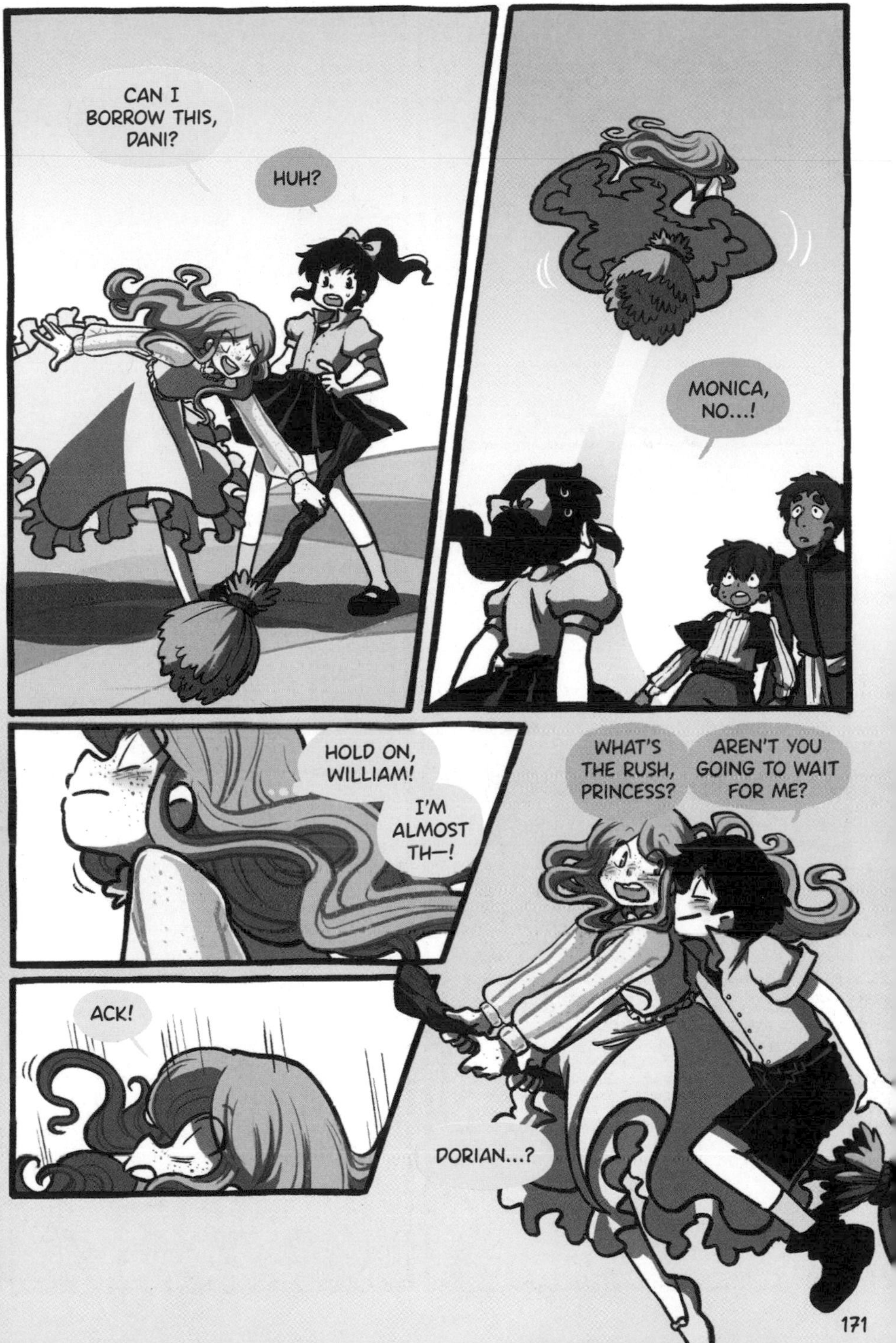
CAN I BORROW THIS, DANI?
HUH?
MONICA, NO...!
HOLD ON, WILLIAM!
I'M ALMOST TH—!
ACK!
WHAT'S THE RUSH, PRINCESS?
AREN'T YOU GOING TO WAIT FOR ME?
DORIAN...?

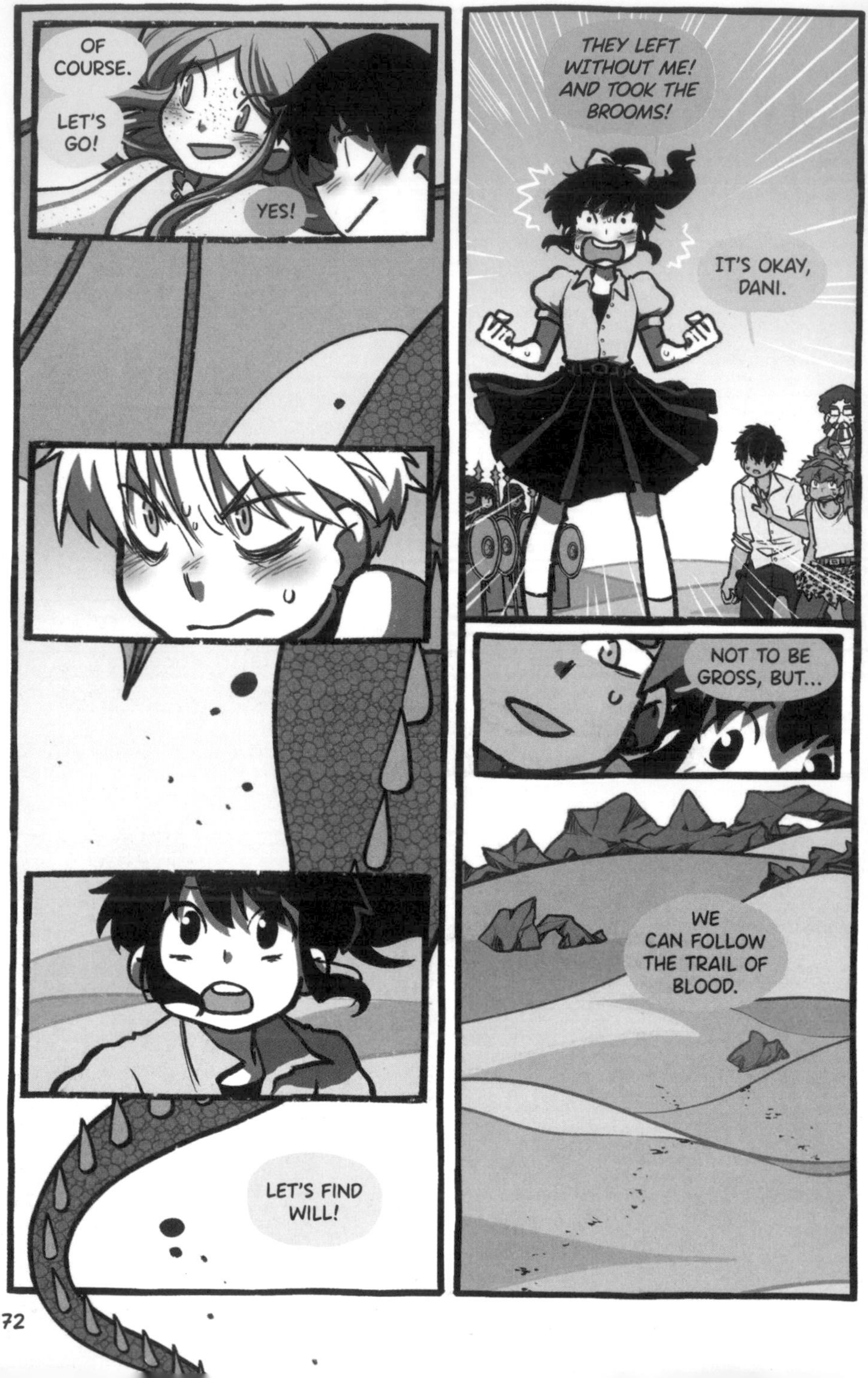
OF COURSE.
LET'S GO!
YES!
LET'S FIND WILL!
THEY LEFT WITHOUT ME! AND TOOK THE BROOMS!
IT'S OKAY, DANI.
NOT TO BE GROSS, BUT...
WE CAN FOLLOW THE TRAIL OF BLOOD.

CHAPTER 43

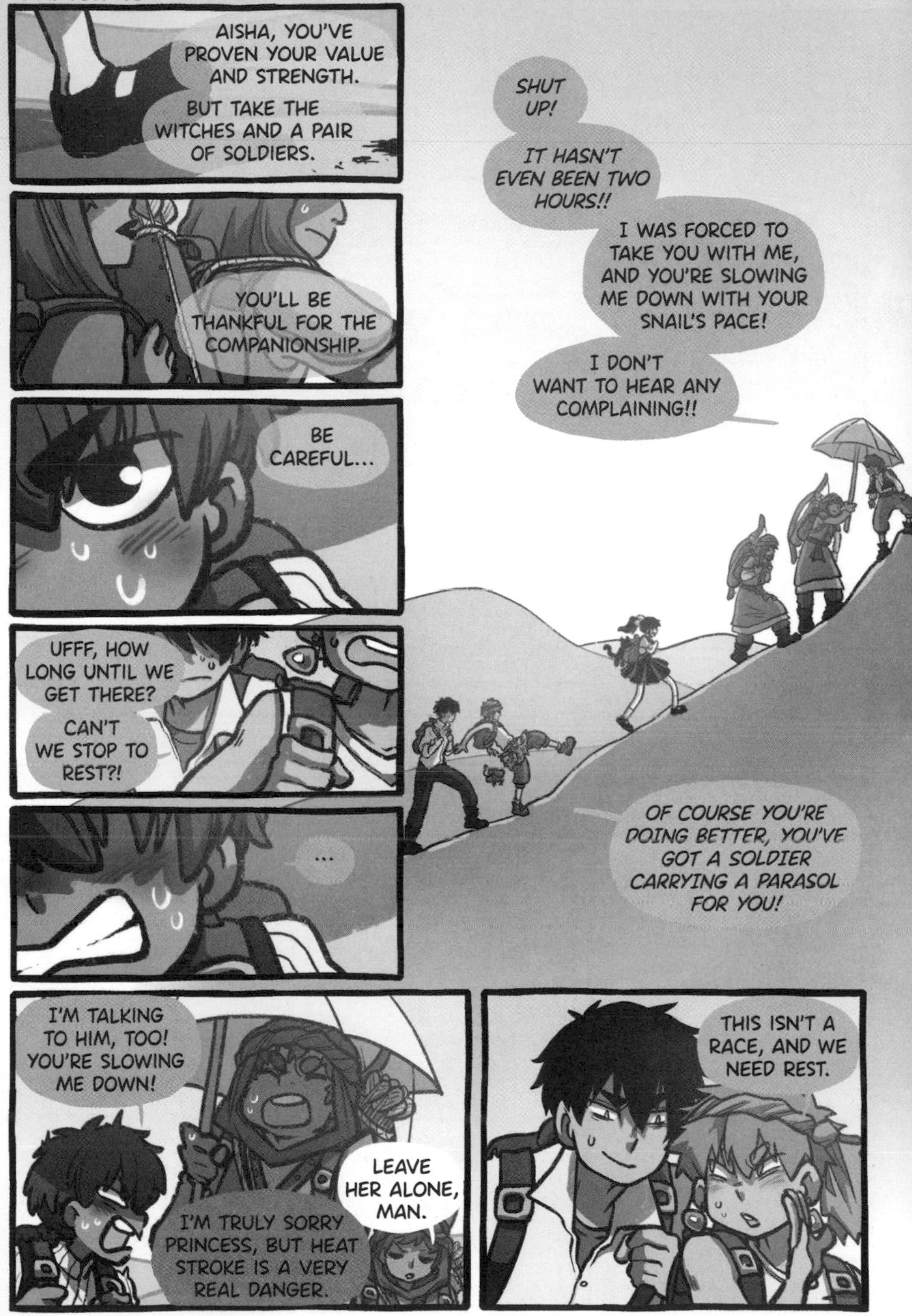
AISHA, YOU'VE PROVEN YOUR VALUE AND STRENGTH.
BUT TAKE THE WITCHES AND A PAIR OF SOLDIERS.
YOU'LL BE THANKFUL FOR THE COMPANIONSHIP.
BE CAREFUL...
SHUT UP!
IT HASN'T EVEN BEEN TWO HOURS!!
I WAS FORCED TO TAKE YOU WITH ME, AND YOU'RE SLOWING ME DOWN WITH YOUR SNAIL'S PACE!
I DON'T WANT TO HEAR ANY COMPLAINING!!
UFFF, HOW LONG UNTIL WE GET THERE?
CAN'T WE STOP TO REST?!
...
OF COURSE YOU'RE DOING BETTER, YOU'VE GOT A SOLDIER CARRYING A PARASOL FOR YOU!
I'M TALKING TO HIM, TOO! YOU'RE SLOWING ME DOWN!
I'M TRULY SORRY PRINCESS, BUT HEAT STROKE IS A VERY REAL DANGER.
LEAVE HER ALONE, MAN.
THIS ISN'T A RACE, AND WE NEED REST.

175

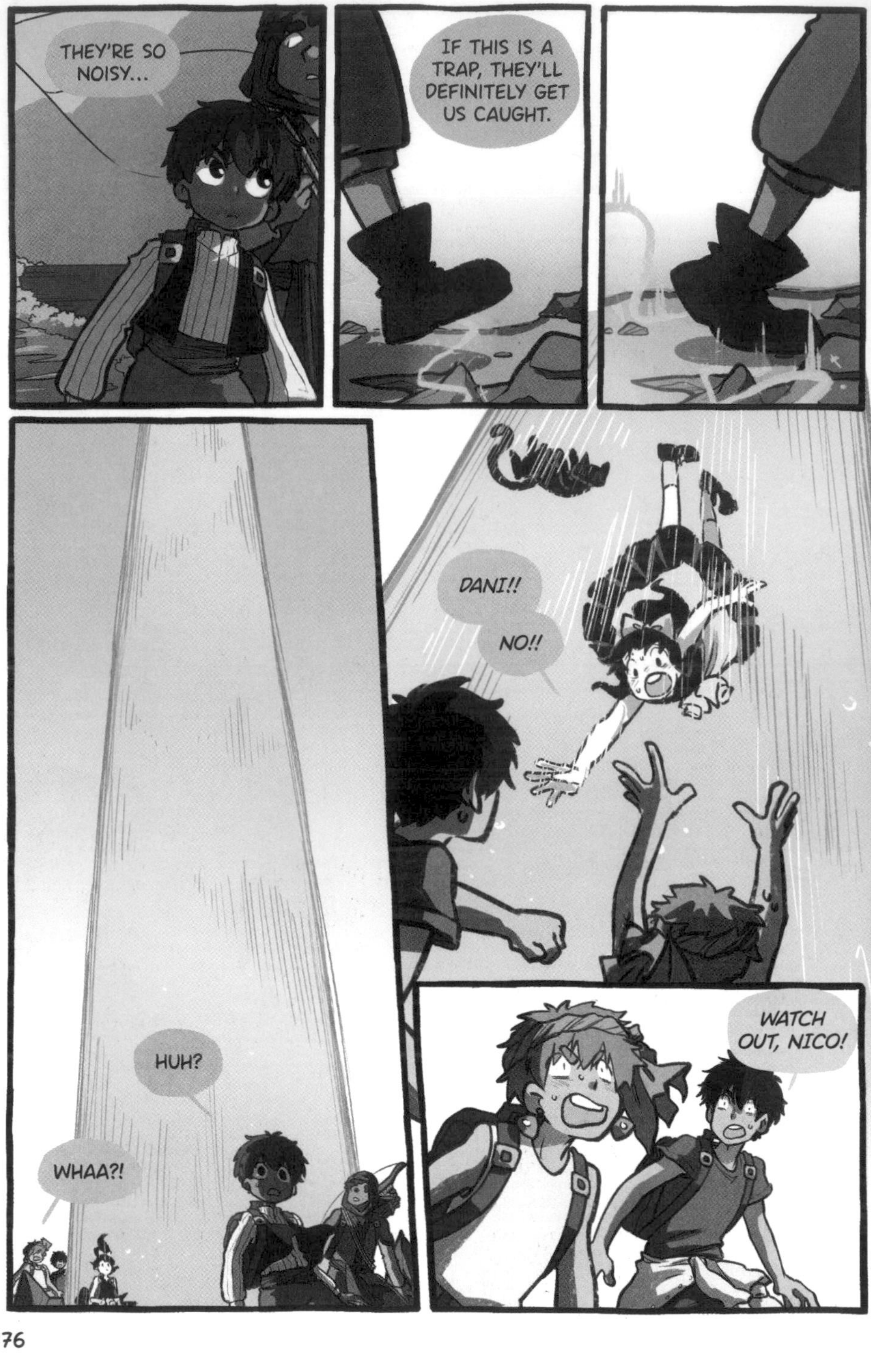
THEY'RE SO NOISY...
IF THIS IS A TRAP, THEY'LL DEFINITELY GET US CAUGHT.
DANI!!
NO!!
HUH?
WHAA?!
WATCH OUT, NICO!

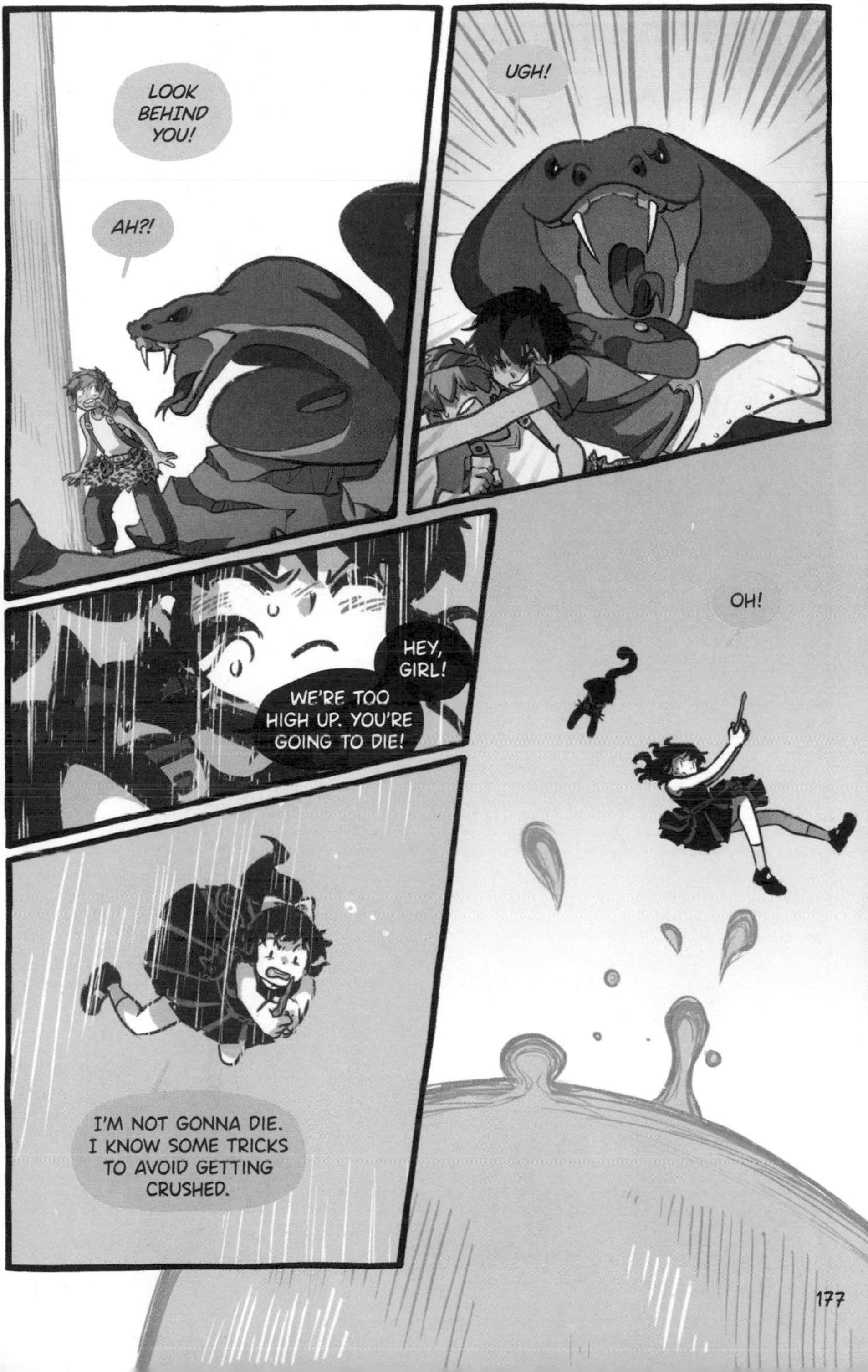
LOOK BEHIND YOU!
AH?!
UGH!
HEY, GIRL!
WE'RE TOO HIGH UP. YOU'RE GOING TO DIE!
I'M NOT GONNA DIE. I KNOW SOME TRICKS TO AVOID GETTING CRUSHED.
OH!

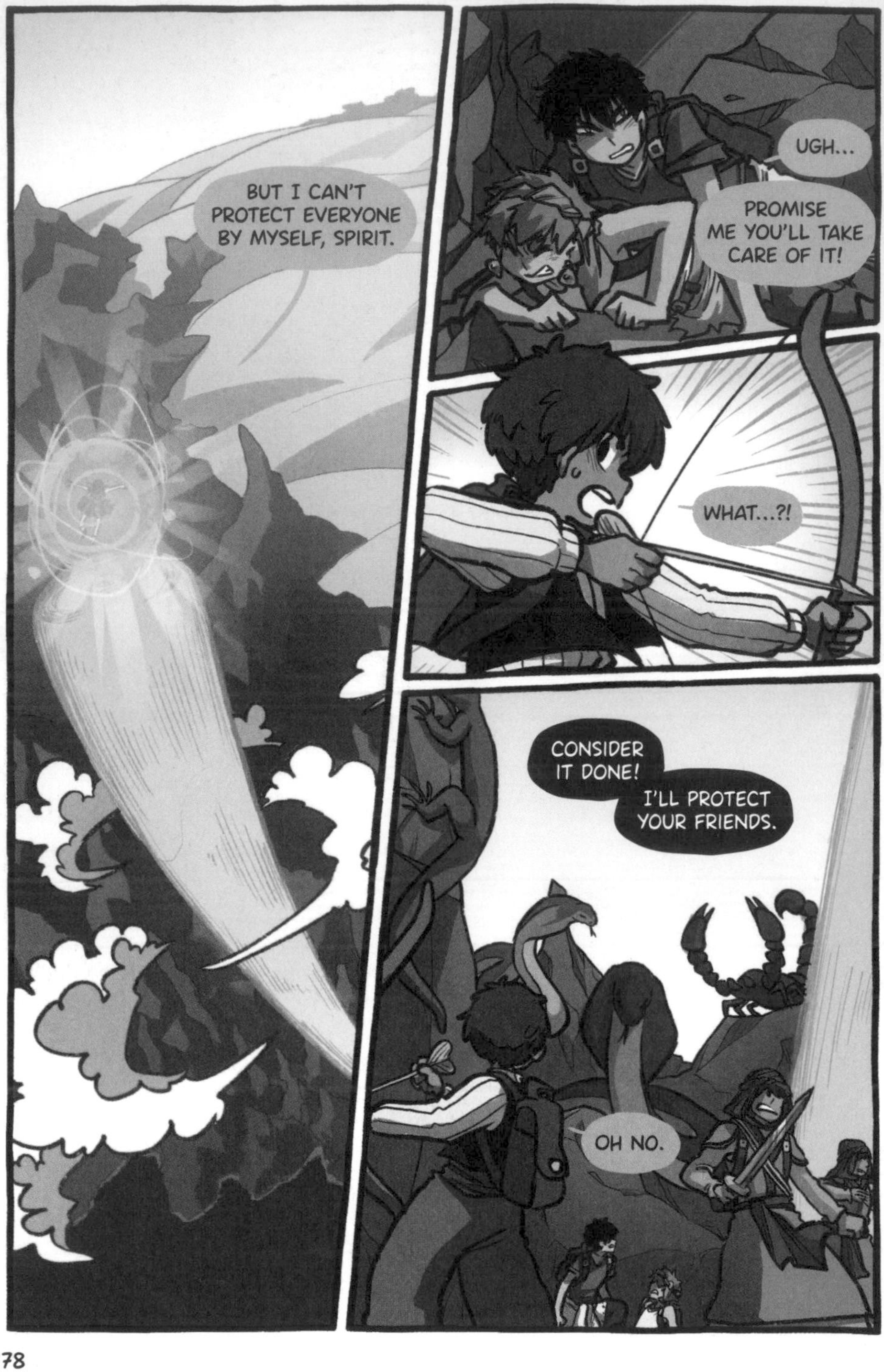
BUT I CAN'T PROTECT EVERYONE BY MYSELF, SPIRIT.
UGH...
PROMISE ME YOU'LL TAKE CARE OF IT!
WHAT...?!
CONSIDER IT DONE!
I'LL PROTECT YOUR FRIENDS.
OH NO.

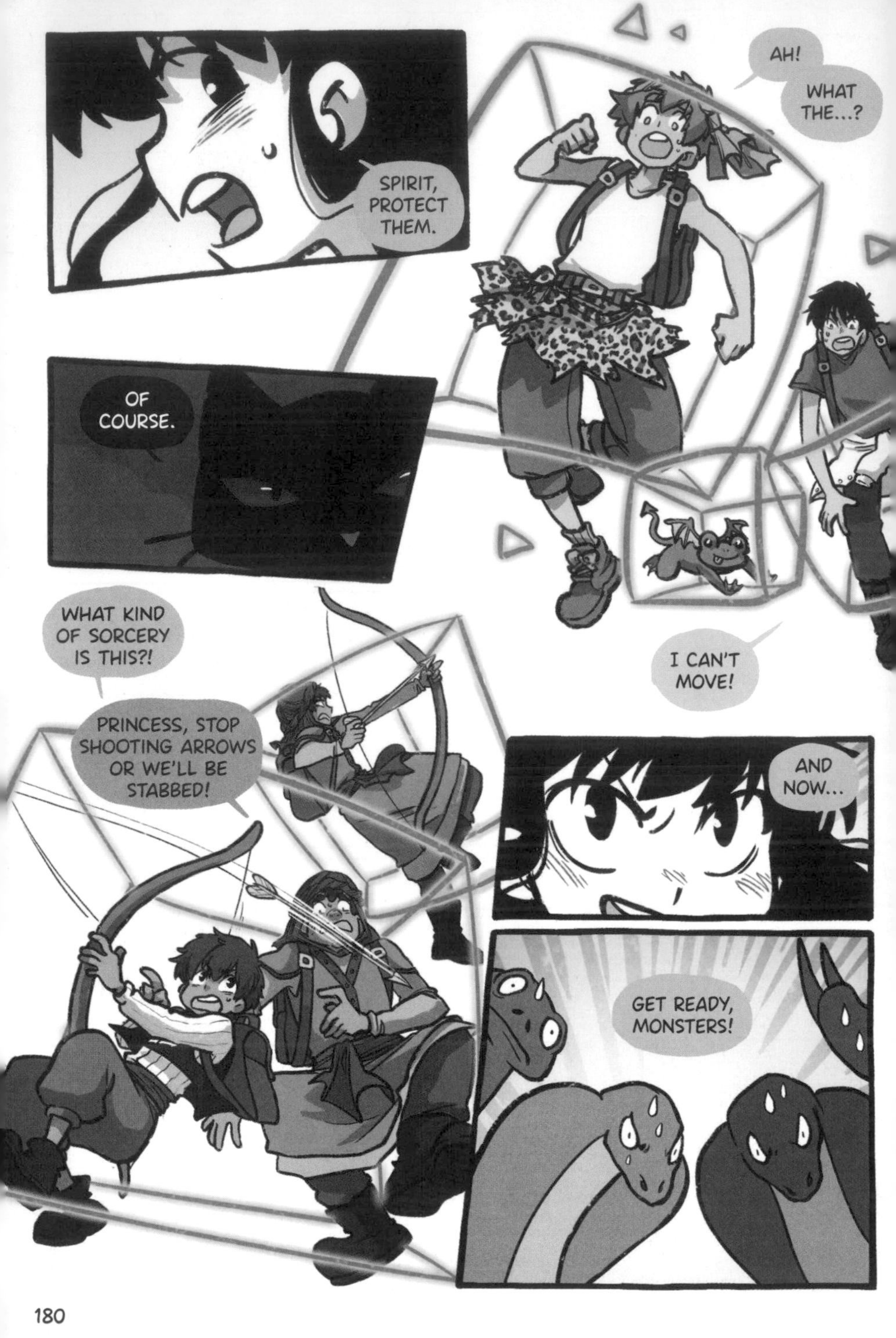
SPIRIT, PROTECT THEM.
AH!
WHAT THE...?
OF COURSE.
WHAT KIND OF SORCERY IS THIS?!
I CAN'T MOVE!
PRINCESS, STOP SHOOTING ARROWS OR WE'LL BE STABBED!
AND NOW...
GET READY, MONSTERS!

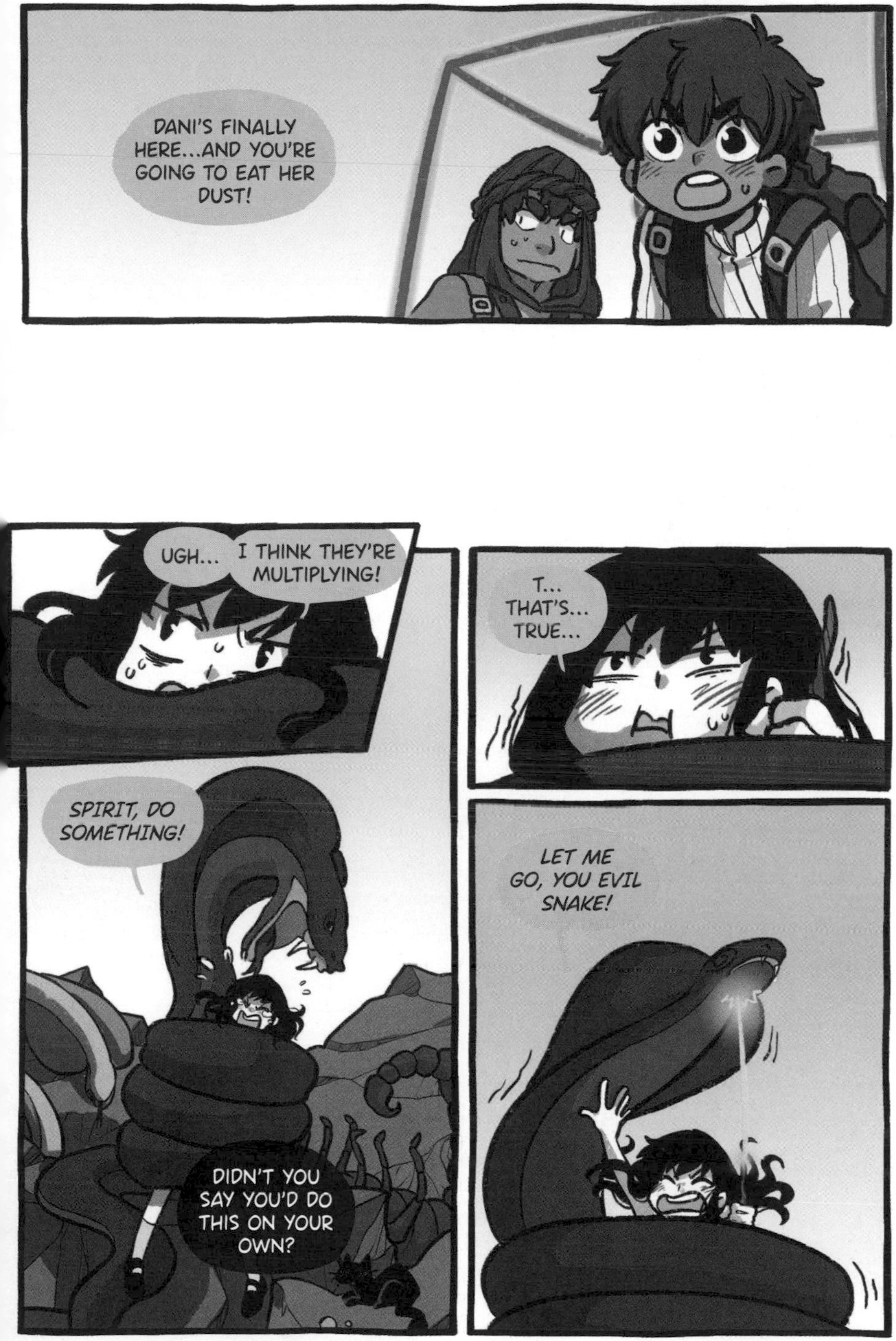
DANI'S FINALLY HERE...AND YOU'RE GOING TO EAT HER DUST!
UGH...
I THINK THEY'RE MULTIPLYING!
T... THAT'S... TRUE...
SPIRIT, DO SOMETHING!
DIDN'T YOU SAY YOU'D DO THIS ON YOUR OWN?
LET ME GO, YOU EVIL SNAKE!

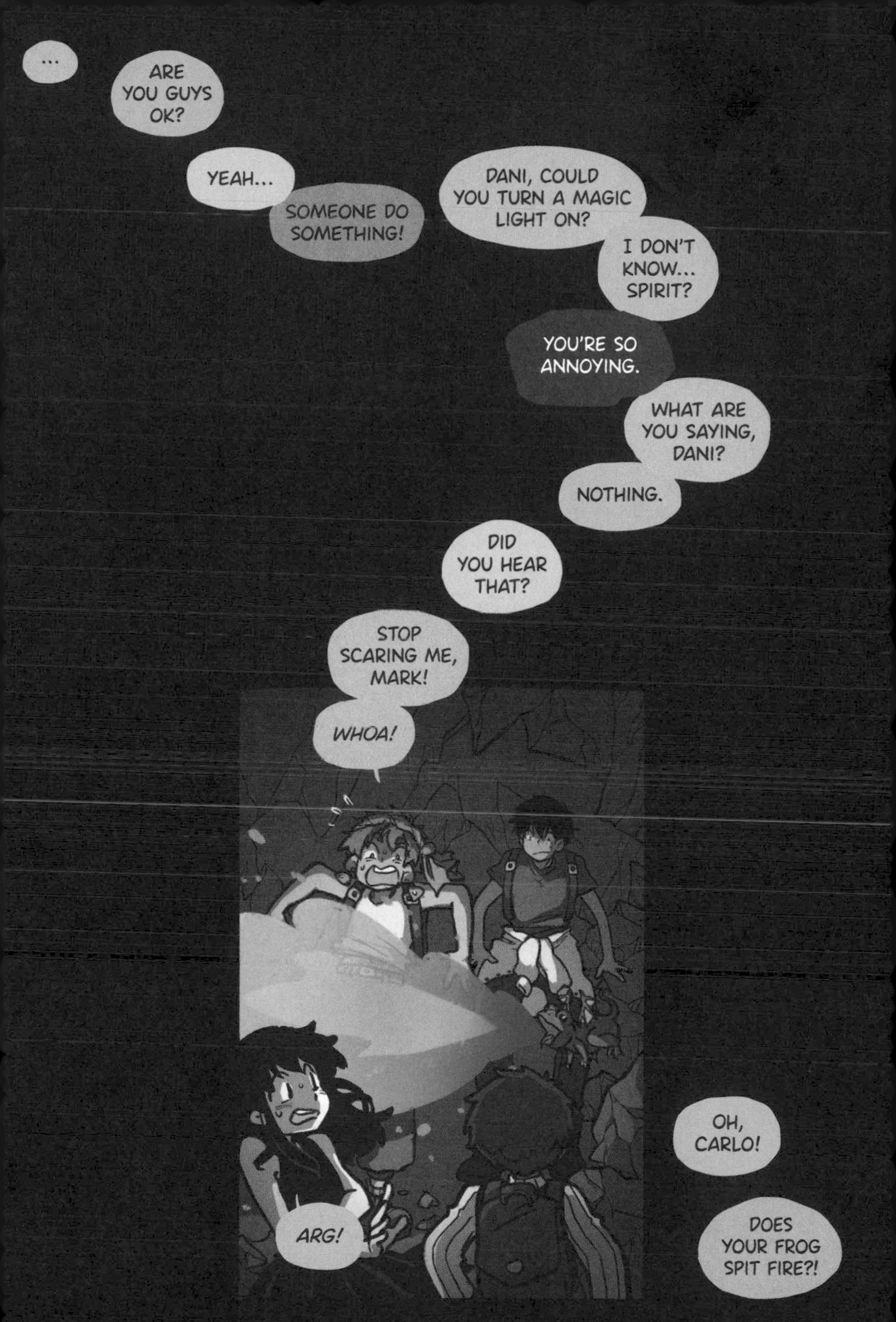
...
ARE YOU GUYS OK?
YEAH...
SOMEONE DO SOMETHING!
DANI, COULD YOU TURN A MAGIC LIGHT ON?
I DON'T KNOW... SPIRIT?
YOU'RE SO ANNOYING.
WHAT ARE YOU SAYING, DANI?
NOTHING.
DID YOU HEAR THAT?
STOP SCARING ME, MARK!
WHOA!
ARG!
OH, CARLO!
DOES YOUR FROG SPIT FIRE?!

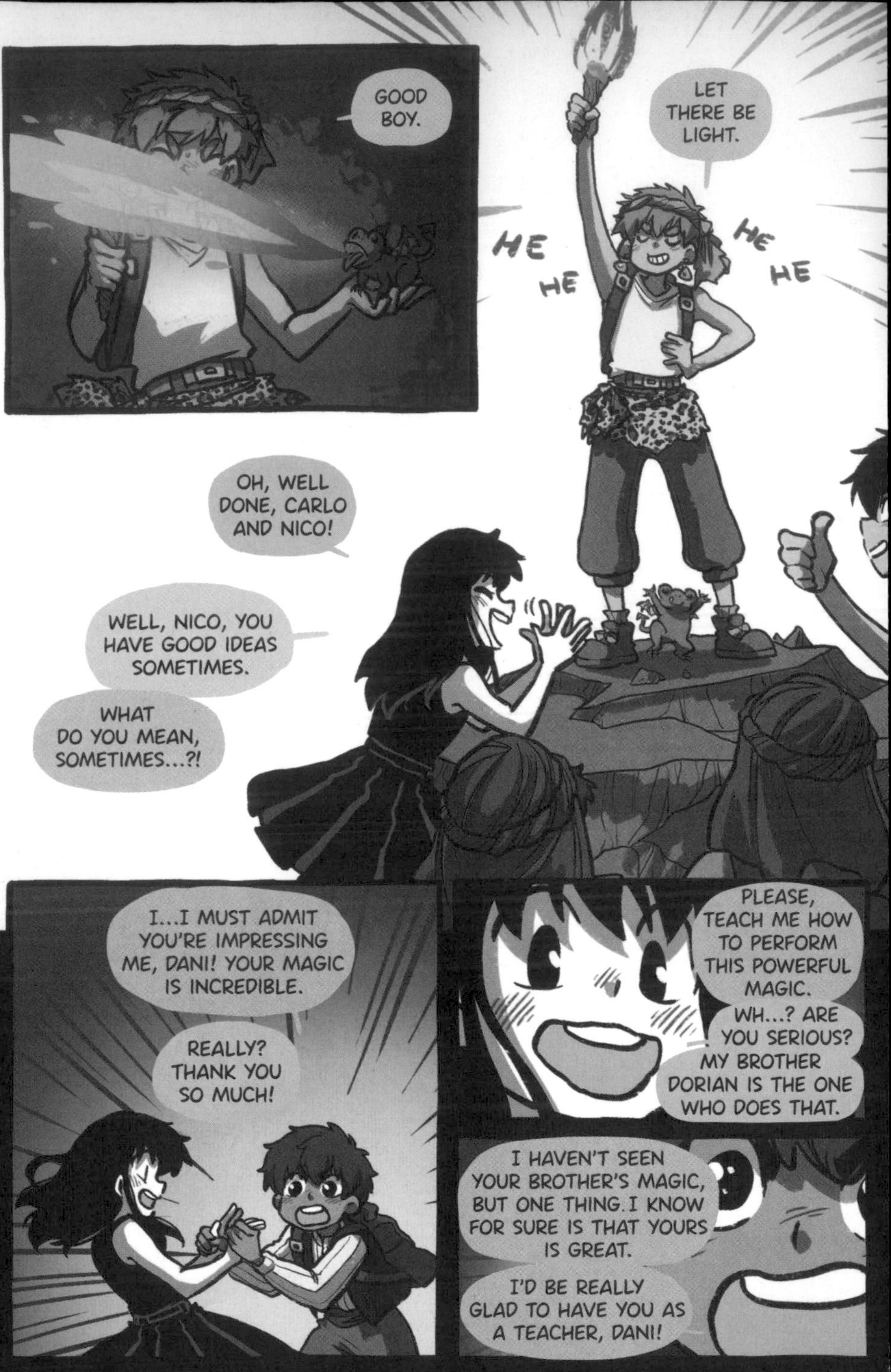
GOOD BOY.
LET THERE BE LIGHT.
HE HE
HE HE
OH, WELL DONE, CARLO AND NICO!
WELL, NICO, YOU HAVE GOOD IDEAS SOMETIMES.
WHAT DO YOU MEAN, SOMETIMES...?!
I...I MUST ADMIT YOU'RE IMPRESSING ME, DANI! YOUR MAGIC IS INCREDIBLE.
REALLY? THANK YOU SO MUCH!
PLEASE, TEACH ME HOW TO PERFORM THIS POWERFUL MAGIC.
WH...? ARE YOU SERIOUS? MY BROTHER DORIAN IS THE ONE WHO DOES THAT.
I HAVEN'T SEEN YOUR BROTHER'S MAGIC, BUT ONE THING I KNOW FOR SURE IS THAT YOURS IS GREAT.
I'D BE REALLY GLAD TO HAVE YOU AS A TEACHER, DANI!

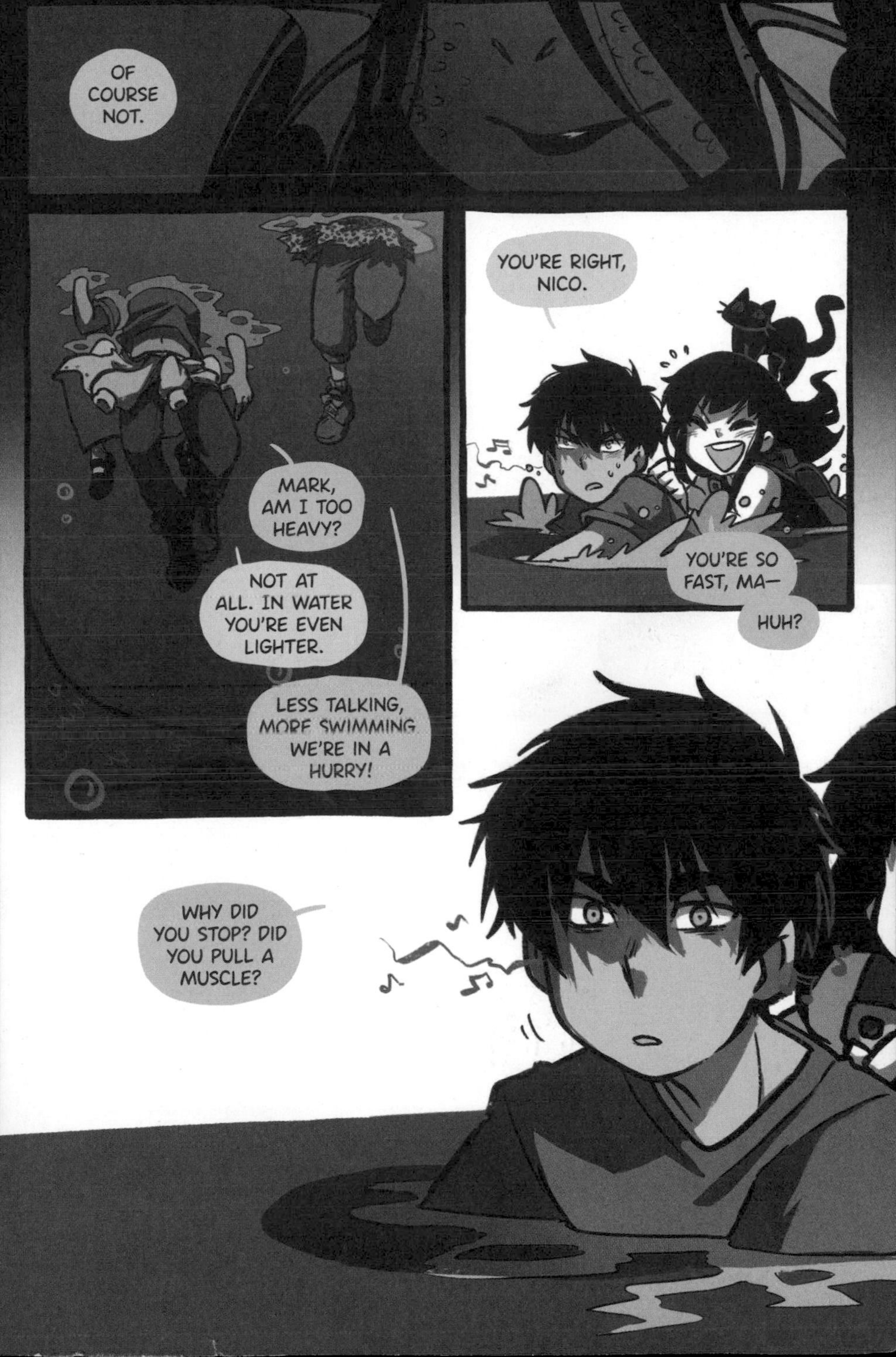
OF COURSE NOT.
MARK, AM I TOO HEAVY?
NOT AT ALL. IN WATER YOU'RE EVEN LIGHTER.
LESS TALKING, MORE SWIMMING WE'RE IN A HURRY!
YOU'RE RIGHT, NICO.
YOU'RE SO FAST, MA—
HUH?
WHY DID YOU STOP? DID YOU PULL A MUSCLE?

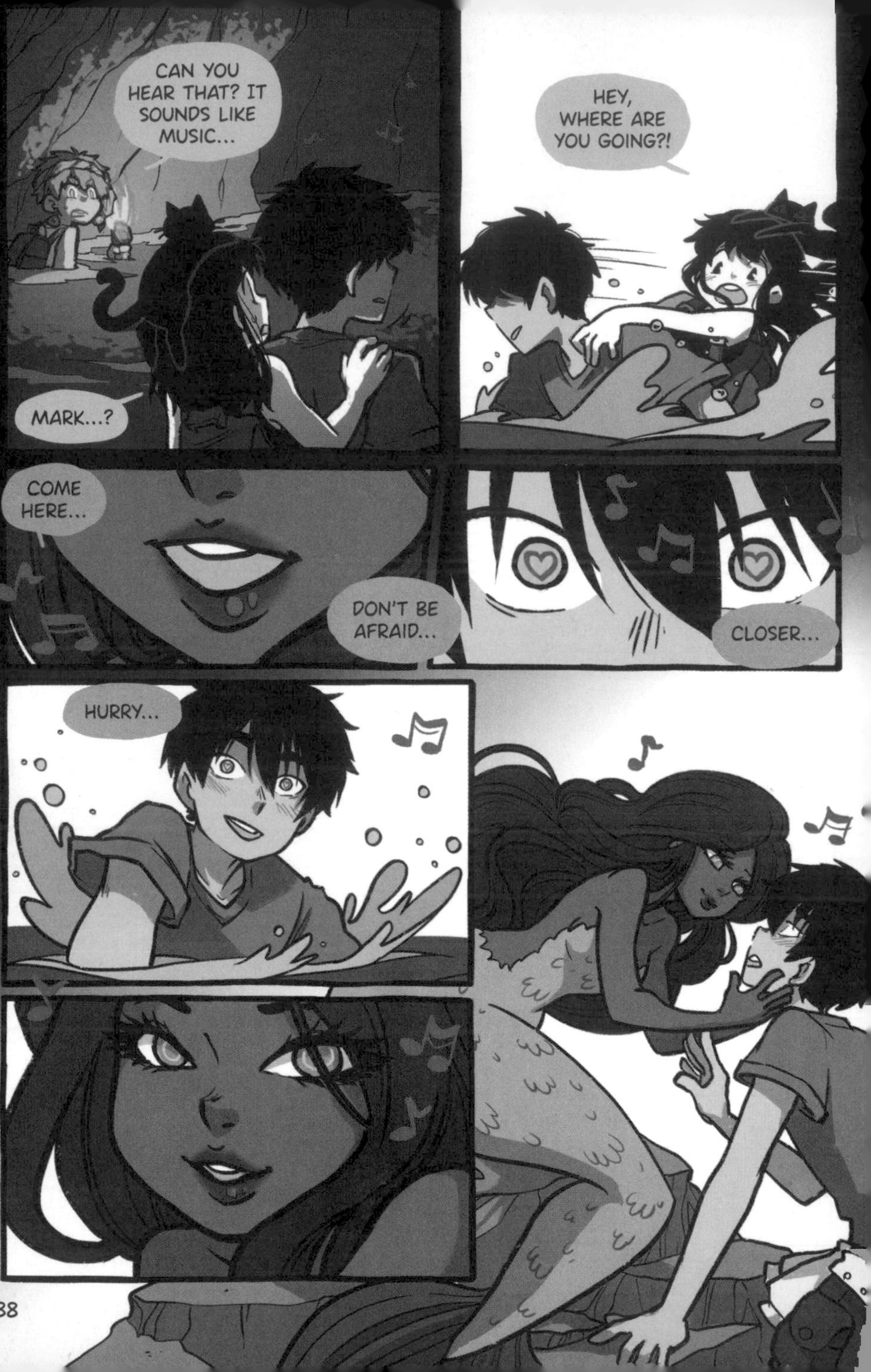
CAN YOU HEAR THAT? IT SOUNDS LIKE MUSIC...
MARK...?
HEY, WHERE ARE YOU GOING?!
COME HERE...
DON'T BE AFRAID...
CLOSER...
HURRY...

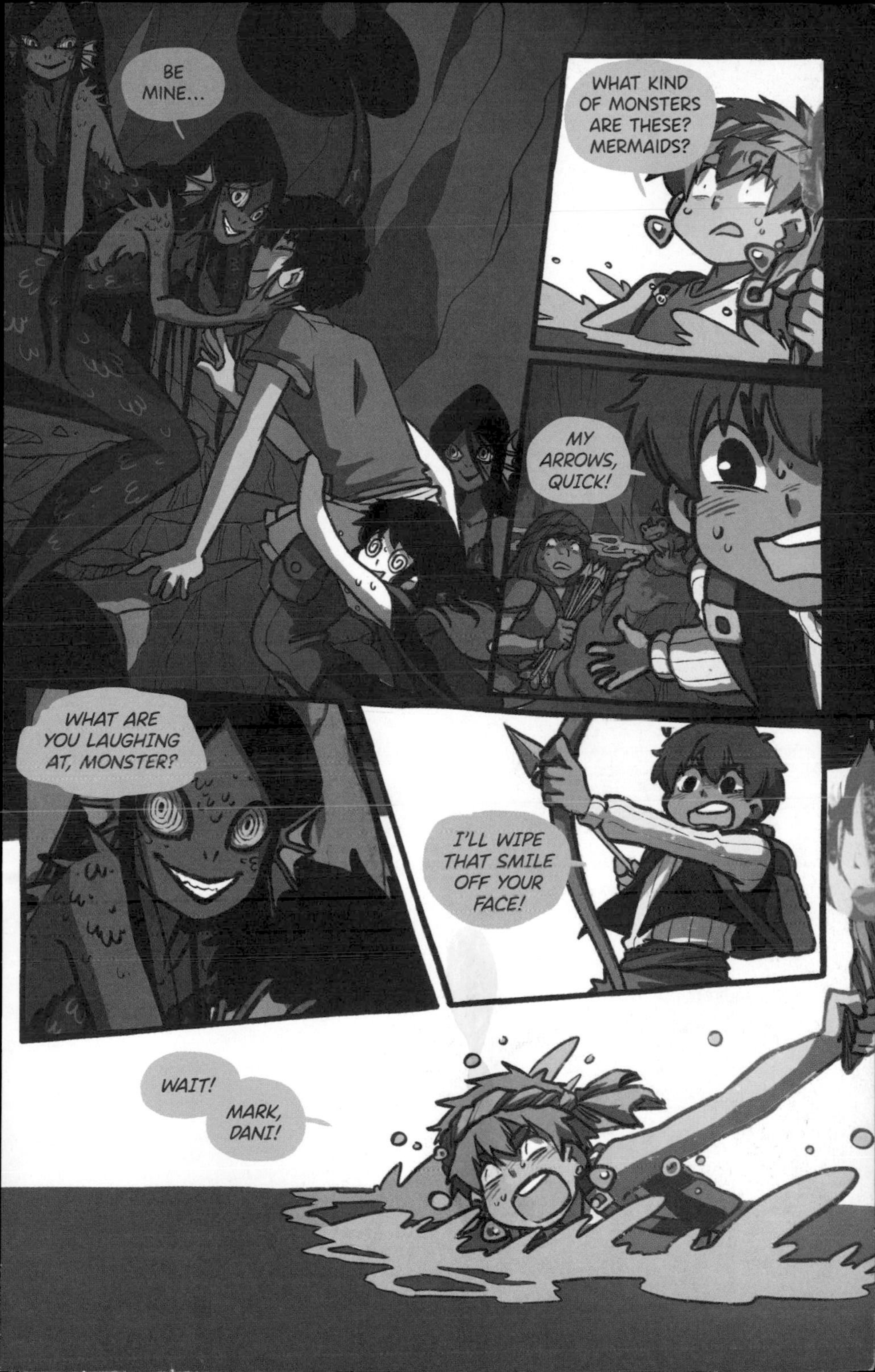
BE MINE...
WHAT KIND OF MONSTERS ARE THESE? MERMAIDS?
MY ARROWS, QUICK!
WHAT ARE YOU LAUGHING AT, MONSTER?
I'LL WIPE THAT SMILE OFF YOUR FACE!
WAIT!
MARK, DANI!

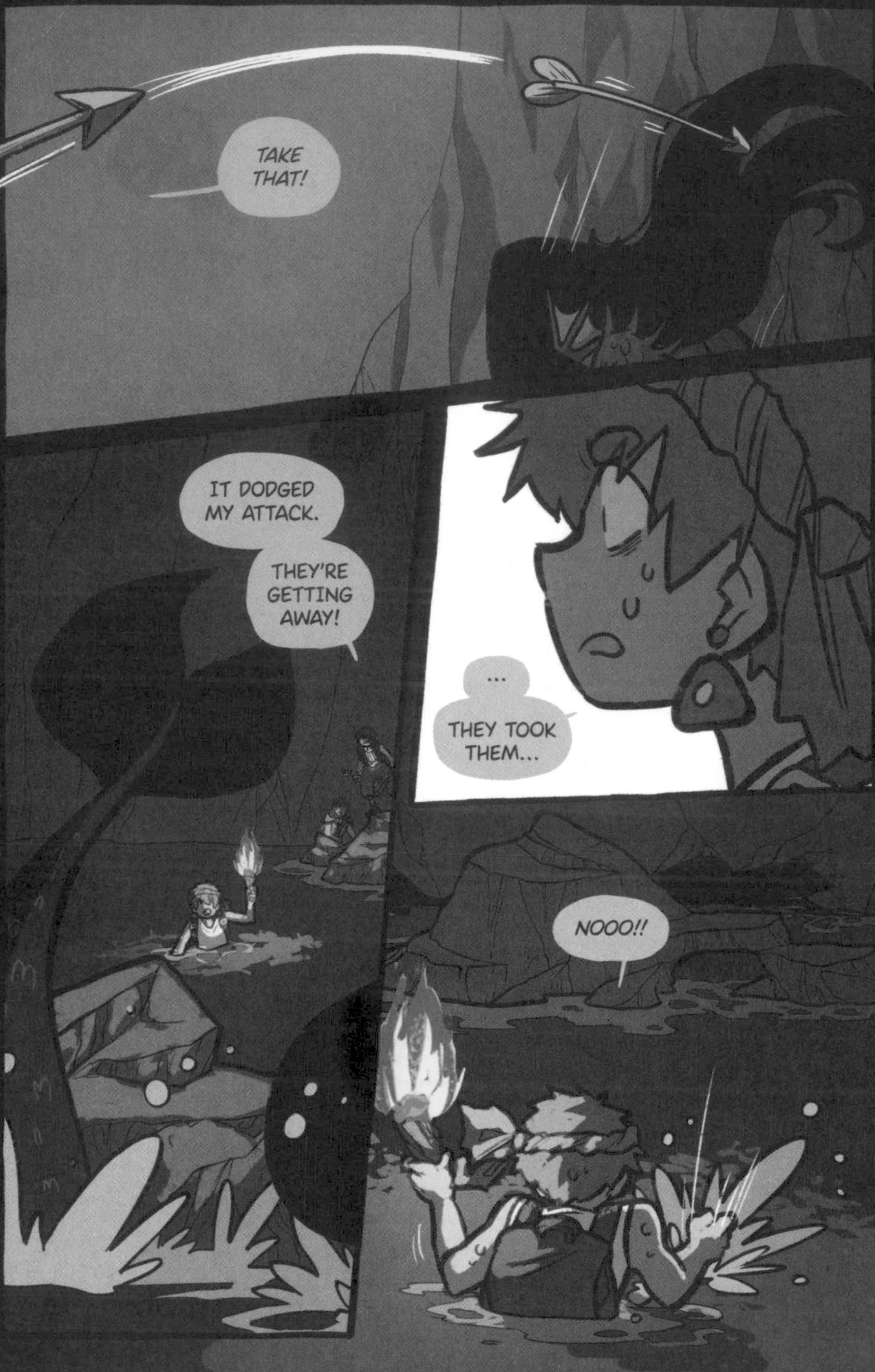
TAKE THAT!
IT DODGED MY ATTACK.
THEY'RE GETTING AWAY!
...
THEY TOOK THEM...
NOOO!!

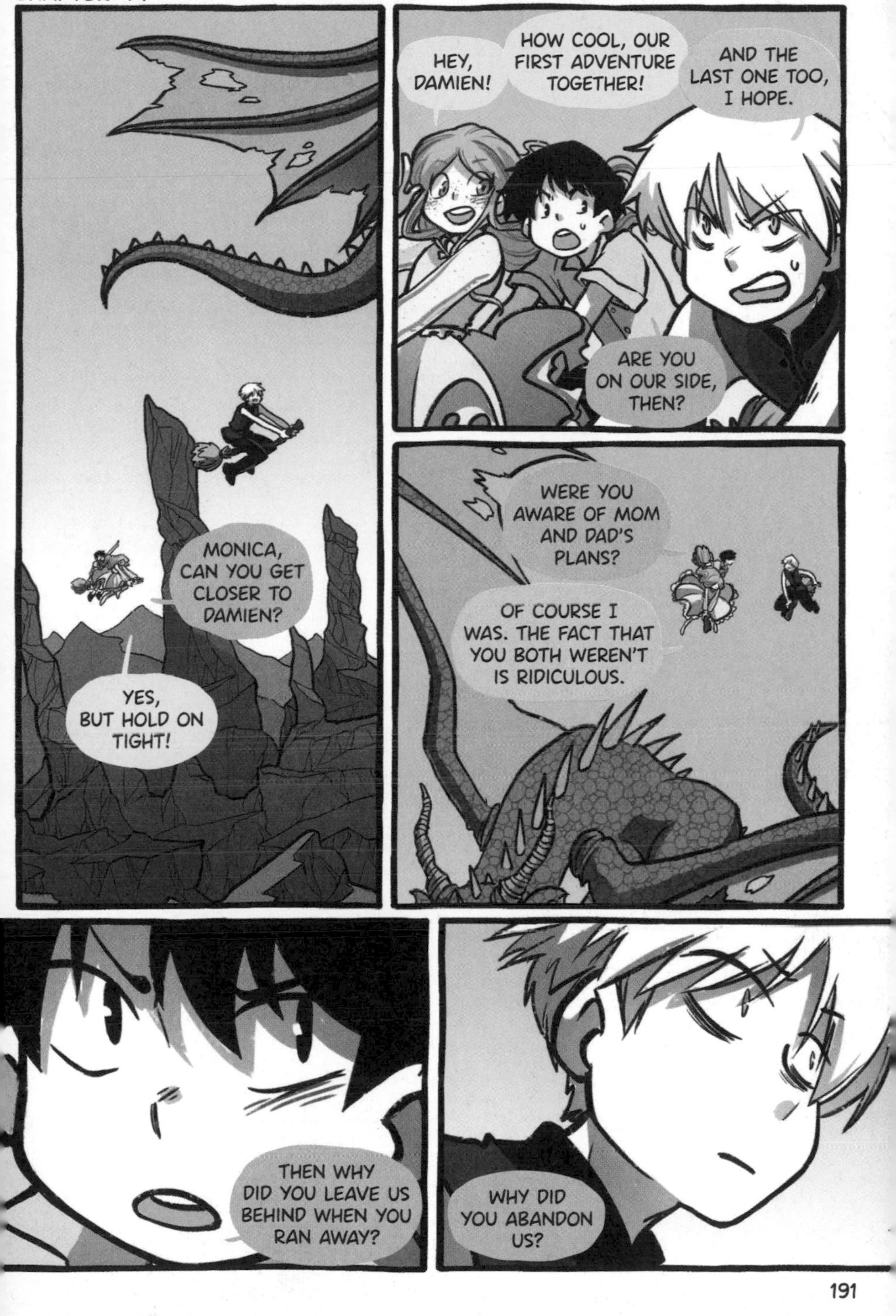
MONICA, CAN YOU GET CLOSER TO DAMIEN?
YES, BUT HOLD ON TIGHT!
HEY, DAMIEN!
HOW COOL, OUR FIRST ADVENTURE TOGETHER!
AND THE LAST ONE TOO, I HOPE.
ARE YOU ON OUR SIDE, THEN?
WERE YOU AWARE OF MOM AND DAD'S PLANS?
OF COURSE I WAS. THE FACT THAT YOU BOTH WEREN'T IS RIDICULOUS.
THEN WHY DID YOU LEAVE US BEHIND WHEN YOU RAN AWAY?
WHY DID YOU ABANDON US?

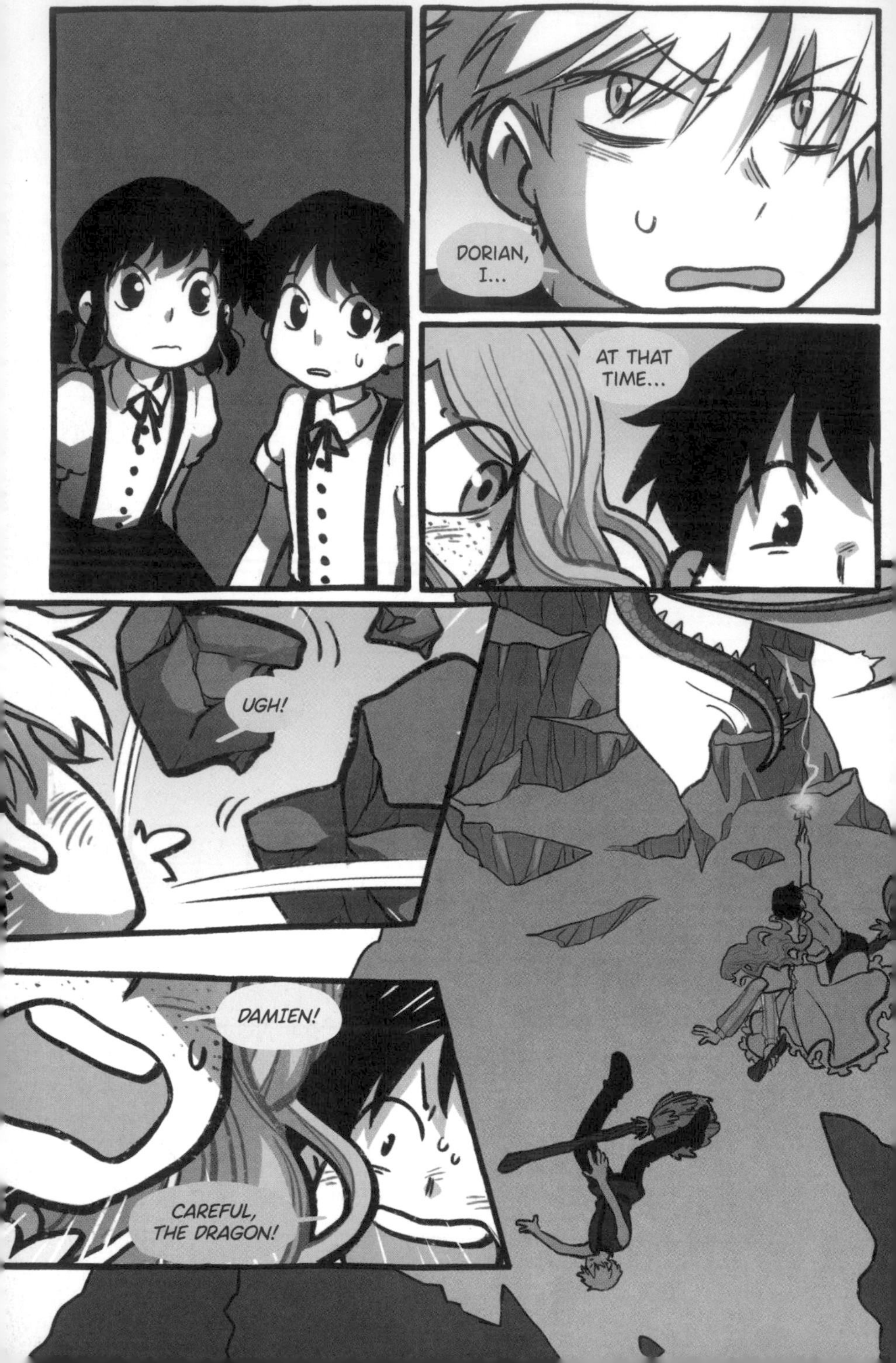
DORIAN,
I...
AT THAT
TIME...
UGH!
DAMIEN!
CAREFUL,
THE DRAGON!

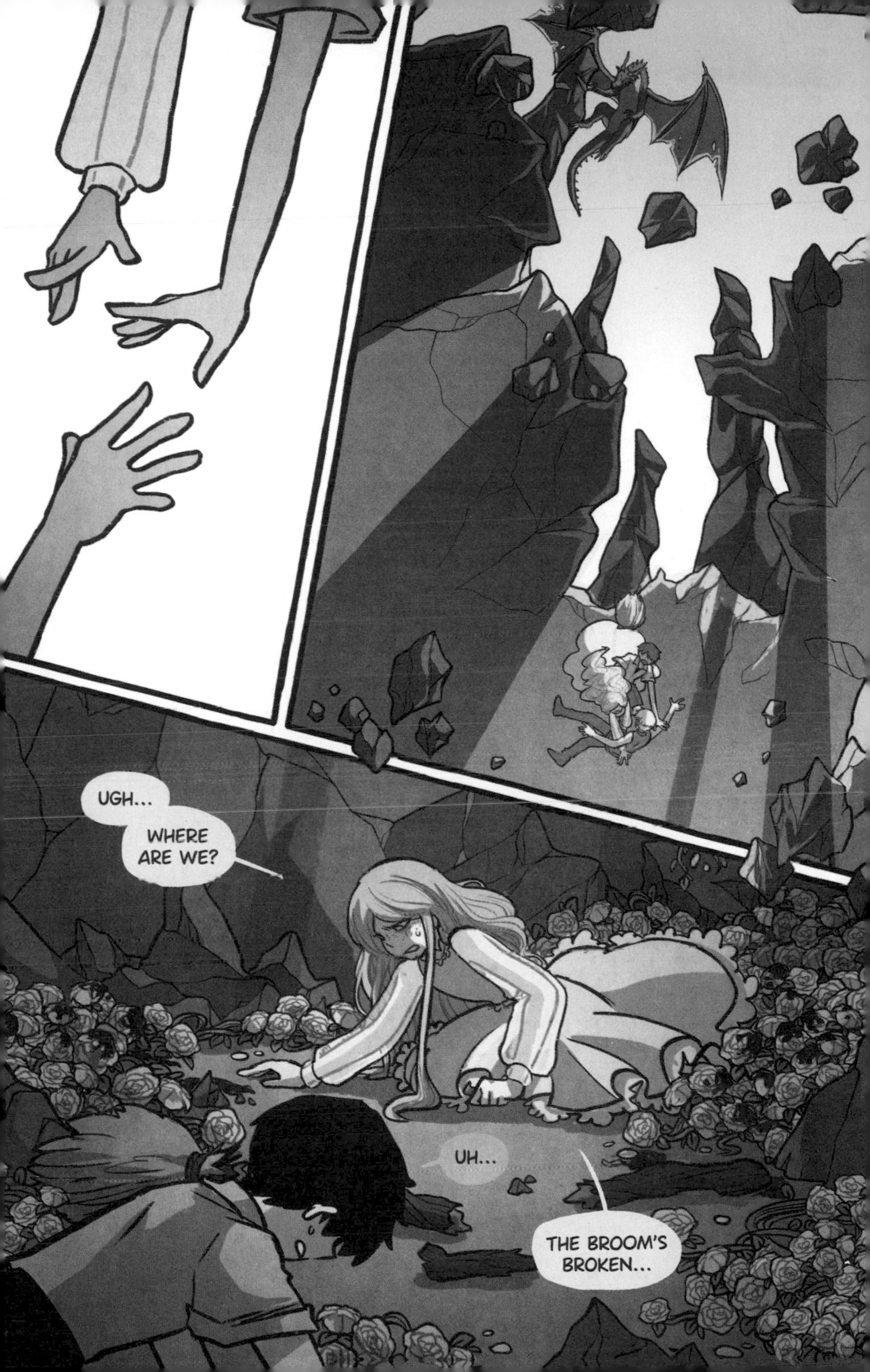
UGH...
WHERE ARE WE?
UH...
THE BROOM'S BROKEN...

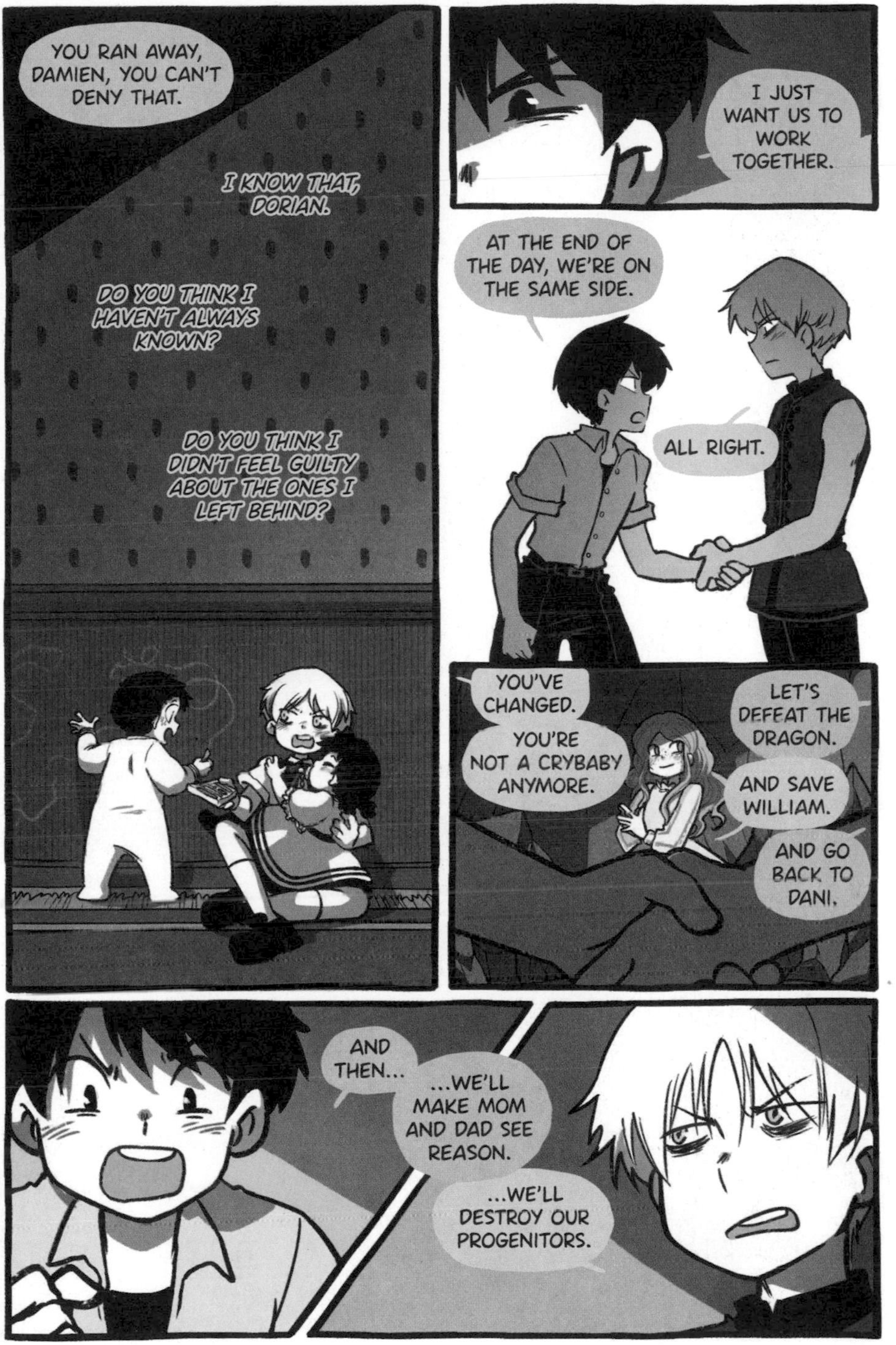
YOU RAN AWAY, DAMIEN, YOU CAN'T DENY THAT.
I JUST WANT US TO WORK TOGETHER.
I KNOW THAT, DORIAN.
DO YOU THINK I HAVEN'T ALWAYS KNOWN?
DO YOU THINK I DIDN'T FEEL GUILTY ABOUT THE ONES I LEFT BEHIND?
AT THE END OF THE DAY, WE'RE ON THE SAME SIDE.
ALL RIGHT.
YOU'VE CHANGED.
YOU'RE NOT A CRYBABY ANYMORE.
LET'S DEFEAT THE DRAGON.
AND SAVE WILLIAM.
AND GO BACK TO DANI.
AND THEN...
...WE'LL MAKE MOM AND DAD SEE REASON.
...WE'LL DESTROY OUR PROGENITORS.

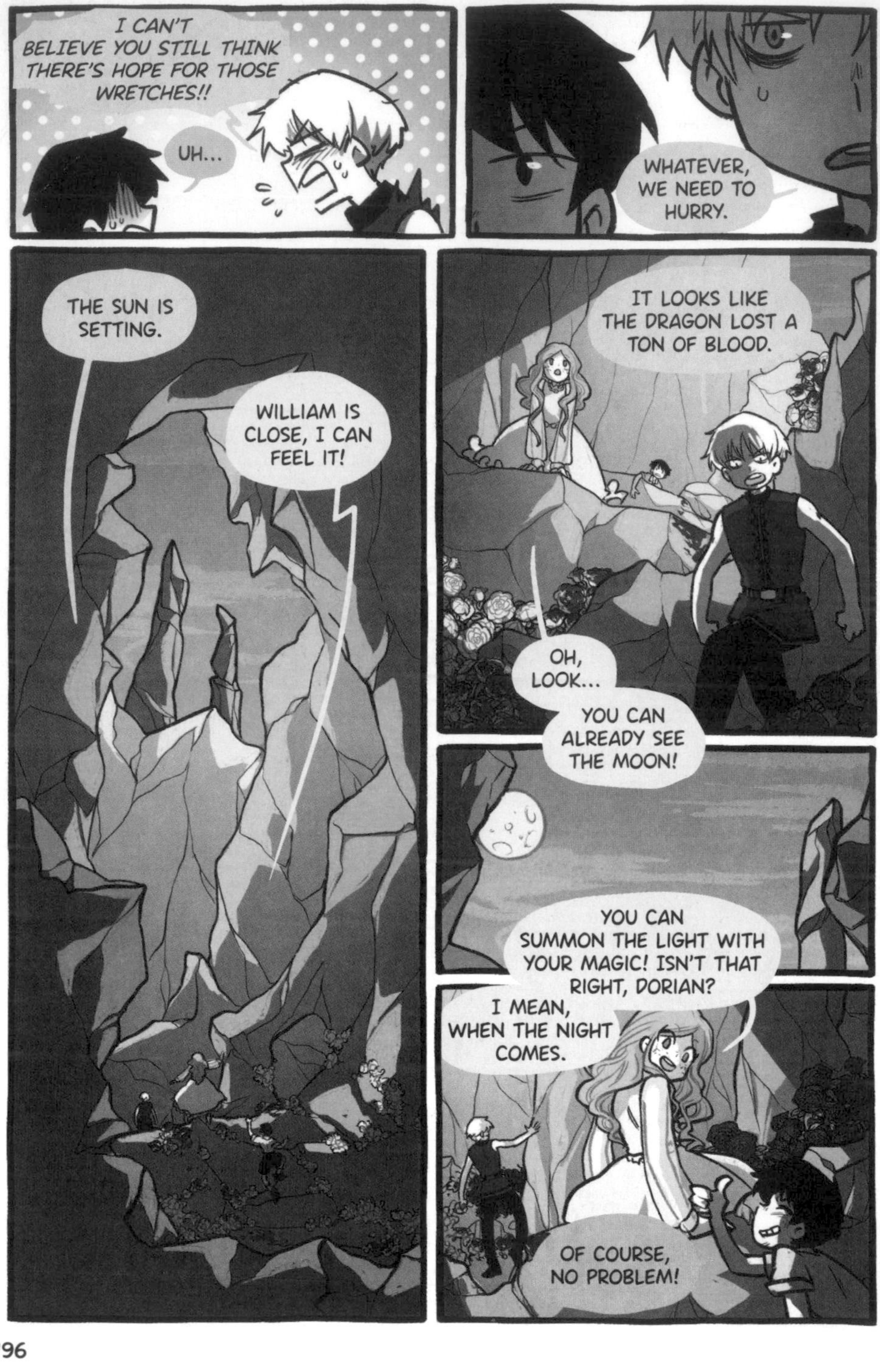
I CAN'T BELIEVE YOU STILL THINK THERE'S HOPE FOR THOSE WRETCHES!!
UH...
WHATEVER, WE NEED TO HURRY.
THE SUN IS SETTING.
WILLIAM IS CLOSE, I CAN FEEL IT!
IT LOOKS LIKE THE DRAGON LOST A TON OF BLOOD.
OH, LOOK...
YOU CAN ALREADY SEE THE MOON!
YOU CAN SUMMON THE LIGHT WITH YOUR MAGIC! ISN'T THAT RIGHT, DORIAN?
I MEAN, WHEN THE NIGHT COMES.
OF COURSE, NO PROBLEM!

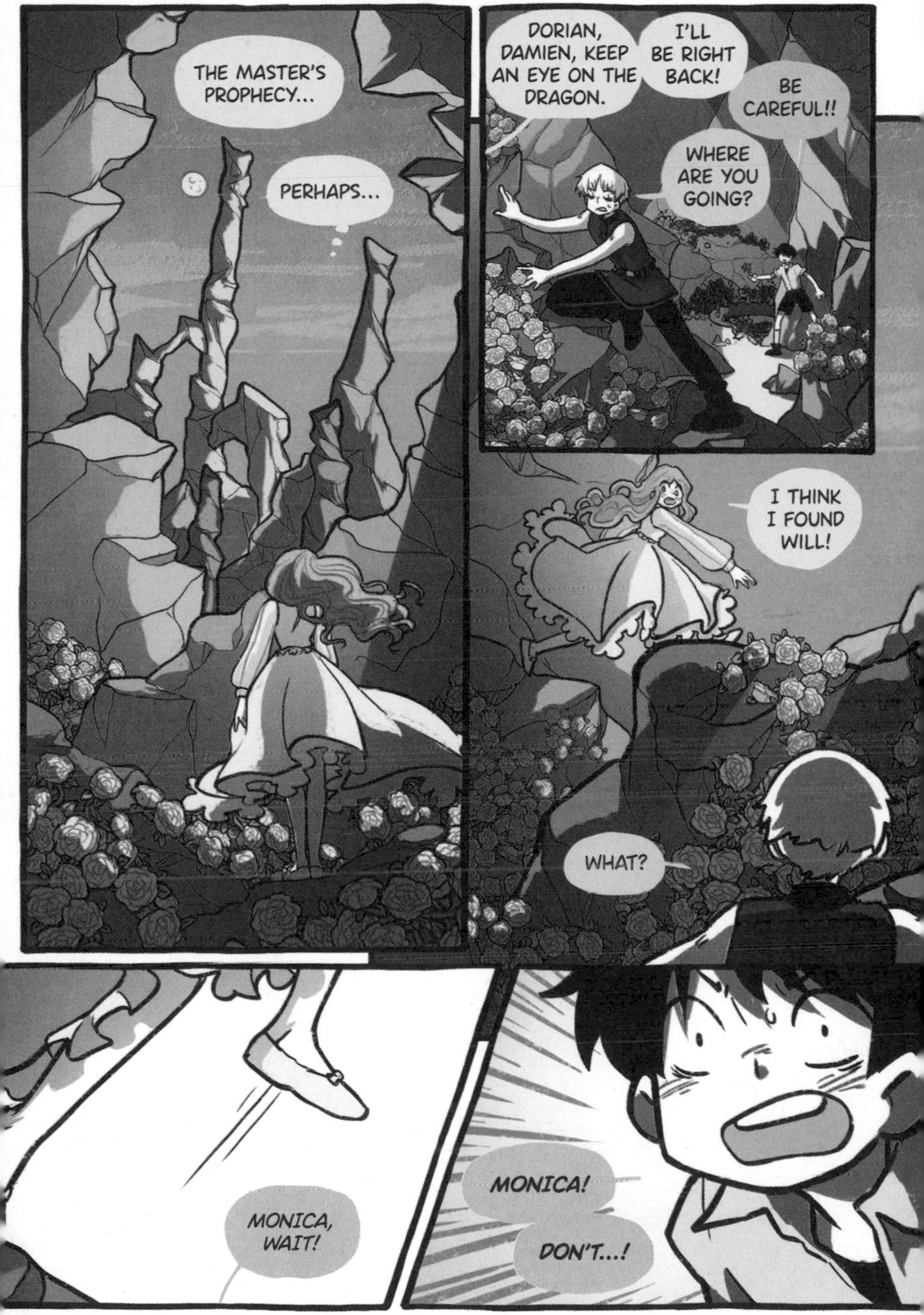
THE MASTER'S PROPHECY...
PERHAPS...
DORIAN, DAMIEN, KEEP AN EYE ON THE DRAGON.
I'LL BE RIGHT BACK!
BE CAREFUL!!
WHERE ARE YOU GOING?
I THINK I FOUND WILL!
WHAT?
MONICA, WAIT!
MONICA!
DON'T...!

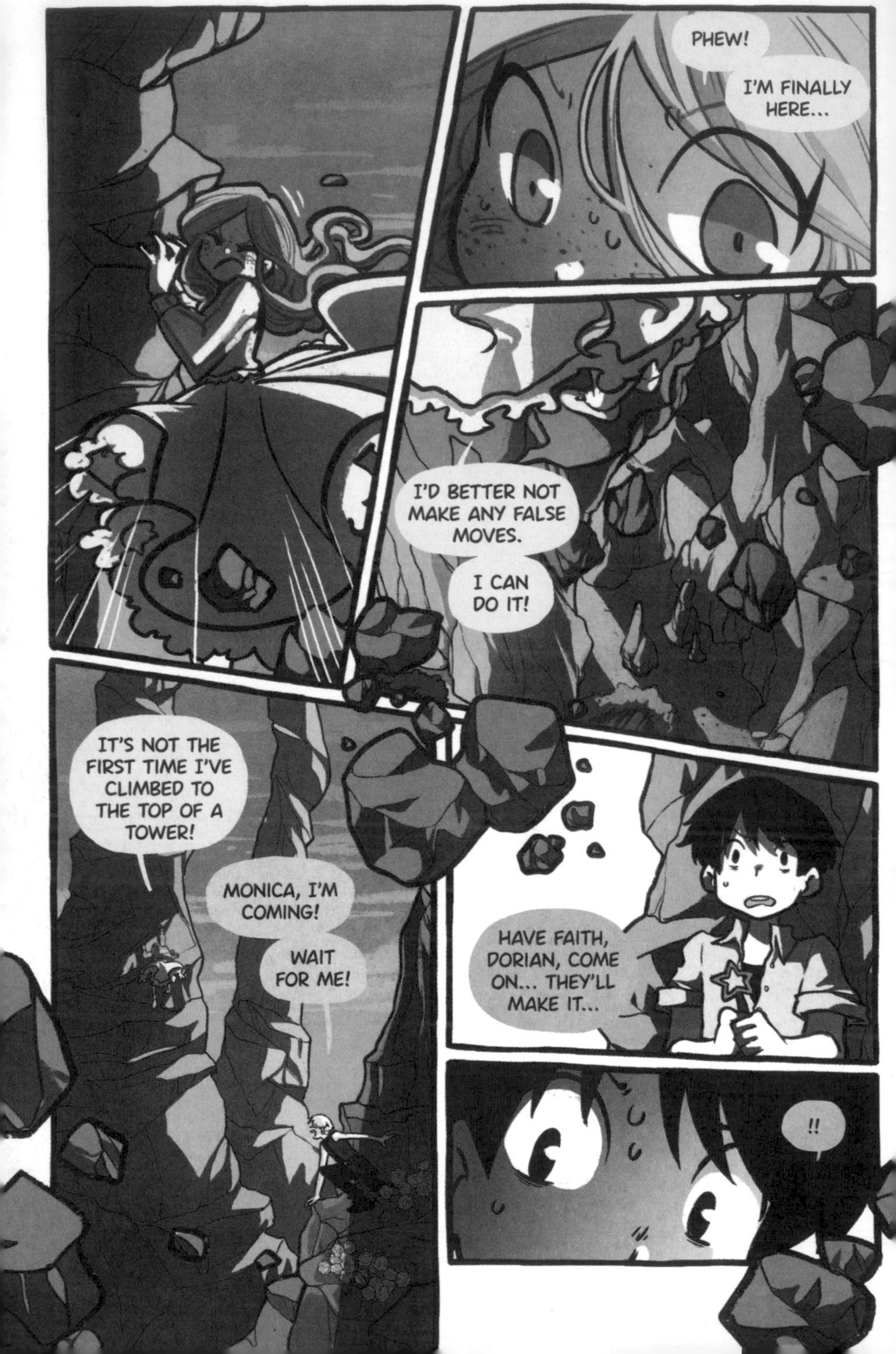
PHEW!
I'M FINALLY HERE...
I'D BETTER NOT MAKE ANY FALSE MOVES.
I CAN DO IT!
IT'S NOT THE FIRST TIME I'VE CLIMBED TO THE TOP OF A TOWER!
MONICA, I'M COMING!
WAIT FOR ME!
HAVE FAITH, DORIAN, COME ON... THEY'LL MAKE IT...
!!

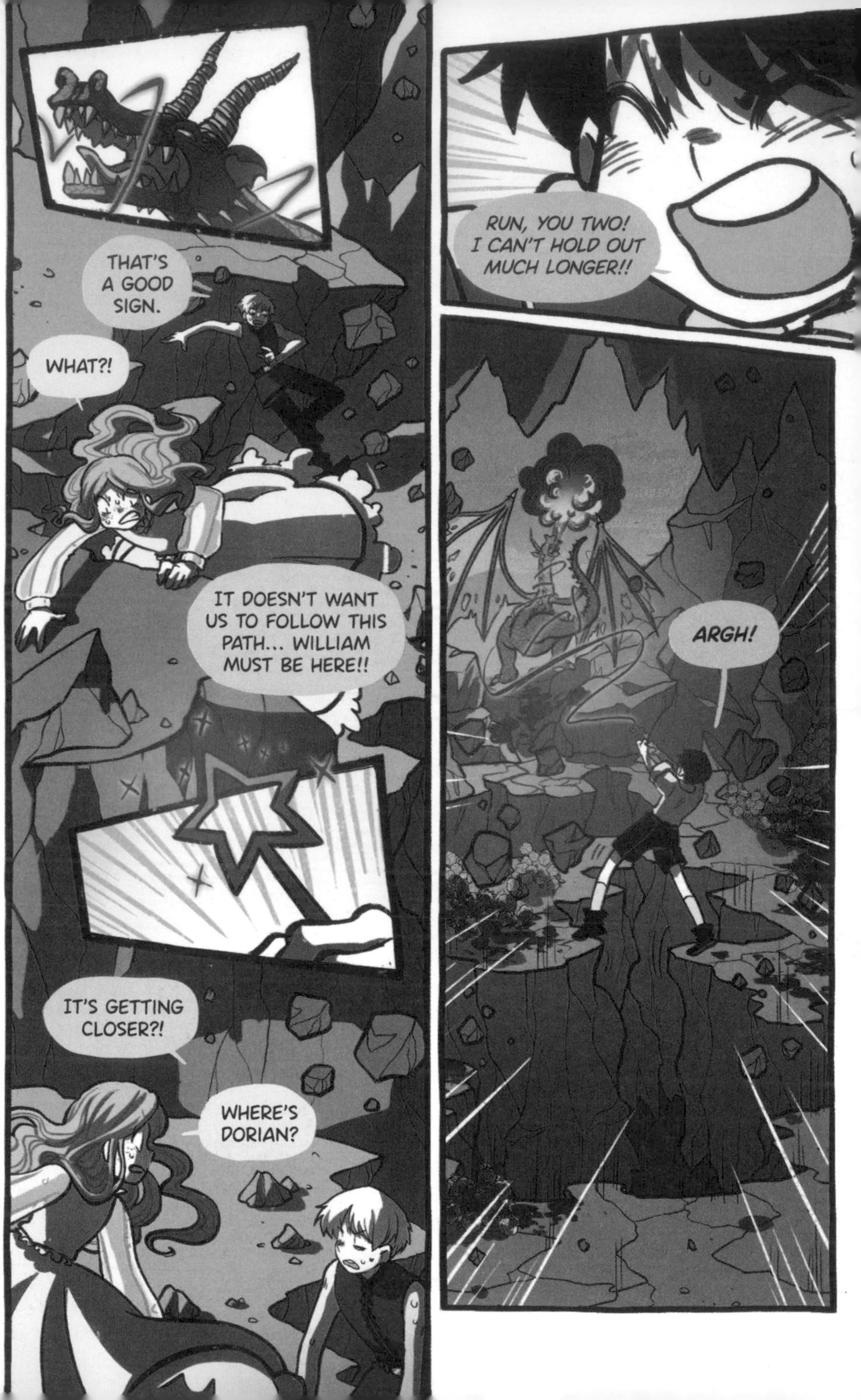
THAT'S A GOOD SIGN.
WHAT?!
IT DOESN'T WANT US TO FOLLOW THIS PATH... WILLIAM MUST BE HERE!!
IT'S GETTING CLOSER?!
WHERE'S DORIAN?
RUN, YOU TWO! I CAN'T HOLD OUT MUCH LONGER!!
ARGH!

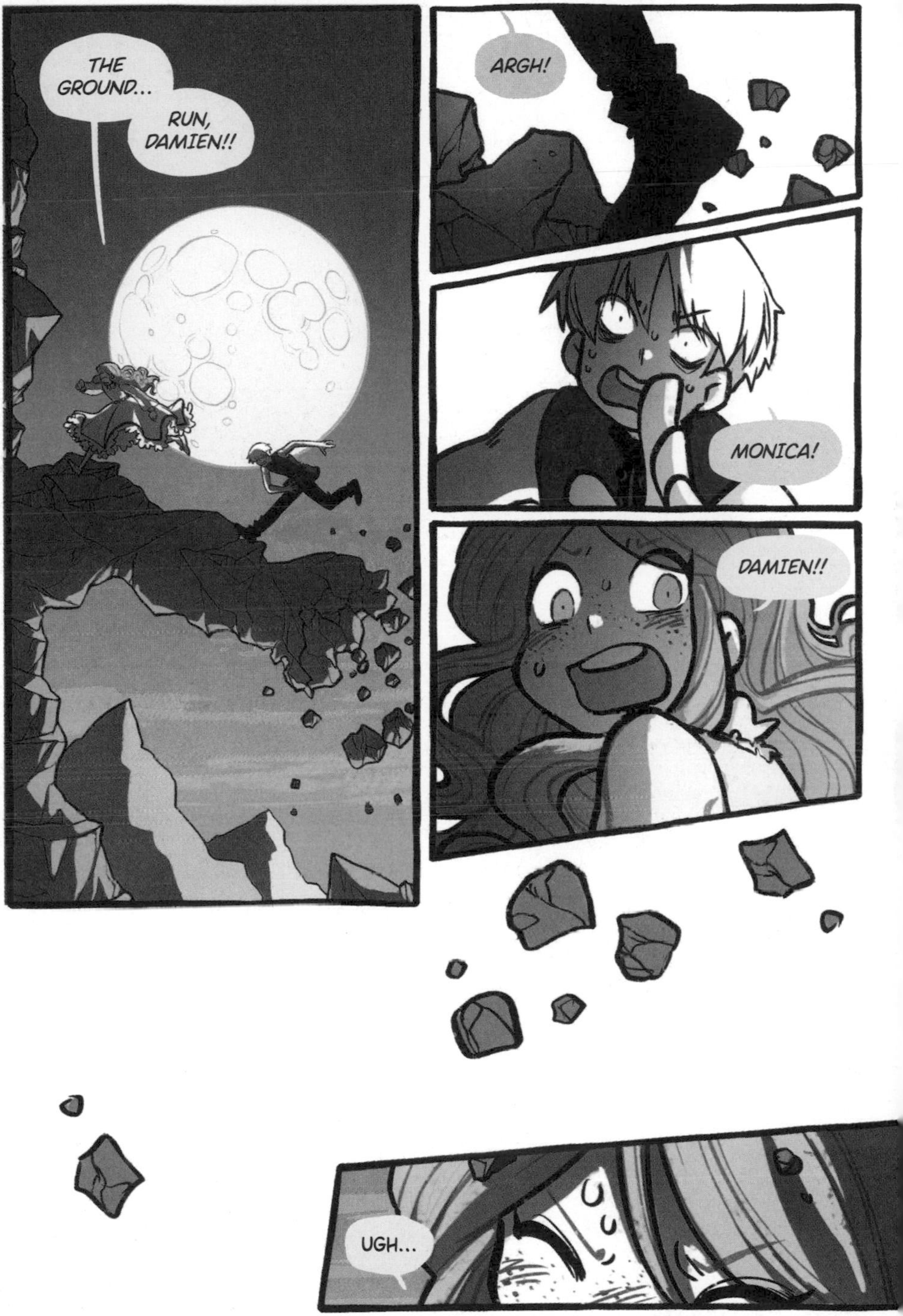
THE GROUND...
RUN, DAMIEN!!
ARGH!
MONICA!
DAMIEN!!
UGH...

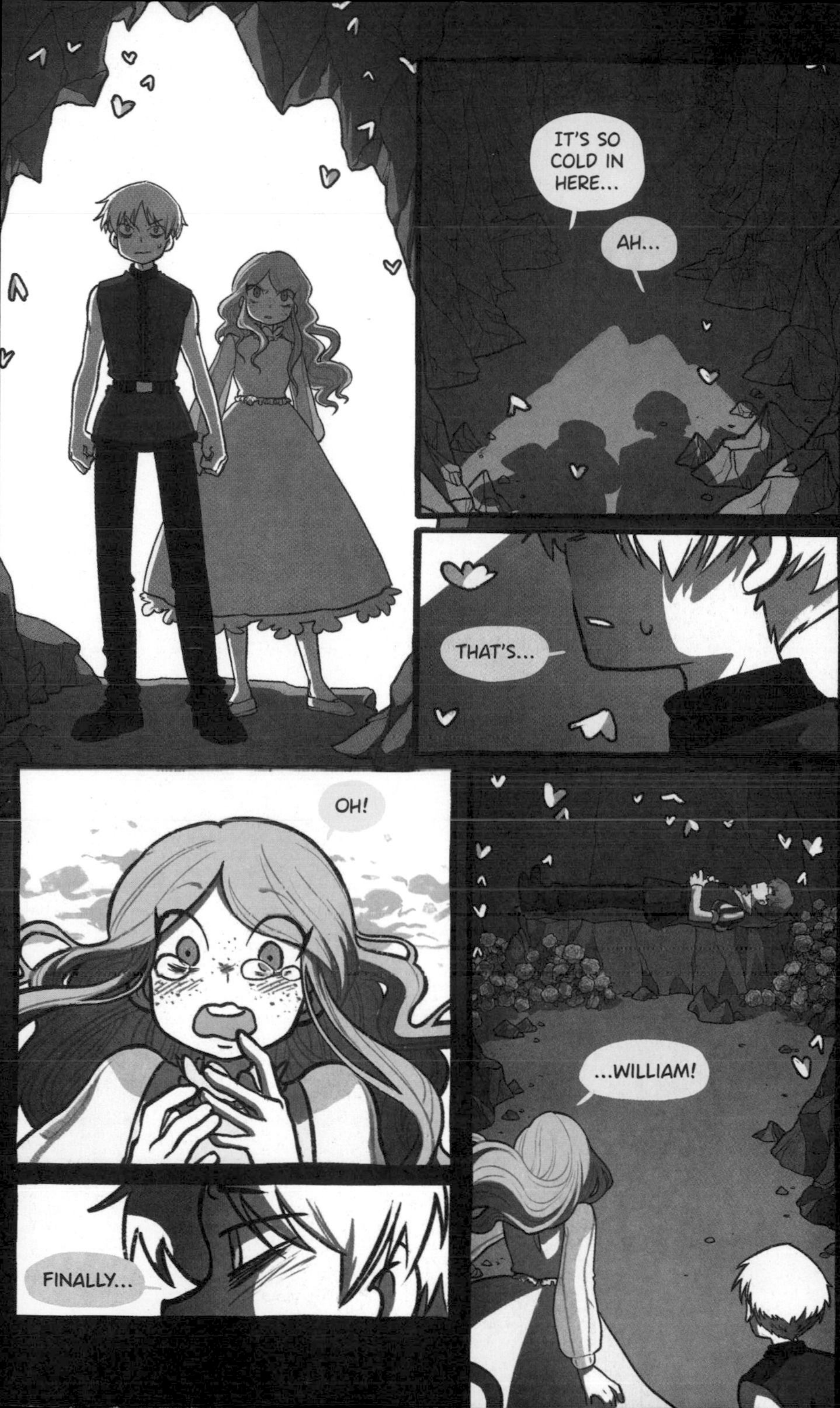
IT'S SO COLD IN HERE...
AH...
THAT'S...
OH!
FINALLY...
...WILLIAM!

212

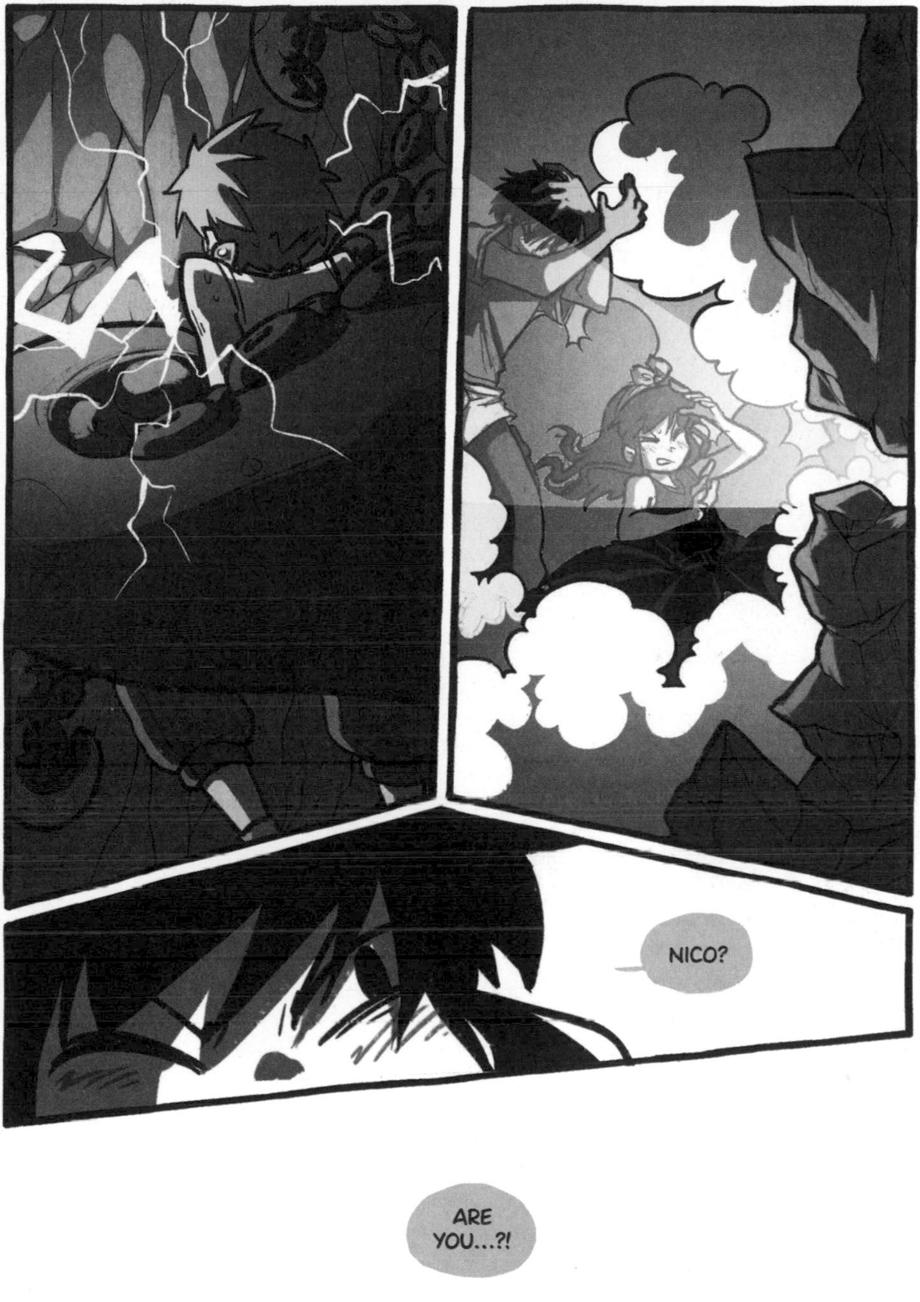
NICO?
ARE YOU...?!

CHAPTER 46

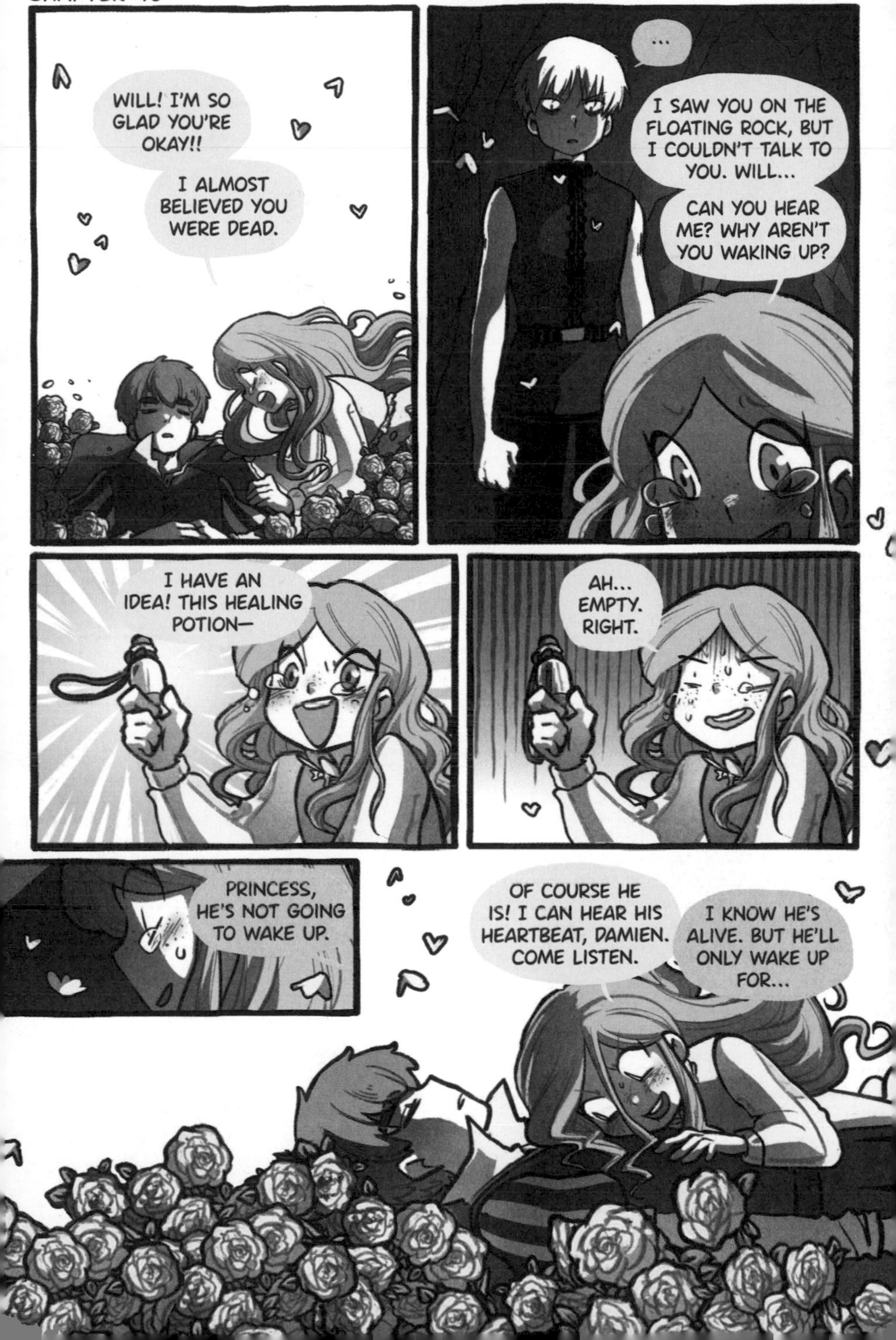
WILL! I'M SO GLAD YOU'RE OKAY!!
I ALMOST BELIEVED YOU WERE DEAD.
...
I SAW YOU ON THE FLOATING ROCK, BUT I COULDN'T TALK TO YOU. WILL...
CAN YOU HEAR ME? WHY AREN'T YOU WAKING UP?
I HAVE AN IDEA! THIS HEALING POTION—
AH... EMPTY. RIGHT.
PRINCESS, HE'S NOT GOING TO WAKE UP.
OF COURSE HE IS! I CAN HEAR HIS HEARTBEAT, DAMIEN. COME LISTEN.
I KNOW HE'S ALIVE. BUT HE'LL ONLY WAKE UP FOR...

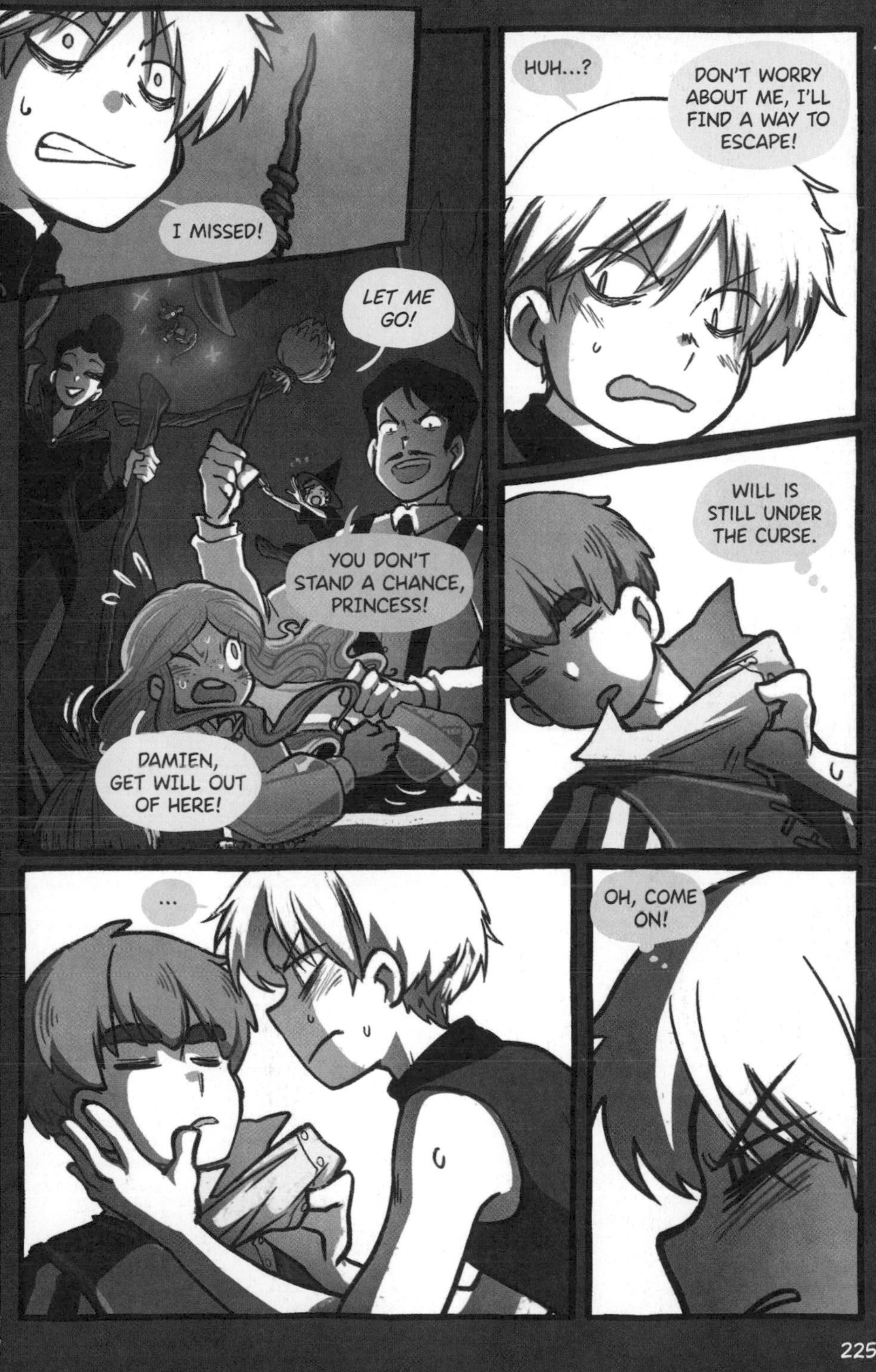
I MISSED!
LET ME GO!
YOU DON'T STAND A CHANCE, PRINCESS!
DAMIEN, GET WILL OUT OF HERE!
HUH...?
DON'T WORRY ABOUT ME, I'LL FIND A WAY TO ESCAPE!
WILL IS STILL UNDER THE CURSE.
...
OH, COME ON!

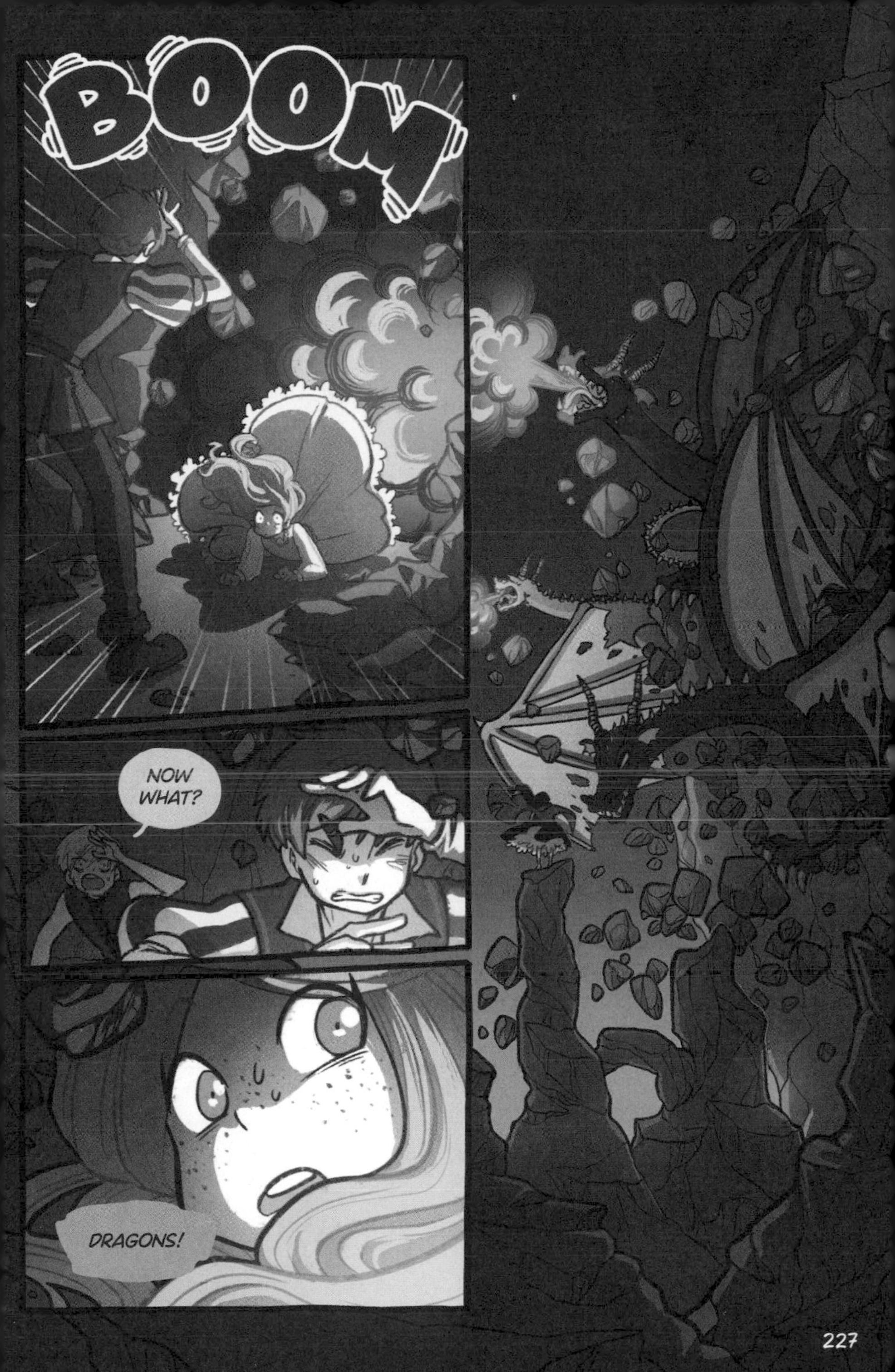
BOOM
NOW WHAT?
DRAGONS!

231

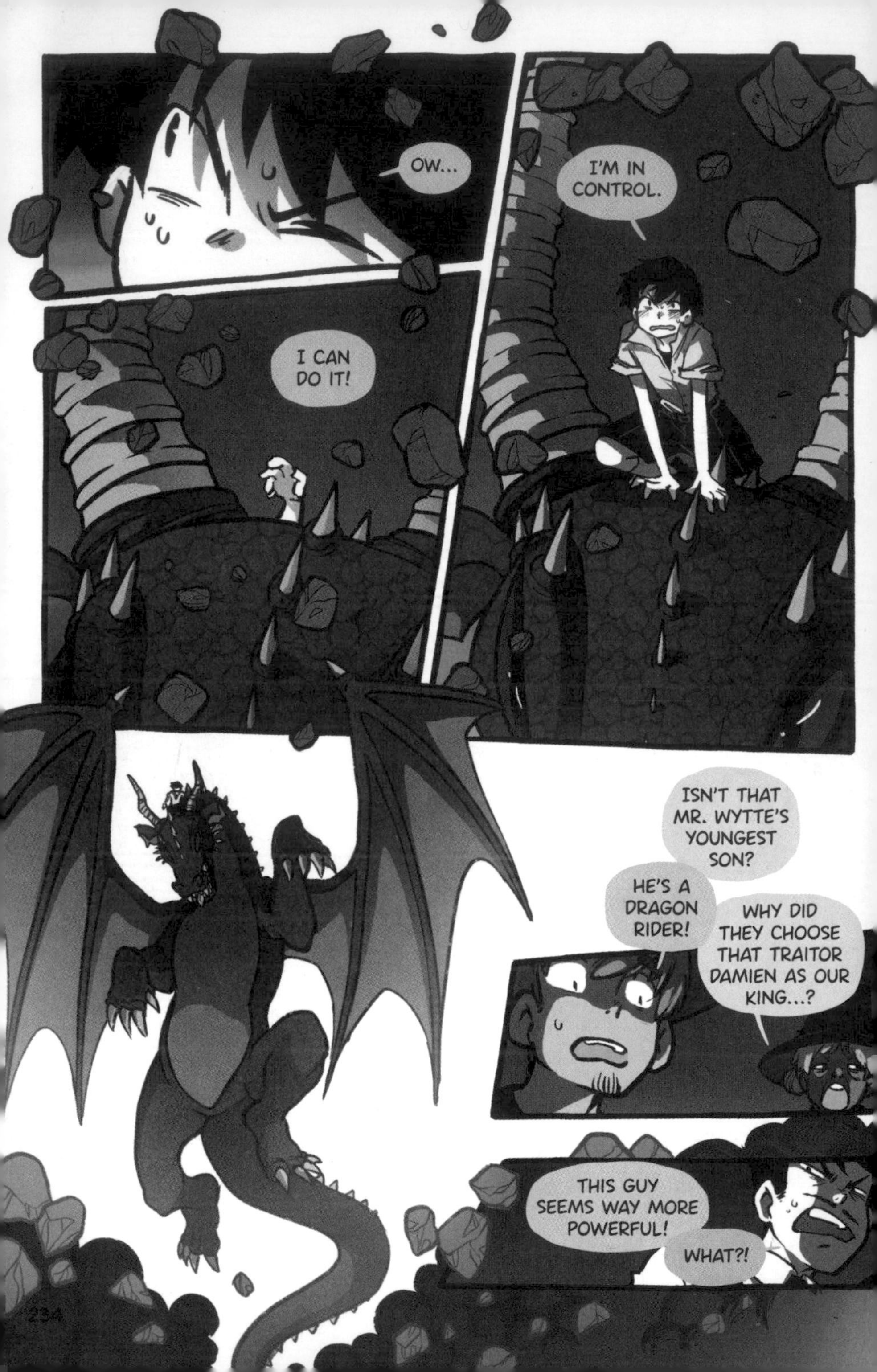
OW...
I'M IN CONTROL.
I CAN DO IT!
ISN'T THAT MR. WYTTE'S YOUNGEST SON?
HE'S A DRAGON RIDER!
WHY DID THEY CHOOSE THAT TRAITOR DAMIEN AS OUR KING...?
THIS GUY SEEMS WAY MORE POWERFUL!
WHAT?!

240

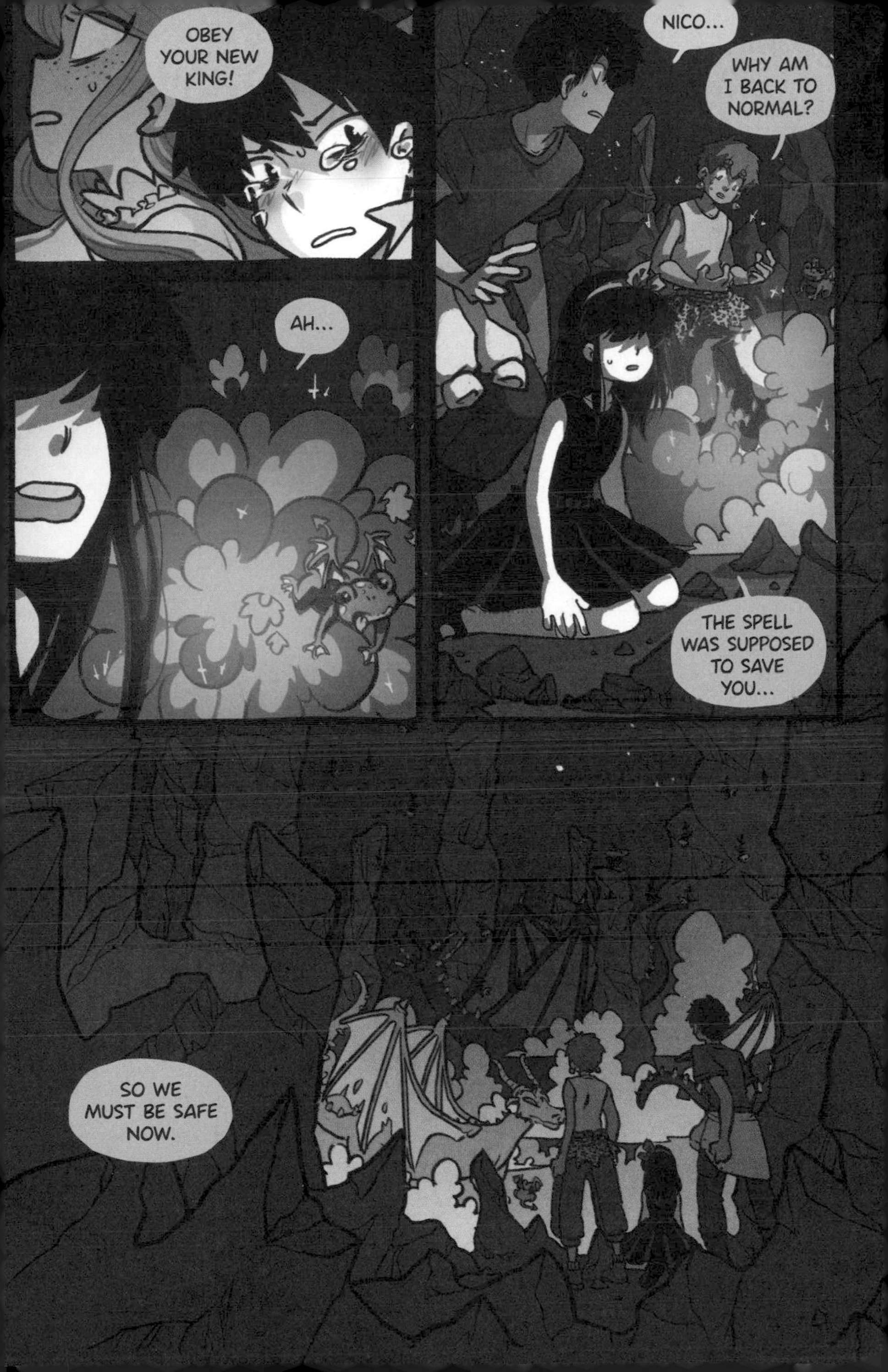
OBEY YOUR NEW KING!
NICO...
WHY AM I BACK TO NORMAL?
AH...
THE SPELL WAS SUPPOSED TO SAVE YOU...
SO WE MUST BE SAFE NOW.

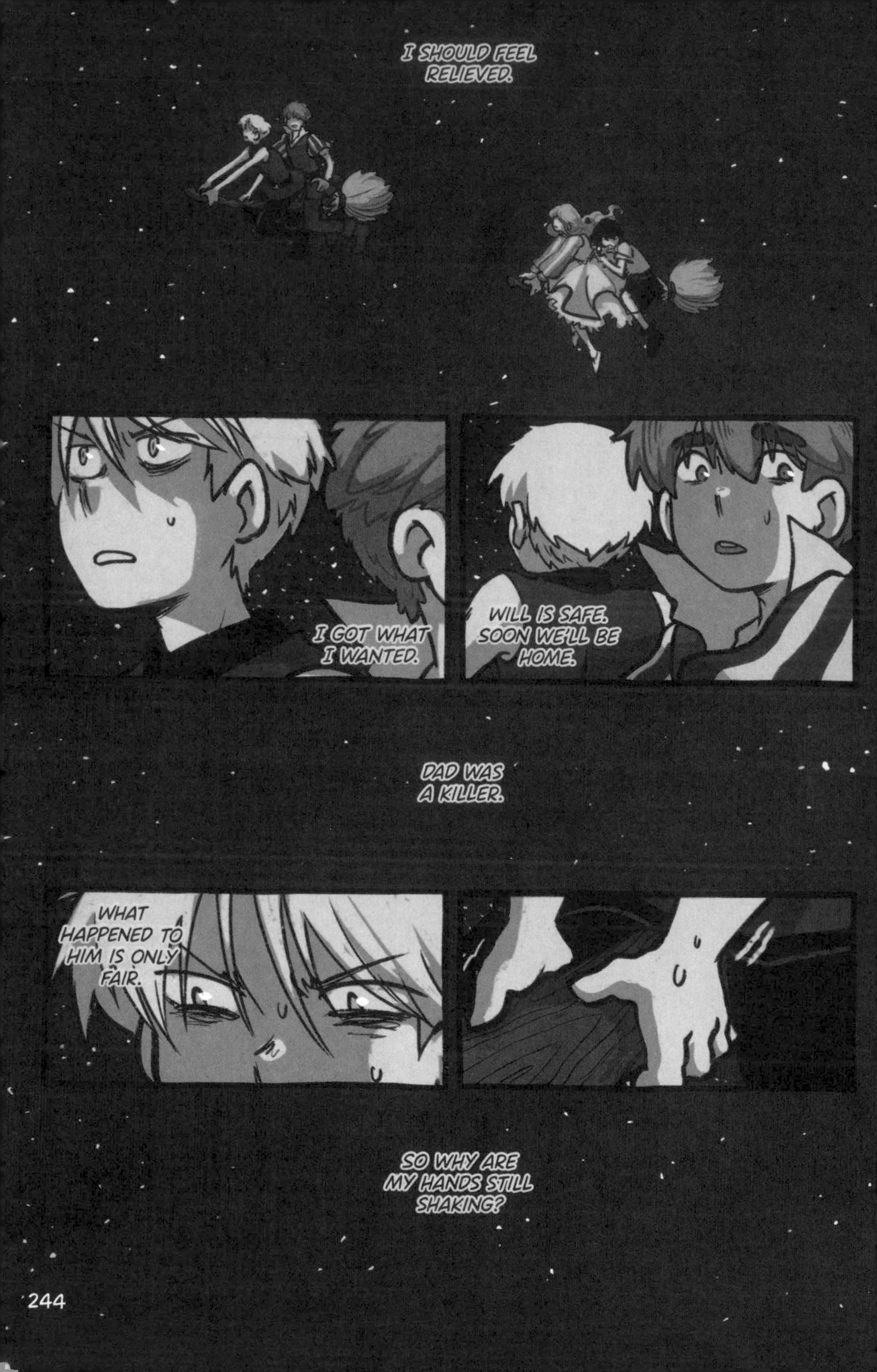
I SHOULD FEEL RELIEVED.
I GOT WHAT I WANTED.
WILL IS SAFE. SOON WE'LL BE HOME.
DAD WAS A KILLER.
WHAT HAPPENED TO HIM IS ONLY FAIR.
SO WHY ARE MY HANDS STILL SHAKING?

249

TODAY WE CAN REST PEACEFULLY OR CELEBRATE JOYFULLY.

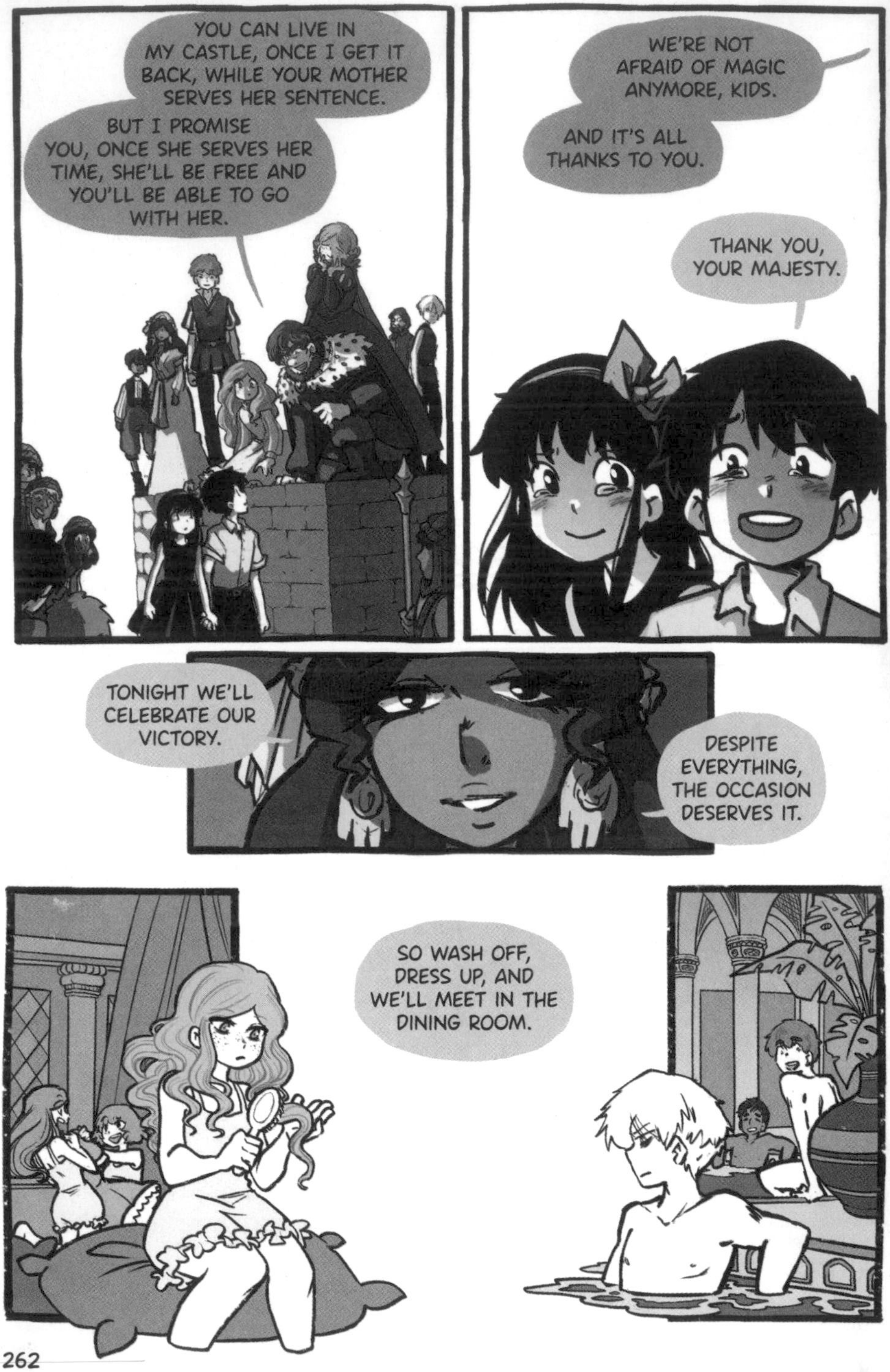
YOU CAN LIVE IN MY CASTLE, ONCE I GET IT BACK, WHILE YOUR MOTHER SERVES HER SENTENCE.
BUT I PROMISE YOU, ONCE SHE SERVES HER TIME, SHE'LL BE FREE AND YOU'LL BE ABLE TO GO WITH HER.
WE'RE NOT AFRAID OF MAGIC ANYMORE, KIDS.
AND IT'S ALL THANKS TO YOU.
THANK YOU, YOUR MAJESTY.
TONIGHT WE'LL CELEBRATE OUR VICTORY.
DESPITE EVERYTHING, THE OCCASION DESERVES IT.
SO WASH OFF, DRESS UP, AND WE'LL MEET IN THE DINING ROOM.

CHAPTER 49

265

WHEN THE WITCHES LOCKED ME UP ON THE FLOATING ROCK.

MONICA ALWAYS WEARS IT TOO, SEE—

AH... WHAT'S THAT?

AN EMPTY FLASK?

IT'S IN MY ROOM!!

NOW WILL YOU PLEASE DROP THE SUBJECT?!

WHAT'S THAT PIECE OF GARBAGE DOING AROUND YOUR NECK, MONICA?

GIVE IT BACK! IT'S NOT GARBAGE!

AND WHERE'S THE RING?

YOU SHOULD WEAR THE RING.

YOU'RE ENGAGED...

CHAPTER 50

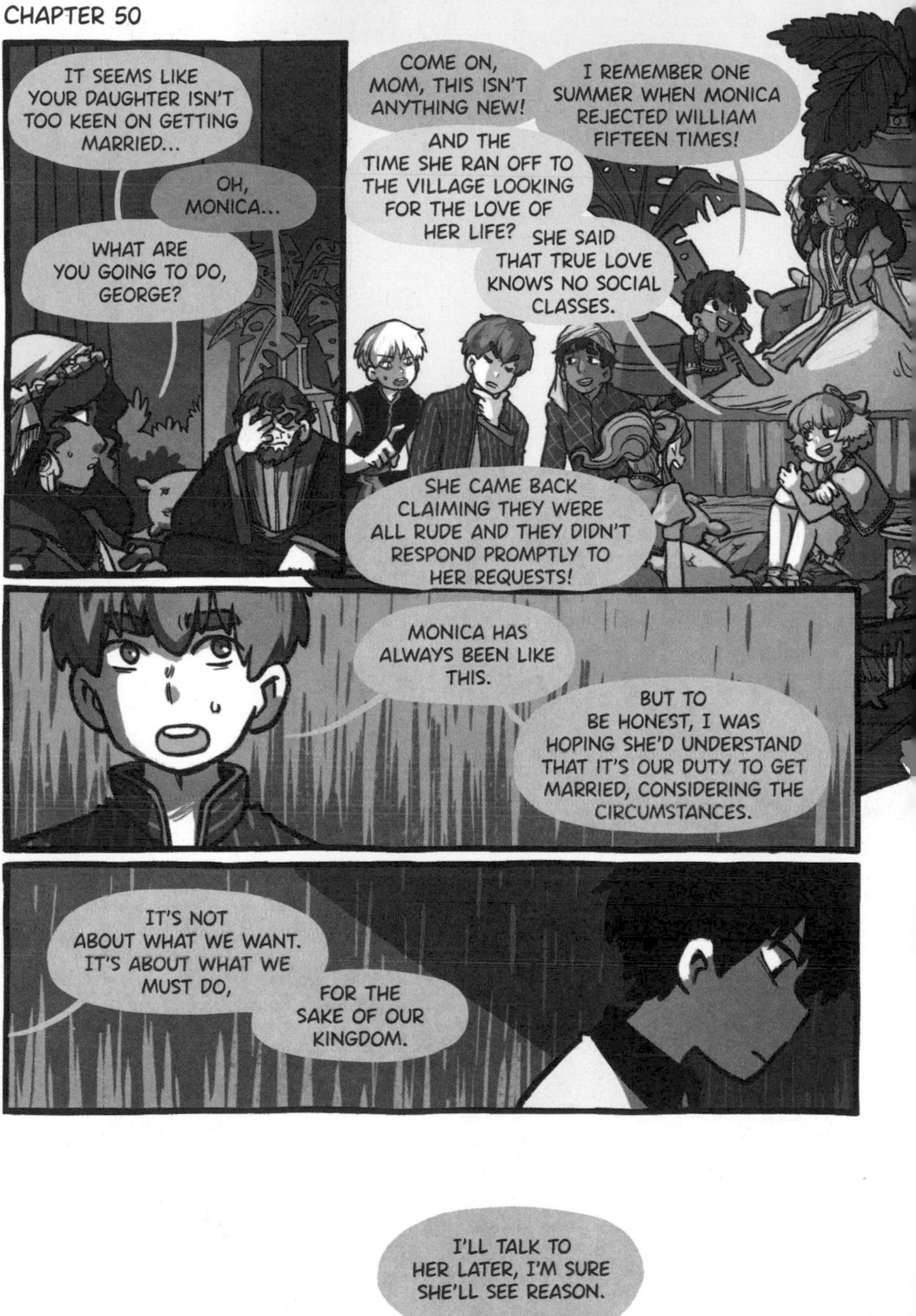
IT SEEMS LIKE YOUR DAUGHTER ISN'T TOO KEEN ON GETTING MARRIED...
OH, MONICA...
WHAT ARE YOU GOING TO DO, GEORGE?
COME ON, MOM, THIS ISN'T ANYTHING NEW!
I REMEMBER ONE SUMMER WHEN MONICA REJECTED WILLIAM FIFTEEN TIMES!
AND THE TIME SHE RAN OFF TO THE VILLAGE LOOKING FOR THE LOVE OF HER LIFE?
SHE SAID THAT TRUE LOVE KNOWS NO SOCIAL CLASSES.
SHE CAME BACK CLAIMING THEY WERE ALL RUDE AND THEY DIDN'T RESPOND PROMPTLY TO HER REQUESTS!
MONICA HAS ALWAYS BEEN LIKE THIS.
BUT TO BE HONEST, I WAS HOPING SHE'D UNDERSTAND THAT IT'S OUR DUTY TO GET MARRIED, CONSIDERING THE CIRCUMSTANCES.
IT'S NOT ABOUT WHAT WE WANT. IT'S ABOUT WHAT WE MUST DO,
FOR THE SAKE OF OUR KINGDOM.
I'LL TALK TO HER LATER, I'M SURE SHE'LL SEE REASON.

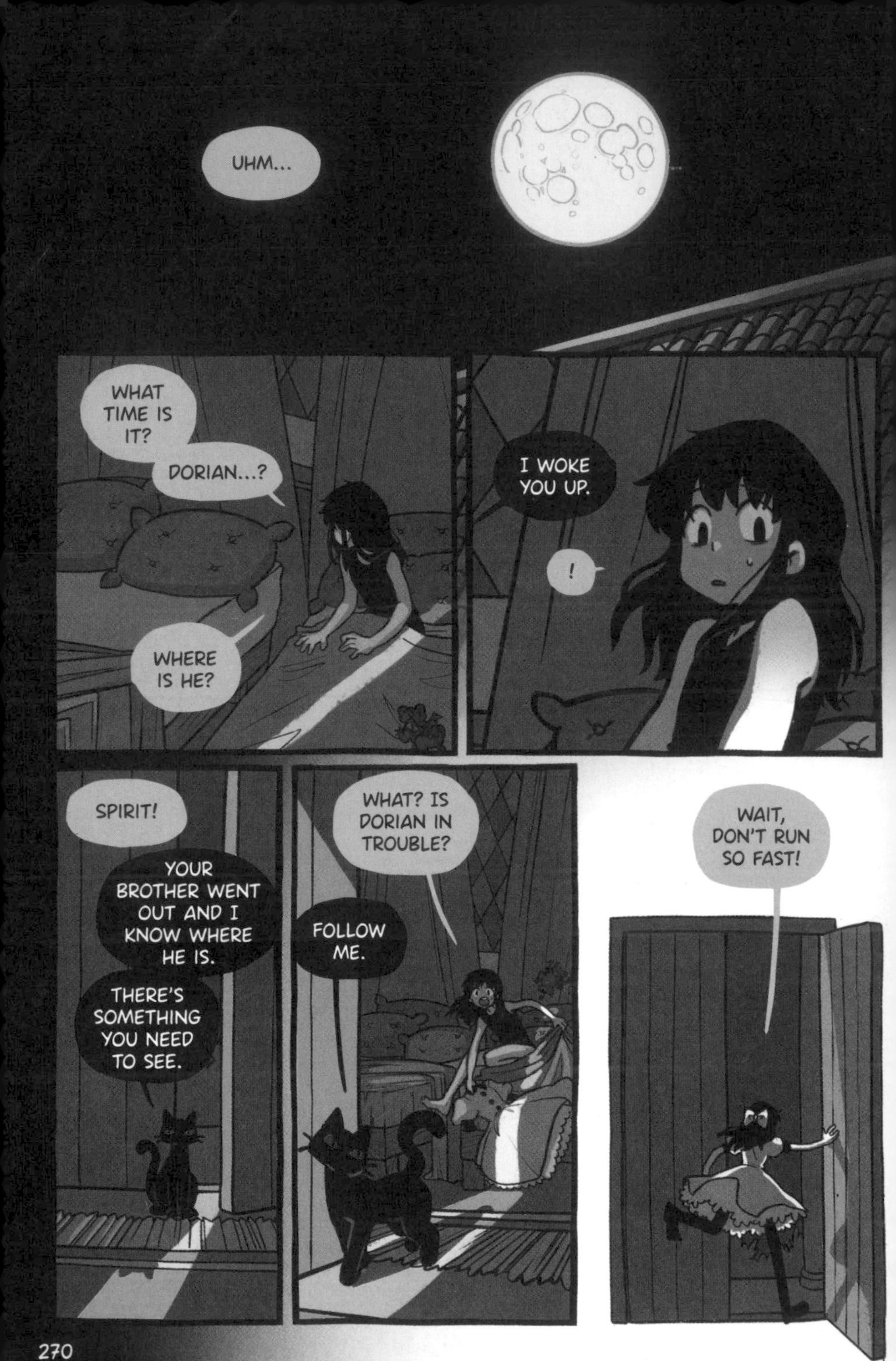
UHM...
WHAT TIME IS IT?
DORIAN...?
WHERE IS HE?
I WOKE YOU UP.
!
SPIRIT!
YOUR BROTHER WENT OUT AND I KNOW WHERE HE IS.
THERE'S SOMETHING YOU NEED TO SEE.
WHAT? IS DORIAN IN TROUBLE?
FOLLOW ME.
WAIT, DON'T RUN SO FAST!

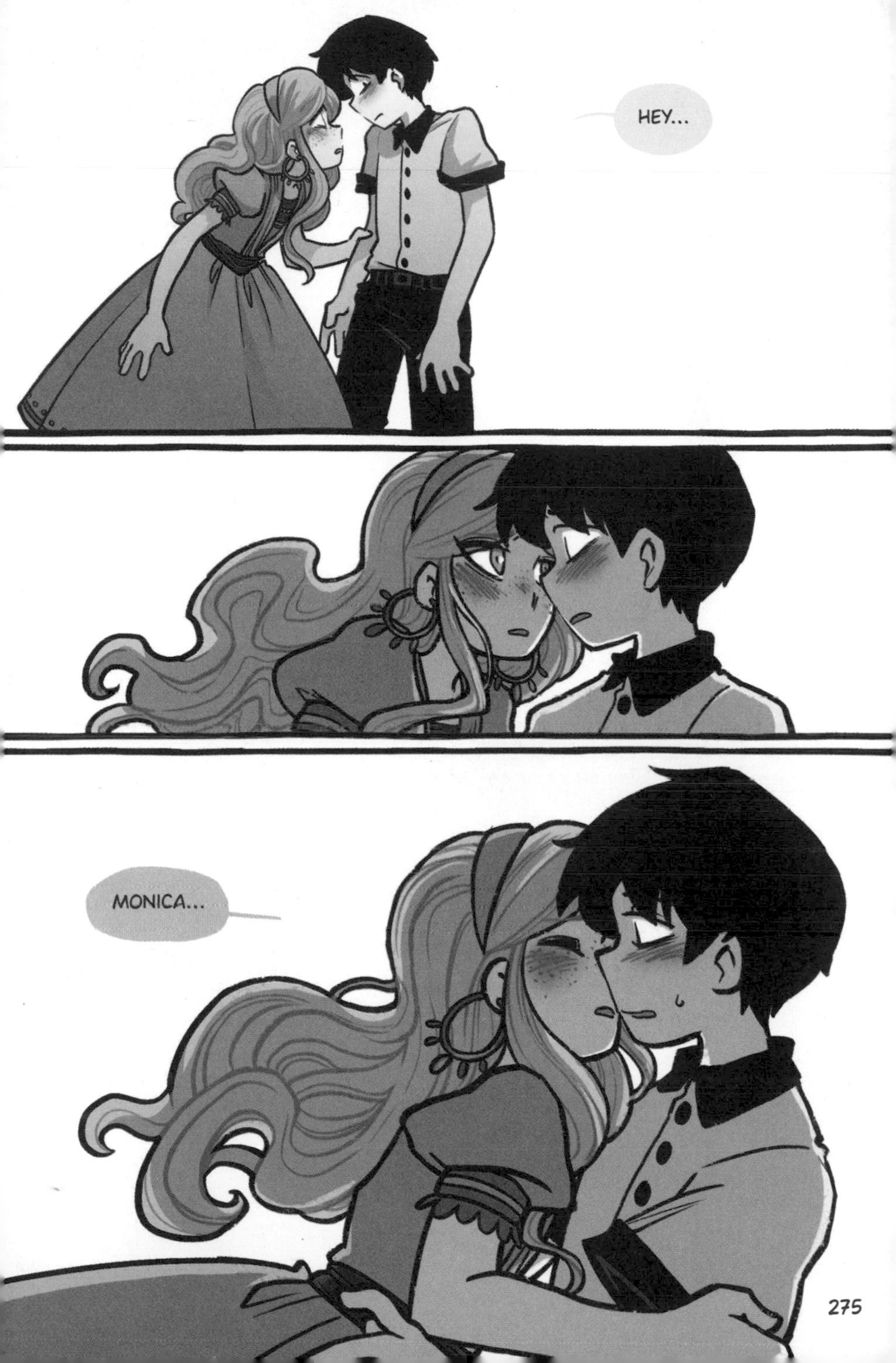
HEY...
MONICA...

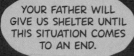
YOUR FATHER WILL GIVE US SHELTER UNTIL THIS SITUATION COMES TO AN END.

I TRULY BELIEVE THINGS MUST GET BETTER FROM NOW ON.

WAIT, SPIRIT!

IS IT HERE...?

ARE YOU SURE DORIAN'S HERE?

CHAPTER 51

WHOA!

MARK, DUDE, WAKE UP!

POW

DANI!!

WHAT A NIGHTMARE!

UGH...

IT'S AN EMERGENCY!

LEAVE ME ALONE, NICO. I WAS DREAMING ABOUT CUPCAKES...

I JUST DREAMED ABOUT DANI CRYING!

SHE WAS WEARING THE SAME WHITE DRESS AS IN THE VISION FROM THE CRYSTAL BALL.

I HAVE A BAD FEELING.

CALM DOWN. SHE MUST BE ASLEEP BY NOW.

I'M GONNA SEE IF SHE'S OKAY!

ZZZZZ...

NOTHING BAD WILL HAPPEN TONIGHT. WE'RE SAFE HERE.

283

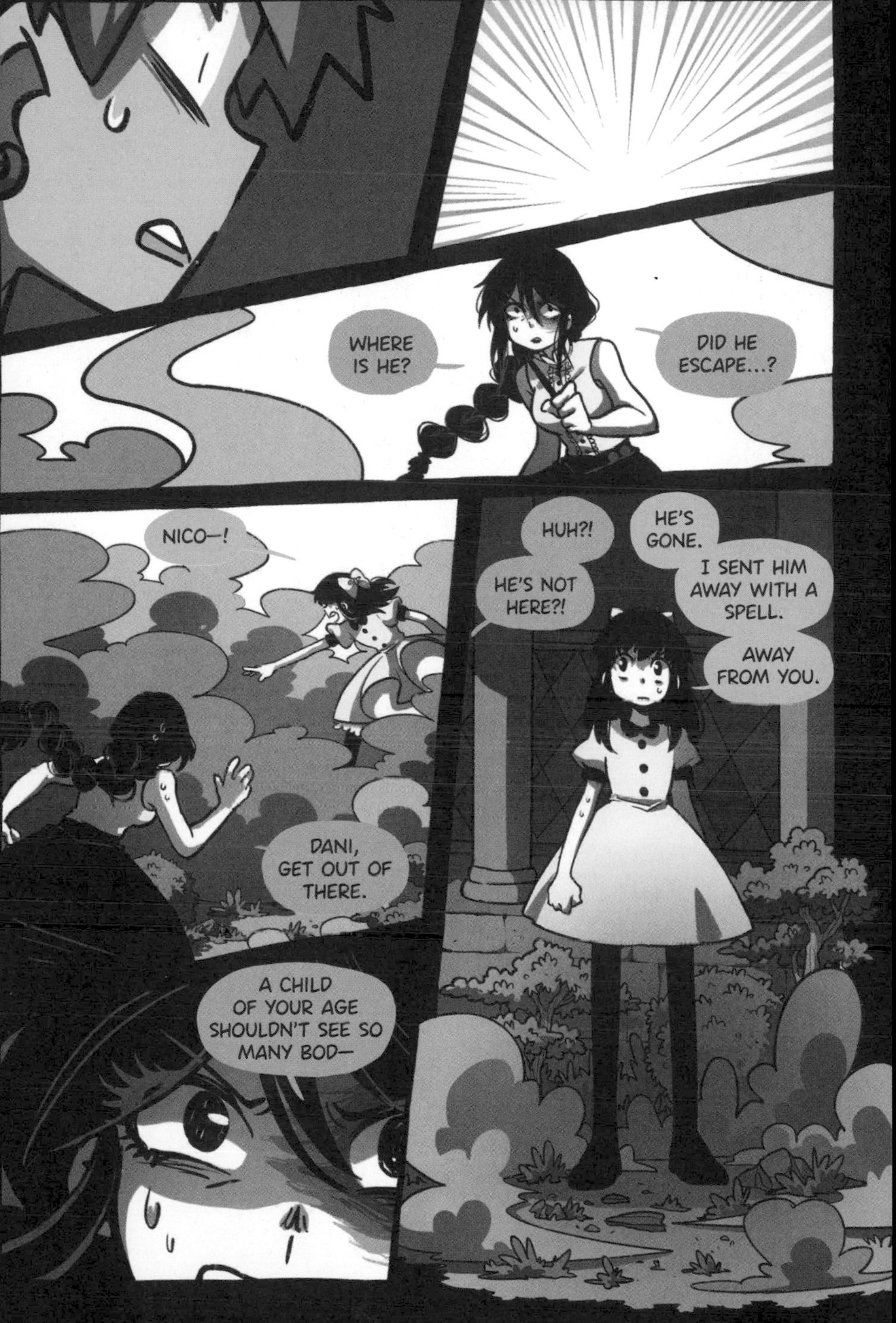
WHERE IS HE?
DID HE ESCAPE...?
NICO—!
DANI, GET OUT OF THERE.
HUH?!
HE'S NOT HERE?!
HE'S GONE.
I SENT HIM AWAY WITH A SPELL.
AWAY FROM YOU.
A CHILD OF YOUR AGE SHOULDN'T SEE SO MANY BOD—

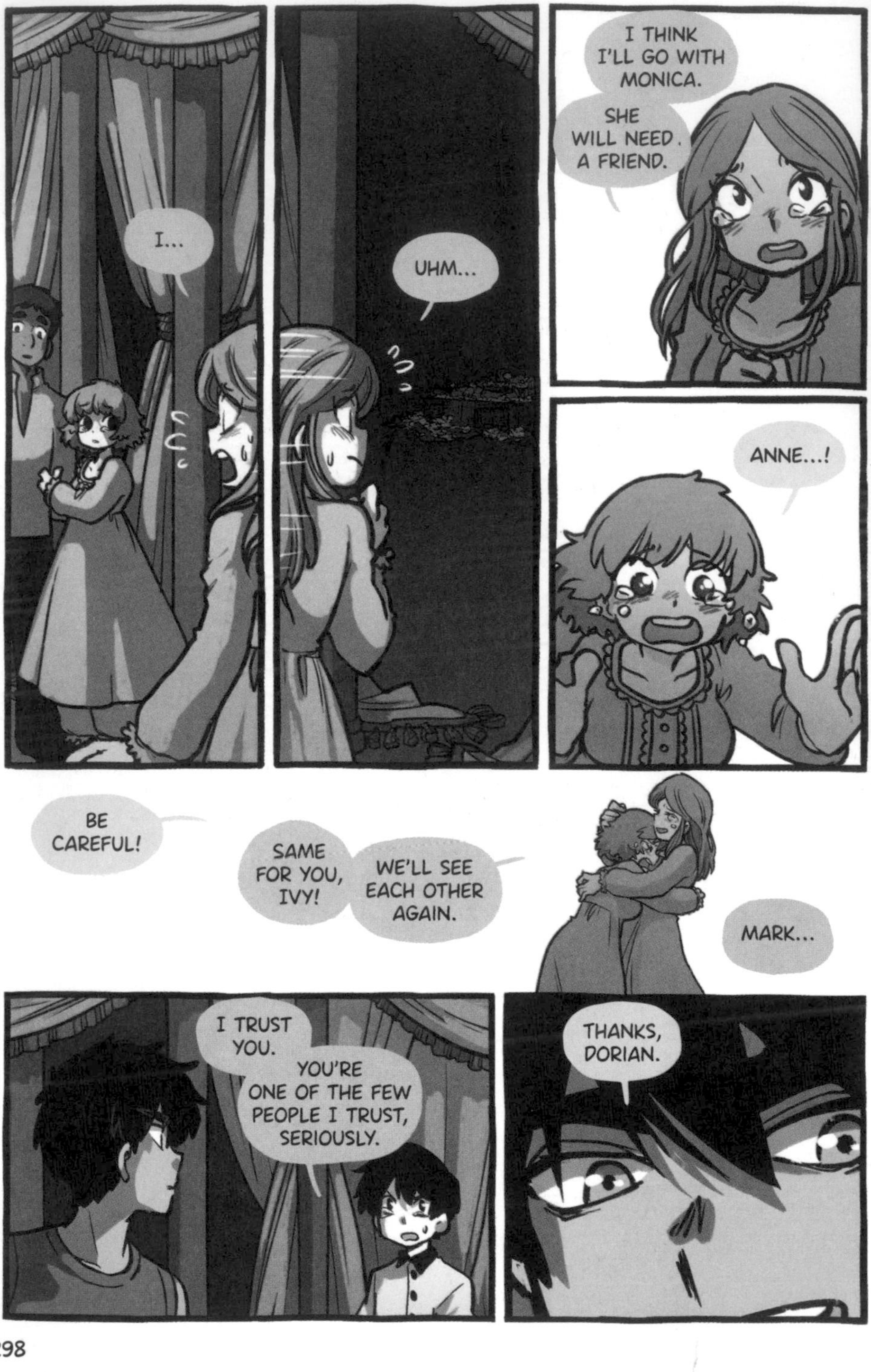
I...
UHM...
I THINK I'LL GO WITH MONICA.
SHE WILL NEED A FRIEND.
ANNE...!
BE CAREFUL!
SAME FOR YOU, IVY!
WE'LL SEE EACH OTHER AGAIN.
MARK...
I TRUST YOU.
YOU'RE ONE OF THE FEW PEOPLE I TRUST, SERIOUSLY.
THANKS, DORIAN.

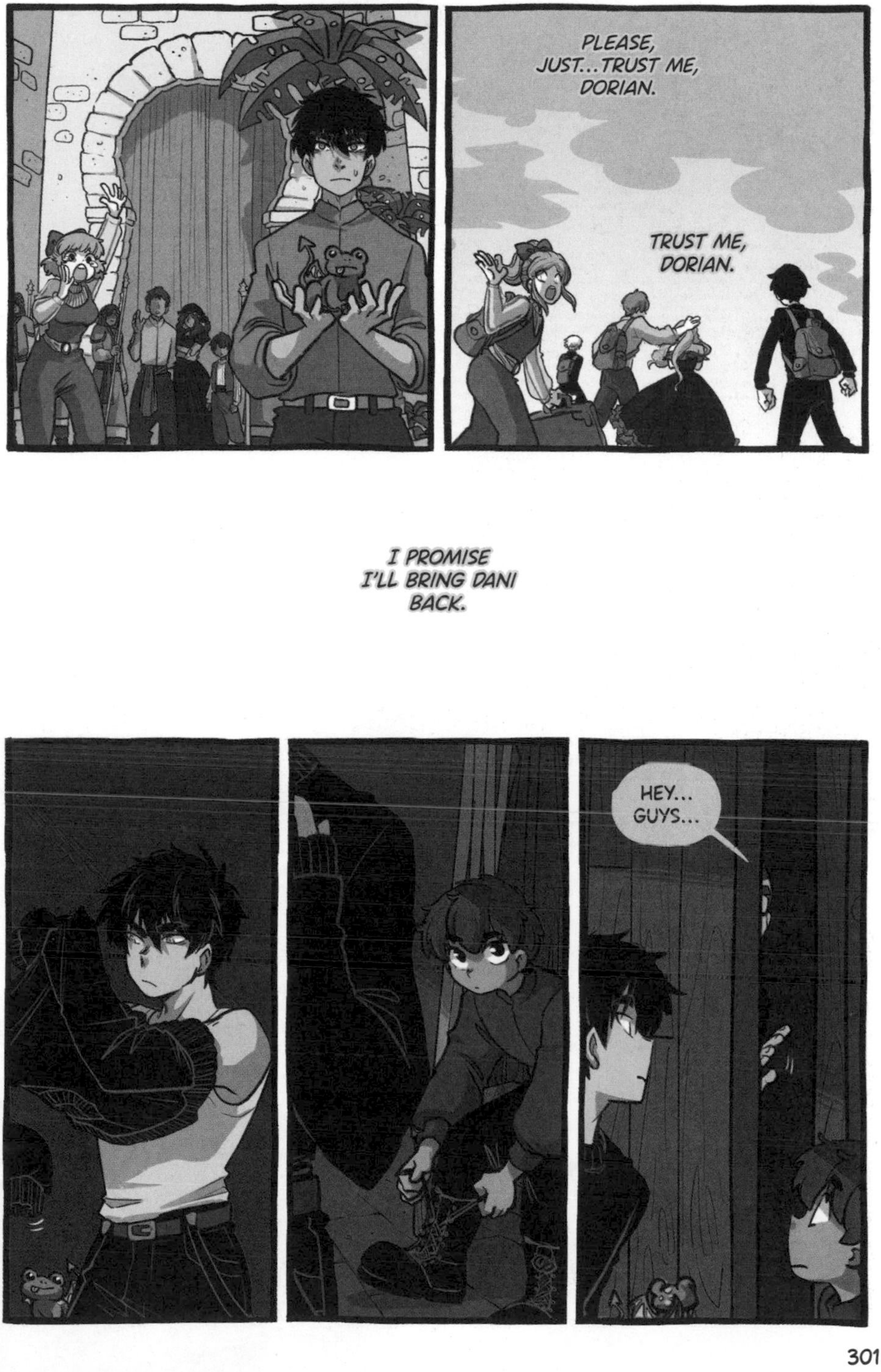
PLEASE, JUST...TRUST ME, DORIAN.
TRUST ME, DORIAN.
I PROMISE I'LL BRING DANI BACK.
HEY... GUYS...

302

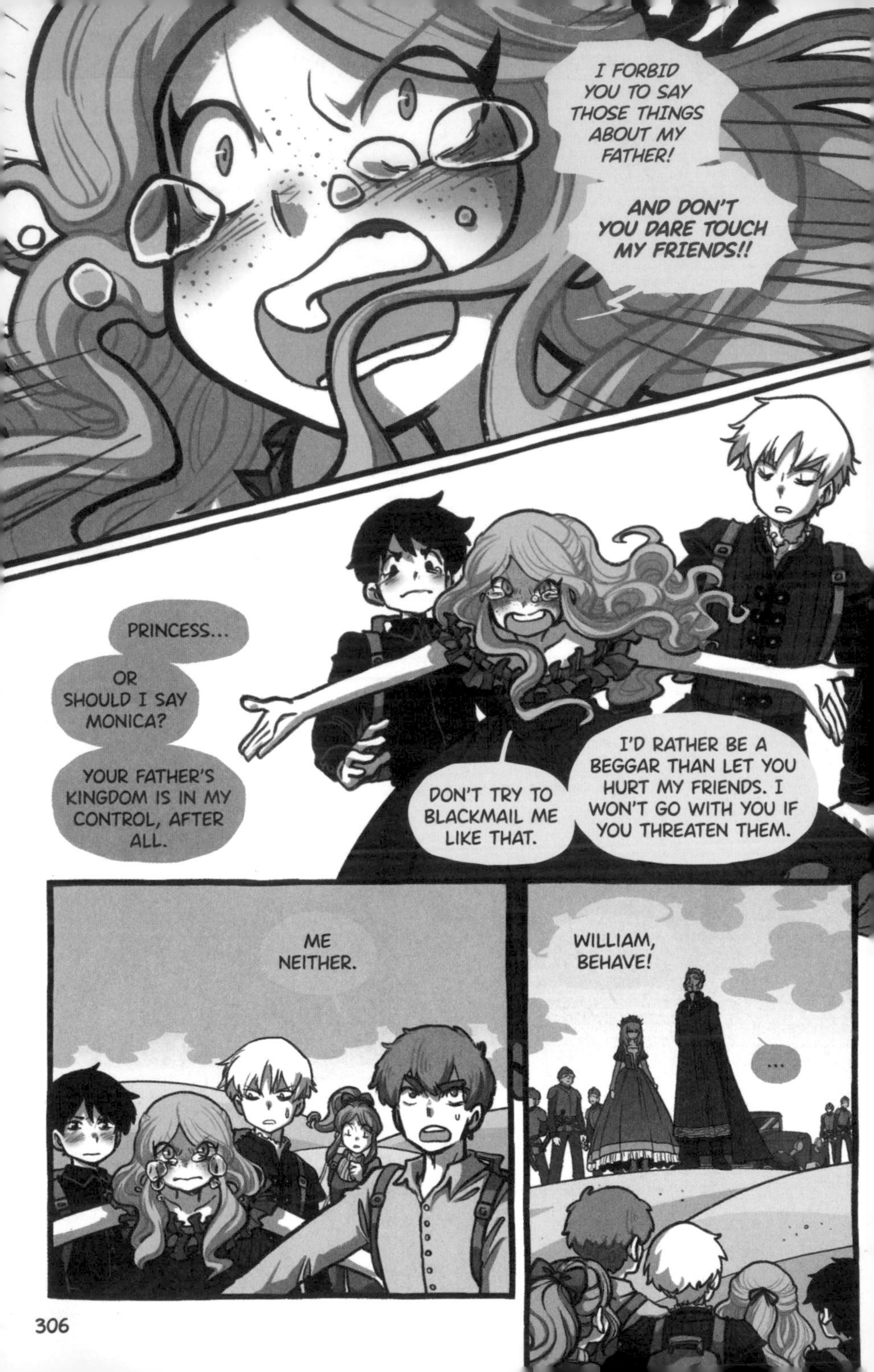
I FORBID YOU TO SAY THOSE THINGS ABOUT MY FATHER!
AND DON'T YOU DARE TOUCH MY FRIENDS!!
PRINCESS...
OR SHOULD I SAY MONICA?
YOUR FATHER'S KINGDOM IS IN MY CONTROL, AFTER ALL.
I'D RATHER BE A BEGGAR THAN LET YOU HURT MY FRIENDS. I WON'T GO WITH YOU IF YOU THREATEN THEM.
DON'T TRY TO BLACKMAIL ME LIKE THAT.
ME NEITHER.
WILLIAM, BEHAVE!
...

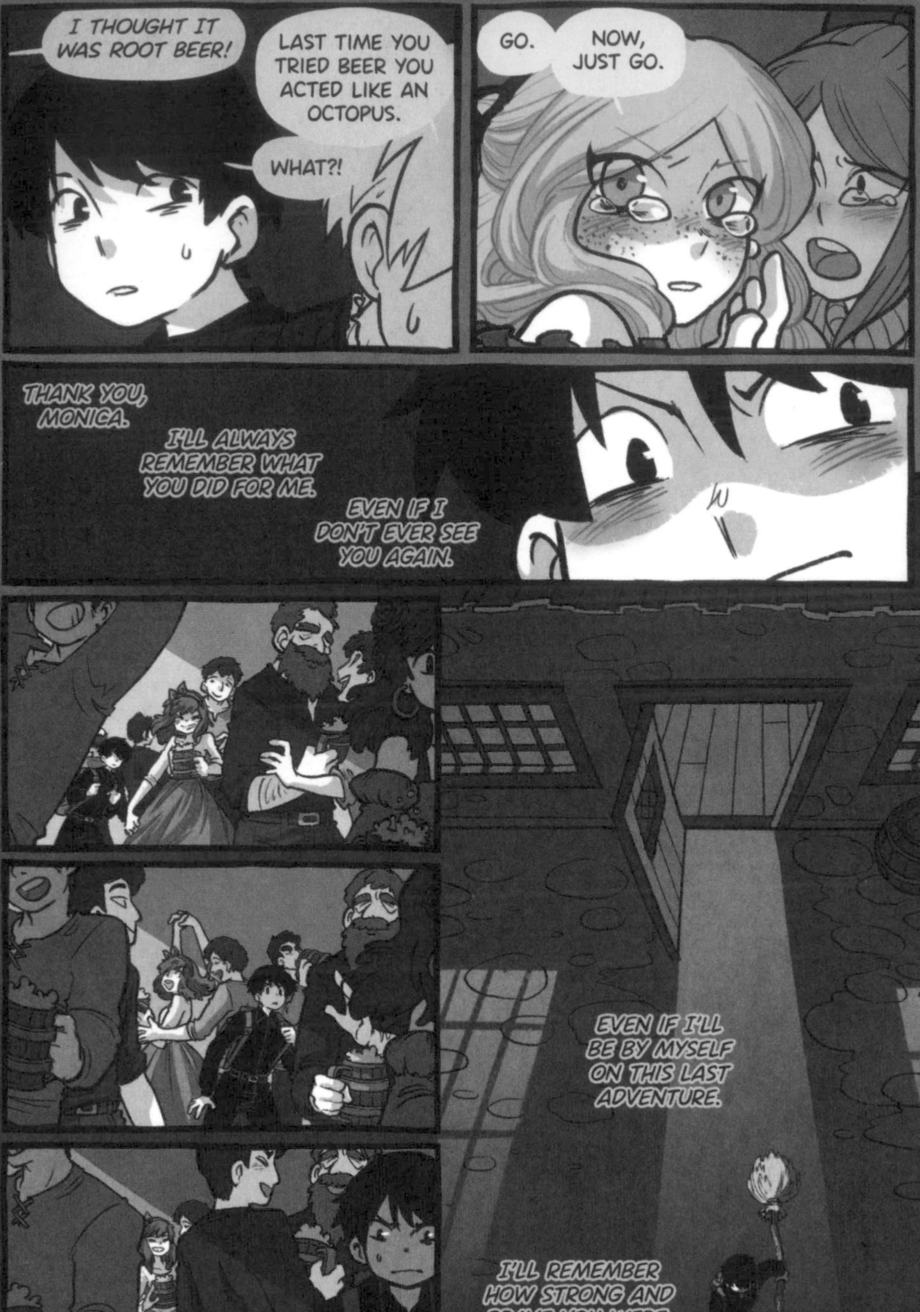
I THOUGHT IT WAS ROOT BEER!
LAST TIME YOU TRIED BEER YOU ACTED LIKE AN OCTOPUS.
WHAT?!
GO.
NOW, JUST GO.
THANK YOU, MONICA.
I'LL ALWAYS REMEMBER WHAT YOU DID FOR ME.
EVEN IF I DON'T EVER SEE YOU AGAIN.
EVEN IF I'LL BE BY MYSELF ON THIS LAST ADVENTURE.
I'LL REMEMBER HOW STRONG AND BRAVE YOU WERE, THROUGH THE DARKEST TIMES.

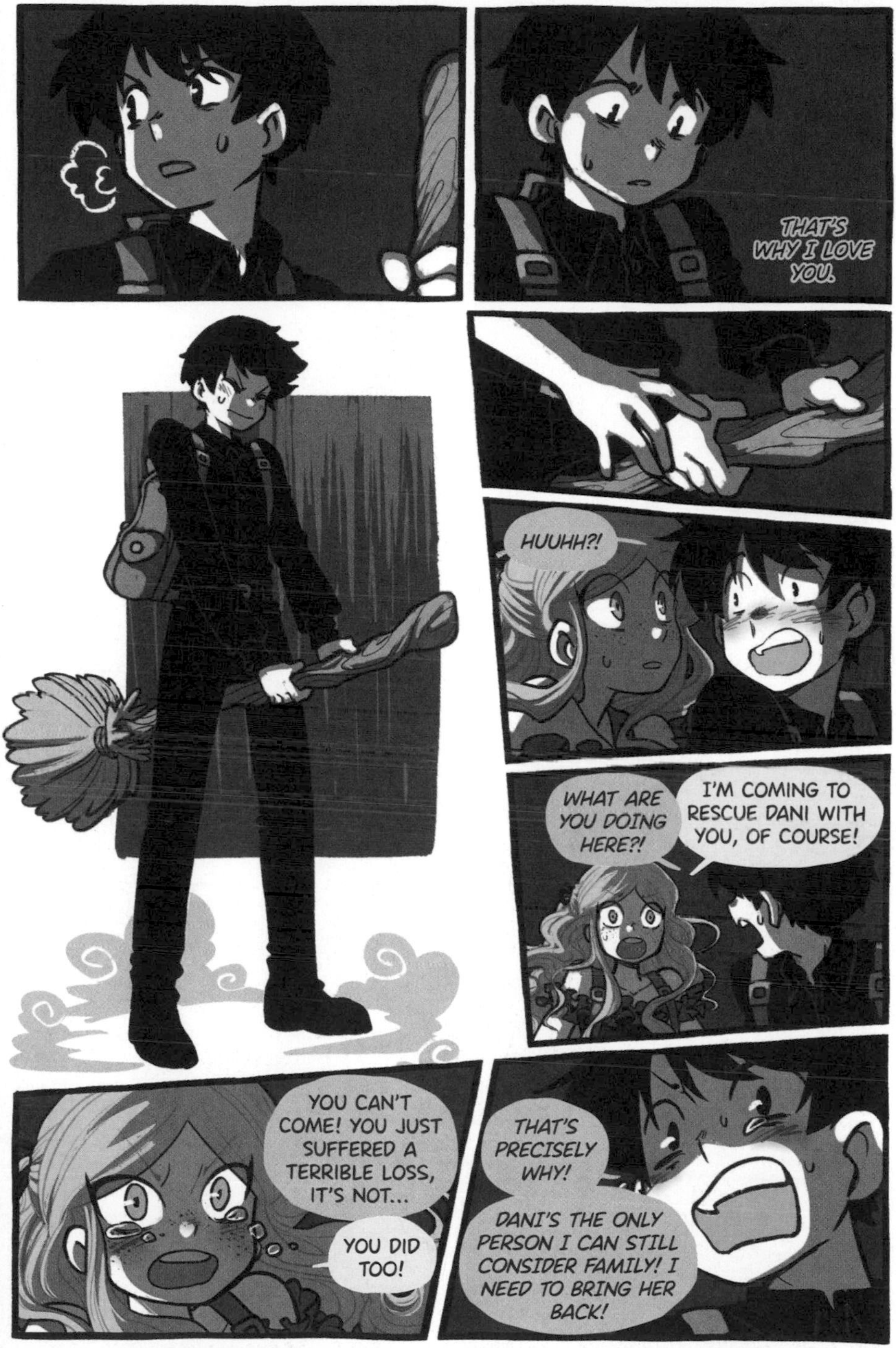
THAT'S WHY I LOVE YOU.
HUUHH?!
WHAT ARE YOU DOING HERE?!
I'M COMING TO RESCUE DANI WITH YOU, OF COURSE!
YOU CAN'T COME! YOU JUST SUFFERED A TERRIBLE LOSS, IT'S NOT...
YOU DID TOO!
THAT'S PRECISELY WHY!
DANI'S THE ONLY PERSON I CAN STILL CONSIDER FAMILY! I NEED TO BRING HER BACK!

CHAPTER 54

317

WE'RE GOING OUT RIGHT NOW, AS SOON AS YOU'RE DRESSED TO ATTEND YOUR FATHER'S FUNERAL.

HUH?

RIGHT... DAD...

MISS, DON'T CRY.

I KNOW THIS IS A HARD SITUATION FOR YOU RIGHT NOW...

BUT THIS EVENT OPENED OUR EYES AND MADE US REALIZE WHO THE REAL KING OF WITCHES IS.

WHAT DO YOU MEAN?

IT'S CLEAR, WE MADE A MISTAKE ISN'T IT? WHEN WE HANDED THE CROWN TO DAMIEN...

HE ENDED UP BEING A TRAITOR.

MANY WITCHES WOULD LIKE TO SEE HIS HEAD ON A STAKE, BUT THE MAJORITY ARE WILLING TO FORGIVE HIM.

WE CANNOT BUILD A SOCIETY UPON THE KILLING OF OTHER WITCHES.

BUT IN THE END, IT WILL BE UP TO THE NEW KING...

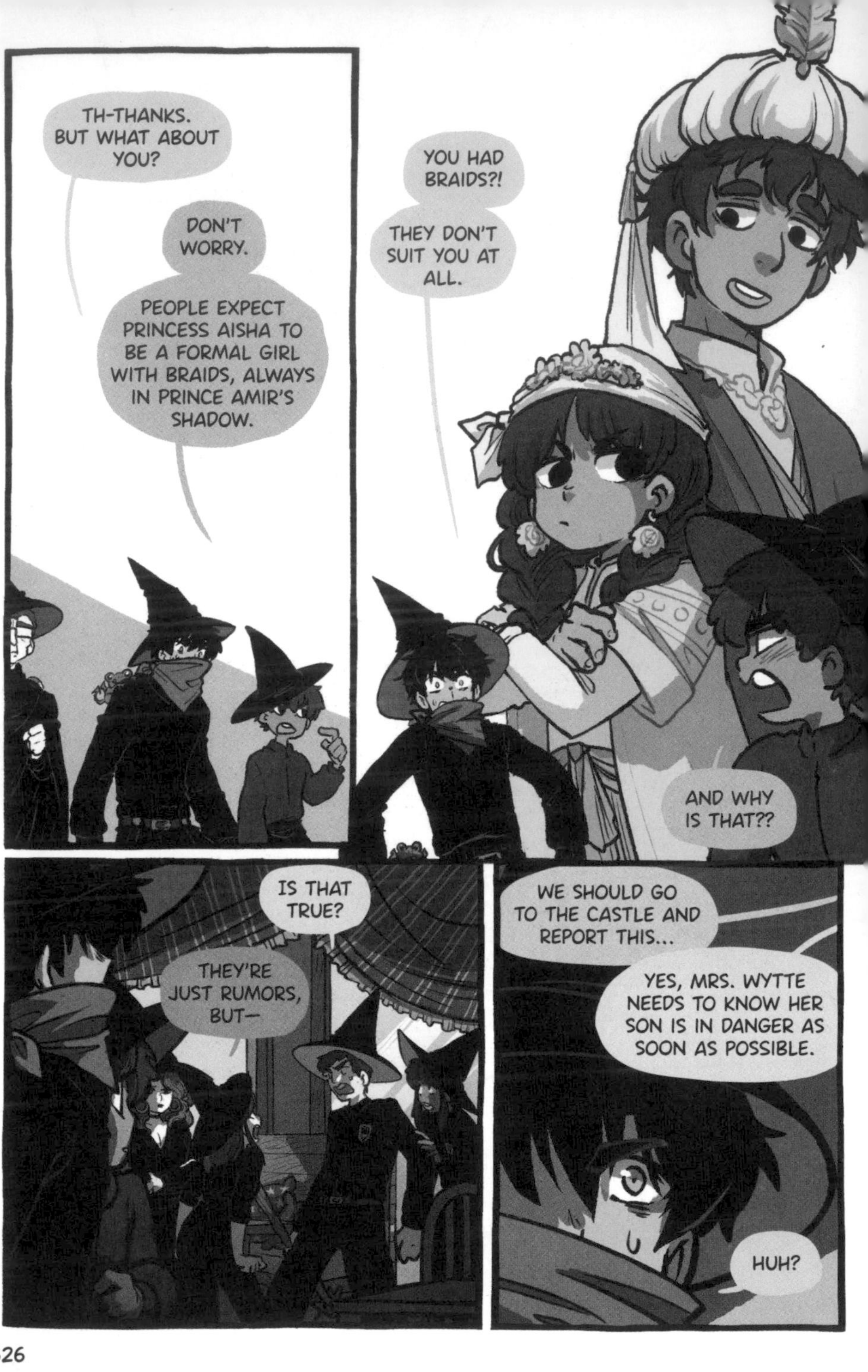
TH-THANKS. BUT WHAT ABOUT YOU?
DON'T WORRY.
PEOPLE EXPECT PRINCESS AISHA TO BE A FORMAL GIRL WITH BRAIDS, ALWAYS IN PRINCE AMIR'S SHADOW.
YOU HAD BRAIDS?!
THEY DON'T SUIT YOU AT ALL.
AND WHY IS THAT??
IS THAT TRUE?
THEY'RE JUST RUMORS, BUT—
WE SHOULD GO TO THE CASTLE AND REPORT THIS...
YES, MRS. WYTTE NEEDS TO KNOW HER SON IS IN DANGER AS SOON AS POSSIBLE.
HUH?

CHAPTER 55

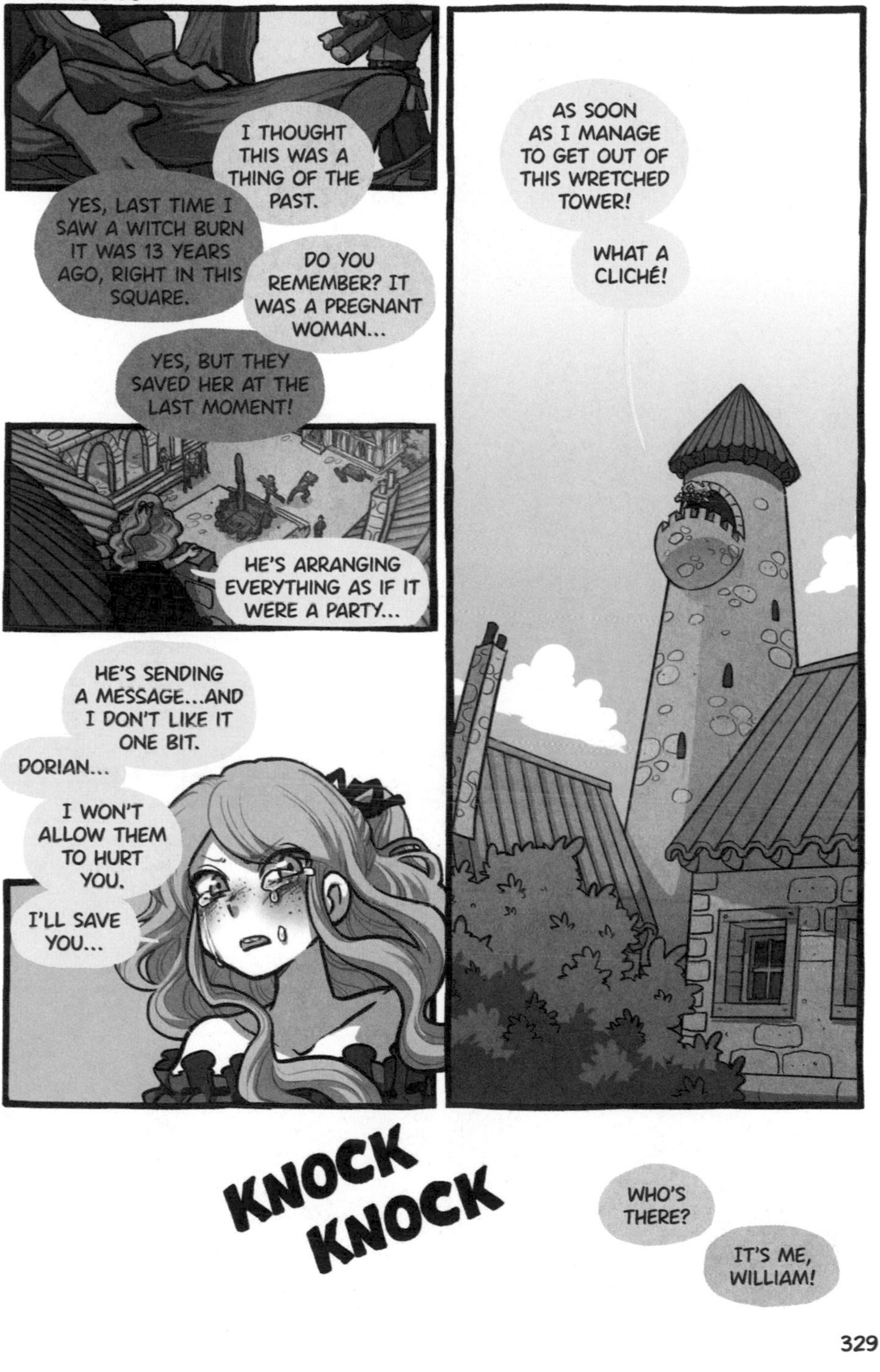
I THOUGHT THIS WAS A THING OF THE PAST.
YES, LAST TIME I SAW A WITCH BURN IT WAS 13 YEARS AGO, RIGHT IN THIS SQUARE.
DO YOU REMEMBER? IT WAS A PREGNANT WOMAN...
YES, BUT THEY SAVED HER AT THE LAST MOMENT!
HE'S ARRANGING EVERYTHING AS IF IT WERE A PARTY...
HE'S SENDING A MESSAGE...AND I DON'T LIKE IT ONE BIT.
DORIAN...
I WON'T ALLOW THEM TO HURT YOU.
I'LL SAVE YOU...
AS SOON AS I MANAGE TO GET OUT OF THIS WRETCHED TOWER!
WHAT A CLICHÉ!
KNOCK KNOCK
WHO'S THERE?
IT'S ME, WILLIAM!

337

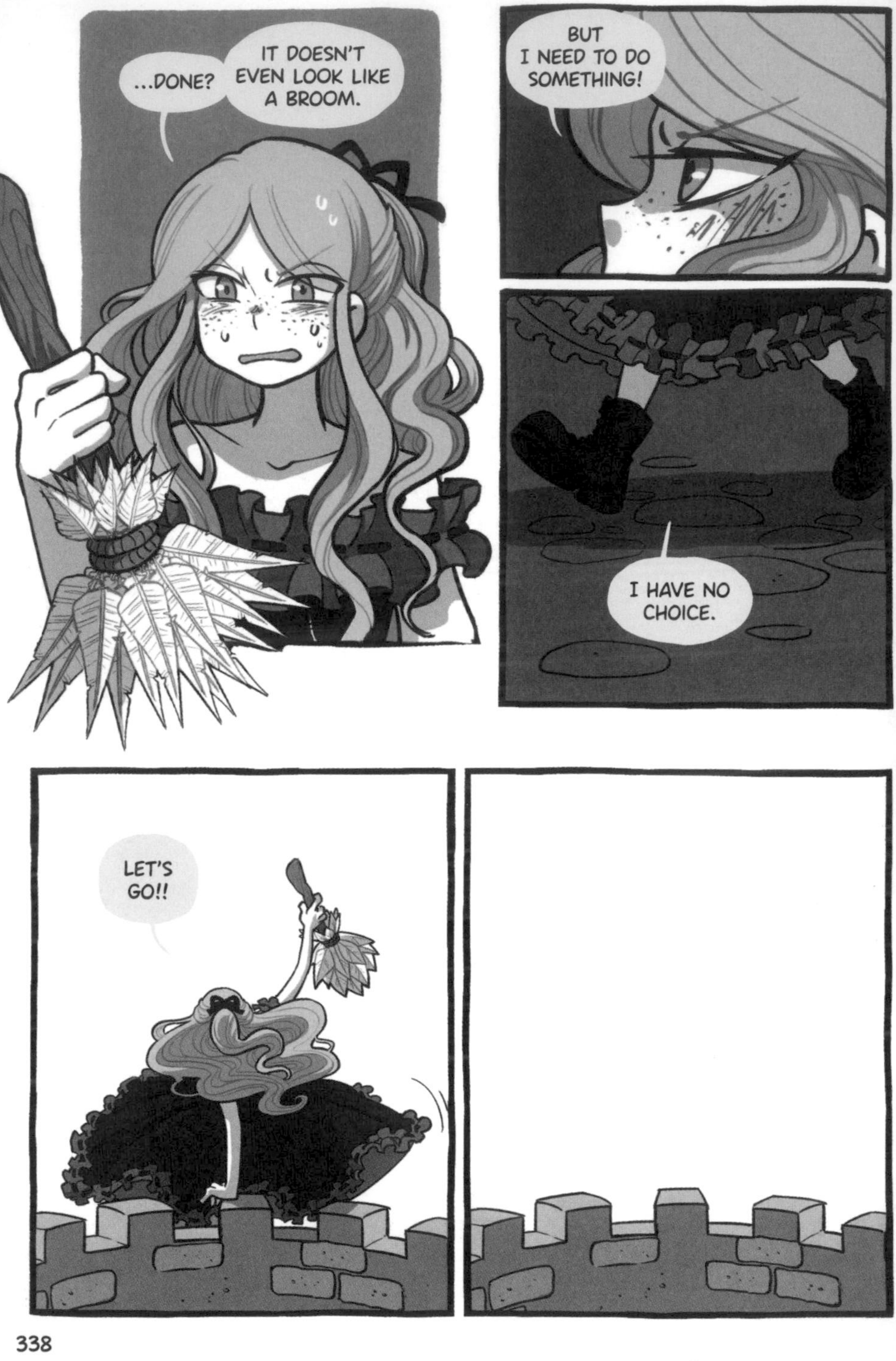
...DONE?
IT DOESN'T EVEN LOOK LIKE A BROOM.
BUT I NEED TO DO SOMETHING!
I HAVE NO CHOICE.
LET'S GO!!

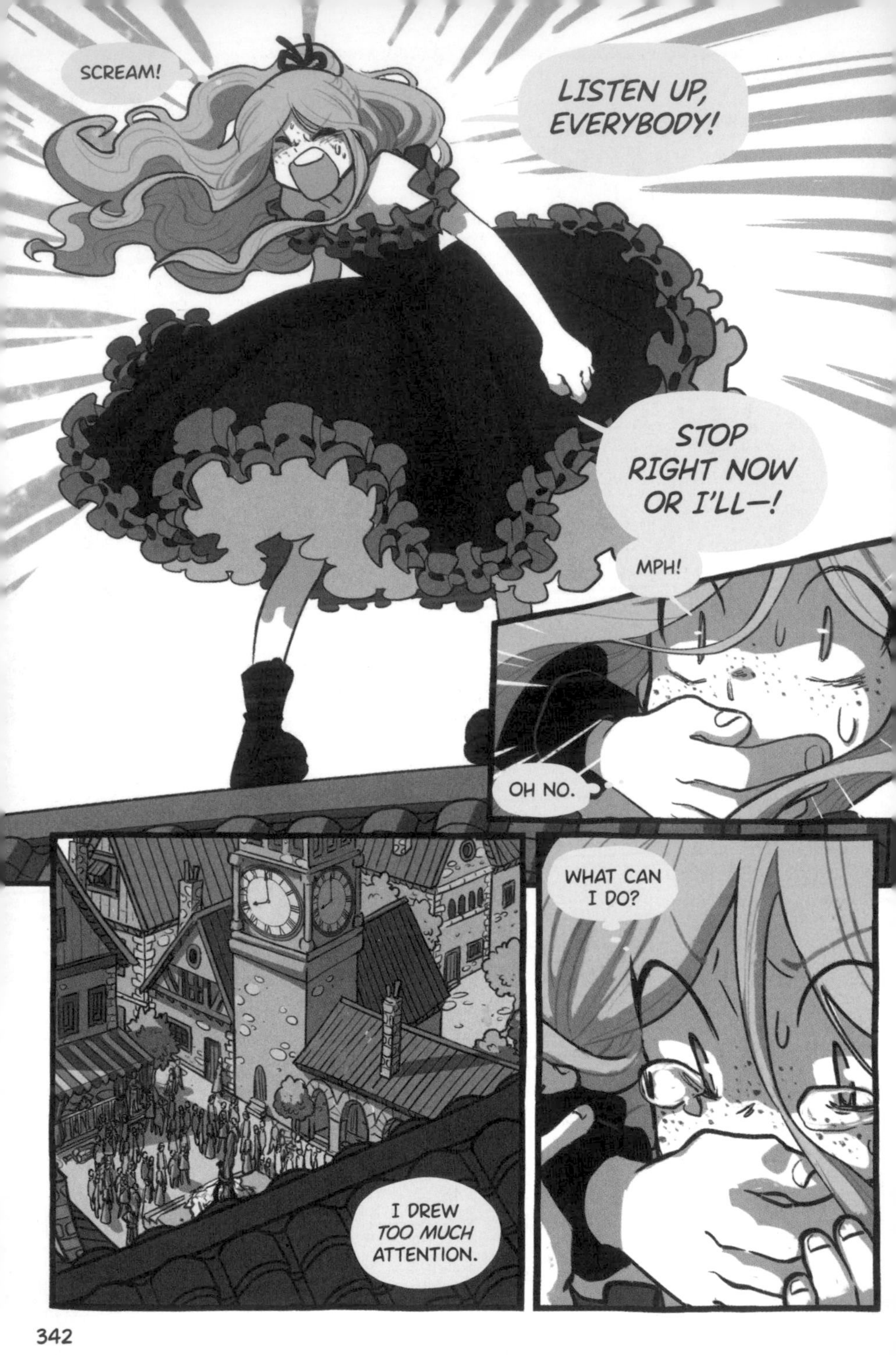
SCREAM!
LISTEN UP, EVERYBODY!
STOP RIGHT NOW OR I'LL—!
MPH!
OH NO.
I DREW TOO MUCH ATTENTION.
WHAT CAN I DO?

343

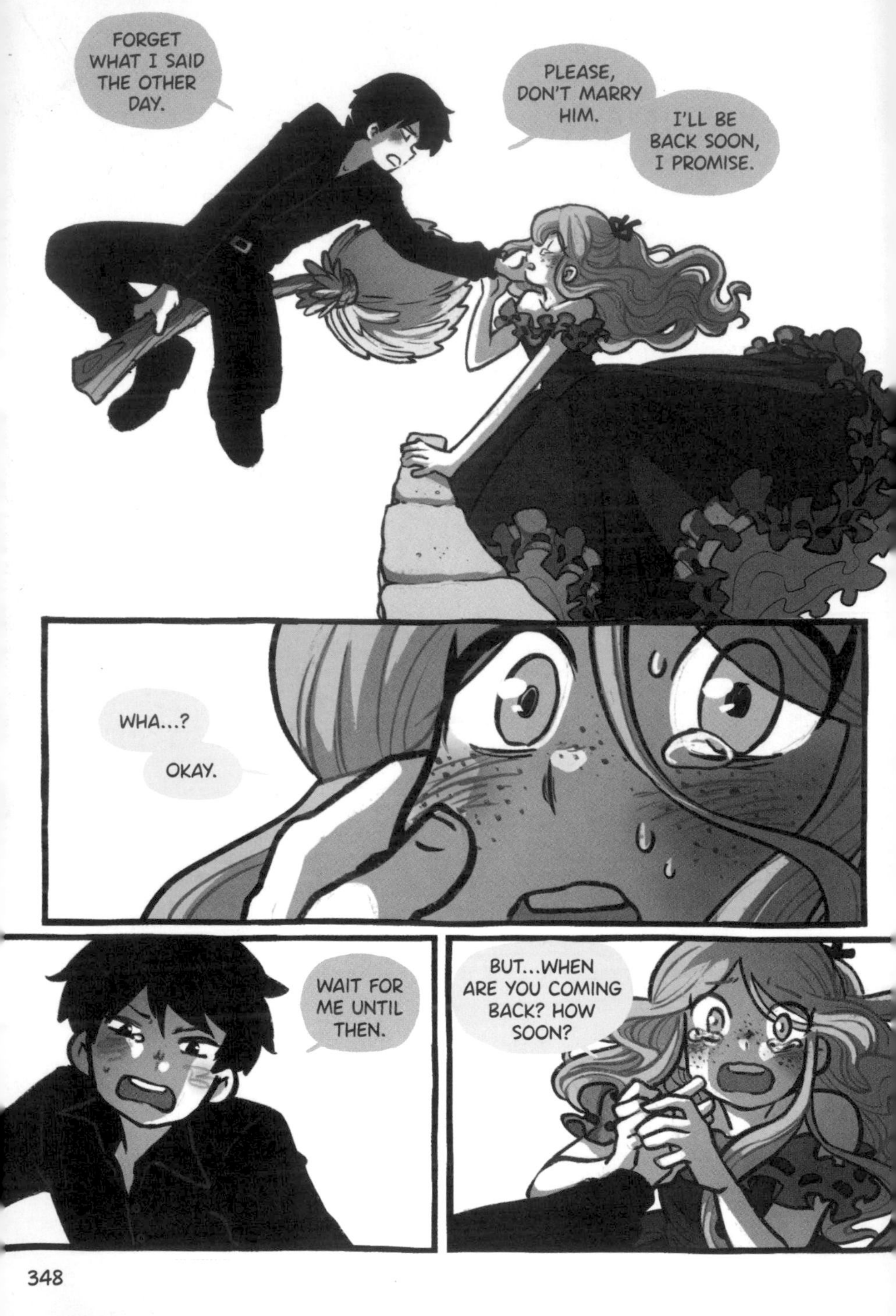
FORGET WHAT I SAID THE OTHER DAY.
PLEASE, DON'T MARRY HIM.
I'LL BE BACK SOON, I PROMISE.
WHA...?
OKAY.
WAIT FOR ME UNTIL THEN.
BUT...WHEN ARE YOU COMING BACK? HOW SOON?

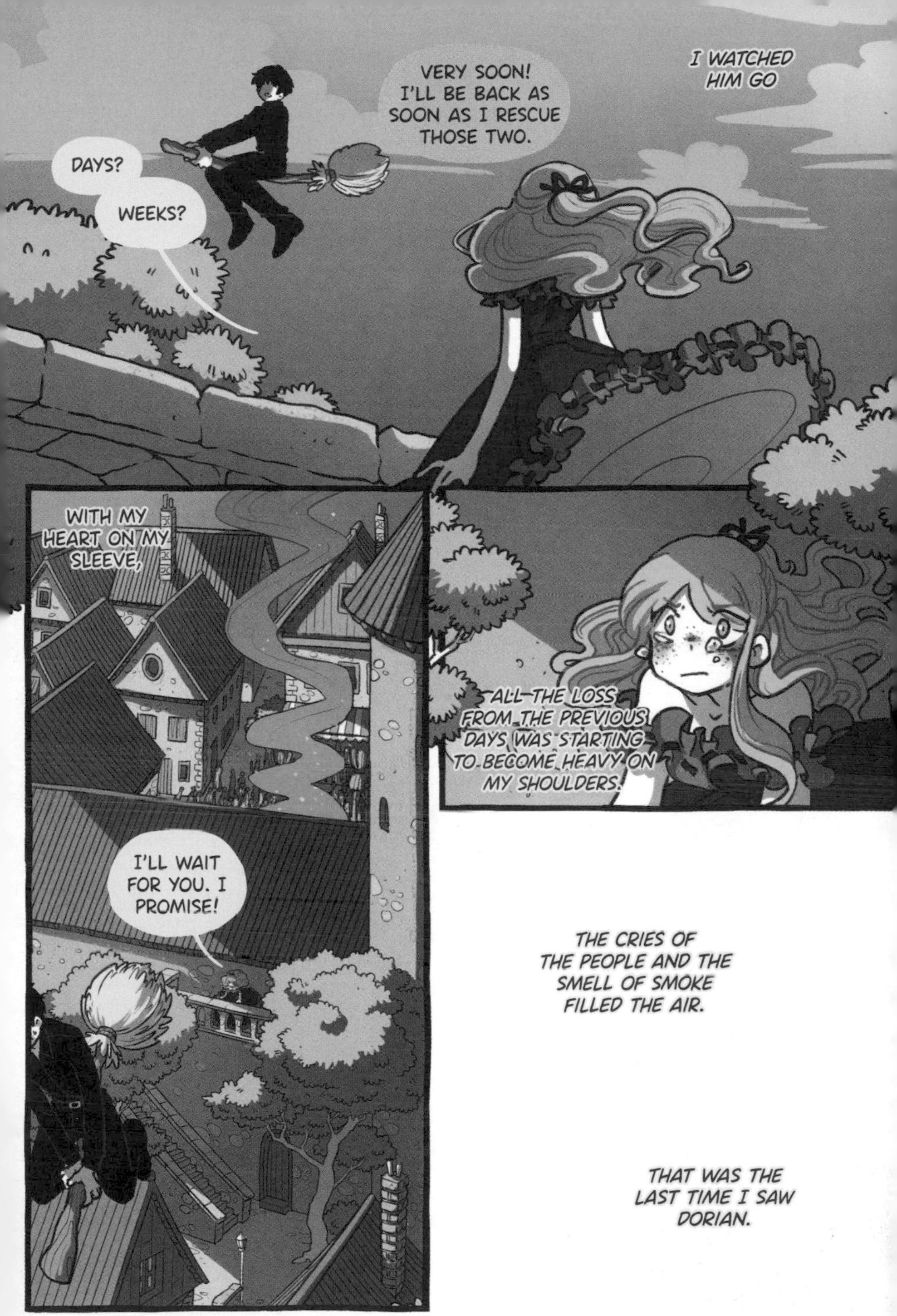
DAYS?
WEEKS?
VERY SOON! I'LL BE BACK AS SOON AS I RESCUE THOSE TWO.
I WATCHED HIM GO
WITH MY HEART ON MY SLEEVE,
I'LL WAIT FOR YOU. I PROMISE!
ALL THE LOSS FROM THE PREVIOUS DAYS WAS STARTING TO BECOME HEAVY ON MY SHOULDERS.
THE CRIES OF THE PEOPLE AND THE SMELL OF SMOKE FILLED THE AIR.
THAT WAS THE LAST TIME I SAW DORIAN.

CHAPTER 57

IT HURTS...

IT HURTS SO BAD,

THERE ISN'T ROOM FOR ANYTHING ELSE.

UGH...

UH...

DORIAN...

...

SNIFF...

THIS CAN'T BE.

MAKE IT STOP.

IT DOESN'T MAKE SENSE.

350

DAD...

DANI...

DANI, I...

AND I CAN'T
GO BACK.

UH...

IT'S TOO
LATE.

352

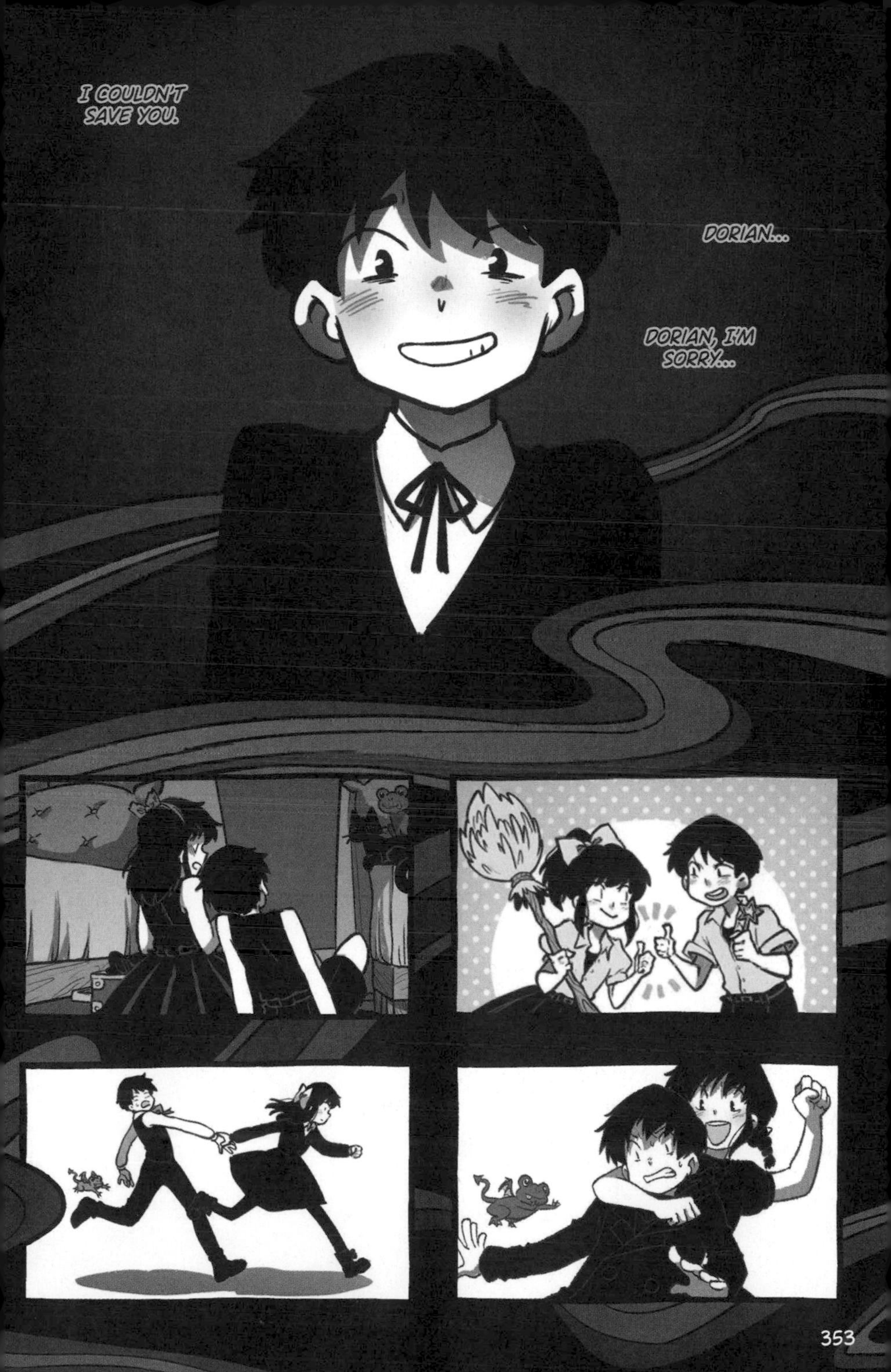
I COULDN'T SAVE YOU.
DORIAN...
DORIAN, I'M SORRY...

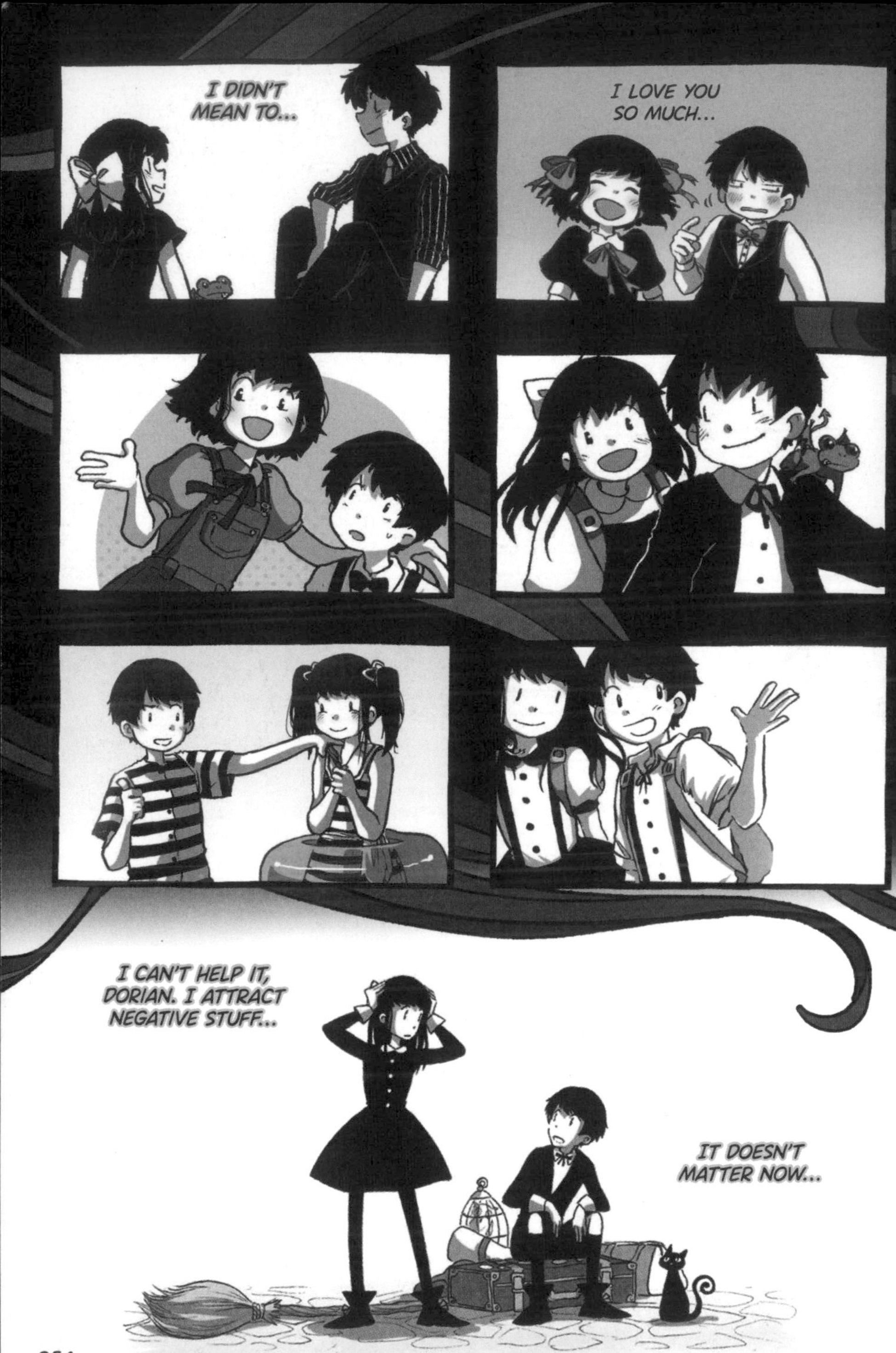
I DIDN'T MEAN TO...
I LOVE YOU SO MUCH...
I CAN'T HELP IT, DORIAN. I ATTRACT NEGATIVE STUFF...
IT DOESN'T MATTER NOW...

355

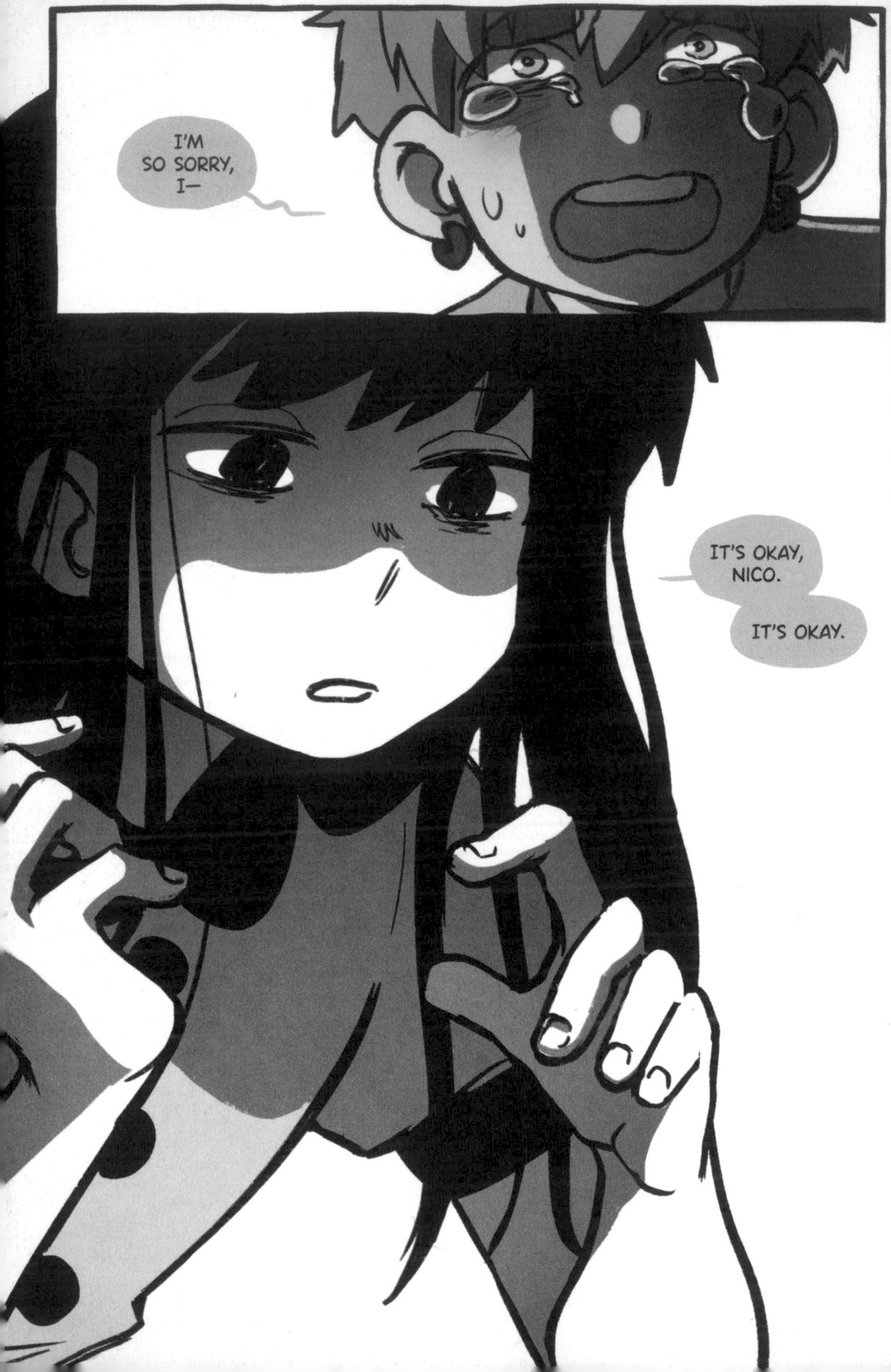
I'M SO SORRY, I—
IT'S OKAY, NICO.
IT'S OKAY.

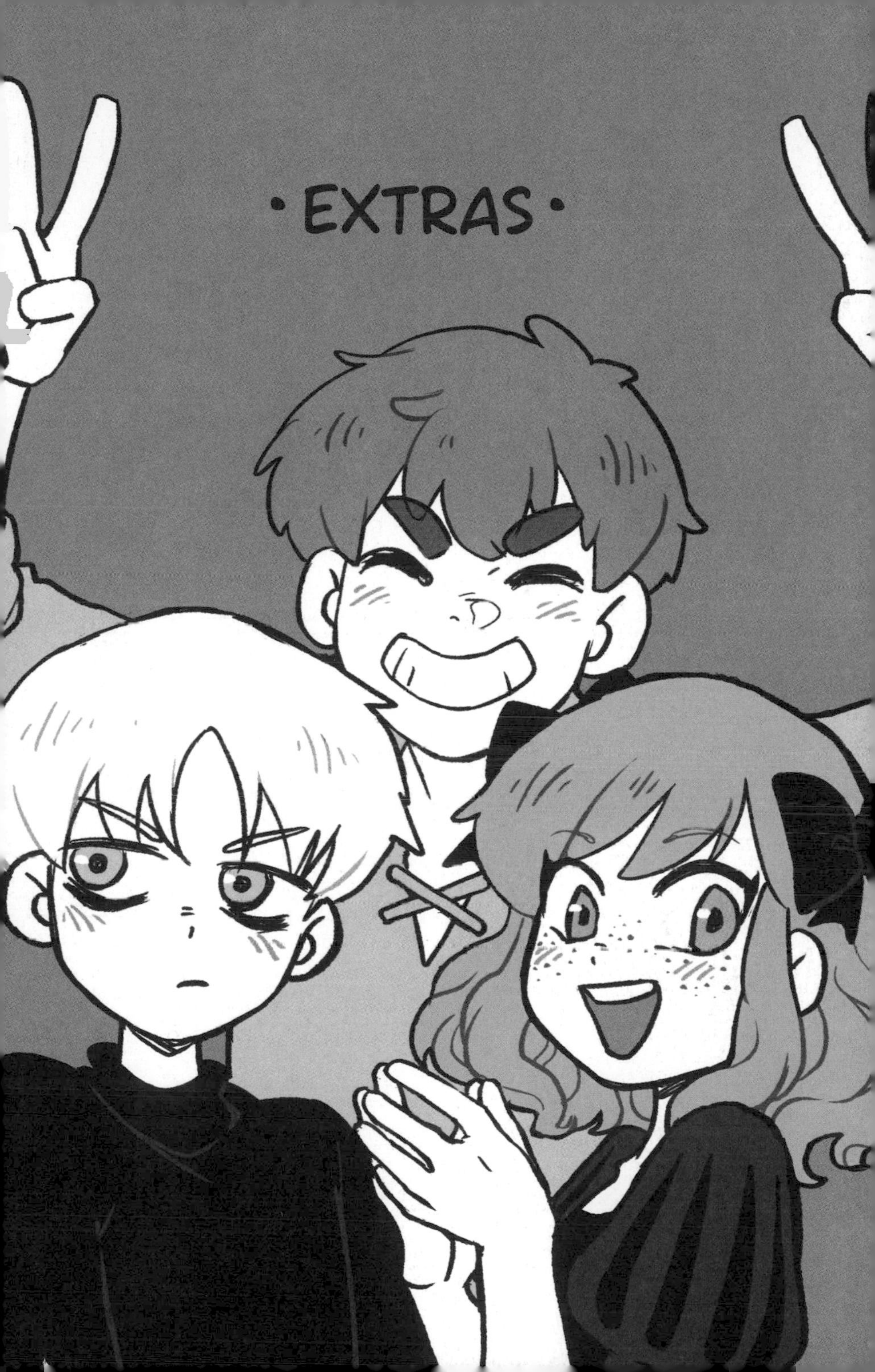

• EXTRAS •

363